Elizabeth Chadwick lives in [...] two sons. Much of her resea[rch...] Regia Anglorum, an early m[...] the emphasis on accurately re[...] the skill of writing historical and romantic [...] novel, *The Wild Hunt*, won a Betty Trask Award. She was shortlisted for the Romantic Novelists' Award in 1998 for *The Champion*, in 2001 for *Lords of the Wliite Castle*, in 2002 for *The Winter Mantle* and in 2003 for *The Falcons of Montabard*. Her sixteenth novel, *The Scarlet Lion*, was nominated by Richard Lee, founder of the Historical Novel Society, as one of the top ten historical novels of the last decade.

For more details on Elizabeth Chadwick and her books, visit www. elizabethchadwick. corn

Praise for Elizabeth Chadwick

'Chadwick's historical grasp is secure and vivid . . . an absorbing narrative that canters along' *Financial Times*

'Wonderfully written, immensely moving and immaculately researched . . . An author who grows in stature with every book she writes' *Lancashire Evening Post*

'The best writer of medieval fiction currendy around' *Historical Novels Review*

'Blends authentic period details with modern convention for emotional drama' Elizabeth Buchan, *Mail on Sunday*

'Compelling historical fiction . . . by the best novelist in this genre' *Driffield Leader*

'One of Elizabeth Chadwick's strengths is her stunning grasp of historical detail . . . her characters are beguiling, and the story intriguing and very enjoyable' Barbara Erskine

'Elizabeth Chadwick knows exactly how to write convincing and compelling historical fiction' Marina Oliver

'Strong, memorable characters, richly realised historic settings and terrific storytelling' *Keighley News*

ELIZABETH CHADWICK OMNIBUS

The Wild Hunt

The Running Vixen

sphere

SPHERE

This omnibus edition first published in Great Britain in 2011 by Sphere

Previously published separately:
The Wild Hunt first published in Great Britain in 1990 by Michael Joseph Ltd
Paperback edition published in 1991 by Time Warner Paperbacks
Reissued in 2008 by Sphere
Reprinted 2009 (twice), 2010 (twice)
Copyright © Elizabeth Chadwick 1990, 2008
The Running Vixen first published in Great Britain in 1991 by Michael Joseph Ltd
Paperback edition published in 2009 by Sphere
Reprinted 2009, 2010 (twice)
Copyright © Elizabeth Chadwick 1991, 2009

A CIP catalogue record for this book
is available from the British Library.

ISBN 978-0-7515-4795-5

Printed and bound in Great Britain by
Clays Ltd, St Ives plc

Sphere
An imprint of
Little, Brown Book Group
100 Victoria Embankment
London EC4Y 0DY

An Hachette UK Company
www.hachette.co.uk

www.littlebrown.co.uk

THE WILD HUNT

Acknowledgements

To my parents for their support,
to Alison King for all her help,
to my husband for his understanding
and to my agent Carole Blake
and my editors Maggie Pringle and Barbara Daniel for
making dreams come true

Author's Note

My first conscious memory of telling stories goes back to very early childhood. I was three years old, sitting up in bed on a light summer evening, making up a tale about the fairies decorating my cotton handkerchief.

Throughout my childhood I entertained myself by inventing stories, generally based on visual prompts from illustrations in books, or from memories of TV programmes I had enjoyed. *Champion the Wonder Horse* was responsible for many an afternoon of involved imagining. At this stage in my life, the tale-telling was always verbal and it wasn't until I was fourteen that I began writing things down – inspired to do so by summer holiday boredom and the BBC's *Six Wives of Henry VIII* starring Keith Michelle as Henry. However, although I enjoyed the writing, my Tudor tale didn't go the distance and was really just a sampler piece.

The following year the BBC aired the children's TV programme *Desert Crusader*, dubbed from the French series *Thibaud ou les Croisades* and set in the Holy Land in the twelfth century. I fell hook, line and sinker for the leading actor, André Laurence, and immediately began to write my own crusading novel. This time I persevered and completed it, realising along the way that I had found my period and my niche. I wanted to write historical adventures for a living – preferably medieval!

It took me another seventeen years and eight full-length novels to achieve that ambition, but I never gave up or saw rejections as a waste. It was all a learning curve and still fun to do. *The Wild Hunt* was the novel that finally gained me both a literary agent and a publisher. It also won me a Betty Trask award, which is an award given to authors under the age of thirty-five for a first novel of a romantic or traditional nature. The year I won, the award was presented by H.R.H. The Prince of Wales at Whitehall. This was a somewhat surreal moment for me as six months previously I had been stacking shelves at the local supermarket to make ends meet while raising my family!

The Wild Hunt has gone on to sell around the world and has been translated into a dozen languages. However, due to the vagaries of the publishing industry, it went out of print in English for many years. When Sphere wanted to reissue it, I was thrilled, but I said that in the light of increased writerly experience and with a bit more historical knowledge under my belt, I would like to go through the novel and give it a spring clean, so to speak.

The Wild Hunt was the first step on the rung of my career as a professional full-time author, and since then I have moved from writing tales of imaginary historical characters set against authentic backdrops, into telling, as fiction, the stories of people who actually lived. However, I remain very fond of this, my first published novel. I hope that my established readers will enjoy revisiting this reworked version and that those who have not come across *The Wild Hunt* before will be delighted too.

CHAPTER 1

ASHDYKE
THE WELSH MARCHES
NOVEMBER 1098

Snow, driven by a biting November wind, flurried against Guyon's dark cloak then swirled past him towards the castle glowering down from the high stone ridge overlooking the spated River Wye. His weary mount pecked and lumbered to a sluggish recovery. Guyon tugged the stallion's ears and slapped its muscular neck in encouragement. Dusk was fast approaching, the weather was vicious, but at least shelter was within sight.

The horse almost baulked at the hock-deep water of the ford, but Guyon touched him lightly with his spur and with a snort, the grey splashed through the swift, dark flow and gained the muddy, half-frozen village road. The crofts were lit from within by cooking fires and the sputtering glint of rushlight. As they passed the church, a cur ran out to snap at Arian's heels. Shod steel flashed. There was a loud yelp, then silence. A cottage door opened a crack and was quickly thrust shut in response to a sharp command from within.

Guyon rode on past the mill and began the steep climb to the castle, grimacing as if a mouthful of wine had suddenly become vinegar. On their arrival, Arian would receive a rub down, a warm blanket and a tub of hot mash to content him through the night. Guyon wished fervently that his own concerns could be dealt with as easily, but he bore tidings that made such a thing impossible.

The drawbridge thumped down to his hail and the grey paced the thick oak planks, hooves ringing a hollow tocsin, for beneath lay a gully of jagged rocks and debris, foraged only by the most nimble of sheep and the occasional cursing shepherd in less than nimble pursuit. Emerging through the dark arch of the gatehouse into the open bailey, he drew rein and swung from the stallion's back. His legs were so stiff that for a moment he could barely move and he clung to the saddle.

'Evil night, sire,' remarked the groom who splashed out from the stables to take the horse. Although there was deference in his manner, his eyes were bright with unspoken curiosity.

Guyon released his grip on the saddle and steadied himself. 'Worse to come,' he answered, not entirely referring to the weather. 'Look at the shoe on his off-fore, I think it's loose.'

'Sir.'

Guyon slapped Arian's dappled rump and walked across the bailey, slowly at first until the feeling returned to his limbs, his shoulders hunched against the force of the bitter, snowy wind. Greeting the guards at the forebuilding entrance, he stripped off his mittens, then climbed the steep staircase to the hall on the second level.

The dinner horn had recently sounded and the trestles were crowded with diners. At the sight of their lord's heir, jaws ceased chewing, hands paused halfway to dishes, necks craned. The men at the trestles marked his long, impatient stride and pondered what new trouble his arrival augured. The women studied his progress with different looks entirely and whispered to each other.

Ignoring the assembly, Guyon strode up the hall to the dais table where sat his father with the senior knights and retainers of the household and also, he noticed with a certain irritation, his sister Emma in the lady's customary place.

Miles le Gallois rose to greet him, an expression of concern on his face. 'Guy! We had not looked for you so soon.'

'A man rides quickly when the devil snaps at his heels,' Guyon answered, bowing to his father. Then he rose, kissed his sister and stepped over the trestle to take the place hastily made for him. His limbs suddenly felt leaden and the room wavered before his eyes.

'The wonder is that you did not fall off. Guy, you look dreadful!' Emma gave a peremptory signal to the squire serving the high table.

'Do I?' He took the cup of wine presented to him. 'Perhaps I have good reason.' He was aware of them all staring at him, their anxiety tangible.

'Surely the King did not refuse to grant you your uncle's lands?' His father looked incredulous.

Guyon shook his head and stared into the freshly poured wine. 'The King was pleased to acknowledge me the heir and grant me all rights and privileges pertaining,' he said in a flat voice. It was three months since his uncle had died fighting the Welsh on the Island of Mon that some called Anglesey. Gerard had been a childless widower and Guyon his named heir, but King William Rufus had been known to favour money above heredity when it came to confirming grants of land. Guyon had gone to Rufus in Normandy to make his claim and he had what he desired – at a price.

'Then why the dark looks for such good news?' his father demanded. 'What else has happened?'

Disinclined to make a public announcement of the news, Guyon tightened his grip around his cup. The ride had been so difficult and cold that he could barely think straight.

His sister set her hand over his. 'You are frozen! What were you thinking to make a journey in such weather? Could it not have waited? I'll have the servants prepare a tub in the solar and you'll come there now where it's warm!'

Some of the bleakness lifted from Guyon's spirit and his lips twitched. Emma still viewed her three years' seniority over him as a licence to command his obedience, more so since their mother had died of the sweating sickness two winters ago. While Emma's husband travelled with the court as an assistant chamberlain, she dwelt here on the Welsh border, terrorising servants and family alike with her demands for a state of gracious domestic order.

This time Guyon chose not to rebel and after a single look, let her have her way. 'You had better stir the cooks to provision for my men,' was all he said as he rose to follow her. 'They will be here within the hour and cursing me to the devil.'

Emma started to scold him about the folly of outriding them when the marches were so dangerous and unsettled, but Guyon let the words tumble away from him like spots of melting snow.

Once the steaming tub was ready, Guyon began to disrobe and Emma dismissed the maids with an autocratic snap of her fingers, causing him to lift his brows. Cadi, his white gazehound bitch fussed around him, wagging her tail and panting. He paused in his undressing to pat her flank and tousle her silky ears.

Miles dropped the curtain behind the two girls. 'I doubt that Guyon has any designs on ravishment just now, Emma,' he remarked drily.

She scowled. 'From what my husband tells me of the court, Guy would have designs on ravishment even if he were tied down and bludgeoned half unconscious.'

'Half the tale and a fraction of the truth,' Guyon defended himself as she snatched his padded tunic out of his hands and nudged Cadi away with the side of her leg. 'It would depend who was doing the tying and what she had in mind.'

As Emma made to cuff him, he ducked with agility, straightened and, seizing her by the shoulders, delivered a smacking kiss to her cheek. Emma glared at him, but her mouth started to curve despite her best efforts to keep it straight. 'You need not attempt your courtier's tricks on me. I know them by rote!'

Falsely crestfallen, Guyon released her with a sigh and began to unlace his shirt. 'I suppose you do.' The teasing look fell from his face. 'But I needs must hope they still have their effect on other women.'

Emma's gaze narrowed. 'Not within this keep,' she said with asperity.

'I was thinking further up the march. Maurice FitzRoger's daughter, to be precise.'

'What?' Miles, who had been lounging against a coffer was suddenly alert.

'Judith of Ravenstow,' Guyon said and having removed the rest of his garments, stepped into the steaming tub. 'On the King's order.'

His father's eyes widened. 'Rufus offered you Maurice of Ravenstow's girl?'

'He did not offer. He said marry her or else.' He looked bleakly at his stunned father. 'He also sold the earldom of Shrewsbury to Robert de Belleme for three thousand marks.'

'What!' Miles's concern became consternation. 'Surely the King would not permit de Belleme to inherit Shrewsbury. Considering what he owns already and the kind of man he is, it is much too dangerous!'

Guyon took the washcloth that Emma silently handed him. 'Every man has his price and de Belleme has calculated Rufus's to a nicety,' he said with a grimace. 'Belleme wanted Ravenstow as well, since it belonged to his late half-brother. He might have had it, too, if someone had not remembered that the heiress was of marriageable age and unbetrothed. The King chose to bestow her himself, and not without malicious amusement,' He began vigorously to wash as if purging himself of the thoughts chasing round his mind.

'You cannot do it!' Emma's mouth twisted with revulsion. 'If you marry the girl, it will make you blood kin to de Belleme. Everyone knows what a monster he is. He robs and tortures for sport and impales those who displease him on greased poles and smiles as they die.' She shuddered and hugged her arms. 'God's mercy, he keeps his own wife locked up in the cells below Belleme with only the rats for company!'

Guyon did not accuse her of hysterical over-reaction. Even the hardest men were horrified by the sadistic cruelty of Robert de Belleme, eldest son of the late Roger de Montgomery, Earl of Shrewsbury. It was not his treatment of the peasants that caused distress – their lives were expendable – but his torture of noble prisoners capable of paying ransom, and he had no respect for any authority but his own.

'If I do not accept this match, I forfeit Uncle Gerard's lands. The King says he will give them to one of his Flemings. I am caught in a cleft stick. Not only does Rufus force a wife into my bed, he makes me pay for the privilege too – five hundred marks. Nowhere near three thousand, I know, but enough to make my tenants squeal when I squeeze them for its payment. It is fortunate for de Belleme that he does not have a conscience as to how he goes about raising his own relief.'

Emma shuddered and crossed herself.

'And of course,' said his father, 'the lands you gain with this match, added to what you own and what you will inherit, make you a suitable counterbalance in the middle marches to whatever schemes of advancement de Belleme may choose to plot.'

'Oh yes,' Guyon said darkly. 'I am to pay for that privilege too, mayhap with my life.'

There was a taut silence. Emma drew a shaken breath and murmuring something about food and wine, fled the room.

Miles sighed and sat down on a stool, his movements easy.

As yet, his fifty-four years sat lightly on his body which remained, through vigorous activity, firm, if more stocky than in his slender youth.

'I know the girl's mother,' he said thoughtfully. 'Alicia FitzOsbern, Breteuil's sister. She was pretty at fifteen, very pretty indeed. If I had not already been married and satisfied with your mother, I might have offered for her myself.'

Guyon grunted. 'I always understood you had no liking for the FitzOsbern clan.'

'The male stock, no. They all were – and are, when you consider Breteuil – snakes, but Alicia was different. She was courageous and gentle and she had eyes like summer twilight. She never forgave her menfolk for selling her in marriage to Maurice de Montgomery.'

Guyon reached for the towel that Emma had left conveniently to hand and stepped from the tub. 'Reason enough for any woman to hate,' he said, thinking of the former lord of Ravenstow who he had always thought resembled a glutted boar atop a dung heap.

'As I remember, Judith was born late into the marriage after numerous slurs of barrenness had been cast in Alicia's direction,' Miles commented, folding his arms. 'I doubt it was all her fault. As far as I know, for all his lechery Maurice sired no bastards.'

Guyon donned a fur-lined bedrobe and called entry to the two servants who came to empty the water from the tub down a waste shaft in the corner of the room.

'At least Ravenstow is a formidable keep from which to establish your dominance,' Miles said. 'Whatever other sins lie on de Belleme's soul, he is a master architect.'

'And I suspect one way or another he will attempt to annex it to his earldom. Ravenstow guards the approach to the Chester plain and all roads east – ideally suited to the purposes of robbery and extortion, would you not say?'

Miles eyed him and said nothing, although his jaw tightened.

'There is always the Holy Land, I suppose,' Guyon added with a twisted smile. 'Freedom from Rufus and de Belleme, and the glory of slaughtering infidels to gild my soul. I—' He broke off and drew a deep breath as Emma re-entered the room followed by a maid bearing food and wine.

Compressing his lips Guyon sat down on the bench near the hearth.

'Rhosyn is in the hall,' Emma announced as she dismissed the woman and poured the wine herself. 'You will have to tell her.'

Guyon eyed his sister warily as he took the cup and drank. 'What of it? She made it plain at Michaelmas she would not dwell as my mistress. She has no cause to complain.'

'She might not have had a cause at Michaelmas, Guy, but she certainly has one now.'

Guyon's wariness sharpened. 'Meaning?'

'Meaning she is not so skilled a herb wife as she thought and the rounding of her belly proves it. Midsummer I would say, to look at her.'

Guyon glanced from his sister's disapproval to his father's blank surprise. He took another swallow of wine to hide his consternation and feigned nonchalance. 'I'll speak to her tomorrow, but I do not see that this marriage will change anything. Willingly I will acknowledge and provide for a child if that is what she wants, but Rhosyn is a wild law unto herself.'

'I am not thinking of wild law, but Welsh law,' Emma said, as he reached for a piece of bread. 'A man's firstborn son, even begotten out of wedlock to a mistress, has equal rights with the other legitimate heirs of his body.'

Guyon discarded the notion with a shake of his head. 'I am Norman born, Em, and Welsh rights do not pertain this side of the border. I could cede a couple of holdings to a chance-gotten child without too much hue and cry, but no more than that. Besides, the child is yet unborn and might well be a daughter, in which case I will find her a good marriage when the time comes.'

Emma's full mouth pursed. 'It needn't have happened at all.'

'Don't be so finicky, sister,' he growled. 'The sin of fornication is a peccadillo compared with the ones I could have perpetrated at court.'

Colour flooded his sister's face. Her husband, as a minor chamberlain, knew most of what transpired in the immediate circle surrounding the King: the scandals, the petty power struggles, the prevalent vices, and Guyon, with his striking looks, disregard for propriety and hint of Welsh barbarity was a magnet to which all three were drawn whether he wished it or no. 'I expect you and Prince Henry keep tallies to compare your ruttings,' she snapped.

'Indeed we do,' Guyon said with a sarcastic flourish. 'How did you guess?'

Miles eased tactfully to his feet and stretched like a cat uncoiling. 'Time enough for discussion tomorrow,' he said. 'I'm for my bed and I'm sure Guyon is too.' He gave his daughter an eloquent stare. Guyon had his trencher piled high enough already without her heavy-handed seasoning of moral chastisement and righteous advice.

'A conspiracy of men,' Emma declared with a sniff, and then gave a tight smile. 'I know when I am beaten.' Going to her brother, she stooped and kissed his stubble-blurred cheek.

He tugged the copper-coloured braid peeping from beneath her veil. 'That does not mean you will give in!'

'Does it not?' She arched her brow at him. 'Let me tell you, I will gladly relinquish the battle to your wife and hope she has better fortune in taming your ways!'

'Know when you are beaten, do you?' he needled as she went towards the curtain. 'Is that why you always have to have the last word?'

CHAPTER 2

In the great hall, Rhosyn rolled over on her lumpy makeshift pallet and sat up, irritated to discover that yet again her bladder was full. Beside her, oblivious, her father snored. He was a prosperous wool merchant these days, with a paunch to prove it. Complacent. They had fared well since their business dealings with Miles le Gallois. There was much profit to be had in wool and the cloth woven from the fleeces. Lord Miles bred it raw on the hoof. Her father sold the clip in Flanders and speculated a little on the wider trade markets – spices and leather, silks and glass – and they prospered.

Beside their grandfather, the children of her first, now widowed marriage slept in a puppy huddle. Rhys was ten, a sturdy, dark-eyed replica of his father. Eluned, seven, resembled herself – slender and fey with raven hair, autumnal eyes and a luminous complexion. This coming child, as yet scarcely realised; well, if a boy, she could only hope by God's charity that he inherited Guyon's beauty married to a less difficult nature.

Stupid, she thought, irritated at herself as she quietly left her children and her father to seek out the garderobe. Stupid to have been so easily caught, she who knew all her herbs and simples, or thought she knew because they had always worked before. Too late now, too dangerous, and not the season for the plants that would have cured her condition.

She had been in two minds whether to make this trip to Hereford with her father, but had reasoned that it would be her last opportunity before the weather grew too difficult for travel. She needed to purchase linen for swaddling bands that she could stitch during the dark, hall-bound months of winter; and winter's threat was already upon them. The knife-bitter wind and the scudding snow squalls had caused them to curtail their journey early in the day and seek shelter under Lord Miles's roof.

Guyon's arrival at dusk had been a surprise, and she was not sure if it was a welcome one. The news of his impending marriage had caused her no grief. She had always known the day would come, indeed, had held herself a little aloof with that knowledge in mind. He had a duty to take a wife of his own status and beget heirs, a wife who would have more in common with him than she ever would.

Rhosyn's practical nature told her there was no point in building upon their tenuous relationship. For all his fluency in the Welsh tongue and his ability to adapt to Welsh ways, he was only one quarter of the Cymru and he was raised to be a marcher lord who would ride into Wales on the back of a warhorse to ravage the land if his King so commanded. He regarded the towering Norman border keeps as home and refuge, not as grey, enclosing prisons that hemmed in the soul.

The latrine was cold and stank of its main function, and she did not linger. Instead of returning to the hall, however, Rhosyn made her way to the small wall chamber where Guyon usually lodged when he stayed here. His gazehound, Cadi, lay outside the entrance, her nose tucked into her tail, but rose with a joyous whine of greeting. Rhosyn paused to stroke the dog and make a fuss of her, before lifting the heavy curtain.

Guyon had been sound asleep, but came immediately to his senses at the first soft clink of the curtain rings and the muffled whine of the dog. This was the keep where he had been born and raised, his welcome here guaranteed, but these days he was so conditioned to react to danger, and complete security was so seldom his, that he was out of bed and across the room in the space of a heartbeat. He lunged at the figure outlined in the glow from the corridor flare. The crown of his captive's head butted his chin, jarring his teeth together. He bit his tongue and tasted blood. A supple body writhed against his and he felt the swell of a woman's breast beneath his fingers.

'It's me, Rhosyn!' she gasped indignantly, her French bearing the lilting accent of Wales. 'Have you lost your wits?'

'More likely you have lost yours!' he retorted, but with amusement now that he was fully awake and enjoying the feel of her body against his own. 'It is a foolish thing to creep up on a man in the middle of the night, *cariad*. Oft-times I sleep with a naked sword at my side. I might have cut off your head!'

'I have seen your naked sword frequently enough for it not to concern me,' Rhosyn replied with spurious innocence and pressed against him in the darkness. She tangled her fingers in his hair and stood on tiptoe to bite his ear and then whisper into it: 'But perhaps it would be safer to sheathe it, my lord.'

Guyon laughed huskily. 'That sounds like a fine idea,' he said, before closing her mouth with a kiss, his fingers busy with the lacings of her gown. 'Do you happen to know of a fitting scabbard?'

Rhosyn stretched languidly like a cat and then relaxed, a contented half-smile curving her lips. 'I had forgotten what a pleasure it was,' she purred, eyeing Guyon sidelong across the tossed coverlet in the glow from a cresset lamp.

'Your fault,' he remarked, but easily, without accusation. 'I wanted you to come with me.'

'I would have stuck out like a sore thumb among those Norman women and been as miserable as sin.'

'Sin is never miserable,' Guyon remarked, thereby earning himself a playful slap. He caught her wrist and pulled her across him and they tussled for a moment, before he let her go and she drew back to study him. With his dark hair and eyes, he could easily have passed for one of the Cymru, although his height and breadth spoke of his Anglo-Norman descent.

'I hear that you are with child,' he said, giving her a serious look now.

Her gaze grew wary. 'What of it?'

'Were you going to tell me?'

Rhosyn bit her lip. 'Probably.' She avoided his eyes. 'My father and yours do too much business together to keep such a matter secret and Rhys and Eluned both chatter like jackdaws. You would have discovered sooner or later.'

Guyon felt a pang at her intimation that had she been able to keep it from him, she would have done so. 'My sister seems to think that you will invoke Welsh law on the child's behalf.'

Rhosyn stared at him.

'In Welsh law the son of the handmaiden is equal to the son begotten on a legal spouse,' he clarified.

She shook her head. 'Your sister is wrong. What good would it do on this side of the border where Norman custom reigns? It would be a hobble of broken straw indeed and I am not sure I would want a child of mine to dwell among *saesnegs* in a great stone tomb like this.' Her eyes roved the comfort of the room with disparagement.

Guyon almost retorted that he was not sure he wanted a child of his to grow up running barefoot over the Welsh hills or huckstering in wool for a living, but he curbed the words, knowing from bitter experience that they too were hobbles of broken straw.

'Emma spoke from the viewpoint of a Norman lady,' he said instead. 'She imagines what she would do in your position, and that would be to fight tooth and nail to have that child accepted as my responsibility.' He reached to twine a tendril of her hair through his fingers. 'Also, I think she said it to put me in dread of ever doing the like again. She disapproves of what she sees as my casual fornications.'

Rhosyn made a face, remembering Emma's frosty expression as her family arranged their pallets in the hall, and then her grimace became a smile as she imagined the lady Emma's response had she witnessed herself and Guyon a few moments ago.

The lamp sputtered in its pool of fat and Guyon gently tugged the strand of hair. 'But our concern is not with Emma, but with you.' His gaze ranged over her body which was just beginning to show the changes of pregnancy.

Rhosyn stared at the coverlet and chewed her lip.

'I try to learn by my mistakes,' he said gently. 'I will not try to hold you; nor, though it be my greatest desire, is it fitting that I should.'

'Your bride, you mean?' she said without rancour.

Guyon made a face. 'You know about that? Ach, how can you not when gossip travels so fast? Rhosyn *cariad*, you are well out of this coil. Take the road to Wales and in the name of God, do not look back.'

'Guy?'

He flashed her a grim look. 'Did you also hear that I am to wed into the house of Montgomery? It is by royal command and the girl's mother is an old family acquaintance. My refusal would put her in mortal danger from Robert de Belleme, the new Earl of Shrewsbury. If he can lock up his own wife in some dark oubliette and put out his own godson's eyes, what need to cavil at tossing his sister-in-law and niece over Ravenstow's battlements? It is about power, my love, and you are well out of it. When your father has finished his business in England, go home, keep to your own hearth and forget about venturing across the border unless you have a well-armed and determined escort. Robert de Belleme and his minions will turn the marches into hell for such men as your father.'

Rhosyn shuddered, wanting to believe he was exaggerating, but denied that comfort.

'I will speak with your father tomorrow before our roads part, make sure he knows not to take short cuts across Shrewsbury's domain.'

'Is it really so dangerous?'

'Yes.' His voice filled with emphasis. 'I mean what I say, Rhosyn. Either go into the heart of Wales and do not venture forth again, or stay here with me, under my protection. There can be no middle path.'

She shook her head numbly and shivered. He drew her back down beside and against his body, pulling the coverlet around them. She pressed herself against him but continued to shiver. This was the end of it. She could no more live in one of these great, grim fortresses than a Norman lady could sit milking a ewe on the slopes of Yr Wyddfa. She needed her measure of freedom and, aside from that, Norman women had entirely different views upon the subject of mistresses and their offspring. She had no desire to feud over a lost cause with Guyon's new wife. If he wanted to see her and the child, then let him come to Wales.

'Ffarwel fy llewpart du,' she murmured against his throat, and kissed him first there in the brown hollow and then raised her head to find his lips. 'R wy'n dy garu di.'

Guyon's arms tightened around her. 'I love you too, cariad,' he muttered, and silently cursed the whole Montgomery clan into the deepest pit of hell.

CHAPTER 3

Judith hissed through her clenched teeth as Agnes, her mother's maid, discovered a hitherto overlooked snarl in the mass of tawny-bronze hair she was combing.

'Stand still, sweeting and it won't hurt so much,' Agnes said, a hint of exasperation in her voice, perspiration streaking her double chin. 'It's nearly done now.'

'I'm not a babe to be cozened!' snapped Judith, shifting from foot to foot.

Agnes's mouth puckered to become another fold in her fleshy face and she turned away to pick up a rope of polished agate beads. Judith sniffed, set her jaw and refused to cry. Tears availed her nothing – a lesson hard-learned in early childhood. Her father had dismissed them as a silly female weakness. Her mother had wept too many herself in grief over lost causes to encourage her daughter in like indulgences.

Judith looked down at her wedding garments. A pale green linen undergown, close-fitting to her slender, almost thin body was topped by a dress of dark green silk damask, gorgeously embroidered with thread of gold at throat and hem and trailing sleeve. Her narrow waist was accentuated by a girdle of jewel-embroidered braid. She felt like the centrepiece at a feast, dressed to be devoured.

In a few hours she was to make her marriage vows in the castle chapel to a man she had never before set eyes upon.

She was to leave her home, go with him, his property to deal with as he pleased; to be bedded by him tonight and perhaps bear his child nine months from now. She was a week short of her sixteenth birthday and terrified. She knew how much her mother had suffered at the hands of her father before his death in September. The growls, the curses, the frequent slaps, the drunken beatings, the disdain that tore at the foundations of confidence. Her mother had borne the brunt, shielded her daughter from the worst of it, but Judith had known, had observed the hell, and could not bear that it might be her own fate.

'Hold still, my sweeting,' said Agnes. 'Let me pin these in your hair, there's a good girl.'

The maid's fingers tweaked and tugged, trailing pain in their wake. Resentment flared in Judith's breast, not just at Agnes, but at everything. She uncoiled her clenched fists and slapped Agnes's hand aside. 'You should have been a butcher's wife, not a lady's maid!' she spat.

Affronted, Agnes clucked like a hen.

The curtain rings rattled, announcing the arrival of Alicia de Montgomery. Taking in the scene before her eyes and sensing the atmosphere, the faint vertical marks between her brows became more defined.

'Thank you, Agnes, you have wrought wonders. Our cygnet is a swan. Will you go and ask the chamberlain's lad to bring fresh candles ready for tonight?'

Head carried high, the maid swept out.

'Agnes is an old besom at times,' Alicia said when they were alone, 'but that is no excuse to strike out. Is it what I have taught you? You will become no better than your father.'

Judith bit her lip and held her chin rigid to stop it from quivering. 'I am sorry, mama,' she said unsteadily, 'but she hurt me. I feel like a filly being groomed for a horse-coper's approval!'

Alicia shook her head and, uttering a sigh, folded her

daughter in a rose-scented embrace. 'I know you do not think it now, but you are most fortunate in this match.'

Judith's response was a stifled sob and her hands gripped suddenly tight on her mother's sleeves.

'Hush now, you'll undo all Agnes's good work.' Alicia stroked Judith's hair. 'This match was made for men's political purposes, but it is a blessing for you could you but understand it. The man whose son you will wed . . . I was almost his bride myself. Would to God that I had been so fortunate.'

Judith wiped her face on her sleeve and stared at her mother.

'Your grandfather FitzOsbern offered me to him, but he chose to wed an English heiress instead because it better suited his plans and besides, he was smitten. Christen had been widowed on Hastings field and she was a grown woman. I was your age and unknowing of the world. Your grandfather was not displeased when the offer was rejected because in the meantime he had received an offer from Maurice de Montgomery.' Who had beaten her for the slightest transgression and behaved with all the finesse of a rutting boar. Occasional baronial gatherings had afforded her glimpses of Miles le Gallois as he grew into middle age. The cat-like grace of his twenties had set, becoming less supple and rangy, but in essence remaining. Maurice had grown ever more to resemble a boar as his waistline overspread the bounds of his belt.

'I know very little of Guyon, but with Miles and Christen for examples I do believe your marriage will be easier than mine.' Alicia gave a regretful shrug. 'If circumstances had been different, you would have had time to know each other before the wedding, but as it is I would rather you had a strong protector when your uncle Robert comes to claim his earldom. Already the vultures are gathering.'

Judith eyed at her mother whose expression revealed nothing – too much of nothing. Judith well knew the rumours surrounding Robert de Belleme. The maids delighted in terrifying each other of a night with tales of his brutality and Judith understood more English and Welsh than was seemly for a girl of her station. They said that he tortured for sport and robbed and murdered without conscience. The more fanciful of them even said that he possessed a forked tail and cloven hooves, but Judith gave no credence to their imagination. What need when the truth was already so lurid?

He had designed Ravenstow himself and loaned her father the money to build it. They were still in his debt to the tune of several hundred marks. She knew her mother was afraid he would come immediately to claim it, being himself in debt to the King. It was the reason that this marriage had been arranged so quickly – before he had a chance to reach out and seize and strangle.

Judith shuddered. The wedding was supposed to be a quiet affair with a select number of guests and vassals – supposed to be, but de Belleme's brother Arnulf of Pembroke had ridden in yestereve and with him had been Walter de Lacey who was a powerful vassal of de Belleme's, a hunting crony of her father's and former suitor for her hand. Her mother had been hard put to find them either house-room or cordiality, for it was obvious they were not present for the sake of wishing joy on the marriage; however, such eminent men could not be turned away and thus guested in the hall with those of official invitation such as Hugh d'Avrenches, Earl of Chester and FitzHamon, Lord of Gloucester.

The curtain swished and Agnes reappeared followed by a youth bearing a basket of fresh candles. 'They're sighted, my lady. Be here within the hour, so de Bec says,' Agnes announced.

Judith began to tremble. The walls seemed to be closing in on her, caging her in a space so small that there was no room to breathe. She felt hot and sick, but her hands were icy. 'Agnes, I'm sorry, I shouldn't have struck you,' she said in a choked voice.

'That's all right, my love,' Agnes said comfortingly. 'Bound to be a bit strung up today, aren't you?' She held out her hand. 'Child, what's wrong?'

Judith knew she would die if she did not escape. Gathering her skirts in one hand, the other clapped across her mouth, she bolted from the room. The chamberlain's lad leaped out of the way, dropping his candles. Alicia and Agnes called out to her, but Judith was gone, fleeing heedless of the dangerous spiralling stairs, fleeing with the wild instinct of a hunted animal to escape. While she was running, she did not have to think. While she was running, she was not fettered.

'Shall I go after her, my lady?'

Alicia gnawed her lip and gazed at the still swaying curtain. 'No, Agnes,' she said after a moment. 'We have hemmed her about too much. Let her be alone awhile. It will be her last chance.'

'She is not ready for this yet,' Agnes said grimly. 'They say he's used to the women of the court – that he plays fast with other men's wives.'

'Gossip!' Alicia snapped. 'And you know better than to listen, Agnes. Do not give me that pitying look. I do not doubt he has owned casual mistresses, but tales are always embroidered to give them colour and I trust to his breeding more than I do to third-hand tittle-tattle. Besides, whatever marriage to him holds for Judith, it can be no worse than a fate at the hands of her uncle Robert, or Walter de Lacey.' Her lips tightened. 'She has to be ready.'

When Judith returned to her senses, there was a tight stitch in her side and she was leaning against a jagged lump of stone. Her breathing rasped in her throat, her recently combed hair was dishevelled and a dark stain was spreading upwards from the hem of her gown where she had splashed heedlessly through the bailey puddles. Her gilded shoes were soaked and her toes clung cold together inside them.

Sleet spattered fitfully in the wind which was as raw as an open wound. Judith's teeth chattered. Her new cloak with its warm fur lining was hanging upon her clothing pole in the chamber she had fled, and not for anything would she return to fetch it.

'I cannot do it,' she whispered miserably, knowing that her words were empty. If she did not agree to this marriage, she exposed them all to the threat of her uncle Robert. Sooner or later she would have been contracted to wed anyway, probably to Walter de Lacey, and nothing could be worse than that, she told herself as she stared at the grey choppy water of the river below.

Guyon FitzMiles, lord of Ledworth. She tested the name on her tongue and tried to envisage the man, but nothing came except sick fear. What if his teeth were rotten or he stank? What if he was gross and balding like Hugh, Earl of Chester? What if he beat her just because his mood was sour? For a wild moment she contemplated flinging herself from the promontory to break like spume upon the rocks below, but she dared not, because such an act would earn eternal damnation for her soul. Gasping, the wind blinding her face with her hair, Judith drew back from the treacherous edge.

A plaintive mew drew her gaze down to the golden tabby cat that was twining sinuously around her skirts, back arched, round head butting and rubbing.

'Melyn!' Momentarily diverted from her unhappy dilemma, Judith bent to scoop the cat into her arms. 'In the name of the saints, where have you been?'

The cat, missing for three days, purred and kneaded Judith's sleeve with her paws, her yellow eyes filled with smugness and disdain.

Melyn was unusual in being a house pet. Usually cats roamed the undercrofts and barns, tolerated to keep vermin at bay, essentially wild, sometimes caught and skinned for their fur. Judith had discovered Melyn last year out on this headland, as a mangy kitten with an infected paw. Alicia had been teaching Judith her herbs and simples at the time and had let Judith develop her knowledge on the kitten, Lord Maurice not being at home to see the little creature destroyed. By the time he returned, Melyn was fully recovered, had become accustomed to life in the bower and had learned manners to suit. Her feline sense of self-preservation sent her either out of the room or into hiding whenever Maurice appeared. Following his death, the cat had stalked the keep like a queen surveying her domain, imperious and aloof. Her disappearance three days ago had been an ill omen. It was as if Melyn knew a new tyrant was coming to Ravenstow and wanted no part of it . . . except that now, when his arrival was imminent, she was back.

Melyn suddenly and painfully dug her hind legs into the crook of Judith's arm and clawed herself on to her favourite perch across her mistress's shoulder. Judith yelped in protest, but bore with the discomfort because she was so relieved by her pet's return. She tugged her hair to one side out of the way. Melyn uttered a strange noise, halfway between whine and growl. Her claws needled Judith's neck as another cat emerged from the tangled dank grass and padded without haste across their path towards the keep. He was sleek, rangy, and as black as jet.

'Sweet Mary!' Judith exclaimed in exasperation, not knowing whether to be annoyed or amused, and most definitely concerned. God alone knew how her future husband would react to a bowerful of kittens. God alone knew how her future husband would react to anything.

CHAPTER 4

Guyon drew rein and, while the herald rode forward to announce him formally, stared up at the limewashed keep, gleaming against the heavy grey clouds and wind-whipped tussocks on its slope.

'I must be mad,' he muttered as the drawbridge thumped down across the ditch and, beyond, the serjeants in the gate-house made shrift to raise the portcullis and open the door into hell. Foreboding scuttled down Guyon's spine. One of the most impregnable keeps along the northern march Ravenstow might be, desirable in the extreme, but for two pins he would have ridden away and left it. But as there were more than two pins at stake, he heeled Arian's flanks and the stallion stepped delicately on to the planks. Cadi bounded joyously forward with no such reservations, and Guyon whistled her sternly to heel.

'The Welsh won't take this in a hurry,' Miles said as they turned at a sharp angle to ride between the outer defences and the palisade of the inner bailey before turning again to enter the inner court through a second gateway.

Guyon grunted in reply and studied the formidable defences with a jaundiced eye, appreciating their strength even while he felt revulsion. If only Robert de Belleme was not so closely connected with the place, he would have been much easier of conscience and mind.

Upon dismounting, they were greeted by an officious little

man in a scarlet silk robe that embraced his paunch and made him look as if he were heavily pregnant. Behind him stood a taller, iron-thewed greybeard in full armour and a welcoming party of what looked like the more prominent vassals and household knights.

'God's greeting my lords, and welcome,' said the paunch in red silk, hands clasped together like a supplicant. 'I am Richard FitzWarren, chamberlain to the lady Alicia, and this is her constable, Michel de Bec . . .'

Guyon forced himself to listen and look polite as he was introduced one by one to all the members of the group. It was politic to remember names, since it was a valuable asset when it came to handling their owners, but it gave him cause to wonder what was amiss that the constable and his underling should emerge to greet them instead of the hostess herself and then freeze them here in the bailey, drivelling of matters that could wait.

Glancing briefly beyond the men while he made acknowledgement, he noticed a woman hurrying from the forebuilding towards them, her manner agitated. Her cloak was fur-lined and her rose-coloured gown shimmered beneath it as she moved. Exposed below her veil, her braids were a handspan thick and lustrous as jet.

'The lady Alicia,' Miles said in a tone of voice that caused Guyon to divert his gaze and eye his father sharply instead.

She approached the men with a fixed smile on her lips and a slightly desperate expression in her eyes. 'I am sorry, my lords, I should have been here to greet you. I apologise for my lack. The more I try, the more obstacles seem to be cast in my path. Forgive me, welcome now, and come within, I pray you.' She gestured with an open hand.

'What is wrong, my lady?' Miles asked. 'Can we be of service?

Alicia drew breath to deny, but then let it out on a heavy sigh. 'Nothing of great import, my lords. The guests are squabbling; the cook has just tipped boiling lard all over the spit boy and the bread is burnt to cinders. The maids don't know their heads from their heels; my constable, when told to play for time, keeps you standing in the ward in the cold as I am doing now; and to season the stew, my daughter has taken fright and run off heaven knows where. Otherwise, everything is as normal as you would expect for a wedding so quickly arranged.'

Miles stifled a grin. Guyon started to ask a question, but the words were driven from his mind as Cadi gave a bark of antagonistic joy and sprang from his side to hurtle across the ward towards a girl who was trying to slink unnoticed around the side of the forebuilding, and would have succeeded were it not for the dog.

The cat that was curled around her shoulders became a hissing arch of erect orange fur. The bitch launched herself at the girl, who overbalanced and sat down hard on the muddy bailey floor. A feline paw flashed. Blood sprang to the accompaniment of an anguished yelp. The cat leaped over the dog, avoiding the belated snap of her teeth, whisked, through the legs of a startled guard and into the keep.

Hampered by her gown, Judith floundered to rise. A swift glance around made her wish that she had been knocked unconscious. The grooms, guards and kitchen maids on errands were gawping in horrified delight. Her mother's face as she bore down upon her was set like stone. Someone sniggered. She closed her eyes, decided that shutting out the situation was not going to make it go away and opened them again upon a neatly built greying man of middle years who had overtaken Alicia to set a hand beneath her elbow.

'I take this for an omen,' he chuckled. 'You and my son are bound to fight like cat and dog and scandalise the entire castle!'

Judith gaped at him too stunned to respond. Her father would have shaken her for this until her teeth rattled.

'No more than you and mama ever did!' a younger man

retorted amiably, appearing beside them, his fingers gripped around the white dog's collar as she strove, forepaws flailing, to pursue her quarry into the keep. 'It is my fault,' he owned with a smile. 'Cadi's still a pup and has yet to learn her manners.'

Judith looked down. He was beautiful and unreal. A courtier, a gilded image with a voice as smooth as dark mead. Her uncle Robert was handsome and smooth too, and rotten to the core beneath the gilding, and her fear increased.

Having delivered Judith to the bower to repair the ravages of the first encounter between bride and groom, Alicia summoned her courage and returned to the hall to attend to her guests.

Miles le Gallois smiled and waved his hand at her apology. 'It is already to be an irregular wedding,' he said. 'I am sure my son's memory of his first encounter with his bride will remain vivid for the rest of his life.'

Alicia cast a glance over her shoulder to where Guyon was giving the dog into the temporary care of one of his knights, then returned her attention to Miles. 'You are laughing at me, my lord.'

'I may be.'

Her mouth began to curve. She straightened it. 'Judith is anxious,' she said. 'Tonight she will be a wife, when this morning she was a child.'

Miles sobered. 'Guyon has a sister and nieces and is by no means green about women.'

'So we hear,' Alicia replied waspishly, and then shook her head. 'No surprise when you consider his looks and the ways of the court.'

'I am not at court now, my lady,' Guyon said, joining them.

Alicia jumped. He moved as softly as Judith's cat.

'You need not fear,' Guyon continued. 'I promise I will treat your daughter with every respect and courtesy.'

'Judith is young, but she is quick to learn and quite capable of managing a household,' Alicia replied, recovering herself. 'If she appeared in a bad light just now, it is because she has been unsettled by her father's death and this sudden change in her situation.'

In other words, Guyon thought wryly, she was a resentful, frightened little girl who would take a deal of delicate handling if anything was to be salvaged from the morass.

The wine arrived, and with it Hugh d'Avrenches, Earl of Chester, thus sparing Guyon the need to make Alicia a reply.

'It is bound to be difficult at first,' Miles said to Alicia as Guyon lent a relieved ear to what his neighbour had to say concerning the Welsh alliances of the region. 'Given different circumstances, there would have been the time we all need.'

'Given different circumstances,' Alicia said with a side-long look at Guyon, 'there would have been no arrangement at all, would there?'

Lost for a reply, Miles lifted his cup and drank.

Guyon looked at the girl to whom he had just bound himself in Ravenstow's freezing chapel, his vows committing him to her protection for the rest of his life, no matter how short that might now be. Her own voice making the responses had been tremulous and more than once swallowed in tears.

He had felt the daggers in men's eyes as they witnessed his marriage. Arnulf of Pembroke had barely been civil in greeting and Walter de Lacey was sneeringly hostile. Judith's face was turned towards him, awaiting the sacrificial kiss of tradition. The high cheekbones gave a distinctly feline expression to her eyes, which were a peculiar mingling of brown upon grey like water in spate.

Dear Christ, what had he sold himself into? Probably an early grave, he thought as he slipped his arm around her waist. She was rigid and trembling beneath the glowing green damask. It was a grown woman's gown cladding the thin frame of a child and he knew that he could no more bed with her tonight than he could with one of his nieces. He kissed her cheek as he would a vassal, the touch brief and impersonal. Her skin smelled faintly of rosewater, and her hair of the rosemary and camomile in which it had been washed for the wedding.

Judith shuddered at the contact and Guyon immediately released her. Together they turned to receive the congratulations of the guests and witnesses; few in number because of the hasty arrangements, to Judith they seemed a claustrophobic throng.

The entire occasion for her was a nightmare endured through a fog. Sporadically the mist would lift to reveal a sharply coloured tableau with herself bound victim at its centre. The awful moment when the dog had sent her flying, her arrival at the chapel, the faces turned towards her, their expressions stamped with speculation, with pity, with predatory greed. Now, clearly, she could see her hand resting upon her husband's dark sleeve, her wedding ring of Welsh gold proclaiming his ownership. She was as much his property now as his horse or that dog, to be used and abused as he chose.

The guests mingled in the great hall. Below the dais they danced in honour of the bride and groom. Guyon watched his new wife perform the steps with one of Ravenstow's neighbours. Ralph de Serigny was another of de Belleme's vassals, a thoroughly disagreeable, parsimonious old ferret who, according to Alicia, was only here in order to eat and drink at another's expense. As his borders marched with Ravenstow's on the Welsh boundary, it had been necessary to invite him lest he take offence. His wife, apparently, was dull-witted and had been left at home tended by her women. At least, Guyon thought half smiling, if Ralph de Serigny was only here to eat, drink and escape his wife, he was a deal more welcome than certain others claiming the right of hospitality at his wedding.

The dance progressed and Judith was passed on to the arm of her uncle, Arnulf de Montgomery. He had a nose like a pitted stone and possessed a dour, unsmiling character. De Montgomery had none of Robert de Belleme's charisma or genius but was the owner of a low, dull cunning. Not having the inventiveness to scheme, he was sufficiently shrewd to attach himself to the plots of others if there was benefit to himself – a man to be watched from the eye corners, frank confrontation not being his style. But how did one look before and behind and to the side at one and the same time?

De Montgomery swept his niece into the clutch of Walter de Lacey who was waiting at the end of the line. The younger man pulled her against his lean body, caught her wrist and turned her around. Judith's face wore a fixed smile. His hand lingered at her waist and he murmured something against her ear.

'More oil than you'd find in an entire olive grove,' muttered the Earl of Chester from the corner of his mouth. Guyon glanced round and up. Hugh d'Avrenches, known as Hugh le Gros on account of his enormous height and girth, was the ugliest man Guyon had ever seen and even now, long acquaintance had not bred the indifference of familiarity.

He had small, hooded eyes of watery pale blue. His cheeks were pendulous red-veined jowls and his mouth was small and soft with a sweet, surprisingly childlike smile, the similarity enhanced by the gap where his two upper front teeth were missing. He cultivated a jolly, bumbling personality to match his gross figure and the unwary stepped in, never thinking of the dangers lurking beneath the shallows. A good friend, an implacable enemy.

'Enough to slip his feet from under him, I would say,' Guyon agreed.

Hugh d'Avrenches folded his arms and regarded Guyon with a twinkling stare. 'Good soldier, though. He led a competent command on the Mon campaign.'

Guyon's lip curled. 'He also amused himself with torture and the rape of girls not old enough to be women.'

The Earl shrugged. 'We all have our own little foibles and sometimes tortured men can be made to sing a very pretty tune.'

Guyon's nostrils flared. 'Yes,' he said without inflection.

Chester laid a hand on Guyon's shoulder. 'Son, you're too finicky and you can't afford the luxury of principles in the present company.'

Guyon watched Walter de Lacey set his hands on Judith's hips and swing her round. The stiff smile on her face threatened to shatter. 'I realise that. De Lacey offered for the girl himself shortly before her father was killed; he had de Belleme's sanction to the suit.'

Chester pursed his soft, small lips. 'Did he so?' He eyed the dancers with interest. 'He'll bear watching then, because it doesn't look as though he's willing to concede you the victory.'

Guyon turned and his gaze narrowed in anger. The music had finished on a flourish and Walter de Lacey had pulled Judith hard to his chest and was kissing her passionately on the mouth, one hand roving and probing the curve of her buttocks. Guyon swore, thrust his wine into the Earl's hastily held out paw and stalked across the room to reclaim his bride.

'The privilege is mine, I believe,' he said icily as he forced himself between de Lacey and Judith. 'I do not want the wedding guests to confuse the identity of the bridegroom.'

De Lacey bestowed on Guyon a snarled smile. 'I doubt they are in any confusion, my lord. Be welcome to the wench while you have the wherewithal.'

'And guard yours if you wish to keep it intact, and mind with whom you drink.' He snapped his fingers at the musicians, who fumbled and then struck up a lively *carole*. Guyon held out his arm to Judith.

She pressed her lips together and shook her head. 'I cannot,' she muttered. 'My lord, I . . . I think I am going to . . .' She clapped her hand to her mouth.

Her face reflected the green of her gown. Taking her arm, Guyon propelled her out of the hall, ignoring salacious remarks and concerned enquiries alike.

Outside it had begun to snow. Judith leaned miserably against the wall of the forebuilding and vomited until her stomach was empty and her muscles ached. The feel of de Lacey's tongue slithering slug-like around her mouth had filled her with shuddering revulsion. She could still taste him, feel his hand digging into her buttocks, forefinger slyly probing, and the hard thrust of his pelvis against her belly and loins. It had been horrible. Tonight she must endure that and worse in her marriage bed.

'Did he hurt you?'

She shook her head, unable to speak.

'There are always men like him,' her new husband said contemptuously. 'It was thrown down to me by way of a challenge. I am sorry that he chose to use you as his gage.'

Judith bit her lip and wished that he would go away. The snow floated down.

'You need not be afraid of me, child,' he said gently. 'I will do you no harm.'

'I am not a child!' she snarled at him, jerking away. Sleeving her eyes, she wondered if he would hit her.

He touched her shoulder. 'I know it is hard for you.'

Judith raised her chin. 'Do you, my lord?' she demanded flatly.

'You have been forced into a match made for the purposes of others and to a partner you had not set eyes upon before today. How should you not be afraid and resentful? I understand more than you think.'

She gave him a surprised look. Whatever else she had expected, it was not this rueful candour. It had not occurred to her that the resentment was mutual, that he might not want her rich lands and the burdens that accompanied them, not least herself.

He applied gentle pressure to her shoulder with his finger-tips until she turned hesitantly to face him.

'I have said you need not fear me for any reason . . . The bedding ceremony, it worries you?'

Judith looked down, wondering where all this was leading. She did not desire a lesson in enlightenment, no matter how kindly meant.

Guyon took her downcast silence for modest assent. 'The first part is something that will have to be borne. The second we can abandon. Rape has never appealed to me.'

'I . . . I know my duty, my lord,' she stammered.

'I have no doubt, but it would be rape all the same and I prefer the pleasure to be mutual. In your own time, *fy Cath fach*.' He lightly brushed a strand of hair from her cheek. She lifted her lids, eyes torn between relief and doubt.

'You truly mean that, my lord?' He had called her a small cat – a kitten.

'I would be a fool if I did not. There is enough on your trencher already without burdening your body so young.'

Judith wiped her eyes again and sniffed. 'I am not always such a wet fish my lord, truly,' she excused. 'It is just that I was so afraid. Before you came, I almost threw myself off the headland . . . And then, when I saw you . . .' she looked at her toes. The snow whispered down. 'I was even more afraid.'

He looked nonplussed. 'I gave you no cause, surely!'

Judith screwed up her face. She could not say that she knew how a flower must feel when it turns towards the sun only to find its blaze too hot to be endured. 'I did not know what you would think of me, sprawled in the mud at your feet.'

'Unique,' he chuckled. 'No girl has ever tried to claim my attention like that before!'

With fortuitous timing, Melyn appeared from one of the

storesheds and walked daintily over to Judith and Guyon,
her ginger tail carried erect. Before Judith could scoop her
up from the settling snow, Melyn came to her own decision
and sprang with practised ease on to Guyon's shoulder,
hooking her claws firmly into tunic and shirt to retain her
grip. Guyon winced.

Judith's eyes widened in dismay.

'You live dangerously, puss,' Guyon addressed the cat, but
he made no move to dislodge her as he turned towards the
steps. 'Your mistress values your life, but I am not necessarily
of the same mind. You may keep your claws to yourself.' He
looked at Judith over his unoccupied shoulder and winked.
'Come,' he coaxed. 'Let us see what our guests think of my
new fur collar.'

Alicia saw Guyon enter the hall with Judith at his side and
breathed a heartfelt sigh of relief. Whatever he had said or
done outside had obviously been the right thing. The
rigidity had left Judith's body and her eyes had lost their
wild expression.

'What in God's name has Guy got on his shoulder?' Miles
laughed.

Alicia gave a cluck of amused annoyance. 'That cat has
no sense of propriety, although how she comes to be there I
don't know. Usually she avoids men. They tend to kick her
or bellow when she gets underfoot.'

'A good sign then,' Miles said.

'Not necessarily. I have heard that women are particularly
susceptible to your son's brand of charm. Melyn is perhaps
just another she-cat bedazzled by her instincts.'

Miles grinned, but shook his head. 'Guy's reputation far
outmatches his deeds. I'm not saying he's an angel, far from
it, but tales become exaggerated in the telling and part of it
when at court is self-defence, the King being what he is.'

Alicia made a gesture of self-irritation. 'Only this morning,
I rebuked Agnes for listening to gossip and here I am no

better. I am a mother hen fussing over her chick.' She sighed and gave him a pensive look. She felt worn out, but knew she couldn't yield to her exhaustion.

'Guyon will treat Judith with all honour,' Miles said. Taking her arm, he led her to a bench set into the thickness of the wall.

'I am sure he will.' Alicia paused, looked at Miles and suddenly poured out her main concern. 'But she is so young and inexperienced. Even if more than half the tales told of your son are untrue, that still leaves a wealth of living in the other part and he is a full twelve years older . . . a man. What do I do if she comes screaming to me on the morrow that she will have no more to do with him? It will break my heart. I remember leaning over the latrine hole, sick with revulsion and praying to die after my own wedding night – after what Maurice visited on me.'

'Then Guy's experience is to the good. He will not force her and, as you have seen, he is capable of charming the birds – or cats – down from the trees.' He frowned at her. 'Have you said anything to Judith to give her a distaste for coupling?'

Alicia drew herself up. 'I am not stupid. More harm than good would come of that, although I fear her attitude has been tainted by her father's behaviour. Slaps and curses and drunken rough handling have not led her to view the state of marriage in a very favourable light. She may find joy; I pray she does, but it is a fickle world.'

'You have little cause to like men, either of you.'

'I do not need your pity, my lord,' Alicia said curtly. Her eyes went to Judith where she stood at Guyon's side. The tawny hair had taken on a fiery glint from the glow of the candles and, with that half-smile on her face and the way her head was tilted, Alicia saw Judith's father for a fleeting instant most clearly. 'No,' she said, a hard smile on her lips. 'I have had my moment of glory and it pays for all that Maurice did to me. My concern is with Judith now. I can see she has a leopard by the tail and must either tame it or become its prey. I know her capable, her blood dictates it so, but she is young for the challenge, perhaps too young.'

Miles gave her a sidelong look and wished that Christen or Emma were here; they would have known instinctively what to say or do, but the former was beyond him for ever and the latter had been summoned to the court by her husband. 'I'll fetch wine,' he muttered, and went to accost a servant.

Alicia drew several deep breaths and controlled herself, aware that Miles was regarding her as he might a skittish horse. If she gained that kind of reputation, she would be shunned or sold off to another marriage and then locked up, conveniently labelled a lackwit like Ralph de Serigny's poor wife.

Miles returned with the wine. She took it from him and looked out over the assembled guests. 'I am not usually so overwrought,' she said ruefully.

'I did not think that you were.'

'Nevertheless you panicked.'

Miles laughed and rubbed the back of his neck. 'A little,' he admitted.

Alicia tasted the wine and set it down. She needed a clear head, for as hostess she was required to mingle among the guests and there was still the bedding ceremony to organise. The humour left her face at the thought and her glance sought out the newly-weds. Melyn had draped herself comfortably around Guyon's neck and half closed her eyes. His hand sat lightly at Judith's waist. She was saying something to him and his head was cocked attentively, although his gaze was elsewhere, sifting and assessing, paring down, focusing on Walter de Lacey and Arnulf of Pembroke even as he answered Judith with a smile. Alicia shivered and offered up a silent prayer. A leopard by the tail indeed.

*   *   *

Judith stood obediently calm, raising and lowering her limbs as Agnes dictated until she stood naked in the bedchamber that had belonged to her parents. The bed had been aired and made up with crisp new linen sheets. Dried herbs to perfume the clothes and promote fertility had been liberally strewn over the bed and the priest had sprinkled holy water everywhere. The droplets on her body made her shiver. Agnes finished combing down Judith's hair and draped a bedrobe around her shoulders.

The female guests crooned and clucked around the bride, turning the room into a hen house. Judith stared at the wall, feeling as numb as the coffer across which her clothes had been draped. Someone giggled a piece of advice in her ear. Someone else of a more practical mind thrust a pot of dead nettle salve into her hand, an ointment used to soothe the female passage after childbed and other rough treatment.

'I won't need this,' she said and looked round in surprise at the laughter. Fear returned to claim her, and uncertainty. She did not know if she could trust Guyon. What if he went back on his word? What if he used her as brutally as her father had been wont to use her mother? Men lied. She couldn't help the whimper that escaped from her throat.

As her mother tried to comfort her the curtain was flurried aside and the room was suddenly full of men, most of them less than sober, their jokes bawdy, crude and raucous. Judith withdrew into the mist again. She did not hear the jests. She did not feel them removing her bedrobe and tugging her to the bed, nor the cup of spiced hippocras that was pressed into her hand to replace the pot of salve. The pink silk of her mother's embrace was a haven but as she tried to cling to it, it was abruptly gone with a sound very much like a sob. Sounds faded to silence. She stared at the wall. The cup of hippocras shook in her hand.

Leaning over, Guyon gently removed the cup. Judith blinked and refocused. Like herself he was naked, his torso lean but powerfully muscled and marked with minor battle scars. Her gaze skimmed over and fled from the curling mat of dark hair at his groin and its nestling occupants. He set the cup down beside the pot of salve, quirking a brow at the latter, then swung on his heel and padded to the curtain. She heard him speak a command in Welsh and then an endearment and her interest sharpened.

'Cadi might hate cats, but she makes an excellent guard dog,' he explained with a grin as he returned to the bed. 'Not that she'll bite anyone, but she'll greet them with such enthusiasm that we'll have warning enough of eavesdroppers.'

Judith smiled wanly. Her eyes flickered again to his crotch. Guyon sought out his indoor cloak, swept it around himself and handed Judith her chemise from an arm's length distance. She took it and struggled clumsily into the garment, feeling all fingers and thumbs.

Guyon paced over to the narrow window and pulled back the hide covering to look out on a slit of whirling white darkness. 'I meant what I said, *Cath fach,*' he murmured without turning round. 'You need not fear me.'

The logs in the hearth crackled and settled. 'I am not afraid,' Judith lied, clutching the bedrobe across her breasts.

'No?' He glanced over his shoulder.

'Well, only a little. I know mama and the others meant well, but they besieged me with their good advice.'

'Such as pots of salve,' he said and, pinning back the hide, turned around. She was watching him anxiously, like a dog desiring desperately to please but afraid of being kicked. Her tawny hair tumbled over the coverlet taking on ruddy highlights from the fire, and was really quite attractive. Her eyes were mingled grey and brown like the muddy water churning beneath the battlements and equally full of turbulence. A veil of honey-gold freckles dappled her face and throat and, for an infinitesimal moment, she reminded Guyon of someone else. The impression, however, was too fleeting to be caught as she moved her head, changing the play of light on the angles of bone.

'My mother is skilled in herb lore,' she said.

'So it would seem,' he said drily. 'Do you have the same competence?'

'She has taught me what she knows.'

He poured himself some wine from the flagon left on the chest and, returning to the bed with it, seated himself on the end and considered her. 'So if I cut my arm with a blade, what would you do?'

'Self-inflicted? I would dose you with valerian to rectify your disordered wits!' she answered with spirit and then, at his silence, sobered and looked down, thinking that she had gone too far.

'No, inflicted by the blade of my wife's tongue!' he chuckled, 'which I hazard is as keen as a sword once unsheathed!'

Judith eyed him warily, but saw nothing in his face to contradict the honesty of his amusement. 'If it was a deep wound,' she said, 'I would sprinkle it with powdered comfrey root to ease the bleeding, then stitch it and bind it with a piece of mouldy bread.'

'Mouldy bread!'

'It is a remedy handed down from Grandma FitzOsbern and it usually works. Deep wounds heal cleanly without going proud or filling with pus. The main danger is from the stiffening sickness. If the wound was only a scratch, I would clean it with water in which pine needles had been steeped and then smear it with honey and bind as necessary.'

Guyon studied her as she spoke so earnestly and fought a battle to keep his amusement from showing on his face. In itself, the information was interesting and her obviously detailed knowledge showed that Alicia was justified in commending her daughter's skill. It was just so incongruous that this slender willow-twig of a girl with all her innocence and uncertainty should hold forth like a grey-haired matron of sedentary years.

The incongruity continued to deepen as he further

explored her knowledge of matters domestic. He learned the best way to salt pork and hang sausages, exactly how much madder was required to dye cloth a certain shade of red and which water to use, the correct ingredients to make a venison ragout, how to buy spices without being cheated. He almost choked on his wine when she began to explain to him the best way to go about honing a sword.

'Your mother taught you that too!'

'Of course not!' she retorted, tone indignant now that she had gained a spark of confidence. 'De Bec showed me last winter when we were snowed in. He showed me how to use a knife too . . . Are you all right my lord?'

Guyon wiped his streaming eyes, speechless between laughter and coughing. 'God's eyes!' he croaked at last. 'When I said that this marriage would kill me, I never thought that you would be the hazard!'

'My lord?'

He waved her away as she leaned towards him, her face full of concern. 'Do you number riding among your many talents too?' he asked after a moment, when he had contained his mirth.

Judith shook her head regretfully. 'Mama prefers to travel by litter and my father said it was a waste of time for a girl to master a saddle when she should be at her distaff. I know a little, but not enough to venture out on more than the most docile rouncy – but I am willing to learn.'

'Good. There are several estates in my honours that are not negotiable by litter.'

'You intend taking me, my lord?'

He lay full length on the bed, plumping up the bolster and pillows to support his back. Judith moved away, but with more wariness than fear. 'My parents always went together and the people have become used to the arrangement. Besides,' he added with a smile, 'there is nothing like the imminent visit of a chatelaine to set a manor humming with industry.'

Judith stirred uneasily. 'My lord, I fear I will not be equal to the burden you lay on me.'

'If you can sharpen a sword and dagger-fight your way out of a corner, you are wholly capable of handling anything else I ask of you!'

She looked doubtful. True, she could manage Ravenstow efficiently. It had been drilled into her without surcease ever since she could remember, but to venture further, tackle people and situations she did not know, that was daunting. It was easy for him to speak. He was a marcher lord with access to the royal ear, his experience far beyond hers.

'Trust me,' he said and kissed her cheek lightly as he might have done to a child. The gesture magically bolstered her flagging resolve and she sat up straight.

Her chemise gaped open at the neck affording Guyon a glimpse of her breasts, scarcely raised from her narrow ribcage. Judith saw the direction of his gaze, and hastily fastened the ties, colour scorching her face.

There was an uncomfortable silence. Guyon bit his tongue to avoid being unkind. He would need to be desperate to take advantage, and he was far from that. Tonight was probably the least amorous he had ever felt when alone with an available young woman.

'Do you have a mistress, my lord?'

'What!' Once more he found himself utterly thrown off balance. 'What kind of question is that!'

'Do not be angry with me, my lord!' She held out a supplicating hand. The fingers were long and elegant and not at all the hands of a child. 'It is only that I do not want to make mistakes. Mama once threw out one of my father's women for insolence and my father beat both of them when he found out.'

Guyon looted disgusted. 'Your father was a fool and a tyrant. I am surprised that with all your knowledge of simples, one of you did not seek to spice his food with monkshood.'

'And have Uncle Robert assure our welfare? How long do you think we would live?'

He grimaced and finished the wine. 'No, *Cath fach*, since you ask, I do not have a mistress. I did have but we parted last month. The borders are no longer safe for her to travel in her father's wool train and, being Welsh, she would not be constrained within one of my keeps.' He shrugged and looked down at his hands, remembering them lost in the black waterfall of Rhosyn's hair. 'A marcher lord and a girl from the Welsh hills. Such matches are fleeting at the most.'

Judith swallowed, wishing that she had not asked the question.

'Even if Rhosyn had agreed to live a Norman life, there are still such things as courtesy and discretion,' he said after a moment. 'It is neither considerate nor far-sighted to have a mistress and a wife beneath the same roof. Grief is bound to come of it.'

Judith nodded sensibly. It never occurred to her that Guyon would be faithful. Her father had been lecherous and indiscriminate in his ruttings and the friends and vassals who dined at his board, the same. Discretion was not a word they knew. Gratitude was an emotion Judith seldom felt.

'You are kind, my lord.'

He shrugged. 'Not necessarily, but I have had no choice but to learn the ways of women. My sister rules her roost and she has three daughters, all of them lively, and Rhosyn has a daughter too, Eluned. One learns to tread with care.'

He spoke with such obvious affection for his womenfolk that another shard of fear broke from the frozen lump at Judith's core and dissolved away. 'Will you tell me about your family, my lord? The marriage was arranged so quickly that I know very little.'

Guyon obliged. It was safer ground than talk of mistresses, or so in his ignorance he thought. Indeed, all went sweetly until he spoke of his half-sister Emma and her marriage to a royal official. From there, the conversation drifted into the murkier waters surrounding life at court.

'De Bec says that the King is a . . .' Judith caught herself just in time from committing another *faux pas*. 'A mincing ferblet' was not a safe remark.

Guyon had not missed her sudden dismayed check. He could well guess the reason. Rufus's tendencies were common guardroom scandal and one did not learn how to sharpen a sword and fight with knife without ingesting gossip.

It was not really amusing, not when the King, who was short, portly and red complexioned, preferred his partners to be tall, honed and possessed of dark good looks. On several occasions the royal groin had stood in imminent danger of damage from Guyon's knee. That had been in the early days before he discovered the amicable company of the ambitious Prince Henry and that the occasional night spent carousing with him amid women of doubtful character, and wine of opposite excellence, was sufficient to dampen Rufus's ardour and send him in pursuit of more co-operative game.

'. . . De Bec says that the King spends more money on clothes in one week than mama would be allowed to spend in an entire year,' Judith amended, regarding him anxiously.

Guyon chuckled. 'Rufus likes to think that he spends more on his wardrobe than other men, but he is outwitted by his own vanity. Last time I was at court my brother-in-law, who was dressing him, fetched him a pair of gilded leather boots. Rufus asked how much they cost, so Richard told him. Rufus was furious and demanded that he go away and find a pair that were worth a full mark of silver, claiming that those he had been offered were fit only for shovelling dung.' His laughter deepened. 'I do not tell a tale like Richard; he had the alehouse in uproar!'

'What happened?'

'Richard went away, found a hideous red pair with green fringing that cost less than the first pair and took them to

Rufus, telling him they were the most expensive boots he could lay hands on.'

'And Rufus swallowed the bait?'

'Well, he paraded round all day in them, thinking himself a peacock and looking like a Southwark pimp and Richard pocketed the profit. God knows if the tale has got back to Rufus yet. I'd hate to be in Richard's boots when it does!'

Judith made a face at his weak pun and then laughed, the sound a delicious feminine tumble of notes, as surprising to Guyon as the fine strength of her hands.

'Tell me about de Bec,' he said when they had ceased laughing at the royal vanity. 'How long has he been here at Ravenstow?'

'He arrived soon after the main keep began to go up, the year before I was born, I think. My father was away fighting the Welsh and it was my mother who employed him.'

'And he has been her man ever since?'

'Whenever it has been possible. If he had defied my father's authority he would have been straight away dismissed and he is too old to travel the roads with his sword for hire.' She gave him a concerned look. 'You do not intend to turn him out, my lord? He is most loyal and he knows this keep better than any man alive . . . saving my uncle Robert of course.'

'No, of course I do not intend turning him out – unless he proves unsatisfactory to my own assessment. Seventeen years of service are not dismissed lightly.' He made a face. 'I am not so sure about your constable however.'

Judith tossed her head. 'FitzWarren's all right. Dry as dust and too full of his own importance by half, but he's loyal and very efficient. He can conjure a feast out of nothing – I've seen him do it, and his accounts are meticulous.'

'I am sure they are. It just troubles me as to where he obtains the wealth to clothe himself in scarlet sarcenet.'

'It was my father's, new last Candlemas. He and FitzWarren were much of a height. Mama gave it to him after the funeral. You can see the account rolls on the morrow if you want . . . Oh, do you read and write?'

'Both. Do you?'

'A little, my lord.' Actually, it was considerably more than a little, gleaned from the household scribe on cold winter days and polished in private moments to an astute skill, but most men preferred their women to dwell in ignorance, or at least in more ignorance than themselves.

'After the hunt tomorrow you can show me – I don't want FitzWarren standing at my shoulder watching me even if he is honest.' He glanced towards the shutters. 'If there is a hunt, with all this snow blowing about.'

Judith stretched and yawned. The wine had made her eyes heavy and it was very late.

Guyon glanced at her. He was not averse to the prospect of sleep himself, for the day had been long and fraught and the morrow seemed set to continue the same. He leaned over and pinched out the night candle and in the darkness removed his cloak. Fabric slid silkily against skin as Judith shed her own garment and burrowed down beneath the covers.

'*Nos da, Cath fach*,' he said compassionately.

'*Nos da, fy gwr*,' she replied in passable Welsh.

Guyon mentally added the skill of language to her numerous talents and wondered how in God's name an oaf like Maurice FitzRoger had managed to beget a child like this. His last thought before sleep claimed him, and not to be remembered in the morning, was that perhaps Maurice had not begotten her at all.

CHAPTER 5

Judith blearily opened her eyes in response to the persistent thrust of a small, cold nose pressing against her cheek and a thunderous vibration in her ear. Melyn uttered a purr of greeting, striped orange tail waving jauntily. Judith groaned and buried her face in the pillow. There was an ache behind her eyes that spoke of an excess of wine and an insufficiency of sleep. The room was lit by weak grey light penetrating the membrane screen across the arrowslit. Given the time of year, it must be well beyond the hour of first mass which meant that there was no time left to turn over and go back to sleep.

Judith pushed Melyn aside, gathered her hair and sat up. The cat stalked across the pillow to the turned back of the other occupant, sniffed the rumpled black hair and patted a playful sheathed paw on the man's face.

'Rhosyn,' Guyon murmured, opened his eyes and received a cold, wet kiss that dispelled all dreaming illusions. 'God's blood!' He jerked upright, seeking his non-existent sword – a man did not come thus armed to his marriage bed. The cat, having achieved her purpose, leaped nimbly to the floor and commenced an inquisitive investigation of Guyon's baggage. Glowering at Melyn's graceful form, he dug his fingers through his hair. Judith decided he was suffering from her own malaise and best left in peace to gather his wits . . . except that this morning there was no time.

She sought her bedrobe and put it on. Guyon pressed his face into his hands. Tactfully, Judith left the bed, scooped up Melyn and went to the arrowslit. 'It is not snowing now, my lord,' she remarked. 'And the clouds are high. The hunt can be held. It will provide fresh meat and it will prevent quarrels from developing. There was a terrible fight last Christmas when Mama's niece got married. The groom's cousin lost three fingers and an ear and the hall was completely wrecked.'

'God forbid,' he said.

'You should watch Walter de Lacey today,' she warned. 'I suppose you know that he offered for me before Papa died and he is one of Uncle Robert's friends.'

'I did not think your uncle Robert had any friends.'

Glancing round, she saw that he had begun to assemble his clothing. His eyes, although bleary were fully open now.

'Do not worry, I know well he is one of the *Cwmni Annwn*. I will be on my guard.'

'The what?'

'Hounds of hell,' he translated, tugging on his shirt. 'The Wild Hunt. Damned souls who hunt in perpetuity and never come to rest. Appropriate, would you not say?'

His flippant tone was a barrier. His father would have recognised it immediately and cut straight beneath it. Judith stood blocked, unsure what to do. She watched him dress, setting aside his wedding finery for a warm, fur-trimmed tunic of green plaid wool, thick hose and tough, calf-hide boots.

Abandoning Judith, Melyn leaped on to the bed and began to wash. Judith's eyes followed the cat and then settled on the linen undersheet. White as the snow that had fallen in the night. Pristine. Unstained. She gave a gasp of panic. Any moment now they were likely to be disturbed by their guests and the first task of the morning would be to display that sheet to all, stained with the sanguine proof of her virginity . . . or lack of it.

Startled, Guyon left off buckling his belt. 'What's the matter?'

'The bed . . . the sheet. They will think that I am impure, or else that you were unable.'

He gaped at her.

'There is no blood!' she almost shrieked at him.

Enlightenment tardily dawned and with it a glint of amusement. 'Ah.' He rubbed the back of his neck. 'I don't make a habit of deflowering virgins.' He shot her a sour grin. 'I wonder which choice they would settle upon.' Pushing Melyn gently to one side, he drew his short eating knife from the sheath at his belt and, forcing up his left sleeve, made a shallow cut upon the inside of his forearm. As the blood welled in a thin, bright line, he smeared it over the centre of the sheet.

'Self-inflicted,' he remarked with wry humour as he stanched the bleeding on his shirt sleeve. 'I beg a cup of valerian to mend my disordered wits, and a pot of honey to smear this slit in my hide.'

Judith handed him the jar of nettle salve. 'This will serve just as well for the nonce.'

His tone was self-mocking. 'And have all the women condemn me for a clumsy oaf and risk your mother's censure? I have a reputation to keep up, you know.'

Judith blushed, for she had not thought of how others would misconstrue the finger marks in the ointment.

'It's a scratch, don't concern yourself.' He rolled down his sleeve and grinned at her. 'I dare say it is not the last wound I'll take defending a lady's honour.'

Before Judith could decide how to reply, Cadi began to bark outside the entrance curtain and a woman cried out in anxiety. On the bed Melyn became a stiff horseshoe of growling orange fur.

Guyon tugged a strand of Judith's hair, gave her an encouraging wink and went to draw aside the curtain and wish good morning to his mother-by-marriage, the small entourage of female wedding guests in her wake and the plump maid bearing a ewer of warm, scented water and a towel.

Cadi greeted her master boisterously. He commanded her down, but although she obeyed him, her forepaws danced on the floor and her whole body quivered with precariously subdued enthusiasm. Alicia returned Guyon's courtesy with a tepid nod and entered the room. At her side an older woman, a second cousin or some such as he remembered, fastidiously brushed white dog hairs from her dark blue gown.

Alicia's gaze went from the bloodied sheet to Judith who was clutching the salve pot in her hand. Judith flashed a dismayed glance at Guyon, caught her under-lip in her teeth and quickly put the salve down, but the damage was already done. Alicia's mouth tightened.

Frightened by the crowd and the dog, Melyn leaped off the bed to make her escape and was immediately spotted by Cadi. Barking excitedly, the hound took a flying lunge at the cat. As Cadi flung past Agnes, the ewer flew out of the maid's hands and a warm deluge christened the two women immediately in front of her. Screams and squawks rent the air, intermingled with a cat's snarls and the hysterical barking of the dog. Melyn streaked for the door and with Cadi hot on her heels, scorched up the thick curtain to cling yowling at the top, claws fiercely dug in.

Guyon seized Cadi's collar, drew breath to speak, saw from the basilisk glares turned his way that it would be a waste of time and beat a hasty retreat with the bitch to the haven of male company breaking their fast in the hall.

Judith, tears of laughter brimming in her eyes, went to coax Melyn down from her precarious refuge.

The breaking of fast was an uncomfortable affair, fortunately not prolonged because the men were eager to be out on the trail of the boar that Ravenstow's chief huntsman assured them lurked in the forests on the western edge.

The bride put in a tardy appearance as the men were preparing to leave, her manner much subdued, the glances she cast at her husband swift and furtive. When the bloodied bridal sheet was displayed by the women, she almost lost control. Her narrow shoulders heaved and she covered her face briefly with her veil while she mastered herself. Alicia's arm went protectively around her daughter's shoulders and she threw Guyon a look boiling with murder.

'Why was Judith weeping, were you clumsy with her?' Miles demanded of his son as they slowed their mounts to enter a patch of bramble-tangled woodland. Ahead of them the dogs could be heard barking as they trailed the rank scent of boar.

Guyon drew himself up. 'Credit me with a little more experience than that. The blasted wench was laughing. I ought to drown that cat of hers!'

Miles raised his brows, justifiably baffled and more than a little worried, remembering Alicia's fear of the previous evening, his own reassurances and then the look on her face this morning. If looks could kill, his son would have been a dead man and himself frozen to stone.

Guyon regaled him with the details of the morning's disaster and Miles's eyebrows disappeared into his hair.

'So there we were,' Guyon said ruefully, 'Judith with the pot of salve in her hand, not daring to look at me lest she laugh, and the sheet all bloody and my mother-in-law itching to geld me . . .' He paused on a breath and turned in the saddle as the constable de Bec rode up to join them on his sturdy dun.

His manner was tangibly cool, his mouth tight within its neat grey bracket of beard. He too had witnessed Judith's struggle for composure in the hall and had been filled with a protective anger, at first so hot that he had almost enquired of Lady Alicia whether she desired to be rid of her new son-by-marriage. Almost, but not quite, for as he had been gulping down his bread and wine and preparing to leave, he could have sworn Judith had smiled at him, a sparkle of mischief in her eyes. Girls distraught to the point of tears did not do such things. Besides, he had reasoned, if Guyon died, the King would only select another man to fill the position, probably of far worse moral fibre and, when he thought about it rationally, the new lord had only had his right and seemed in public gently disposed towards the child.

'Judith tells me that you have been teaching her to hone a blade and use it,' Guyon remarked pleasantly to the constable.

De Bec rubbed his fist over his beard. 'She asked me so I showed her, my lord. Nothing wrong in knowing a bit about weapons, especially here in the marches.'

'No,' Guyon agreed, hiding a smile at de Bec's stony expression and his father's sudden wide stare. 'Did her parents share your opinion?'

'Lord Maurice never knew. Lady Alicia wasn't keen, but she knew when to give a little and when to rein in.'

'So you have been a nursemaid as well as constable,' Guyon needled gently. 'Devotion to duty indeed.'

De Bec glinted him a look. 'Mistress Judith is the daughter I never had the opportunity to settle down and sire. Don't be deceived by what you saw yesterday. She is one of a kind.' He cleared his throat. 'Have a care, my lord, or you may wake up one morning to find yourself gelded.'

'She is maiden still,' Guyon replied. 'I have no taste for rape. The blood on the sheets is my own and freely given.'

De Bec cleared his throat. 'It is your right,' he muttered gruffly into his chest.

'Indeed so,' Guyon answered, 'but one I exercise at my peril. I hazard that if I harmed so much as one hair of her head, I'd not wake up at all the next morning.'

Their eyes locked and held for a moment before the older man dropped his gaze to the smooth muscle of his mount's shoulder, knowing he had gone as far as he dared with a man

he did not know. Guyon turned his head. Distantly the
hounds gave tongue in a new key, a sustained tocsin, belling
deep.

'Boar's up and running,' Miles said, jerking his courser
around.

Guyon swung his own horse.

De Bec spoke abruptly. 'Keep your eyes open, my lord.
You have as many enemies among your guests as you have
allies and when I see men huddling in corners and glimpse
the exchange of silver in the darkness, I know that no good
will come of it.'

Guyon smiled thinly. By disclosing his suspicions when
he could have held silent, de Bec had accepted his new master,
even if the man had yet to realise the fact. 'I was not blind
myself last night, but I thank you for the warning. The sooner
this mockery of a celebration is over, the better.' He set his
heels to his courser's flanks and urged him in pursuit of the
dogs. De Bec wrenched the dun around and followed.

Guyon bent low over his mount's neck to avoid the tangled
branches that whipped at him. Shallow snow flurried beneath
the chestnut's hooves. The frozen air burned Guyon's lungs
as he breathed. His eyes filled and he blinked hard to clear
them, and braced himself as the horse leaped a fallen tree in
their path. Ahead he could hear the loud halloos and
whistlings urging the dogs on and the excited belling of the
dogs themselves.

The hunters pressed further into the depths of the forest.
Thorns snagged their cloaks. Hoofbeats thudded eerily in
the echo chambers created by the vaulted span of huge
beeches, the daylight showing luminous grey through the
fretwork of empty black branches. They galloped across a
clearing, the snow fetlock deep, splashed through a swift-
flowing stream, picked their way delicately round a tumble
of boulders and plunged back into the tangled darkness of
the winter woods. A branch snapped off and snarled in
Guyon's bridle. He plucked it loose, eased the chestnut for

an instant, then guided him hard right down a narrow avenue
of trunks pied silver and black, following the frenzied yelping
of the dogs and the excited shouts of men.

The boar at bay was a sow, a matron of prime years,
weighing almost two hundredweight. She had met and
tussled with man before. A Welsh poacher had lost his life
to her tushes when he came hunting piglets for his pot. The
huntsmen had found his bleaching bones last spring when
they came to mark the game. The sow bore her own scar
from the encounter in a thick ridge of hide along her left
flank where the boar spear had scored sideways and turned
along the bone.

She stood her ground now, backed against an overgrown
jut of rock, raking clods of beech mast from the forest floor.
Her huge head tossed left and right, the vicious tushes threatening to disembowel any dog or human foolish enough to
come within their reach.

Guyon drew rein and dismounted. The senior huntsman
tossed him a boar spear which he caught in mid-air. It was
a stout weapon, broad of blade, with a crossbar set beneath
to prevent the boar from running up the shaft and tearing
the hunter to pieces. A dog ran in to snap at the sow's
powerful black shoulder, was not swift enough to disengage
and was flung howling across the path of the other dogs, a
red slash opening in its side. Cadi barked and darted. She
was a gazehound, bred to course hare, not boar, but her
narrow-loined lightness made her too swift to be caught.

The men began cautiously to close upon the sow, their
spears braced, knives loose in their belts, every muscle taut
to leap, for until the moment she charged no man knew if
he was her intended victim. It was exhilarating, the tension
unbearable. She raked the leaves with her trotters, rolled her
small black eyes and tushed the ground, smearing her bloody
incisors with soil.

'Come on girl, get on with it,' muttered Hugh of Chester
licking his lips. Another man whistled loudly, trying to

attract her attention and waved his spear over his head. Ralph de Serigny wiped his mouth, a pulse beating hard in his neck. Walter de Lacey remained immobile, his only movement a darting glance of challenge at Guyon. Guyon returned the look with glittering eyes and crouched, the spear braced.

The sow paused, quivering; the massive head went down; the damp leaves churned. A squealing snort erupted through her nostrils and she made a sudden powerful lunge from her hams, straight at Guyon. Driven by her charging weight, the levelled spear reamed her chest. Guyon braced the butt against the forest soil, the muscles locking in his forearms and shoulders as he strove to hold her. The barbed tip lodged in bone and the shaft shuddered. Guyon heard the wood creak, felt it begin to give as the sow pressed forward, and knew that there was nothing he could do. The spear snapped. Razored tushes slashed open his chausses and drew a bloody line down his thigh. The sow, red foam frothing her jaws and screaming mad with pain, plunged and spun to gore him, the broken stump of the spear protruding from her breast. Guyon rammed the other half of the boar spear down her throat. A fierce pain burned his arm. Miles's hunting knife found the sow's jugular at the same time that de Bec's spear found her heart.

Silence fell, broken only by the eager yelping of the dogs and the whimpers of the injured one. Blood soaked the trampled soil and snow. The chief huntsman whipped the hounds from the dead pig, his face grey. He darted a look once at de Lacey and Pembroke behind, and then away. They ignored him.

'Are you all right?' Anxiously Hugh of Chester laid hold of Guyon's ripped sleeve to examine the pulsing gash.

Guyon nodded and smiled for the benefit of those who would have been only too pleased to see him seriously injured or killed and wadded his cloak against the wound to stanch the blood.

De Bec crouched beside the broken spear shaft and examined it. Then he rose and stalked to the senior huntsman and thrust the stump beneath his nose. The man shook his head, his complexion pasty. De Bec began to shout. Arnulf of Pembroke moved between the two men. Guyon shouldered him aside.

'Let it go,' he commanded. 'There was a weakness in the wood. It could have happened to any one of us.'

'A weakness in the w—?' de Bec began indignantly, but caught the look in Guyon's eye and realised that the young lord was totally aware of the situation. 'Faugh!' de Bec spat, threw down the shaft and stalked to his horse, muttering under his breath.

'My lord, I did not know, I swear I did not!' stuttered the huntsman, his throat jerking as if a noose was already tightening there.

'Oh stop gibbering, man, and see to the pig!' Guyon snapped and turned away. There was time enough later to grill him for details, and the wilds of these border woods was no place to hold an impromptu court with tempers running high and blood lust rife.

Miles picked up the shaft, saw how it had broken, and narrowed his eyes.

Guyon whistled Cadi to heel, stepped over a rivulet of pig blood and went to mount up.

Judith sat in the solar, distaff in hand, longing to set about her companions with it. They had offered her all manner of advice, both well meaning and malicious and had asked her some very intimate questions that made her realise how innocent she really was. All she could do was blush, her embarrassment scarcely feigned. The women's curiosity was bottomless and avid and at least one of them with connections at court knew things about the groom that were better left unsaid. It did not prevent her from relating the information with grisly relish. Alicia parried frostily. Judith retreated behind downcast lids and wished the gaggle of them out of the keep.

Steps scuffed the stairs outside the chamber and the curtain was thrust aside. The women rose, flustered and twittering at the sight of the bridegroom whose reputation they had just been so salaciously maligning. Guyon regarded them without favour. 'Ladies,' he acknowledged, and looked beyond them to Judith. She hastened to his side. There were thorns and burrs in his cloak and a narrow graze down one cheek. There was also, she noticed, a tear in his chausses.

'My lord?'

He reached his right hand to take hers, an odd move since his left was the nearer. 'I need you to look at a scratch for me.'

'Your leg?' Her eyes dropped to his chausses.

'My arm. I fear you may need your mouldy bread.' He spoke softly, his words not carrying beyond the air that breathed them. All the women saw was his hand possessively on hers, the movement of his lips close to her ear and the sudden dismayed widening of her eyes.

'Go to the bedchamber,' said Judith. 'I will bring whatever is necessary. I take it that you do not want them to know.'

'No.'

Her lips twitched. 'You are begetting a foul reputation, my lord.'

'Not half as foul as their minds.' He cast a jaundiced glance at the women.

'Is there a difficulty, my lord?' Alicia enquired, coming forward, prepared to do battle. She was furious. It was bad enough that he should have used Judith roughly last night as attested by the bridal sheet and her daughter's trembling fight with tears, but that he should stride in here, dishevelled from the hunt and demand her body again, using her like a whore to ease his blood lust, was disgusting.

'I should be grateful for a word if you can free yourself from your duties.'

Alicia stared at him. 'Now, my lord?'

'Come above with Judith, I will explain.'

Her eyes flickered with bewilderment as the ground of expectation was swept from beneath her feet. Guyon bowed formally to her, saluted the others with mockery and left the room, drawing Judith after him. Alicia collected her reeling wits, made her excuses and left them to think what they would.

Judith snipped away the blood-soaked sleeve from his left arm. Guyon clenched his fist on his thigh and winced.

'Boar?' Judith peered at the jagged tear. It was not deep to the bone, but neither was it superficial enough to just bandage and leave. 'It will have to be stitched.'

He gave a resigned shrug. 'At least I am testing your abilities to the full.' He managed a weak grin as she soaked a linen pad in a strong-smelling liquid decocted from pine needles.

'Just pray that they do not fail. It's a nasty wound. What happened?'

Guyon almost hit the rafters as she pressed the pad to his arm and began to clean away the dirt slashed into the wound by the boar's tush.

Alicia walked into the room to hear her daughter breathlessly apologising, a quiver in her voice.

'Get on with it!' Guyon gasped through clenched teeth. 'If you stop every time I flinch, we'll be here all day, and that really will set the fat into the fire!'

Judith bit her lip. Alicia looked down at the raw, still seeping wound. 'You will need the mouldy bread,' she said neutrally.

'I have it, mama.'

Alicia eyed Guyon thoughtfully. 'I have just heard from one of the beaters. He says the boar spear snapped and that you were lucky to escape with your life, let alone a few small scratches.'

'This is more than a small scratch, Mama!' Judith protested, staring round.

'I can see that. I am only repeating what the beater said, and he had it from your uncle's squire.'

'They were both right,' said Guyon.

The women stared at him. After her first startled declaration, Judith's wits quickened. Plainly Guyon was not disclaiming this tear as a mere scratch just to be manly. He wanted the wound kept a secret, or at least reduced to nothing.

'Boar spears do not just snap,' she said. 'My father was always very strict about the state of the hunting equipment, particularly when it came to boar. He had the spears checked regularly.'

'By your senior huntsman?'

Alicia reached for a roll of bandage while Judith threaded a needle. 'Maurice never made any complaints against Rannulf's efficiency,' she said carefully. 'I cannot say that I know him well myself. He came to us from Belleme on Robert's recommendation.'

'Would he be willing to commit murder for the right amount of silver?'

'Truly I do not know, my lord. Anything is possible if my brother-in-law has his hand in the pie.'

'Has someone then offered Rannulf silver to give you a weakened spear?' Judith asked to the point.

'Probably. De Lacey was talking to him most earnestly in the hall last night and he's not the kind to mingle with servants unless it be for a specific purpose. I will know more when I have had an opportunity to question Rannulf and . . . ouch!'

'Hold still, my lord, and it will not hurt as much.'

'I think you are enjoying this,' he grumbled.

Judith wrinkled her nose at him. 'Tush, my lord. So much complaint for such a "little scratch".'

'Insolent wench,' he growled, eyes laughing.

Baffled, Alicia watched the two of them as she prepared the poultice of mouldy bread. Here was no frightened child flickering nervous glances at the world through a haze of tears and, despite Guyon's obvious pain and preoccupation, he was handling Judith with the ease of a man accustomed to women, not one who would deflower her savagely in a fit of unbridled lust.

Guyon clenched his teeth and endured in stoical silence until Judith and Alicia had finished with him. Judith wiped her hands and brought him a cup. He sniffed the contents suspiciously. 'Valerian, yarrow and poppy in wine,' she told him. Guyon tasted, grimaced, put down the cup and began to ease his sleeve over the bandage.

'It will relieve the pain.'

'And dull my wits,' he retorted.

Judith sighed and went to find him a fresh pair of chausses and some salve for his grazed cheek and thigh.

'It seems that I have misjudged you,' Alicia said to him softly.

Guyon finished arranging his sleeve. 'I hope I have enough common sense to realise that rape is not the best way to begin a marriage. I haven't touched her and I won't until she's ready . . .' He stopped and looked round as his father swept aside the curtain and strode into the room.

'Your huntsman's bolted,' he announced starkly. 'Snatched de Lacey's courser from a groom and was out over the draw-bridge before anyone could stop him.'

Guyon's eyes darkened. 'God's teeth!'

'That is not the worst of it. De Lacey's gone after him and with every right to kill. Pembroke's with him and de Serigny. Chester's taken de Bec and some of the garrison and ridden after them.'

Guyon swore again and reached for his swordbelt.

'I'll meet you in the bailey,' Miles said.

Guyon struggled to tighten the belt with his injured left arm. Judith hastened to help him. 'Have a care, my lord,' she said anxiously. 'I fear that Rannulf may not be the only quarry.'

He looked down at her upturned face and with a humourless smile, tugged her braid. 'Forewarned is forearmed, so they say,' he replied. 'I promise you I'll do my best to stay alive.'

Riding hard they caught up with de Bec and Chester a little beyond the village and de Lacey upon the track that led eventually across the border into Wales.

'I thought I had him!' de Lacey growled, 'but the bastard's doubled back on me. Bones of Christ, when I catch him I'll string him up by the balls. Do you know how much that stallion is worth?'

'Nevertheless, I will have him alive,' Guyon said curtly.

'God knows why,' Arnulf de Montgomery snorted. 'First that "weak spear" and now Walter's best courser. The man's guilty, no doubt about it.'

'Yes,' Guyon said, 'and I want to talk to him about why.'

Pembroke flushed. Ralph de Serigny looked puzzled. De Lacey drew his sword and turned his horse, momentarily blocking the road.

Guyon and his father exchanged glances. Without a word Miles dismounted and disappeared into the woods bordering the road. He had spent his boyhood among the Welsh hills and, saving the supernatural, could track anything that trod the earth, including a rat that smelled so bad the stench of it was all pervading.

'Put up your sword,' Guyon said to de Lacey, 'Rannulf will meet his end in justice, not hot blood, when the time comes.'

De Lacey returned his stare for a long moment before breaking the contact. The sword flashed again as he shrugged and began sheathing it. 'This is justice,' he said.

Unease prickled down Guyon's spine. He began reining the chestnut about. Simultaneously there was a warning shout and the whirr of an arrow's flight. He flung himself flat on the courser's neck and the arrow sang over his spine and lodged in a beech sapling on the other side of the road.

De Lacey drew his sword again and spurred his stallion into the forest. De Bec bellowed and kicked the dun after him while Hugh of Chester rammed his own mount into Montgomery's horse, preventing him from pursuit. Among the trees, someone screamed. Guyon hauled on his rein and urged the chestnut in pursuit of de Lacey and de Bec.

He was too late. The huntsman Rannulf sprawled in sightless regard of the bare winter branches. Walter de Lacey, his tunic splashed with blood, stood over him, his eyes blazing and his whole body trembling with the aftermath of violently expended effort and continuing rage. Miles was leaning against a tree, face screwed up with pain and arms clutching his torso.

Ignoring his injured arm, Guyon flung himself down from the courser and hastened to him.

'I'm all right,' Miles said huskily. 'Just winded. I'm not as fast as I was . . . more's the pity.' He flashed a dark look at de Lacey and pushed himself upright.

Guyon glanced him over and, reassured, swung to the other man. 'I said I wanted him alive!' he snapped.

De Lacey bared his teeth. 'Should I have let him knife your father and escape?'

'If you were close enough to kill him, you were close enough to stop him by other means, but then dead men don't talk, do they?'

De Lacey's sword twitched level and the red edge glinted at Guyon, who reached to draw from his own scabbard. Hugh of Chester, moving swiftly for a man so bulky, placed himself between the men, his back to Guyon, his formidable blue glare for de Lacey. 'My lord, you forget yourself,' he said coldly.

'I forget nothing!' de Lacey spat, but lowered his blade to wipe it on the corpse before ramming it back in his scabbard. He turned on his heel to examine the stolen horse, running his hands down its legs to check for signs of lameness.

Guyon compressed his lips and struggled to contain his fury.

De Lacey mounted the black, looped his other mount's reins at the cantle and after a contemptuous look at Guyon, rode over to where Montgomery waited.

Guyon watched de Lacey with narrowed eyes and with conscious effort, slowly unclenched his fingers from the hilt of his sword.

Chester bent down beside the dead man and picked up the bow. 'You were drawn here to be killed, you realise that, lad?'

Guyon grimaced. 'I suspected it back at the keep and knew for certain the moment we caught up with them. A man so anxious to retrieve his horse would hardly lag to wait for us. Did you see the way he blocked my path to make me a sitting target for this poor greedy wretch?'

'It was all arranged last night,' de Bec said, leading over Guyon's courser and Miles's grey. 'I'm sure of it now. If you search his pouch, you'll probably find the cost of his betrayal.'

Chester reached to the purse threaded upon the huntsman's belt, unlatched the buckle and delved. The small silver coins, minted with the head of the Conqueror, gleamed on his broad, fleshy palm in mute evidence of treachery. He trickled them from hand to hand, eyes following their flow and then looked up at Guyon. 'Will you take it further?'

Guyon gingerly remounted. 'How can I? Oh, I know that's proof in your hands, but it's not damning. It could easily be claimed that Rannulf won it at dice. Besides, with this arm I'd be mad to risk challenging de Lacey or Montgomery to a trial by combat which would be the sure outcome of a public accusation. No, let it be. Each of us—' He broke off and looked around as his father, who had reached for his mount's bridle, uttered an involuntary hiss of pain. 'Sir?'

Miles made a face. 'I think I must have a couple of cracked ribs – and my pride is sore wounded. In the old days I'd have taken Rannulf like a wraith from behind and him none the wiser until my dagger was at his throat. The flesh grows old and the mind forgets.' He shook his head regretfully. 'De Lacey has come out of this coil with a halo of glory, hasn't he?'

'Shining with corruption,' Guyon agreed. 'But at least I know where his intentions are nailed.'

CHAPTER 6

Alicia fetched the comfrey salve and a fresh dressing and went to Miles where he sat on the bed. He was stripped to the waist and she had just unbound the yards of swaddling bands from his injured ribs in order to treat again the nasty graze that swept over his left side, legacy of yesterday's scrimmage.

'You and your son between you seem determined to exhaust our supplies,' she remarked to break the silence.

'Entirely unintentional,' he said ruefully and stroked the head of the white bitch sitting at his knee. Now that their guests had departed – some of them in haste following the incidents of yesterday – Guyon and Judith were in a wall chamber examining the account rolls. Since Melyn was tucked around Judith's shoulders, Cadi had been banished.

Alicia flicked him a swift glance. 'Hold this for me.'

He took the ointment and sniffed its green herbal aroma. 'It's only a scrape and a couple of cracked ribs. You need not go to all this trouble.'

'It could have been your life!' She dipped two fingers in the jar and began to smear the salve over his ribs. He tensed at the first, cold touch. Alicia murmured an apology, her colour heightening. He made a disclaimer and slowly relaxed. The light touch of her fingers was soothing. He fondled the dog's ears and gazed at a colourful hanging on the wall.

'What happens now?'

Miles shrugged. 'Nothing. We keep a close watch on all future moves of Walter de Lacey and our new Montgomery kin.'

'You are not going to pursue the matter? Murder and twice attempted murder?'

'And no proof. You cannot make a corpse speak. It is Guyon's word against de Lacey's with an equal number of witnesses to swear for either side.'

'But . . .'

'I like it as little as you, but our hands are tied. If it went to justice, it would end in trial by combat. You've seen Guy's arm. Every marcher lord is bred from the cradle to fight. The odds are too close to load them in de Lacey's favour. Perhaps I'll just stick a knife in his ribs on a dark night. My Welsh blood permits me such lapses of honour.'

'You'll do no such thing!' Alicia's eyes widened in fear as she wiped her fingers on the edge of one of the swaddling bands. 'He is Arnulf's friend and de Belleme's vassal. Robert would impale you on a stake at the Shrewsbury crossroads and leave you there until your flesh rotted off it!'

He flashed her a brief, distorted smile. It was at moments like this that he realised the true depth of his loss. Christen had been one of four within the keep to succumb to the sweating sickness. It came, it claimed haphazardly and it moved on. Even now, two years later, the wounds were unhealed and inadvertently Alicia was laying them open again, reminding him of what he no longer had.

He was drawn from his introspection by the awareness that she was trembling. 'What's the matter? I was jesting, I swear it.'

'You would not jest if you had lived beneath Maurice's code of cruelty,' she said bitterly. 'You have not had to sit at meat with Robert de Belleme and Walter de Lacey when they have come red-handed from torturing some poor wretch out of his life and wonder if you or your daughter might be their next victim!' Abruptly she pressed the end of the swaddling band against his ribs. 'Hold this,' she commanded.

'Alicia . . .'

She reached around him. He felt the warmth emanating from her body and smelled the drifting scent of attar of roses. He let go of the bandage, slipped his arm around her waist and kissed her.

He felt her quiver. She hesitated as if on a brink, and then she made a soft sound in her throat. Her lips parted beneath his and her arms circled his neck, the bandage falling to the floor at their feet.

As impulse gave way to a deeper need, Miles forgot that he had been going to give her detailed reassurances about himself, Guyon and Robert de Belleme, forgot everything but the quickening beat of his blood responding to the feel and taste of her – like fresh water after a long drought.

Alicia gasped and pressed against him as he unwound her braids and threaded his fingers through the thick black twists of her hair. He took his time, kissing her face and nuzzling her throat before claiming her lips again. He ran one hand lightly up her ribcage, found the soft curve of her breast and lightly stroked.

'Tell your maid to keep watch so we are not disturbed,' he muttered hoarsely against her temple.

She heard his words through a haze of sensual delight, and it took a moment for them to reach her brain, but when they did the effect was as immediate as a deluge of frozen water. The thought of Agnes listening outside while she coupled with a man she barely knew, the notion of instructing the woman with her hair all unbound and her lips swollen by kisses, the memory of a time almost seventeen years ago when she had done just that . . . The images coagulated and all the magic was lost. She removed her arms from around his neck, averted her mouth from his kiss and pushed him away.

'I am not a whore,' she said flatly.

'What?' He sought her blindly for a moment and then his eyes opened and slowly refocused. 'Alicia . . .'

'If you want a woman to tumble, there are plenty of serving girls accustomed to Maurice's ways who would relieve your need.' Gathering her hair, she began clumsily to rebraid it.

'I don't want another woman, I want you.' His hand extended in supplication, he took a step towards her. Alicia backed away.

'You would make a whore of me in my own household before my servants and vassals!'

'Of course not! Why do you think I told you to speak to your maid?'

'What would you have me say to her?'

'Anything. That we wish to discuss a private matter concerned with the wedding or dowry.'

'With my hair all unbound?'

Miles turned away with an oath and scraped his fingers through his hair. 'You led me to believe you were willing . . . more than willing.'

Alicia worked frantically at her braids. There was no answer to that, for she had indeed been eager to couple with him until brought abruptly to common sense, and her body still tingled with thwarted desire. 'You took advantage!' she said accusingly, and suddenly her throat was tight and her chest heaving.

'Yes,' he snapped. 'Blame me, because you dare not blame yourself!'

Alicia began to cry, deep-rooted sobs that shook her body from head to toe.

'God's sweet life, don't . . .' Miles started towards her, then hesitated.

Cadi whined and wagged her tail as Guyon swished through the curtain, a roll of parchment in his hand. His grim expression changed on the instant to comical, slack-jawed amazement. 'I'm sorry, I did not realise . . .'

'There is nothing to realise!' Alicia responded through her

tears and, gathering her skirts, pushed blindly past him and out of the room.

Guyon stared at the curtain as it fell, then back at his sire.

'Do not ask me,' Miles groaned, subsiding on to the bed and putting his head in his hands. 'I seem to be making mistakes hand over fist these days. Where's Judith?'

'Ensuring the cooks know what they are about.' He eyed his father, wondering how to interpret what he had just seen. As Alicia had pushed past him he had not missed the detail that the front of her dress was smothered in green unguent.

'Are you any good at binding cracked ribs?' Miles handed him the length of swaddling, his expression giving nothing away. Guyon took the linen from him and set about the task.

'What's this?' Miles took the parchment and squinted at it.

'The amount owed to Robert de Belleme for the stone and craftsmen to build this place.'

'The what?'

'According to that document, de Belleme lent Maurice five hundred marks to purchase men and materials. There are still three hundred owing and, knowing de Belleme, I doubt he will waive the sum as a wedding gift to his niece. In fact, it gives him the excuse he needs to claim Ravenstow if I cannot pay. With Maurice it did not matter – it was a convenient hold on his loyalty – but there is no profit to be had from me except in full payment, and he knows it.'

'Can you raise the silver?'

Guyon finished banding the linen around Miles's chest and secured it. 'Probably, but it will be no small inconvenience and will leave my new vassals considerably poorer than when they swore me homage.'

'Providing of course that they are willing to pay in the first place.'

Guyon smiled thinly. 'They are obliged by custom to render a relief on Judith's marriage and I will have that from them at the oath-taking tomorrow before they leave.'

Miles glanced uneasily at Guyon. He did not doubt his son's ability to wring the relief from his vassals, nor his ability to hold them loyal to their oaths of fealty. What did disturb him was the glint of devilry lurking beneath the surface of Guyon's thoughtful expression. He had seen that look before, usually preceding some act of rash lunacy. 'What are you plotting?' he demanded.

Guyon smiled. 'Naught, as yet. I'm a newly married man, or had you forgotten? Speaking of which, that's a very pretty lover's bruise on your throat.'

Miles heard the warning behind the flippancy. He was being told to mind his own business and for a moment resentment flared. He fixed his son with a hard stare. Guyon's eyes returning the look were a melting luminous brown, edged with silky, thick lashes. They masked a will as flexible and strong as a willow wand. You might bend it, but the moment you let go it sprang back to its original way of growing, usually striking you into the bargain. It was useless to argue.

Miles dropped his regard to the parchment and heaved a sigh. 'As I said, I seem to be making mistakes hand over fist.'

CHAPTER 7

The sky was the colour of a wild harebell, its expanse interrupted by small flocks of cloud herded west into Wales by
a scudding wind. Judith clicked her tongue to the sedate
brown gelding she was riding, and somewhat reluctantly he
increased his pace. The wind gusted at their backs, flapping
her cloak, threatening to snatch off her veil. She released the
reins to feel for the pins holding it in place and secured them
anew. It was a mark of her confidence astride a horse and
her swift ability to learn new skills that she felt sufficiently
safe to trust to balance while she performed her toilet.

Before her as they crossed the heathland between Guyon's
manor of Oxley and his keep at Ledworth, rode his shield-
bearer, Eric Godricson and six serjeants, with a like number
behind. An attack by the Welsh or other hostile factions was
unlikely but it was still better to be safe than sorry, particularly with Guyon absent raising revenues among his other
manors.

Judith stared at the dark trees beyond the heathland
without really seeing them as she evaluated the three months
that had passed since her precipitous marriage.

The oaths of fealty sworn two days after the boar hunt had
mostly been sincere, with the occasional protest at the steep-
ness of the marriage relief. Guyon had dealt smoothly with
complaint. He had the silver tongue of a courtier and a
merchant's shrewd acumen – men smiled and agreed with him,

then scratched their heads and wondered how they had been manoeuvred into parting with their coin when they had intended fiercely to resist.

The incident with de Lacey and Arnulf de Montgomery had sunk out of sight like a rotten log into a quagmire. Guyon's arm had healed cleanly to leave a thin, pink scar. He seldom spoke of the boar hunt although occasionally, in repose, his expression gave her cause to wonder at his thoughts.

Arnulf de Montgomery was busy in south Wales. De Lacey was sitting on his lands like a disgruntled rook on a nest – God alone knew what he was hatching. Ralph de Serigny was ailing with pains in the chest, brought on by a severe winter cold from which he had not properly recovered. The harsh weather of January and February had also prevented Robert de Belleme from travelling further up the march than the seat of his new earldom, where an array of defences was being constructed beneath his critical architect's eye . . . And defences cost money.

Judith was aware of Guyon's concern because he was as tense and alert as a hunting cat. For the most part, he kept his worries to himself, although occasionally he would snap. The first time she had recoiled, awaiting the blow that was certain to follow, but he had lowered his gaze to the tallies over which he was poring, set a pile to one side and continued to work. After a while, when her frightened silence had registered, he had raised his head, apologised briefly and told her to leave him alone. Since then, she had learned to recognise the warning signs and would keep well away, attending to duties elsewhere.

A month ago, when the weather had eased enough to make travelling possible, they had moved down the march to Guyon's main holding of Ledworth, recently inherited from his uncle who had died in battle during the ill-fated summer campaign in north Wales.

The stone and timber castle was imposing, built upon a

high crag to dominate the growing town below and the drovers'
roads leading from these middle borders into the heart of
Wales. It was also, despite its recent construction, musty and
uncomfortable. The former lord had neglected the domestic
side of keep matters when his wife had died. The seneschal's
wife was crippled by stiff hips and the maids had taken advantage of her infirmity to do much as they pleased, which was
very little.

Three weeks of purgative chaos had ensued as Alicia and
Judith set the worst of the rot to rights so that at least the
place was habitable. Alicia in particular had thrown herself
into the exercise, chivvying the maids remorselessly,
addressing them all as sluts and hussies, her tongue as abrasive as the brushes and lye with which she made them scour
the dairy floor and slabs.

Judith was concerned, for the shrewish woman with whom
she shared the bower was not her gentle mother. The bouts
of feverish activity spoke of panic and a deeply troubled
spirit. Once she had come across Alicia choking back tears
in Ledworth's private chapel and begging whispered forgiveness. Forgiveness for what? Her mother was more sinned
against than sinning, her confessions to the priest usually of
oversights and peccadilloes, nothing that would stain the
soul with such guilt.

Judith guided her mount with her knees and frowned, trying
to remember when she had first noticed the change in her
mother's manner. A couple of days after the wedding, it would
have been. Alicia had retired to her chamber with a vicious
headache and stayed there for two days, refusing all ministrations save those of Agnes. She had emerged on the third
day a full hour too late to wish Guyon's father God-speed on
his road home. Miles, as she recalled, had been perturbed at
her absence and by Agnes's firm declaration that her mistress
was still asleep and had left instructions not to be woken.

'Riders to the rear!' cried one of Judith's escort, inter-
rupting her thoughts.

'My lord is expected soon,' Eric said with a frown, 'but it is not the direction from which I would expect him to come.' He rubbed the side of his nose, considering. 'Best play safe,' he decided. 'If it is my lord, he'll take no offence at our caution. If it's another, we owe them no excuses. Are you able to gallop, my lady?'

Judith's heart began to thump but she gave a nonchalant shrug. 'If this nag is, then yes,' she responded and gathered the reins.

The serjeant who had first cried the warning circled away behind them to discover the identity of their pursuers. They quickened their pace. A distance of about nine furlongs separated them from the safety of the keep, but much of that route was uphill.

Judith's gelding started to flag. She dug her heels into his sides and heard him wheeze.

'It's Robert de Belleme and Walter de Lacey!' yelled the serjeant, his voice indistinct but explicit with panic.

'Blood of Christ!' Eric spurred his horse afresh and laid his whip across the rump of Judith's gelding.

The drawbridge was down over the ditch. The wet winter and spring had raised the level of the water table and instead of the noisome sludge that usually offended the nose, there was a glistening moat of sky-blue water. The hooves drummed on the planks. Judith glimpsed the glittering ruffles. She flung a look over her shoulder but the wind whipped her braids across her face and all she could see between the tawny strands were the heaving horses behind her and the solid mailed protection of her escort.

Her mount stumbled as they rode beneath the portcullis and into the ward. She pulled him up, his ribs heaving like bellows, his legs trembling, spent. Without waiting for aid to dismount, she kicked her feet from the stirrups and slipped over his side to the ground.

The last man pounded across the bridge at a hard gallop. The guards on duty began winching the bridge the moment he clattered on to it. The black fangs of the portcullis came down and Ledworth snarled defiance at one of the most powerful men in England and Normandy.

Eric spat and crossed himself as they heard the drawbridge thud flush with the outer wall. 'It is called burning your bridges,' he said grimly. 'Do you go inside, my lady, and join your mother.'

Judith frowned and laid her arm upon Eric's mail-clad sleeve. 'Wait,' she said. 'If we deny him entry we offer him unpardonable insult and he never allows a slight to remain swallowed for long.'

'But mistress—'

'I was prey to be snatched when I was outside the keep, but within he must preserve the civilities. I know why he is here. My lord husband has been expecting him all winter.'

Eric looked unhappily at the chequerboard spars of the portcullis and the security of the solid oak planks beyond. Faintly from without there came a hail. 'My lady, I am reluctant to admit him. Lord Guyon would string me from the highest tree on the demesne if ill should come of this.'

'Let me worry about Lord Guyon,' she replied with more than a spark of bravado. 'How many men does my uncle have with him . . . Thierry?'

The young serjeant cleared his throat. 'About thirty at a rough guess, my lady,' he replied and fiddled with the hilt of his sword, eyes shifting from her to the closed drawbridge.

'Then admit my uncle and his five most senior companions,' she said. 'Eric, take custody of their weapons and put the guards on alert. Have a messenger ride out and find my husband – one of his Welshmen, by preference; they have the stealth to go unseen.'

Eric spread his hands. 'What if the seigneur de Belleme refuses to disgorge his weapons and abandon his men outside?'

'He won't refuse,' she said. 'Delay them awhile until I am fittingly dressed to receive them.'

'But my lady . . .'

She was gone, skirts gathered to reveal her ankles as she ran, her plaits dishevelled and snaking to the movement of her spine. Eric swallowed, muttered a prayer, and set about giving commands, although he was not at all sure he should be obeying Judith.

Alicia gaped in disbelief as her daughter seized a comb and began to mend her hair. She had discarded her riding dress in favour of a tunic of dark gold wool lavishly banded with embroidery in two shades of green.

'You have done what?' Alicia gasped. 'Are you mad? You might as well open the chicken run and let the fox run amok inside!'

'Mama, I am not mad. I would as lief not grant him entry, but on this occasion, at least, he means us no harm.'

'It is not experience of years that has gained you such foresight!' her mother said acidly.

'I thought he and my father were fond kin and allies,' Judith answered in a preoccupied manner, fingers working with nimble haste.

Alicia sighed and looked at Judith with a mingling of sacrifice and exasperation. 'I suppose I will have to go down and face him now that you've been foolish enough to grant him entry.'

A spark of resentment flared in Judith's breast. 'It is my responsibility, Mama,' she said. 'Besides, he does not know me, and it will be easier than you greeting him with hatred when I can plead the ignorance of youth.' She returned to her toilet, clipping the ends of her braids with bronze fillets and smoothing her fresh gown.

Alicia stared at her daughter. The change from child to woman had accelerated rapidly since her marriage to Guyon. There was command in her voice and the same authority that made men perform her father's bidding, or else back off with frightened eyes. She had his way of looking, too. An open, fearless stare, locking will with will.

'Be careful, daughter,' she warned. 'Snakes bite slyly.'

'And cats have claws,' Judith retorted tossing her head, then belied her self-assurance by turning to her mother and hugging her fiercely.

Alicia returned the embrace full measure and prayed that they would emerge unscathed from what was to come.

Robert de Belleme, Earl of Shrewsbury, ranged his gaze over the construction of Ledworth's great hall and considered how to go about the matter of besieging the keep. Not that it was anything personal – yet – merely a constructive and pleasant pastime while he awaited his hostess. One never knew when such ruminations might be called upon to bear fruit.

His eyes were without expression and almost without colour. A beautiful light glass-grey set beneath straight-slashed black brows. He was thirty-eight years old yet looked little more than twenty-five. Some men in their ignorance said he had sold his soul to the devil in exchange for the earthly trinkets of youth and power. Others, more know-ledgeable, said that he had no soul. Robert de Belleme cared not what anyone thought, contemptuous to the core of all his fellow men.

He tapped his whip against his leg and eyed with amuse-ment the scuttling avoidance of the servants, their sidelong stares, and their limbs poised to leap if he should uncoil to strike. It was sweet to see their terror which was, of course, totally justified.

A girl crossed the length of the hall and came towards the fire where he and his companions stood warming themselves. Her pace was confident, her head carried high, her eyes making direct contact with his. It was such a contrast to the twittering fear he so usually encountered that his interest sharpened and he narrowed his eyes to appraise her.

'I am sorry we kept you waiting, my lord, but the times cause us to err on the side of caution,' Judith said in a low, sweet voice as she curtsyed.

He looked down on her bent head, and the long, fine-boned hands clutching the folds of her gown. 'Indeed, it is difficult to judge enemy from friend,' he concurred and cupped her chin to raise her face to his scrutiny.

There was naught of his half-brother to be seen. Her brow, cheekbones and softly curved lips belonged to Alicia, but the narrow nose, cleft chin and strange, grey-agate eyes were completely individual.

'It was a pity your marriage took place while I was occupied elsewhere. I would have liked to attend.' He raised her to her feet. She was as slender as a willow stripling, thin almost, with scarcely a figure to mention. If FitzMiles had got a child on her, it did not yet show. Probably as poor a breeder as her dam, which was a pity. If the lord of Ravenstow were suddenly to die, the widow's lands would revert to the crown. Not that he foresaw any particular problem in wheedling them out of Rufus's pocket and into his own, but should FitzMiles die with a babe in the cradle, the estates of both parents would devolve upon that child's head and the wardship of such wealth would be power indeed to whoever owned it. Still, there were more ways than one to milk a cow.

He circled Judith's wrist in a grip of steel. 'Your husband should be here to take care of a prize so valuable,' he remarked. 'Is he always so careless?'

Behind him, Walter de Lacey sniggered. Judith was reminded of her mother's panic-stricken remark about the fox in the chicken run. Her mouth was dry, but she permitted no fear to show on her face and retained a façade of blank innocence. 'He had business elsewhere, my lord. I would not presume to question him . . . Do you care to wait?' She signalled to a servant who crept forward with a flagon and cups.

Robert de Belleme released her wrist and lounged against a low table. 'Playing at chatelaine,' he mocked as she waved the terrified creature away and served him and his men herself. 'How old are you, my dear?'

'Sixteen, my lord.'

'And sweet as a ripe apple on the tree.' He rotated the cup in his fingers to examine the interlaced English design. 'Tell me, Judith, does your lord hope for an heir before the anniversary of your marriage?'

Heat scorched her face and throat. 'If God wills it, my lord,' she managed, feeling as though the pale eyes had stripped her down to the truth.

'And if your husband can restrain himself from the company of his Welsh paramour and other whores and sluts,' de Lacey sneered.

Judith set the flagon carefully down. Anjou wine was too expensive to be flung, she reminded herself, and it was her best flagon. 'I do not interfere in my lord's private business,' she said stonily. Her look flashed over de Lacey and quickly down before her revulsion betrayed her. 'He treats me well, and I thank God for it.'

De Belleme smiled. 'I have yet to meet a woman who is not taken in by Guyon's charm.'

'Or a man for that matter!' guffawed de Lacey. 'It is not every bride can count the King as her rival for her husband's body!'

'Shall I instruct the cooks to make a feast, or is this just a passing visit to express your joy upon my marriage?' Judith demanded in a choked voice.

De Belleme shrugged. 'I have to be in Shrewsbury tonight. I have a matter of business to discuss with your husband, but it can wait and in the meantime I have brought you a belated wedding gift.' He stood straight and half turned to pat the stitched bundle lying on the table behind him. De Lacey, a sudden sly grin on his face, presented his overlord with a sharp dagger to slit the threads.

Shaking inside like a custard, outwardly composed, Judith watched him apply the blade. The strands parted in staccato hard bursts of sound and the skins spilled out on to the table, glossy, supple, jet black against the coarse woven linen of their coverings.

'Norwegian sables to grace your gowns . . . or your bed,' de Belleme said with an expansive sweep of his hand and presented her with one of the glowing furs.

The sable still possessed its face and feet. Judith swallowed her aversion – the thing looked as though it had been squashed in a siege – and thanked him. It was a costly gift, fit to grace the robes of a queen.

Her uncle dismissed her gratitude. 'It is nothing,' he said, and meant it. In the fullness of time he expected them to return to his keeping and all they had cost him was a little joyful exertion of his sword arm. 'Is your lady mother here with you?'

'Yes, my lord. She pleads your indulgence. She has a megrim.'

'I have that effect on her.' Smiling, he toyed with the blade of the knife still in his hand.

Judith shivered, suddenly thankful that the majority of her uncle's men were outside the keep.

'Are you afraid of me, Judith?' He admired his reflection in the mirror-bright steel.

'Has she cause to be?' Guyon's voice was as soft as his entrance had been.

De Belleme spun round, his expression momentarily one of shocked surprise before he schooled it to neutrality. For all his height and breadth, Guyon FitzMiles moved like a wraith. It was a trait that irritated the Earl, for God alone knew what the man was capable of overhearing in his stealth.

'Christ's blood, no!' He tossed the dagger back to de Lacey. 'But you know how reputations travel.'

Guyon's eyes fell to the sables puddling the board. His nostrils flared and his luminous gaze struck de Belleme's. 'I know the very roads,' he answered and unpinned his cloak. 'I have granted your men a corner of the bailey. They may have their weapons when they leave.'

'Your hospitality dazzles me, nephew,' said de Belleme drily.

Guyon tossed his cloak on to the table and rested one haunch on the wood. 'Yours would blind. I wonder what you would have done had you caught up with my wife before the drawbridge?'

'Nothing improper, I assure you.'

'By whose code?'

'My uncle has brought us a wedding gift of these fine sables,' Judith said quickly. She could feel Guyon's hostility and knew they could not afford a rift with the Earl of Shrewsbury. There was a moment's silence. The balance teetered. Judith held her husband's gaze and silently pleaded. Joining him, she grasped his right arm possessively as a bride might do, but actually to prevent him drawing his sword. His muscles were like iron and rigid with the effort of control, and his eyes were ablaze. Frantically she stood on tiptoe to kiss his tight lips, trying to break the terrible concentration.

Through a fog of rage Guyon became aware of her desperation and the spark of sanity that had prevented him from leaping at de Belleme's throat kindled to a steadier flame. He dropped his focus to her upturned face and filled his vision with her shining honesty instead of the contemptuous challenge of his uncle-by-marriage. 'I would set your worth even higher than sables, *Cath fach*,' he said with a strained smile as he slipped his arm around her waist and kissed her cheek, knowing that she had drawn him away from the edge of a very dangerous precipice.

'As it happens,' said de Belleme pleasantly, 'I do have other fish to fry, nothing too important. Indeed I am embarrassed to make mention of it.'

Guyon doubted the lord of Shrewsbury had ever been embarrassed in his life. He lifted a brow and looked enquiringly blank, pretending not to see de Lacey's lounging smirk. Beside him Judith had clenched her jaw and he knew that she realised what was coming next.

'*Cariad*, go and bestow your wedding gift safely and organise some fitting repast for our guests,' he said.

Judith gave him a keen look. He extricated himself from her grip and ran one finger lightly down her freckled nose. 'If you please.' It was a charming, light dismissal, but a dismissal nevertheless. His gaze flickered to the sables and then quickly away.

Judith curtsied – she could do little else – and excused herself.

'You were saying?' Guyon folded his arms.

'It is a small matter of silver owed to me by my late brother Maurice for the building of Ravenstow . . .' said the Earl of Shrewsbury with a smile

Judith smoothed one of the sables beneath her palm, staring down at the glowing fur without really seeing her action or feeling the luxury beneath her caress.

The midday meal had been more elaborate than their customary bread, cheese and watered wine, the flustered cook having organised additions of roasted pigeons, mutton in pastry coffins, herrings seethed in milk and sprinkled with almonds and small honey cakes, crusty with chopped nuts and dried fruit.

Judith did not know if it was fare fit for an earl, but it was the best she could provide at such short notice. Certainly her uncle had not complained. Indeed, he had settled to the meal with a hearty appetite which was more than could be said for her husband, who had attacked the wine as voraciously as others attacked the food, seeming set to drink himself beneath the table in as short a time as possible. Barely a morsel of food had passed his lips and every time his cup neared the dregs he would signal the lad serving to replenish it to the brim. He had begun to slur his words and his voice had grown over-loud.

Robert de Belleme had watched Guyon's disintegration with a contemptuous eye and a scornful smile. No more than a cupful of wine had flowed over his own tongue, which remained mellifluous and precise.

Judith's tentative plea to her husband had met with a snarl to mind her distaff, and a half-raised fist. At this juncture she had begged leave to retire, having no desire to bear the humiliation of a public beating. She could remember only too well how it had gone with her father in the past. He would drink. Someone would make a remark that he misliked and the blows would fall, cutting if he happened to be wearing rings.

Steeped in misery, she sat waiting now for she knew not what and wondered what had happened to drive Guyon over the brink like this. Her uncle was owed a large sum of money. Guyon had been thoughtful about that for some time, deeply thoughtful and busy, but certainly not depressed. She knew he enjoyed the taste of good wine, but in three months of marriage she had yet to see him merry, let alone drunk. It was beyond her to fathom the reason for such deviation and her fear was all the more potent for her lack of understanding.

There was a sound outside the door. Melyn, coiled in a warm ball upon the bed, popped her head erect and uttered a soft greeting miaow. Judith dropped the sables and hastened to the door, unbarring it to admit Eric and one of the serjeants bearing Guyon's upright weight between them. Stinking of hippocras, he swayed on the threshold.

'Traitors!' he bellowed for all and sundry to hear, taking a wild swipe at Eric and almost overbalancing as he staggered into the room. 'I'm sober 'nough to see my guests on the road . . . Lemme go!'

He continued to utter loud protests as they manhandled him to the bed. Judith watched him, her fingers at her throat, her whole body tensed to avoid him if need be.

Eric glanced at her and gave her of all things a wink and a smile. 'Don't you worry, mistress, he'll sober up quicker than you think,' he said comfortingly and, his grinning companion in tow, left her alone with her dread.

Melyn leaped on to Guyon's wine-drenched chest and kneaded the spoiled cloth with splayed claws. Guyon scooped her up and, depositing her on the coverlet, sat up.

'God help me,' he grimaced, pulling the garment over his head. 'I stink like the morning after in a Rouen brothel!' He slung the richly embroidered wool across the room and followed it with his shirt.

Still standing near the door, Judith's eyes were round with astonishment. 'You're not drunk!' she said.

'Sober as a stone, *Cath fach.*' Going purposefully to his clothing chest he rummaged among the contents. Sunlight rayed obliquely through the shutters and gilded his skin. It picked out the scar from the boar hunt on his arm and the marks of stitches neatly made.

'But why?' she enquired in bewilderment. 'Why did you want us all to believe that you were sodden drunk?'

'You did not have to pretend your responses and they were more convincing than you could have feigned. Your uncle as well as most of the keep thinks that I have drowned in hippocras my despair at losing so much silver into his wanton care.'

'But I saw how much you swallowed. Your back teeth must be awash!'

Guyon flashed her a grin. 'A gut full of red-dyed water, and just enough hippocras to reek my clothes and skin. It was Eric's lad serving at table, did you notice?' He took a shirt and an overtunic of coarse, patchily dyed linen, devoid of embellishment, and threw them on the bed.

'But in God's name why? Why would you want my uncle to believe that you are a swiller?' Judith moved away from the door and picked up the wine-soaked tunic and shirt to put them on the chest beside the sables.

He glanced at her from beneath his brows. 'He has my silver. I am a distraught weak reed and, as far as anyone knows, saving a precious few, I shall wallow abed in a drunken stupor for the next full day at least.'

'What are you planning?' Judith began to feel frightened again. 'And why are you dressing yourself in those disgusting rags?'

'An exercise in stealth, *Cath fach*. The less you know, the better.'

Her eyes flashed. 'I am not stupid!'

'No,' he agreed. 'You are too clever by half. And do not scowl at me like that. I mean it as a compliment. It is very hard to deceive you on any matter for long.'

'Such as your Welsh paramour and other sluts and whores!' she snapped and then pressed her hands to her mouth, wondering in shock what on earth had made her quote de Lacey at him like an accusation.

His gaze held hers steadily. 'If I have been over the border of late, it is for reasons other than the pursuit of pleasure.'

Judith dropped her lids and felt heat scorch her face. She would not apologise. She picked up one of the sables to rub the cool pelt against her hot cheek. 'Why were you so angry when you first arrived?' she asked after a moment, as association brought sudden remembrance.

Guyon latched the buckle of his belt and for a moment frowned as though he was not going to answer. But then he shrugged and spoke. 'I passed a pack train two days ago, heading for Shrewsbury. The merchant, Huw ap Sior, was a likeable man. I've traded with him before now, my father too. If he had a fault, it was that he could talk the hind leg off a donkey and he was heedless of danger where he thought there might be gain . . . They found his body in a ditch this morning, choked by the binding of his own chausses and his limbs carved off, and of course not a sign of his goods. I believe the sheriff is blaming Huw's servant for the deed because the lad has vanished into thin air and, being in de Belleme's pay, he's not going to look further than the easiest scapegoat.' He drew a hard breath to steady his rising revulsion and anger.

'Huw knew that there were men of high import in

Shrewsbury at the moment. He was taking his pack of silks and Norwegian sables there to sell . . . only the poor idiot never arrived . . . Look at the canvas in which your bride-gift is wrapped. Do you think those brown stains are merely blotches of mud from the road?'

Judith swallowed and flicked her gaze to the pack and its tell-tale pied markings, 'No,' she whispered hoarsely. 'It is not true.'

He turned from her to pull on a rough sheepskin jerkin and brown woollen hood. 'Then look the other way,' he said. 'Tell yourself that your husband has an over-active imagination.'

Shuddering, Judith dropped the sable back among its companions and pressed the back of her wrist to her mouth, feeling sick. Tight-lipped, Guyon continued to make his preparations. After a moment, he straightened, alerted by a faint sound from behind. Her breath was shaking from her throat in small, effortful gasps as she fought to stifle her sobs. It was on his lips to snarl at her that grief came cheaply, but he remembered in time, reminded by her white, pinched face, that for all her cleverness she was still a child.

He swore beneath his breath and went to take her in his arms. She gripped his jerkin, struggling for control. 'My mother was right,' she gulped with loathing. 'Snakes do bite slyly.'

'Unless you pin them behind the neck and draw their fangs.'

Her head jerked up and she looked at him through her wet lashes. 'My lord, I do not know what is in your mind save that it be more than dangerous. In God's name, have a care to yourself!'

'You worry too much.' He kissed her cheek. She moved her head. For an instant their lips met, hers soft and unprac-tised; his gentle without possession or demand, and he was the first to disengage from the embrace. 'As far as everyone else in this keep is concerned, I am confined here in a drunken stupor. I trust you to keep up the pretence for a day at least.'

'When will you be back, my lord?'

'By moonlight I hope.' He drew up his hood. His face disappeared into brown shadow. 'God be with you, *Cath fach.*' He tugged her braid and slipped silently from the room. She stared at the door he had just closed, then went to drop the bar. Sitting down beside the bundle of sables, she set her mind upon what to do with this gift culled from murder.

To keep the sables was impossible. She could scarcely bear to look at them. The sight of the bloodstains upon the bindings curdled her stomach. Burn them? That was waste upon waste. Throw them back in her uncle's face? No. Guyon would have done that had it been feasible. Give them away? She steepled her fingers under her chin, deep in thought.

CHAPTER 8

The Earl of Shrewsbury lounged in his saddle, his legs loosely straight, heels crowned by gilded prick spurs, supple boots reaching to mid-calf and laced by tasselled green thongs. His sword rode lightly in its scabbard, his left hand relaxed upon the curved pommel.

Behind him, sweet on the ear, the pony bells jingled, the sturdy bays laden with the Earl's travelling accoutrements. Flanked by two guards, another pony bore a load of scarred brown leather sacks. Three hundred marks in sweet silver pennies. Guyon FitzMiles had been sufficiently wise to pay up. The only element that had surprised de Belleme was the bridegroom's ability to pay in full, although he suspected the effort had nigh on beggared the young man.

Magnanimous in victory, he had offered to take two hundred marks now and leave the balance until the Michaelmas rents had been paid, and for his pains had been told on a swallowed snarl where to put his largesse. A solicitous suggestion that FitzMiles could sell his mother-in-law to cut his losses had for a moment held them on the edge of an exciting precipice. He had felt his sword arm tingling with anticipation and de Lacey had begun to reach for his dagger, but FitzMiles, holding to the control he was later to lose in wine, had stalked from the room, crashing his fist into the door as he went.

De Belleme gave a superior smile, remembering the young man swilling his wine like a street drunkard, the loose-limbed grace growing clumsy, the cultured accent slurring, the eyes becoming slack-lidded and glazed. He had half expected it to happen. On more than one occasion at court, FitzMiles had roistered away the night with Prince Henry, drinking himself beneath the table, a woman on each arm. The lack of moral fibre was of no consequence to the Earl; it was the lack of self-discipline that gave him cause for scorn.

The bleating of sheep roused him from contemplation of a ripe future to the more immediate contemplation of the road before his eyes which was blocked by an enormous cloud of baaing, smelly sheep.

His horse lashed out as de Lacey's mount, brought up short, collided with its rump. De Lacey swore and wrenched on his bridle.

'God's eyes!' snarled de Belleme. 'Get these stinking, tick-ridden beasts out of my way!'

His words were smothered in a chorus of mournful bleating as the sheep advanced and closed around the troop. His destrier began to plunge in earnest. The pack ponies kicked. Cursing, his men attempted to control them and their own mounts and draw their weapons at the same time.

Walter de Lacey swung his sword at a sheep, but stopped in mid-motion, his wrist arrested in response to the nocked arrow aimed at his breast. A range of ten yards made death a certainty.

There were men among the sheep, rising to their feet, their tunics wrong side out affording them a sheepskin camouflage, unseen until it was too late. Welshmen, dark and slender, with short swords at their hips and the deadly longbows in their hands.

'Yr cledd,' said the nearest Welshman gruffly, jerking his nocked bow at de Lacey's sword. The Baron's mouth tightened. For a moment the blade gleamed in his hand as he turned it, contemplating folly and then, as the Welshman adjusted his line of sight, he spat and threw it down among the sheep.

'You'll die for this,' he said thickly.

Without reply, the Welshman gestured him and his over-lord down from their horses.

Robert de Belleme was not afraid. It was an emotion he seldom experienced even in the teeth of death, but his fury at being trapped and helpless to extract himself, surrounded as he was by bumping, bleating sheep, raged so hot that he was incandescent. His hands were lashed behind his back. A black hood was forced down over his head and tied there, clogging his sight. Barbarian Welsh jostled his muffled ears. De Lacey's invective was cut off by the sound of a dull blow and then retching. Someone laughed. Rage stuck in de Belleme's gullet and almost choked him. Small coarse hairs from the cloth hood clung to his lips and tongue. He writhed and struggled and felt the bonds saw into his wrists.

Guyon lowered the bow, his eyes sparkling with laughter. His throat quivered as he controlled the impulse to shout his triumph aloud. Commands flickered in Welsh. Fresh pack ponies were brought and the loads transferred. Sheep, destriers and the now unladen ponies began their escorted journey deep into the wilds of Powys where, except by Welshmen, they would not soon be found.

Guyon murmured something to one of his companions, his voice warm with triumph as he studied the two men, bound like caterpillars in a web. In a single swift motion, he straddled the mount that Eric had brought him.

The words were lost upon his victims, but not the rich delight with which they were spoken and, had de Belleme not seen with his own eyes Guyon FitzMiles sliding beneath the trestle, overcome with drink and had not his assailant been so obviously Welsh, he would have known immediately at whose feet to lay the blame.

As it was, he lay in the road, struggling within his cocoon, hearing the curses of men similarly encapsulated fighting to win free. Horses circled and plunged around him. The Welsh tossed banter cheerfully hither and yon in dips and swoops of singsong language, haranguing each other and their victims alike and then, like autumn swallows, they were gone. A hoof caught de Belleme's side as the last horse departed and involuntarily he arched at the sudden buffet of pain.

Silence descended and it began to rain.

CHAPTER 9

Rhosyn listened to the rain as an eddy of wind drove it against the hafod shutters. One of several spring squalls. In between, the stars would peek through the scudding clouds in pinprick points of diamond light.

The fire, banked for the night, gave off a low, comforting glow, glints of red jewel warmth winking beneath the aromatic logs of the diseased pear tree that Twm had cut down last year.

Rhys and Eluned were newly abed. She could hear their conspiratorial whispers behind the curtains. Her son had turned eleven last week and thought himself very grown up. At fourteen, in Wales, he could claim his manhood. She would be thirty then, Eluned ten and this new babe, if it survived the early months, would be rising from helpless infancy into sturdy childhood.

She picked up her sewing, took a few half-hearted stitches and, with an irritated cluck, put it down again. The rush-light was too poor for this kind of delicate work and her mind was restless tonight, fluttering purposelessly like a moth at a candle flame. The baby turned in her womb, busily flexing new, delicate limbs. She felt the thrust and flicker with a protective hand. With almost four months of carrying left before the birth, she had not yet burgeoned into ungainly discomfort. Her ripening body was still a pleasure and she was lost in the wonder of it.

The old dog sitting with its moist nose at her knee suddenly growled deep in its chest and stiffened. Rhosyn stood up to face the cottage door, one hand reaching for the rake that Twm had earlier been using on the floor rushes.

It was Twm's voice she heard outside now, gruff and questioning. A horse snorted. A man replied with amusement, the tone deeper than her servant's and edged with a foreign inflection to the Welsh she would have known anywhere. She bade the dog lie and, dropping the rake, flew to the door and unbarred it to the night.

'Guyon!' she cried and flung herself into his arms. Twm arched a knowing resigned brow and, completely ignored, dismissed himself to his bed. Rhosyn withdrew from the hard clasp of Guyon's arms and tugged him inside the hafod. Gelert whined and thumped his brindle tail on the rushes. She reset the bar and came once more into the circle of his arms.

'You smell of sheep,' she said against his mouth.

He nuzzled her cheek with a stubbly jaw. 'What kind of greeting is that for a man who has ridden hard for your sake?'

'Not for your own?' Rhosyn queried pertly, her eyes laughing, as green and gold as moss agates. 'You are overblown with vanity indeed.'

Her dark hair spilled down over his hands in a fine, cool cloak. Her breasts were ripe and warm against his chest. Within her belly the child kicked.

'How goes it with you?' he asked, his face suddenly all tenderness and concern.

Rhosyn gave a little shrug. 'I'm not sick any more, indeed, I've an appetite like a bacon pig. When I start to waddle like one, I will curse you and a certain hot, harvest night . . . Have you come alo—' She stopped. Guyon lifted his head from contemplation of her glowing skin and brilliant eyes just in time to be almost bowled over by the two children.

They were like puppies, gambolling and clamouring; Rhys's new-found manhood had flown out of the window to leave only the excited child. Guyon bore with it very well, riding out the first storm with wry, rueful humour, curbed behind a half-turned head as their mother calmed them with dire threats and a voice suddenly grown as sharp as the flick of a lash.

Subdued, but not defeated, Eluned went to fetch Guyon something to drink and Rhys sat down before the banked fire, hugging his knees, a dark scowl on his face.

'How long will you stay?' he demanded, slanting Guyon a hard glance.

'Rhys!' his mother reprimanded more sharply than she had intended. It was a question she herself wanted to ask but dared not.

Guyon waved aside her anger with a grin. 'I am accustomed to it by now. If he was not so obviously a boy, I would think it was my wife sitting at my feet. She has that way with her too.'

There was a strained silence. Rhys's question was just the crust of the loaf, one of a thousand questions Rhosyn longed to ask him, but would not do so in the presence of the children and for the sake of her own pride.

'A few hours only, Rhys,' Guyon answered the boy. 'I have dared to pull the devil's tail and I must be in my own bed before dawn lest he scorch me with his pitchfork.' He smiled at Eluned and took the mead she offered him. It was strong and sweet and as honey-golden as the fragrant harvest evening on which the unborn child had been conceived.

Rhys looked blank for a moment and then his quick mind took in the implications of the rough Welsh garb and coupled it with his knowledge that Guyon had skills most Normans did not. Something clandestine had been afoot and Lord Guyon did not intend the blame to lie lying at his door. Eluned, younger and impressionable when it came to tales, took his words at face value and regarded him wide-eyed.

'And precisely where is your own bed?' Rhosyn asked, setting a platter of bread and cheese before him and thinking with a hint of bitterness that they were like courtiers, fêting him with adulation.

Guyon gave her one of his quicksilver glances. 'Ledworth,' he answered and did not elaborate. Instead, he tossed something to Rhys.

The boy caught the item deftly and transferred it to his lap. It was a leather sheath, lined with raw wool to hold in place the knife it contained and keep it naturally oiled. The knife itself was almost a weapon. Eight inches long with a blade gleaming as bright as fish scales against the blue herringbone pattern that fanned from its centre. The hilt was carved from a narwhal tooth.

'I know it is a month after Candlemas, but I had not forgotten your year day,' Guyon said as Rhys examined the knife with speechless delight.

Rhosyn eyed the gift with mixed feelings. Childhood was almost behind the boy and the knife was a symbol of the man too soon to emerge. 'You should not,' she said to Guyon with a frown.

'Grant us both the indulgence,' he answered, his voice light, but his gaze eloquent as he drew Eluned into the circle of his arms. 'And I had not forgotten that it is your own year day come Easter and, since I am unlikely to be here, I have brought your gift early. Guess which hand.'

Delighted, Eluned played the game with him and he teased her, knuckles clenched, his sleight of hand eluding her. At length she pounced on him, giggling and he conceded defeat, begging abjectly for mercy and presenting her with a small cloth pouch containing a string of amber beads. Eluned flung her arms around Guyon's neck and delivered him a smacking kiss. 'The surest way to a woman's heart,' he chuckled as he fastened the beads around Eluned's slender throat.

'You buy us all,' Rhosyn agreed and, blinking, turned away to mend the fire. Guyon watched her over the child's tumbled black hair.

'That is not true, *cariad*,' he said softly. 'I have never had the price of you and I doubt I ever will.'

Rhosyn savagely poked the logs. 'You have always had the pretty words to cozen what you cannot buy!' she snapped. 'Rhys, Eluned, it is long past time you were asleep. Go on, get to your beds now!'

'But Mam . . . !'

Her eyes kindled with wrath. 'Do as you are told!'

Guyon lifted his brow at her tone, shot her a speculative look and squeezed his warm, rebellious armful. 'Obey your mother, *anwylyd*,' he said gently. 'It is time she and I had a private word. Go now.'

Eluned pouted, unconvinced. Rhys stood up, the knife in his hand, his expression a mingling of childhood and maturity as selfishness warred with duty. After a hesitation, the latter dominated. He thanked Guyon most properly for the knife, kissed his mother on the cheek and crossed the hall to withdraw behind the bed curtain.

'It's not fair!' Eluned complained.

'Life never is, my love,' said Rhosyn bending to hug her daughter. 'You'll discover it time and again as you grow older. Now say good-night and be off with you.'

The child sighed heavily but did as she was bid. Her grip around Guyon's neck almost throttled him. 'I wish you could stay,' she said, her lips warm on his cheek.

'So do I, *anwylyd*,' Guyon replied and meant it.

When they were alone, Rhosyn again mended the fire even though it was unnecessary. The silence stretched out and the old dog whined. When she could bear it no longer, she threw down the poker and spun round to face him, her words almost a cry. 'Why have you come?'

'I thought you would be pleased to see me.'

Rhosyn drew breath to snap that he thought wrong, but changed her mind before the words were spoken. 'I am too pleased. You disrupt our lives. You come with your gifts and your ensorcelments, you beguile us into adoration and then you leave. I cannot bear it!'

'You have it in your power to change that,' he answered

gently. 'You are welcome to make your home at one of my manors.'

'A pretty caged bird to sing at your pleasure!' she flung, turning back to the fire.

'I did not come here to quarrel, *cariad*. Nor do I intend to leave upon one. We know each other better than that. If I have rubbed salt into a wound then I am sorry. You never gave me cause to believe that it ran any deeper than a mutual pleasuring.'

Rhosyn bit her lip and dug her nails into her palms, striving for the control to smile lightly and say that yes, he was right, it had not run any deeper. She felt his hand lightly on her shoulder turning her to face him. 'I needed to know how you fared.'

'Well, now you do,' Rhosyn would have drawn away except that he held her fast and kissed her averted temple, the corner of her eye, her cheek and her mouth, refusing to release her and, indeed, her struggles were only half-hearted and soon ceased.

'I am foolish, Guy,' she murmured, setting her arms around his neck. 'I see the moon in a pool and I am disappointed when my hand despoils the illusion instead of grasping the reality. Be welcome for whatever time you choose to stay.'

Their embrace deepened, warm, sweet and poignant, desire sweeping but hard-held by the presence of the children a thin curtain away and, in Guyon, by a reluctance to cause Rhosyn a deeper wound than she had already suffered. He broke away first, his breathing ragged, and prowled to sit at the fire. His body protested. It had been a long time since he had lain with a woman and his hunger was keen. Keen, but not desperate. Whatever his detractors said, sexual liaisons were not to Guyon an immediate necessity of life. Given the leisure, the right circumstances and a willing partner, he enjoyed indulging his senses. But as now he possessed only the latter, he drew several deep, slow breaths and made his mind busy with other thoughts.

'Where is your father?'

Rhosyn sat down beside him, just out of touching distance and picked up her distaff. Her fingers were trembling. She concentrated on the raw wool until the hot weakness left her limbs. 'Gone to Bristol. We expect him home tomorrow or the day after. I worry about him, Guy. He is not well. He gets pains in his chest and Rhys is too young to take more than an apprentice's responsibility.'

Guyon turned his head, eyes sharpening. 'The pack routes are no place for a woman,' he warned.

She did not answer, but the line of her mouth grew mulish and she gave all her attention diligently to the distaff.

'Rhosyn, so help me, if I hear you have stirred from your hearth to go tramping about the borders in a drover's cart, I will carry you off to Oxley myself and lock you up like a caged bird, in truth!'

'You have not the right!'

'I have every right. You carry my child. I will not see you dead in a ditch like Huw ap Sior!'

'I won't . . . What did you say?' Her fingers ceased their nimble twirling. Her eyes opened upon him, wide with shock. 'Huw, dead?'

'At the hand of Robert de Belleme and his gutter sweepings. Huw's pack-load of sables was brought to myself and Judith as a blood-smirched wedding gift.' Sparing her nothing, he gave her the details.

'He was my father's best friend,' she whispered jerkily when he had done. 'They were boys together . . . Oh sweet Virgin!'

Their bodies closed again of necessity as Guyon grabbed hold of her, afraid that she was going to faint. She leaned her cheek against his jerkin, shivering, sick to the soul with grief and fear and shock.

'Promise me, *cariad*,' he murmured, stroking her hair.

She made a little movement against his chest. Her fingers gripped his arms.

'Promise me.'

'What good is an oath given under duress?' Rhosyn replied shakily. 'I could give you my word and it would be worthless.' She uttered a desolate laugh. 'Welsh oaths always are.'

'Rhosyn . . .'

She pushed gently away from him and, having wiped her eyes, poured herself a cup of mead. 'I might be fickle, Guy, but I am not about to step deliberately within de Belleme's ring of fire. I will swear you this much honestly: that I will not stir from here until after the child is born and only then by necessity. And I will send to you for an escort.'

Guyon studied her through half-closed eyes but did not seek to persuade her further. He had her concessions in his grasp and was not going to jeopardise them with bitterness and anger.

'Very well, *cariad*,' he said quietly. 'I do not suppose I would care so much were you not so cursedly independent.' He sat down beside the fire and picked up the mead that Eluned had poured for him earlier.

Rhosyn stared at him in the firelight. With his Welsh clothing and dark complexion he might have been of her own race and class – no barrier but the fire's glow between them. It was a bitter-sweet illusion. Merchant's daughter and marcher lord, already married for the sake of convenience and dynasty. He looked tired, she thought. The shadows beneath his eyes were not all the result of the dull light.

'Does your wife know your whereabouts, Guy?'

He took a swallow of mead, swirled its golden surface and looked at her with rueful amusement. 'She may have a suspicion,' he admitted. 'For sure, if I am not over the drawbridge come dawn, I'll have to deal with a hellcat . . . and not for the reason I can see on your face.' The amusement became a wry chuckle. He drank the remainder of the mead and did not offer to elucidate.

Rhosyn swallowed the temptation to ask. If Guyon was on this side of the border after dark, dressed in native garments and murmuring about scorching the devil's tail, then it was best to know nothing. 'What is she like?'

'I think she would surprise you.' He put down the cup to fondle the cold thrust of Gelert's nose at his thigh. 'God knows, she certainly surprised me . . . and continues to do so.'

'Is she pretty?'

A curious, casually spoken woman's question with tension lurking beneath the surface.

'Not as you are pretty, *cariad*, but striking in her way, I suppose, or she will be when she grows into her bones. She's a child Rhos, man-shy and half wild.'

Rhosyn knelt at the hearth and felt the heat glow on her face. She had thought about him at the time of his marriage, imagined him abed with his unwanted young Norman bride and wondered if the skills of the bedchamber and sweet grass meadow had stood him in good stead then.

'I have not bedded her,' he said into the small silence of her thoughts. 'She has the frightened eyes of a lass half her age. She knows nothing of men except what her father was and her uncle is.'

Rhosyn turned her head in surprise.

'Even if she opened to me for the sake of duty, it would be little less than rape. She is as flat as a kipper before and behind and the crown of her head scarce reaches to my armpit.'

'Jesu, Guy!'

'Wishing you had not asked?' He gave a mocking smile, then shook his head. 'The match is not entirely a disaster. Judith has abilities beyond most young women of her station.'

Rhosyn lifted her brows. Guyon laughed, this time with genuine mirth. 'It is not given to every wench to be able to handle a dagger, or hone it to perfection on a whetstone. She has a wicked sense of humour, too. I would not put it past her to grease a slope for the joy of seeing someone slide down it – probably me. I do not believe I shall grow bored – if I live. Walter de Lacey would dearly love to dance on my grave and rule in my stead and Robert de Belleme merely bides his time. Fool that I am, it offends my sensibilities to murder the pair of them in stealth as they would do to me without a qualm of conscience.'

Rhosyn considered him. He had spoken lightly, but his eyes were hard and the fine mouth was set in a straight grim line. She realised how trivial her own complaints must seem when set against his various burdens. Crossing the space between them, she laid her hand on his shoulder and her cheek to his in a wordless embrace, her black hair spilling down over his rough jerkin and hood.

His own hand reached to grip hers, long-fingered and graceful. She wished suddenly that the child she carried should inherit those hands.

They sat like that while the silence of the night settled around them. Rain thudded against the hafod walls, rhythmic and heavy. Guyon closed his eyes, meaning only to rest them for a moment and instead fell asleep.

Rhosyn gently, stealthily, disengaged her hand from his and stared at him. Vulnerable and slack-limbed, his jaw was fuzzed with dark stubble, his eye sockets smudged with weariness. Swallowing the lump in her throat, she remembered the time she had first seen him.

She had been a bride of fifteen with her proud new husband indulgently buying her trinkets in Hereford. Guy had been nineteen then, awkward with his limbs, still filling them out but even then, coltish and immature as he was, his beauty had been striking. He had not noticed her then, nor yet in the times that she visited his father's keeps with her husband and her father. Not until four years ago when, widowed, she had personally bargained with him over the price of the wool clip. His wide brown eyes, so melting and innocent, had almost been her downfall. She had believed that innocence until realising belatedly that she was being ruthlessly manoeuvred into a corner from which the only extrication was agreement to his price. *Yr llewpart du*, they called him – the black leopard – and, like a cat, there were claws beneath the soft pads and the tuned instincts of a hunter.

She had not let him catch her; not then, nor when she went to his bed, and especially not now. She rubbed her sleeve over her damp eyes and gave a small, self-deprecatory smile as her practical merchant's mind surfaced from the maelstrom of emotion in which it had been bogged down. She took his cloak and spread it across a stool to dry and prepared a small costrel of mead, her movements brisk but silent. In an hour, she would wake him and he would go, and their meshed worlds would slide apart like two sword blades gliding off each other in a spangle of sparks.

She sat down again when all was done and took up her distaff, and listened with pleasure to the slow, even rhythm of his breathing while she wondered idly what had brought him over the border in so clandestine a fashion.

Twenty miles away and some hours later, wondering was also the preoccupation of another who waited, vacillating between terror and rage at Guyon's continued absence. Judith's emotions were raw. The very touch of a thought agitated them to agony.

It was almost dawn. A glimpse through the arrowslit repeated several times this last hour had revealed the sinking stars and a milky glimmer to the east. The words she hissed as she peered out on the imminent morning were hot with fury and filled with guilt lest she was cursing a dead man to hell for his tardiness. The thought of him staring sightless into the dawn, his body sword-cloven caused her to whirl from the arrowslit with a gasp.

Eric and the others had ridden in through the postern

shortly before midnight. She would not have known of it had not Melyn yowled to be let out, thus disturbing her from a restless sleep. The arrowslit which looked out on the postern had revealed the stealthy entry of the men and ponies. She had expected Guyon then, but he had not come. The ponies had disappeared promptly like beasts of the Wild Hunt into the hollow hills and when she had let Melyn out and gone down to Eric, he had been taciturn and evasive. Lord Guyon had business in Wales. He would be back soon enough. He advised that she retire.

Judith knew that when she recovered her equilibrium she would be thoroughly chagrined at losing her temper, but for the nonce, like a drunkard, she did not care. Eric had recoiled from the lash of her tongue, eyes wide in shock. When Guyon returned, she intended to do more than just make him recoil. He told her nothing, left her to worry, treated her like a child who did not have the skill to understand.

'Nor shall I if he does not give me the chance!' she said through clenched teeth as she flounced away from the arrowslit and began to dress.

She had just pulled on her stockings and shift and was scrabbling about on all fours searching for a wayward shoe, when Guyon entered the room as silently as a cat.

'Good morning, wife,' he said, grinning at the sight of her upturned posterior.

For a long moment she was still and then she rose to her feet and faced him, her complexion flushed with anger.

'Strange moonlight,' she said sarcastically. 'I have been sick with worry! Eric rode in before midnight matins. Where have you been?'

'I went to see Rhosyn and I fell asleep,' he replied matter-of-factly and came further into the room to sit on a stool and begin unlacing his boots.

'You went to see Rhosyn?' she repeated and swallowed the urge to hurl her newly found shoe at him. 'Have you changed your mind?'

'About what? Fetch me a drink, there's a good lass.'

Judith dropped the shoe and turned away, her back as rigid as a lance, her voice choked with the effort of controlling her rage. 'You said you had no mistress.'

Guyon flashed her a glance. 'I don't. Huw ap Sior was a close friend of her family. I took her the news of his death and a warning to be on guard. I am sorry if you are vexed, but expect apology for naught else.'

'Vexed is not the word!' Judith sloshed wine into a cup with a shaking hand. 'I could kill you myself!'

'No doubt . . . Pass me those clothes over there.'

'Those?' She swung to him, lids widening. 'But they stink!'

'I know.' He grimaced, took the wine she offered, drank a mouthful and then set it down. 'Spike it, will you?' he said. 'With white poppy.'

'What for?'

'To make me sufficiently difficult to rouse when Robert de Belleme hails at our drawbridge.'

'And why should he do that?' Judith had a strong inkling as to the reply, having had plenty of time to think during the long watches of the night while her absent husband enjoyed another woman's company without thought for his terrified wife. However, she wanted to hear the words from his own lips, not be treated like an imbecile who would give the game away if possessed of knowledge.

'He might think I was involved in a Welsh raid upon him and his men that took place on the Shrewsbury road yestereve,' he answered. 'I did not tell you before in case we failed. At least you could truthfully have claimed your innocence.'

'What good would that do?' Judith was not impressed. 'You know what my uncle does to "innocents".' Her mouth tightened, but it was because he had been ensconced at another woman's hearth, perhaps even in her arms, while she paced the floor at Ledworth in a cold sweat of terror for his life.

'Look,' he said wearily, 'I do not expect you to go into the kitchen details of how you make a particular dish, but I will praise it or otherwise when it comes to table, and it is the same with certain of my doings. I told you what was needful.'

'What you thought was needful.'

Guyon swallowed and cast around for a fresh reserve of patience. A day of pretence and fencing with men he loathed, a night of clandestine work, an hour's sleep in a hard chair and some chancy riding over rough terrain in the pitch dark made it difficult to find. 'Judith, don't push me,' he said softly.

A trickle of fear ran down her spine. The gentle tone was far more frightening than a bellow to mind her business, or a raised fist. She turned abruptly away to begin preparing a draught of the poppy syrup.

Guyon continued to strip. 'What about the rest of the keep?' he asked after a moment. 'What do they think?'

She looked round at him, her expression impassive. 'Some of them believe that it is good for you to release your tension in a surfeit of drink, all young men do it. Others say they always knew you were wild and incontinent. Mama is desperate for my safety. My father used to beat us both when he was in his cups . . . He split my lip once . . . Mama cannot act to save her life. I dare not tell her the truth.'

He snorted with brusque amusement. 'You accuse me and then do the same to your mother!'

Judith drew breath to retort that it was not the same at all, but clenched her teeth on the words. Do not push me, he had said, and she had no way of knowing how close to the edge he actually was.

'I am sorry your mother should be deceived in me, but there is no help for it. So much depends on de Belleme believing my innocence, or at least being unable to refute it.' Guyon came to take the cup from her, tilted her chin, and kissed her gently. 'Trust me, *Cath fach*.'

His lips were as subtle as silk, his beard stubble prickly

on her tender skin. Warmth flowed through Judith's veins as if her blood had turned to wine. Disturbed, she drew quickly away from him. 'Will you tell me how you retrieved the silver?'

Guyon eyed her closely, but could read very little in her expression, so carefully was she guarding it. His own fault, he knew, for warning her off, but one contrary woman a night was enough on any man's trencher. He looked down into the wine and swirled it thoughtfully around. 'It was worth every drop of this foul brew,' he said after a moment and took a gulp so that the heavy sweetness would not cloy his palate. And then, beginning to laugh, he told her precisely what they had done.

Foul-tempered, all insouciance flown, Robert de Belleme demanded hoarsely to see the lord of Ledworth.

'He's still abed, m'lord,' Eric answered staunchly. 'It'll be the devil of a job to rouse him.'

'Do it!' snarled de Belleme, 'or I'll flay your hide and use it for a saddlecloth!'

From another man, the speech would merely have been picturesque. But as it was the Earl of Shrewsbury who spoke, Eric knew the threat was not idle.

'If you will wait a moment, my lord—'

'Make haste, peasant!' growled Walter de Lacey from his place at the Earl's left shoulder and wiped his hand across his bruised mouth.

Eric bowed low, mouth tightening under cover of his full brown moustache, and left the two men at the fire, a wine flagon close to hand.

It was late morning, the servants bustling. The smell of new bread wafted past the men's dust-caked nostrils as a maid laid out the dais table.

'Returning for hospitality so soon, my lords?'

De Belleme whirled to regard the icy glance of his former sister-in-law, Alicia de Montgomery. A bitch in blue silk with a milky collar of pearls at her still surprisingly young throat.

'Recovered entirely from yesterday's malady, I see,' he answered with mock pleasantry, continuing to look her up and down. 'You are remarkably well dressed for a drudge.'

'You should take a gazing-glass to yourself,' Alicia retorted, the pearls jumping hard on her collarbone. 'What can we offer you to be on your way this time?'

His right hand flashed out to grip her wrist and tighten over the knobs of bone. It was so sudden and so painful that involuntarily she cried out. A servant with a pitcher in his hand hesitated. De Belleme flashed him a red-rimmed glare that sent the man scuttling for cover.

'You always were a clapper-tongued bitch too clever for your own good!' he hissed at her. 'My brother was a fool not to silence your jabber with the blade of his knife!'

'It runs in your family,' she retorted, struggling in his grip, feeling as if her bones were about to snap beneath the grinding pressure.

'Where was Guyon FitzMiles last night?' he demanded, his face so close that she could see the small open pores pinpricking his nose and feel the flecks of spittle on her face as he spoke.

'Blind drunk in his bed!' she gasped. 'My lord, you are breaking my arm!'

'And so I will if you do not tell me the truth, you whore!'

It was no idle threat and Alicia knew it. The pain was making her feel sick. One more slight twist and her bones would snap like dry twigs. 'It is the truth. You saw him carried away yourself!'

De Lacey muttered a warning from the side of his mouth and the Earl flung her several paces away from him with a routier's oath.

Gasping, tears of pain and fury in her eyes, Alicia glared loathing at him.

De Belleme returned the look in equal measure and turned

away to view the man staggering across the hall, supported on one side by the captain of the guard and on the other by his anxious wife.

De Lacey swore in dismayed surprise. The Earl stared blankly at Guyon who was stained and rumpled, ungroomed, still stinking of wine and completely without co-ordination.

'Whatever you want,' Guyon enunciated slowly, his tongue stumbling round the words, his eyes owlishly squinting and unfocused. 'I pray you be quick before I am sick all over your boots.' He swayed alarmingly. Eric propped him up. Judith bit her lip and, looking tearfully concerned, clung to her husband's wine-soiled sleeve.

De Belleme gazed round the circle of hostile faces. 'We were attacked on the road, pillaged, tied up and left for the wolves,' he snapped. 'I thought you might know something.'

Silence. Guyon's sluggish lids half lifted. 'Lost your silver too?' he said with a slow smile. It almost became a laugh but the movement of his shoulders brought on a sudden bout of nausea and he folded retching against his wife and his bodyguard.

Judith looked across at the enraged men. 'I am sorry to hear of your misfortune,' she said sweetly. 'Is there anything we can do? Horses? Food? Are there wounded among you?'

Impotent, beaten, Robert de Belleme stared into her hazel eyes with all their innocence and Eve-like deception and then flicked his gaze to the huddled man at her feet, the feline grace gone, the lank black hair grazing the rushes.

'Pray,' he snarled. 'Pray very hard that you are innocent.' He swung on his heel. De Lacey followed him, sneering over his shoulder. Alicia flinched and crossed herself.

'Oh God,' Guyon groaned, half raising his head. 'You wretched girl, I ought to kill you before you kill me.'

'Perhaps I put too large a measure of the potion in your wine, but at least your display was convincing,' Judith answered judiciously. 'Do you feel sick, or are you able to stand?'

Alicia, about to set her foot where angels feared to tread, once more found herself a baffled outsider to the understanding that existed between Judith and the green-faced man now gingerly rising to his feet.

'You'll be all right by this evening,' Judith consoled him and gestured one of the household knights to help him back to bed.

'Witch,' he muttered, but managed a wan smile over his shoulder.

'I do not suppose you are going to explain any of this to me?' Alicia asked, a line of exasperation between her brows.

'No, Mama,' Judith agreed, her smile the secretive one that was all her father's legacy.

CHAPTER 10

The shadows of the June evening had begun to lengthen. The sunlight was as golden as cider, but the wind that cut across the marches and ruffled the slate feathers of the peregrine on its eyrie was edged with cold.

Guyon stood upon Ravenstow's wall walk and inhaled the clean, meadow-scented air with appreciation. Below, the hall was hazed with the smell of the smoked fish that had been the main dish of the evening meal, it being Friday. A lingering aftermath of the deception practised upon de Belleme – a punishment and a penance – was the delicacy of his stomach where such food was concerned.

Cadi thumped her tail, eyes cocked adoringly, alert to move if he should, but he remained staring out over the demesne. The water meadows gave way to the peasants' strips sown with oats and beans, green-blowing in the wind that chased a contrast of shadows and amber sunlight over the land. A harsh land, filled with the dangers of sudden Welsh raids and the slinking shadows of wolves.

As the summer advanced, the Welsh had grown bold in their raiding. A flock of sheep here, a bull there, a woman in one of Guyon's border hamlets. He had, of course, retaliated. An eye for an eye. Everyone knew the rules . . . except Robert de Belleme who rampaged up and down his earldom like Grendel of the marsh, destroying and torturing. Doggedly the Welsh retreated into the hills where he could not follow, taking everything with them and letting their flimsy hafods burn. Reconstruction took only a matter of days and de Belleme was too great a lord to occupy his entire summer chasing shadows through wet Welsh woods. He left that to his vassals, men such as Walter de Lacey and Ralph de Serigny.

The latter had died last month during one such foray into Wales. He and his men had been ambushed and, while fighting his way out, he had suffered a seizure and fallen dead from his horse. Guyon and Judith had attended the funeral as a mark of respect but, circumstances and the other mourners being what they were, had not remained beyond the ceremony.

Guyon had dealt efficiently with the raids on his own lands and kept a jaundiced, watchful eye on de Lacey's efforts to do the same. He did the rounds of his vassals and castellans, holding manor courts, advising, solving, replacing and recruiting, granting, denying, his finger firmly on the pulse.

He began to move slowly along the wall walk. Cadi leaped to her feet, shook herself and followed, nose grazing his heels. A young guard saluted him. Guyon paused a moment to speak, remembering from long training the man's name and family circumstances. It was a little effort that never failed to repay more than double its expenditure in willingness and loyalty.

The guard paused in mid-reply to Guyon's query and saluted again, this time flushing scarlet to the tips of his ears.

Guyon turned to find his wife, pink and breathless from her climb, strands of hair escaping her braids and blowing wild. The guard's blush he attributed to the fact that women seldom came aloft and certainly not as informally as this. It never occurred to him to think the young man might find Judith attractive.

'I've found her!' Judith panted, clutching Guyon's arm, her eyes as bright as two polished agates. 'She was in one of the bailey storesheds nestled among a heap of fleeces.'

He slipped his arm absently around her waist and kissed her cheek. 'I told you she would not have gone far,' he said with a superior air.

Judith stiffened. 'You groaned the words at me from the bed because you wanted to be left in peace to sleep,' she said tartly. 'You could not have cared less!'

'Well, not at the time,' he conceded with a grin. 'But I knew she was bound to turn up. I've never known a beast with a life so charmed.'

'She's taken a lover. The same one that sired her last lot of offspring. A great black mannerless leopard of a tom that lives wild on the slope!'

Guyon smiled and leaned upon the limewashed sandstone to watch the clouds chase past on the wind. 'Well, it is spring after all,' he said with amusement.

Judith blushed. He had been very patient with her thus far, his embraces light and fraternal, teasingly affectionate and 'safe'. Her stomach no longer lurched sickeningly when they retired of a night. She knew she was not about to be raped. Once, unconsciously he had reached an arm across her naked body and murmured a name into her hair, his lips nuzzling her nape and her blood had prickled, moved by something alien and unsettling that flushed her loins with moist heat. Afraid, she had tossed vigorously and coughed and, the pattern of his breathing had broken; he had removed his arm with a wry, half-waking apology and rolled over away from her.

The time would come, she knew, when she would have to know his flesh. He was his father's sole heir, the duty pressing upon him to beget more branches on the tree than Miles had done.

'If I was barren would you divorce me?' she asked curiously.

He left the merlon and walked onwards until they could overlook the river and its bustle of traffic at the toll as boats sought to moor before nightfall. 'Come now, *Cath fach*, where else would I find a wife capable of besting me at dagger play?'

'I do not suppose it would matter if she bore you half a dozen sons.'

'Kind of you to offer,' he grinned, deliberately miscon-struing her words. 'I have the patience to wait on your ripening lust.' She pinched him. He recoiled with a protest, and then suddenly craned forward, narrowing his gaze the better to focus on the distance. 'Visitors,' he said.

Judith came to his side and stood on tiptoe. Below them, a long barge had just nudged into its mooring and the crew were making her secure.

'Your father!' she exclaimed as Miles stepped on to the wharf.

'Cat among the pigeons,' Guyon said with a thoughtful smile.

'Who is that with him?' Judith bobbed against her husband and a stray tawny wisp of her hair cobwebbed his face.

'My half-sister, Emma. If you remember, she could not attend our nuptials because she was in London.'

'Those girls with her are your nieces?'

'Christen, Celie, and Marian,' he agreed, looking wryly amused.

Judith regarded the group for a moment. The older woman, even from this distance, was obviously lovely, and rich. The white fur lining of her cloak gleamed like silk on snow as it caught the sunlight and her braided hair was the precise colour of a sweet chestnut new-hulled from its case. The girls too were elegantly robed and pristine. Delicately bred, gentle young ladies.

Dismayed, Judith bit her lip, aware that she was wearing her oldest gown and that it was rough with Melyn's moulting fur. Her hair was unkempt and there was nothing prepared to make them a fitting welcome.

'What am I going to do?' she asked.

Guyon turned, looked her up and down from the bird's

nest crown of her head to the scuffed toes of her leather slippers and grinned. 'And yet you can face down Robert de Belleme with never a qualm.' He tilted her chin on his forefinger and kissed her nose before whirling her about to face the stairs down. 'Em's all right, she won't eat you.'

'She might if there's naught else on her trencher,' Judith responded.

'My sister has a heart of gold. She'll fold you to her breast like a waif and stray and I'll be the one to receive the scolding. She still thinks of me as a brat of six filching griddle cakes from the bakehouse door and putting headless mice on her trencher.'

Momentarily diverted, Judith flashed him a glance compounded of horror and amusement. 'And things have changed?' she said saucily and ducked adroitly beneath his playful cuff.

'Headless cats now,' he retorted and hugged her.

They had reached the bottom of the stairs. 'I am very fortunate,' Judith said on a sudden, blushing impulse. 'And very grateful. My lord I—'

'Do not set your worth too cheaply,' he said and tugged her braid in an affectionate gesture with which she was now thoroughly familiar.

'Your wife is contrary to my expectations, Guy,' murmured Emma, reaching a well-tended hand to pick up her cup.

Guyon smiled and stretched out his legs to lounge more comfortably in his chair on the dais. 'What did you expect?' He followed her gaze to the fire and the four girls who crouched there, heads close, intent over a game of knucklebones. Christen possessed her mother's chestnut-red colouring. The two younger girls were plain brown like their absent father. Judith's hair sparkled bronze-blonde like the pelt of a young vixen. Christen said something. Judith capped it wittily and her laughter rang.

Emma sipped her wine. 'Well she's certainly not a

Montgomery to look upon. I can see her mother's bones, but where on earth did she get those eyes and that hair?'

'From her grandam perhaps?' Guyon said with a shrug. 'Maurice was only a bastard son of the house. By all accounts his mother was a Danish widow out of York.'

'Yes, perhaps. I thought she would be slight and dark . . . and less of a child. At her age I was extremely conscious of my appearance and how to use it on men to gain my own ends.'

'Oh, Judith has her ways and means,' he said easily. 'And if I ever had a yen for women who primped and preened, I lost it swiftly enough at court. The difference between those harpies and Judith is the difference between dross and pure gold. No insult to yourself intended, Em. You use your talents with subtlety.'

'Thank you,' she retorted archly. 'I'll treasure the compliment.'

'Christen does not appear to have inherited your discretion,' he added as Christen looked up from the game and slanted a long-lashed glance at one of the youngest knights in the hall.

Emma sighed. 'You have noticed it too? There is a devil in her, Guy and it will destroy her unless it can be exorcised.'

'She is scarcely yet fourteen,' he said, all humour flown.

'And older than Eve.'

'And I hazard part of the reason you were summoned to London and are here now instead of with Richard at court?'

She gave him a sidelong look. 'I had forgotten how sharp you are. It seemed a sound idea to send her to housekeep for her father while my duty kept me here in the marches after Mama died. The girls see so little of him that I thought it would be of benefit to them both.'

Guyon grunted. 'You see little enough of Richard yourself.'

Emma shrugged. 'It is not given that every match should scorch the soul. We are content, Guy.'

'Have you spoken to Richard about her?'

'He says the sooner we match her the better, but I do not know. Perhaps she is merely playing at what she sees the court concubines do and, because she is pretty and men respond, she does it the more, never knowing how close to the fire her fingers are.'

He was silent for a time, considering the circle of girls. A serving lad replenished his cup and moved on. Cadi stirred restlessly at his feet. 'You were right to bring her away,' he said at length. 'Christen has always been swayed by the actions of those around her. Do you remember when she was nine and wanted to become a nun because one of the maids took the veil?'

A pained smile curved Emma's lips. 'And last year the crusade. I caught her sewing a cross on her best cloak, her belongings packed in a travelling bundle and vowing to see Jerusalem or die.'

'So what she requires is a spell of gentle domestic harmony with myself and Judith for examples?'

Emma grimaced at him.

Eyes laughing, he said, 'I thought you had serious doubts concerning my state of grace?'

'That was just irritation at the weakness of all men,' she said impatiently. 'I know why you act the rutting stag at court and you and Rhosyn have long had a private understanding. You handle Christen better than any of us. She might listen to you . . . and she might listen to your Judith. There is not so much difference in age and they appear to like each other.'

'It depends upon what you want her to learn in lieu of coquetry,' Guyon chuckled, thinking of Judith's repertoire of dubious skills. He rose to his feet and, still smiling, left the table. Emma followed him.

His father and Eric were locked in mortal combat over a game of merels beside the hearth and neither paid any attention to Cadi's inquisitive nosings.

'Have you noticed any difference in our father these last few weeks, Em?' Guyon asked in a low voice.

She shook her head. 'Not really. Perhaps a little quieter, but you know how he broods. Before we set out, he spent a long time kneeling at Mama's tomb and then complained that his knees were stiff. Why do you ask?' Her voice sharpened. 'Is there something wrong?'

'No, nothing.' He set a reassuring hand on her arm. 'Just filial interest. 'What he needs is another wife . . . or a mistress.'

Emma scowled at him. 'You don't seriously mean that, Guy.'

'Why not?'

'Would you welcome another woman in Mama's place – a stepmother?'

'You are deluding yourself if you think he has lived like a monk since her death.'

'I know he has taken casual women for comfort and pleasure,' Emma said with asperity. 'But they were in no wise partners for life.'

'That's what I mean. He needs something more. Our mother was his anchor and he is in danger of going adrift without one.' Having gained the information he sought, he went to play knucklebones with his wife and nieces.

'Rannulf Flambard has officially been granted the bishopric of Durham as payment for his tireless endeavours,' said Miles, his face studiously blank.

The lantern swung gently on its hook and shadows lumbered upon the stable walls. Guyon looked up from the delectable golden mare he had been examining. The horse was a gift for Judith, the furtiveness of this night visit to the stable because she was to be a surprise. He stared at his father with bright interest. 'God preserve the devil when he gets to hell.' His mouth twitched. 'What's he going to do, strip the church from within and give it all to Rufus?'

'Of a certainty, weasling little runt.'

The mare lipped Guyon's tunic. He scratched her beneath

the chin. 'But shrewd and clever with it. At least if he's snatching food from the mouths of monks, he's not snatching it from us.'

Rannulf Flambard, a common cleric, had risen by his own diligent efforts from obscurity to the ranks of the most powerful men in the land. He had become indispensable to Rufus and a menace to every member of the barony; a tax collector with a Herculean grip on men's financial affairs and the ability to tighten that grip and squeeze his victims dry.

Guyon thoroughly disliked the man, for his attitude rather than from any squeamishness concerning his lowly birth or his task of crown revenue raiser. Indeed, with a numerical talent of his own, he had the good sense to respect Flambard's extraordinary skills and step warily around them.

'Of course,' Miles added sarcastically, 'Flambard is not the only hazard to our coffers. The Welsh take their tithe of silver too.'

Guyon eyed his father nonchalantly across the mare's satin withers. 'I thought you might have heard about de Belleme's misfortune,' he said with a hint of regret in his voice.

'And yours too?'

Guyon said nothing. He could not dissemble with his sire who knew him too well and saw too clearly. Silence was by far the better line of defence.

'Have a care, son. Step very softly around the Earl of Shrewsbury. His rages are all the more deadly for being silent and the remains of his victims are not a pretty sight. He is stronger than ever now. Did you know that he has paid Rufus another relief to take Roger de Bully's lands?'

The flippancy vanished, replaced by startled attention. 'No, I didn't.'

'Blythe and Tickhill straight down the devil's throat. He's likely to be short of coin and temper. Don't try any more clever tricks like that last one . . . You know what I mean.'

'So if he wants to eat the world, I just stand aside and let him?'

'You don't fling your gage in his teeth!'

'I haven't. A trip rope across his path perhaps, in revenge for a parcel of bloody sables.'

Miles scraped his fingers through his hair and reminded himself that Guyon was almost thirty years old and the mould was too firmly set to be broken or altered by an exasperated lecture.

'Just be careful, that's all.'

'Meek as a virgin,' Guyon answered lightly.

'Just don't get deflowered,' Miles said curtly. 'I'm going to bed.'

The lightness left Guyon's face. 'Chance would be a fine thing,' he said to the horse and followed his father.

CHAPTER 11

Judith gasped and wriggled around in the bed, squinting through her lids as the brightness of daylight flooded the room.

Guyon wrenched the covers aside. 'On your feet, you lazy baggage, or are you going to sleep until noon?'

She sat up, glowering.

Guyon laughed. 'You'll miss a surprise if you do.'

Judith rubbed her eyes and regarded him blearily. He was wearing his hunting tunic of green plaid and leather hose. She had not heard him wake and dress, but then he could be as soft-footed as Melyn when he chose.

'What kind of surprise?'

'The kind that will not wait for ever.' He hooked his thumbs in his belt and studied her. Her hair spilled down. A freckled white shoulder gleamed through the untidy tresses and a small, apple-sized breast. Flank and leg were lithe and long. Flustered, she lowered her eyes, a pink flush staining her throat and face. Abruptly he turned away to her clothing pole and, selecting garments, tossed them on the bed.

'I'll send in your maid. Don't be too long, *Cath fach*.'

His tone was light and his face wore its customary good humour so that her momentary qualm dissolved into an impudent grimace as he reached the door.

Most of the household was still asleep and, as Judith indignantly discovered on entering the hall, it was not long after dawn. A yawning boy was arranging the side trestles for the serving of bread and curd cheese. Guyon was leaning on the edge of the dais, deep in conversation with the steward and the reeve, Cadi as usual glued to his side.

The two standing men bowed. Judith smiled a greeting to the steward. To the reeve she spoke. He had not long been appointed to the position – a young man with small children, well able to cope with the task of mediating between the lord and his tenants, but still finding his feet.

Guyon listened to her enquiries after the health of the man's family with whose every name and circumstance she was familiar and was once more amazed at her scope.

'I didn't know his aunt Winifred suffered from gout,' he chuckled as he led her out of the forebuilding and into the early morning bustle of the bailey.

'She doesn't.' Judith regarded him with grave clarity. 'She just likes their attention. There's nothing wrong with the cantankerous hag. I could think of several effective if drastic remedies to cure her condition. Cutting out her tongue, for one.'

'Judith!' he spluttered.

'It is the truth and only you to hear it. Why should I lie?'

Guyon shook his head, unable to think of a response or reprimand because in essence she was right

A lanky youth of about Judith's own age was forking soiled straw into the yard. Hens pecked and scratched near his feet. Balls of yellow fluff twinkled hither and yon, imitating in miniature the actions of their parents, miraculously avoiding the lad's stout boots and the sweeps of the fork.

'Good morning, Hob,' Judith greeted him. He turned a dusky campion-pink and mumbled into his chest.

'What's the surprise, Guy?' She smiled up at him as she had smiled at Hob.

'You are, constantly,' he replied, then said in English to the boy, 'Where's your father?'

'Just coming, sire. He's walking her round to stop her getting cold.'

'Who?' asked Judith.

Guyon took her arm and turned to face his head groom who appeared around the edge of the building with a harnessed mare following behind in a well-mannered fashion.

'Guyon?' Judith twisted to look up at him and then back at the delicately stepping palfrey.

'I thought it was time you had a more mettlesome mount than that old bay nag you've adopted. Her name's Euraidd. She's five years old and from the stud herd down at Ashdyke.'

Judith stared at the vision filling her eyes and it swung its head to return the compliment with limpid black eyes. Euraidd – golden. A mare the colour of the sun. Darker dappled rings like gold coins shimmered on the silken haunches and contour of shoulder and belly. Her mane and tail were a flossy blonde, the former braided with tassels of scarlet silk. The harness, like the horse, was expensive.

'She's beautiful!' Judith gasped, more than a little awestruck. 'Are you sure you want me to have her?'

'How else do you expect to keep up with me when we go riding?' Guyon grinned. 'That bay bag of bones might as well have been standing still the other day.'

'He ran his heart out for me when we were fleeing Earl Robert,' she said, and stepped forward to stroke the soft tawny nose. The mare had a white star between her eyes and two small trails of stardust dribbled beneath. She lipped Judith's fingers, seeking a titbit, and the groom obligingly produced a wrinkled apple.

The under-groom emerged from the stables with Guyon's grey saddled up and ready.

'Care to try her paces?' Guyon cupped his hands.

'You should not make such an open display of your wealth,' she reproved, faintly troubled even in the midst of her joy.

'My father has one of the best stud herds in the land. Even impoverished as I am, I still have access to good horseflesh. Besides, you should know not to look a gift horse in the mouth.'

Judith made an agonised face at the literal pun and set her foot into the bowl of his linked fingers.

They rode far and wide over Ravenstow's demesne. The mare's gait was like silk, her muscles flowing like water beneath a cloth of golden satin. Her mouth was sensitive to Judith's slightest touch on the reins. She moved effortlessly from walk to pacing trot, to canter and back to a walk and Judith felt not so much as a jolt as she changed step.

Guyon considered Judith's seat in the saddle with a critical eye and discovered that, as with all skills, she had mastered this one in a very short time.

'My mother used to hate riding horseback,' he said finally as they rode side by side for home. 'For my father's sake she bore it, but it was a sacrilegious waste of good horseflesh. The best in England and she appreciated it not one whit.'

Judith looked down at the mare. There was exhilaration in riding such smooth power, a tingling of triumph in the knowledge of mastery.

'He misses her, doesn't he?' she said thoughtfully.

'My mother was the light of his life,' Guyon said, his eyelids tightening with pain. 'They fought on occasion fit to bring down the keep around our ears, but I remember the love. She would have given him her lifeblood to drink if he had asked, and vice versa.'

Judith gnawed her lip, unable to contemplate such a depth of feeling and trust. Her own parents had spent their time damning each other's souls into the pit of hell. Slaps, blows, ill-treatment, degradation, cruelty. She knew only too well the nature of marriage . . . or thought she knew. She looked through her lashes at her husband's arrogant features and tried to imagine cutting her own veins at his command. No, she thought. I would take up a knife and defend myself to the last bitter drop of blood.

Hard on that thought followed a wave of guilt. He had

been so good to her, tolerating her whims, handling her with
patience and consideration, gifting her richly, not least with
this beautiful horse. She liked him well enough, knew that
she had been more fortunate than her mother as a heifer in
the ring, but it was too great a trust to give her soul into
another's squandering.

'You are quiet, *Cath fach*,' he said.

Judith smiled and tossed her head. 'Foolish thoughts,' she
laughed, her mouth twisting. 'Not worth a penny for their
time. Does she gallop, is it safe to give her free rein?' Without
waiting for his reply she used her hands and heels to
command the mare into a sudden spectacular burst of speed.
Guyon muttered a startled oath beneath his breath and
spurred the grey in pursuit across the meadow.

Geese scattered honking from beneath the flying hooves.
The swineherd, out with the keep's pigs, shaded his eyes
against the slant of the sun and watched the horses hurtle
past. Ground-nesting plovers broke cover and took hasty
wing. A blackbird chipped at them from a stump.

The golden mare flew lightly over the ground like a faery
beast, her tail rippling like combed flax.

Inch by inch the grey gained on her, his stride that slight
bit longer, but it was a slow process. The weight he carried
was greater and the mare was determined to keep her head
in front. He reached her shoulders, his neck outstretched,
his shoulders and hindquarters working like pistons and
slowly his nose began to draw level with hers.

Judith glanced round, her braids whipping her face, her
eyes blazing with exhilaration and met Guyon's laughter,
white-edged with triumph.

'Oh no!' she cried, laughing back at him. 'Not this time,
my lord!' And as they pounded on towards the edge of the
meadow, she leaned as far forward as the saddle would
permit, gripping like a monkey, the reins clutched hard on
Euraidd's neck. From somewhere the mare found an extra
thrust of speed and, aided by Judith's forward weight, once

more pulled ahead of the stallion to reach the marshy end of the meadow a length ahead.

Mud splattered up around the mare's forelegs and dappled her glowing coat with brown splotches and freckles as Judith breathlessly wound her down to a halt and hung over her braided mane, laughing with delight.

Guyon reined round beside her, drawing the stallion's head hard into the wide grey chest.

'That was wonderful!' Judith gasped, her eyes shining like two coins, her face flushed and vibrant.

'And you are a madwoman!' he answered, half angry, half amused. 'What if you had fallen off?'

'I would have broken my neck, but I didn't and it was wonderful. And if you are going to scowl at me like that, I'd rather ride on my own anyway!'

'Minx,' he chuckled despite himself.

'Fusspot,' she retorted, poking out her tongue.

Guyon's eyebrows shot up. It was the first time anyone had called him that! Before he could think of a suitable retort, Judith clicked her tongue to the mare and shook the reins, urging her across the stream and towards home. At a safe distance, she looked over her shoulder to where he sat staring after her and grinned impishly.

Guyon steadied his grip on the reins. He was painfully tumescent and very tempted to ride after her and soothe the irritation where it would do him the most good . . . and her the least. She is a child, he reiterated to himself. It had been too long an abstinence, that was all. After a moment, the impulse and its source subsided. He walked the stallion meekly in her wake while he consolidated his hold on things rational.

At the keep they had visitors. Tethered in the bailey were a dozen sturdy pack ponies tended by an equally sturdy black-haired youth. He was loosening the pack of the foremost pony and speaking to a frowning, middle-aged man who was unloading what looked like bales of cloth.

The youth lifted his gaze and met Guyon's as the latter dismounted. Unlatching the last buckle, he spoke a quick word to the servant, and came across the ward to greet them. Judith looked curiously at the lad as he arrived and stood smiling before them. He was as solid and stocky as a young oak tree and darkly Welsh, his eyes onyx black and extravagantly fringed. His wide-planted stance exuded the confidence of a man, the flush in his cheeks the uncertainty of boyhood.

'I'm here with my grandfather,' he said in rapid Welsh. 'We've brought cloth to trade and we need new ponies, and grandfather has other business besides.'

The grooms took the two mud-smirched horses.

'How fares your mother?'

'She had a baby girl two days since,' Rhys said, gaze darting to Judith, obviously wondering how much Welsh she understood. 'She is well and so is the baby . . . Eluned is jealous.'

Before Guyon could compose himself to reply, Madoc ap Rhys himself strode out of the forebuilding and clapped a brown, knotty hand on Rhys's shoulder.

'I thought you'd have finished unloading by now!' he declared, but his hazel eyes were laughing and his tone was indulgent. 'God's greeting, my lord. I see that you've had the good tidings. A fine, healthy babe and blessed with your grandsire's red hair and, to judge from the sound of her lungs, his temper too!' His manner was affable. Rhosyn's liaison with Guyon FitzMiles and the resulting child were useful bonds to future profit as far as he was concerned.

Judith opened her mouth to speak, but changed her mind and compressed her lips instead, not trusting herself.

Guyon invited the merchant into the hall to drink to the infant's health and discuss the business he had brought with him upon the back of a dozen ponies. Belatedly, he remembered to introduce Madoc and Rhys to his wife.

Master Madoc made the proper responses in impeccable

Norman French and concealed his curiosity and surprise behind deep-set lowered lids. The girl who tepidly smiled her duty was not the fey, frightened thing that Rhosyn had led him to expect. Her agate-coloured eyes were cool, her voice clear and firm. Slender, yes, with barely a curve to her name, but possessed of a certain gauche grace and also a certain coldness of manner and, from the quick look she had tossed at Guyon as they entered the forebuilding, it did not take much of his merchant's shrewdness to guess the cause.

At first he and Guyon discussed the merits of the new downland rams that had been introduced to Guyon's herds and the effect they would have on the quality of future wool clips.

'It will make your fleeces whiter and increase the length of the staple. The Flanders looms are crying out for good-quality wool. If God grants me my health, I should be crossing the sea after harvest to see for myself.'

'Rhosyn said you had been unwell.'

Madoc gave a dismissive shrug. 'I lack breath occasionally and my chest gripes, but the bouts are usually when I've done more than I should, or the weather grows too cold. A few more years and Rhys will be old enough to shoulder much of the burden.' He smiled at his grandson, who smiled in return as he plied his meat with a fine, ivory-hilted knife.

Madoc applied himself to his own meal for a while, then turned his shrewd gaze upon Guyon's young wife who had been silent throughout the previous conversation. 'My lady, if you permit, there is a matter I would like to discuss with you.'

Judith inclined her head. 'Master Madoc?'

'I believe you wrote to the widow of Huw ap Sior, offering to her the sables that had come by underhand means into your possession. She has asked me to act for her in this business and gratefully accepts your generosity.'

'It is naught of generosity, it is her rightful due,' Judith said with a grimace. She had put the sables away at the bottom of a chest, wrapped in fresh canvas, and had thrown the bloodstained coverings on the back of the fire. Even to think of them made her shudder.

Guyon looked at her with surprise and approval. He had not asked her what she had done with the furs, merely assumed that their disappearance marked their disposal.

Madoc too studied her and wondered if she knew her own power. Probably not; she was still very young and her eyes were innocent of all guile. One day she would be formidable. A black leopard and his golden mate. He smiled at the whimsy.

'You will need an escort,' Guyon said. 'Sables these days are worth their weight in blood.'

'Is Rhys yours too?' Judith enquired a trifle acidly when they were alone in their bedchamber.

Madoc and his grandson were asleep on bracken pallets in the hall among the other casual guests and travellers seeking a night's hospitality.

Guyon scratched the sensitive spot just behind Melyn's ginger ears. The cat purred and kneaded his tunic with ecstatic paws. 'No,' he said, giving his attention to the cat.

'You look alike.'

'Colouring mainly. His father was black of hair and eye. You're not the first to assume my paternity. I wish it were true. He's a fine lad.'

'You have a daughter of his mother's blood,' she said, watching him through her lids.

Guyon's fingers stilled in the cat's thick cream and bronze fur. 'Not one who will know me as more than a shadow,' he said carefully.

'Why did you not tell me about the child before?'

'Where would have been the point? It is not as though she is going to be raised beneath my roof. Rhosyn will give her a Welsh name and raise her to be Welsh.'

'And you have no say in the matter?' she demanded incredulously.

Melyn leaped from his knee and lay down to wash beside the hearth. 'What should I do?' he growled testily. 'Snatch her from her mother's arms and bring her to Ravenstow and salve my pain at the expense of Rhosyn's hatred and a blood feud with her people?' He rose and, going to the flagon, splashed wine into a cup. 'My say has been said. I once asked Rhosyn to stay with me and she refused. I could no more constrain her to live with me, or give up the child, than I could bear one of those caged birds in my bedchamber.'

'Will you go to her tomorrow?'

He looked at Judith over the rim of the cup. Her expression was guarded, her face milk-pale, the stubborn chin lifted in challenge.

'Probably.'

Judith's fingers were claws. She fought a completely new and unsettling emotion that left her wanting to shriek at him that she was not going to stand for him riding off into the arms of another woman, and longing to scratch out that woman's eyes and call her whore.

Frightened, she turned away and busied herself unlocking the chest that contained the sables. True to his word, Guyon had not taken a maidservant or mistress into his bed, or if he had, it had been discreetly elsewhere without insult or humiliation to herself. Having lived beneath the cruelty of her father's code, she should have been grateful and was both confused and chagrined to find that instead she felt betrayed. Desperately she scrabbled in the chest.

'Why ask me if you do not want to know?' Guyon said and crouched beside her to put his arm lightly across her shoulders. 'I have known Rhosyn for many years and her father since I was your own age. You cannot expect me to sever those ties.'

The package of sables came into her hands. She lifted them and turned. 'I do not, my lord.' She gave him one swift look before lowering her lids. 'It is just that you pat me on the head and give me presents and laugh when I amuse you, but

I wonder if you ever see me as more than a troublesome child with whom you are saddled.' She put the furs on top of the chest and stood up. So did he, a frown between his eyes.

Her gaze was still lowered. After a moment, he tilted up her chin and kissed her gently. 'Come, *Cath fach*, look at me.'

Her lashes flickered up to reveal a shine of tears. She pushed herself away from him. 'Don't patronise me!'

Guyon let his hands fall to his sides and drew a slow breath. Then, carefully, he let it out. 'How should I treat you?' he asked with baffled exasperation. 'You are not a woman, you are not a child. You waver over the line between the two like a drunkard. You laugh and play knucklebones with my nieces and skip around the keep hoyden-wild. You tease me like an experienced coquette, but were I to take up the offer in your smile you'd bolt in terror. In God's name, Judith, make up your mind!' He swallowed down the wine and picked up the flagon.

Her gaze widened. 'Where are you going?' she said breathlessly.

'To think,' he said with a twisted smile. 'Don't wait up for me.'

The curtain dropped behind him. Melyn stretched in a leisurely fashion, eyed her mistress from golden agate slits and padded to sit expectantly at her feet. Judith scooped her up, buried her cheek in the thick, soft fur and refused to cry.

In the event, Guyon did very little thinking. He took his flagon to the guardroom, sat down, propped his feet on the trestle and with relief, was soon thoroughly absorbed in the convivial, vulgar gossip of his soldiers. It was a long time since he had spent an evening thus and, besides relishing the salty, masculine conversation, he was able to bring himself abreast of current marcher gossip.

Walbert of Seisdon's wife was pregnant yet again. One of the mills at Elford had a broken grindstone. The remains of a butchered deer had been found in the woods on

Ravenstow's border with Wales. Robert de Belleme had brought a grey Flemish stallion to run with his native mares. Robert de Belleme had offered the widow of Ralph de Serigny in marriage to Walter de Lacey.

Guyon's face emerged abruptly from the depths of his cup. 'What?'

'It's true, sire. My sister's married to a Serigny retainer and is a seamstress up at the keep. Regular upset it has caused, I can tell you.'

Guyon wiped his mouth and removed his feet from the trestle. 'You are telling me that Walter de Lacey is to marry Mabel de Serigny?'

'Yes, sire. Not common knowledge yet, but it soon will be.'

'Imagine waking up wi' that in bed beside you.'

'De Lacey won't be too impressed himself!' quipped the joker in their ranks to a response of loud groans.

De Bec leaned over to refill Guyon's cup. 'De Serigny's estates are rich,' he said. 'Mabel's dowry was huge and Sir Ralph a regular miser.'

Guyon sent him a look that said far more than words, then he drank. 'Do you think he'll invite me to the wedding?' he asked.

'More likely the funeral,' grunted de Bec. 'Mabel's not likely to outlive her second husband, is she?'

Guyon pursed his lips. The Serigny lands and the keep at Thornford lay on Ravenstow's south-west border, separated from Wales by a deep, defensive ditch. There were other keeps in the honour too, forming part of the fortifications ringing Shrewsbury and, coupled with what de Lacey already possessed, it would make him a baron of some considerable standing along the middle marches and increase threefold the threat he posed to Guyon's interests.

One step forward and two steps back, Guyon thought, staring at a puddle of wine on the trestle. 'You'd better tighten up on the patrols,' he said to de Bec. 'I don't want him cutting his new-found teeth on my borders.'

'You reckon he would, sire?'

'Depends on how much backing he gets from de Belleme and how good a grievance he can find to start a war. Knowing our respective overlords, I do not suppose an excuse will be long in presenting itself.' Grimly, he held out his cup to be refilled. 'Do you think de Lacey will celebrate his nuptials with a boar hunt?' Prudently, de Bec forbore to answer.

CHAPTER 12

Judith stared into the Saracen hand mirror and found nothing that pleased. Her eyes were dark-circled for want of sleep and her complexion was pallid, bedevilled here and there by blemishes. Her women's courses which for the past two years had been an erratic inconvenience seemed to have settled down into less than welcome four-weekly visitations of cramp and messy discomfort. That it was supposedly Eve's curse and thoroughly sanctioned by the church was no comfort; nor was the kind of information imparted by Christen, her fourteen-year-old niece-by-marriage – that they would cease as soon as she conceived.

'I should have been a man!' Judith said rebelliously.

'They don't live as long,' Christen pointed out. 'And they are easy enough to handle once you have learned the knack.'

'If you had known my father, you would not say that.' Judith began combing her hair. 'His remedy for everything was a bellyful of wine and the thrashing of the nearest scapegoat. Has your father ever beaten you?'

'Sometimes,' Christen answered with a dismissive shrug.

'And left bruises that took weeks to fade?'

Christen made a swift gesture. 'That was your father. Guy's not like that and his needs are obvious if you know where to look.'

'Indeed?' Judith arched her brow, wishing the precocious child would leave her alone. Her thoughts skimmed back over the last few hours. Guyon had come late to bed, smelling of drink and had fallen asleep the moment he lay down with never a word in her direction. Probably he assumed she was already asleep and she had done nothing to contradict that assumption, afraid of what he might do in his cups.

The morning saw him in possession of a splitting headache, a rolling gut and numerous duties to carry out. The cramps in her stomach had made her feel sluggish and sick. They had scarcely exchanged a word. Neither of them had the time or inclination to be civil and his kiss on her cheek before he rode away had been a matter of form. He had looked through her to the waiting grey and the train of pack ponies and had omitted to tug her braid as was his usual wont. *Don't patronise me*, she had said. Perhaps last night he had thought and decided how he should treat her. She blinked very hard. 'Where then do I look?' she challenged the other girl.

Christen eyed her thoughtfully. 'Guyon likes to hunt,' she said after a pause. 'You must twist and turn and evade and, even if he catches you, refuse to give in.'

Judith's wayward eyebrows rose higher.

'And of course,' Christen added with a knowing look at the bed, 'there is always that particular method of persuasion.'

'You know all this from experience?' Judith snapped.

'Of course not! I had it from Alais de Clare. She used to be his main solace at court until her husband found out.'

'I see,' said Judith, tight-lipped.

'No you don't,' Christen giggled. 'Her husband wanted her to sweeten Prince Henry, not waste her time on a minor fish like Guyon . . . only she preferred Guy's looks and got waylaid, so to speak.'

'And she told you, his niece, all about it?' Judith said scathingly.

Christen blushed beneath the scorn in Judith's voice. 'It wasn't like that.'

'If Guyon offered me to another man by way of a bribe,

I'd make hell seem cold by comparison!' Judith replied savagely. 'God help me, I'd kill them both before I'd be sold like a slab of meat!' And then she clamped her bottom lip in her teeth, remembering that being sold like a slab of meat was precisely the manner of most marriages.

'But you love Guy, and Alais's husband is fat and getting old and—'

'Do not be so sure about the love!' Judith spat.

Christen stared at her with round eyes. 'I do not think Guyon really wanted Alais,' she said anxiously, afraid that she had roused Judith's jealousy and that it would cause trouble for her uncle. 'It was just that the King was chasing him and Guy literally had his back to the wall. He would not have looked at Alais otherwise.'

Judith firmed her lips. There was no malice in Christen; she meant well enough, but her perception was a trifle clouded. However, she had given Judith pause for thought here. There were lessons to be learned, both from Christen and this Alais de Clare who had been bartered by her husband for the favour of a prince. Subtle persuasion. The use of her body as weapon and defence. It had not occurred to her to think in those terms before and, now that it did, she required leisure to digest the notion. She looked covertly at Christen, some of her irritation waning. The girl was only just fourteen, but already she had a ready command of the art that Judith was suddenly aware of lacking.

Subtlety. The chestnut eyebrows were plucked, but only to remove the straggling hairs, and the well-defined, strong lines went unaffected. Her hair was plaited in one shining, heavy braid threaded with gold ribbon and her gown was of a flattering holly-green wool, moulded to display her figure to its best advantage and embellished only by a girdle of silk braid. She looked exquisite with very little effort and Judith knew how those blue-green eyes could angle across the hall, hiding a wealth of promise and refusal behind the down-swept lashes.

It was not an area Judith had previously dared consider, but perhaps in the light of last night's conversation, she ought to do so. Did she want to attract Guyon's notice in that sense? That was something else to be pondered at leisure rather than panicking in his presence. He was susceptible to the persuasions of the bed. She coloured and, over her shoulder, eyed the object with disfavour, wondering how one acquired such skills. Through practice, she supposed, and shuddered at the thought, remembering two of the keep dogs copulating in the hall and the bawdy shouts of the men egging them on. She knew all the words for what male and female did together, precious few of them mentioned in the Bible, and was reluctant to join the circus. If only she could see the thing as power, not a humiliating subjugation.

'Perhaps you are right,' Judith conceded, frowning. 'Honesty may be the best policy, but a crust slips down better if it is spread with honey first . . . I think I have a great deal to learn.' She put the comb down and stood up. 'For the moment, I've to instruct the cook and see about employing a new seamstress and I need to check the spice cabinet and fabric chests. Master Madoc promised to fulfil any commissions I had for him . . . and then,' she added, drawing a deep breath, 'I will consider the matter of subtlety.'

Christen smiled in return without knowing why and decided in future to keep her mouth firmly closed.

In her own chamber, Alicia shook out the drab-coloured gown she had worn in the first weeks of her widowhood. A linen bag of dried lavender and rose leaves fell from its folds along with severe evidence of moths. She clicked her tongue and tossed the garment on the bed.

'Not taking it, my lady?' enquired Agnes, reaching to inspect the damage.

Alicia shook her head and regarded the half-packed baggage chest. She had gowns enough for her retirement upon her dower manor, indeed too many. Her estates, although prosperous, were a backwater compared to the border violence of her former husband's holdings. At least she could be alone with her unseemly hunger.

'What about this belt, my lady. Shall I put . . . ?' Agnes stopped and bobbed a curtsy.

Alicia turned round and her heart began to drum to a battle beat.

Miles le Gallois studied the travelling chests, open to reveal their neatly packed contents – clothes, cups, vials, combs and embroidery. His eyes ranged over the strewed bed and the bare clothing pole, then returned to Alicia. 'If it is on account of me,' he said, 'there is no need. I am leaving tomorrow.'

Alicia mutely shook her head.

'I need to talk to you alone,' he said and as she answered him with stricken eyes, added, 'you may tie me up if you wish, but I swear on my honour not to harm you.'

Alicia carefully folded the veil she had been holding and, after a hesitation, drew a deep breath and gestured Agnes to leave. The maid's mouth thinned, but she dropped a curtsy and retreated beyond the thick woollen curtain.

Miles sat down on the bed and picked up the veil that Alicia had so painstakingly folded. 'Last time we were alone I acted like a green youth in rut,' he said. 'I have come to apologise if you will accept.'

'There is no need of apology,' she said in a low voice, 'unless it be mine.'

'Alicia, look at me.'

Wearily she raised her lids. Her eyes were the colour of twilight and storms and full of vulnerability.

'Do you think that it has gone unnoticed? For the sake of our children, we must come at least to a truce.'

'Why do you think I am going to my dower lands?' she replied.

'Because you are running away?'

Her mouth twisted. 'Not for the reasons you think.'

Miles unfolded the veil. It was made of fragile gauze, the embroidery edging it skilfully worked in gold thread. 'You will miss her,' he said gently.

'She has her own life to live and will the sooner grow into a woman without me for a leaning post. In time I would become the child. Indeed, it has begun already. She shuts me from her thoughts and she is very strong willed.'

'Not a whit like her father, is she?' he mused.

There was a hesitation that made him look up. Alicia's face had blenched. Then she rallied, smiled and drew a shaky breath. 'I wouldn't say that.' She turned her face into the shadows. 'There are many similarities.'

Something rang false. Memory searched and pieced disjointed fragments. 'Who is he?' Miles asked.

He saw the silent vibration of her shoulders. 'That is my own affair,' she answered in a choked voice.

'And mine too since it will touch the blood of my grand-children.' He rose and went to her and turned her to face him.

'And if I say a baseborn groom or a passing pedlar?' she challenged.

'If that were true, you'd not have denied me the day of the boar hunt.'

Alicia shook beneath his light touch, knowing what she risked if she told him the truth.

'Does he still live?'

'Yes.'

'Does he know?'

'No,' she said. 'To him it was a night of pleasure, a comfort along the road to be forgotten in the dawn.'

'And to you?' He watched her with checked tension.

She laughed at some private bitterness. 'Expedient. When your cow fails to calf, get a different bull to service her.'

Miles released her and, folding his arms, frowned.

'Not pretty, is it?' she said. 'I cuckolded my husband in his own keep and deceived him with my lover's child. You see too much, my lord, or perhaps I have just grown care-less of late.'

'I see too much,' he said, smiling painfully, 'because I want you.'

'You don't know me.'

'Well enough to see too clearly.' He tried to decide from her expression the approach he should take. 'I've known you for a long time, ever since you were Judith's age and defying your father's will. And in the years since then, I've watched you from a distance grow and change.'

'And wanted me?' she challenged.

Miles saw the trap yawning at his feet and skirted it deftly. 'I had Christen,' he said. 'There was no space in me to want another woman. You know that.'

Some of the hostility left her eyes, but she remained strongly cautious.

Miles shrugged. 'It is two years since I lost her. Sometimes it seems as close as yesterday. Sometimes the loneliness rides me so hard I think I will go mad. I have taken women to my bed so that I do not have to sleep alone, but there is no lasting solace in that. What I need is another wife and, if I can get a dispensation, your consent.'

Alicia stared at him, dumbfounded. 'It is impossible!' she said huskily.

'The dispensation or your consent? Rannulf Flambard will perform any miracle for the right amount of gold and I will not take no for an answer from you . . . not without excellent reasons.'

Alicia sat down. 'I could give you them,' she said shakily.

Miles persisted. For every protest that she made, he had an answer ready, a reasonable solution. He made a nonsense of her fears . . . all but one. She told him the name of Judith's father.

Miles drew breath, held it, stared at her in dawning amaze-ment, and very slowly exhaled. She saw his mind make that final, vital connection, saw his eyes flicker.

'Yes,' she said harshly. 'He was fourteen years old and I was twenty-eight, and in one night he taught me everything that Maurice did not have the imagination to know.'

'Sweet Christ and his mother,' Miles swore, staring at her while he tried to assimilate what she had just told him.

She watched his face, waiting for the revulsion, but it did not come. It was a blank mask behind which any thought could have lurked. She covered her face and turned away.

After a moment, Miles mustered his wits. She was trembling so hard that he thought her flesh would shiver free of her bones. He laid a firm hand on her shoulder. 'It makes no difference to me,' he said finally. 'It is in the past and, knowing him, even at fourteen he was no innocent to be seduced unless he so wished.'

Alicia swallowed, remembering how it had been. She with a plan half formed, afraid to dare, and he with his mind already made up.

'So you will marry me?'

Alicia removed her hands tentatively from her face and looked at him. 'How can you say it makes no difference? I set out deliberately to cheat my husband. I bedded with a boy whose voice had barely broken, I—'

'You flay yourself with guilt,' he interrupted, capturing her hands in his. 'I do not doubt you. The Welsh have a saying: *Oer yw'r cariad a ddiffydd ar un chwa o wynt.* Cold is the love that is put out by one gust of wind. I have taken women to my bed for the comfort and the pleasure they offer, never out of forced desperation. I account your sin the lesser.'

Alicia's mouth trembled with a smile. 'You are very persistent, my lord.'

'It's the mix of Welsh and Norman blood,' he agreed cheerfully.

She shook her head and sniffed. 'I cannot give you an answer. I am so confused that I do not know my head from my heels.'

He put out his hand as if to touch her, but let it drop again to his side, aware of how much was at stake. It was like stalking a deer. Softly, slowly and no sudden moves. 'Perhaps you should remove to your dower lands,' he said thoughtfully. 'It will give you time to think.'

Alicia stepped away from his disturbing proximity. It was obvious that his own mind was made up. She had shown him the black secret lurking at the bottom of her soul and he had dismissed it as of no consequence, still valuing her enough to offer her marriage. It was the first time she had felt her worth to be above that of a mere chattel. A pity it was thirty years too late.

'I hazard you do not often lose an argument,' she said.

'It depends on the subject.' He gestured. 'I could escort you home if you wish it. I have business with Hugh of Chester, but I could take you when I return, say in four days' time'

'And if I say no?' Her tone was sharp, for she received the distinct impression that she was being manipulated in the direction he desired her to go.

'I'll have to think of something else, won't I?' he replied, still smiling.

CHAPTER 13

It was fortunate for Guyon that the journey into Wales proved uneventful, for he felt as though his brains had swollen to twice their size and were thumping the cage of his skull in a vigorous attempt to escape. It was a long, long time since he had fallen victim to an overindulgence of wine. Since quitting the court, he had held to sobriety and his capacity to drink had thus diminished.

He knew he had not been considerate of Judith, but her sulky expression, her frown as he mounted up to ride out and his own malaise had not lent him the inclination to tug her braid or smile and bear with her. The guilt and the knowledge that he would have to make amends and somehow smooth their differences when he returned only made his headache worse, while his stomach churned like a dyer's vat.

By the time they reached the hafod it was full noon, the sun shimmering the men's mail to fish scales of light, dazzling the eye. Madoc, in his heavy woollen gown with coney trim was as red as clay, sweat dribbling down his face so that he looked as if he were melting.

Guyon tethered his grey to a post in the yard and then, his skull feeling as if it would split asunder, removed his helm and followed Madoc over the threshold.

Eluned ran to her grandfather and embraced him with enthusiasm. Tossing back her silky black hair, she saw Guyon and went to him. 'Mam's had the baby,' she announced. Her eyes, bright hazel like Rhosyn's, were anxious. 'It's a girl.' She clung tightly to his arm.

'I know, *anwylyd*.' He kissed the top of her head.

The midwife paused in ladling a cup of broth into a wooden bowl and looked at Guyon. 'Birth went easy enough,' she said to him with a curt nod. 'Babe's small, but she'll thrive.'

'May I see them?' he asked in Welsh, his tone deferential, for one did not trifle with the great respect in which these women were held. Other than the will of God, it was upon their skill that the life of a mother and child often depended.

'Take this in to her, lord,' she said, giving him the cup of broth. 'But do not be too long; she is tired.'

Eluned made to follow, but her grandfather caught her back and asked her to find him a drink.

Guyon pushed aside the curtain that screened Rhosyn's bed from the main room, and put down the bowl of broth on the coffer beside it. His movement stirred the air and Rhosyn raised her lids. For a moment she thought she was dreaming or that she had contracted the deadly childbed fever and was hallucinating. Then she rallied herself because Guyon was too travel worn and sweat-streaked to be an illusion. He was watching her with dark, pensive eyes as if he did not know how she would receive him. She sat up and softly spoke his name.

'Beloved.' He knelt beside her and took her hands in his.

He was wearing his mail shirt, the rivets glistening a sullen grey in the dim light. His business over the border this time was official.

'I am glad you have come,' she said and was annoyed by the betraying wobble in her voice.

'Did you doubt I would?'

'There was no obligation on you to do so.'

'No obligation?'

She watched his gaze turn to the wooden crib at the bedside

and the swaddled scrap of life it contained and she bit her lip, afraid, knowing she did not have the strength to fight him if he chose to make of his daughter a battleground.

Oblivous, the baby slept, a fluff of red-gold hair peeping from beneath its swaddling cap.

'There will always be an obligation, *cariad*.'

'Guy . . .'

'No,' he said softly, touching the baby's fledging fuzz before giving Rhosyn a look filled with pain. 'I am as leashed to your bidding as that hound out there . . . Just don't kick me out of the door without giving me a chance. Does the little one have a name?'

Rhosyn shook her head.

'Permit me?'

'I . . . I do not know.'

He took her hand. 'Why do I receive the impression that you do not trust me?'

'Because I don't. Naming is a kind of possession for life.'

'What else am I ever likely to have of her, Rhos? A distant glimpse from a tower top. A snatched meeting here and there. From babe to child to woman in the blink of an eye. She is yours. I accept that, but at least grant me the grace of her naming.'

'Your way with words has always been your deadliest weapon,' Rhosyn accused him, shaking her head, her eyes brilliant with unshed tears. 'Very well, I grant you that grace. Do not abuse it.'

'Not Hegelina or Aiglentine then,' he agreed incorrigibly, but kissed her tenderly, almost but not quite with reverence, before he leaned over the cradle again to look at his sleeping daughter.

'Have you told your wife?' Rhosyn wiped her eyes on her shift.

'Judith knows,' he said without inflection.

'And is not best pleased?'

He rubbed his aching forehead. 'She's developing a

sense of possession,' he said ruefully, 'and sometimes it is uncomfortable.'

'I read her letter to Huw's wife. They were not the words of a child. Children grow up, especially at that age. It may be that suddenly you have a woman on your hands.'

His mouth twisted. 'It would still be rape,' he said laconically. 'Not that much of a woman.'

'Even so, bear it in mind, Guy,' she said and then was silent, drinking her broth before it went cold.

'Heulwen,' he said after a time. 'What do you think?'

She put down the cup, looking surprised. 'Heulwen?'

'I promised no Norman monstrosities.'

'I thought you would choose Christen, for your mother.'

'I already have a flighty niece to bear that name. No, let her be called for my Welsh grandmother, Heulwen uerch Owain. Besides, she has the colouring to suit the name.'

Rhosyn cocked her head, considered, and then slowly smiled. 'Yes,' she said softly, 'I approve, Guy. I approve very much.'

The midwife appeared to shoo him out of the room and Madoc was waiting to usher him to the table, still short of wind but a better colour and full of self-satisfied bonhomie. Eluned clamoured for his attention and he gave it with half a mind and smiled at Madoc with another portion, locking away what was left until it could be reviewed without tearing the fabric of his soul. Heulwen. Sunshine. Clouds across his vision.

Travelling home, he would have been at Ravenstow's gates by compline had not Arian cast a shoe and begun to limp. The fine weather had broken up, the innocent, fluffy clouds of early morning displaced by a seething mass of charcoal grey, laden with rain.

'Best rest up for the night, my lord,' said Eric. 'There's a village not far and there's bound to be a farrier.'

Guyon blinked through the downpour. The ground

beneath his feet was a brown tapestry of mud and puddles and his boots and chausses had long since become saturated. Despite it being summer, he felt chilled to the bone. Beyond the lush June-green of the trees and against the lowering sky, a church tower reared through the rain. Further away, dominating its knoll, crouched the timber keep formerly belonging to Ralph of Serigny, but now the property by marriage of Walter de Lacey.

'You reckon it safe?' Guyon said wryly to his captain and slid the wet reins through his fingers, eyes half closed against the rain.

'No, we'll bide at the alehouse if they have one while the farrier sees to Arian, then we'll be on our way. I'd rather ride whole into Ravenstow than carved into joints and stuffed into my saddlebags.'

Eric grimaced. The Chester road at night in this deluge was not a heartening prospect, but his lord was right. They were too close to the Serigny keep at Thornford for comfort and Walter de Lacey, if he discovered their proximity, would not baulk at murder.

The village proved substantial enough to own not only a smithy, but a good-sized alehouse and while Arian was shod, Guyon and his men repaired to the latter to fortify themselves for the damp miles remaining.

The floor of the main room was covered in a thick layer of rushes upon which were set two well-scrubbed long trestles. Rush dips gave light of a kind and a fire burned cleanly in the hearth. The ale-wife was a florid, handsome woman of middle years whose voice bore a strong Gwynedd lilt. Her husband, bluffly English by contrast, sent their son outside to tend the horses.

The only other customers were a young couple seated unobtrusively in the darkest corner of the room, quietly attending their meal. The girl raised her head at their entrance and stared at the armed men with wide, frightened eyes. She had fragile bones and delicate gauzy colouring. Her husband was a plain, wide-shouldered young man, somewhere between twenty and Guyon's own age. He looked warily at the newcomers and put his left hand protectively on top of the girl's. His right stayed loose, within easy reach of the long knife at his belt.

Guyon, after one startled glance at the girl's luminous beauty, ignored the couple and sat down. Water dripped from his garments and soaked into the rushes. Eric gingerly eased himself down beside his lord and rubbed his aching knees.

The woman brought them bowls of mutton stew, fairly fresh wheaten loaves and pitchers of cider and ale, her manner deferential but briskly efficient. 'Foul night to be travelling, sire,' she addressed Guyon. 'You can bed down here if you've a mind to stay.'

He thanked her and shook his head. 'You've a new lord over at Thornford and I'd as lief not encounter him.'

'Worse for business than the plague!' complained the landlord, adding a bowl of honey cakes to the table. 'Started already it has and Sir Ralph barely in his grave. He could be a bastard, but he was so mean that it was good for business. Folks would come here rather than claim a night of hospitality up at the keep, what with him and mad Mabel for hosts.'

'Now folk don't come at all,' his wife sniffed. 'Or if they do, they're like yourselves, here and gone for fear of Lord Walter and his routiers.' She hitched her bosom and stalked away.

Guyon and Eric exchanged glances. The couple in the corner finished eating and went out into the deluge, the man's arm curved around the girl's narrow shoulders.

One of Guyon's men gave an appreciative whistle. 'Pretty lass,' he said.

'Her father's one of the grooms at the keep,' the landlord volunteered, helping himself to a mug of cider, one eye cocked for the reappearance of his wife. 'The lad's a huntsman there, or he was. Had an argument with the new lord and didn't see fit to stay beyond packing his belongings. He's a proud 'un, young Brand, and his wife's a rare beauty as you all saw. Sir Ralph was never one for the women. Too old and not enough steel in his sword to bother getting it out of the scabbard, but Lord Walter . . .' He paused for effect and a gulp of cider and wiped his hand across his mouth. 'Nothing in skirts is safe from his pursuit. Best gamekeeper he'd got, that young man. New lord's an idiot if you ask me to throw away talent like that for lust. Mind you, I can see why he was tempted. I'd . . .' He stopped, hastily put down his mug beside Eric's arm and stepped away from the trestle, pretending bustle as his wife returned, her mouth puckered, although not for a kiss.

Eric chuckled into his moustache. Guyon pushed his bowl aside and finished his ale, hiding his own smile behind his mug. 'I'm away to the smithy,' he announced, biting his lip to keep a straight face as their host grimaced like a goblin behind his wife's back. 'The farrier should have finished with Arian by now.'

'I'll come with you,' said Eric. 'There's safety in numbers in this neck of the woods.'

Guyon threw him an amused look, saw that his shield-bearer was grimly serious, and stopped smiling.

'We're in need of a huntsman at Ravenstow,' Guyon said thoughtfully as they crossed the street, which was deserted in the rainy evening. 'I haven't properly replaced Rannulf yet. Perhaps I should go after the lad and offer him employment.' He flicked a mischievous glance at Eric and was not disappointed.

'You are courting danger if you do, my lord,' Eric warned. 'You heard what the landlord said. Sir Walter won't let them go, you know that. Don't you think you've chanced enough just lately?'

'And not so much as a boar in sight,' Guyon teased as they reached the smithy.

Eric inhaled to remonstrate, but stopped before the

damage was done. Having been Guyon's marshal for fifteen years, he was all too aware that his lord could be a devil incarnate when the mood was upon him: witness that escapade with the sheep and the silver. Arguing with him only made him the more determined to follow his course. Hold to silence, and sense might just prevail.

Guyon glanced along his shoulder at Eric, almost laughing to see the poor man choking on words he was longing to utter. 'Surely I am not so unamenable to reason,' he jested and picked up Arian's forehoof to examine the new shoe.

'My lord, you know you are not,' Eric said, not in the least mollified.

The stallion's coat steamed gently as it dried in the heat from the forge, the dapple reddened to a flickering roan. Guyon put down the hoof and, with a nod to the farrier, paid him the halfpenny fee. In the act of putting the coin in his pouch, the man stopped, his gaze darting into the gathering twilight.

Eric swung round, right hand going to his hilt. Hand on the bridle, Guyon stiffened. Hooves thudded on the dirt road and harnesses jingled. A man swore bawdily in Flemish and a woman cried out. Guyon spoke quickly to the farrier and, taking the reins, led Arian out of the enclosure and into the village street. At the crossroads twenty yards away a group of mounted, mailed Flemings had surrounded the young couple from the alehouse and were refusing to let them pass.

'I'm a free man,' Guyon heard the young huntsman say hotly in accented French. 'You've no right to bar my path.'

'Go on then, you're free!' laughed one of the men, teeth flashing. 'We've no quarrel with you that your little wife won't be able to mend. Lord Walter wants her back.'

'On her back!' corrected someone with a snigger.

'He has no right,' the young man replied, guarding his wife with his body. 'We are free to leave as we choose.'

'You're free to die,' replied the spokesman. Suddenly a

blade sparkled. The girl screamed as a Fleming groped for her bridle. Her husband felt for the dagger at his belt, but subsided in mid-motion to duck beneath the murderous sweep of the drawn sword.

'Let them pass,' commanded Guyon, his own sword free and confidently held, his knees commanding Arian to thrust forward between the couple and their tormentors.

The Fleming measured Guyon and the older man behind. Two of them to their nine and only the foremost mounted, but the grey was solidly boned, the man astride exuded the confidence of ability and they were probably not alone. 'Don't meddle in what's not your business,' he growled.

'Sound advice,' Guyon retorted. 'Apply it to yourselves and let them pass.' A swift glance revealed that the mercenaries were spreading out to encircle himself and Eric. Strained ears caught the sound of a shout from the alehouse end of the street.

The Fleming wasted no more time on words, but lunged at Guyon, whose arm was jarred to the shoulder as he warded the vicious blow, not with the safety of his shield but the blade of his own sword. Bluish-white the sparks glanced off, and he realised grimly that his assailant was left-handed. A man was taught from the cradle to crouch behind the shield worn on his left arm, to let it take the blows and to counter-strike with his sword in his right. Sword to sword was a nightmare. You parried and risked snapping the blade, or you missed the parry and you died.

Behind him, Eric gasped as a blow caught him beneath his guard, splitting his mail but not cutting through the thick quilting of his gambeson. The girl was crying. Someone snatched the dagger from her husband's hand and pinioned his struggling arms like a coney prepared for the table.

Guyon thrust his shield against a sword blow on his left and felt the blade score and slide off the toughened lime-wood. With his knees he commanded the stallion to pivot and lunge against the mount of the left-handed Fleming, their leader, and brought his sword across, unexpectedly hard and low. It almost worked, but the mercenary was too experienced and at the last moment intercepted the move with a slicing sidelong slash. Guyon twisted and parried. Pain seared his thigh as the Fleming's blade bit flesh. He locked his wrist against the pommel, sweeping the other sword sideways, changed his grip, and slashed. The Fleming grunted, lost his grip on the reins, and hunched over his saddle.

Guyon swung Arian. The end of a flail grazed his hair. He slammed his shield into the backswing, kneed Arian forward, and was rewarded by the shriek of someone unexpectedly unhorsed.

'*Ledworth!*'

Guyon heard with relief the rallying cry of his own men. '*A moi!*' he bellowed, hacking about him. Arian lashed out, and another horse neighed high and shrill with pain. The leader of the Flemings toppled from his saddle, hit the churned mud, shuddered and was still. His second in command looked around, saw that they were now outnumbered and, with panic in his voice, yelled the order to retreat.

A rearguard attempt to bring the huntsman and his wife away with them was aborted as Guyon spurred Arian between their horse and that of the Fleming tugging on its bridle. The sword chopped downwards, cleaving leather, flesh and bone. The mercenary shrieked as he was parted from three of his fingers. Guyon grasped the gelding's broken reins and pulled the horse hard about. One of his men took the bridle from him and passed the couple through to safety.

Guyon turned Arian around. The horse was bleeding freely from several slashes on his neck and forequarters and was jittery, still spoiling for battle, so that Guyon was forced to stay in the saddle. There was blood running down his leg. It would have to wait. Undoubtedly reinforcements would be summoned from Thornford and set on their trail.

The young huntsman had taken control of their mount

and was busily knotting the reins to make them whole again. 'There is no way we can thank you enough, my lord,' he said to Guyon. 'We owe you our lives.'

Guyon smiled bleakly. 'Walter de Lacey is no friend of mine. You owe me nothing. It was a pleasure. I'd advise you to be on your way as soon as you can, though. He tends to nurture grudges.'

'You do not need to tell me that, sire!' the young man snorted. 'I'm a free man and I'll not work for the likes of him. Lord Ralph was mean and sour, but he'd not lay about him with a whip for the pure pleasure of it, nor take a girl to his bed if she were not willing!'

Guyon shifted his gaze to the delicate blonde young woman watching them anxiously. Probably she was about Judith's age but she looked no more than twelve, just the kind that de Lacey enjoyed. 'Where are you and your wife bound?'

'I have relatives in Chester, my lord. They will take us in while I find work. I thought I would seek employment with Earl Hugh.'

'There is work nearer to hand at Ravenstow if you desire it. I've been a huntsman short since last winter. Make up your mind as we ride,' Guyon offered. 'Ravenstow is on your road anyway and you would do well to take advantage of an armed escort off Serigny lands. If you decide against staying, I'll recommend you to Earl Hugh. He's a personal friend.'

The young man considered him from beneath a tumble of wet brown curls. Guyon FitzMiles was a huntsman short because Sir Walter had almost beheaded the man in a fit of fury during a hunt to honour the marriage of Ravenstow's heiress, or so the rumour went. Something about the theft of a horse and a broken boar spear. 'Thank you, my lord,' he replied, turning to his horse. 'We are grateful.'

CHAPTER 14

Judith ceased combing her hair and regarded her mother across the space that separated them. 'I thought you might,' she said without surprise.

It was not quite the response Alicia had expected to her announcement that she was going to her dower lands as soon as Guyon's father returned from his business with Hugh of Chester to escort her there. She had come to her daughter's room prepared for tears and pleading and was completely thrown by Judith's aplomb.

'I do not want you to think that I am discontented here with you and Guyon, but you have your own life to live . . . and I have mine.' She wondered if she should test that aplomb by telling her daughter what else she intended besides.

Judith put down the comb, went to her mother and wordlessly hugged her. They were much of a height now, almost eye to eye, for Judith had grown since the early spring and had put flesh on her bones.

Alicia returned the embrace. 'Of course, I will visit you often and you will know where to find me should the need arise,' she said, feeling guilty, but then guilt was nothing new and was about to be consolidated.

'You will always be welcome, you know that!' Judith answered, kissing her. 'But why do you speak as if you intend your stay to be permanent?'

'Because I do.'

Judith lifted her head from Alicia's shoulder, her eyes filled with shock and anxiety. 'Is there something wrong? Something that I or Guyon can do?'

Alicia stroked Judith's shining tawny hair. 'Understand when the time comes,' she said pensively, 'and do not judge me too harshly.'

'Mama?' Judith looked up at her, beginning to feel worried. Her mother would not meet her gaze and her lids were red-rimmed as they so often were these days.

Beside the fire, Melyn gave a leisurely stretch, then stalked past the two women to the door. Alicia sniffed and gained control of her precarious emotions. Mother and child. She could sense the reversal.

Judith was staring at the cat and the entrance, her tension palpable.

'What's the matter?' Alicia said.

The curtain parted and Guyon entered the room.

'Mother of God!' exclaimed Alicia because water was dripping from every portion of him and puddling in the rushes. Leaving her daughter to deal with him, she hastened from the room to see that the fire was built up in the hall and dry blankets provided for the men.

Guyon squelched to the fire. His gait was far from its customary lithe prowl, Judith noticed. Indeed, he was limping badly.

'What's wrong with your leg?' Judith hurried to his side.

He unfastened his sodden cloak and handed it to her. 'A sword arm that was too slow,' he answered wearily.

'You were attacked?' she said, her eyes flicking over his soaked chausses and the rain-washed streaks of blood channelling down them.

'Clever girl.' His tone was sarcastic. 'Have you any wine?'

Judith fetched the flagon, a small vial of aqua vitae and two cups. 'Do you want a bath?' she asked cautiously.

'Does it look like it? God's death, we nearly drowned at Elmford. Our mounts were in the river belly-deep and the current was like a wild horse.' He took the wine from her and swallowed it down, coughing a little at the strength of the aqua vitae. His face was grey.

She put her own cup down, fetched a linen towel and knelt to unbuckle his swordbelt. 'What happened?'

The weight of the belt slid from his hips into her hands and he sighed with relief. Flatly he told her of their encounter with the Flemings, its reasons and its likely consequences.

'It is true then. I thought it was just rumour that de Lacey was going to marry Mabel.' Judith disposed of the belt and returned to help him off with the hauberk. 'Mama says that she's not really mad. Her mouth's deformed and what she says comes out as gibberish unless you know her well.'

'I doubt it will trouble her new husband for long.' Guyon put down his cup so that she could draw the hauberk over his head.

Judith frowned, for he was shivering violently. Her knuckles touched his throat as she drew the garment over his head. His skin was cold and clammy to the touch. 'I'd better look at your leg,' she said and began to unlace his gambeson.

'One of the men bound it for me,' he said with a shrug. 'Let be, Judith. I'm so tired I could fall asleep on my feet. The last thing I need is you poking at me with your tortures and nostrums.'

'Nevertheless you will drink what I give you.' She threw him a stern look from beneath her brows.

The faintest twist of humour curled his mouth. 'Oh God,' he said. 'What have I ever done to deserve this?'

'You married me,' she retorted, her own lips curving for an instant from their severity before she took the wet gambeson from him and the clinging damp linen shirt he wore beneath it.

Guyon eyed Judith, his vision throbbing to the lead weight

pressing down on top of his head, sensing a change in her but unable to fathom what or where. She returned with a sheepskin bed covering and flung it around his shoulders then turned away to mix a brew composed of poppy and feverfew in wine.

'So I did,' he said softly and bent to remove his boots. The room swam before his eyes. He reached to brace himself against the clothing chest and missed.

Judith spun round and, with a cry of consternation, ran to him. She saw a brighter red stain spreading on his chausses and his breath was coming in harsh, effortful gasps. He was on his knees. She knelt down and unlaced his chausses.

'Lie down,' she commanded.

'I don't—'

'Lie down!' she snarled and pushed him. Guyon subsided as though she had struck him with a mace and not the flat of her hand.

Efficiently she stripped him, her lips tightening at sight of the ineptly bound linen strip, newly wet and red. 'How long have you been riding with this?'

'Five . . . six hours,' he muttered from between clenched teeth.

'You fool!' She left him to fetch a wad of clean linen which she folded into a pad and pressed hard to the leaking edges of the wound.

'No choice, not with Walter de Lacey and his cohorts howling for my blood.'

'It looks as if they got it!' she snapped, 'and perhaps your life with it.'

'I've taken worse.' He tried to smile and failed.

'I doubt it.' She leaned on the pad. 'You've lost more blood than a stuck pig, to look at you.'

'I knew it would come back to boars in the end,' he said and lapsed into semi-consciousness.

Judith was almost panicked into running for her mother.

Almost, but not quite. There was nothing Alicia could do that she could not and he was her charge. 'So much for subtlety,' she said shakily, looking down at her wet, bloodied bedrobe and smeared hands. Seeing that the bleeding had eased she left him in order to fetch the powdered comfrey root and fresh bandages, and sent her maid Helgund for a bowl of mouldy bread.

Returning to him, she shook the comfrey root into the wound, wondering with grim laughter how the fair Alais de Clare would have coped with such a situation. And the humour died as she wondered what Rhosyn ferch Madoc, mother of his child, would have done.

The maid returned with the bread and was told to fetch sheets and blankets. Judith braided her hair, pinned it out of the way and set to work with needle and thread. The Fleming's sword had caught Guyon's inner thigh where the hauberk was slit to allow for riding and there was no mail to protect his flesh. It was not a long wound, but it had pierced deep and, had it been two inches higher, she would not have needed to worry about the matter of subtlety, and neither would he. Indeed, as she worked, the hysterical urge to giggle almost overcame her again, for kneeling between his legs she had a very intimate eyeful of what had previously so terrified her. Not so daunting now for the simple reason that she had control. If she wanted, she could leave him to bleed to death. It was a sobering thought. She swallowed her sense of the ridiculous and attended single-mindedly to her purpose.

Having dressed the main wound as best she could, for it was in a difficult position to bind properly, she examined him for signs of other injury.

Surprisingly, for a man so dark, Guyon was not hirsute; there was just a ridge of hair running from the centre of his breastbone down into the thick bush at his groin and she was able to scrutinise his flesh closely. It was something she had never done before, preferring to dwell in deliberate ignorance and he, sensing her fear and awkwardness, had seldom stripped naked in front of her.

It had never occurred to her to think of a man's body being attractive. A source of pain and brutalisation, so her previous experience said. Now, almost in wonder, she traced with light fingers a thin white line scoring one muscular pectoral and one higher up, just grazing his jawbone.

Guyon groaned and opened his eyes. Judith sucked a sharp breath between her teeth and quickly withdrew her hand.

'*Cath fach,*' he said weakly and found a smile from somewhere; this time his tone was not patronising. 'How bad is it?'

She could see his pulse racing in his throat and the sweat sheening its hollow. 'Bad enough. You've lost so much blood that there's scarcely a drop left in your body and you're quite likely to develop wound fever. There were flakes of rust in the cut. I've packed it with mouldy bread, but it's hard to bind. I can't move you for fear that you'll open it again. You are going to be uncomfortable for no small time . . . if you live . . . and no, I am not japing with you. You had best prepare your soul.'

'What kind of comfort is that?' he said, tried to laugh and desisted, eyes squeezing closed.

Judith used the moment to scrub her face with her sleeve, refusing to be seen in tears. 'The only kind you'll get from me!' she snapped. 'And don't go to sleep. You've to drink this first.'

He lifted his lids, then with an effort widened them at the sight of the stone pitcher full to the brim and the cup she was filling from its bounty.

'All of it,' she said with a certain satisfaction.

'God's death, you evil wench. Robert de Belleme does not have sole monopoly on torture after all. What is it?'

'Boiled water, a sprinkling of salt and three spoonfuls of honey. It is to make up for the blood you've lost.'

'I'll be sick,' he said faintly.

Judith propped him up on the bolster and pillows fetched by the maid and rammed the cup under his nose. 'Drink it!' she commanded in a voice of steel that gave no indication that her knees had turned to jelly.

Something like surprise flickered across his pallor as he looked at her. 'I'm not worth it, *Cath fach*,' he said huskily.

'You are when I think of the alternative,' she answered, and lowered her lids over betraying tears.

As Judith had predicted, the wound fever struck and sent Guyon's temperature soaring out of bounds and with it his grip on reality. Steadfastly she did what she could to bring the fever down, Alicia giving her aid and relief between times.

During one of his lucid periods they moved him to the bed and Judith forced him to drink ox-blood broth in an effort to give his body the strength to fight back. He was promptly sick and she went away and wept in a corner, then returned and gave him more of the salt and honey water.

Once, his eyes glittering like black glass, he looked through her and spoke in Welsh as if holding a conversation. 'It would still be rape. Not that much of a woman.' And another time, 'She's developing a sense of possession and it's becoming uncomfortable.'

Bouts of raving showed her facets of his life that he had previously hidden from her. His relationship with Rhosyn, twisting like the current of the Wye, bitter-sweet as gall and honey. Once he laughed and called her Alais and made a suggestion that both flustered her and filled her with curiosity. She had not known that such a position was possible. During an occasional lucid spell, he would recognise her for her own self. *Cath fach*, he would say and smile ruefully at his own febrile weakness. If she had ever desired revenge for his treating her like a child, she had it now and the taste of it was sour as vinegar.

After the second night, his condition worsened. Miles rode in at dawn to find his eldest granddaughter gulping tears and clinging to her mother for comfort and the priest bending over Guyon's fever-ravaged body, administering the last rites. Judith, her face waxen, stood opposite Father Jerome, her hands clenched upon the cloth with which she had been wiping Guyon down in a vain attempt to lower the raging of his blood.

Miles came to the bed and gazed down upon his son's fight for life as he had gazed down on his wife's. Guyon's hair was lank with sweat, his cheekbones like blades with blue hollows beneath.

Miles looked at Judith. She returned his gaze evenly with eyes that were full of fear. It had gone beyond what she could do for him. In God's hands his life now lay and the odds against his recovery were not favourable. Beyond the moment she dared not think. Life went on; she knew it all too well.

Miles stood a moment longer and then, unable to bear the room, turned and strode out. Judith hastened after him and found him leaning against the rope-patterned pillar of the cross-wall's arch, his fist clenched upon the stonework, staring blankly at nothing. She set her hand on his arm.

Miles closed his eyes, opened them again and faced her. 'How did it happen?'

She told him. 'Eric won't be using his arm for some little time. I have scarcely spoken to the girl or her husband, but he told me they owed Guyon their lives and their gratitude. I need not tell you that at the moment it is no consolation.'

'No,' Miles agreed bleakly.

Judith bowed her head and returned to her vigil.

Two hours later, de Bec came grim-faced to tell her that Walter de Lacey was waiting in the outer ward.

She put down the mortar in which she had been grinding herbs. 'And what could he possibly want?' she said sarcastically as she made sure that Guyon was as comfortable as

his condition allowed, and bade her maid Helgund stay close
by him.

De Bec lifted his craggy brows at her. 'Mistress, when he
saw our new huntsman, he didn't know whether to leap for
glee or fall into apoplexy.'

'What a pity he couldn't decide,' Judith said viciously.

De Bec cleared his throat. In this kind of mood his young
mistress was lethal and the man to best deal with her was in
a raving fever at the gates of death. He took a deep breath.
'From what I have heard, you had best bring the lass up here
out of sight until Sir Walter's gone.'

Judith considered, nodded and sharply bade one of the
maids fetch Elflin of Thornford to her chamber.

The girl arrived from her duties in the kitchens. There
was a smut of flour on her cheek and her hyssop-blue eyes
were filled with terror.

'Oh my lady, please don't send me back to him, for the
love of God, I beg you. I'll kill myself, I swear I will!'

Judith looked at the bent flaxen head, the clenched small
hands that were as delicate as a child's. 'Get up,' she said
neutrally. 'Do you think that I would give you up to that
scum when my lord has perhaps sacrificed his life that you
should go free?'

The girl stood up and wobbled a curtsy.

'You say you would kill yourself?' Judith said coldly. 'You
would do better to take a knife to the tryst and put it through
his black heart.' Her voice seethed on the last words. She
eyed the girl with contempt. 'Elflin, is it not?'

'Yes, my lady.' Her voice quavered, thin and reedy with fear.

'Well then, Elflin, stiffen your spine and stop snivelling.
There is no room for a wet fish in my household. He won't
have you, I promise. Now, do you take up that distaff over
there and that basket of carded wool and work awhile. Ask
Helgund if there is anything you need to know.'

Elflin squeaked assent and bobbed another curtsy.

Milk and water, thought Judith impatiently, then

checked herself, recalling her own fear of the unknown in the early days of her marriage to Guyon and remembering too, with a guilty pang, his patience and good humour during that time. If she was not afraid now, it was because of him.

In the hall, Walter de Lacey was standing before the hearth. The chamberlain had furnished him with a cup of wine and she saw with a sinking heart that he was deep in conversation with Father Jerome, who had about as much guile as a newborn lamb. From the smirk on de Lacey's face as he watched her come forward, it was obvious that he knew and delighted in the news of Guyon's grave illness.

Stifling the urge to be rude until given grounds, Judith made a stilted, traditional speech of welcome.

De Lacey's smile was supercilious. He looked at his nails. 'I am sorry to hear that your husband is so grievously wounded, but the fault is his own. He should not have meddled in my affairs on my lands.'

Father Jerome frowned at him. 'My lord, as I understand matters, he came to the aid of innocent travellers being wrongly molested.'

'A jumped-up gamekeeper and my groom's wayward daughter?' De Lacey's laugh was caustic. 'Guyon FitzMiles prevented my men from carrying out their lawful duty. Indeed, I am sorely tempted to seek compensation from him for the death of my captain.'

'Your former gamekeeper is a free man to sell his services where he desires and his wife is a free woman,' Judith said, looking at him with repugnance. 'You have no right.'

'So you refuse to turn them over to me?'

'It gives me the greatest satisfaction to deny you both them and your compensation,' she said, her chin high. 'Drink your wine and go. There is nothing for you here.'

His lids narrowed. 'I do not think that with your husband on his deathbed you can afford to annoy me. After all, who knows where these lands will be bestowed next and my wife

is growing old and not in the best of health. I expect soon
to be bereaved.'

'Rot in hell!' Judith hissed.

He smiled at her. 'There'll be more pleasure in taming
you than that bag of bones I've got at the moment. My
compensation is already assured.'

Father Jerome made a shocked exclamation.

'If you want to be a gelding, that's your own choice,' Judith
retorted, her fingers itching to draw her eating knife from
her belt and do the deed there and then. 'I think we have
nothing to trade but threats and insults. Excuse me if I do
not see you on your road. My husband needs me.'

He raised his cup to her in a mocking salute and looked
her insolently up and down as if she was already a piece of
his property.

In the bedchamber, Judith collapsed beside the hearth,
her teeth chattering and her hands icy. Helgund fetched a
sheepskin from the foot of the bed, wrapped it around her
mistress's shaking shoulders and hunted out the flask of aqua
vitae.

Judith choked on the strong liquor. 'I'm all right,' she
reassured the maid, finding a wan smile from somewhere.
'Lord Miles will need to know. Have you seen him?'

'Not recently, my lady. He did not come here while you
were gone.'

'My lady, he was talking to your mother in the hall before
Lord Walter came,' Elflin offered timidly from her corner
where she sat deftly spinning the wool, her manual dexterity
far in advance of her mental. 'But they had gone when you
summoned me to your chamber.'

'I'll try his chamber in a moment,' Judith said and,
finishing the aqua vitae, cast off the sheepskin and went to
look at Guyon.

He was sleeping deeply and his temperature, although
still raised was, she fancied, not as high as it had been, or
perhaps it was just wishful thinking. She turned round and

saw the dainty English girl watching her with a wide-eyed mingling of expectancy and fear.

'Our visitor has gone,' Judith said. 'I think it will be safe for you to seek your husband now.'

'Thank you, my lady!' Elflin dropped her work and, blushing, bobbed a deep curtsy before departing the room at a near run.

'What it is to be young and eager,' smiled Helgund, addressing Judith as if she were a staid matron beyond love's first sweet violence.

'Yes,' Judith agreed flatly and smoothed the coverlet. 'What it is.' Her chin quivered. She mastered the urge to weep and straightened up. 'I must find Lord Miles and tell him what has happened. Let me know if there is any change.'

'Yes, my lady.'

Judith left the room almost as swiftly as Elflin had done, got halfway down the stairs, stifled the familiar panicky instinct to run and continued at a more sedate pace across the great hall and up the stairs to the small chamber that was her father-in-law's when he visited.

She could hear the murmur of voices as she approached, one deep and hesitant, the other her mother's and breathless. Then the voices ceased. At the curtain, Judith paused, warned by some sixth sense that to clear her throat and just walk into the room would not be wise.

Cautiously she drew aside the merest fold of material and peered within to assess whether she should go or stay. Set into the thickness of the wall, the room was tiny with space only for a bed, a small clothing pole and a brazier for use against the cold. Before the brazier, blocking it from view, her mother stood locked in Miles's embrace, her blue gown melding into the dark green of his tunic and chausses, his hands lean and brown against the snowiness of her wimple. Her mother's arms were locked around his neck and they were kissing as, only yesterday in the hall, she had seen Elflin and her husband kissing.

Judith dropped the curtain, stepped away and wondered why she had not realised it long ago. There had been enough beads to make a necklace if one had the eyesight to pick them up. The swings of her mother's moods, the looks and counter-looks cast across the hall, met and avoided. What had her mother said? Understand when the time comes and do not judge me too harshly. No more harshly than Alicia had judged herself, she thought and wondered if Guyon, less naïve than herself, had known.

At the foot of the stairs, she encountered the lady Emma about to ascend and quickly blocked her way.

Emma's gaze sharpened.

'I should not bother him until later,' Judith said, her voice slightly constricted. 'He is otherwise occupied.'

Emma searched Judith's face for meaning. 'With a woman, you mean?' Judith hesitated and Emma grimaced. 'That always was his source of oblivion.' She sighed, turning with Judith to go back down to the hall. 'He's not much use at getting drunk and he's too slightly built to go out and pick a fight. I've known him ride a horse half to death, but a woman by preference is his usual form of solace. At first after my stepmother died there was scarcely a night when he slept alone . . . God knows some of the sluts Guy and I had to tolerate in the early days!'

Judith coloured. 'He is with my mother,' she said quietly, 'and they still have all their clothes on.'

Emma's eyes rounded. She stopped and turned. 'Your mother?' The thought seemed to have blocked her brain.

Judith stared her out. Emma drew a long breath between her teeth and let it out again slowly. 'Well then, I am sorry if my words gave offence but in the past it has been true.'

'The past is not now,' Judith said, not quite keeping the coldness from her tone. For all that Emma was Guyon's sister and he maintained that she had a heart of gold, Judith was hard pressed to find it beneath the layers of iron and ice.

Emma bit her lip. She and Judith were never going to be more than tepidly cordial. Their natures had too many similarities, subtle shades apart and, within this keep, like two stones in close proximity on a riverbed, they had begun to grate against each other. Emma began to think with new longing of her dower estates and how, when Guyon's crisis was resolved one way or the other, she would go there with her daughters.

Christen seemed to be cured of her affliction to flirt. No more was 'Alais says' the bane of their lives. In part she knew it was due to the seriousness of Guyon's condition. That, in itself, was sufficient to put meaningless frivolity in its true perspective, but part was also due to Judith's steadying influence. Guyon's wife might laugh and play childish games with her nieces, might have a puckish sense of humour and an impudent tongue, but attracting men appeared scarcely to interest her. Nor did she wish to gossip about them to the detriment of all else and her domestic skills were more than competent, as was her knowledge of healing and sickbed nursing. Christen, receiving an indifferent or bored response to most of her tattle, had steadied her own giddy attitude and begun to think a little for herself. What profit there was in that had yet to be seen. 'No,' she agreed, 'you are right. The past is not now.'

CHAPTER 15

A week came and went. So did the priest. Twice. Guyon wavered on the narrow brink between life and death, teetered and stepped back from the edge. Another week passed. There was a terrific thunderstorm. Three sheep in the bailey were struck by lightning and one of the store sheds caught fire. Guyon's temperature descended to normal. He recognised those who stood at his bedside and spoke to them, but he was as weak and dependent as a newborn kitten and even the effort of speech left him exhausted.

In August they received the news that Jerusalem had fallen to the crusaders. The people of the town held a great bonfire and rejoiced for two days. Guyon got out of bed for the first time, walked three paces and collapsed. Judith made him swallow iron filings in wine and more of the disgusting ox-blood broth and gave him a stick to help him walk.

Emma and her daughters left to go first to Emma's dower lands and then return. At the end of the month too, Alicia departed for her own dower lands with Miles for escort, her leave-taking of Judith somewhat tearful, but there was a new peace behind the emotion and Judith did not begrudge the cause of it, only hoped it would last.

By late September the wound in Guyon's thigh had healed to a livid pink scar that he would bear for the rest of his life, but, precluding the success of any schemes that her Montgomery uncles and Walter de Lacey might have in store, his life was not now measured in terms of hours and minutes.

Currently, Robert de Belleme was in Normandy conducting a private war against a neighbour who had offended him and was not expected back in England this side of spring. Walter de Lacey had been occupied in a localised but savage war against the Welsh, persuading them to stay on their own side of the border and leave his herds alone. The patrols went out from Ravenstow, but their own borders, due to the vigilance of Eric and de Bec, remained secure.

Outside, the wind was gusting a carnival of brown and yellow dead leaves against the keep walls. Pigs rooted in the woods for acorns, or snuffled among the windfall apples in the garths and orchards attached to the cottages. In the fields, men ploughed over the stubble and prepared the land for its winter lying while women and children were out gathering the blown-down dead twigs and branches for kindling in the long dark months ahead.

In the main bedchamber, Guyon closed his eyes and buried his head on his forearms, lulled by the soothing motion of Judith's strong fingers on his back, massaging stiff muscles with aromatic oil of bay. It had been his first time on a horse since his illness. He had discovered that although his recently healed tissue protested, he was not overly uncomfortable and had thus spent longer in the saddle than he should. 'Learning to ride before you can walk,' Judith had said with exasperation.

Peevish with exhaustion, he had snapped at her that he knew his own limits.

'Then why overstep them?' she had smartly retorted with a toss of her head and left him to struggle upstairs on his own.

She had been right of course – as usual. He stirred beneath her touch as she found a strain and thought that he owed her his life. Without her knowledge of simples and her care in the early days, he would have died. In between, she had faced down and seen off Walter de Lacey and, with the aid of his father and the keep's official machinery, had run the demesne with commendable efficiency.

One of the maids murmured something and Judith replied softly. A slight shift of his head and a lazily lifted lid showed him the huntsman's wife Elflin for whose sake he had almost got himself killed. She was striking in a strange, ethereal way, her bones bearing the fragile delicacy of frost on glass. Brand, her husband, had been holding Guyon's courser's bridle this morning, a smile of welcome on his taciturn features. They had decided to remain awhile, he said. Judith had confirmed that Brand was indeed a skilled huntsman, quick, willing and conscientious. Judith had brought the girl upstairs to train. Kitchen work was too heavy for her and her beauty was the kind to cause trouble among the general mêlée of servants who visited the kitchens, or had recently been finding cause to do so. Here, within Judith's immediate governance, she was safe.

Guyon's thoughts drifted drowsily. Judith's hands worked lower over the small of his back. She paused for a moment, and then there was the cold touch of the herbal oil and the slow, undulating motion of her fingers.

Long abstinence, the slow pressure of her hands above and the mattress below, made his reaction inevitable. Heat flooded his loins and burgeoned.

Judith felt the change in him. Quite suddenly, beneath her kneading palms, the fluid muscles were rigid with tension.

'Are you all right, my lord? Did I hurt you?' Anxiously she leaned over him. The ends of her braids tickled his back. Her movement released a waft of gillyflower from her garments, spicy and warm.

'No,' Guyon muttered, voice choked. 'No, you did not hurt me, but I think it would be best if you made an end.'

'I was nearly finished anyway,' she said with a shrug, thinking that he wished to be left to sleep. 'Do you turn over and I will anoint your leg.'

There was a strained silence. Judith began to worry. 'Guy, what's wrong?'

He closed his eyes and willed the offending member to subside. It did nothing so charitable. The feel of her breasts, warm and round against his back as she leaned over him, was only making matters worse.

After a moment, he raised his head from his buried arms and said with agonised amusement: 'What's wrong, *Cath fach*, is that the condition I'm in won't do either of us the least bit of good if I give it free rein now.'

'What condition?' She looked blank.

'Oh God, Judith, just give me the ointment and get out!'

'But your thigh, it needs . . .' Her voice trailed off and her eyes grew as wide as goblet rims as belatedly she made the connection and with a gasp sprang away from him, her face flaming. Picking up the jar of oil, she thrust it down beside him and fled the room in panic.

Guyon looked at the little pot by his head and, with a groan, buried his face again in his forearms.

It was impossible to run down the sharply twisting narrow stone steps when hampered by an undergown and thick woollen tunic. As Judith slowed her pace, the racing of her mind began to subside as well. Chagrin swept through her. She had been a fool to panic. More than ever now he would think of her as a child. Wherein lay the point of washing her hair in herb-scented water and perfuming the points of her body, tempting fate, only to flee in terror the moment that fate appeared briefly on the horizon?

And if I had stayed, she wondered and gave a small shudder, half fear, half something else. It was like snatching hot chestnuts from the fire and hoping not to get burned. Was the prize worth the pain? *And if I go back* . . .

Poised at the foot of the stairs, her dilemma was resolved for her by FitzWarren stooping to inform her that the lord of Chester was here and asking hospitality overnight for himself and his retinue.

'I have found accommodation for most of his men, but the cook says we have not enough bread and no oven space to bake more with all the new preparations he will have to make.'

'There's an oven in the village, use that,' she said, her present problem abandoned for one of literally far greater dimensions. Where in the name of Holy Mary were they going to lodge Earl Hugh? The great bedchamber it would have to be, and Guyon could have his father's tiny wall chamber. She would make do with the maids in her mother's chamber on a straw pallet. Mentally clucking with irritation, she sent one of the girls scurrying aloft with the news and went forward wreathed in smiles to greet the lord of Chester.

He was even more huge and solid than she remembered and the kiss of peace he stooped to bestow on her cheek was as warm and gluey as melted pig's trotters. 'Well well!' he chuckled in his husky voice, looking her up and down and quite misconstruing the breathless pink flush on her cheeks for something less innocent, 'I see that marriage is suiting you!'

Judith's colour darkened and the Earl gave a phlegmy chuckle of delight, and then proceeded to view with approval the way she mastered her embarrassment and with commendable efficiency set about making him comfortable. 'I remember when you were a tiny maid at your mother's knee,' he grinned, as she drew him to the fire and bade a servant take his cloak. 'Mind you, it also reminds me that I was still slim enough then to chase women for the fun of it!' He patted his enormous paunch ruefully.

'Don't believe a word,' Guyon said behind her, setting his hand lightly on her shoulder and giving it a gentle squeeze. 'He's still frighteningly fast when he chooses.'

'Faster than you, so I hear,' said Earl Hugh, the blue eyes disconcertingly shrewd.

'I was rash and I paid for it.'

Chester grunted. 'Not for the first time. Watch him, wench. He'll run rings round you both and you'll end up tangled in knots.'

Judith's laugh was more than wry. 'Do you think I do not know it!'

Guyon tugged her braid. She risked a glance at him. His face was a little fine-drawn with tiredness, but his expression was light enough and there seemed no change in his usual manner. Involuntarily her eyes went lower and colour flamed her face anew.

His mouth twitched. 'Do not be too sure of the outcome, Hugh,' he grinned. 'She's an awesome gaoler.' He led the Earl towards the small solar behind the dais. Judith excused herself to consult with the cook and see if she could get the carpenter to strengthen the guest's chair so that it would not collapse beneath the strain of so great a weight, as it had almost done during his last visit at their wedding.

'You have been very busy making yourself enemies,' Chester remarked, hunching his powerful shoulders.

'Have I?' Guyon eased himself down on to a padded stool.

The Earl considered him. He had come to know Guyon well during last summer's difficult Welsh campaign: a competent leader of men and an excellent scout with an innate knowledge of the workings of the Welsh mind. If he had failings, they were composed of an unpredictable wild streak – probably due to the Welsh blood – that resulted in a disturbing inclination to go his own way if not minutely scrutinised and checked. 'You know damned well you have!' he growled. 'Hardly Robert de Belleme's favourite nephew, are you? He has some very nasty suspicions concerning your involvement in a raid on the Shrewsbury road back in the spring.'

'Nothing he can prove.'

Earl Hugh lifted a flagon from the cupboard against which he leaned and examined the intricate Byzantine workmanship.

'When has lack of proof ever stopped Bellteme from pursuing his intended victim?'

'I might as well be impaled for a sheep as a lamb,' Guyon said and smiled with private amusement remembering the incredulity on the Earl of Shrewsbury's handsome, narrow face.

'It is no game, Guy,' Chester warned.

'Did I say that it was?'

The Earl's eyebrows lifted towards his thinning hair. 'Don't be obtuse with me!' he warned. 'I'm not a woman to be deceived by the twists of your tongue.'

Guyon propped his leg on a footstool. 'I admit it was fool-hardy to risk de Belleme's rage, but at the time I was raging myself. Since then I've been a model of propriety.'

'Excluding this recent escapade?' The Earl pointed the flagon at Guyon's leg. 'Antagonising the new lord of Thornford by fighting in his village and stealing his servants?'

Guyon snorted. 'Yes, look at me. Do you think I fight odds of nine to two because I enjoy flirting with death and rousing a wasps' nest of trouble? Bad fortune, nothing more. If Arian had not cast a shoe, I'd have been nowhere near his territory – and I didn't steal his servants. They were leaving him anyway.'

Chester put the flagon down on the cupboard. Guyon's lids were heavy, but it was not all the aftermath of fever. Part of it was concealment. 'Walter de Lacey wants Ravenstow, Guy . . . and he wants Judith.'

Guyon snorted. 'Tell me something I do not know. He's had a dagger at my back ever since my wedding.'

'I won't share my boundaries with such a one as him if I can help it. No control over himself, for a start. Half a brain and too much cunning, and he's in de Belleme's pay.' He gave a breathy laugh. 'The Welsh nibbling me one side and him the other. It behoves me to keep you alive and in a state of grace!'

'Is that why you're here?' Guyon raised his lids to reveal a glint of humour. 'To protect me from the worst of my own nature?'

Chester shook his head. 'To make sure you know how close to the fire your fingers are!'

'You sound like my father!' Guyon laughed.

'Is he not wise?'

'Oh, very.'

Chester's restless fingers toyed with his heavy circular cloak brooch. He had heard several rumours in Shrewsbury concerning Miles and Maurice de Montgomery's widow. Well, and why not? She was well preserved and her dower lands, although not vast, were pleasant and fertile. A man could find it in him to plough both with ease. Perhaps it would be entertaining to pay Miles a visit in the near future and see about the purchase of another horse . . .

'I know how close to the fire I am,' Guyon said into the Earl's ruminative silence. 'But "uncle" Robert will have his eyes on a broader arena than mine now that Jerusalem has fallen into Christian hands. I hazard that for the moment he'll leave my demise to fate and expendable tools such as Walter de Lacey.'

Chester pursed his lips. The King's older brother, Robert Curthose, had pawned the Duchy of Normandy to Rufus in exchange for the necessary silver to go on crusade and had departed forthwith. The Christian force had been successful and, barring mishap to Robert's ox-like frame, a few more months would likely see his return and an ensuing broil of trouble. Rufus was not going to smile sweetly and hand over Normandy like meat on a trencher.

'De Belleme will thrust his sword where it will cause the most mischief,' Guyon continued. 'I'll wager you five marks to a single penny that the moment Robert sets foot on Norman soil, the Earl of Shrewsbury will hare to his side and offer him all assistance. You know what he thinks of Rufus.'

'You think that too,' Chester pointed out drily.

'But I have held my oath to him, have I not? Therein lies the difference. De Belleme doesn't give a pot of piss for his own fealty. I can see it coming as clearly as a thunderstorm over Ledworth ridge. Brother Robert returns from the Holy Wars mantled in glory and demands the return of his earldom. Rufus refuses. De Belleme joins the side that is most advantageous to himself and merry havoc holds sway. All we need then is for the Welsh to come hotfoot over the border aflame with raiding fever and it'll be worse than a drunken brawl at Smithfield fair! It won't matter about me because everyone's fingers will be in the fire then.'

The white bitch at Guyon's feet raised her head and nuzzled his hand. Chester absently admired her narrow-loined conformation and considered Guyon's words. Most of what he had said had already occurred to Chester and doubtless half the other barons in the country. Stormy weather lay ahead and those with sense were making preparations to endure it, or else seeking a new shelter, as in the case of the powerful de Clare family who were quietly cultivating the third brother.

'And Prince Henry?' he said. 'What about Prince Henry?'

'What about him?' Guyon rubbed his thigh. 'He'll watch us all burn for a while, toss the occasional twig on the fire and, when he's had enough, he'll either douse it or walk away, whichever suits his purpose best. Probably he'll side with Rufus. He wants him to obtain Edith of Scotland for his bride and he wants Rufus to name him the heir.'

'You know a great deal for a man who's been on his sickbed since before harvest time,' Chester remarked drily.

Guyon shrugged. 'My brother-in-law writes letters to his wife, my sister, and she shows them to me to relieve the boredom.'

'Your brother-in . . . Ah yes,' said the Earl. 'He assists the chamberlain, doesn't he?'

'Along those lines. We all have our ways and means.

Speaking of which, is there a purpose behind your visit, or is it truly just to comfort my convalescence?'

'That depends upon how sick you still are,' Chester said and cocked a glance at the propped leg.

Guyon shook his head and laughed. 'Sick only of being wrapped in swaddling. If I so much as sneeze, Judith appears at my side with some noxious potion or other.'

'She's a young wife, eager to show off her skills,' Chester said, momentarily diverted. 'Considering the life she led before her marriage, you ought to be grateful she's not spiked your wine with monkshood.'

Guyon's laughter deepened and seamed the corner of his eyes. 'You don't know the half of it, Hugh. Monkshood is far too swift a revenge!'

Chester looked a question.

Guyon sobered. 'I owe her my life,' he admitted. 'And more than twice over.'

'She's a fine-looking girl with a sound head on her shoulders. You are luckier than most.'

Guyon clasped his hands behind his head. Fine-looking? Well, yes, perhaps she was growing that way as her body filled into womanhood and he would not deny her intelligence; but as to his being luckier than most? He thought back to her reaction in the bedchamber, the fear in her eyes, the way she had run as if from rape.

For close on a year now he had held himself in check. The first months it had been easy for she was still so obviously a child, but time had blurred the division between girl and woman. He was aware of his hunger and the fact that unless he resorted to force, it could not be appeased. Whatever the change in her body, it was obvious that she was not mentally prepared to accept his flesh. Monkshood was indeed too swift for revenge.

'What did you want to talk about?' he asked abruptly and brought his hands down.

Chester darted his brows at the sharpness of Guyon's tone

which was quite at odds with the amusement of a moment since. 'Where your land borders mine, up on Llyn Moel ridge, there is a blind spot between the hills, and the Welsh ride down the valley to raid. A keep is needed and the best site is within your bounds. When you see it, I think you will agree.'

'Within my expense as well?' Guyon asked. 'I know the place you mean. Lord Gruffydd's men came through the gap this spring and carried off some of our herds.'

'I am sure we can come to an amicable agreement,' Chester said with a benign smile.

'It might be possible,' Guyon fenced, knowing that look of old. Hugh d'Avrenches was no man's fool when it came to arguing prices and what he did not know the canny officials he kept around him did.

Chester's smile became a rich chuckle and his eyebrows flashed swiftly up and down. 'I thought we could ride out tomorrow, your health and your wife permitting. There are some fine hunting grounds up there on my side, too. I've recently built a lodge.'

'I may be able to escape for a few days,' Guyon answered cautiously. 'Providing your quarry is not boar.' His eyes went to the door. 'I don't hunt them for pleasure.'

'Does anyone?' Chester said, taking his meaning immediately, and changed his expression to one of beaming welcome as Judith entered the room followed by a maid bearing a flagon and cups.

CHAPTER 16

LONDON
WHITSUNTIDE 1100

The cry of a boatman floated up from the river. Judith set her sewing aside and went to the casement. Blossom was drifting down from the apple trees in the garth, as green-tinted through the glass as the bright feathers of the popinjay regarding her beadily from its perch. Being momentarily high in the King's favour, Emma's husband could afford to waste silver on such rare frivolities as green glass windows and exotic foreign birds.

She and Guyon were in London to attend the Whitsuntide gathering of the court, held this year at the newly completed Palace of Westminster designed by Rannulf Flambard, who took men's money and spent it in the name of the crown. The city was crowded, as packed to bursting as a thrifty housewife's jar of dried beans, and only the highest magnates in the land were granted sleeping space within Westminster and its immediate environs. The rest had to manage as best they could. Conveniently for them, Richard, Guyon's brother-in-law, owned a house on the Strand but a few minutes' walk from the new palace and was able, with a bit of a squeeze and a great deal of organising from Emma, to house Judith and Guyon and their immediate servants for the length of their sojourn. They were uncomfortable and cramped, but more fortunate than most . . . fortunate being a relative term, Judith thought and scowled over her shoulder at the bed in the corner of the curtain-partitioned room.

It was Richard and Emma's and they had insisted on giving it up to herself and Guyon during their stay. A kindness that was a cruelty in disguise. Last night Guyon had sat up until the early hours talking to Richard and used the excuse of not disturbing Judith and the other sleepers across whose pallets he must step in order to reach his own bed as a reason to roll himself in his cloak among the other men in the hall.

Judith leaned her head against the wall and folded her arms, her eyes troubled. Ever since that incident in the bedchamber at Ravenstow, when his body had reacted to her touch and she had run from him in terror, he had taken pains to avoid the physical contacts of their relationship.

The morning after Earl Hugh's arrival, he had ridden out with him to inspect the proposed site of the new keep. Judith, her mind and emotions in turmoil, had not been so foolish as to try and stop him. Indeed, when he told her of his intentions, after one brief, involuntary denial she had listened quietly to his reasoning and to Earl Hugh's jovial bluster and agreed with them that they must go; she had even found a smile from somewhere and the will to be interested in what they intended.

In the morning she had served them both the stirrup cup and wished them good fortune with a smile on her lips, and when Guyon had leaned over Arian's neck to tug her braid she had suffered it with humour and forced a smile. It was only for a week at most that they would be gone, only a week she told herself, but it might as well have been a lifetime. She had sobbed furiously into her pillow. The mastery was no longer hers. She had lost it the moment she ran from him in panic, her hands slick with aromatic oil and the feel of his skin still imprinted on hers.

In the event, it had been a full ten days before he returned, looking positively refreshed by his freedom. His skin had

worn an outdoor glow and his manner had been ebullient as
he discussed the plans for the intended new keep. It was
literally a stone's throw from the Welsh border. There were
merlins nesting on the lichened rock face and wolf pugs in
the mud of the river crossing at its sheer, boulder-tumbled
face. To the west, the hills of Gwynedd were a purple dragon-
back in the distance. To the east lay the fertile Chester plain.

A price had yet to be haggled and the costings worked
out, but both men professed themselves content that the
project should commence by the early spring. So much Judith
had heard from Guyon, his manner enthusiastic, nothing
concealed. In a roundabout way, as it went from guardroom
to hall servants to her personal maids, she also heard that
Earl Hugh not only kept an excellent table at his hunting
lodge, but also provided a comprehensive list of other creature comforts for the benefit of his guests. Apparently the
girl had been well endowed and willing and Guyon's enthusiasm as boundless as that which he displayed when
discussing the proposed new keep.

At first Judith had been hurt and jealous, but these
emotions had been replaced by irritation with herself and a
certain wry acceptance. At least he had not sought his relief
with Rhosyn. She did not think she could have borne that.
And, the remedy she knew lay in her own hands could she
but bear to reach out and grasp it, thorns and all. He still
called her *Cath fach* and pulled her braid, but he was more
wary of touching her now. Fewer hugs and kisses. Sometimes
he would look at her in a way that made her insides melt
with fear and on those occasions his eyes were not on her
face.

He lingered more with his men. Some nights he did not
come to bed at all. He spent much of his time away, some
of it genuine, concerned with the new keep and mainten-
ance of those he already held, some of it an excuse to
avoid her. The easy camaraderie of the early days was gone.
The thread that bound them was taut, vibrating with

tension and stretching a little further each day. And if it
snapped . . .

Stifled by her thoughts, Judith opened the casement and
looked out. The apple blossom, prematurely detached by a
frisky breeze, drifted in pink-tinted snow across her vision.
The sound of laughter silvered her ears and she saw that a
boat was being manoeuvred into the steps at the foot of the
garden, a private riverboat with protective bright canopy and
furs piled within against the nip of the spring breeze.

The source of the laughter was an exceptionally pretty
young woman wearing a cloak lined with vair. She sat on the
nearside of the canopy and was leaning intimately into
Guyon's shoulder. Her braids, exposed beneath her veil,
were the colour of new butter against his dark cloak. He was
laughing too and the woman leaned further to kiss him playfully on the lips as he rose to leave the boat. Richard, his
brother-in-law, followed him, chuckling a remark and
receiving a jesting slap from the woman in punishment. The
last to leave was a slender young man who bent with polished
courtesy to kiss the beringed white hand offered to him.

'That's Prince Henry's private craft,' Christen said,
nudging her way in to lean beside Judith and watch the boat
steer out into the swift, grey current of the river. 'He still
sees Alais on occasion.'

'That is Alais de Clare?' Judith narrowed her eyes, but
the blonde figure was too far away now to be freshly
appraised.

'There's no cause for concern,' Christen said blithely. 'She
flirts from habit and Guy was never really that interested.'

'I'm not concerned,' Judith said with far more nonchalance than she actually felt. 'Who else was there with Guyon
and Richard?'

Christen turned pink and smoothed her already immacu-
late gown. 'That was Simon de Vere, one of Papa's assistants.
He's heir to an estate just outside the city, but Papa
thinks he will rise to much higher things in the King's service.'

So much higher that Richard was hoping for a match between Simon and his eldest daughter. Christen was amenable to the idea, for Simon was nineteen years old, likely to be rich and already an accomplished courtier.

The women heard masculine voices raised in jovial conversation and Christen hastened to open the door, almost tripping over Cadi who was determined to be first.

Richard strode into the room laughing and wiping his eyes at some joke and tossed his cloak casually on to a chest, Emma being absent among the stalls of Cheapside with her maid and not there to take him to task.

The popinjay screeched at the men and bobbed on its perch. 'You ought to get one, Guy, they're good company when your wife's not around.' Richard grinned, as Guyon paused beside the perch to eye the bird dubiously. 'Mind you, so is Alais de Clare, eh?'

'Not much to choose between the two,' Guyon answered neutrally as he walked around the bird. 'But I rather fancy that Alais bears more resemblance to a coney than a popinjay.'

Richard snorted and turned to take the wine that his daughter brought for him.

Guyon looked round at Judith, who still stood at the open window, her expression censorious. 'Where's your cloak, *Cath fach*?'

'*Cath fach*?' Richard looked round, still laughing. Familiar with Latin, French and Flemish and even a smattering of English, he was totally nonplussed by the Welsh that his wife's marcher relatives used so freely.

'Kitten,' Guyon translated in the same, neutral tone. 'She might look sweet, but don't try picking her up unless you want to be scratched.'

'A coney, a popinjay or a kitten,' Richard mused. 'Which would you rather?'

'A kitten any day,' Guyon smiled across at his wife. 'They know how to fend for themselves.'

She looked at him and then away, crossly aware that she was blushing. 'Why do I need my cloak?'

'Simon's grandfather has a house this end of the Holborn road and he's renting breathing space if we want it.'

Judith glanced around the room. Christen and Simon had drawn aside and were talking in stilted formal fashion, painfully aware of Richard's approving but amused paternal scrutiny. Tonight there would be straw pallets laid out over every portion of floor space and not even the privacy to piss in the chamber-pot without alerting half the household to the event. Besides, the crowded proximity in which they were forced to dwell was straining the lukewarm tolerance between herself and Emma to the limit. She nodded to Guyon and went to pick up her cloak from the foot of the bed.

'Get your cloak, Christen,' Guyon said across the room to his niece. 'You might as well come too. Simon's grandfather won't object. He enjoys company.'

'He'd be delighted,' Simon confirmed, his face alight with that particular emotion before he turned a pensive look in Richard's direction. 'With your permission, sire?'

'Dare I trust you for a chaperon, Guy?' Richard enquired, lifting a sardonic brow. 'Emma will have me chopped into gobbets and fed to that damned bird if anything untoward happens.'

'Papa!' cried Christen indignantly, as if his concern had not, at one time, been warranted.

'I will have every respect for Christen, sir,' said Simon with earnest, stilted courtesy.

Guyon considered the bright ludicrous bird upon its perch. 'Does it eat meat, anyway?' he asked.

Christen hit him.

Simon's grandfather was a garrulous old man, in his seventieth year but still hale and hearty, delighted to greet company. He teased Simon unmercifully about Christen, pumped him and Guyon for court scandal, sucking his gums with relish over the juicier bits and making acid remarks about the brains and breeding of the people involved. He gave them wine and honey cakes. The tables board came out and a set of dice and counters. He invited Christen to play and swivelled a jaundiced eye towards Guyon.

'I heard about you from the Prince last time he was here. "Never play tables with anyone from Flambard's household, or with Guyon FitzMiles," he said. "They'll strip you naked in less time than it took you to dress in the first place!"'

'That's untrue!' Guyon protested, laughing. 'I'd leave you your braies for decency at least!'

The old man dismissed him with a disgusted wave. 'Nay, but you're not as pretty to look at across a trestle as your niece here and I've a close interest in her, since she's likely to be future family. Take your wife above and show her the rooms awhile.'

Simon, not about to miss the opportunity to study Christen's dainty profile, drew up a stool so that he could watch her as she played.

Judith and Guyon went outside and climbed the wooden outer staircase to the rooms above.

'What did he mean about the Prince?' Judith asked as Guyon opened the door and drew aside a heavy curtain.

'Oh, Henry occasionally stays here, or he used to before the new palace was finished. Sometimes he games with old Walter to humour him.'

Judith examined the room with renewed interest. The walls were plastered and illuminated with seasonal scenes – hunting, plouging, reaping, women dancing at a feast, a man catching fish. The colours were rich and vibrant. There was a brazier in the room and in a niche in the wall stood a small alabaster statue of the Virgin. There was a bench, an oak chest and a long trestle table.

'He would hold meetings here sometimes,' Guyon said, glancing round at the familiar surroundings. 'That mark on the table is where he propped his feet with his spurs still on.'

'Dicing, wenching and carousing?' she said archly.

'Not often. There are places on the Southwark side for that kind of sin.' He followed her through the second curtain into the slightly smaller bedchamber, which was empty of its main item of furniture. 'I expect Henry's had the bed transferred to Westminster, but I dare say we can find one from somewhere.'

'One?' Judith looked over her shoulder at him.

'As the need arises,' he answered with a shrug, as if the matter was of no consequence.

Judith examined the rest of the room. The windows, like Richard's, were glazed and the walls as in the first room were plastered and illuminated. Rushes strewed the floor, scattered with lavender, and on a coffer was a folded blanket that was obviously a bed covering. She looked down at a second tableboard set upon a cloth-covered trestle and uneasily moved one of the polished jet counters.

'We can remain with Richard and Emma if you'd prefer,' Guyon said, picking up one of the other counters, tossing it in the air and catching it on the back of his hand as if playing knucklebones.

She shook her head, eyes stubbornly lowered, fingers toying desperately with the smooth, cold lump of jet whose twin was lodged in her stomach. 'You have seen how cramped we are. Emma will not thank us if we refuse and it would be a discourtesy to Simon and his grandfather.'

Guyon studied her for a moment, then set his counter down and tilted her face on his fingertips. Judith raised her eyes, feeling hot and weak and frightened, and wished that they had stayed downstairs.

'That is their preference, not yours,' he said gently.

'It is mine too,' Judith stood her ground as he traced the line of her jaw until he reached her ear, skirted it and feathered his fingertip down her throat. Her scalp prickled.

'There is nothing to fear,' he said softly. 'I won't hurt you. You know that, or you should by now.'

A chill ran down her spine. The finger became a hand that slipped slowly down to her waist, curved there and drew her lightly against him. He brushed her temple with his lips, her cheekbone and jaw, slanting to seek her earlobe beneath her braid and nibble it gently. Judith gasped and arched at the sensation.

He nuzzled the sensitive hollow behind her ear, kissed her throat, returned to her face, his lips light as a butterfly travelling the same path again to return to her earlobe. He held her loosely, not compelling her to the embrace, stroking her as he might stroke Cadi or Melyn, soothing her while enticing her to want more. At length, he moved his other hand from her back and slowly took it up the side of her ribcage to the small, neat outer swell of her breast. Softly he touched her lips with his own, applying no demand, then moved on, kissing her chin, trailing the tip of his tongue over her throat.

Judith began to respond. One hand came up tentatively to rest on his belt, the other, palm flat, smoothed the dark wool tunic on his back. She moved closer. Guyon forced himself to a patience he was far from feeling. His body, responding to instinct and abstention, was eager for release. It had been a long time since Earl Hugh's hunting lodge, but Judith was so edgy and afraid that one step too soon or too clumsy and he would lose all the ground he had thus far gained. Besides, a hasty coupling on the floor with one ear cocked for a tread on the stairs was hardly the best method of initiating a frightened virgin and, while it might satisfy his current appetite, it would do nothing for his abiding need.

Judith's lips parted beneath the gentle insistence of his own. She felt as if she was drowning beneath flowing warm waves of sensation. Her breasts tingled. Her loins were moist and aching, her whole body a boneless supple mass.

Downstairs there was a shout of laughter from the old man and loud exclamations from his two young companions. The spell shattered. Judith leaped like a doe and

Guyon's arms involuntarily tightened to hold her. Judith struggled and tore free, her eyes wide, a gasp catching in her throat.

Guyon slowly let his hands fall to his sides. He was breathing hard, as if he had just run up a tower in full mail. 'You see what happens when you stir a banked fire,' he said ruefully. 'I've been wanting to do that for a long time.'

Judith swallowed. He was melting her with that burning brown stare. Their relationship was paused on the brink of another plane and it terrified her. Snatching hot chestnuts from the fire indeed!

Guyon paced to the window, braced his forearms on the thick wooden ledge and looked down at his hands gripping the dusty edge while his blood cooled. He had seen the fear in her eyes and did not know how to deal with it aside from schooling himself to further patience. There were remedies of course, none of them satisfactory. There was no pleasure in drinking water when it was wine you wanted.

Judith hastily sleeved her eyes as Simon walked into the room, grinning broadly, a half-eaten apple in his hand. Christen had just defeated his grandfather in a move that was as much a surprise to herself as it had been to the old man. 'Is it all right?' he asked, nodding around the room and taking another bite of the fruit. 'Don't worry about the bed. Grandfather says he knows where he can get hold of one.'

His back turned. Guyon muttered something at his spread hands and then laughed without humour.

'It belongs to the Abbess of St Anne's,' Simon added, brow cocking curiously. 'It's got a feather mattress and silk hangings and everything else. It was part of her dowry, but the Bishop says she has to give it up . . . What's wrong, Guy, have I said something funny?'

'No,' Guyon said, turning round. 'It's not funny at all. Do I have to say grace before I get in?'

'Depends on what you have in mind,' Simon said. 'For what we are about to receive and all that.' He smiled round at Judith. She turned pink and, choking an excuse, she gathered her skirts and hurried from the room.

'I didn't think that she would take offence. I'm sorry,' Simon said, staring at the still moving curtain with a perplexed frown on his face.

'How many Hail Marys does it take to work a miracle?' Guyon asked wearily.

CHAPTER 17

Judith lifted the goblet. It was made of the finest silver gilt delicately incised with a scrollwork pattern of vine leaves. The wine within was sweet-sharp and cold from the well in which it had been chilled prior to being brought to table.

The King's new hall of Westminster blazed with rich colour, the walls painted in a bold, angular design that glowed red and blue, gold and shadowed matt black. Banners sparred the walls in vivid primary colours. Candles flamed and dripped, cream and gold, reflecting the napery on the long trestles. The high barony of England glowed like a mobile, flowing tapestry.

Judith sipped her wine and watched the weaving men and women – her uncle Arnulf de Montgomery, as objectionable as ever; her maternal uncle William Breteuil was with him and they were talking amiably enough, although the frequent flicker of their eyes betrayed their mistrust. Her most notorious relative, Robert de Belleme, was not here at this gathering, preferring to hold his own court in Arundel prior to taking ship for Normandy, but Arnulf, among others, was his informant as to the happenings at court during his absence.

Further down the room Gilbert de Clare, lord of Tunbridge, was deep in conversation with his brother Roger and with Robert FitzHamon of Gloucester who had been at her wedding. Guyon himself stood on the edge of the group

that included them, having just arrived from the direction
of the latrine. He was resplendent in a gown of garnet-red
wool embroidered with thread of gold. The tunic, unlike the
ones worn at knee length for the rigours of everyday life in
the marches, swept the tops of his ankles. He was a lord of
some importance and at court, if nowhere else, had perforce
to dress as one, even down to the heavy rings encumbering
his fingers.

A man on his way from the hall paused in the act of
pinning his cloak to speak with the group of men. Prince
Henry. She had seen him sitting on the high dais beside the
King, his brother. He was of middling height and girth with
a shock of soot-black hair and narrow features. Guyon replied
to something the Prince said and Henry laughed aloud. The
plain features lit up, became attractively mischievous and he
thumped Guyon's shoulder and walked on. Guyon bowed,
then straightened to glance across at her. Caught in the act
of her own scrutiny, Judith blushed and quickly attended to
her wine. A youth refilled her cup to the brim and passed
on down the board with the flagon.

She drank in deep gulps until her panic had subsided. She
could not forget the delightful, unsettling sensations aroused
in her by the skilful play of his hands upon her. The body
as a weapon. It was a two-edged sword and she had yet to
learn how to handle it. What was it the Welsh said? *Arfer
yw mam pob meistrolaeth*. Practice is the mother of mastery.
Guyon had a vastly unfair advantage and he knew it. It was
there in every look he had given her since that afternoon.
He had not touched her again. He did not need to. The
tension between them was a palpable entity crackling the
air. The eye sufficed, speaking all that the tongue avoided
and the body suppressed.

Some tumblers leaped before the trestle, their costumes
parti-coloured and sewn with bells. One of them between
gyrations juggled with six flashing knives, catching them
expertly by the hilt.

'Enjoying the experience?' Hugh of Chester said in her ear.

Judith jumped and turned round. The Earl was opulent in blue silk, loose cut for comfort over his great belly. Roped gold winked across the width of his breast and there was a huge round Welsh brooch pinned to one shoulder.

'I am glad to have come, my lord,' she said with a smile, 'but I think I prefer the clean air of the marches to that of the city.'

An elderly man at the Earl's shoulder was staring at her with frank, almost startled curiosity. Chester introduced him as Sir Hubert de Caen, a veteran of Hastings and aide of the late King William. Judith smiled and responded politely.

'Ravenstow's wife?' Sir Hubert murmured, taking Guyon's place at the trestle. 'Forgive me for asking, but surely you are related to the Conqueror?'

'Well yes,' said Judith, looking doubtful, wondering at his intention. 'My grandfather and King William were cousins.'

He looked disappointed. 'The tie is no closer than that?'

'I'm afraid not.' She glanced up at Earl Hugh, who shrugged his flesh-padded shoulders and surreptitiously tapped his head.

'It is curious,' pursued Sir Hubert. 'You are the living image of Arlette of Falaise, the old King's mother. She had freckles too, you know, and hair of your colour in her youth and that same way of looking.'

'I am sorry to disappoint you, but the lady Arlette is no part of my bloodline. My grandfather was related through the male line.'

'Remarkable,' Sir Hubert murmured, shaking his head as he rose stiffly to his feet.

The juggler nearly missed one of the knives but swooped and recovered. On the dais, Rufus roared with laughter at a joke. Hugh of Chester moved on with his companion. Judith drank her wine, looked for Guyon and choked on it when she noticed that Alais de Clare had accosted him by one of the stone arches supporting the roof of the hall. A blue and gold banner drifted in the haze above their heads. Alais had her arm linked proprietorially through his, her face upturned and dazzling. He dipped his head to listen to what she was saying. She giggled and flashed a glance around and then stood on tiptoe to whisper in his ear, her hand going boldly down between them.

Judith sat in stupefied amazement, watching her, and then the wine in her blood exploded into rage. She jerked to her feet, shivering the surface of the remaining drink in her cup, walked around the startled juggler and stalked over to her husband and the courtesan.

Taking hold of Guyon's free arm, she stood on tiptoe in mimicry of Alais, but instead of whispering, she bit him. Guyon jerked with a stifled yelp. 'Just thank Christ I chose your ear,' Judith said and looked at the startled older woman. 'You must be Alais,' she said. 'I have heard much about you, so I won't waste any more of my time, yours, or my husband's,' and, in guardroom English, purloined from childhood escapades, she told Alais de Clare precisely what she could do.

Guyon spluttered. Alais gaped at Judith in horrified astonishment. Judith, taking her rival's rooted shock for defiance, raised her arm to strike her, but Guyon seized her wrist and bore it down in a grip of steel.

'It is best if I go, Guy,' Alais cooed in a pillow-soft voice and patted his arm. 'You can give me your reply later.' Ignoring Judith's dagger-bright stare, indeed ignoring Judith altogether, she left him and moved on to intercept, with a ready smile, a young baron attached to Chester's household.

'What in God's name do you think you are doing?' Guyon hissed at her. 'You're a marcher baroness, not a fishwife and the sooner you remember that the better!'

'And she's a high-bred gutter whore!' Judith spat in return. 'I suppose you have arranged to bed with her!'

'You've hardly grounds for complaint, have you?'

For a moment they glared at each other, the air between them charged with tension. And then Guyon released his breath on a hard sigh. 'I wasn't making a liaison behind your back,' he said and tugged her silk-twined braid. 'Jesu God, don't you think I have enough trouble controlling the woman I've got without noosing myself to a featherbrain like Alais de Clare?' He grimaced and rubbed his bitten ear.

Judith lowered her lids and looked down at her soft gilded shoes. The impetus of the wine was beginning to wear off. She felt foolish and a little sick. 'But I thought . . . Christen said that you and she used to . . .'

Guyon snorted. 'Once, twice, no more. I was too drunk the first time and too desperate the second to make better provision and Alais was so pleased with herself that she made the whole court a party to her conquest until her husband clapped his hand over her mouth and pushed her at Henry. He's very partial to brainless blondes.'

'And you are not?'

'I have a marked preference for tawny-haired vixens.' He slipped his arm around her narrow waist, drawing her close to his side.

On the dais, William Rufus laughed again and clapped a brawny arm across the shoulder of the slender young man seated next to him. He was dark-haired and dark-eyed with a mouth like a freshly bitten strawberry.

'His latest toy,' Guyon said. 'He's called Ernoul and comes from Toulouse. It's fortunate that Anselm of Canterbury isn't here, he'd have a seizure.'

'Who's the priest on the dais with him, then?' Judith asked and shifted her hip from the intimate sidelong pressure of his thigh.

Guyon pretended not to notice. 'Rannulf Flambard, Bishop of Durham. He wouldn't flinch if Rufus led a goat in here and held a black mass before his very eyes, providing there was money in it of course.' He cast his gaze around.

'Flambard designed this hall. Rufus says it's too big for a room and too small for a great hall, but that's just his nature.'

'As is Ernoul?'

'As is Ernoul,' he said and tried not to think of how it felt to have the King's arm draped heavily across the back of your neck, or to feel his breath hot on your cheek and know that any moment you were going to be sick. Probably Ernoul didn't mind. Probably Ernoul was being paid a lot of money.

Judith shuddered. The royal court was twice as dangerous and barbaric as life in the marches. As in nature, the bright colours were a warning not to touch. She too knew how to stalk and snarl in all that jungle of colour, but inwardly it worried her. When everyone was a predator, someone was bound to get eaten.

The evening continued. Yet another course of the interminable feast arrived. Things disguised as other things, stuffed and gilded and caparisoned in mimicry of the great gathering they were intended to feed. The wine changed from cold, sharp Anjou to a cloying French red. The dishes ran the gamut of the head cook's heat-sweated imagination. Decorated roast meats served with spicy perfumed sauces, pies filled with fruit and chopped meat and one full of tiny live birds that flew amok and twittered around the hall, soiling the new hangings in their panic. The King sent to the mews for his sparrowhawks.

Musicians played with varying degrees of skill. A jester told some bawdy jokes. A sword swallower amazed the gullible. The knife juggler attempted a refinement that did not quite work and was carried off bleeding like a stuck pig. Rufus did the rounds of his vassals, full of a bluff, jovial bonhomie, the force of it hinting at the choleric temper that lay close to the surface.

The King was a squat, compact barrel of a man with a round, sanguine face and short, powerful limbs. None of the Conqueror's sons were able to boast their sire's inches, although all of them possessed his breadth and inclination towards middle-aged corpulence. Florid and strutting like a barnyard cockerel, Rufus chucked Judith beneath the chin as though she were a kitchen maid. 'So,' he grinned, 'this is Maurice FitzRoger's wench, eh?'

'Sire.' Judith lowered her lids. His fingers were as thick and clammy as raw sausages, but instead of being limp they gripped powerfully, pinching her flesh.

'Skinny little thing, isn't she?' Rufus mused to Guyon as if Judith was deaf. 'No sign of a belly on her yet either?'

'I'm in no hurry, sire,' Guyon responded with a lazy smile. 'A flat furrow's easier to plough than one with a slope.'

Rufus let out a great guffaw and his variegated grey-brown eyes squeezed into puffy slits. His sense of humour was crude and boisterous and it was the kind of remark that he whole-heartedly appreciated.

Judith lifted her taut jaw off his fingers, feeling like a market beast on a block. Rufus opened his eyes and she glared back at him.

'God's blood!' He chuckled softly. 'I remember my grandam Arlette giving me that look when she was wrath.'

It was the second time that evening that she had been compared to the dead Countess of Conteville and it disturbed her not a little. 'Probably you deserved it,' she said.

There was a momentary silence. The bonhomie slipped a little. 'You've a saucy tongue,' the King remarked sharply.

'It's the teeth you have to watch.' Guyon grinned, touching his bitten ear, and kicked her hard beneath the trestle.

Rufus chose suddenly to laugh. 'I can see that! Speaking of which, Hugh d'Avrenches told me a good one just now: "If you were a knight, you'd not have done that." "If you were a lady, you'd not speak with your mouth full!"'

Guyon snorted and laughed. Judith looked blank.

'I thought that knowing Alais de Clare, you'd appreciate it,' Rufus chuckled. 'Meet us tomorrow at Clerkenwell if you desire to hunt. I've a new Norway hawk I want to fly.'

Slapping Guyon's shoulder, Rufus moved on to accost another victim.

'Christ, are you trying to get me exiled?' Guyon demanded with exasperation.

Judith drained her goblet. 'I am not a lump of meat on a trencher to be poked and prodded and discussed intimately as if I have neither ears nor feelings!'

Guyon shrugged. 'Rufus cares little about such niceties where women are concerned.'

'I did not understand his joke.'

Guyon crumbled a piece of bread and watched the action of his ring-bedecked fingers. 'It is probably best you did not. It was very crude, and no, I am not going to give details.'

Judith narrowed her eyes at him. Her thinking processes were by now badly impaired by the wine and it was a struggle to remember how to control her limbs let alone set about cajoling Guyon into explaining what he did not wish to explain, or solve it for herself. She smiled hazily at the servant who refilled her goblet and raised it to her lips. 'Rufus still fancies you, doesn't he?' she said instead.

'Fancies is as far as he will get.' Guyon quirked his brow at her. If she had been less than sober before, she was now well and truly on her way to being gilded. It was seldom that she took more than two cups of wine at the evening meal and frequently they were more than half water. Tonight, he had lost count of the quantity she had swallowed.

He wondered if Judith was anxious in the midst of such an important gathering, although it was not in her nature to soothe herself with drink. He had a strong suspicion that the opulent bed manoeuvred that evening into the bedchamber of the house they had rented was the main reason for her attitude now. Terrified of what the night held in store, she was taking the advice of many a mother to her daughter on a wedding eve and drinking herself insensible.

'Judith, no more,' he said compassionately, staying her hand as she reached to her cup.

'Why not?' she protested. 'I'm enjoying it now. It was hob . . . hobbir . . . horrible at first, but you get used to it, don't you . . . like a lot of things?'

'When you're drunk,' he agreed wryly.

'Who's drunk?' she demanded in a loud voice. Heads turned. Fortunately, at that juncture the King chose to leave the hall and amid the etiquette of rising and reseating, Guyon succeeded in calming his belligerent wife to a muttering simmer. That mood did not last long. The wine had reacted upon her blood to produce aggression. Now it reacted against the contents of her stomach and she began to feel very sick indeed. When Guyon drew her to her feet she lurched against him, her balance awry, her hand to her mouth.

Guyon took one look at her green face and propelled her out of the hall and into the cool, blossom-scented night where she was violently sick, shuddering against his support.

'Sorry,' she gulped weakly.

'I can see that,' he said with exasperation.

After it was over, he swung her up in his arms and took her lolling and semi-conscious to where Eric waited with their horses.

'She won't want her head in the morning, my lord.'

'She doesn't want it now,' Guyon replied. 'And certainly not her stomach.'

'Poor lass,' said Eric with sympathy, recalling many a night of his own misspent youth. 'You'll not be needing the mare then.'

'No.' Guyon gave Judith to his captain while he mounted his horse, then reached to take her up before him. 'God's bones,' he muttered, trying to settle her so that she would not give him a dead arm on the ride home. 'You'd think to look at her that she weighed less than a feather.'

Judith merely groaned and flopped against him like a dead doe.

Helgund unbarred the door to him and exclaimed in horror at the sight of Judith's wan face.

'Too much wine,' Guyon said, sweeping past the servant to the capacious scarlet-bedecked bed, where he deposited Judith.

Clucking like a mother hen, Helgund leaned over her mistress. Judith's eyelids fluttered but did not open. Another maid goggled around the curtain, received a sharp command from Helgund and disappeared again.

'I'll sleep below with Sir Walter,' Guyon said, aware that he was now redundant, but oddly reluctant to leave. Judith looked so vulnerable, her hands pale and long-fingered against the cover of stitched beaver skins, her profile flushed and delicate. He knew how her nose would wrinkle when she laughed and that one of her teeth was chipped where she had fallen down the dais steps as a child. He knew that her waist was slender and her breasts as round and resiliently soft as the breasts of the white doves in the cote at Ravenstow. She had also quite deliberately drunk herself into a stupor rather than share the intimacy of this bed with him.

Helgund arranged the cover and looked around at him, her broad features creased with concern. 'My lady has been very unsettled of late,' she ventured.

'I know, Helgund.' The same could be said of himself, he thought and for parallel reasons. He looked thoughtfully at the maid. She owned a position of considerable trust and as a result knew most of what did, or rather did not, transpire between himself and Judith, and must also be aware of the undercurrents and tensions that existed as a result.

Helgund returned his scrutiny beneath the deference of half-lowered lids. 'She is like a vixen confronting food in a trap, sire. She wants the meat, but dare not attempt to snatch it for fear of paying the price.'

His brows twitched together. 'Am I the meat or the price?' he enquired.

'Both, sire. She fears lest she become reduced to the status of bitch or brood mare, or cast-off wife. It is rumoured at court that you prefer the chase to the kill.'

Guyon's frown deepened. Helgund swallowed, but continued doggedly. 'It is not her fault, sire. If you had seen what Lord Maurice did to her lady mother in front of us all, and mistress Judith no more than a mite of three years old. Said he would fill her belly with enough seed to plant a dozen children and dragged her to the bed there and then before us all and used her like a whore . . . Happened more than once too and sometimes he was in too much of a hurry to draw the hangings. We protected the child as best we could but . . .' Helgund drew a shaken breath and fell silent beneath the onslaught of his stare.

'Thank you, Helgund.' His voice was frighteningly quiet, belying the anger she saw in his eyes. 'Thank you for telling me. I can see the kind of obstacles across my path now. Before, I just kept treading on them. Go back to your bed now. I'll seek mine in a moment.'

Relieved, Helgund curtsied and made herself absent.

Guyon drew a deep breath and controlled his ire. Maurice de Montgomery was already dead; the Welsh had got there first.

'Well, *Cath fach*,' he said softly, brushing a stray wisp of tawny hair away from her eyelids and the thick, downswept bronze lashes, 'how do I avoid these obstacles of yours?'

He knew she was not indifferent and that the times when her guard was down, he would have sold his soul to keep her that way. The times when her guard was up, she was impossible to reach.

Never once of her own accord had she offered him a sign of affection or endearment. Jealousy, yes, but that was an emotion born of insecurity and mistrust. The moves were all his, and they were straining the bounds of her acceptance. Today he had stepped beyond the limit. Tonight she was blind drunk. So what else was left? He shied from the thought.

'*Nos da, Cath fach*,' he murmured softly, tugged her braid and quietly left the room.

CHAPTER 18

On the crest of the hill, Guyon reined his courser to a halt and shielded his eyes to watch the goshawk assault the air on dark, swift pinions, gaining height against the hot blue sky before stooping like a wind-ruffled stone upon the desperate flight of a round-bodied partridge.

Prince Henry, triumphant owner, fisted the morning air as the partridge tumbled over in a puff of feathers and was borne to earth beneath the goshawk's talons. The falconer and a huntsman ran towards the two birds, one to be retrieved in proud prowess to Henry's wrist, the other to be added to the mound of soft bodies already culled that morning. The King's Norway hawk was a skilled killer too.

Henry stroked the breast of his own bird where she perched, dark wings folded, and deftly replaced the leather hood over the fierce golden eyes. Then he looked at Guyon.

'I hear your wife made quite an impression last night,' he remarked with a laconic grin.

'She is not accustomed to quite so much wine, my lord,' Guyon excused and eased himself in the saddle. He had back-ache as a result of sleeping on a lumpy, makeshift pallet within range of a sly draught.

Henry's grin deepened. 'I didn't mean that business with Alais, although I wish I had been there. I meant her resemblance to my grandmother, Arlette. Old Hubert couldn't believe his eyes, thought he'd seen a ghost and Rufus remarked on it this morning at mass . . . and he told me an appalling joke.'

Guyon lifted his stiff shoulders. 'As far as I know, the only blood she shares with your family is that of her maternal grandsire, and, even then, the Countess of Conteville is not of that line.'

'Maurice FitzRoger's girl, isn't she?' Henry looked thoughtful. 'How old is she now, Guy?'

'She was born in the November of 'eighty-three, my lord.' Guyon squinted against the sun at the Prince whose look had suddenly grown secretive, the way it sometimes did after he had been closeted with Gilbert and Roger de Clare. Still waters ran deeper than anyone could fathom.

'Any girl of seventeen who looks like my grandmother deserves closer examination,' Henry said, still stroking his hawk, his gaze intent upon the action of his fingers.

'Angling for an invitation sire?' Guyon jested with the familiarity of long acquaintance and the occasional deeper friendship.

'How did you guess? Anyway, I used to rent the house. You cannot refuse. Is tonight all right? After the hunt?'

Guyon's gaze flickered and sharpened, for Henry's interest was perhaps a little too keen for comfort.

'I did wonder,' Henry said softly to the bird, 'but she never sent word. Perhaps it was just as well.'

'Sire?'

Guyon's tone must have given him away, for Henry uttered a forced laugh. 'God's blood, Guy, stop thinking wild thoughts! With a face like yours, is it likely that I'd be able to seduce your wife before your eyes, or even behind your back! I want to meet her, no more than that. Look, Rufus has started a hare!' He turned to the falconer, gave him care of the goshawk and clapped spurs to his courser's sides.

Guyon followed more slowly, aware of a niggling doubt at the back of his mind. Henry could lie the hindleg off an ass if expediency demanded. Guyon did not believe that he was lying now, but he was sure the Prince was concealing something. The problem with such a devious man was knowing what.

Judith would need to know that they had guests. He had looked in on her this dawn before departing to hunt and found her huddled beneath the pelts in a heavy sleep. He knew the symptoms and how dreadful she would feel on awakening. Renewed nausea, a tight, swollen drum where her head should be and a raging thirst. Hardly the best equipment with which to organise food and entertainment for a prince of the realm who was coming to visit her because she resembled his grandmother. In her present state Judith would doubtless give a commendable imitation of the said lady risen untimely from her crypt.

He muttered an oath beneath his breath, bent a scowl upon Henry's fast-disappearing back and, calling Eric to him, sent him off with a message.

Judith woke late in the morning with all the vile after-effects Guyon had predicted and more besides. Half an hour voiding in the latrine made her swear a miserable oath that she would never again drink the seemingly innocuous wines of Anjou, whose potency was so wickedly concealed. She had meant to drink enough to dull the edge of her fear and instead she had swallowed her way into hell. Of the night before she remembered little except being ill.

Green-faced, she directed Helgund to mix a valerian posset to ease her rolling gut and skull. It tasted disgusting and, fighting the urge to retch because by now her stomach was so sore, she retired again to bed to let the herb do its work. She had been there perhaps an hour when Eric rode in with his message, half a dozen limp partridges over his saddlebow.

Panic ensued. Judith, her headache aggravated to a megrim of titanic proportions, presided over a household that resembled a disorganised corner of hell. However, gradually, her tenacious common sense reasserted itself. This had once been Prince Henry's house. Well and good, let the Prince's machinery do what had to be done. Mustering her wits and drinking another cup of the valerian brew, she tidied her hair, put on a clean overgown and went below to visit Sir Walter and explain her predicament.

By noontide, the kitchen shed was bustling, the cook in receipt of the recipes for Henry's favourite dishes and two servants sent off to the markets to fetch whatever was not available on the premises. A minstrel had been engaged, Helgund and Elflin were busy with brooms and beeswax polish and Judith had retired to the sinful luxury of a hot bathtub, the water scented with attar of roses, in order to compose herself for the coming ordeal.

Her gaze on the bed as she soaked, ignoring Helgund's dire warning that all the goodness would come out of her body, she wondered how she had been brought home last night and where Guyon had elected to sleep, for there had been no imprint in the bed beside her. Probably below with Sir Walter. A memory came to her, hazy and thick as wine dregs. Alais de Clare had been whispering in Guyon's ear and pressing herself against him. Perhaps he had shared a feather mattress last night, and not for the purposes of sleep.

Alais de Clare would give Guyon what he wanted without baulking or complaint, as would many other of the women who frequented the court. She had seen the way they looked at him . . . and at her, the amused patronising hostility, their thoughts naked in their eyes as they wondered how long she would hold him faithful.

She looked down at her body and then at the sinewy freckled forearm and wrist resting on the edge of the tub. She did not have Alais's natural advantages of a lovely face and ripe, lascivious curves, nor her amoral aptitude for coupling, but she probably had at least as much imagination if shown the right direction and she had always been quick to learn. The only problem was overcoming the fear of pain and subjugation, of

being held down and used as no more than an object on which
to breed sons. She knew Guyon would not treat her thus, but
knowing did not prevent the thought from occurring. It was
no light thing to step off the edge of a precipice with only a
tenuous, recent trust for support.

Her mind plodded a fruitless circle. She cursed with soft
vehemence and called for Helgund to bring her a towel.

Henry sniffed appreciatively as they passed the bakehouse
door. Rich, savoury scents wafted to his nostrils. The sound
of the cook paddling the spit boy's behind for failing to turn
the spit at the crucial moment made him smile.

Simon's grandfather hobbled out to greet the hunting
party, wrinkled face bright with pleasure. Henry stopped to
speak with him. Guyon cast a suspicious look over his
shoulder at the industry within the bakehouse, then back at
Sir Walter, who winked at him.

'Resourceful lass you've got there,' he chuckled as Guyon
followed Henry up the stairs.

Helgund and Elflin stood to one side, their working gowns
covered by fresh, snowy aprons, their hair tidied beneath
pristine wimples. Henry turned from their anxious obeisance
before their bobbing up and down made him seasick and
was welcomed within by Judith.

She was very slender; he could have spanned her waist
with his mount's noseband. Her breasts were high and small,
her flanks long and lithe and her voice clear and low. The
years fell away and for a moment it was a different woman
who welcomed him into a different room, a woman with
raven-black braids and twilight-coloured eyes. Judith of
Ravenstow had the same eye shape, but more variety of hues,
and her hair was a warm sandy-bronze, bordering on red.

'I hope I have not put you to any trouble, Lady Judith,'
he said with a smile as he raised her to her feet. It was a
meaningless civility. Henry had long ceased to care about
putting people out in order to have his own way.

Judith made a sincere-sounding disclaimer and, taking his cloak, gave it to Helgund. Guyon handed his own directly to the maid while looking his wife up and down. 'I'm glad to see you are better,' he said. She was wearing a plain cream undertunic and a long-sleeved gown of copper-coloured silk. A girdle of gold links and shaved, amber oblongs hugged her waist. Her expression was calm, bearing no trace of the previous evening's excesses.

'Patched up and surviving on valerian.' She sent him a rueful smile. 'I've still got a raging headache for my sins, but thank you for the warning. At least I have had the time to prepare.'

'More than time,' he murmured, tugging one of her braids and glancing round at the white linen cloth upon the trestle, the fine cups and flagon, the wax candles surrounded by fresh flowers and greenery.

Judith gave him a secretive smile and Guyon's fingers left her braid as though one of her gold fillets had scorched him. His gaze flickered between herself and Henry.

'Dear God,' he said softly.

'What's the matter?'

Guyon shook his head and mutely went past her into the room. Henry paid Judith a compliment concerning her domestic abilities. Guyon snapped his fingers at one of Sir Walter's servants, drafted in for the evening. The man hastened to pour wine. Guyon watched him without noticing his actions, absorbing the shock of what he had just seen and deciding that it was patently impossible. Henry was only thirty-two now.

He thought of himself at fourteen. Sexual congress had been an undiscovered mystery then. Fumblings in dark corners, snatched kisses and giggles, pleading persuasion, his mother's sharp eye upon the younger maids. The dry throat, the anticipation, the blinding flash finished too quickly to be savoured until familiarity lent refinement and control. And Henry at fourteen? Henry at fourteen had already possessed the assurance and technique that came of long acquaintance with the act.

'Penny for your thoughts, Guy?' Hugh of Chester nudged him.

'You'd need more than that,' he said with smile that was not a smile and, taking his wine, went to join Henry.

Hugh d'Avrenches frowned, but after a moment shrugged and followed him.

The evening progressed and so did Guyon's doubts. The similarities were infinitesimal, mainly in the smile and the tilt of the head, and fleetingly seen, but the Prince's attitude gave them credence. He was acting on two levels. Superficially, he was the charming, genial guest, fluent of phrase and gesture; underneath, though, he was studying Judith, drawing her out, examining her piece by little piece, using both his eyes and his expert sleight of mouth. Warmed by his subtle attention, Judith responded as all women responded to Henry, opening like a rose to the warmth of the sun.

Towards the end of the evening when the men were relaxed with food and wine, the conversation was pleasantly upon the merits of Irish hounds for coursing deer and the minstrel was softly plucking out the notes of Stella Maris on his harp, one of Henry's messengers arrived and was shown upstairs.

Henry, drawn from indolent comfort, listened to the kneeling man, his features impassive, but the wine in his hand rippled and a flush darkened the stubble edging his jaw.

His older brother Robert, sauntering glory-clad home from his crusade, had paused in Sicily to take to his bosom a wealthy young bride, one Sybil of Conversano, daughter of an Apulian count with strong Norman ties. The name did not really matter, nor the rank, but the girl's considerable wealth would enable him to buy back his pawned duchy from Rufus and the marriage itself made the prospect of Robert's heir an imminent possibility. Henry's proximity to the crown was suddenly seen distantly across a smoky hall instead of glittering above his cupped hands.

Silence descended in the wake of the messenger's news. No one looked at anyone else. And then Gilbert de Clare muttered something at his boots and Henry flicked him a sharp glance and warningly shook his head. 'A toast,' he said in a brittle voice and raised his cup. 'To my brother and his bride, may they find safe harbour.'

Cups clinked. The toast was mumblingly repeated.

'What will you do now?' Earl Hugh folded his hands comfortably over his paunch, body slack, eyes as sharp as shards of blue glass.

Henry pursed his lips. A look flashed between himself and Gilbert de Clare. 'Rufus won't make me his heir,' he said softly, 'and Robert's got the anvils and hammers to beget his own brood now. I suppose I needs must follow the example of my father.'

Chester waved a gnat away from his face. 'If it's civil war you're suggesting, count me out,' he said, tone still comfortable. 'Got enough problems with the Welsh warring over who inherits what without looking down this end for trouble.'

'Civil war?' Henry's eyes widened innocently. 'No, who would back me?'

'You have friends, sire,' said Roger de Clare, voice low but full of fierce meaning.

'It's not friends I need, but opportunity and the right kind of backing . . . Would you give it to me, Guy?' There was bitter mischief in his eyes.

'A feudal oath is sacred unto death, my lord,' Guyon said quietly after a moment. 'It might cause me pain, but I'd shut my keeps to you.'

'Precisely.' Henry twisted a smile. 'Excellent building material were it but mine. Can I offer you no inducements?'

Their eyes met and held. 'Not even if you were related, my lord,' Guyon said deliberately.

Henry stretched like a cat and his smile deepened.

'I thought not. But supposing it came to a choice between myself and Robert? What then?'

'Then I hope I would make the right choice,' Guyon said, refusing to be drawn.

'Where does your father fit into all this?' enquired Earl Hugh politely.

'No one handed him his meat on a platter, so he went out and shot his own deer.'

Judith decided that this conversation had sailed quite far enough into murky waters and deliberately let her cup slip from her fingers. Exclaiming in distress, she set about collecting the fragments and accidentally caught the finger-bowl with the trailing end of her sleeve, tipping it into Henry's lap.

The Prince dragged a shocked breath over his larynx. Earl Hugh gave a great bellow of laughter, slapped his hand down on the table and drove a dagger of glass straight into his palm. Blood spurted. The bellow became a howl of pain. Judith grabbed a napkin from the table and sought to staunch the wound but, in her flustered haste, knocked over a candle-stick and set fire to Gilbert de Clare's sleeve.

Guyon, his eyes filled with hilarity, snatched the flagon and doused their guest with a great deal of enthusiasm and a very poor aim for a man who was so skilled a warrior. Gilbert's hound snarled and tried to bite Guyon's ankle and was kicked across the room to fetch up yelping against the wall. Pandemonium reigned. Stella Maris faltered, twanged and stopped. The minstrel sidled out of the room, de Clare's abused dog snarling at his heels. Judith flapped around like a headless chicken, creating more chaos than she was clearing up, but at last, Chester's wound was thoroughly, if clumsily, staunched with the napkin, she looked around at the wreckage with brimming eyes, then covered her face with her hands, muffling little sounds into them, her shoulders shaking.

Guyon flicked a look at his wife, spluttered and quickly

bent to retrieve a dish from the floor while he mustered his control. 'I suggest, madam, that you go and find some fresh garments for my lord Prince,' he said in a choked voice.

Judith squeaked and fled. Gilbert de Clare saw an embarrassed husband struggling manfully to control his rage at the shortcomings of his foolish wife. Hugh of Chester in contrast saw a man striving to contain his mirth and banishing its giggling catalyst from his presence until he should be capable of controlling himself. He also saw why it had been done and, looking down at the wad of embroidered linen screwed ineptly round his cut and, knowing how her competent medical skill had saved Guyon's life, concluded that Judith of Ravenstow would take some holding if she ever decided to take the bit between her teeth.

Judith re-emerged, biting her lower lip, her shoulders still displaying a disturbing tendency to tremble as she handed Henry tunic and chausses. Henry quirked his brows, not quite as befooled as his bland expression suggested.

'Do not fret yourself, Lady Judith,' he said magnanimously. 'Accidents will happen.'

Gilbert de Clare coughed and, after a quick glance at Henry, pretended great interest in the rushes strewing the floor. Henry ignored him and changed into the garments. He and Guyon were of a similar breadth, but whereas Guyon measured around two yards in height, Henry fell a full six inches short of that mark and the chausses had to be extensively bound with cross-garters to take up the surplus material. Consequently, the evening ended in laughter and a deal of good-humoured jesting.

Henry swung to horse in the torchlit courtyard, his face open and smiling, black hair tumbling in an unruly shock over his broad forehead, grey eyes shining with the remnants of a good joke. 'You are most fortunate in your wife, Guy.' He glanced over his shoulder to where she stood outlined in the doorway. His tunic reached almost to his fingertips in the new style of the court women and the chausses, even with the bindings, were appallingly wrinkled.

'I know, my lord,' Guyon answered, smiling. 'Although, as you have seen, most of her ploys have a sting in their tail.'

Henry chuckled. 'To be expected when she is under the sign of the scorpion,' he said.

Guyon looked up sharply.

Henry leaned down over his saddlebow and said impishly, 'Remember me to Alicia when you next see her. Tell her I approve.'

The horse lunged forward. Guyon stepped back and watched the glossy bay stallion trot out of the yard. Gilbert de Clare followed on his patchy, raw-boned roan, his brother in tow, and then came Earl Hugh and the bodyguard.

'What was all that double talk about being related?' the Earl asked.

'Nothing,' said Guyon, uncomfortably aware that Hugh d'Avrenches missed precious little. 'A private joke. I am not sure that I understand it myself. What's more to the point, my lord, is Henry's closeness to the de Clares. There was a deal of double talk there, too.'

'Keep your nose out, Guy. Judith was right to drop that cup when she did. What the eye does not see and the ear does not hear cannot be a source of grief in time to come.'

'Oh yes,' Guyon said a trifle bitterly. 'I am an expert in the art of diplomacy.'

'Well then, don't fall foul of the de Clares. They bid fair to be as powerful as the Montgomery line one day, and one day soon at that. Hunting tomorrow? I'll see you there.'

Guyon watched him leave, then, frowning, went to the stables to check his courser which had a suffered a leg sprain during the day's hunt.

Upstairs, Helgund bustled around the bedchamber, lighting the night candle, folding and tidying, setting matters to rights. Judith slowly removed the gold fillets that clasped the ends of her braids and unwound her hair. Helgund helped her unlace the tight-fitting overgown and, after Judith had drawn it off, hung it tidily on the clothing pole and fetched her mistress an ivory comb.

Judith was thoughtful. The evening had not passed without incident, but at least a potential disaster had been avoided. A pity that the Prince possessed a sharper vision than Gilbert and Roger de Clare, who both obviously saw her as a muddle-headed juvenile. She had the impression that Henry had been amused because he was already several steps ahead of her and could afford to laugh. It was not a comfortable thought, but then neither were the other ones that jostled for space and recognition.

Slowly she combed the kinks from her hair until it hung in a glowing, fiery fan to her thighs and tried to coax her tense muscles to relax. In a quiet voice she thanked Helgund and bade her go to bed. The maid curtsied and left. A soft silence descended and was infiltrated by the sounds of the spring night. Judith sat in the stillness and fiddled with the drawstring of her shift.

When Guyon finally came up to the room, he found Judith sitting on the bed buffing her nails, the candlelight making a golden halo behind her head. She looked up and gave him a strained smile and, rising, padded barefoot across the room to pour him wine.

He took it from her, his expression blankly preoccupied, drank, looked at the delicate glass and seemed to come to his senses, for suddenly his eyes refocused and he concentrated upon her face.

'What's the matter?' she asked. 'Why are you looking at me like that?'

It was there. You could see it when you knew. The expressions, the occasional mannerisms, the way her hair sprang from her brow. 'Nothing,' he said, wondering if his father knew. Perhaps. If it became common scandal the results would be disastrous. She was not Maurice of Ravenstow's daughter, therefore the barony was not hers by right of birth but belonged instead to her Montgomery uncles – Robert de Belleme, Arnulf and Roger. He suddenly felt very cold.

'Guy?' Feeling frightened, Judith touched his arm and, when he did not move, his brow also. He started at her touch and looked at her, but as if she was a complete stranger he had never seen before.

'What's wrong? Has Prince Henry taken offence at me? Did he realise that I . . . ?'

'Prince Henry?' He gave a humourless laugh. 'Prince Henry will take no offence. How could he?' Oh no, it was very much to his advantage. The halter, yoke and hobble of blood. He stared at the cup in his hand, set it down and paced over to the shutters. The catch was loose and he pushed them open. The scent of hawthorn was thick and sweet. He could see the blossom gleaming softly white in the garth. A breeze ruffled his hair and eddied one of the wall hangings.

'Is it something so terrible that you cannot tell me?' Judith asked at his elbow. 'Do we face ruin?'

Guyon gathered his reeling wits and turned to face her. 'I cannot tell you, love. Call it a political secret if you will, or just plain discretion. It is a confidence I think I would rather die than break.' He kissed her freckled forehead and tugged a burnished strand of her hair.

Judith frowned. Henry had told him something in the courtyard, of that she was sure, and she could only hope it was not along the lines that she had earlier curtailed by her deliberate clumsiness. 'It is not a wise hold to have over a man of power,' she said doubtfully.

He stepped away from her proximity where the scent of the hawthorn had been replaced by the more dangerous beguilement of gilly and roses. 'Henry intended me to know. He deliberately turned a vague suspicion into a certainty.'

'Is it very important that you say nothing to anyone, even to me?'

He picked up his wine, drank it and glanced over the cup's rim to where she stood, her breasts outlined by the yellow gilding of the night candle. 'Especially not to you, *Cath fach.*' Putting down the goblet, he moved towards the curtain.

'Where are you going?'

'Below to Walter. There's a pallet made up in an alcove for me and it's getting late.' He picked up his cloak.

'But the bed . . .' She gestured around, her heart thumping. 'It's big enough.'

'Not for us both,' he said with certainty.

'Yes it is . . .' She drew a deep breath, her eyes enormous.

Guyon looked at her frightened bravery and his heart turned over. 'When I made contract, my love, I did not want you. Now I do. If it were lust, it would not matter, I'd either slake it elsewhere, or take you without thought. Being as it isn't, I'll sleep downstairs.'

Judith swallowed, but the lump in her throat did not go away.

'Good-night, my love,' he said to her with a tight smile and, cloak over his shoulder, snapped his fingers at Cadi.

She waited until he had almost reached the curtain, struggling and struggling until at last she forced her voice beyond the choking lump of fear.

'Guy!' she croaked, holding out her hand. He turned. She cleared her throat. 'Before you go, can you do this for me? I've dismissed Helgund and it seems a shame to waken her for a mere knotted lace.'

Guyon hesitated for a moment, then put the cloak down. She padded over to him and showed him the tangled drawstring on her shift.

'I'm not a lady's maid,' he growled, stooping over the knot. 'Perhaps you should rouse Helgund, or just sleep in it.'

'I would be too hot and I have run poor Helgund off her feet all day. Let her sleep.'

He turned her to the light the better to see what he was doing and began to realise that the task was impossible.

Even the maid's skill would have been unable to undo the knot, so tightly was it pulled. The fact that his fingers, usually so clever and deft, were serving him with as much dexterity as a platter of sausages, did not help matters either, nor the fact that the scent of gilly was drowning him in its spicy waves as it rose from the warmth between her breasts. Her hair kept tangling with his efforts.

Impatiently he reached to the sheath at his hip and drew his knife. 'I'll have to cut it. How in hell's name did you snarl it up like this, Judith?'

The blade tugged against the material, jerking her against him. She did not resist the pull, but flowed towards him. The newly oiled and sharpened blade sliced cleanly through the knot and the shift dropped to cling precariously to her shoulder edges, held up by the merest whim of fate.

Guyon's throat was dry. He was aware that if he did not pick up his cloak and leave, he was going to do something very stupid. 'In God's name, Judith,' he said hoarsely, 'do you think I am made of stone?'

She raised her eyes to his. They were wide and afraid and full of stout determination. 'Show me.' She set her arms around his neck, craning on tiptoe. 'I want to know.'

The chemise fell from her body, leaving her slender and naked, pressed against him. Guyon closed his eyes, fighting the urge to throw her down flat beneath him and take her there and then. That was lust as he had said, not love. Besides, if the best wine was served, you drank it slowly, savouring it on the palate, not swilling it down your gullet in one fast gulp. Very difficult when you were dying of thirst.

'Hadn't you better sheathe that blade?' she said against his jaw.

The wheel had come full circle. He remembered Rhosyn saying that to him, twined in his arms, only her voice had been ripe with amused experience and Judith's was innocent, devoid of innuendo. The message, however, was the same. He put up the knife. She buried her face in his neck. Gently he held her away so that he could look at her.

'Well, *Cath fach,*' he said quietly. 'I am not sure that this is the right moment, coming to it so intent of purpose.'

'Guyon I . . .'

He put his finger to her lips, took her icy hand in his and led her to the bed. He sat her down upon it, then he sought around the room, found her bedrobe and gave it to her. 'Put it on,' he said gently. 'You're too much of a temptation without it.'

Tears filled Judith's eyes, but she did as he bid in order to bring some control to her limbs. 'You say you are not sure,' she sniffed. 'But I am. I've had time enough to think and if I have any more, I will go mad, I swear I will. I feel like an ox on a treadmill and there's only one way to end it!'

Guyon shook his head, torn by doubt and desire, by reluctance and need. 'I do not even know if I can show you,' he said. 'I do not know the limit of my control.

Judith blushed and smoothed a crease in the coverlet. 'We have all night,' she offered timidly.

He laughed and looked away. 'You have a blind faith in me, do you not?'

'What else is there?'

Folding his arms, he sat down on the bed and considered her.

Judith cast round for something to say that would sway the balance or lighten the difficult weight of his stare. The silk coverlet was cool to her touch and as red as blood. She remembered that it had belonged to a bishop. 'You haven't said grace yet,' she reminded him, forcing her mouth to smile.

Guyon let out his breath on a heavy sigh. 'I haven't said any Hail Marys either,' he replied, but after a moment's hesitation unfolded his arms to curve one around her shoulders and draw her within the dim red shadows of the hangings.

* * *

At first, stricken by the enormity of what she had done, Judith did not respond except to shiver against him, her breathing swift and shallow with fear. He held her, stroked her gently as he might have stroked Melyn or Cadi, spoke to her of trivia, whatever came into his mind, making of his words a soothing flow.

Gradually, Judith calmed and started to relax, allowing languorous pleasure to filter through her. The rigidity left her body, and she stopped shivering. She snuggled against him while he brushed his lips over her temple and cheek and the corner of her mouth, twisting his head slightly to trail small kisses along her jaw until he reached her earlobe. He paused there to play and then sucked the small, tender hollow behind it.

Judith gasped and pressed closer. Her loins felt as if they were dissolving. Hesitantly she nuzzled his throat where the tunic parted and moved her arm a little further so that her hand touched not cloth, but the hair at his nape. His hand stopped at her waist and tightened and the molten feelings tingled through her pelvis. She tasted his skin.

When he slipped his hand inside her bedrobe she stiffened, more with surprise than fear, but Guyon stopped immediately and made as if to withdraw. She dug her fingers fiercely into his nape, drawing him down, and lifted her face. 'Show me,' she said again, eyes bright with concentration.

He studied her doubtfully and she returned him a look that was at one and the same time wanton and innocent and full of a strange, wild tension, and then she broke the gaze and leaned into his body. Her lips touched the hollow behind his collarbone and her tongue flickered out. Guyon drew a sharp breath and pulled her close, seeking her mouth with his own. Hesitant at first, Judith quickly mastered the skill and pushed herself forward with a soft, impatient sound, lips clinging and yielding sweetly.

He ran his hand up her side, lightly brushed the small curve of her breast, sought inwards with his thumb and

feathered it over her areola and nipple. Judith broke the kiss
to cry out at the intensity of the sensation and surged against
him, craving, but as yet ignorant of precisely what. Applying
gentle pressure to her waist with his free hand, he drew her
down and over until she was lying on top of him. 'You have
the advantage, *Cath fach*,' he said softly. 'Do with me what
you will.'

Judith considered him, her swift breathing no longer a
mark of panic, but of increasing arousal. She gave a mischievous smile. 'Do you mean that?' Sitting up she reached to his
belt buckle.

'Within reason,' he qualified dubiously as she began
slowly unlatching it, her eyes never leaving his face.

He arched so that she could slide the belt from beneath
him and drop it with a slithering clink on to the floor. Hearing
his breath catch in his throat, watching the expression of
pleasure-pain cross his face as she rubbed herself against
him, her own sensations were heightened by the knowledge
of her effect on him.

He drew her back down, lips replacing his fingers. Judith
cried out at the sharper intensity of feeling and wriggled
upon him, seeking to ease the core of sensitive pressure
between her thighs.

'Wait,' Guyon said breathlessly and shifted her so that he
could sit up and pull his tunic over his head and then his shirt.
Judith flickered appreciative eyes over his chest and shoulders
admiring the lean, toned musculature. They were face to face.
Guyon circled her waist and drew her against him, fingers
lacing her hair and running over her skin. He kissed her throat,
the white valley between her breasts, found the cord of her
bedrobe and gently tugged it undone, pulled her down upon
him again, his hands cupping her neat, round buttocks,
squeezing her against him.

Judith purred and rubbed herself upon him like a cat. She
kissed his throat and chest, twisted her head to follow the
line of hair that ran from the centre of his breastbone and

over the ridges of his flat belly, her breasts lightly grazing his flesh. He groaned softly and tightened his hold on her and Judith felt her excitement growing as the knowledge of power triumphantly redoubled. She sought the drawstring of his chausses, continuing to nibble the line of hair as it descended.

Suddenly he gasped, banded his arms around her and rolled her hard beneath him. 'Jesu!' he exclaimed hoarsely against her mouth. 'What need have I to show you anything?'

Judith had cried out at his lightning pounce. Now she shuddered beneath him. The rippling twinges of desire radiating from her loins faltered, for there was the hint of savagery and lust in his voice, the threat of what he might do, and she did not know how to deal with it. 'You're hurting me!' she cried, going rigid in his arms.

Guyon stopped and braced his weight on his elbows to look down at her. He drew a deep, shuddering breath, then let it out again slowly while he mastered himself. 'Judith, I'm sorry,' he muttered, brushing a wisp of hair from her face. 'It is only that I did not expect you to learn quite so quickly. You outpaced me.'

She sniffed and swallowed, rubbed the back of her hand across her eyes and looked at him warily.

'I wouldn't hurt you for the world, you know that.' He bent his head to kiss her eyelids and then tenderly her mouth, playing with her, stroking and nuzzling until her tension subsided and her body once more began to undulate against his own. 'Trust me,' he murmured, pressing small kisses over her throat, then delicately brushing lower, deliberately tickling. 'Trust me, Judith?' Laughter edged his muffled voice.

'No!' she cried, wriggling. 'Stop it, Guy . . . don't.' Laughing herself, she struck out at him. He trapped her fingers, kissed them one by one until they unclenched, then turned them over, tongued her palm and nibbled his way up her arm, along her shoulder to her throat and back to reclaim her mouth. Slowly, lightly as a drifting feather, his fingertips trailed over her pubic hair.

'Trust me?' he repeated against her lips.

'Yes,' Judith whispered, twining her arms around his neck and arching her hips.

Guyon fondled her gently now, stroking her body, the sensitive zones in particular; the tips of her breasts, her inner thighs, then higher still. Judith writhed and cried out, striving towards his teasing, knowledgeable fingers. She pushed against his hand and arched.

With firm purpose and great care, Guyon entered her, and held her there, his hips pressed down flat, unmoving while her parted flesh settled around him. 'Judith, look at me.'

She opened her eyes which had been squeezed closed against the moment. The feeling of him fully within her was strange. The dreaded intrusion was accomplished and, although not stricken, she was disturbed and uncomfortable.

'Have I changed?'

She searched his face. His eyes were open and shining in the dim candle glow, his expression tender. She could see the gleam and trickle of sweat on his chest and feel the trembling of hard-held restraint.

'No, my lord,' she said. Smiling, she touched his face and shifted her hips to ease the pressure. The movement pressed him deeper within and involuntarily her muscles tightened around him. A keener sensation arced across her loins and was gone. Seeking its source, she pushed against him in a movement older than time. Guyon's head went back, his eyes closed and his breath emerged in a drawn-out groan. She moved again, her own pleasure sharpened by the knowledge of his and, conceding her the battle, he started to thrust in slow counterpoint.

It was like the first time she had galloped Euraidd – wild and exhilarating and a terrifying, delightful risk. The pace increased by steady degrees and so did the imperative needs of her body. She gasped and dug her nails into his shoulders, sought his mouth, demanding with her own, clung to him dizzied, her only thought to hold on to something solid as the world began to tremble and dissolve. And then she did not think at all. She cried his name, unaware that she did so, as her body totally submerged her mind, shattering the barriers to storm-tossed flotsam.

Guyon seized her hips and held her still, panting at her to stop, his forehead pressed into the curve of her neck, but Judith did not heed him and struggled against the restraint, desperate to regain the friction where she needed it.

'Judith, I cannot . . .'

Her nails clawed him with sudden urgency and she arched her spine and thrust down hard on him. He felt the small convulsions ripple through her, and, with a gasp of relief, surrendered his own control to the exquisite pulses of climax.

Slowly Judith became aware of his weight on her, no longer taken on his elbows, of his harsh breathing and of his body pressed hard against and within her own. The pleasure still flickered in dying twinges, promising renewal. She slid her hands over the sweat-damp ridges of his ribcage and moved a little beneath him, made uncomfortable by his weight.

Guyon sighed and rubbed his lips over her throat. Then he raised his head and looked her in the eyes.

'You are squashing me,' she complained breathlessly and stifled the urge to giggle as his face fell.

'Did I hurt you? I thought . . .' He narrowed his eyes, considering her. The clawing of her nails could be misconstrued, perhaps even the muffled cries, but not the tremors of her inner flesh. 'Wanton!' he pronounced, rolling over and drawing her with him. 'I shall not call you *Cath fach* again. *Cath wyllt*, perhaps!'

Judith moved sinuously upon him. 'It is better than getting drunk,' she admitted, giggling openly now. 'Just.'

'Remind me to ask you in the middle next time, not afterwards.'

'Next time! You mean we have to do all this again?' She widened her eyes in mock horror. 'Where's the nettle salve?'

'For my back you mean? You must have clawed it to shreds!'

'You should not be so clumsy,' she retorted swiftly, poking out her tongue and then using its tip to flick over his throat, her hips surging playfully.

Guyon laughed. 'Then I needs must practise,' he said and caught her down to him.

Judith awoke to the noise of a flock of sheep being driven down the road on their way into the city and the sharp whistle of the shepherd commanding his dogs. They were sounds with which she had grown up and it brought to her now the image of the marches greening lushly into summer and filled her with longing to be out of the city and home.

There was a warm weight across her body – Guyon's arm, the fingers in relaxed possession of the curve of her breast. He was still sleeping deeply, sprawled upon his stomach, and had not moved since their last pre-dawn bout of love-making. Her mouth twitched. It was her fault, she knew. She had told him that it was better than getting drunk. Well, indeed it was but, just like wine, it could become addictive.

So great had been her fear of the sexual act as a result of witnessing her mother's degradation at the hands of her violent, contemptuous father, that her own survival of the deed, indeed her enjoyment and satisfaction, had led her to prove to herself several times that it was no illusion. It was not. The last time, Guyon had asked her, groaning, if she was trying to kill him. Her gaze flickered over his lean, sleep-relaxed body. Coaxed and cajoled, he had become aroused, but it had taken him a long, long time and it had been wonderful. There was a low, dull ache in the small of her back and her body was languorous with content. It was certainly a better aftermath than a drink megrim.

She heard Sir Walter speak to the shepherd and make a

fuss of one of the dogs. Secure, and reluctant to break her mood of drowsy contentment, she snuggled back down into Guyon's embrace and closed her eyes.

When Guyon finally roused sufficiently to lift his lids, the morning was high and hot, first mass a memory and the hunters long gone on their quest. Sunlight slanted dustily through a warped gap in the shutters and shot the red silk bed hangings to the colour of flame. The night candle was burned to a puddle of congealed wax. He empathised. He flicked a wary glance at the sleeping innocence beside him ... Innocence! Good Christ, Rhosyn and even the inimitable Alais de Clare were mere novices compared to the supple, oblivious girl in his bed. Rape. She had feared rape. He stifled a chuckle at the irony.

Gently he touched a tendril of her hair and looked at her curled form, remembering when she had cowered from him, a half-grown starveling with terror-filled eyes. They had come a long way since then, not always along the same road, but converging here at a new crossroads. The Conqueror's granddaughter with the Viking blood of Duke Rollo and the common tanners of Falaise mingling in her veins.

In the light of what he had realised last night, he pondered her immediate parentage, wondering what had driven Alicia to mate with a boy of half her age and twice her experience. Probably he would never know and there were good reasons for keeping such knowledge private, not least the needs of this vulnerable wanton at his side.

As if aware of his musing regard, Judith stretched and opened her eyes, and yawned at him.

'Good morning, my wild cat,' he greeted her with a kiss.

'You missed the hunt,' she said with a sleepy smile.

'No I didn't,' he contradicted with a grin. 'I just had no inkling that I was the quarry.' Judith blushed. 'No matter, I can think of better ways to spend the day than aiming a bow at a driven deer or whatever. Besides, I'd rather not straddle a horse today.'

Her blush deepened and extended to include her throat and shoulders. 'Are you angry with me about last night, Guy?'

'Which part?' he teased. 'Where you froze Henry's manhood in the fingerbowl, or when you drained mine to a husk?'

Judith bit her lip. Against her scarlet chagrin, her eyes were brilliant, almost topaz. 'It was like drinking that yellow wine, I did not want to stop,' she excused herself, hanging her head.

'Drunk two nights in a row!' he chaffed her. 'What am I to do with you? No, don't tell me, I haven't the strength. Just don't ask me to show you anything ever again, even if you are desperate to know! God's life, it nearly killed me!'

Judith fisted him in the ribs and he yelped.

'But if you were content, it was worth it.' He sobered, looking at her rosy, flustered face. 'I have no objection to dying like that, unless it be four times a night!'

She slanted a quick glance through her lashes. 'At least there will be naught left of you for Alais de Clare,' she said with a return of her accustomed tartness and, sitting up, shook back her hair. The sunlight lit her eyes with sparkling glints of mica.

'I don't want Alais de Clare,' Guyon answered, stretching. 'Why settle for dross when you can have gold?'

Judith looked at him. 'I am dreaming,' she said pensively. 'One day I am going to wake up alone and cold and realise I have been the dupe of illusion.'

'What has happened to last night's blind faith?' He tugged a strand of her hair. 'Isn't it enough now?'

'It's not that, Guy,' she answered, frowning. 'It is the opposite. I have too much. It isn't true.'

'Never satisfied, are you?' He put his arm around her. 'What do you want me to do? Cut my other wrist for you as well and swear an undying oath?'

Judith shook her head, refusing to be cozened. 'It is I who

have bled this time,' she said softly, turning back the covers
to look down on the dried blood smearing the insides of her
thighs and the sheet.

'Trust me?' He kissed her shoulder. 'Trust me, Judith?'

She could feel his lips smiling there in remembrance. 'Did
Rhosyn trust you?'

He had not been expecting it. She felt his lips pause and
then leave her skin. He sat up and pushed his hands through
his hair and muttered beneath his breath. 'You know where
to kick, don't you?'

Judith pleated the coverlet beneath her fingers. Guyon
linked his hands around his upraised knees and studied her.
'Rhosyn was not prepared to trust me,' he said after a
moment. 'We were never committed in that kind of way. It
would have been too dangerous and she saw it, even if I did
not.'

Judith regarded him sombrely. 'Guyon, I cannot give you
my soul.'

'Nor would I want it,' he said. 'It is too private a thing to
give into another's possession. Keep it whole, *Cath fach*. I
understand more than you think.'

Judith impatiently scrubbed her forearm across her eyes.
Outside she heard Elflin speak to Helgund and the sound
of milk being poured into a container. By the door Cadi
whined. Judith put her arms around Guyon and kissed him
as if the kiss itself was a talisman. 'I do believe that you could
wheedle your way through a thorn thicket,' she sniffed.

He returned the embrace and then drew away to search
for some garments in the scattered creased heaps on the floor.
'What do you think I'm doing now?' he said with a wry
smile. 'You are the thorniest thicket I've ever encountered.'
He paused in his dressing to lean over the bed and kiss her
warmly on her lips. 'And the sweetest rose.'

'And you cannot grasp one without risking the other,' she
agreed gravely, trying to put all dark qualms behind her while
her own words rang like a prophecy in her head.

Guyon stood up, finished buckling his belt and headed towards the door. 'I'll send in Helgund,' he said and paused in fondling Cadi's thrusting head to stoop and pick up her discarded shift with its knife-slashed lacing. 'You did this apurpose, didn't you?' He tossed the garment on to the bed.

Judith leaned back against the bolster and smiled exactly like her father.

CHAPTER 19

AUGUST 1100

Thunder rumbled in the distance where the sky hung in purple billows like mulched grapes. On the wall walk, Judith squinted into the distance. Lightning zigzagged. The trees were brilliantly green and the stone of the merlon against which she leaned was a rich, warm gold. Most of Caermoel's defences were still timber, but the keep wall was almost completed, as was the gatehouse containing the portcullis and winding gear.

The messenger had ridden in an hour ago while the sun still shone, bearing the news that Guyon would be here before nightfall and she had set herself to make all ready in the way of food, warmth and comfort and had then hastened up here to look out for his return.

It had been five days since the young men in their hot blood had ventured across the border to steal cattle and corn from the English side. Five days since the alarm had been raised, and Guyon had gathered his immediate troops and ridden out in pursuit of a fine dairy herd, three Flemish mares with foals at foot belonging to him and the contents of one of Earl Hugh's grain barns.

She looked down as Melyn twined an erect tail around her skirts and mewed plaintively before clawing her way aloft on to her shoulder to settle there, oblivious to the storm that was blowing in from the south. A cry from the far side of the wall walk caused Judith to strain her eyes in that direction and then to smile and hasten towards the bailey steps.

The edge of the storm hit as the men dismounted. Lightining snarled across the sky. Several cows bellowed and baulked as they were penned in a corner of the ward. A groom was taking custody of the three mares and their foals and a belligerent Welsh pony stallion that was lashing out indiscriminately.

Guyon turned from speaking to his groom and saw Judith running towards him, her face alight with welcome. She moved unaffectedly, like a man, but her gown moulded itself to her slender curves, marking her all woman. The time-wrought changes of her mind and body never ceased to amaze him. A year ago she would have greeted him gravely and stood just out of his reach as if anticipating a blow. Six months ago they would have avoided each other with eyes downcast to conceal hunger and tense fear. Now, laughing, she flung herself into his arms and drew his head down and kissed him. Melyn, jolted from her perch, gave a feline growl of displeasure, leaped vertically from Judith's back and stalked off in the direction of the living quarters.

'It is only five days!' Guyon chuckled, delighted at the warmth of the greeting. 'What will you do when it has to be forty?'

Judith relinquished her grip and blushed, aware of the amused glances of his men. 'I shall take a lover,' she riposted smartly. 'There's a tub prepared and food at the ready. How did you fare?'

Guyon followed her, ducking his head and increasing his pace as the rain began to cut down. 'We took back what was ours and also a little of what was theirs. You know the rules of border warfare. They won't come raiding again . . . not for a while at least.'

'Unless they come *en masse*,' Judith pointed out as they entered the wooden building in the bailey that was their private living quarters whilst the castle was being built.

'Could we withstand a full Welsh assault, not just the prickings of their hot-blooded young men?'

'Probably, but it's not a notion I want to test just yet. Has all been quiet here?'

'Mostly. Madoc came two days ago with Rhys and a distant relative from Bristol who's helping him with the business. They brought that new ram you asked Madoc to get. He says that Heulwen's walking now and chattering like a magpie, and that she's already strewing the road with broken hearts. I think he wanted to remind you of the bond.'

'I hardly need reminding of that,' he said, half under his breath. 'Did he mention Rhosyn?'

'Only that she was well and sent you her duty. If there was more, he probably thought it unwise to confide it to me.'

'How could there be more?' Guyon teased, squeezing her waist. 'You leave me neither the energy nor the inclination to play games with other women. What's this?' He moved the polished agate weight and picked up the letter from the trestle.

'From my mother,' Judith said, going to pour hot wine. 'She asks when we are going to leave our eyrie and make her a visit.'

Guyon took the wine and kissed her hand. 'Somewhere between Michaelmas and Martinmas,' he replied, expression thoughtful as he drank. 'I want a word with her anyway.'

'What about, Guy?'

He tossed the parchment down and finished the wine. 'Nothing. A minor detail concerned with your inheritance.'

Judith's lips tightened in response to his casual tone and the blank innocence of his eyes. The reality was upon her, warm and secure as a duck down mantle, but now and again she pondered the difference between belief and blindfold. Guyon was dissembling. She knew that look by now and also the method. A smattering of sugared truth and eyes warmly guileless to conceal what he wished to conceal.

Dutifully she unbuckled his swordbelt but her hands were

jerky. Guyon looked at her mulishly set lips. His own mouth
curved and then straightened. It was not really funny, for he
had no defence save to tell her the truth and the shock of
that would probably do far greater harm than the with-
holding. If he had not been so road- and battle-weary, he
would never have permitted his tongue the mistake of
speaking an absent thought aloud.

'What kind of minor detail?' Judith challenged, stepping
away from him, the belt in her hands, sword and dagger still
attached.

Guyon busied himself removing his garments. He was
not wearing the customary Norman war gear of mail hauberk
and gambeson, but hunting clothes topped by a sleeveless
sheepskin jerkin. When in Wales it was wisest to do as the
Welsh did. It was impossible to cross a swiftly flowing
torrent and pursue winding, scant paths if weighed down
by armour and slowed by supply trains which were vulnerable to attack.

'The kind that is your mother's private business. If she
wants to tell you, then well and good,' he answered more
evenly than he felt, wondering how to extricate himself before
the thing got out of hand.

'I am surprised that your brain does not burst with all the
little matters you cannot confide to me for fear of breaking
your oath!' she snapped.

'So am I.' Guyon gave her a wry look. 'Judith, I don't
want to quarrel.'

'That is up to you.' She tossed her head and turned from
him to lay his swordbelt aside. Whe she turned round again,
she gasped aloud at sight of the clotted red diagonal line
across his chest. 'Holy Mother!' she cried and ran to get her
basket of medicines.

Guyon drew breath to say that it was only a scratch and
the Welshman who had given it to him was in much worse
case, but quickly thought the better of it. Closing his mouth,
he contrived to look as wan and limp as rude health and a

summer tan would permit. Unresisting, he let her lead him to the bed and push him down.

'How did you get this?'

He looked at her through his lashes and saw the terror in her eyes and felt a flicker of guilt for his deceit. Last time he had come to her wounded he had almost died and the memory had obviously left its taint of fear. 'The raid leader didn't want to relinquish his gains and he was faster than I thought. He's gone to Chester as a hostage – if he does not die of his own wounds on the way.'

'Why not bring him here?'

'I don't want to encourage Welsh hordes to come visiting, not even to parley, until the defences have grown a little, and I haven't the time to – ouch!'

'Lie still then. You are lucky it is so shallow. Some comfrey and marigold salve should suffice. Are you hurt anywhere else?'

'Yes.' He closed his eyes as though faint.

'Where?' Anxiously she leaned over him.

Fast as a closing trap, his hands circled her waist and pulled her down on top of him. 'Where only you can ease me,' he murmured, subduing her retort with his lips.

Judith struggled briefly in order to satisfy her conscience, but with no real enthusiasm; in a moment, with a soft sound of capitulation, she yielded herself up to the pleasure. Three months of intensive, inventive tuition had taught her the refinements of this new and delightful skill and how to use it to its best purpose. How to provoke and tease and taunt him to the brink and then hold him there suffering, until she herself could bear it no longer and took them both over the edge.

Of course, she reminded herself hazily, it was a double-edged weapon and Guyon was an adept, as demonstrated by the dextrous manner in which he had just divested her of clothing. Frequently he gave her the control, knowing that it heightened her pleasure, but if he chose to take the initiative, as now, he was quite capable of submerging her in a welter of pure, fierce sensation that made everything else insignificant until well after the event. The acrid smell of horse and sweat sharpened her hunger, as did the nibbling play of his stubble-surrounded mouth on hers and the feel of his hands seeking down over her belly.

Lightning zigzagged and dazzled and the rain beat down, thudding the ground like the footsteps of an army running. In the bailey, Simon de Vere swung from the saddle of his trembling, near-spent horse. He had been in the saddle for such a long time that his legs at first refused to support him and the groom had to help him up from the mud as he fell.

'Lord Guyon is, er . . . busy,' said de Bec to the young man as he was helped, limping, into the hall. 'Best sit down and recover yourself awhile first. We've not long ridden in ourselves.'

'He won't be too busy to hear these tidings,' Simon said, pushing his fingers through his rain-sleek hair and wiping a drip from the end of his nose. 'The King is dead, slain in the New Forest and Prince Henry's claimed the crown. I've half killed my horse getting here.'

De Bec's bushy brows shot into his silver fringe. 'God have mercy,' he said, crossing himself. 'Here, sit down by the fire. You, wench, bring food and drink for Sir Simon and tell mistress Helgund to fetch my lord and lady.'

Judith looked at her husband as the sweat dried on their bodies and their breathing slowed. Outside the thunder rumbled and the lightning blinked against a gap in the shutters. For a time she had felt as if she was riding in the midst of the storm and she could still feel small flickers on the periphery. 'When Madoc came, he told me something else too,' she said after a moment. 'Apparently, Mabel de Serigny is with child.'

Guyon had been sleepily nuzzling her shoulder, but now he lifted his head and gazed at her with widening eyes. 'Impossible! She's ninety if she's a day, Judith!'

She laughed at the incredulity on his face. 'Not quite. She's only a few years older than Mama. Eight and forty or some such. Oh, I know it's old to catch for a babe, but not impossible.'

'And I thought Walter de Lacey was a coward,' Guyon said facetiously, but a frown forked his brow. He wondered what would happen if the same God's grace was granted to Alicia. Even if she and his father did obtain a dispensation to marry, it would be the devil's own work to sort out the resulting blood ties.

'I suppose it is all in his favour,' Judith added, stretching sinuously, and rolled on to her stomach. 'If she carries the babe successfully then he gets an heir out of her; if she dies, then he's free to look elsewhere and because he is rich, he will be able to pick and choose. He cannot lose.'

There was a soft knock on the door and Helgund's voice came impassively from without. 'My lord, my lady, you are sought in the hall. There is important news from Winchester.'

Guyon groaned. Judith scrambled from the bed and hastily donned her bedrobe. 'Can't it wait?' she snapped, feeling like a serving wench caught coupling in the straw.

'It is Simon de Vere, my lady. He says that the King is dead.'

'What?' Judith stared over her shoulder at Guyon. He swore and reached for his discarded clothes.

'Messire de Bec sent me to fetch you both, my lady. I do not know any more.'

'All right, Helgund. Thank you.'

Judith abandoned both bath and bedrobe to find her shift. 'If Rufus is dead, who is King in his place?'

'Who do you think?' Guyon snapped because it was such an obvious question. 'I'd better have one of the lads scour my hauberk because I'm going to need it.' He stood still long enough for her to smear his wound with salve, then dragged on his shirt and tunic, tugged one of her combs through his hair and strode muttering from the room. Judith glared after

him, then subdued her anger. She knew he had been tired
when he rode in, and wounded, and the energy expended
just now between the sheets would further have drained his
resources. Small wonder if his mood was sour when instead
of sleep and recuperation, he received a summons of this ilk.
Heaving a sigh, she called for Helgund to help her dress.

'An accident,' said Simon, whom Richard had sent from
Winchester on the morning of the funeral. 'A hunting accident last Thursday evening. Walter Tirel shot at a deer and
missed and hit the King in the chest. He died instantly. Prince
Henry was with the hunting party, but not near the scene of
the death. He rode straight to Winchester and secured the
treasury. He claims the right of being born the son of a king
over his brother.' Simon knuckled his bloodshot eyes. 'He
expects your feudal oath as soon as you may.'

Guyon pressed his own eyes with the heels of his hands.
It was too late to set out tonight, but arrangements would
have to be made for the following dawn and riders sent on
ahead to organise their nightly stops. From here to London
was a good six to seven days' ride; more if the weather
continued dire.

'Myself and Richard must have been the last to see him
alive, except for the hunting party,' Simon added into the
silence, compelled to speak by renewed ripples of shock. 'I
still cannot believe it. If only he had stayed abed and not
taken up de Clare's suggestion to hunt, he might yet be alive.'

'Gilbert of Tunbridge?' asked Judith.

'Yes, and his brother too. The King had been plagued by
a queasy gut, the reason he didn't want to hunt in the
morning, but he was fully recovered by noon. After the
dinner hour, de Clare said he would not mind clearing his
head by riding out to see what he could bring down and it
seems to me that he was not talking of deer and that his head
had never been clearer in his life.' Simon attacked his
trencher. Rufus had had his failings, but he had never found

him a hard taskmaster and Richard had been moved openly to tears at the news of his untimely death.

'Are you saying he was murdered?' de Bec demanded.

'I'm not saying anything.' Simon avoided looking at his companions. 'Tirel has fled the country squawking his innocence like a dust trail. He says he was nowhere near the King, that it was not his arrow.'

'And the de Clares are his brothers-by-marriage.' Judith's voice was as colourless as her face.

'I suppose the inquest will decide the truth of the matter,' de Bec said, stretching out his legs until his heels pressed Cadi's white rump.

'What inquest?' Simon demanded sourly. 'Henry's not holding one.'

Guyon paused eating to stare at Simon, then continued to chew, but slowly, as if ruminating. 'Who else went out to hunt, Si?'

'Rannulf des Aix en Louvent, your lady's uncle William Breteuil, Gilbert de Laigle and William de Monfichet.' Simon shook his head. 'Rufus must have been mad. He might as well have ridden out with a pack of wolves. They didn't even stop to bring his body back to the lodge in decency, but rode straight for the treasury at Winchester. It was left to me and Richard to take charge of the body from the back of a charcoal burner's cart and compose it decently for the return to Winchester. It's wrong, I . . .' He swallowed convulsively and clenched his fist on the trestle. 'Anyway, Henry's claimed the crown and you'd best be quick about swearing your allegiance. He hasn't stopped since the arrow was loosed.'

Judith rose from the board, her eyes blank and, without excuse or explanation, drifted away from the men like a sleepwalker. No one took much notice. Guyon cast her a sidelong glance of surprise, but his mind was occupied with Simon's budget of news and its implications and what now had to be done. The Welsh situation was stable for the nonce and could be left to cook awhile unattended and Henry, whatever the blots on his soul, had the makings of a strong monarch. Besides, with the private connections of bloodline, Guyon knew that providing he did nothing wildly asinine or treacherous, he was guaranteed the royal favour . . . for as long as Henry remained King.

'There'll be a flaming barrel of pitch when Robert Curthose gets to hear of this,' he said and rubbed his hands slowly together, feeling the calluses on his palms where he had recently grasped sword and shield.

'And de Belleme will be delighted to light torches from it,' said de Bec.

'Oh yes. We will need to work very hard indeed to make sure Henry keeps his crown, no matter the manner of his obtaining it. Curthose has about as much control over Robert de Belleme as a wrung chicken has control of its limbs. You've seen what he's done in Normandy. God forbid he should get to wreak his worst on our lands too.'

'Want me to increase the patrol on our boundary with Thornford? It's been very quiet there of late.'

'It won't harm, but don't stretch the patrols too thinly elsewhere to compensate.' Guyon shoved his trencher aside and called for a scribe to be brought so that he could inform his vassals of the news.

Judith picked up Guyon's swordbelt and examined the strip of buckskin without really seeing its embossed golden leopards or the elaborate twists of gold wire decorating the buckle, or indeed the article itself. The sword lay sheathed on the bed. She had had one of the boys clean and oil it, for it had seen recent hard use against the Welsh. The sharpening of the two edges she left to Guyon. She could have done it herself, she was perfectly capable, but the feel of it in her hands would have frightened her with suggestions of what she should do with it.

Sitting down on the bed she stared at the rumpled sheets,

remembering a warm spring night and the laughter of high-born men carousing in a candlelit room, drinking out of green glass cups; feasting with murder on their minds. The Prince and the de Clare brothers had all been members of the fatal hunting party and Walter Tirel was married to Gilbert and Roger's sister.

Malwood, the royal hunting lodge, was only sixteen miles from Winchester, the seat of the treasury. Tirel had fled with all eyes on him, when folk should have been looking at those men left behind. And Guyon knew, and had known since that May evening. She remembered him coming to her in the bedchamber when their guests had gone, his expression preoccupied, and when she had questioned him, he had avoided the answer. What had he said? A confidence he would rather die than break, especially to her. And if he knew, then he was implicated. He had long been a companion of Henry's and his apathy towards Rufus was no secret.

Judith frowned. The disarrayed sheets reminded her all too clearly of that first night, only now the memory was not tender, but obscene. He had come from plotting a man's death and lain with her. It was a violation. She felt sick and wished suddenly that the bathtub was still in the room so that she could scrub herself free of his touch, the very thought of his touch. His seed was deep within her body. She put her hand to her mouth, striving not to retch.

Guyon entered the room, stretching and yawning. 'I could sleep for a week,' he complained as he dropped the curtain, 'but I suppose a few hours will have to suffice. I never realised Richard was so fond of Rufus. Then again, it's probably his position at court he fears to lose.' He picked up the scab-bard, examined it absently and held out his hand for the swordbelt. She dropped it on the bed and, rubbing her arms as if frozen to the bone, turned her back on him.

Guyon eyed her from beneath his brows and busied himself with fastening the thongs. 'We're stopping at Ravenstow tomorrow noon. It's safer if we escort you there on our way south. I do not think the Welsh will attack Caermoel, but you never know how this news will affect them. I've already spoken to Elflin and Helgund about the packing.'

Judith did not speak because she could not trust herself to do so. Guyon put down the belt, his scrutiny sharpening, for neither of his remarks had been granted a reply and he had not seen her stand like that, clutching herself protectively, since the early days of their marriage.

'Judith?'

The night candle flung lumbering shadows at the walls. Melyn leaped at a moth, caught it deftly in a flashing paw and bore it triumphantly away to a corner to devour.

'It can't be helped. I'll come home as soon as I can,' he added and then, aware that without saying anything she had put him on the guilty defensive, he tightened his mouth and began to remove his garments.

'Don't flatter yourself!' she snarled. 'Stay as long as you choose!'

Guyon pulled off his shirt, swearing as the linen caught the rough line of the dagger scratch on his chest. He wondered briefly if it was near her time of the month again. Her tongue was apt to be sharper then and her moods liable to swing without warning. After a moment when she remained aloof and contained, he relented and tried again, coming up behind her and setting his hand on her shoulder. 'Judith, love, what's wrong? Tell me.'

She shrugged away from him, fighting nausea, and flung round to face him. 'Rufus was murdered, wasn't he?' she challenged.

Guyon shrugged, feeling puzzled. 'Probably.'

'Do not play the innocent with me, my lord. You knew what was going to happen!'

'That's preposterous!' He reached for her. She avoided him. 'I haven't been near the King or the court for a full three months and Henry knows that whatever the de Clares would do for him, I certainly would not!'

'No? You had reason to dislike Rufus and you have long associations with Henry.'

'Christ, girl, what do you take me for? I might not have liked Rufus or wanted to be a party to his private habits, but that is hardly a reason to plot his death or barter my honour.'

'Then tell me what Prince Henry told you when he dined with us at Whitsuntide,' she challenged.

She saw it: the flicker of his lids, the bunching of muscle in his jaw before his face went blank. 'He told me nothing,' he said tonelessly.

'Liar!' she flung at him. 'It was less than three months ago. Do you think I am so besotted by your charm that I cannot remember? You said there was something you could not tell me, a political secret, a confidence you would rather die than break, and you were shaken by it. There was cold sweat on your brow.'

'That was nothing to do with Rufus's death.'

'What was it then?' Her mouth twisted. 'After all, nothing can be much more damning than plotting a king's death.'

His face remained expressionless. 'I will not tell you, Judith. It is not my place and perhaps it would do more damage than it would resolve.'

She gave him a look compounded of triumph and defeat. 'I thought you would have an answer,' she said with contempt.

He gripped her arms. 'Judith, I swear to you on my soul . . . on my mother's soul, that whatever was plotted against Rufus, I had no part in it. I have no defence except my word. The words that would absolve me, I will not speak. It would only shift burdens and guilts to shoulders less able to bear them.'

'You're hurting me,' she said dully.

He swore and relaxed his grip, but only to soften it to an embrace and pull her against him. 'Judith, what do I do if you won't trust me?'

She stood quivering within his arms, torn between doubt

and doubt. Shield or blindfold, she dreaded to make the decision. He was adept with words, fashioning them to his needs, could convince her black was white if only given the opportunity. 'What do I do if you betray that trust?' she responded and slid her hand over the fine black hairs of his braced forearm, denuded by the ridge of scar tissue where the boar had tushed him, and on up to the smooth curve of his bicep. 'Prove me wrong.'

'How?' he asked bleakly. 'If I fulfil your trust I break another.'

She refused to relent. 'And which is more important?'

Leaving her, he sat down on the bed and rubbed his hands over his face. 'I don't know. Neither. The edge is so finely balanced I dare not tip the scale. All I can swear to you again is that I was not involved in any plot to murder Rufus.' He looked across at her where she stood braced as if waiting to receive a blow and let out his breath on a heavy sigh. 'It's late. Are you going to come to bed or stand there glaring at me all night?' He held out his hand.

She looked at his outstretched graceful fingers, knew how they would feel gliding over her body, trailing fever in their wake, knew how they looked holding reins or a sword, knew their tensile strength and of what they were capable.

'Neither,' she said, and walked out of the room.

CHAPTER 20

Rhosyn looked at the crocks of brawn on the trestle, product of a long morning's work. She sealed the last one with a thick layer of melted lard.

'All done?' queried Heulwen, beaming up at her. Rhosyn smiled and lifted her younger daughter to sit on the trestle. Heulwen was a chubby bundle of energy with a bright crop of red-gold curls and green-blue eyes, the legacy of her Norman great-grandfather, so Madoc, who had known him, had said. The legacy of her Norman father was her ability to cozen warm approval and adulation from smitten members of the opposite sex.

Rhosyn had not seen Guyon since immediately after Heulwen's birth. Messages passed with Madoc. The trading bond remained strong, but the gossamer ties that had bound herself and Guyon for four years had dissolved into the wind, saving this one living, finespun thread.

'All done,' she confirmed and, straddling the infant on her hip, left the kitchen quarters and set off across the small, withy-enclosed compound towards the hall. After ten strides she stopped short as if she had been poled with an ox-mallet.

Eluned was jumping up and down at Guyon's stirrup and his chestnut courser was sidling restlessly and rolling a white eye. Beyond, she saw Eric and the men of the guard. Guyon leaned over the pommel, one hand on his thigh, the other drawn tight on the reins as he spoke to Eluned. She tossed her head mutinously, but after a moment stepped aside from the horse. Rhosyn's heart began to thud. As if it did not matter, as if she had only seen him last week, she went forward with a cordial greeting on her lips.

Guyon dismounted and took hold of the chestnut's bridle. Rhosyn saw that his clothes were powdered with dust and that the points of his cheekbones and the bridge of his nose had caught the burn of the late summer sun. 'May we claim the hospitality of a drink?' he asked. 'And water for the horses?'

'You know you are always welcome,' she responded and her face grew warm beneath his stare. The luminous brown gaze flickered to Heulwen, who struggled against her mother's confining arms.

'I did not know,' he said, giving the horse to one of his men. 'It has been a long time. Where's Madoc?'

'Away with Rhys and my second cousin Prys to Bristol, but we expect him home any day now. Did you especially want to see him?'

'I've a few commissions for him. How's his health?'

'He works too hard, but I might as well try butting down a stone wall with my head as try to stop him. He struggles to breathe sometimes and he gets a pain in his arm, but he won't give up.' She turned to lead him into the hafod. 'I hear he spoke to your wife recently.'

'Yes.'

Rhosyn did not miss the lack of inflection and looked at him curiously. Her father said that Lady Judith had been glowing with the contentment of being well loved and secure. Guyon had not come here in over a year. She had begun to assume he would not come again and that the contentment must be mutual.

'You are growing tall, *cariad*,' Guyon said to Eluned as he sat down. The amber bead he had given her gleamed against the dark wool of her gown. 'And pretty as your mother.'

'Am I prettier than your wife?' she challenged him.

'Is an apple prettier than a pear?' he countered and drew her down to him, lightly kissing her cheek, his eyes meeting Rhosyn's troubled stare over the child's narrow shoulder. 'No one can answer that.'

'Not even you?' Rhosyn mocked before calling one of the serving women. 'Do you want my father to visit?'

'No, I've instructions for him here.' Guyon produced a roll of parchment and took the cup of mead that was given to him. 'Payment in raw wool as usual, unless I hear otherwise.'

She nodded briskly. Their eyes met again, examining, searching. Heulwen, released from her mother's grasp, wobbled towards him, lost her balance and plonked down squarely on her bottom. Undeterred, she struggled up again, grasping Guyon's cross-garter for support.

'*Da*,' she said, and smiled disarmingly at him. It was the Welsh word for father.

'She says that to everyone,' Rhosyn muttered quickly, her colour high.

Guyon looked from the engaging fire-haired child to her mother who was obviously struggling to retain her equanimity in his presence. It had been a mistake to come, he thought, born of his own pain, and he stirred restlessly as if he would rise and leave.

Rhosyn was on her feet before he could make the thought a fact. 'I want to show you something,' she said with forced brightness. 'Can you spare a moment?'

He looked slightly taken aback. 'Of course.'

'Eluned, look after Heulwen for me.'

Eluned made a face but was not so foolish as to refuse.

Guyon raised a brow as she led him into her private chamber, but forbore to utter the ambiguous remark that came first to mind. Matters had changed since then. Whether or not for the better, he no longer knew. Rhosyn selected a key from the bunch upon the ring at her waist and looked over her shoulder at him. 'We hear you are pushing into Wales now. A new keep, no less.'

'To protect the border against Lord Gruffyd's raiding. It's no use breeding good raw wool only to have it disappear into the mountains.'

'I sometimes think that you Normans would eat the world if you could.'

'A nibble here and there,' he answered, refusing to be drawn, for there was no heart in him to argue. 'What did you want to show me?'

She unlocked a stout oak coffer and withdrew from its depths a bolt of fabric. 'What do you think of this? My father bought it in Flanders on the last trip, from an Italian merchant who owed him a favour.'

The cloth flowed on to the bed. It held the rich amber and russet tones of autumn leaves and where the light was trapped by the pile, it shimmered like a sunlit pool. To the touch it was soft and thick and springy, like sun-warmed moss or cat's fur. Having never set eyes on the like before and being thoroughly curious, Guyon sat down on the bed and sought to discover everything that Rhosyn knew.

'So all this is done with shears,' he murmured, smoothing the pile.

She looked at his slender fingers on the nap of the cloth. Heulwen's were chubby little stars, formless as yet. 'It is a detailed skill and not many have it. My father thought of selling it in Winchester at the next court gathering.'

'Next court gathering's in London in November,' Guyon said. 'What price for a Flemish ell of this stuff?'

Her hazel eyes met his and locked. His crinkled at the corners. She suggested a sum. He laughed and responded with an amount much lower.

'What's happening in November?'

'King Henry's marriage to Edith of Scotland. Judith suits autumn colours.'

'Your new King is to wed?'

'It's been under negotiation for a while, since before Rufus died. I think that they have only met once or twice. Still, that's more than Judith and I had.'

Rhosyn gave him a considering look. 'Is she still a child, Guy?'

'Neither child nor virgin, but as vulnerable as blown glass.' His brow furrowed. 'God knows, Rhos, I think I have her and then she eludes me with a twist of her mind and we are back where we started.'

'I know what you mean,' she said with a pained smile and then named another sum a little lower.

His brow cleared. 'I can get two ells of silk damask for that price!'

'But then silk damask is not so rare.'

'And you are priceless.' He glinted her a look and made another bid. She snapped a response. He pretended to ponder before answering.

Rhosyn began folding the bolt back upon itself.

'I'm not even sure that I want it,' he added with a grimace. 'Judith will probably think I am offering it to her as a sweetener. We quarrelled before I left and I had no defence except my word and that, apparently, is not good enough.'

Rhosyn straightened and stared at him. 'And is it a sweetener? Are you buying because you cannot have for the asking?'

'I don't think so.' He frowned. 'The King's marriage will throw her into the royal circle. Henry's new Queen will be fêted by the wives and daughters of the English barons and Judith will need to dress according to her rank. It is a practical luxury, I suppose.' His expression lightened and his eyes sparkled with devilry. 'And since Judith will be wearing it at court among all those other envious rich men's wives who will nag their husbands to death for a gown of the same, it behoves you to be generous in your dealings with me!'

Despite herself, Rhosyn was forced to laugh. 'Guy, you wretch!'

He grinned at her. Her heart melted but she did not show it. 'Very well, I'll meet you halfway.'

'As ever,' he said gravely, his eyes alight, and stood up.

She had forgotten how tall he was and the mail he wore made him seem twice his actual breadth. Her body craved him. Her mind, cold and clear, prevented her from making a fool of herself. Her time was past. Out in the hall she could hear his men and Heulwen's crow of laughter. She moved towards the sounds of sanity.

'Robert de Belleme is back in the marches,' he warned, catching her arm as he followed her out. 'Alert your father if he does not already know. De Belleme is in a savage humour. Henry's much harder to handle than Rufus was and he'll take it out on those least able to defend themselves. Have a care to yourself and the children and remember what I said about an escort if you should need to travel.'

'How could I forget when you keep ramming it down my throat?' She rolled her eyes heavenwards. 'Guy, I am not a half-wit.'

He squeezed her waist and gave a deprecatory smile. 'No, *cariad*, but I am.'

CHAPTER 21

LONDON
NOVEMBER 1100

Alicia muttered an oath beneath her breath as she inadvertently stabbed herself with the embroidery needle for the third time in as many minutes. Sucking her finger, she bade Agnes light the candles. Then she looked across the brazier towards her daughter who sat with her shoulder pressed into the wall, unseeing eyes on the fading rain-spattered light through the open shutters.

It had not escaped Alicia's notice that her daughter and Guyon were barely on speaking terms these days. Judith behaved as if she loathed the sight of him, would not even let him near enough to lay a hand on her shoulder and refused if possible to make eye contact. Sometimes when he turned away, she would look at him, her eyes filled with bewilderment. Alicia's only conclusion thus far was that Guyon had consummated the marriage and that Judith had reacted badly, but it did not satisfactorily explain all the other tensions she felt boiling around them. Judith seemed to feel she had a genuine grievance. Guyon defended himself like a man with his hands tied behind his back, desperately but without effectiveness. Occasionally she had seen temper flash in his eyes and then extinguish, doused by Judith's cold contempt and his own control.

Indeed, since Henry had granted Guyon more lands

following his coronation and marriage to the Princess Edith last week, Judith's mood had been vicious and there had been no living with her. Guyon had chosen to remain absent, attending upon Henry in council at Westminster. Judith, who should have been with him visiting the Queen, had professed a headache and declined to come and now sat shivering on the window seat, staring blankly into the distance.

'Come away to the brazier, love,' entreated Alicia with a worried frown. 'If there's a draught, you'll catch a chill.'

Judith gave a wordless shake of her head. Alicia carefully set the needle into the fabric, put her sewing down and crossed to the window. Close to, she saw why Judith had not answered. Her throat was jerking convulsively as she fought down the sobs that were struggling to tear their way to the surface and in the fading light, tears tracked glistening trails down her cheeks.

Alicia's own eyes prickled with pain at the sight of her daughter's suffering. Filled with worry, she folded Judith in a tender embrace.

The feel of her mother's arms around her, the secure, familiar smell of her, and the outpouring of love and sympathy were too much and Judith yielded to a turbulent storm of grief. Alicia held and rocked her, soothed her with murmured words and reassurances, stroked her hair and, when the first violence had passed, drew her away to a seat near the brazier. She dismissed the hovering, worried Agnes with a brief nod and a request for more charcoal.

'Now then,' she said as the curtain dropped behind the maid. 'What is wrong between you and Guyon? Sweeting, can it not be mended? Is it a matter of pride? Another woman?'

Judith shook her head and blew her nose on the square of linen that was handed to her. 'They would be easily overcome,' she said shakily. 'No, Mama, it is a matter of trust. He looks me in the face and lies. I cannot bear it!'

'Most men lie at one time or another,' Alicia said

ruefully. 'Are you sure you are not making a mountain out of a molehill?'

Judith lowered the linen square to her lap and wrung it into a rope. Her chin wobbled. 'I am sure. There is something he will not tell me. I have asked and asked him, but he just backs away, walks out of the room if I persist and the stupid thing is, Mama, that if he did tell me, admitted to my face what I already know, I think I would die.'

'Daughter, what do you mean?' Alicia looked at her with increasing anxiety, sensing deeper water than a mere lovers' misunderstanding or jealous quarrel. Judith bent her head and began to cry again and shiver. Through the tears, muffled, a little incoherent and punctuated by long hesitation, Alicia received the tale and her own stare became as desolate as her daughter's. She put her hand to her mouth, feeling not just queasy but dreadfully sick.

'Mama, what am I going to do?' Judith wept brokenly.

Alicia stood up and moved stiffly to the flagon. It was almost empty but she splashed dregs into a cup and, ignoring the sediment, gulped it down. 'Your husband is innocent,' she said abruptly. 'The guilt is all mine. Lay the blame at my door, child, not his.'

Judith turned her head and stared at her mother in bewilderment.

'Yes, you do have a right to know, but not from your husband's stumbled-upon knowledge.' Assailed by shock and dizziness, she reached for and grabbed the back of the bench chair. She had not believed in her wildest nightmare that it would come like this, so suddenly without time to prepare. What was she going to say? Mary, mother of God.

'Judith . . .' She swallowed hard, lifted her chin and forced out the words as if they were scalding her tongue. '. . . Judith, Maurice de Montgomery was not your father . . . I should have told you long since, but it was never the time . . . And now I fear it is too late.'

Judith stared at her struggling mother, as if she had suddenly grown two heads.

Alicia put her hand to her breast. 'I know it is difficult for you to understand, but if Maurice had ever found out—'

'Then who is?' Judith interrupted.

'Judith, I . . .' Alicia extended her hand in a pleading gesture.

Judith leaped to her feet, ignoring it. 'Who, Mama?' she demanded again.

Alicia made a small, frightened gesture. 'Henry . . . Prince Henry . . . the King.'

'That's not possible. He is only Guy's age now!' Judith stared at her mother, appalled and disbelieving.

'Even at fourteen he was no novice to the game,' Alicia answered wearily. 'He knew more than a woman twelve years wed.' Of necessity, she held Judith's gaze, but the feelings of guilt were almost more than she could bear, and her daughter's anguished look seared her heart.

'Why, Mama, why?'

Alicia gripped the bench until her knuckles whitened.

'Why?' Judith repeated, and dashed her sleeve across her eyes.

'Maurice blamed me for being barren. Every month when I bled he would beat me and the times in between he used me as if we were dog and bitch . . . and for nothing. Maurice had more sluts and casual whores than I can recall, but not one of them quickened. He was unable to beget children.' Her mouth twisted. 'Prince Henry came visiting on a hunting trip. Maurice was away. I had the fading remains of a black eye and bruises on my arms and his latest whore was flouting my authority in the hall. It did not matter that Henry was so young. I was so sick of Maurice that I'd have lain down for a leprous beggar in order to get myself with child and shut his filthy mouth. We had a night and a morning and you were conceived. For a time things were better. He did not beat or abuse me lest I miscarried, but after you were born, a daughter, matters went from bad to worse. He expected me to conceive again and when I did not the beatings increased apace.'

Judith's voice cracked. 'Mama, why didn't you tell me before?'

'I meant to, truly I did, but the time was never right and I knew how much you hated Maurice. At least when he beat you, you thought he had the right. I was afraid what you would reveal to him if he drove you too far.'

'And Guyon knows the truth of my begetting?'

'Not all of it,' Alicia watched her daughter anxiously. Judith's expression was now unreadable, but her hands were clenched at her sides and much as Alicia desired to cross the gulf and embrace her, the fear of rebuff was greater and held her rooted to the spot. 'Probably he has Henry's version of the event . . . I was not even sure until you spoke that Henry knew of your existence.'

'There have been remarks passed in court concerning my likeness to Arlette of Falais,' Judith said flatly as the control to understand warred with the need to strike out. Her marriage had been ripped apart by this murky secret from the past – her mother's past. She remembered the accusations she had flung at Guyon in her pain, and how he had absorbed them, swearing his innocence, but unable to give her the facts. And now it might be too late to set matters to rights. The pain was physical. 'Mama . . .' She stopped and looked round as Cadi trotted into the room and shook herself, spraying water from her close white coat. Guyon followed her, diamonds of rain winking on his fur-lined cloak. His hair had begun to curl at the edges. He was clutching a roll of parchment in one hand and his expression was at first blank, then wary as he looked at the two women and sensed the tension.

Alicia gave a soft gasp and her knees buckled. Guyon did not quite reach her in time and her head struck the sharp side of the brazier as she fell. Judith was rooted to the spot, unable to move, all her being still caught up in shock. Guyon bent over Alicia and felt for the pulse in her throat. It beat there steadily enough – in rhythm with the blood welling through her dark hair. He swore and propped her senseless form against him and pressed the cuff of his tunic to the side of her head.

'Judith, for God's love, don't just stand there like a sheep, go and get your medicines – make haste, she's bleeding hard!'

The snarled urgency in his voice jerked her into movement. She snatched up the nearest thing available to help him staunch the flow – her mother's painstakingly worked embroidery – thrust it at him, and sped to find her nostrums.

Grimly, quickly, she worked, ruining her beautiful gown, her commands to him terse and authoritative and he did as she bade him without complaint or demur. At last, finished, she sat back to regard her handiwork. The stitches were not as neat as they might have been, for the light was poor and she had been in a hurry, but it would not matter. Alicia's hair would cover the scar.

Her mother was dazed, but her colour was reasonable, her breathing and heartbeat steady and her pupils responded to the candle flame passed in front of them. Gently, they undressed her to her shift and Guyon carried her to the curtained bed and laid her in it. Together they looked down at her and then at each other, and slowly Judith walked into Guyon's embrace and laid her head against his chest.

'I can see why you kept it from me,' she said in a small voice. 'Guyon, I know it is not enough, but for what it is worth I'm sorry.'

'She told you, then? I was going to speak to her about it, but Henry has kept me too busy for leisure these last few days and, truth to tell, I could not bear the atmosphere in this house for longer than it took to change my clothes.'

'Guy . . .'

He studied her capable blood-caked fingers gripping the dark stuff of his tunic. 'Hush, love, we've all made our mistakes, yes, and paid for them.' He grimaced. And perhaps still were paying.

She lifted her eyes to him. 'Do you think that Henry will openly acknowledge me?'

'Christ in heaven, I hope he has more sense! Mischief prompted him to tell me. He likes to call the tune and watch men dance, but if he officially recognises you as his child, what do you think Robert de Belleme will do? Aside from the insult your mother's adultery would cast on the Montgomery bloodline, there is the matter of your birthright. You hold lands that are not legally yours. If your uncles ever discovered the truth, we'd have a war on our hands.'

'But they wouldn't . . . not with Henry . . .'

'De Belleme is backing Robert Curthose for the crown and so are more than half the other barons. I've letters with me, rough drafts as yet, commanding out the fyrd, the common men of the shires and my own feudal levies. Henry is preparing for war with the ordinary English people as his backbone because he does not know how many of the smiling faces at his table are also smiling at Curthose. If Curthose, with de Belleme at his right hand, carries the day, then God help us!'

Judith shuddered. 'Guy, stop frightening me!'

'Our lives have been a misery these last three months because you thought I had lied,' he said with wry humour.

'I know.' She shivered. 'I do not really mean it. I suppose I would rather be scared to death than so miserable I want to die.'

'So, I am innocent, *Cath fach*, but what of Henry? Rufus was his own brother.'

'I do not feel as though Henry is my father,' she said slowly after a moment. 'I only know it is so because I have been told and even now my wits are bemused. But I do not believe I care what Henry has plotted. My father . . . Lord Maurice I mean, committed crimes equally foul, I am sure.'

'But you cared that I might have done so?'

'That was different.' In the light from the brazier and the candles her complexion deepened to a rosy gold. 'I don't . . . love them as I love you.' She half turned away, still fighting it even though the words were spoken. Thorns and roses. You could not have one without risking the wound of the other.

Guyon drew her back against him, within the circle of his arms, raised his hand to smooth her hair and, seeing the blood caked under his fingernails, set it instead on her shoulder and angled his head to kiss her tenderly. 'Then we have everything, and the rest does not matter.' Which was not entirely true, but appropriate to his thoughts at the time.

'My lady, I've brought some fresh char—' Agnes paused on the threshold, basket clutched to her ample bosom and stared goggle-eyed at Guyon and Judith as they turned to face her. Judith's gown was blotched and spoiled by blood, Guyon's cloak less obviously so, but nonetheless smirched, and, behind them, Alicia's form lay still on the bed, gleaming in the white shroud of her shift.

Guyon, more knowledgeable by now, moved with the necessary speed to catch her and after the staggering weakness of sudden shock Agnes rallied and sat down to mop her wide pink brow on her sleeve while Guyon explained what had happened.

'Shall I fill a tub, my lady?' Almost recovered, Agnes wallowed to her feet and went to fuss over her sleeping mistress.

Judith sighed with obvious regret. 'No, Agnes. She needs rest and quiet and all the fuss of organising a bath would make too much noise. Tomorrow, perhaps. A good wash will suffice.'

'How long before your mother rouses, do you think?' Guyon asked.

'I don't know. Her colour is good, but she is deeply asleep and she will need watching.'

'Agnes is competent to do that? And Helgund?'

'Yes, but . . .'

'Good. Then put on your cloak.'

'But Guy, I can't go out like this and – oh!' She broke off to catch the garment as he threw it at her.

'Find something else to wear and bring it with you.'

She stared at him, or rather at his back, for he had turned away to rummage in his own clothing chest for a decent tunic. 'Guy, where are we going?'

'Wait and see. I've told you before about looking gift horses in the mouth.' He swung around and pinning his own cloak, advanced upon her.

'Guy?'

'Trust me?' His expression was a mingling of laughter and tension. 'Trust me, Judith?' He put his arm around her waist and pulled her close, or as close as the bunched cloak trapped between them would allow, and kissed her in a fashion that sent Agnes bustling to a far corner of the room on the pretext of some overlooked task.

'I don't know if I should,' Judith said, tilting her head. 'What awaits me if I do?'

'A fate worse than death?' he suggested, draping the cloak around her shoulders and fastening the pin.

She felt a warm glow in the pit of her stomach. Her lips curved and then parted in a full smile; her eyes danced. She would think about everything later. This moment belonged to her and Guyon. 'Show me,' she said, a catch in her voice. 'I want to know.'

Judith was sitting beside Alicia when she woke, her fingers nimbly weaving a needle in and out of a tunic she was stitching for Guyon, her manner one of demure domesticity. She had never been inside a Southwark bathhouse before, indeed had almost refused when she discovered their destination, but Guyon, grinning, had dragged her protesting through the doorway and the rest had been too interesting for her to want to leave.

Mention a Southwark bathhouse and most people would raise their eyebrows and utter knowing laughs, or purse their lips and shake their heads. Many of the stews warranted such censure, but Guyon's particular choice, which she suspected came of long acquaintance, appeared to cater for those with the wealth to buy privacy and discretion. She had seen several people she knew from the court, two of them alone, another in the company of a very pretty girl who was most certainly not his wife.

She and Guyon had soaked themselves clean and warm in a spacious tub and had drunk effervescent wine – not in any great quantity. They had played floating tables – and other less intellectual games, the kind associated with the Southwark stews and knowing laughs and pursed lips, and lent an added spice because of that.

She stifled a giggle and bit off the thread, and became aware that Alicia was watching her.

'Mama?' For an instant Judith was startled, but she recovered quickly and leaned forward. 'How are you feeling?'

'As if my brains have been squashed,' Alicia said faintly and put up her hand to touch her bandage-swathed head. 'What happened?'

'You fainted and cut your head on the brazier as you fell.'

From the other room, muffled by the heavy curtain, came the reassuring sound of male voices in conversation. Alicia strove to sit up, then desisted with a gasp of pain.

Judith pressed her gently back down. 'I had to stitch the wound and quickly,' she apologised. 'It is not my neatest piece of work.'

Frowning with pain and concentration, Alicia studied her daughter. Her rich gown had been replaced by a neat, serviceable homespun. The tawny hair was woven into a simple thick braid and looked almost as if it were damp.

'Judith, how long have I been asleep?'

She placed a cool hand upon her mother's forehead. 'Not long, do not fret yourself.'

'I seem to recall that I have cause to fret.'

Judith shook her head in wordless denial.

Alicia moistened her lips and groped towards what she wanted to say. 'I would have told you, truly I would. I believed in my innocence that Henry would want to do the same. I never thought that . . . is he using it to leash Guyon to his cause?'

Judith looked over her shoulder at the curtain. 'Guy is no tame dog to trot to heel, unless it be his wish.' She smiled towards the sound of his voice, while a conflict of pride and anxiety churned within her.

Her mother's voice was small and timid. 'You do not hate me, then?'

'Hate you?' Judith was astonished. 'Mama, of course not!'

Alicia's mouth trembled. Judith leaned over and hugged her mother. Shakily Alicia returned the embrace and then, drained, fell back against the pillow, nauseous with pain but feeling as if a great burden had been lifted from her soul. 'I thought you might. Or else be disgusted. Jesu knows, I have felt those things for myself many times over.'

Judith squeezed Alicia's hand. 'Mama, let it rest. It has caused enough grief. You had your reasons. I think when I have had the time, I will understand them.'

'Is all well between you and Guyon now?' Anxiety flooded back into Alicia's eyes.

The dim light masked Judith's blush. 'Yes, Mama,' she said, voice choked with laughter. Her mother might have cuckolded her husband with a fourteen-year-old youth, but she would be horrified if she knew where her daughter had just been.

Alicia looked doubtful. 'Are you sure?'

'Very sure, Mama.' Judith gave her mother a dazzling smile in which there remained a hint of secret laughter. 'Miles has been twitching about outside like a cat with a severe dose of fleas. I'll send him in.' And without waiting for Alicia's yea-say, she went to the curtain.

CHAPTER 22

AUGUST 1101

At his father's keep at Ashdyke, Guyon leaned his head against the cushioned high back of the chair, closed his eyes and within moments was asleep. It was an ability he had cultivated of a necessity since Whitsuntide. He could even doze in the saddle, although that was less than safe. Bred to ride from birth, he would not have fallen off, but there was always the danger of a Welsh attack or a surprise assault from one of de Belleme's vassals.

He was sorely beset. Henry was demanding men, money and supplies that Guyon was hard pressed to find or persuade out of others; Curthose was threatening across the Channel, perhaps even at sea by now; de Belleme and his wolfpack were poised to strike the moment it was politic and, to twist the coil, Earl Hugh of Chester had suffered a seizure and was lying paralysed and close to death in a Norman monastery. His heir was a child and the Welsh were understandably gleeful. Already a few experimental raids had tested the earldom's somewhat fluid boundaries. The garrison at Caermoel had been involved in skirmishes twice that week.

Guyon was doing his best, but was fearful that it was not enough. Last night he had dreamed that he was tied hand and foot and drowning in a sticky lake of blood and had woken drenched, gasping and terrified to discover Cadi lying on his chest, licking his face, demanding to be let out of the room.

It had been a grim year thus far and very little light to hold at bay the yawning cavern of de Belleme's ambition. In January, Mabel de Lacey, former wife of Ralph de Serigny had given birth to a healthy son and, against all odds, mother and child had survived the ordeal. De Lacey had used the excuse of his son's christening to host a council of war, chaired by the Earl of Shrewsbury who was openly plotting treason. Henry, without the support of more than half his barons, was for the moment constrained to swallow it.

In February, Rannulf Flambard had escaped from confinement in the Tower of London and had hastened to Normandy as fast as his sandals could carry him in order to promote the cause of Robert Curthose. Flambard was an able, persuasive prelate, capable of squeezing blood out of a stone and an excellent manager of that blood once squeezed. If Henry had been the kind of man to panic, he would have done so. As it was, he continued calmly to muster the resources and supporters he possessed into an efficient fighting unit, although Guyon had his doubts about how efficient some of them actually were. The fyrd was the backbone of Henry's army and it was composed of ordinary villagers and worthies who hadn't a hope in hell against the men who would come at them, men who made war their profession – the mercenaries of Normandy and Flanders, paid to rake the heat from hell and scatter it abroad.

He thought back to one hot midsummer afternoon when King Henry had been personally overseeing the training of his peasant-bred troops. Guyon had suggested that he would do better to instruct them in the use of the quarterstaff and spear rather than seek to imbue them with the warrior skills that were attained only by instruction from birth.

Henry, his forelock wet, dark patches on his inner thighs where he had sweated against his saddle, had looked at Guyon and given that familiar, engimatic smile. 'Robert's amenable to reason,' he said. 'He doesn't really want to spill my blood and he's usually swayed by whoever has the most persuasive tongue at the time . . . particularly when they are in possession of a large, efficient army. Mutton dressed as wolf, you might say.' And he had laughed softly.

'You mean I'm sweating my guts out for a mummers' show?'

'I certainly hope so, Guy, although it is hard to tell how deeply the rot has set in.'

How deep, how far? And all they had was Henry's guile and a terrible gamble on Curthose's nature.

The sound of wine splashing from flagon to goblet and the weight of Cadi's rump as she settled inconveniently across his toes, jolted his lids open.

'Go to bed,' his father advised, pouring a second cup and handing it to him. 'Alicia remarked to me how tired you look. I know she's apt to fuss, but this time I would say she is right.'

Guyon shook his head. 'I can't. I only stopped here because it was convenient to water the horses and eat a meal without being stabbed in the back. I've got to be in Stafford by tomorrow night.'

'You will burn yourself out,' Miles warned.

Guyon arched his free hand over his eyes. 'Do you think I do not know that?'

'At least roll yourself in your cloak for an hour.'

Guyon took his hand away and smiled at his father. 'Now who is fussing? I was going to do that without your urging, providing of course that I can trust you to wake me up. I've to skirt Quatford and Shrewsbury. I'd rather not saddle-sleep in such inhospitable territory.'

Miles sat down in the chair opposite. 'Is there any more news from the south?'

Guyon shook his head and dragged his feet out from beneath Cadi's weight. 'Not news, only commands.'

'Surely there are more resources than yours to draw upon?'

'Yes, but not in the marches. De Belleme is for Curthose; Mortimer sits on the fence and smiles; Earl Hugh is dead, or as good as, and Arnulf of Pembroke is a Montgomery. FitzHamon, Warwick and Bigod are bearing the brunt of the work elsewhere. Who else is there except me?' He made an eloquent face. 'It cannot go on for much longer. Did you notice the direction of the wind from the battlements? It's been blowing to our disadvantage for the past three days. If Curthose does not come now, he never will.'

'The Queen is due to be brought to bed any day now, isn't she?' Miles said.

'Next month. She's confined at Winchester with the treasury.' Guyon's words were bereft of inflection. 'His wife, his heir and his money. I know what I would do if I were Curthose.' He finished the wine and put the cup down. 'Henry expects him to land near Hastings. It is both expedient and symbolic.'

Miles grunted. 'Do you think they will really fight? I was always under the impression that Curthose treated Henry as his wayward baby brother – deserving of the occasional sharp slap, but never a complete crushing.'

Guyon shrugged. 'If Flambard and de Belleme have anything to do with it, then yes, they will fight, but as you say, they are up against Robert's nature. He has always nurtured a soft spot for Henry and he's so determined to be a perfect knight that they'll have an almighty struggle persuading him to act otherwise. But then they can be very persuasive men . . .'

'Yes,' Miles said, his expression revealing what the word did not. He grimaced. He was prepared for war because, living on the Welsh border, one was never not prepared for it, but sparring with the Welsh was not the same as resisting men such as Walter de Lacey and Roger Mortimer.

'Judith is coping?'

Guyon's mouth softened. 'Better than I,' he said with grim humour. 'She's a superb quartermaster and deputy. Every time I put an obstacle in her path, she floats effortlessly over it. Jesu, sometimes I am hard pressed to stay with her, she learns so quickly. When I think of her two years ago on the day of our marriage, a gawky, frightened waif and then I look at her now, holding the reins of our estates in her hands, not just holding but controlling, I sometimes wonder if I am dreaming. And then she looks at me and smiles and I know I am not.'

'Blood will out,' Miles said with a faint smile.

Guyon chuckled sourly. 'Oh yes, blood will out,' he agreed and, leaning back his head, closed his eyes.

'She shows no sign of breeding yet?' Miles asked hesitantly. 'Alicia worries . . .'

Guyon's eyes remained closed. 'Judith's reasons can hardly be hers, can they? After all, I've already proved my worth at stud, even if the outcome has been a daughter.'

'That's not what I meant,' Miles reproved. 'But your lands and titles are far greater than mine and Judith has royal blood in her veins.'

'And it would be a pity if no crop was sown from it to benefit,' Guyon said expressionlessly.

'Well it would,' Miles defended and rubbed the back of his neck. 'It would please Alicia greatly to be blessed with grandchildren. She is afraid that the payment for her sins will be Judith's inability to conceive.'

'Then tell her I shall apply myself with diligence – chance permitting. I can count on the fingers of one hand the occasions we have shared a bed since Easter and most of those I was unconscious the moment my head hit the bolster. Besides, these are not safe times to bring a child into the world. I'd not damn an offspring of mine to death in Shrewsbury's dungeon. God knows, I worry enough about Rhosyn and Heulwen.'

'I saw Madoc last week,' Miles said, memory jolted by Guyon's mention of his former lover and their child.

'Did you?' Guyon's words emerged as a sleepy mumble.

'Hurrying too much as usual and full of bluster, you know Madoc. I swear his lips were as blue as blackberry juice, the fool. He had a young man with him – distant kin from Bristol – Prys ap Adda.'

'Mmmm?'

Miles eyed his son thoughtfully. The name obviously meant nothing to him. 'A young man who talked a great deal about Rhosyn and her children. I got the impression that he'd like to be closer to Madoc than a mere distant relative . . . son-in-law, for example.'

Guyon's eyes opened. He turned his head.

'Madoc's amenable,' Miles said, exploring Guyon's slightly startled expression for hints of any deeper emotion. 'He knows his body is failing him and soon he won't be able to travel any more. Rhys is not old enough yet to take on the graver responsibilities, so it behoves him to find a willing, energetic younger man and bind him to the family.'

'Madoc always did have a need for ropes and grapnels,' Guyon said humorously, but then his smile slipped. 'Rhosyn has never seen herself as a rope.'

'Madoc thinks she will consent . . . providing of course that Prys is not a complete idiot in the way he sets about convincing her. He did not seem an idiot to me.'

Guyon thought of Rhosyn and their warm, stolen moments together – the brevity of those encounters, an hour here, a half-day there, scattered in disjointed fragments like pieces of a stained-glass window, shattered and strewn down a path four years long. Beautiful, jewel colours that even now, when he had Judith, possessed edges sharp enough to pierce the heart. 'He won't be if she accepts him,' he said quietly, 'if the children accept him.'

'Your Heulwen included?'

Guyon's lower lids tensed. He drew a deep, steadying breath and controlled himself before he spoke. 'She is still a babe in arms. Belike she will cleave to him and the better so.' He manoeuvred his shoulders until he was comfortable and shut his eyes again. 'Forgive me. I'm very tired.'

Miles said nothing, because there was nothing more to be

said that would ease or comfort the situation. His footsteps soft, he walked away and left Guyon to sleep.

Guyon roused with a start to the feel of someone violently shaking his shoulder. He was so stiff that for a moment he could not move and, when he did, it was to discover that his feet were completely numb where the dog's weight had pressed all feeling from them.

'What's the matter?' he demanded groggily. 'Is it time to go?' And then his gaze focused on his father. 'Why are you wearing your mail?'

'Henry's messenger has just ridden in on a half-dead horse. Curthose has landed, and not at Pevensey as we all expected.'

'What? Where then?' Guyon shoved Cadi off his feet, pushed himself out of the chair and began automatically to don the hauberk that Eric was holding out to him.

'Portsmouth,' Miles said grimly. 'Some English sailors were persuaded to pilot Curthose and his ships into the harbour.'

'Then the road to Winchester is open?'

'Yes.'

Guyon cursed as he picked up his swordbelt and fumbled to attach the scabbard to its thongs. The Queen, the heir, the treasury.

Alicia hovered in the background, looking as if she might burst into tears. Guyon glanced round the room for his spurs and lifted them off the coffer. 'Look after Cadi for me,' he said to her, 'I cannot take her with me.'

Alicia nodded distantly, but her eyes were all for Miles, devouring him. Guyon flicked a look from one to the other. 'I'll meet you below,' he murmured to his father, kissed Alicia on the cheek, thought briefly of Judith and left the room, Eric stamping in his wake.

Alicia gave a small, despairing sob and cast herself into Miles's mail-clad arms. He smoothed her glossy black braids and buried his face in the pulse beating in her white neck. The sword pommel intruded between them, butting up beneath her ribs. It might as well have been through her heart, blade end on.

CHAPTER 23

If Robert de Belleme had been the kind of man to tear out his hair and swear and curse, he would have done so. Those who knew him well enough recognised the signs of agitation with sufficient clarity to take evasive action before it was too late. Those who did not, found they had a scorpion by the tail.

As the troops made ready to disperse, he sat in his tent and stared blank-eyed at the rough canvas wall. A muscle ticked in his cheek. His fists tightened. After a moment he glanced down at the dirty yellow colour of his clenched knuckles, then gently flexed them, placing his hands palm-flat upon his thighs.

He had picked his horse, he had nurtured it, fed it from his own hand, cajoled it, coaxed it sweetly down to the water trough. It had dipped its muzzle and at the last, impossible moment had refused to drink because the water was not as crystal clear as it had imagined. By rights he should have taken his sword and hewn the beast into gobbets there and then.

Outside the tent, he heard Walter de Lacey and another of his vassals joking together, something about the young age of the whore currently appeasing de Lacey's lust. A red mist floated before de Belleme's eyes. They were laughing about a slut when months of careful planning and hard work were unravelling around them like a loom weaving backwards. But then what did he expect of fools? When he was sure of his temper, he rose and stalked purposefully out into the open.

'Aren't those other tents down yet?' he snarled.

'Nearly, m'lord,' a serjeant answered fearfully.

He shoved him aside and snapped his fingers at the soldier who held his stallion. De Lacey and the other man stopped laughing and exchanged wary glances. He did not even look at them, although they were part of his personal escort who were to ride with him to the signing of the peace treaty between the brothers. Peace treaty – hah! For what it was worth to Robert Curthose, he might as well use it to wipe his backside.

De Belleme mounted his stallion and drew in the reins, pulling the horse's mouth against its chest. 'When you are ready,' he said icily.

De Lacey cleared his throat, muttered an apology and swung into his saddle.

The King and his brother sat side by side at a long, linen-spread trestle. Guyon, seated further down the board, watched the banners flutter in the warm breeze. Behind and before, two armies were amassed, one of English shire levies, commanded by the barons who had remained loyal to Henry and one of Normans and Flemings, bulked out by the vassals and retainers of such men as Robert de Belleme, Arnulf of Pembroke and Ivo Grantmesnil.

The smell of so many bodies was distinctly middenish, as was the language. The English were merely insulting the Normans because it was a traditional pastime. The Normans were swearing because their leader had decided to make peace with his brother when it was crass stupidity to do so. Better by far to fight.

Guyon and Miles had reached Winchester with their troops close on dusk of the day following the messenger's arrival, had been momentarily mistaken for the enemy and

almost set upon. Cursing, Guyon had roared his name at
the men on the walls, his shield flung up and furred with
arrows and, after the captain of the guard had been sent for
and emerged hitching his chausses and complaining that he
could not even go for a piss in peace, they were admitted to
spend the night there.

Curthose's army had bypassed Winchester, so the captain
had told them, his eyes cynical with disbelief. Guyon sent
a glance along the board to the bearded, stocky form of
Robert Curthose. The kind of man who forsook such a prize
when it was his for the taking was the kind of fool who was
unfit to govern.

Curthose lived in a world of chivalric unreality, an
illuminated page that had little to do with worldly practi-
calities. It was the reason he never had any money. He was
constantly frittering it away in the interests of distributing
làrgesse. His misplaced sense of knightly generosity had
led him to declare he could not possibly be so much of a
brute as to disturb the Queen when she was so near to her
time.

Robert de Belleme, who could indeed have been so brutish
without a qualm, was left gnashing his teeth at Curthose's
inability to maintain both his sense of purpose and the anger
at Henry that might have kept his fervour burning.

Those barons who had counted on being able to make
Curthose fight for the English crown were now watching
Henry, avoiding his eye if he watched them in return and
anxiously counting the cost of misjudgement. Henry was
not his easygoing brother to forgive and forget, unless it was
politically expedient to do so.

They were all gathered here now, enemy and ally, on the
London road at Alton, so that Henry and Curthose could
hammer out their differences and come to terms. De
Belleme and Flambard and Grantmesnil had advised
Curthose to fight. His position was good and would never
be stronger. Henry had smiled into his brother's childishly

innocent eyes and asked why resort to bloodshed when diplomacy was by far the better way?

Curthose had been only too willing to listen to Henry's sweet-talk, which was, of course, Henry's deadliest weapon. Curthose's intention to war with Henry had considerably cooled since its first indignant eruption and, besides, he was now embarrassed for funds. All he wanted was some money to cover his expenses and to go back to Normandy and let the dust settle. Henry was most amenable. All that remained to be discussed was the sum Curthose would be paid annually in return for his acknowledgement of Henry's right to the crown.

Guyon studied the assembly. Grantmesnil, de Belleme and Roger de Poitou had arrived looking like a trio of warlocks, their minions swarming behind. The lord of Shrewsbury was wearing a blood-red gown. His eyes were as pale as shards of glass and stabbed everyone they encountered.

When the look slashed over Guyon, the latter answered it impassively. He shielded himself from the malevolence by recalling their last encounter and the gratifying sight of de Belleme and de Lacey parcelled up in the road among a herd of bleating, stinking sheep. His mouth twitched and he quickly lowered his eyes before he laughed. When he dared to look up again, the Earl's gaze was stalking FitzHamon with vicious intent and Walter de Lacey was watching him instead.

Without qualm this time, Guyon smiled at him.

De Lacey stiffened and his right hand twitched towards his sword; except of course that he wasn't wearing one. No man came armed to a parley. He transferred his fist to his empty belt and clamped it there instead.

The annual sum to be forfeited by Henry was set at three thousand marks. Robert appeared delighted with the bargain. Henry's own smile was wry, but with a secretive undercurrent that Guyon well recognised. Judith looked like that when matters had not gone entirely her own way but she intended them to do so in the fullness of time. Curthose might get his payment this year and next, but as soon as Henry's hold on his kingdom was less precarious, he would set about seeking a way to extricate himself from the agreement.

Twelve barons from each faction ratified the treaty with their seals. Henry and Robert clasped each other. Curthose's hug was ebullient and affectionate, Henry's a pale imitation. Affection in Henry was reserved for those who did not threaten his crown and even that these days was sparingly given. He was in love with the task of ruling and it left precious little room for softer emotions.

Guyon was in the act of accepting a cup of wine and a heel of bread from his father's captain while around him the men made shrift to load the packhorses, when Henry himself approached, picking his way carefully around the campfire and assorted heaps of baggage. FitzHamon was with him, the sun reflecting off his pink, freckled scalp.

Guyon bowed, his mouth full of bread. Miles appeared from the tent, breath drawn to speak and, startled, made his own obeisance.

Guyon swallowed hastily. 'Breakfast, sire?' he asked with a touch of humour. The bread was stale and the wine was warm and stuck to the palate. It was all they had left.

Henry made a gesture of refusal and came straight to the point. 'I have to put a curb bit on de Belleme, his brothers and their allies,' he said, 'and I need your help, Guy, and yours too, Miles.'

'If it be in my power, sire,' Miles answered gracefully, eyes full of suspicion.

Guyon glanced at FitzHamon whose face was unhelpfully blank. His heart sank. All he wanted to do was go home, bury his head beneath a pillow for six months, sleep and rediscover the pleasure of a bathtub and Judith fragrantly soft in his arms. Judith, who was Henry's daughter. 'Sire?'

'I've had the exchequer gathering evidence against Surrey and Grantmesnil since the late autumn, but I need more information on de Belleme and his brothers. There is much groundwork to be done in the marches and until I am ready to cast the noose, I do not want my prey to know how tight I intend to draw it.'

'You want us to spy for you?' Miles demanded.

Henry pinched the end of his blunt nose. Miles, half Welsh by birth, had been one of his father's most valued scouts, a master in the arts of reconnaissance and stealth, one of the props of the Norman army during the notorious northern campaign of 'sixty-nine. 'Not personally,' he said with a tepid smile. 'I'd not lose either of you to one of Shrewsbury's little pastimes, but you must have contacts from the old days, Miles, men you can trust.'

'To have their entrails pierced in my stead?' Miles said with quiet contempt.

'Don't be so awkward, Miles,' said FitzHamon. 'Someone has to recruit the men and collate the information gleaned. Would you rather have de Belleme ravening about the borders like a mad wolf for the next thirty years?'

Miles snorted. 'A knife in the dark would work just as well,' he said, 'and would probably be a lot simpler to accomplish.'

Henry shook his head. 'I had thought of that, but it wouldn't really serve. If Robert de Belleme dies, then the lands go to his son, or to one of his brothers. If, on the other hand, he is stripped of his fiefs for flouting the law of the land beyond all redemption, then the estates and revenues come directly to the crown.'

'But first he has to be found in official error of the law,' Guyon said, beginning to understand. His mouth twisted. 'And then it will come to war.'

FitzHamon shrugged. 'You cannot make wine without treading grapes and one way or another it will still come to war in the end.'

'Blood and wine, they're both red, aren't they?' Miles said, his expression blank.

'I'm sure you would rather be a treader than a grape.' Henry said with a glimmer of amusement. 'Think about it. If you decide in favour, send to me, or get a message to Beaumais in Shrewsbury. You do know him, don't you?'

'Beaumais? but he's . . .' said Miles.

Henry's smile was feline. 'Yes, he's a justiciar in de Belleme's household and he's been in my pay for the past year. You'll be working closely with him if you choose to take on this task.'

Miles stared at Henry, the hairs prickling his scalp. Guyon, more accustomed to the devious workings of his sovereign's mind, quirked him a wry, 'should have known it' look. Henry conceded a genuine laugh and reached up to slap his shoulder. 'Think about it,' he repeated. 'I'll talk to you later.'

'Will you do as he asks?' FitzHamon said as he made to follow Henry across the camp.

'I do not think we have a choice,' Guyon replied. 'And there's no point in cutting off your nose to spite your face.'

'That doesn't stop him from being as much a bastard as his father was,' Miles grunted with considerably less charity. 'Only William's was a matter of birth. His is a matter of nature.'

'That's why he's King and Curthose isn't,' Guyon said.

CHAPTER 24

SUMMER 1102

Rhosyn drew rein and let the leather hang slack in her capable fingers so that old Gwennol could graze the dusty roadside grass. Beyond them, pocked and rutted, the road cut through fields and forest and past formidable fortresses – the marcher eyries of Robert de Belleme – until it reached Shrewsbury, crouched within the protection of the Severn bend. Behind her on the drovers' road lay Wales and safety, as far as anything could be termed safe these days. Guyon had been right, Robert de Belleme and his vassals had turned the marches into hell for men who had to travel them for a living. The war in the south where King Henry sought to bring his most voracious earl to heel sent disturbing rumours scudding north. If Arundel fell to the royal forces, then the storm would burgeon here in the heart of de Belleme's honours and blight the land she rode.

She considered now the left fork and felt a surge in her solar plexus. She always did when she thought of Guyon and not just because of what had been between them. He would be furious when he realised she had risked crossing the border with only a drover and his market-bound herd of sheep for protection.

Her father had been in Flanders when his heart had finally failed his driving will and he had died in a hostel on the Bruges road. Prys had sailed from Bristol to fetch his body home for burial. They would mourn him, and then, because time did not stand still, they would marry. Rhosyn bit her lip, beginning to regret the impulse that had driven her from the hafod towards the market at Ravenstow. There were items she needed, she told herself, items for her wedding. The item she most wanted, she could not have. Better to settle for the same thing in a serviceable day-to-day mould without the gilding, but knowing what was better and sensible did not ease the pain.

'Why have we stopped, Mam?'

Rhosyn looked round at her daughter and the fine lines fanning from her eye corners deepened into a deprecatory smile. 'I am beginning to wonder if we should have come at all.'

'Too late now,' declared Twm sourly, riding up from behind, the pack ponies jingling behind him.

'Won't Guyon be pleased to see us then?' Eluned looked anxiously at her mother and then at Heulwen cradled sleeping in Twm's broad embrace.

'Probably not,' Rhosyn admitted ruefully. 'He may not even be there, not with the war down in the south.'

'What about his wife, will she?' asked Rhys, thinking of the young woman he had met on several occasions during trading visits with his grandfather. Despite himself he liked her. Beneath her wariness dwelt a sense of humour and a genuine interest in people whatever their station.

'Perhaps.' Rhosyn's fingers twitched on the reins and Gwennol raised her head and backed restively. Guyon's wife. How would she react to their presence at Ravenstow and what in God's name was she going to say to her if they met? Neither child nor virgin, Guyon had said, but as vulnerable as blown glass, and there had been an expression in his eyes that she had never seen before.

'I don't want to meet her,' Eluned said with a mutinous pout. 'She's probably a haughty Norman bitch.'

Rhosyn turned to her daughter. 'Whoever we meet and whatever happens, you will remember your manners and not disgrace my name or your grandfather's. Is that understood?'

'Yes, Mam,' Eluned said with a scowl.

The market at Ravenstow was in full cry, the booths hectic despite, or perhaps because of, the unrest and warfare swirling around the county. Men had to make a living and even with their lord absent at the siege of Arundel, the Ravenstow lands were still safer than many.

There were stalls of pies, breads and sweetmeats to tempt the hungry. Spice vendors cried their wares. One of the Ravenstow guards was having a tooth drawn, the efforts of the sweating chirurgeon observed with grisly relish by a critical crowd. A performing bear lumbered in pawing, shaggy circles to the music of an off-key set of bagpipes played by a man with a paunch that could have supported a cauldron.

There was a cacophony of livestock. Women sat with baskets full of surplus home produce to barter or sell – cherries and root vegetables, butter and cheese. The potter was there with his green-glaze wares, as was the salt chandler, the shoe-smith, the basket-weaver, and the other tradesmen of the town.

Judith did her duty by the senior merchants and townspeople, pausing to speak and smile and discuss, setting their fears at rest before making her purchases. At the bronze-smith's booth, she bought a new chappe for one of Guyon's belts and a collar for Cadi, the bitch having deposited the last one somewhere on a ten-mile stag hunt, and then she repaired to the haberdasher's stall to obtain needles and embroidery silks for the hanging she intended to warm the solar wall.

Another woman was already there, intently scrutinising a length of ribbon. A small child clutched her skirts and peeped up at Judith from a pair of round, kingfisher-blue eyes. An older, black-haired girl at the woman's other side shifted impatiently from foot to foot. Behind Judith, de Bec muttered a startled, stifled oath.

'What's wrong?' Judith asked, half turning. In that same moment, the boy Rhys stepped from the crowd and joined his mother and sisters at the stall. There was no mistaking the relationship. They all had variations of the same blunt nose and their hair grew to a similar pattern.

'*Heulwen, dewch yno*,' said the mother absently as her red-haired youngest one moved from the safety of her skirts towards Judith.

Judith's stomach turned over as the child smiled at her. She put her hand to her mouth and bit on the fleshy side of her palm. Guyon's mistress, Guyon's daughter, here in the heart of their lands. Here, where she had thought she was inviolate. What did one do? Fight? Back away like one cat sighting another? Brazen it out? Judith lowered her hand and drew herself up. She was no longer a child beset by unfocused emotions, bereft of weapons or defence. She had the knowledge now and the confidence to use it. All that this woman had were the ties of the past . . . and the child. Involuntarily, Judith's hand went to her own flat belly before she crouched to the infant's level. 'Heulwen,' she said with uncertainty and smiled.

Rhys turned his head, dark eyes widening. Rhosyn looked round, the ribbon twined in her neat, capable fingers, her expression first surprised, then anxious. It was a pleasant face with glossy arched brows and full-lidded autumnal eyes. Pretty, but not strikingly so and there were faint weather lines seaming her eye corners.

'I am Judith de Montgomery, Guyon's wife,' Judith introduced herself with an impassivity that gave no inkling of the seething emotions beneath. 'If you have come to see him, I am afraid you will be disappointed. He's down at Arundel with the King.'

Heulwen smiled coyly at Judith before turning to her mother and pressing her face into her skirts.

Her heart thumping, Rhosyn stared at the woman who now rose to her feet and confronted her. Were it not for her cool statement of identity, she would never have connected the imagination to the reality. Here was a striking young woman, as slender and straight as a stalk of corn in her golden wool gown and not an inch of vulnerability in her attitude.

'I am pleased to meet you, my lady,' Rhoysn responded in excellent accented French marred by the crack in her voice. 'You are not as I thought.'

The gold-grey eyes fixed on her in cool appraisal. 'Neither are you.'

Rhosyn swallowed. 'I have not come to make of Guyon a battleground,' she said, trying to defend herself against Judith's gaze which owned the properties of winter sunlight – bright but killingly cold.

'But nevertheless you are here, and I do not think that it is because you intend buying trinkets or watching the bear dance.'

'No, there is more to it than that,' Rhosyn admitted. 'Some of it is a matter of trade. I have those spices you asked my father to obtain for you last time and I needed some trimmings for a new gown . . .' She drew a shaky breath. 'My father went to Flanders last month and died there. Prys has gone to bring him home. I was hoping to ask Guyon for an escort back into Wales – he did promise me one should I need it – and I thought he should know of my father's death . . . and other things.' Her voice stalled into silence.

'Then you had best come up to the keep,' Judith said stiffly. 'There will be tallies to settle and you will need a place to sleep. I am sorry to hear about your father. We had become friends.' She wondered what she would do if Guyon came unexpectedly home now and lavished all his attention on Rhosyn and their small, engaging daughter. It was an area they had left well alone. Judith had never enquired beyond the superficial and he had seldom volunteered insights, both of them avoiding what might cause them too much pain. She saw now, too late, that they had been wrong.

The tension between the two women remained palpable, although Judith relaxed her guard sufficiently to haggle prices with Rhosyn, who responded vigorously to the challenge as soon as she realised Judith's astuteness. Eluned was sulky and intractable and de Bec took her and Rhys off to the stables to show them Melyn's latest batch of kittens before the child's rudeness became inexcusable. The two women were left alone in each other's company, except for the infant.

'Eluned has lost her father and now her grandfather,' Rhosyn sighed, 'and this new babe has not made matters any easier.' She looked tenderly down at the child curled sleepily in her lap. 'I did not mean to conceive, you know – a slip-up with the nostrums that would have prevented such a thing. She is a tie with Guyon I could well do without.' Gently she touched the feathery whorls of red-blonde hair and smiled. 'She takes her colouring from Guyon's grandsire, Renard de Rouen. He married a Welsh girl, old Lord Owain's daughter, Heulwen. My father was at their wedding, although of course he was no more than a child himself then.'

Judith was silent, not knowing what to say. Spoken in a different tone, Rhosyn's words might have been a challenge, yet crooned softly like a lullaby to a drowsing infant, there was no threat but, Jesu, they stung all the same. A vision of Guyon's lithe, muscular body filled Judith's inner eye. She knew exactly how his skin would feel beneath her fingertips; the gliding, sensual promise of joy. So did Rhosyn, the child in her arms a visible, living reminder of the pleasure Guyon had taken on her body. And as yet she had no such reminder to comfort herself.

Glancing up from her sleepy daughter, Rhosyn glimpsed Judith's expression before it was masked to neutrality, and her stomach lurched. Behind that controlled façade there stalked a wild beast.

'Perhaps it would be better if you gave me my escort now,' she suggested with dignity.

Judith parted her lips to snarl an agreement, caught her voice in time and, hands clenched in her lap, looked away towards the space upon the solar wall where she intended to drape the hanging. The jealous anger she felt was corrosive and damaging. She had to face it and force her will through it. Turning back to the small, dark Welsh woman, she laid her hand on her sleeve.

'No, please stay. It is too late in the day to set out for Wales. You would not reach your home before dark. Besides, we have not concluded our business. Can you obtain some more of that rich cloth for me? The last gown was ruined in London.'

'I will try. We've been swamped by demands for it since last winter, but of course you and Guyon have priority. I'll speak to Prys.' She studied Judith warily. They were navigating a deep, narrow channel and where there were not jagged rocks to be avoided, there were currents and whirlpools.

Ignorant of adult strivings, Heulwen slept, a heavy warm weight in her mother's arms, and Rhosyn was only too glad to accept Judith's invitation to put her down in the upper chamber with Helgund and Elflin.

The room was well appointed and reasonably warm, for in addition to the braziers it boasted a hearth. The maids whispered delightedly over the sleeping child. Rhosyn laid her daughter in the huge bed which dwarfed the small form to the size of a doll and, after tenderly smoothing her curls, gazed around the room. The walls were bright with hangings that stayed the draughts and combated the seeping coldness of the stone walls. The narrow windows were covered by slats of wafer-thin ox horn so that at least some daylight was permitted into the room, but rush dips still illuminated the corners and unseen things seemed to lurk there. She shivered and hugged her arms.

'Is there something wrong?' Judith enquired.

Rhosyn shook her head and smiled wanly. 'I hate these places.' She shuddered. 'No light, no air save that it be musty and tainted with damp. The walls hem me in. I never sleep well when I'm lodged in one of these keeps. I need to be free. Guy could see it, but he never understood. He loves the stones. Perhaps they grow warm under his touch as they do not under mine. It is one of the reasons I would not stay with him. In time the nightmare would have swamped the dream.' She looked round at Judith and dropped her arms to her sides. 'You are like him; content to dwell here. You do not feel the hostility. I could no more make my home in a keep than you could live rough in Wales.'

Judith took her coney-lined cloak from the clothing pole and handed Rhosyn hers across the space separating them. 'Then you do not know me,' she responded with a glimmer of fierceness. 'Yes, I do enjoy the security of these walls and caring for those within their bounds, but it is not all my life and, if it was, I would go mad.'

She led her out of the room and on up the twisting stairway to the battlements, her tread making nothing of the steep, winding steps. Almost defiantly she added between breaths as they went, 'I know how to track and snare game. I can make a shelter from cloaks and branches. I speak a fair degree of Welsh and I can use a dagger as well as any man. When Guy goes on progress to his other holdings, I go with him and it is no hardship for me to sleep beneath a hedge or hayrick wrapped in my cloak. I need to feel the wind in my hair and the rain on my face. Sometimes I come up here for precisely that purpose.'

Rhosyn, her calves aching, put her hands on the stone and leaned between the merlons while she rested to gain her breath. A guard saluted the two women. Judith greeted the

man by name and stood beside Rhosyn, her tawny hair
wisping loose of its braids.

'You have it in you to keep him,' Rhosyn said, seeing now
the promise. Not just a strikingly attractive young woman,
high-bred and Norman with all the domestic and social skills
that a man of Guyon's status required, but one who beneath
the cultured exterior was still only half tame, a thing of the
woods, wild for to hold. Guyon was not about to grow bored
with such a complex, complementary blending of traits.

A few late swallows swooped the sky, their cries poignantly
sharp, like needles darting through blue cloth. Judith looked
down at her hands. 'If we are granted a life together,' she
said with a hint of bitterness and stared at a blemish on one
of her nails until her eyes began to sting. 'Since last
Martinmas, I have scarcely seen him. Either he is with the
King, or about the King's business and the times he is home,
he just eats and sleeps and his temper is foul . . . but then I
suppose it has reason to be. There is no guarantee that Henry
will win this war. If he fails it won't matter whether I have
the ability to hold him or not . . . in this life at least. De
Belleme knows whose work was behind half the charges he
was summoned to answer.'

Rhosyn leaned with her and watched the swooping birds.
A trickle of foreboding shivered down her spine. 'Is he in
serious danger?'

'I have never known my lord when he has not been in
serious danger,' Judith said with a reluctant smile. 'From his
own contrary nature, if nothing else. He sets out to court
trouble sometimes and I have the devil's own job to persuade
him that he should be courting me instead!'

It was spoken with humour, but it was in no wise amusing,
as Rhosyn well knew. Leopards did not make good hearth
animals. They were liable to tear out your heart.

The watch changed, spears scraping on stone, jocularities
bantered. Some sheep were driven into the bailey from the
surrounding fields for slaughter the next day. Below them,

the market was packing up as folk began wending their way home. Leaning over the battlements, Judith saw the guard who had been having his tooth pulled weaving this way and that over the drawbridge, clearly the worse for drink. She made a mental note to check with de Bec that he was not on duty that night.

'I was foolish to come,' said Rhosyn in a soft voice that Judith had to strain to hear. 'Only I wanted . . . I wanted to see you for myself. If I am honest, that at least was the half of it.'

Taken aback, Judith stared at her. 'I would call it a very dangerous indulgence,' she said.

Rhosyn made a face. 'Do you think I have not said the same thing to myself a hundred times over?' She smiled sadly. 'But it has been like a sore tooth, nagging me and nagging me until it had to be drawn. I had to know. Well, now I do and I am glad it is over, but that is not the sole reason I am here.' She drew a deep breath, her eyes on the horizon towards which the sun was now angling. 'My second cousin Prys, who lives in Bristol and with whom we have strong business ties, has asked me to marry him and I have agreed.'

'Congratulations,' Judith said courteously. 'When is the wedding to be?'

'We don't know yet. Before Christmastide, I suppose. We have my father to mourn first and the business to sort out.' She frowned and pressed the heel of her hand into the gritty stone. 'I've known Prys since we were children and Rhys and Eluned are fond of him . . . but it is Heulwen, you see. After all, she is Guyon's daughter and for the sake of what was between us, he should know my decision. Prys has no heirs. Perhaps in the fullness of time I shall bear him children, but he is willing to take Rhys, Eluned and Heulwen for his own.'

'I do not think Guyon will stand in your way,' Judith said slowly after a pause for consideration.

'Neither do I.' Rhosyn blinked. 'It has run its course, for
him at least. We never had enough in common to make of
it more than a dry grass fire. I wish . . .' Rhosyn shook her
head and turned away, her chin wobbling.

Judith had imagined Guyon's mistress to be dark and
mysterious and beautiful with all the wiles at her fingertips.
Only the first was true. The reality was a straightforward
practical woman with a generous, gentle spirit. She could see
why Guyon had held on to the bond for more than four years
and also why it must now be severed. And Rhosyn saw
too, or else she would not be crying here beside her on the
battlements.

Rhosyn sniffed and, wiping her eyes on her sleeve, gave
Judith a watery smile. 'I am sorry, I was being foolish. Will
you and Guyon come to the wedding?'

Judith looked doubtful. 'Will it not cause trouble?'

Rhosyn shook her head. 'Prys knows my past. You will
be most welcome.'

Judith inclined her head. 'Then gladly we will come,
circumstances permitting.' She watched the drawbridge
being drawn up for the night. One of the men on watch
shouted a cheerful insult across to the guards at the winch
and was answered in kind.

'I hope Guyon will still see her on occasion,' Rhosyn
added. 'She is his daughter.

'She will always be his firstborn,' Judith agreed with a
judicious nod. 'It would be wrong to try and prevent him.
That far I will permit you to tread on my territory because
I cannot change it, but seek further at your peril.'

From the inner bailey, the dinner horn sounded and
someone cheered with irony.

Rhosyn stared at Judith. The challenge was there in
Judith's strange, stone-coloured eyes, but leavened by a
twinkle of humour. 'I do not think you will see me at
Ravenstow again,' she replied.

* * *

Rhosyn rode out the next morning on to a sun-polished road
with an escort of eight serjeants and her manservant, Twm.
The pony hooves echoed on the dusty drawbridge planks.
She looked beyond the rise and fall of their loaded backs to
where Judith stood between the bridge and portcullis, one
arm shading her eyes, the other raised in farewell. Rhosyn
returned the salute briefly and turned in the saddle so that,
like her mount, she faced Wales.

At noon they stopped to water the horses and eat a cold
repast of bread, cheese and roasted fowl. Heulwen, as usual,
ate the cheese, spat out the bread and made a thorough mess.
Eluned in contrast, nibbling as daintily as a deer, considered her mother, swallowed and said, 'He was forced to marry
her, wasn't he, Mam?'

Rhosyn looked at her daughter in concern. Eluned had
been very quiet since yestereve's rudeness, a brooding kind
of quiet that would not yield to cozening. 'At the outset,
yes,' she answered cautiously.

'He does not love her.' Eluned fingered her amber
necklace.

Rhosyn bit her lip. The child's eyes were her own – hazel
green-gold and full of pain. You grew up and learned to hide
it, that was the only difference. 'You cannot say that, Eluned,'
she said. 'It is what you would like to be true, not truth itself.
You should wish them joy in each other, not strife.'

'She's ugly!' Eluned thrust out her lower lip.

'Eluned!'

Heulwen choked and Rhosyn unthinkingly rescued the
half-chewed piece of chicken wing from the back of the
infant's throat, her attention all focused on her elder
daughter.

'I hate her, she's a Norman slut. Guyon belongs to us,
not her!'

Rhosyn's hand shot out and cracked across Eluned's
cheek. Eluned gasped. The men of the escort looked round
from their oatcakes and ale. Eluned put her hand to her

face, stared at her mother with aghast, brimming eyes as the mark of the slap began to redden. Whirling round, she fled beyond the startled men into the thickness of the brambles and trees.

'No, Mam, let her go.' Rhys caught Rhosyn's arm as she made to pursue. 'She's leaving a trail a blind man could follow. I don't think she'll go very far.'

Rhosyn subsided with a sigh. 'It is my fault. I did not realise it ran so deeply. She used to say that she was going to marry Guyon. I thought it was a child's game.'

'So did she,' Rhys said with a wisdom beyond his years.

Rhosyn reseated herself upon the spread skins to finish her meal, but her eyes kept flickering towards the trees.

Rhys considered her for a moment and then gave an adolescent sigh, heavy with impatience, and hitched his belt. 'All right, Mam, I'll go and find her.'

Rhosyn gave him a grateful smile. She wondered how to go about dealing with Eluned when she returned. Diplomatic silence as if it had never happened? Detailed, careful explanations? A scolding? Sympathetic affection?

Heulwen was rubbing her eyes and whining. Rhosyn bent her mind away from the problem of her elder daughter to persuade her younger one to take a nap beneath one of the skins.

Two greenfinches dated across the clearing, their song a chitter of alarm. A horse snorted and, throwing up its head, nickered towards the trees, ears pricked. One of the men put down his drink and went to the restless beast.

Sounds of something crashing blindly through the undergrowth came clearly to their ears, and then a cry. Rhosyn sprang to her feet, her heart thudding against her ribs. She stooped and covered Heulwen, by now asleep, with another of the skins, concealing her as best she could.

Her escort drew their swords. Shields were reached for and slipped on to men's arms. One of the escort turned to give Rhosyn a command but she ignored him, transfixed by horror as she watched her son stagger towards them, hugging the trees for support, his tunic saturated with blood.

'Rhys!' she screamed. Lifting her skirts, she started to run towards him. A young serjeant, Eric's brother, caught her back.

The boy looked in the direction of her voice, but his eyes were blind, his mouth working, pouring blood. 'Mam!' he gasped frothily and then, choking, 'The *Cwmni Annwn!*'

'Rhys!' she screamed again and tore free of her captor to run stumbling to where he had fallen face down in the turning crisp leaves. He was dead. She could see the rents in his clothing where a blade had been plunged and his blood was hot and dark on her hands.

Bent over her son, she did not hear the horrified warning yelled by her escort, nor see the riders of the wild hunt advancing through the trees, following the trail of lifeblood to their victim.

CHAPTER 25

Soon after Rhosyn had left, Judith fetched her cloak and departed Ravenstow with her own escort, her destination one of Ravenstow's fiefs. The lord of the small, beholden keep at Farnden had recently died and she had promised his son, the inheritor of the holding and its military obligations, that she would attend a mass in the church there for the soul of his father before he rode out to rejoin Guyon. Also, there were the customs and rights of the new tenancy to be confirmed and the oath of fealty to be sworn.

Thomas of Farnden was a pleasant, not particularly bright young man, but he knew his feudal duties and was capable of performing them stoically and well. He lacked imagination and ambition but that was no reason to neglect him. A horseshoe nail was just as important as the horse and Judith gave him her sincere attention for the duration of the visit.

The mass was performed in the tiny Saxon church and attended by all members of the keep and the villagers of most senior authority. Alms were distributed, and bread. Dinner was eaten outside in the orchard, the trestles spread beneath the lush summer green of the trees. It was so pleasant and a poignant far cry from the war in the south that it brought tears to Judith's eyes, and she had to set about reassuring a worried Sir Thomas that she was really all right.

Shortly before mid-afternoon, her business completed, she made her farewells to Sir Thomas and set out for home.

With his eye on the dwindling height of the sun, de Bec took the short cut across the drovers' road and through the forest to reach the main track.

The day had been hot and the green forest air was humid, catching earthily in the throat and nostrils as it was breathed. Judith's chemise clung to her body. Beneath her veil her head itched as if it harboured a thicket of fleas. Now and then a rivulet of sweat trickled down between her breasts or tickled her spine, and her thighs were chafed by the constant rubbing of the saddle. She thought with longing of a refreshing, tepid tub, of a clean light robe and a goblet of wine, chill from the keep well.

Such thoughts set her to bitter-sweet rememberings of a raw November night, of drinking wine in a bathtub, of Guyon's eyes luminous with laughter and desire. Her longing abruptly changed direction. Heat moistened her loins. She shifted in the saddle and tears returned to prickle her eyes. It had been so long since there had been the time or opportunity for that kind of dalliance. The inclination had been swamped – or so she thought – by a combination of worry and sheer physical exhaustion. There had been odd occasions together, but snatched and unsatisfactory because there was no real enjoyment in assuaging a need that intruded inconveniently upon other needs and was tainted with fear.

Two pigeons clapped past them and a blackbird scolded. When a spotted woodpecker followed, crying alarm, de Bec ceased lounging at ease to reach for his shield. These were not birds immediately startled by their approach, but already alarmed and winging from some earlier disturbance. This band of woodland was within Guyon's jurisdiction but at the north-western edge lay a boggy ditch marking the Welsh border and the standing stones on the south-western side were the boundary between Ravenstow and Thornford. It was for the latter reason in particular that de Bec muttered soft imprecations as he drew his sword and ordered his men to surround Judith.

A horse flashed through the trees in front of them. Both Judith and de Bec recognised the striking red sorrel immediately, for it was one of Guyon's own crossbreeds, belonging to Eric's younger brother Godric who had been in command of Rhosyn's escort. A cold hand squeezed Judith's heart, for although Godric was in the saddle, he was hunched over, clutching the pommel and did not answer their hail. The horse, however, threw up its white-blazed head and, nickering at sight of its own kind, picked its way towards them.

De Bec leaned across to grasp the reins. 'Godric, Christ man, what's happened?' His voice was hoarse with shock.

The young man raised his eyes but remained hunched over. 'De Lacey,' he croaked. 'Hit us out of nowhere . . . Too many of them. We never stood a chance . . . I managed to save the little lass.' He swayed, his face grey. Against his body, tied within his cloak for security, Heulwen began to cry and push against her confines, her little face as flushed as her tangled fiery crown of curls.

A knight unfastened the child and lifted her out of Godric's cloak, then uttered an oath of consternation for she was smeared in blood from head to toe.

'Not hers, mine,' said Godric huskily and tumbled out of the saddle to sprawl unconscious at their feet. Judith dismounted in a flurry of skirts and bent down beside the young soldier to examine his injuries. He had taken a nasty slash to the midriff. Fortunately, as far as she could see, it had not pierced the gut, but it was still deep and it had bled a great deal. She unfastened one of his leg bindings to use as a temporary bandage until they could reach the safety of the keep and she could tend him properly. Two of her escort set about constructing a crude stretcher out of branches and horse blankets.

Heulwen sobbed and screamed for her mother in broken Welsh. Fortunately the serjeant who held her had five children of his own and was used to dealing with infant tantrums. A borderman, he also spoke fluent Welsh and soothed

Heulwen in that language until she calmed into hiccuped sobs and then poked her thumb into her mouth.

Godric's eyelids fluttered. Judith put her hand on his brow. 'Rest easy now,' she soothed, 'help is here.'

'Mistress, we could do nothing,' he fretted. She held a wine costrel to his lips and he took a convulsive swallow. 'De Lacey outnumbered us at least four to one. The child was asleep beneath some skins. They missed her and they left me for dead . . . Dancer bolted in the fray but he came back when I called him.' He clenched his teeth and groaned.

De Bec's eyebrows drew together in a worried scowl. 'How far back, son?'

'No more than a mile . . . just off the road. We had stopped to eat and they came out of the trees at us.' He closed his eyes and swallowed. 'I lay for dead and they thought me so. I heard de Lacey say that there was less gain than he had hoped and they had best be on their way . . . Thornford they were headed for . . . Myself and the child are the only survivors . . . The other little maid . . . Oh Christ, they took her with them!' He gasped and strove not to retch. Judith fought her own gorge and set a steadying hand to his brow.

'Lie quiet, Godric,' she said gently and raised her head to meet de Bec's granite stare. There was no way their own troop could pursue, and the attack was more than three hours old. De Lacey would be safe within his keep by now.

'The bodies will need to be brought back to Ravenstow,' she said. The coldness of shock and fear, the knowledge of what had yet to be done, made her feel queasy and tearful, but she controlled herself. 'We had best bring them away with us now before the wolves and foxes have their chance at them.'

De Bec shook his head. 'My lady, it will not be a sight to be viewed save by necessity, and Godric and the child should be got to Ravenstow as soon as possible.'

Judith considered for a moment, then nodded curtly. There was nothing to be gained by going to the scene of the slaughter herself. De Bec could note the details for Guyon and the sheriff. There would be enough trauma in washing the corpses and laying them out decently . . . and in sending this news to Guyon. What was she going to say? How was she to face and tell him when he returned? It did not bear thinking about and yet, like the laying out, it had to be done and it was her responsibility.

The reality proved far worse than Judith had imagined. She stitched Godric's wound, poulticed it with mouldy bread, dosed him with poppy syrup and left him to sleep. Heulwen kept crying for her mother, but, apart from being fractious and bewildered, seemed none the worse for her ordeal.

Judith's own ordeal began when de Bec rode in, his face waxen and his expression so stiff that he might have been one of the ten corpses bundled in cloaks and roped like game across the backs of some pack ponies borrowed from Thomas of Farnden. The men who rode with de Bec all wore variations of that same look on their faces and, when the bodies were brought to the chapel, Judith understood why. The abomination beneath Rhosyn's cloak bore no resemblance to the woman she had encountered yesterday. The spirit had flown and the mortal body was so mutilated that it was difficult to know if it had once been human at all.

Her belly heaved. She clapped her hand to her mouth and staggered to the waste shaft where she was sick to the pit of her soul. It was not just murder, it was obscene desecration.

De Bec gently touched her elbow, handed her a small horn cup of aqua vitae and waited until, choking and spluttering on its unaccustomed strength, she had swallowed it.

Shaking, Judith leaned for a brief moment against his iron-clad solidity. 'He is not a man, he is a devil!' she said and shuddered.

De Bec folded a mail-clad arm around her quivering shoulders, feeling a wave of paternal protectiveness. 'Have you sent a messenger to Lord Guyon yet?' he rumbled. 'He needs to be here.'

Judith shook her head. 'I don't know what to write,' she gulped. 'And I don't know if he is still at Arundel.'

'Tell him naught, only that he is needed swiftly. A messenger will find him sooner or later. I'll get FitzWalter to do it for you.'

Judith stiffened her spine and pulled away from him. 'No,' she said firmly. 'I'll do it myself.' A wan smile strained her lips. 'You feel like a rock because you are one.'

De Bec's eyes began to sting and he had to blink. In all but name, he had regarded Judith as his daughter from the day of her birth and to see her struggle with her fears and doubts and force them down beneath her will filled him with a fierce burst of tenderness and pride. He could have crushed her between his two hands – it did not seem possible that she could house such strength.

He watched her return to the horror in the chapel and murmur to the priest, her face so pale that every freckle stood out as a deep, golden mottle, her manner composed, and knew that if he was a rock, then she was surely as resilient and strong as the best sword steel.

CHAPTER 26

Guyon shifted in the high saddle and loosened the reins to let Arian pick his way between the trees. The afternoon light was as golden-green as the best French wine. Coins of sunlight and leaf shadows scattered and sparkled among the troop of men who rode with steady haste towards Ravenstow and preparation for war in the marches.

Now that Arundel was theirs and de Belleme effectively cut off from his support abroad, the King intended to move upon de Belleme's chain of grim Shropshire strongholds with the purpose of clearing them out one by one and Guyon was returning to Ravenstow to support him in that endeavour.

As they emerged from the trees on to the waste land, all eyes were drawn to the gleaming lime-washed walls of the keep dominating Ravenstow crag. Guyon's gaze at this, the core of his honour, was both admiring and rueful. It was de Belleme's design and it followed that winkling the Earl of Shrewsbury out of the other strongholds he had also designed, but held in his own hand, was going to prove difficult. God knew, Arundel had been a tough enough nut to crack.

A cowherd touched his forehead to Guyon and tapped the cattle on their mottled backs with a hazel goad to keep them moving. His dog went wagging to investigate the horsemen and was whistled sharply back to place. At the mill, the miller was transferring sacks of flour to an ox-drawn wain; he paused to wipe his brow and salute the passing soldiers, cuffing his brawny son into similar respect. His wife ceased beating a smock on a stone at the stream to curtsy, her expression apprehensive. She touched the prayer beads on the belt at her waist and raised them to her lips.

Guyon eyed the woman curiously and wondered anew at the speed with which news of impending war travelled. He did not believe de Belleme would attack Ravenstow – he was too busy strengthening his own fortifications – but the Welsh were always ready to harry, loot and burn and de Belleme had several Welsh vassals who would be only too pleased to stock their winter larders at Ravenstow's expense.

The drawbridge was down to admit them and the portcullis up. Guyon shook the reins, urging Arian to a trot and they emerged again into the late sunshine of the shed-crowded bailey. A woman was feeding twigs beneath a giant outdoor cauldron, the girl beside her plucking a wrung chicken to go into the pot. She looked up at the men, nudged her companion and made the sign of the cross upon her breast. The older woman straightened and crossed herself too, her eyes full of pity before she turned to stare at the forebuilding from which Judith was running.

Cadi barked and sprang joyously to greet her, tail swishing like a whip. Guyon dismounted and threw the reins to a groom. The young man said nothing but, with a look over his broad shoulder at Judith, dipped his head and led the grey away to his stall.

Guyon watched his wife hurry towards him and felt his spirit lighten. Her braids trapped the sunlight and glowed like molten bronze and her face was becomingly flushed from the effort of running down several flights of twisting stairs and across the ward.

And then she was facing him and his admiration fell away as he saw the look in her eyes and the set of her mouth.

'Rhosyn's dead,' she said without preamble. 'I have been

wondering how to tell you, but there is no way to make it any easier.'

He looked at her blankly. The sun was warm on the back of his neck but suddenly he felt frozen from crown to toe.

'They were attacked on our land, on the Llangollen drovers' road yestereve. I gave her the escort she requested but they were all cut down. Father Jerome is in the chapel attending to what needs to be done . . .' Her words stumbled to a halt.

He stared at her while everything slowed down and ground to a halt. 'Dead?' he repeated in a blank voice.

She grasped hold of his sleeve like a sighted person taking hold of someone blind. 'Guyon, come within and I will try to tell you what I know. Heulwen is safe. Eric's brother Godric saved her. They were the only two to survive . . .'

He allowed her to lead him. Most of her words washed over him like an incoming tide, leaving only a residue of scouring grit and the words 'Rhosyn's dead' indelibly printed on his mind.

Judith gave him wine, lacing it liberally with aqua vitae. He sat down mechanically, looked at the cup, set it aside and raised disbelieving eyes to her.

'Tell me again,' he commanded. 'I don't know what you said.'

She repeated her words. His face never changed but, as she finished, he covered it with his hands.

'I am sorry, Guy,' Judith whispered. 'Truly I am.'

He did not respond.

'At least you have Heulwen.'

He looked up at that. 'Yes,' he agreed tonelessly, 'at least I have Heulwen.' And then he laughed and shook his head and buried his face again.

Judith knelt beside him, her arm across his mail-clad shoulder. 'I wish I knew what to say, or how to ease the pain, but I don't . . .'

'Then don't say anything,' he muttered and, after a

moment, withdrawing from her grasp, he stood up and moved towards the door.

'Where are you going?'

'To the chapel, where else?'

'No, Guy!' She sprang after him. 'Wait at least until you have rested. I'll have a tub prepared and see to your comfort.'

'Do you think I care about that?'

'No, but I do.' She took hold of his sleeve.

'Let me go.' Shrugging her off, he continued on his way.

'Guyon, no . . . It's not . . . I mean . . .' She drew a shuddering breath and momentarily closed her eyes. 'She did not die cleanly.'

'Stop treating me like a nursling!' he snarled and lengthened his stride.

Judith caught up her cloak and went after him. He might not be a nursling but he was inadequately prepared for what would greet him in the chapel.

Guyon looked at the row of shrouded pallets laid out before the altar, ten in all, white mounds of recent humanity.

Father Jerome fussed anxiously in the background. 'A terrible business,' he ventured, 'but they are at peace now.'

Guyon drew back one of the sheets to look upon the face of Herluin FitzSimon, a promising young man who had served with him during the Welsh campaign and who would one day, in his middle years, have captained a keep garrison. All wasted now on the edge of a sword. The linen shift in which he had been clothed did not cover the gaping wound in his throat or the sword slash that had laid his face open to the bone.

'At peace, are they?' Guyon enquired icily, replacing the sheet.

Father Jerome blenched. 'You must not doubt it, my son,' he said, putting out his hand to comfort.

Guyon stepped aside. 'I would rather you left me alone.'

The priest hesitated. Judith lightly touched his arm. 'Go to,' she said. 'It may be that he will need you later. I will stand surety for now.'

Relieved, the priest pressed her arm and quietly left her alone with Guyon. Judith squared her shoulders and went to her husband. He was staring down at Rhys.

'If Godric had not survived, the bodies would not have been discovered for some time. I was not expecting the escort back for at least three days and no search party would have been sent out before five.'

'You are telling me that this is fortunate?' he said huskily, as he drew the sheet back over Rhys's face.

'It could have been much worse. At least they were saved being despoiled by foxes and crows. Heulwen owes her life to Godric.'

'Sensible Judith,' he snarled.

'Guyon, stop it!'

'Do you interfere for pleasure or because you cannot help yourself?' he demanded savagely. 'In Christ's name, Judith, leave me alone!'

'In Christ's name, no!' she retorted with equal vehemence. 'I'll not be your scapegoat!' Going to the last pallet, she drew back the cover herself. 'Look and have done and come away!' she said brutally.

He flinched and his complexion turned the colour of ashes. Despite the work of Judith and the priest, Rhosyn's body was still not a sight for the squeamish. She had fought hard for her life and her beauty was marred by the livid bruises and distortions of strangulation. Her body beneath the shift was mauled and mutilated and her braids hacked off. Judith covered her up again.

Guyon swallowed jerkily. 'Where's Eluned?' he asked, fighting his gorge.

'De Lacey took her with him.' Judith compressed her lips.

Guyon whitened further at the implications.

'My lord . . .' said Father Jerome and was barged aside before he could say more by a wild-eyed, travel-stained young man.

'Where is she?' the newcomer asked hoarsely, his French

so thickly accented with Welsh and filled with raw emotion
that at first Judith stared at him without comprehension.
His gaze flickered over the row of bodies and the vigilance
candles. 'My Rhosyn, where is she?'

'*Your* Rhosyn?' Judith's expression sharpened. 'Then you
must be Prys—'

'I went to fetch her father for burial and now I am told
that I must bury her too, and the lad . . .' The wild eyes fixed
on Guyon with bleak loathing. 'Couldn't you leave her alone?
If not for you, she'd still be alive and my wife!'

Guyon flinched. 'I did not know that she was coming to
Ravenstow,' he defended himself. 'If I had, I would have
stopped her. Christ knows, I tried to warn her.'

'You should have tried harder!'

'How much harder?' Guyon spat. 'How much would you
have tolerated? Short of locking her up, there was nothing I
could ever have done to hold her.'

'Then what in Christ's name was she doing here at
Ravenstow?'

'She came to invite us to your wedding,' Judith said, trying
to calm the sparks between the men that were threatening
to flare into violence and violate God's altar and the dead
who sought sanctuary there, 'and to talk of Heulwen's future.'
It was not the whole truth, but she felt no remorse at with-
holding what could not safely be said.

'Neither matter was so pressing as to warrant this!' Prys
gestured towards the row of corpses, and it came to Guyon
that the young Welshman was as filled with guilt as himself,
for he too had not been there to prevent this dreadful crime
and rage was a bolt hole to be dived into rather than face the
unfaceable.

Prys pushed past him and Judith. 'Which one?' he
demanded. Judith opened her mouth to say that he should
not look, but Guyon forestalled her by pointing to the nearest
shroud.

'Walter de Lacey was the man responsible,' Guyon said

softly. 'I'm going to tear Thornford down stone by stone and make of that keep a burial mound.'

The young man drew back the sheet and fell to his knees at the side of the bier. 'Ah Rhosyn, *cariad*, no!'

Father Jerome set a comforting arm around Prys's shoulders, although there was nothing that could comfort the sight laid out before their eyes.

Guyon gently drew the cover over Rhosyn again. Prys shuddered and crossed himself. Trembling, he rose to his feet and stared at Guyon.

'I'm a merchant,' he said, voice unsteady with unshed grief, and savage. 'I wear a sword for my protection, but I'm clumsy using it . . .'

Judith drew a frightened breath, thinking for a mad instant that the Welshman was going to challenge Guyon to a trial by combat in order to assuage his grief. Guyon must have thought so too, for she felt him tense beside her.

'I want you to teach me to wield it properly. If you are going to march on Thornford, I am coming with you. They told me outside . . . about Eluned. No worse can be done to Rhosyn, she's beyond it now . . . but God alone knows what he will do to the child . . .' He choked and compressed his lips.

'Be welcome,' Guyon said, his own voice constricted. 'I'll lend you a hauberk from the armoury.'

The chapel was cold and almost entirely dark. The candles on the altar and around the biers made splashes of light in the pre-dawn blackness. Guyon stared at the flames until his vision blurred and repeated the prayers he had known by rote since childhood. Rote without meaning. The reality was the flagged church floor pressing cold and hard against his numb knees, the smell of incense cloying his nostrils and Rhosyn's desecrated body stretched out before him.

He had tried time and again to believe it was a dream, nothing more than a nightmare from which he would wake up sweating with relief. *Ave Maria, gratia plena* . . . He had only to lift the linen sheet to know it was not.

The candles flickered in a draught and light rippled over the bier, giving Rhosyn's shroud the momentary illusion of movement. His hair rose along his spine and he stopped breathing. A gentle hand squeezed his shoulder and he jumped and stared round.

'Guyon, come away,' Judith entreated. 'It is all but dawn now and if you are to lead the men, you need to be rested. Prys sought his pallet an hour ago.' She held out his cloak and he saw that she was wearing her own over the gold wool gown of yesterday. She had been kneeling in vigil with him most of the night, but he had not marked her leaving, or indeed Prys's.

'There is a tub prepared above. You must be frozen stiff.'

The words *'sensible Judith'* floated amongst the disjointed flotsam of the upper layers of his mind. He was suddenly aware of exhaustion seeping through his body just as the iciness of the flagged floor was seeping into his knees. 'To the soul,' he muttered, genuflecting to the altar and rising stiffly to his feet. 'To the pit of my soul.'

Staggering with weariness, he let her lead him up the stairs to the main bedchamber. She dismissed the maids with a swift gesture and, as the curtain dropped behind the last one, began unbuckling his swordbelt.

As the belt slipped into her hands, he took her by the shoulders and tipped up her chin to examine her face. The dim light concealed some of the ravages, but not all. Mauve shadows marred the clarity of her eyes and the bones of her face were sharp, suddenly reminding him of the first time he had seen her.

He was a sleepwalker, jolted awake. 'Ah God, Judith,' he said on a broken whisper and pulled her tight and close.

'I met her on the day before it happened,' she said into his breast, her voice cracking. 'God's love, Guy, I was so jealous, I wanted to scratch out her eyes, but I couldn't. She was so . . . so honest, and she did not deserve what they did to her!' She burst into tears, digging her fingers so hard into Guyon's hauberk that the rivets cut deep semicircles against her knuckles.

'Judith, love, don't!' Guyon pleaded, kissing her wet face while tears spilled down his own. 'Do you want to break me?'

'I can't help it!' she sobbed. 'Since that night in Southwark, we have not had a moment to ourselves that has not been marred by fear and strain and war!' She struck his hauberk with her clenched fist.

Guyon seized her hand in one of his and clamped the other around her waist, holding her tightly, aware through his own shuddering of hers.

At length, sniffing and tear-drenched, she pulled away to look at him. 'I meant to be calm and strong when you came home,' she whispered, 'and instead I shriek like a harpy. The tub is growing cold and you are still in your mail.'

'Never mind the tub,' he said, his whole body shaking with cold and the delayed reaction of shock and fatigue. 'I have lived without creature comforts for so long that another night and day does not matter. Just help me unarm and come to bed.'

Judith wondered whether she should persuade him to eat some food and decided that, for now, she just did not possess the energy. The battle could be taken up again once they had both slept.

'Judith.' He stretched out his hand to her in supplication. With a soft cry she returned to his embrace, stood tightly enclosed within it for a brief moment, then set about helping him remove his mail.

CHAPTER 27

The dawn sky on the horizon was barred grey and cream and oystershell, striated like marble. Smoke from cooking fires hazed the immediate air. Fatty bacon sizzled. A loaded wain of new bread from Ravenstow creaked into the camp.

Men were hearing mass, their bellies rumbling.

Guyon watched the mangonel launch another boulder at Thornford's curtain wall. There came the crash of stone splintering on stone and a high-pitched scream from within.

'It is a great pity to see such fine new defences reduced to rubble before we take them,' Eric murmured at his side.

'Do you have a better suggestion?' Guyon growled. 'If not, go and find out what's taking those miners so long and get me a cup of wine before my throat closes!'

Eric lifted long-suffering eyes towards heaven and fetched the latter first accompanied by a mutton pasty. Then, face studiedly impassive, he went in search of the sapper's foreman. Lord Guyon had been the very devil to please of late, the knowledge of what lay behind those walls goading him to frustrated rage like a baited bear. Unable to come to grips with de Lacey, he was venting his spleen on those around him instead. It was understandable, of course. All of them were sickened at what had happened to Rhosyn and her escort. Casualties of war were one thing; wanton destruction and rapine of a child were another, especially when the victims were people with whom one had shared companionship and hospitality and had always complaisantly assumed one would see many times again.

Having found the foreman of the sappers who had paused in his endeavours in order to eat his breakfast, Eric asked him Guyon's question.

The small man wiped his earth-smeared hand across his mouth and grimaced. 'We been working all night fast as we can, see. What does he expect, miracles?'

These men were a law unto themselves, their invaluable skill setting them above the conventions of rank. Mainly Welshmen and brought up to the craft since birth, working open-cast coal seams, they were digging a tunnel underground to a point directly beneath the wall, supporting their work with wooden props. Once completed, the tunnel would be filled with pitch-soaked furze and dry wood and bladders of pork fat, then set ablaze. As the props burned away, the tunnel would cave in, bringing down the wall above, in this case a section of the eastern rampart. It was dirty, difficult work and the rate of pay reflected it. Dai ap Owain and the men literally beneath him earned a shilling a day, which was as much as a fully accoutred knight could expect to command.

'What do I tell him, Dai?'

'Tell him we'll be done by prime and that we need more oil and brushwood.'

Eric looked doubtful. 'No sooner?' he mistakenly asked, envisaging Guyon's displeasure.

'If my lord desires such a thing, let him come down and dig himself. *A fo ben, bid bont!*'

Eric retreated. 'Prime,' he said to Guyon, 'and they need tinder and oil. I'll go and see to it,' and he disappeared before Guyon could flay him alive with the edge of his tongue.

By mid-morning, the grey light of dawn had brightened into a strong blue heat and the arrows that swished between besieger and besieged were hard black shafts raining down from a cloudless sky. Guyon shot a glance at his archers. Half of them had set aside their bows and had begun preparing their short swords and round shields for the imminent assault. This was the lull, the still before the storm. Guyon's fingers twitched on Arian's reins. He made a conscious effort to relax as the stallion side-stepped, soothing him with soft words and a smoothing hand on the sleek, silk neck.

It had taken three weeks to come this far, and not without trials. Walter de Lacey might be a fool in the political sense, might be a child-molesting murdering pervert, but it did not prevent him from being a skilled soldier and tactician. Their siege machines had been sabotaged by a daring night raid and a couple of attempts to take the keep with scaling ladders had been repelled. The enmity was intense, each foothold gained paid for in blood.

Guyon rubbed his sweating palms on his chausses. He had never wanted a thing so much in his life as to take Thornford and tear its occupant apart piece by little piece. He did not think of Eluned. To have done so now would have overset his balance and thus far he had kept it well on the level.

Over by the water butts two sappers were swilling water down, their bodies lithe, hard and small. He had never met a man of the trade much above five feet in height. Indeed Dai, their foreman, frequently stood on a mounting block or a keg so that he could address Guyon at eye level. Fiercely independent and forthright, Dai saw no reason to back down from a point of view just because he lacked stature, and the men who knew him had long since ceased to make the mistake of patronising him.

He was at the mine now, supervising the blaze which had been kindled an hour since. Guyon switched his hungry gaze again to Thornford's defences, a muscle bunching and releasing in his jaw. The stone curtain wall had replaced a wooden palisade about ten years ago when Welsh raids had been particularly savage. The original wooden keep had been rebuilt in stone and now stood three levels high. It did not approach the impregnable grandeur of Ravenstow – few strongholds did – but it was certainly stout enough to repel the Welsh and several weeks of determined, conventional siege.

'It's going to go,' Dai ap Owain lilted, appearing out of nowhere to stand at Guyon's stirrup.

'Thank Christ for that,' Guyon said and signalled his captains to take up their places and make ready their men. They knew what was to be done. Plans had been discussed last night and in more detail this morning while they waited for the miners to complete their work. If any man bungled it now, it was his own fault, but Guyon did not anticipate problems. Eric and de Bec were experienced, dependable men, quite capable of extricating themselves and those beneath their command if a crisis arose.

He looked over his shoulder. Godric was guarding his back, his sorrel fretting and dancing, as anxious as his rider for the action to be upon them. Beside Godric, astride one of the remounts, sat Prys ap Adda, sword drawn, shield held in tight to his body. For all his declaration that he was a clumsy swordsman, Guyon had found little lacking. The Welshman might not have the bulk of the men he would be facing, but he was as fast in motion and ferocious as summer lightning and he, too, had a personal cause to lend vehemence to his sword arm. Had the man been trained to war from birth, Guyon doubted that he could have bested him.

A dull rumbling sound like the roll of summer thunder grew gradually louder and the ground shook. Horses started and shied. The bailey wall collapsed, crashing down into the tunnel, sending loose stones and mortar bounding across the courtyard floor. Smoke and thick dust mingled upwards, in an obscuring cloud.

'There's pretty for you!' Dai breathed exultantly.

Guyon was not listening. 'Forward!' he roared, flinging

all his pent-up tension into the cry as, clapping spurs to Arian's flanks, he bolted for the gap.

He, Godric and Prys erupted simultaneously through the gaping hole, Guyon driving straight ahead, his companions to right and left. Eyes streaming, lungs choking on the boiling fog, Guyon rode down three of the defenders who were not swift enough to scatter before his rage. Arian barged past them, felling two among the debris. Guyon cut down the third. The stallion killed one man before he could rise. Guyon brained the other with his shield, dealt with another on a vicious backswing and swung the horse towards the inner bailey, the entrance to which was defended by two iron-bound gates, four fingers thick and secured on the inside by a massive bar which took the strivings of at least four stout men to lift from its slots.

'Ravenstow à moi!' Guyon bellowed and the men of his group disengaged so they could to run or ride with him, leaving the soldiers under Eric's command to take care of the outer ward. From the direction of the western wall walk, the wind fed them the yells of de Bec's group on the scaling ladders and the deadly whiz of arbalest quarrels.

'The ram!' Guyon shouted and the order was passed swiftly down the line. The huge oak trunk with its reinforced pointed iron head was run forward by fifteen men-at-arms, coughing and sneezing in the clogged air. One of them screeched and fell, an arrow in his leg. Guyon leaped down from the stallion and took his place, the exhilaration of battle coursing through him.

'Heave!' he cried and the ram thrust forward and smacked against the gate, boomed and rebounded. 'Back . . . heave . . . back . . . heave . . .' And the rhythm was taken up and echoed down the line. Much to the appreciation of the men, Guyon began a crude song in English about the broaching of a difficult virgin.

A sword clanged on a nearby shield as Prys felled a defender. An arbalest bolt crashed into the ram hard by

Guyon's thrusting shoulder. A moment later another one swished past his ear.

'Get that sniper!' he broke off singing to bellow furiously. 'Before he gets me! No dolts, don't stop! God's death, you weren't as hesitant as this when you hit the London stews last summer!'

Bawdy guffaws, capping remarks and renewed efforts greeted his outburst. The dinted head of the huge oak log pounded against the solid planks. Guyon began to sweat with effort. His breath grew harsh in his throat; his mouth was dust-dry. With salt-stung eyes he glanced around, assessing the ward. Behind and around them many of the lesser combatants had begun to cry quarter rather than die and Eric's men were effectively dealing with those who preferred to fight on.

'Lord Guyon!' rasped the soldier beside him. Sunlight glinted from his helmet as he jerked his head energetically at the gates. Guyon squinted at him and then at their target, and abruptly stood up and raised his hand. The singing raggedly ceased. The men rested the ram and stared with their lord towards the scuffed, surface-splintered but otherwise intact gates. Guyon hefted his shield, wiped his hand across his upper lip and commanded forward his two most accurate archers to train their sights upon the gap as the great, thick planks began to swing inwards.

A dour soldier wearing a leather gambeson filled the entrance, grey-streaked hair falling to his shoulders. He was weaponless, not even an eating knife about his person and behind him, like the contents of a stoppered wineskin, cowered what seemed to be all the inhabitants of the inner ward.

'My lord, we yield ourselves and this keep to your mercy,' he said formally, eyes betraying all the fear that his deliberate deep voice did not.

Guyon said nothing but gestured the men at his back to slip within and take up defensive positions. Prys spoke to him quickly in Welsh. Guyon answered with a single terse word and did not look away from the man they were facing.

'It is no trick, lord,' the spokesman said with dignity. 'I would rather open to you now and spare the lives of good men, than fight to the last drop of blood for such a one as Walter de Lacey. If that is treason, then so be it.' His head came up proudly. There was a rumble of assent from the crowd behind him.

'And precisely where is Walter de Lacey?' Guyon asked in a hard voice.

'He went over the west wall in the early hours of this morning, and his guard with him. I am Wulfric, the constable's deputy and former bodyguard to Lord Ralph. There is no one else here of any higher authority. You killed the man he left in command on the first charge.' He shrugged his broad shoulders. 'Lord Walter knew he could not hold this place, not without aid. He's gone down the border to look for it, but with the King's forces stretched across Wenlock Edge, I doubt he'll find it, sire, unless it comes from Wales.'

Guyon's sword hand twitched and the blade came up in response to his rage and frustration. Over the wall and through his fingers like a fish through a hole in a net. 'Eric,' he said over his shoulder. 'Find out who was on duty at the west wall last night and bring him to me.'

Eric acknowledged, a chill running down his spine as if it was his own back that was laid bare to the lash.

Guyon returned his attention to the Saxon. 'What about the child?'

The man shook his head. 'He is here my lord, but not well, not well at all. He and his mother are both suffering from the bloody flux and like to die of it.'

Guyon gaped at him stupidly. In his mind there was only one child, his Eluned, but of course to this man the query could only pertain to de Lacey's heir. 'Not the boy,' he said: 'the Welsh girl.'

The man looked perturbed. 'My lord, she's dead. On the first night it happened. She managed to escape him and jumped off the wall walk yonder.' He looked behind him at the faces shielded by his bulk. 'Nick there was on duty and tried to grab her, but he was too late, just missed the edge of her shift.'

The young man nodded, his Adam's apple bobbing up and down. 'Did my best, but she was slippery as an eel.'

'No!' Prys shouted, shaking his head in violent denial. 'He's lying. It is not true, it is not true!' He lunged at the spokesman, who staggered and put up his hands to protect his head. Guyon intercepted him, but his mind was detached as he separated Prys from his victim and braced himself against the Welshman's onslaught. Then Eric pinioned Prys in his frenzy and led him aside. As if from a distance, Guyon heard Prys vomiting. His own body trembled with a deadly mixture of fury and fatigue. Somewhere at the back of his mind, he supposed that it was a mercy Eluned was dead.

The old man wiped a streak of blood from the corner of his mouth, his eyes going sidelong to the retching Welshman. 'We buried her in the garth near the churchyard, me and Nick. Lord Walter said to throw her in the ditch, but we couldn't do that. Lady Mabel gave us a sheet to wrap her in . . . we did our best, lord.'

Guyon bit the inside of his mouth. 'For which you have my thanks,' he acknowledged. 'It will not go forgotten, I promise you.'

They parted to let him through and he went across the ward and up the forebuilding stairs into the hall, his step no longer light with the spark of battle, but heavy, as though the spurs clipping his heels were fashioned of lead. It was all for nothing. De Lacey still owned life, limb and liberty. He was suddenly aware of the myriad minor cuts and bruises he had sustained in the heat of the fray. The keep had still to be cleared and inspected and shored up against a possible counter-attack, and a report made to Henry whom he was to join as soon as all was finished here. Only it was not finished, and perhaps never would be.

Sitting in the rushes a few yards from where he stood, one of the servants' children was playing with her straw doll, expression intent as she decorated its ragged sacking dress with a necklace of delicate amber beads.

Guyon put his face in his hands and wept.

CHAPTER 28

When Judith arrived at Thornford in response to an urgent summons from her husband; it was sunset of the second day and work still hard afoot to repair the worst of the miners' ravages.

In the outer ward, scene of so much previous destruction, small cooking fires burned as normal, tended by the soldiers' women and the smells of bread and pottage wafted enticingly on the evening wind. Judith guided Euraidd between the fires. A bat swooped low overhead, casting for insects in the gloaming. Broken arrows and lances littered the ground.

A groom held Judith's mare and Guyon himself stepped from the shadows to lift her from the saddle. His lids were heavy and dust-rimmed. Sweat and battle dirt gleamed in the creases of his skin, but the narrow semblance of a smile glinted before he stooped to give her a scratchy kiss.

'You made good speed, *Cath fach,*' he approved. 'I had not thought to see you until tomorrow noon at least.'

'Needs must when the devil drives,' she answered lightly, her eyes full of concern.

His smile vanished. 'Yes,' he agreed blankly and turned, his arm around her waist, to face the keep. 'Needs must.'

Judith eyed him thoughtfully. His letter had informed her of the victory and asked her to come quickly, little else, and she had hailed the messenger back from his refreshment to

reassure her that Guyon was not wounded. First qualm of
terror dissolved, she had set out to pump the man for the
information not contained in the letter.

'I'm sorry, Guy,' she said softly and pressed his arm.

He made a rueful gesture. Faced by the thought of being
unable to go on, he had felt a desperate need for the comfort
of Judith's forthright, astringent presence and, despite its
stilted brevity, his letter had come straight from the heart.
Indeed, had he paused for rational thought at the time of
writing, he would have left her at Ravenstow rather than
command her here to the shambles of a recent battleground
– but yesterday there had been little room for reason.

'I suppose it is for the best,' he owned as they entered the
inner ward. 'When you crush a flower it falls to pieces. God's
eyes, Judith, if only I had—'

'Guyon, no!' She stood on tiptoe to press her palm against
his lips. 'You must not shackle yourself with guilt. Rhosyn
would have taken her chances on the drovers' roads far more
recklessly were it not for your warnings. At least you sought
to protect her and the children.'

'But it was not enough.'

The stubble prickled her palm as his lips moved. Judith
studied him narrowly. 'When did you last eat and sleep?'

Guyon took her hand away to grasp it in his. 'You sound
like my mother,' he said with a hint of weary amusement.

'Who by all accounts was a woman of sense,' she retorted.
Her brow wrinkled. 'Why send for me if you did not want
to be nagged?'

'Because . . .' He drew a sharp breath as if to change his
mind, then stopped and faced her, scraping a hand distract-
edly through his hair which was in sad need of cutting. 'Oh
curse it, Judith, because you are the most infuriating, stubborn and capable woman it has ever been my misfortune to
know!'

She burst out laughing. 'Is that a compliment or an
insult?'

'To be honest, I do not know!' He set his hands on her shoulders. 'All I do know is that I need you as I've never needed anything in my life.'

Judith gasped and staggered. He was pungent with horse and sweat and smoke. His armour could have stood up of its own accord so strong were the mingled aromas.

'And why precisely should you need me?' she demanded archly. 'Apart from the obvious.'

He grinned at that, shaking his head at her tart perception, but sobered quickly as they began to walk again. 'Apart from the obvious, I need you to organise this shambles so that more than just cold pottage and dried meat graces the table. The servants don't know their heads from their heels and Lady Mabel is in no fit state to organise them. I do not have the time.'

'Lady Mabel is here?'

'And her son.' A frown drew his brows together. 'They are both sick with the bloody flux. Look at them if you will, but I suspect it is in God's hands now.'

There was something in his tone, a harshening that made Judith regard him with sharp curiosity. He paused at the foot of the forebuilding steps, fist gripped tightly on the hilt of his sword, as if holding it down in the scabbard.

'What is to become of them if they survive, Guy?'

He followed her gaze to his clenched fist and removed it carefully from the grip before he answered, his nonchalant shrug belied by the grim set of his jaw. 'The lands will be forfeit because de Lacey has rebelled against his King, but they were only his by right of marriage anyway. I suppose the child will inherit them when he is of an age to do so and in the meantime Henry will appoint a warden. The convent is the best place for Lady Mabel.'

'And de Lacey?' she asked.

'Is bound for hell!' he snarled. 'The reckoning is only postponed, not abandoned.'

* * *

Judith found Lady Mabel and the child in a chamber off the hall. The floor was strewn with new rushes and the bed had been made up with clean linen, but the air was still fetid with the stench of bowel sickness. Judith went to the shutters and threw them back, opening the room to an arch of smoky twilight sky. Helgund always swore that night vapours were bad for the lungs, but Judith had slept too often beneath the stars to give any credence to such superstition. Besides, night vapours were a sight more sweet-smelling than the human ones of the moment.

Sounds drifted up from the bailey; the good-natured raillery of two serjeants, the outlandish Welsh singing at the miners' fire, the neigh of a truculent destrier.

The woman on the bed thrashed and moaned. Judith went to her and laid a gentle hand on the hot forehead. Mabel de Serigny raised sunken lids and struggled to focus. Her head rolled on the pillow and a shudder racked her wasted body. Red stars of fever burned on the points of her cheekbones and her breath laboured in her lungs: a matter of time only, Judith thought, and short at that.

The child in the crib was awake and alert. As she approached him, his eyes locked on hers and tenaciously followed her movement. They were his father's eyes, ale-brown in colour, the tone echoed in the thick, straight hair. He drew his knees up to his chest and wailed hoarsely. Judith bent and picked him up. He was hot to her touch, but not burning and, as far as she could see, his condition was not yet mortal.

'Poor mite,' muttered Helgund as she set down Judith's basket of medicines. 'What kind of life is he going to make with the start he's had?' She came to peer into the infant's face and crossed herself at the marked resemblance to his sire.

'Better than the life he would have had otherwise,' Judith answered as she laid him back down and set about mixing a soothing potion to ease Mabel's pain. 'A mother who cannot speak, who never wanted him and a father who has bullied, deceived and butchered and who harbours a vicious lust for young girls. What kind of example would he have had as he grew up? At least now he has a chance to learn honour and decency.'

'Mayhap you're right,' said Helgund, but she still looked dubious. 'I cannot help but think that wolves breed true.'

'He is only half wolf,' Judith said gently. 'And there is good blood on his mother's side. Come, help me lift her and then I want you to fetch the priest.'

'No hope then?'

Judith shook her head. 'There are others afflicted like this too. My guess is that the well water is to blame and that the weakest have succumbed. My lord has set the servants to cleaning out the shaft.'

'I wondered why you had left the shutters wide.'

'What do you mean?'

'To let her soul fly free, m'lady.'

Judith said nothing. Let Helgund believe that she adhered to that old custom if it would stop her from lecturing on the ills of open shutters at night. Mabel coughed and choked on the bitter nostrum and most of it dribbled down her chin.

The infant was dosed with more success than his mother and his soiled linens changed. Unlike Heulwen, he was slow to smile and exuded not one iota of her engaging charm. His stare was solemn, almost old . . . but then, she thought, throat tightening, Heulwen had known only love and affection down the length of her short life and this child never had. Mabel had rejected him, so the maids said, and left him to the wet-nurse who had been a dim-witted slatternly girl from the village with more interest in her trencher and the attentions of one of the grooms than in the infant she was supposed to be suckling.

Judith blinked away the suspicion of tears and sat by the crib, smoothing the child's thick hair until his lids drooped and his breathing came slow and soft and then she rose and, leaving him with Helgund, went to administer similar comfort to her husband.

Guyon stepped into the tub, hissing softly through his teeth as the hot water found cuts and bruises he had forgotten he possessed until now. Slowly, he eased himself down into the herb-infused water until it lapped his shoulders and, tilting back his head, closed his eyes.

Clouded visions danced before his darkened lids. The imagined image of Eluned's death and the reality of the raw earth mound in the garth behind the churchyard. Rhosyn's mutilated body. Heulwen asking in bewilderment for her mother. Heulwen smiling at him through her lashes in the exact manner that had been Rhosyn's, her pudgy hand curled trustingly in his. He swore, opening his eyes, and jerked forward in the water. Judith cried out and backed away from him, almost dropping her basket of medicines.

'What's wrong?' She looked at him askance.

Guyon subsided with a shake of his head. 'Nothing,' he said, tight-lipped.

Judith set down the basket. 'Strange behaviour for a nothing,' she remonstrated. 'That's a nasty graze on your shoulder. You had better let me look at it before you dress.'

His mouth softened. 'Yes, madam.'

She bent to sort through his baggage and find him some presentable garments, clucking in irritation at the dismal state that three weeks without female attention had wrought on his clothes.

'What of Lady Mabel and the boy?' he asked far too casually as he busied himself with his wash.

Judith looked round, a pair of leg bindings dangling between her fingers. 'Lady Mabel will die,' she said bluntly, 'probably before dawn. There is naught to be done. The child will likely survive.'

There was a long silence. Judith came over to the tub, drawn by the quality of his tone. He looked up at her, then bleakly away into the middle distance. 'Do you know, Judith, when they told me that Eluned was dead and that the boy and his mother were still here in the keep, in my power, I wanted to kill them both?' He swallowed hard. 'The little boy . . . he looks so much like his father . . . I actually found myself unsheathing my sword and standing over him . . . and then where would be the difference between myself and Walter de Lacey?'

Judith had put her hand over her mouth. Quickly she took it away as his gaze shifted towards her. She knelt beside the tub and gently touched his tense arm. 'You would have derived no pleasure from it, Guy, not like him.'

'You think not?'

'You did not do it, however much you desired,' she replied steadily, 'and that is the difference.'

His look was bleak. 'No,' he said. 'But I thought about it so hard that it might as well have been the deed. If Eric hadn't been in the room with me . . .' He broke off the sentence.

Judith was filled with burning anger – at Walter de Lacey, at Robert de Belleme, at this whole war and at how far Guyon had been pushed and pushed and pushed. Suddenly she understood his need of her and that she must not fail him. 'You were overset and there is no point in brooding upon it.' She shook his shoulder. It was his grazed one and his breath caught. 'Guy, look at me.'

He turned his head. 'You did not do it. You held back,' she said slowly and clearly.

'Yes,' he agreed in a toneless voice, gaze slipping wearily from hers and back to the middle distance.

'Oh, in the name of the Holy Virgin!' Exasperated and cross because she was frightened, Judith thrust herself to her feet. 'Go on then, wallow until you sink in your own guilt. Just do not expect me to follow you!' She flounced away towards the flagon and reached jerkily for a cup.

Guyon shut his eyes and, with a soft groan, leaned his

head against the rim of the tub. 'Judith, let be. I can't argue with you, not now.'

'And that is half the problem,' she diagnosed tartly. 'You are so tired that your wits are not serving you as they should. You don't want to argue with me because you dare not. You need time to rest and recover.'

He gave a crooked smiled. 'There is need and need, *Cath fach*. Henry needs my report and then he needs me. My own needs can wait.'

'You will be worse than useless to him.'

'Stop pricking me, Judith. I'll manage.'

'And you have the gall to call me infuriating and stubborn!' she retorted. When he chose not to respond, she narrowed her eyes and, mouth set, reached for her vial of poppy syrup and laced his wine with it, adding a hefty splash of aqua vitae to disguise the taste. Her eyes brightened with tears at the memory of the last time she had poured him wine while he lounged in a tub and she contrasted it bitterly with the present. This time there was no brimming laughter, no electric charge of sexual tension. This time there was only fear-tinged determination and exhaustion.

Returning to the tub, she handed him the spiked wine. 'Speaking of needs,' she said, changing the course of her attack, 'the men at least will have to be released for harvest very soon.'

'Such as are necessary,' he agreed. 'I suppose I will have to hire mercenaries to replace them. I'll send to Ravenstow for the strongbox.' He took a gulp of the wine and choked on the underlying bite of the aqua vitae.

'Drink it!' she commanded, eyes fierce, cheeks flushed, terrified that he would discover the taste of the opium.

His lids flickered wide at her peremptory tone and then he smiled slowly. 'Dare I? he asked. 'Last time you shoved a cup beneath my nose and commanded me like that, you were hell-bent on torture.'

Judith felt her whole face scorch fiery red. 'I saved your life, didn't I?'

'Yes you did, *Cath fach*.' His look became quizzical. 'Why are you blushing?'

Judith's heart began to gallop. 'I'm not,' she croaked. 'It is the summer heat.'

Guyon gaped at her over the goblet rim with undisguised astonishment. Hot without it might be, but the keep walls were several feet thick, the gaps filled with rubble and, even in the summer months, it was comfortable to have braziers in the private chambers.

'I'll fetch food,' she muttered breathlessly, and detached herself from his scrutiny to dive for the doorway.

Guyon shook his head and then ducked it beneath the water to wet his hair and clear his thoughts, wondering how on earth Judith had the temerity to suggest that his mind was not serving him as it should when her own was quite obviously addled. He continued his wash and, frowning, took another swallow of the wine. That remark about the heat had been a flustered idiocy, her exit rapid before he could investigate further; or at least, he thought, until she had invented a more plausible excuse for her blush.

It was after she had given him the wine. Until then she had been simmering at him like a cauldron on a blaze. After a moment, a glimmer of enlightenment caused him to taste the wine again and roll it experimentally round his mouth. Smooth, high-quality Anjou and rough border aqua vitae and . . . ! He spat it out into the bath water and swore with soft vehemence, staring with furious eyes at the curtain through which she had vanished. Anger sparkled along his nerve endings, an invigorating anger, buoying him up, subduing fatigue. Lace his wine, would she?

Judith returned with a tray of cold roast pigeon and fresh white bread, a new flagon of wine and an excuse for her previous flustered behaviour ready and credible on her tongue, for it was in part the truth. She intended saying that she had been swept by desire at the sight of him in the bath along with the association of pouring him wine, and knowing how tired he was, had not wished to burden him further. It was therefore with a mingling of vexation and relief that she discovered he had fallen fast asleep in the rapidly cooling water.

Eyes raised heavenwards, she set the tray down on a clothing chest, gave Cadi a firm, low command that flopped the bitch down on her belly at the door, eyes still cocked in distant hope on the food, and went to the tub to pick up the empty goblet from the floor.

'In Jesu's name, Guy, you might have gone to bed!' she complained with exasperation, then shrieked as Guyon surged from the water like a pike, seized her and dragged her down.

'And you might refrain from poisoning my wine!' he growled as she tried to thresh out of his hard grip.

'I wasn't, Guy, truly!'

'You deny there was poppy in that wine?'

'Only enough to give you a sound night's sleep. You need it.'

'You did it in deceit!'

'It was for your own good.'

'Ah yes, my own good,' he said silkily. 'Swaddle me up like a babe while you are at it.'

'Guyon please, you're hurting me!' Judith half sobbed, more afraid of the cadence of his voice than the grip on her arm.

'I ought to beat you witless!' he complained, but let her go. She floundered from the tub, the front of her gown drenched, the ends of her braids dark bronze and dripping. 'Don't ever try that trick on me again.'

Judith took her courage in both hands. 'I'll make sure that next time you don't know!' she retorted. 'My only fault was that in my haste I did not disguise the taste enough.'

Guyon jerked to his feet in a swish of angry water. 'Dare it at your peril.'

'Threat or promise?' she asked with a saucy confidence she was far from feeling, aware that she was playing with fire and that one step too far would ignite a totally different conflagration from the kind she was nurturing now. 'Will you unlace my gown? It's soaked and I'll catch a chill.'

'Your own fault. Call your maids.'

'I can't. Helgund's sitting with Mabel and the child and if you glare at Elflin like that, you will terrify her, not to mention what Brand will do to you if he thinks you have been making improper advances to his wife.'

'What?' Guyon spluttered. He knew by now that he was being led a merry dance, but was too interested in its destination to halt the devious steps of its progress.

'Well, if I sent for Elflin and she saw you in that condition, the Lord alone knows what she might misconstrue. You know how timid she is of all men, saving Brand.'

'What cond—' Guyon followed the direction of her amused gaze, then flicked his own back to her face. Laughter was tugging at the corners of her mouth. She raised her eyes to his. They were round and innocent and she kept them on him as she raised her arms to remove her circlet and veil.

'Shall I leave that uncomforted, too?' she enquired with spurious solicitude. 'Or would you let me close enough to rub it better?'

'Judith!' Guyon choked, laughing despite himself. Half an hour ago he had been so weary and soul-sick that he could have lain down and died. Now the energy was flowing through him like a vigorous stream in spate. 'What am I going to do with you?'

'Get me with child?' she suggested, slanting him a provocative glance. 'Women are supposed to dote and soften when they are breeding.'

Guyon snorted. 'Since when have you ever done what other women are supposed to do?'

'There is always a first time. You might be pleasantly surprised.'

'For a change,' he said with a grin.

She gave him a lazy, answering smile. 'Unlace me, Guy?' she requested again.

He reached to the side fastening of her gown and began to pluck it undone. 'You are naught but a hussy, do you know that? Summer heat indeed!'

She stepped out of the drenched garment and turned in his embrace to twine her arms about his neck and meet his lips with her own. He reached for the drawstring of her shift. 'I have practised better deceptions,' she admitted impishly against his mouth. 'It's not knotted this time.'

'I did not think it would be,' he said wryly as the garment slid down from her shoulders and pooled at her feet and her body blended itself with his.

CHAPTER 29

Guyon stirred in response to a dazzle of light across his eyelids and squinted them open. The chamber was dim; sunlight lanced across the bed from a gap in the warped shutter. He moved his head and idly watched the motes of dust glitter in its bright rainbow bars. It took him a moment to remember where he was and why. Then came the familiar feeling as of a cold stone in the pit of his stomach, immediately dissolved by the awareness of Judith's body curled at his side, sleeping with the innocent abandon of the kitten that was her nickname. Hard to believe in the scheming seductress of the night.

He stretched and relaxed, smiling at the incongruity. Flowers and thorns. Sharp claws sheathed in soft padding. He turned towards her and nuzzled his chin on the crown of her head. She murmured and nestled closer. Her lips moved in a sleepy kiss at the base of his throat.

He glanced beyond the luxurious comfort of his bed and wife to the shifting strands of light and the smile still on his lips became rueful as he realised that it was the first time in three days that he had woken at dawn instead of noon. As usual she had been right, he acknowledged. He had not known the depth of his exhaustion until he had succumbed to it, and succumb he had with a vengeance. The last three days had passed him by like distant scenes from an illuminated psalter and he an illiterate turning the pages. He vaguely recalled rising to eat in the hall and speaking to people, although what he had eaten and what he had said were now a complete mystery. He also remembered going out to inspect the repair work on the curtain wall, but Judith had apprehended him with some specious excuse that had drawn him back within . . . and inevitably to bed where, by unfair means, she had enticed him to stay.

Restlessly he shifted his position, aware of a need to be up and doing that was born of renewed energy, not dull-edged desperation. The grief, anger and guilt were still with him, but no longer intruding upon his every waking thought. Raw, but bearable and probably a burden for life.

Lady Mabel had died on that first night. God rest her soul, since it had not had much rest on this earth. Judith had been tearful about that, although he suspected the tears were more a relieving of tension than any deeper grief for the dead woman. The child still lived. His fever was gone and he had stopped passing blood, or so Judith told him. She kept the babe from his sight and he had no desire to go and see for himself – not yet; perhaps never.

He thought of the incident with the spiked wine. He had always known she was mettlesome, but sometimes she was almost too quick for him to handle. Get me with child, she had said. He was not sure that he could imagine Judith soft and doting. It was not in her nature, or at least not yet. Perhaps children would gentle her, but he doubted it. Kittens did nothing to make a cat less feral. In fact the reverse.

The sound of a horn interrupted his ruminations: a hunting horn, but the notes were not in the sequence that summoned the dogs or blew the mort and they cut through his sense of well-being. He bolted upright in the bed and reached instinctively for his sword. In that same instant, Michel de Bec clashed aside the curtain without courtesy or preamble and strode into the room.

'My lord, it's de Lacey,' he said curtly. 'He's got

lightweight siege equipment and an army of Welsh behind him and he's about to storm the walls.'

'De Lacey?' Guyon repeated. Beside him, Judith sat up, the sheet clutched to her breasts, her eyes filled with sleepy bewilderment.

De Bec wiped his hand across his beard and looked sick. 'We did not see them before. There was a thick mist at first light and they concealed themselves among a flock of sheep being driven up to the keep.'

'Sheep?' Guyon slanted his constable a look. 'Sheep?' he said again and gave a bark of bitter laughter at the irony. 'Do you think it is the same flock, perchance? Thirty pieces of silver?'

'My lord?' De Bec looked at him sidelong.

'Hell's death, Michel!' Guyon shouted. 'He gets out over the wall without being seen and returns in the same wise. God in heaven. I ought to blind every last man on duty. It's quite obvious the bastards have no use for their eyes!' He flung back the bedclothes, tossed his sword on top of them and began swiftly to dress.

'Cadwgan's men, I suppose?'

'I do not know, my lord.'

'God's teeth, what do you know?'

De Bec swallowed. 'They came on us from the west, from across the border, my lord. I do not think they are part of the Shrewsbury force.'

Guyon pulled on his chausses. 'That doesn't make them any less likely to murder us all,' he said in a voice that was husky with curbed temper. 'How far are we outnumbered?'

'About three to one, my lord, but half of them at least are little more than bare-legged Welsh rabble.'

'Don't underestimate them,' Guyon said sharply. 'They might look like peasants, but they fight like wolves, and a weakened keep, like a new lamb, is game for their sport.' He gave his constable a calculating look. 'They won't sit beyond a couple of days for a siege – it's all got to come on the first or second assault. If we can beat them back so that they lose heart, then we have a chance.'

'The women . . .'

Guyon followed de Bec's gaze. Clothed by now in a clinging white woollen undertunic, her hair spilling to her thighs, Judith was a sight to rouse the lust of any man in battle heat and rank offered no protection when Walter de Lacey was leading the assault.

Judith unsheathed Guyon's long knife from his sword-belt. 'I can look after myself,' she said quietly, holding the knife in an accustomed, confident grip.

Guyon opened his mouth to tell her not to be so ridiculous, but snapped it shut again. There was no point in warning her that most Welshmen were adept dagger-fighters and that she might strike once and succeed by dint of surprise, but not again. Probably she knew it already, but the die was cast and it was too late, whatever happened.

'The women will have to take their chance with the rest of us,' he said to de Bec as he struggled into his hauberk, feeling that it was a prison and punishment rather than security. He looked round at Judith again and held out his hand for his swordbelt. She fetched it and he stroked her cheek lightly with his knuckles.

'Organise the servants as best you can, love. The women can care for the wounded and boil up whatever we have – pitch, oil, water. Let the men douse whatever is burnable and carry supplies to the battlements. I'll send you word in more detail when I've seen for myself how the situation stands. At all costs, Judith, keep them from panicking.'

She nodded more staunchly than she felt. Panic was like fire when it spread – difficult to contain and very destructive. She would have to make sure that everyone was kept far too busy to give in to its ravages, including herself. Her chin came up. She looked Guyon proudly in the eyes and he drew her against him, arm hard around her waist. Her fingers tightened on his back, on the iron rings of war when not

fifteen minutes before they had been resting contentedly on
his warm, naked skin.

'Guy, have a care to yourself,' she whispered, suddenly
feeling very frightened as it began to hit her. 'Don't go after
de Lacey at the cost of all else.'

He released her to buckle on his belt. 'I'll take that as fool-
ishness, not insult, *Cath fach*,' he said. 'I know what is at
stake.' He latched the ornate buckle, hitched the scabbard,
then kissed her again, this time lightly and tugged a strand
of her hair.

She watched him leave, fear squeezing her heart. With icy
fingers she braided her hair and pinned it out of the way.
The fear intensified and with it came a rallying anger. She
yanked on her overtunic, belted it and thrust the knife down
against her left side. It was an act of bravado, but at least it
gave her the confidence to stalk from the chamber like an
Amazon and begin organising the half-hysterical servants
into something less reminiscent of a chicken run with a fox
amok within.

Guyon peered down from the wall walk battlements on a
scene of utter chaos below and, tight-lipped, rapped out
several commands. 'Get the sling stones to the wall and stop
their pick before that section of shored-up wall comes down
. . . the same for the ram. And there aren't enough grappling
hooks up here. De Martin, get one of the boys to fetch some
up from the stores, and arrows too if we have them. Soak
them in pitch and set them alight and see if we can get that
mangonel.'

'Christ's bloody bones,' Eric cursed beside him. 'It looks
as though half of Wales is howling out there.'

Guyon smiled grimly. 'Not quite,' he said, 'but enough
to send us out of this world if they break through; de Lacey
will make sure of that.' He donned his helm and his expression vanished behind a broad nasal bar and patterned bronze
brow ridges. He stabbed a finger. 'The trebuchet wants

moving over there. It's not a bit of good where it is now. Michel, see to it and you take that section of wall as your command. Choose the ten men that you think will best serve your needs. Eric, come with me.'

'Do we have a chance, my lord?' Eric looked doubtfully at the ant's nest of Welsh below. They were preparing an assault by scaling ladder with remarkable rapidity and making no attempt to conceal their intentions. Walter de Lacey was present, out of arrow range, talking with several of his captains and vassals.

'A fighting one, literally,' Guyon said, as he watched the small knot of men break up and take their positions. His eyes followed de Lacey with narrowed concentration before he turned and, hand on hilt, stalked to inspect the rest of the perimeter.

The attack came with the searing fury of a summer storm – fast and wild, and as difficult to contain. Stones and molten pitch were dropped upon the ram and boiling water was spouted down on the men scaling the ladders. An exchange of arrows swarmed the air. An arrow tipped off Guyon's helm as he strove with Eric and another knight to grapple loose a ladder. Thirty feet long and set at an angle of about sixty degrees to the wall, they were extremely difficult to dislodge, particularly when loaded with fifteen determined, rapidly scrambling men.

'It's going!' panted Eric, face crimson with effort as he struggled for all he was worth. The foremost Welshman had reached the top and had begun straddling the wall, his round shield held before him, sword already swinging for Eric's throat. Eric was forced to duck and relinquish his hold on the grappling hook. Guyon swept beneath the Welshman's guard, slashing open his leather jerkin as if it were made of parchment, and kicked him back over the wall. He slammed his sword pommel beneath the second man's jaw, snapping him backwards and then kicked him off too.

The ladder scraped and grated on the stone as it started to slip. Another of the enemy reached the top and met his death on Guyon's blade. His cry mingled with the shrieks of his companions on the rungs as the ladder toppled sideways and crashed into the ditch below. There was no time to congratulate each other, or even to lean weakly against the stone to regain breath and stop their hearts from bursting, for ladders were up either side of the one just dislodged and from one of these the Welsh had gained the parapet and were dispersing along the wall walk.

For a time the fighting was so desperate that Guyon could scarcely hold his own without time to think of the defences elsewhere; when there was a lull in his section, it was only because the wall had broken on the other side and de Lacey was drawing men away to force the breach.

Guyon sprinted in full mail towards the new danger and was tripped by a wounded Welshman. A knife glittered. Guyon blocked the thrust on his shield and then slammed it into the man's face, rolled and regained his feet. Eric bellowed a warning. Guyon ducked and a hand axe connected with the side of his helm instead of splitting his face, and sent him to his knees. The second blow he caught on his shield, which splintered beneath the impact. The third never landed, for he backswiped the blade across his opponent's shins and brought him screaming down. But there was another to take his place, and then another, and he could not break through.

CHAPTER 30

'I want the Welsh put out of the reckoning, Miles.'

Miles set down the destrier's hoof he had been examining and slapped the stallion's powerful glossy shoulder.' 'Easier said than done, sire,' he said to King Henry. 'When we make war among ourselves, it is the time of their greatest profit.' He wiped his hands on his chausses and reached for his shirt.

'Perhaps I should have said the Welsh who are allied with de Belleme. The last thing I need when we march on Shrewsbury is for Cadwgan's rabble to come hurling out of Wales and attack from the side.'

Miles donned the garment and, hands on hips, signalled the groom to lead the destrier round so that he could assess how well the strained foreleg had mended.

'You want me to go to war against the Welsh, sire?' he asked with deceptive mildness.

Henry studied the stallion's long, fluid stride. His lips twitched. 'I want you to negotiate with them, my lord – bring them to the trestle and make them see sense.'

Miles snorted. 'Anyone who sits at a trestle with you, sire, usually ends up being the meal,' he said drily.

Henry's smile deepened with appreciation and he made no attempt to deny the remark. 'They'll be susceptible to bribery. Offer Cadwgan whatever he wants – within reason. He's not particularly intelligent, but he's greedy and astute with it. With your Welsh connections and other skills you should be able to persuade him off my back and on to de Belleme's.'

Miles looked wry. 'And what happens to be in it for me?' he asked. 'Apart from the warm glow of knowing that I am a loyal servant of my King?'

Henry pursed his lips. 'A dispensation perhaps?' he said, raising his eyes to Alicia as she came down towards them, a packet in her hands.

Miles's mouth tightened. He nodded to the groom and the horse was led away. 'When do you want me to leave?'

'As soon as you may. I want possession of Shrewsbury before the winter frosts stop the grass growing.' He turned to Alicia with a gracious smile. Her braids were still as black as midnight and she smelled wonderfully of attar of roses. 'Worth it, isn't it?'

Miles said nothing, but the tight line of his mouth was eloquent.

Alicia lowered her eyes before Henry. Of necessity he was occasionally a visitor, but she felt awkward before him and tried to keep their contact to a minimum. There had been desperate reasons behind her adultery. Henry's own need had been a simple, adolescent lust.

Mischievously, Henry reached for her hand to kiss it, but she evaded him and placed the packet in his grasp instead.

'What's this?' he enquired.

'I do not know, sire. The messenger has only just ridden in.'

Henry looked at the seal. 'Your son,' he said to Miles as he broke open the wax and then quickly perused the contents. Alicia went to slip her arm through Miles's, seeking the reassurance of his body.

'Hah! He's taken Thornford,' Henry said with satisfaction. 'Says he'll shore up and garrison and move down to Bridgnorth via Ledworth and Oxley to gather fresh supplies.'

'What about de Lacey? Is he dead or prisoner?'

Henry shook his head 'No. Apparently he slipped out before the last assault, to Shrewsbury so one of the garrison said, but Guy cannot be sure. De Lacey's wife and son are at Thornford, both sick of the bloody flux.'

'Does he mention a Welsh girl?'

Henry shook his head and passed the letter to Miles. 'Some special concern of his? Didn't he have a Welsh mistress once?'

'De Lacey murdered her and her son and abducted her ten-year-old daughter to serve his lusts,' Miles said brusquely. 'Her other child, Guyon's daughter, is being cared for at Ravenstow. By a hair's breadth, she was spared her mother's fate.'

'I'm sorry, I did not know.' For a moment Henry's expression was stripped of its customary aplomb to show pity and complete surprise.

'Guyon would not make a parade of it, sire,' Miles replied. 'It was too deep and personal a matter and it happened little more than a month ago.'

Henry tapped a thoughtful forefinger on his chin. 'Perhaps, in view of what you have just told me, it might be as well if you take a detour through Thornford on your way to parley with the Welsh.'

'I was going to do that anyway, sire. He is my son.'

Henry smiled. 'Well, now you have the royal sanction, don't you? It's starting to rain. Let us go within and discuss what I want of Cadwgan in more detail.'

Miles stared in consternation at the serjeant he had sent ahead to notify Guyon of his imminent arrival, for the man was spurring his courser back towards the troop, not sparing the horse or himself in the late summer heat. Even if Guyon had returned to Ravenstow or already set out for Ledworth, there was no cause for this tearing haste unless there was serious trouble.

Gasping almost as much as his labouring mount, the man gave his report. 'The keep's under attack, my lord, by the Welsh as far as I can see, and it's going hard for the defenders!'

Miles's expression, grim at first, slowly brightened into

savage amusement. 'The Welsh, eh?' His lip curled. 'And in search of a little Norman hospitality. Well, why not?'

'My lord?'

Miles shook his head and rode to the front of the column, increasing the pace from a steady walk to a ground-eating lope.

The sun had moved almost an hour's position in the sky by the time they reached Thornford, and the defenders had reached a state of *extremis*. Miles took in the scaling ladders clumped against the wall, the lack of men on them suggesting that most were engaged within the boundaries of the keep; took in too the broken section of the wall and heard on the breeze the sounds of desperate skirmish. Turning his stallion, he swiftly addressed his men who were expectantly threading their shields on to their left arms and readying their weapons for a charge.

'You can see for yourselves what we're in for. You are all experienced, you should know the ways of the Welsh. Watch your destriers' bellies, they'll slit them open if you force them to fight in close. Remember, a Welshman does not wear armour. He's vulnerable, but he's faster than you. Kill if you must to save your own skin, but if you engage in combat with any man who seems important, try to take him prisoner. Lives will be useful to barter for Cadwgan's favour and whoever takes a useful hostage will find himself handsomely rewarded. Understood?'

As they acknowledged this, Miles threaded his own shield on to his left arm, checked the secure fit of his helm, unlooped his mace from his saddle and with a yell, spurred his destrier into a gallop.

The Norman charge burst into the outer bailey creating mayhem among the attacking Welsh. A bare-legged hill man flew from the roan's shoulder and was trampled by the destrier following on behind. The mace caught a Fleming's face beneath the brow of his helm and crushed his cheekbone. He fell, screaming. The Welshman behind him tried to protect his head but was too slow and took a splintering blow to his temple. As Miles had said, very few of the Welsh wore armour and the Norman charge went through them like a hammer through a trough of ripe plums.

Miles felt a hard blow on his shield as he emerged into the daylight of the inner ward. He gasped as his left arm was jarred and in retaliation, launched a blow over his shield rim. A solid thud and a cry answered him. He reined his stallion around and, amid the fighting and chaos, saw a bare-legged Welshman running towards a group of his comrades who were fighting furiously with someone they had surrounded. Bare-legged the warrior might be, but the pommel of his short sword was set with jewels, and his belt was tooled and gilded with gold leaf. A Norman helmet was set jauntily askew on his straggling black curls. With a yell of triumph, Miles rode him down.

The group of Welsh exploded outwards like ripples from a flung stone in a pool. One of their number rolled on the ground, clutching his ripped belly and screaming. Guyon followed through hard, iron shield-boss jabbing dangerously, sword swinging low at the enemy's unguarded legs. At his back, feet wide-planted, Eric's battleaxe hewed the air and any Welshman daring to venture within the path of the blade's glittering arc.

Miles's destrier ploughed into the Welsh and the mace narrowed the odds.

Guyon spat out a mouthful of blood from a cut lip and pressed forward. He was functioning on instinct now, not finesse, and it took him a moment to recognise his father's stallion and even longer to realise that help, no matter how miraculously, was at hand.

Miles reined the destrier round to block the retreat of the Welsh noble he had marked. The young man's eyes darted between the plunging shod hooves threatening to brain him and the suggestively swinging mace. 'Throw down your sword and yield,' Miles commanded in Welsh. 'I promise you will not be harmed.'

Guyon cast a rapid glance around the inner bailey, saw that the advantage of the battle had swayed back in his direction, glanced further and saw that the forebuilding doors had been broached. Commanding a handful of his soldiers to follow him, he ran for the keep.

Miles looked towards his son and the Welshman thought he saw his opportunity and bolted for freedom. Miles spurred to block his path and the mace came down on the man's skewed helmet, rattling his wits round his skull and knocking him half senseless to the ground. With a snort of disgust at the man's folly, Miles set about securing him from further attempts at escape.

Within the keep, Judith listened to the screams of men receiving a face full of scalding water, the war cries, the death cries, the thud of the ram, and felt sick to the soul with fear lest one of those screams was her husband's.

She had done all that was possible for her to do, short of joining the men on the battlements; indeed, she might have even dared that were she not so fettered by her responsibilities to the wounded and those within the core of the keep who looked to her for succour and guidance.

She knew their situation was desperate. The Welsh alone they could have fought off, but with Norman leaders the matter was not so sure. Guyon had had to batter Thornford hard to take it and four days had not been long enough to shore it up to withstand the kind of punishment it was taking now. She could only thank Christ that she had left Heulwen at Ravenstow, for she had been in half a mind to bring her and only the doubt of what she might find here had made her leave the child behind . . . perhaps to be raised an orphan.

Judith's belly heaved as she contemplated her future at the hands of Walter de Lacey should he prevail. She swallowed. What had Guyon said about panic? The room started to close in on her and the wounded man she was tending groaned and jerked. Chagrined, she apologised to him and finishing with the salve, reached for a roll of bandage. There was none and a swift investigation among the maids showed that there was very little left. She took a swaddling band from Helgund to bind the man and, relieved to have an excuse, left the hall to raid Lady Mabel's linen chest in the solar.

She was kneeling by the chest, cutting a tablecloth into strips with Guyon's knife, when she became aware of how much nearer the battle sounded to the keep. The shouting was no longer an amorphous muddle; she could distinguish actual words now and hear the blows and thuds of sword upon shield. From without there came a tremendous crash and then the screams of women and the grating screech of sword on sword. She ceased her task and rose to her feet, her breath catching in her throat. Weapons clashed together outside the curtain. She heard grunts of effort and a hissing curse, and tightened her fingers on the grip of her knife.

There was a solid thud, a grunt, and then a bubbling groan. The curtain clashed aside and she was confronted by Walter de Lacey, his mail shirt glistening like snakeskin as he breathed in heavy gasps. His sword was edged with blood and his eyes were aglow with triumph.

Her throat closed, but not before a whimper had escaped her lips. Rape and a living hell. She could see her future clearly imprinted in his voracious stare.

'You're not properly attired for a wedding, but you'll do,' he said with a smile.

'Keep away from me!' Judith snarled.

He shook his head at her. 'Is that any way for a wife to speak to her husband? It seems that I am going to have to lesson you into meeker ways.' Sheathing his sword, he advanced.

Judith backed. Her thighs struck the chest and pressed there. She was cornered, no retreat, and he was going to do all the things to her that Maurice de Montgomery had once done to her mother. She thought of Rhosyn and Rhys and Eluned, of what had happened to them. She thought of Guyon sprawled sightless in the ward, for surely de Lacey would not be gloating here otherwise and, as he reached for her, her eyes flashed and her chin came up.

Guyon ran, not feeling the weight of his mail or weapons, only filled with a dreadful sense of foreboding. A Fleming, intent on pillage, barred his way and Guyon cut him down like swatting a fly. The maids were screaming and cowering. The wounded who had been unable to run away were all dead. A Welshman was swigging raw wine straight from the flagon. He was still clutching it to his chest when Guyon ran him through. Blood and wine soaked into the rushes. Guyon seized Helgund's arms. 'Where's your mistress?' he demanded.

'She went . . . solar . . . fetch more bandages!' Helgund gulped through a mask of tears and terror as around her men skirmished, chasing each other over and around trestles, hacking and slashing, killing or being killed.

Guyon released her arm and ran the length of the hall. Prys was sprawled across the solar entrance. He stooped and turned him over, but the life had flown and Prys was as limp as a rag. Guyon's blood froze. Standing straight, he parted the curtain and made himself enter the solar.

A shaft of sunlight slanted across the room to the wall above the prie-dieu and illuminated a splash of blood and a beadwork of sprayed drops above it. He followed the pattern up and then down to where it disappeared into the deep corner shadows beside the open linen chest, the napery it contained spilling untidily over the edge and embroidered erratically with great scarlet flowers of blood. Hesitantly he trod in the wake of his gaze until he was looking down on the body of Walter de Lacey and beneath it, the russet home-spun of Judith's oldest working gown.

If his blood had run cold before, now he felt it congeal, and for a moment he was unable to move. A wet, cold nose nudged at his hand and Cadi whined. Her tail swished against his chausses and he broke eye contact with what he dreaded to face to look at the dog. She sniffed at de Lacey's hauberk and growled.

The power of movement returned to Guyon's limbs, although they seemed to belong to a total stranger. He stooped and, grasping de Lacey's shoulder, rolled him over and to one side. There was a jagged tear in his throat and his eyes were fixed in a baleful stare.

Judith was drenched in blood, but how much was her own he had no idea. Her face was unsmirched except for one small streak that only served to emphasise her pallor. Her eyes were closed and for a heart-stopping moment he did not know if she was dead or alive.

'Judith?' he said softly and, kneeling, lifted her and braced her weight against his shoulders. 'Judith?' He patted her face and she flopped against him like a child's cloth doll. Frightened, he hit her harder and then, by pure reflexive instinct, shot out his arm and grabbed her wrist before she could do to him with the knife what she had just done to Walter de Lacey.

'Guy?' Her eyes cleared. She looked at him and then at the knife and let it drop before turning into his arms with a shuddering sob.

'Judith, are you hurt, love? I cannot tell for all this blood.'

'Hurt? . . . No . . . It is all his. He did not know I had the knife until I struck – it was hidden under these bandages . . . I thought when I saw him that you must be dead . . .' Her breath caught in her throat and Guyon smoothed her hair and kissed her. She kissed him fervently in return, then pushed him away to look at him. 'You talk of my hurt, as if your own were of no consequence!' she gasped, pointing to a bloody rent in his mail.

'It's nothing,' he answered, not entirely telling the truth.

'I've taken worse in practice. And it doesn't matter now. It is all over.'

His tone was so weary that she panicked. 'What do you mean? Surely with de Lacey dead, the Welsh will be willing to talk ransom?'

'That is what I am hoping, although at the best of times they can be contrary bastards and I'm in no state to negotiate myself.' His eyes flickered to the doorway.

Judith stared at Miles in open-mouthed astonishment as he stepped over the corpse on the threshold and entered the chamber.

'I thought you did not have the time to send for succour,' she said to Guyon in utter bewilderment.

'I didn't, love.' Guyon released her to wipe his sword on de Lacey's leggings, then wished he had not, for as he bent, his vision fluctuated and he felt as if he were on the deck of a ship in the midst of a storm. He straightened slowly and, with great care, sheathed the blade. 'It was sheer good fortune, or the will of God . . .' He looked at his father. 'If you had not come when you did . . .'

'The will of the King, you mean,' Miles said wryly as Guyon fumbled to remove his helm. 'And as it happens, this situation could not have profited him better.'

Guyon looked blankly at his father. 'Forgive me. I've fought my way to the gates of hell and back. I can't think.'

Miles went out into the hall, returning with a jug of wine that had miraculously survived the onslaught. 'Henry wants me to negotiate with the Welsh. Well, thanks to you and Walter de Lacey, I've a nice fat collection of caged birds to lure Cadwgan to the table . . . including his own son.'

'Cadwgan's son?' Guyon gulped the wine straight from the flagon, spilling more down his mail than he actually got into his mouth. 'You mean that idiot with the jewelled sword and no notion of how to use it is Cadwgan's son?'

Miles grinned wolfishly. 'The very same. Do you think that his father values him above his loyalty to Robert de Belleme?'

Guyon shook his head in wonder. His gaze moved to the sprawled corpse of Walter de Lacey and a tremor ran through his body. He put the wine down. 'It is a pity he is dead,' he muttered. 'I would have borrowed one of de Belleme's greased stakes and let him dance on it awhile. He escaped too cleanly.' He rubbed his hand over his face and swore as his palm opened up a cut and it began to bleed again.

Concerned, still trembling herself with shock, Judith rose and went to him.

He stroked her cheek. 'Don't fret, love,' he said. 'The shoring up of Thornford will take some little while to accomplish this time. I won't be going to Bridgnorth just yet, so you can stop scheming how you're going to disguise the white poppy this time.' He tugged her braid, smiled at her and slowly slipped down the chest to the floor.

CHAPTER 31

ASHDYKE
AUTUMN 1102

Below Ashdyke Crag, between it and the River Wye, the common grazing land was illuminated by a huge bonfire around which the people from the surrounding villages clustered and capered. The water glittered with gemstones of firelit colour, the sharp autumnal breeze skimming the jet surface with creases and pockets of ruffled gold.

Judith looked down on the scene from an arrowslit in the small wall chamber overlooking the river, and smiled as she replaced the hide screen. There was so much to celebrate that it was hard to believe that less than a season since they had been caught up in the violent ugliness of death and war.

She turned away and picked up her new, marten-lined cloak. Helgund was moving quietly about the chamber, tidying and setting to rights. The night candle softly illuminated the faces of the two sleeping children. The King had given Guyon the wardship of Adam de Lacey and thus the infant and his inheritance were Guyon's responsibility until Adam should reach manhood. Guyon had baulked at first, but Judith had managed to persuade him otherwise. The boy was not responsible for the crimes of his sire and in the years that they had him they could mould him to their own pattern and codes. Guyon had consented, because at the time he did not have the strength to argue with her and she had taken shameless advantage of his weakness to install the child in their household. Adam was still slow to smile and solemn, but he had gained in flesh and confidence and followed Heulwen everywhere that she would tolerate him.

Heulwen. She looked so angelic and innocent with her rose-gold curls and delicate features that it was impossible to believe in the hellion of her waking hours. In all but her physical appearance and her ability to flirt, Heulwen might have been a boy. She romped and climbed and swung and already straddled a pony with more confidence than either of Helgund's grandsons.

'Are they asleep now?' asked Alicia, tiptoeing to look over Judith's shoulder at the children.

'Soundly.' Judith smiled in response. She considered her mother. Alicia was wearing a fetching gown of rich blue wool that turned her eyes the colour of hyssop flowers. Her hair was braided with pearls to match those worked at the neck of her gown and up the hanging sleeves:

'I suppose,' Judith said mischievously, 'that I ought to be organising the bedding ceremony.'

Alicia's face grew slightly more radiant as she blushed and then laughed. 'Do not you dare!' she cried. 'It might be sport for everyone else but . . . well, the bedding ceremony with Maurice was enough to give me a lifelong dread of that ritual and with myself and Miles . . . it is hardly the first time, is it? We are not likely to repudiate each other.'

Judith embraced her mother. 'I was only teasing,' she laughed. 'I am pleased to see you so happy.'

Alicia returned the embrace warmly. 'I never thought to be. I was so frightened that I would lose him in this war.'

For an instant they clung, women aware of the fragility of their present joy, for even now it was not entirely over. Banished from England de Belleme might be, but for how long? Banishment could be revoked on the whim of a king.

Alicia was the first to step away. She looked Judith critically up and down. 'Does he know yet?'

Judith's hand went instinctively to her belly which was still tight and flat. It was early yet to be sure, the symptoms vague, more a knowledge of the body than of the mind.

'How did . . . ?'

'You've put on flesh. Oh, not there yet, that will not show for some time, I think, but you never filled your gowns so well before.'

Judith's gaze flicked down to her bosom. 'I suppose I ought to make the most of it before the rest catches up,' she sighed with false regret and smiled as they left the room and began to wind their way downstairs. 'No, Guy doesn't know. I suggested to him that the best way to handle my waywardness was to get me with child, and he took me at my word . . .' The smile became a giggle at her weak pun, but then she sobered. 'I conceived at Thornford some time between Lady Mabel's death and the second siege. In a way, I suppose it is a new beginning, a light out of darkness and all the more precious for being so.'

She found Guyon standing alone by the riverside, watching the reflection of the flames dazzle in the water, and picked her way carefully over to him across the autumn grass. Hearing the rustle of her approach, he turned quickly, then his expression relaxed into a smile and he held out his hand.

'Brooding alone?' she asked in a light voice, but with a qualm, lest he was mulling over the private losses of the last year.

'Not now,' he answered easily enough, drawing her close. Their breath frosted the air and mingled. The water lapped near their feet, tipped with light. 'I was wondering what will happen in Normandy now that de Belleme is banished there.'

'It is not our concern now.' Her fingers anxiously tightened in his.

'No, but I cannot help but pity Duke Robert and the rest

of the Norman lords. He will eat them alive.' And then Henry would interfere and there would be war again, but in Normandy, not England.

'I do not care, just as long as he leaves us alone.' She was fully aware of everything that he was not saying. He had been very ill after the battle for Thornford – not unto death as the last time, thank Christ, but enough for Bridgnorth to have fallen and for Miles to have negotiated his treaty with the Welsh before he was capable of taking the field again and, in her ignored opinion, it had been too soon. He still tired easily. He had been at the bitter siege of Shrewsbury, one of the barons present to witness Robert de Belleme and his brothers ride away to exile in Normandy. For the nonce at least, they were safe.

'Are you weary?' She rubbed her cheek against his cloak.

He shrugged. 'A little.'

'Perhaps we should retire,' she suggested, then looked anxiously up at him as she felt him shudder, only to realise that he was laughing.

'Before the bride and groom? Shame on you, you hussy.'

Her lips twitched. 'Yes,' she sighed meekly. 'Shame on me.'

'Judith, you are never seeking to agree with your husband?'

'Well, if I am, it is all your fault.'

'Mine! Why?' he gave her look filled with indignation.

'Why else should I grow soft and doting?'

That stopped him as if he had walked into a keep wall. He gaped at her like a peasant drunk on rough cider.

'Late spring, I think,' she added, eyes wide and guileless. 'Aren't you pleased?'

Guyon took her by the shoulders. A wondering smile gradually replaced the dazed expression on his face. '*Cath fach*, I love you,' he murmured.

She put her arms around his neck. 'Show me,' she said. 'I want to know.'

THE RUNNING
VIXEN

Acknowledgements

As always, I would like to say a big thank you to my agent Carole Blake at the Blake Friedmann agency. Also my editor Barbara Daniel at Little, Brown. They have not only shared this journey with me, they have made it possible.

My thanks and love to my husband Roger. He lets me be who I am with quiet support and without complaint, and that is something without price. For long-term readers of my work – yes, he is still doing the ironing!

My thanks too, to numerous friends and e-groups online who keep me sane and thoroughly enrich my moments of procrastination, especially the members of historicalfictiononline.com, Friends and Writers and the RNA.

Author's Note

My first publishing contract was for two novels – *The Wild Hunt* and this one, *The Running Vixen*. When I signed the contract I had yet to write the latter. Due to the vagaries of the publishing industry, not least the death of media tycoon Robert Maxwell, *The Running Vixen* was published in a very small print run in hard cover for the libraries. The paperback, although it came out, was on and off the shelves faster than the sell-by date of milk in a supermarket, and the paperback imprint under which it was published crashed soon after.

Down the years readers have often asked me whether it was going to be reissued and until recently I had to say, sadly not. However, my current publishers decided it would be good to make my out of print novels available again – and I wholeheartedly agreed with them, naturally! My only proviso was that I be able to take a look at the material with the eye of increased experience and historical knowledge.

Inspired by such films as *The Vikings*, *The Warlord*, *El Cid* and even (blushing) Errol Flynn's *The Adventures of Robin Hood*, I set out writing at the romantic adventure end of historical fiction and through a steady career path graduated to writing fiction where the star players had actually lived. In earlier works, my protagonists are fictitious, but woven into a firm historical backdrop. *The Running Vixen* falls into the former category and is a stand alone follow-up to *The Wild Hunt*.

Readers often ask me if I had a specific location in mind when writing the backdrops to *The Wild Hunt* and *The*

Running Vixen. The answer is that I took my inspiration from the area of the middle Welsh marches as a whole: Chepstow, Ludlow, Shropshire, the former Montgomeryshire. I didn't have one 'set' place in mind, but almagamated many into a general description.

As far as the historical backdrop to the story is concerned, I have embroidered my tale on the known details. In 1120, King Henry I's only legitimate son was drowned while crossing from Normandy to England. The only other direct heir of Henry's blood was his daughter, Matilda, and she was dwelling in Germany as wife of the Holy Roman Emperor, Henry V. When Henry died in 1125, her father recalled her and made his barons swear an oath of allegiance to her. He also planned a second marriage for her with the house of Anjou. This was not a popular move and there was plenty of muttering and some outright resistance. Henry had a nephew – William le Clito, the son of his older brother, and le Clito's claim was just as good, if not better than Matilda's. Political wheeling and dealing was every bit as underhand and murky as it is today. Despite changes in mindset and social habits, many things remain exactly the same!

1

The Welsh Marches, Autumn 1126

On the day Adam de Lacey returned to the borders after an absence of more than a year, the monthly market at Ravenstow was in full, noisy cry, and thus numerous witnesses watched and whispered behind their hands as the small but disciplined entourage wound its way through their midst.

The young man at the head of the troop paid scant attention to their interest, to the bustling booths and mingling of scents and stenches, the cries and entreaties to look, to buy – not because it was beneath him to do so, but because he was preoccupied and tired. As Adam rode past a woman selling fleeces and sheepskin winter shoes and jerkins, the lilting cadence of the Welsh tongue pleased his ears, causing him to emerge from his introspection and look around with a half-smile. Of late he had grown accustomed to heavy, guttural German, spoken by humourless men with a rigid sense of rank and order, their lifestyle the opposite of the carefree, robust Welsh, who had few possessions and pretensions and set very little store by those who did.

The outward journey to the mourning court of the recently deceased German Emperor had been filled with the violence and hardship of long days on roads that were often hostile, and the route home had been even worse owing to the querulous temper of his charge. Adam was an accomplished soldier, well able to look after himself where the dangers of the open road were concerned. The lash of a haughty woman's tongue – and she the King's own daughter and Dowager Empress of Germany – was a different matter entirely. Her high estate had prevented him from defending himself in the manner he would have liked, and the obligation of feudal duty had made it impossible for him to abandon her on the road, forcing him to bear with gritted teeth what he could not change; but then he was used to that.

A crone cried out to him, offering to tell his fortune for a quarter-penny. His half-smile expanded and developed a bitter quality. He flung a coin towards her outstretched fingers but declined to wait on her prophecy. He knew his future already – the parts that mattered, or had mattered once until time and grim determination had rendered them numb. Abruptly he heeled his stallion to a rapid trot.

Ravenstow keep, the seat of his foster father's barony shone with fresh limewash on the crag overlooking the busy town. It had been built during the reign of William Rufus by Robert de Belleme, former Earl of Shrewsbury and now King Henry's prisoner, his evil rule a fading but still potent memory; too potent for some who had lost their friends and family to the barbaric tortures he had practised in his fortress strongholds a generation ago.

Adam's own father had been de Belleme's vassal and accomplice, his name stained with the overspill from de Belleme's infamies. Adam knew from servants' tales, whispered in dark corners, the kind of man his father had been: a dishonourable molester of women and young girls, tarnished with murder and guilty of treason. Not an ancestor to claim with pride, but one to bury deep with guilt and shame.

The drawbridge was down but the guards on duty were swift to challenge him, and only rested their spears when they had taken a close look at his banner and the face revealed to them as he removed his helm by its nasal bar. Then they let him pass with words of greeting on their lips, and speculation rife in their eyes.

Eadric, the head groom, emerged from the stables to take the dun and deployed his underlings among Adam's men. 'Welcome, my lord,' he said with a half-moon grin. 'It has been a long time.'

Having dismounted, Adam stared around the busy bailey which looked just as it always had. The smith's hammer rang out clear and sweet from the forge against the curtain wall. A soldier's woman was tending a cooking pot tripoded over an open fire, and the savoury steam drifted tantalisingly past his nostrils, reminding him that he hadn't eaten since well before prime. Hens pecked underfoot, doves from Countess Judith's cote cooing and pirouetting among them. A curvaceous serving girl carried a tray of loaves across the ward and was whistled at by a group of off-duty soldiers playing dice and warming their backs against a sunny timber wall.

3

'A long time, Eadric,' he agreed, with a sigh and a wary smile. 'Is Lord Guyon here?'

'Out hunting, sir, and the lady Judith with him.' Eadric looked apologetic, and then brightened. 'Master Renard is here though, and Mistress Heulwen.'

The smile froze upon Adam's face. He set his hand to his stallion's reins as though he would mount up again, but then glanced round at his men. He could hear their groans of relief and see the way they stretched stiff muscles and rubbed sore backs. They were tired, having ridden a bone-jarring distance, and it would be foolish and grossly discourteous to ride out now that their presence was known.

A young man with a stork's length of leg came striding towards him from the direction of the mews, stripping a hawking gauntlet from his right hand as he advanced. He had pitch-black hair and strong features just beginning to pare out of childhood's unformed roundness. It took Adam a moment to realise that this was Renard, Lord Guyon's third son, for when last encountered the lad had been a lanky fourteen-year-old with less substance than a hoe-handle. Now, although still on the narrow side, his limbs were beginning to thicken out with pads of adult muscle and he moved like a young cat. 'We thought you'd gone for good!' Renard greeted Adam with a boisterous clasp on the arm and a total lack of respect. His voice was husky and a trifle raw, revealing that it had but recently broken.

'So did I, sometimes,' Adam answered wryly, and took a step back. 'Holy Christ, but you've grown!'

'So everyone keeps telling me – but not too old for a beating, Mama always adds!' Renard laughed merrily,

4

displaying white, slightly uneven teeth. 'She's taken my father hunting because it's the only way she can get him to relax his responsibilities for a day, short of spiking his wine – and she's done that before now. There's only myself and Heulwen here. She'll be right glad to see you.'

Adam lowered his gaze. 'Is her husband here too?'

They went up the forebuilding steps and entered the great hall. Sweet-scented rushes crackled underfoot, and sunlight shone through the high window spaces and illuminated the embroidered banners adorning the walls. Renard bade a servant bring wine, then tilted his visitor a speculative look from narrow, dark-grey eyes. 'Ralf was killed at midsummer by the Welsh.'

'God rest his soul.' Adam crossed himself, the words and gesture emerging independent of his racing mind.

Renard grimaced. 'It was a bad business. The Welsh have been biting at our borders like breeding fleas on a dog's back ever since it happened. Warrin de Mortimer chanced on the attack, drove the Welsh off and brought what was left of Ralf home. Heulwen took it badly. She and Ralf had quarrelled before he rode out, and she blames herself.'

The maid approached them with a pitcher and two cups, her eyes flickering circumspectly over Adam. He stared through her, a muscle bunching and hollowing in his cheek. The wine was Rhenish, rich and smooth, and he almost retched, remembering Heulwen's wedding day and how he had drunk himself into a stupor on this stuff and Lady Judith had forced him to be sick in order to save his life. Afterwards, the incident had faded into a memory recalled with wry chuckles by everyone except

5

himself. Sometimes he wished that they had been sufficiently charitable to let him die.

Renard sat down on a fur-covered stool before the
hearth, dangled his cup between his knees and said
disgustedly, 'De Mortimer's been buzzing around
Heulwen like a frantic wasp at an open honey jar. It's
only a matter of time before he formally asks my father
for her.'

'Is he likely to agree?'

Renard jerked his shoulders as if ridding them of
something that chafed. 'Admittedly it's a useful bond,
and as Warrin was once one of my father's squires, he'll
probably get a generous hearing.'

Adam filled his cheeks with the wine, then swallowed
it. He remembered the rasp of dust against his teeth,
the sensation of a spur-clad heel grinding on his spine,
a mocking voice telling him to get up and fight. The
bruises, the humiliation, the tears swelling painfully in
his throat and choked down by fear of further scorn;
the effort to rise and face his adversary, knowing he
would be knocked down again. Training, it was called:
a thirteen-year-old facing a man of twenty, whose sole
concern was to display his superiority and put the most
junior squire firmly in his place. Oh yes, he well knew
the glorious Warrin de Mortimer.

'And Heulwen herself?' he asked with forced neutrality.

'Oh, you know my sister. Playing hard to get as only
she can, but I think she might have him in the end.
Warrin offered for her before, you know, but was turned
down in favour of Ralf.'

'And now Ralf's dead.'

'Yes.' Renard cocked him a curious look, but something

in Adam's manner made him change the subject. 'What's Matilda like?'

Adam gave him a rueful look. 'That would be the "Empress Matilda",' he said. 'Woe betide anyone who doesn't afford her the full title. She's as cold and proud as a chunk of Caen stone.'

'You don't like her then,' Renard said with interest.

'I didn't get close enough to find out – I didn't want to end up as stone too!'

The younger man grinned over the rim of his goblet.

'It's no cause for laughter, Ren. Henry hasn't just summoned her home to comfort his dotage or her widowhood. She's to be our future queen, and when I see her treating men like dirt under her feet, it chills me to the marrow.'

'Just how did you end up in the entourage sent to fetch her?' Renard asked.

Adam smiled darkly. 'I've served at court, so I suppose Henry knows I'm discreet and stoical – unlikely to boil over in public at being called a mannerless oaf with mashed turnip where my brains should be.'

'She said that to you?' Renard bit his lip in an unsuccessful effort to conceal his mirth.

'That was the least of her insults. Of course, most of them were in German, and I didn't ask to have them translated. Even a mannerless turnip-brain has his pride. I—' He stopped and stared across the hall, suddenly transfixed.

Heulwen stood in a shaft of sunlight that fired her braids beneath the simple white veil to the precise colour of autumn oak leaves. Her russet wool gown was laced tightly to her figure, and as she approached the hearth the delicate gold embroidery at the throat and hem of the dress glittered with trapped light.

Adam closed his eyes to break the contact, swallowed, and prepared to endure. He would rather a hundred times over have undergone the haughty scorn of the Empress Matilda than face the woman who approached him now: Heulwen, Lord Guyon's natural daughter out of a Welsh woman whom his own father had murdered during the dispute for the crown more than twenty-four years ago.

He rose clumsily to his feet and some of the wine slopped down his surcoat, staining the blue silk. He could feel his ears burning and knew he had coloured like a gauche youth.

'Adam!' she cried joyfully, and with complete lack of self-consciousness flung her arms around his neck and drew his head down to kiss him full on the lips. The scent of flowers engulfed him. Her eyes were the colour of sunlit sea-shallows – azure and aquamarine, flecked with mica-gold. His throat tightened. No words came, only the thought that the Empress's remarks were perhaps not insults but the truth.

Heulwen released him to step back and admire the new style of surcoat he wore over his hauberk, and the ornate German swordbelt. 'My, my,' she teased, 'aren't you a sight for sore eyes? Mama will be furious to have missed greeting you. You should have sent word on ahead!'

'I was in half a mind to ride to Thornford first,' he said in a constricted voice, 'but I have a letter to your father from the King.'

'Churl!' she scolded, eyes dancing. 'It's fortunate that

some of us are not so lacking in courtesy. There's a hot tub prepared above.'

Adam stared at her in dismay. He was accustomed to bathing at least once in a while. Indeed, he enjoyed the luxury and relaxation it provided, but he was filled with dread, knowing that Heulwen, as hostess, would be responsible for unarming him and seeing to his comfort. 'I haven't finished my wine,' he said woodenly, 'or my conversation.'

Renard said unhelpfully, 'You'll only have to repeat it all later to my parents, and there's no law against taking your wine upstairs.'

'And since I have gone to the trouble of preparing a tub, the least you can do is sit in it. You stink of the road!' It was hardly the way to speak to a welcome guest, and Heulwen could have bitten her tongue the moment the words emerged. Since Ralf's death she had found herself being irritable and snappish. People made allowances – those who knew her well – but it was a long time since she and Adam had shared the closeness of childhood friendship.

Adam stared obdurately at the wall beyond her head, refusing to meet her eyes. 'Well that's because I've been on it for a long time – too long, I sometimes think.'

She touched him again with eyes full of chagrin. 'Adam, I'm sorry. I don't know why I said such a thing.'

'Because you have gone to the trouble and I am not suitably grateful?' he replied with a grimace that just about passed for a smile. 'Well if I am not, it is because I've had a crawful of being ordered around by a woman.'

'Straight to the middle of the target!' crowed Renard at his blushing half-sister.

'No insult intended in my turn.' Adam put down the cup which was still more than half full of wine, and went towards the curtain that screened off the tower stairs. 'Bear with me awhile until I've found the grace to mellow.'

'Jesu,' Renard said to her with a shake of his head. 'He hasn't changed, has he?'

Heulwen looked baffled. 'I don't know. When I mentioned the bath, I thought he was going to turn tail and flee.'

'Perhaps the Germans mutilated him below,' Renard offered flippantly, then shot her a shrewd glance. 'Or perhaps they didn't.'

Renard was like that. The unwary were lulled into seeing a likeable, shallow youth, wallowing through the pitfalls of adolescence towards a far-distant maturity, and then he would suddenly shatter that assessment with a piercing remark or astute observation far beyond his years.

'Then he's a fool.' Heulwen tossed her head. 'I've bathed enough men in courtesy to know what sometimes happens if they've been continent for too long. I won't be embarrassed.'

'No,' Renard quirked his brow, 'but he might.'

Adam stood in blank contemplation of the steaming tub, while around him the maids bustled, checking the temperature of the water, scattering in a handful of herbs, laying out towels of thick softened linen, setting more logs on the fire and fresh charcoal in the braziers to offset the seeping cold from the thick stone walls.

'I'm sorry if I made a mistake,' Heulwen said, lowering

10

the curtain behind her. 'I thought that a bath would be a comfort after a long day on the road.'

His mouth smiled, but his eyes remained on a distant point beyond her. 'And so it is. As you said, I was just being a churl.'

She considered him. There had been no engagement in his voice; she might as well be speaking to a tilt yard dummy for all the response she was receiving, and her irritation flared. 'Is it just a matter of venting the heat?' she asked in a practical tone. 'Shall I summon one of the soldiers' sluts?'

That at least elicited a gratifying widening of his eyes. 'What?' The pitch of his voice revealed that he had heard her perfectly well, but did not quite believe his ears.

'Well, what other reason could you have for refusing a bath? You can't be shy and you are not the kind to take vows of abstinence in order to purify your soul.'

'I didn't refuse.' He compressed his lips.

'You tried.'

'Because I'm tired and I haven't the wit or patience to match bright talk with you!' he snapped, and through the anger and shock, realised she was baiting him to see just how far his temper and credulity would stretch. As of old.

'That's better,' she approved. 'I was beginning to think you had remained in Germany and sent a wax effigy home in your stead, and were afraid of it melting in the bath water.'

Adam suppressed the urge to throttle her out of hand; and then his sense of humour fought its way to the surface and stepped carelessly upon the ruins of his pride. He snorted. 'You did that apurpose.'

11

'I wanted to destroy that mask you're wearing, and I've succeeded, have I not?' Her head cocked to one side, she studied him. 'Was the Empress so awful, then?'

'I've experienced worse,' he said, smiling now.

'Churl!' she repeated, and laughed. 'All right, I'll stop plaguing you for the moment. Here, give me your surcoat!' Efficiently, she whisked the garment from him, then exclaimed with pleasure at the quality of the silk, and with regret that it was snagged and marked with rust from his hauberk.

'It keeps the sun off your mail,' he said, laying aside the swordbelt, 'and it's good for impressing the peasants – essential to the escort of an empress.'

Heulwen helped him remove his weather-stained mail shirt. 'This needs scouring before you can wear it again,' she tutted as she dropped it on the floor and spread it out. 'I'll have it sent to the armoury. There have been several Welsh attacks this year, including the one that killed Ralf and you might need it.' Carefully she rolled the hauberk into a neat but bulky bundle, and before he could protest that he was not intending to stay and that there was no need, the garment had been spirited away for refurbishing.

He sat down on a low stool to remove his boots and hose. 'When I left, the Welsh situation was fairly quiet, otherwise I wouldn't have gone.'

'Well it's fluid now. They have a new lord over the border and he's been cutting his teeth on your lands during your absence and on Ralf's since early summer. My father hasn't had the time to engage him properly. Miles would have been of an age to take some of the burden, but Miles is dead – we can't even mourn his grave because he drowned.' She bit her lip and steadied herself. 'John's chosen the church because he's blind as a bat, so he's little use. Renard's shaping up well, but he's not old enough to bear any serious responsibility yet, and Henry and William are still only children.' She gave him a taut smile. 'Still, now you are home you can set the worst of it to rights, I am sure.'

'Oh, there's nothing I enjoy better than a good fight,' he said flippantly, and lowered his eyes to the unwinding of his garters.

Heulwen's smile dropped, and faint vertical lines appeared between her brows. Adam had always been difficult. Although not her brother by blood, she had always regarded him as such. She had romped with him in childhood – climbed trees and swung from a rope in the stables, stolen apples from the undercroft and honey cakes from beneath the cook's nose. They had shared a passion for the fine blood-horses that her father and grandfather bred. A bareback race for a dare had resulted in a thrashing. She had been confined to the bower for a week and Adam had been sent in disgrace to one of her father's other keeps to ponder the folly of his ways.

Adolescence had caught them both unawares. She had matured quickly, and at fifteen had married Ralf le Chevalier, a neighbour of theirs who was a past master in the art of training her father's destriers. It had been her admiration for his dextrous handling of all that power that had first brought them together.

As her love for Ralf blossomed, Adam had retired into uncommunicative sulks, his natural reticence becoming a full-blown unwillingness to interact with anything or anyone. She could still see him now, his expression surly, his face cursed by a red gruel of spots, his body long-shanked and uncoordinated. Ye withal, he had had a peculiar grace, and a way with a sword. And even if he wore a constant scowl, he was always reliable and diligent.

Taking his shirt now, she clucked her tongue over its threadbare state. 'I notice the Empress was not so finicky about garments not on display,' she remarked. 'You must let me measure you and get the seamstresses to stitch you some new clothes.'

'Organising my life for me?' he needled her.

Heulwen laughed and handed his remaining garments to the maid. 'What else are sisters for?' As she looked teasingly over her shoulder at him, the laughter left her face and her stomach wallowed. Her mind had been talking to the lanky, spotty boy of her childhood. Now the illusion was stripped bare, as if shed with his garments, and she found herself confronting Adam the man, a stranger she did not know. Renard had warned her and she had not listened, and now it was too late.

The spots had gone, replaced by the ruddy glint of beard stubble prickling through his travel-burned skin. His hair was sun-streaked, the russet-brown bleached to bronze where it had been most exposed, and his eyes were the colour of dark honey. His thin, long nose was marred midway by a ridge of thickened bone where it had been broken and reset slightly askew, and a faint white scar from the same incident ran from beneath his nose into the lopsided long curve of his upper lip. Her glance flickered lower, taking in a physique that was no longer out of proportion. There were a few scars on his body too that had not been there before. One of them,

14

obviously recent and still pink, curved like a new moon over his hip. Hastily she looked away and gestured him to step into the tub. Her throat was suddenly dry and her loins, in contrast, were liquid. Never would she have thought to apply the term 'beautiful' to Adam de Lacey, but the cygnet had shed its down, and more besides. 'You have seen some hard fighting recently,' she said hoarsely, and busied herself finding a dish of soap.

He stepped into the oval tub and sat down. The water was hot, making him gasp and flinch, but at least it concealed the more unpredictable parts of his anatomy from her view. 'We were attacked several times on the road by routiers and outlaws. They picked the wrong victim in me, but some of them took the devil of convincing. Am I supposed to use this?'

She took back the soap dish she had just handed to him with a puzzled look.

'I shall smell as sweet as a Turkish comfit!' he elaborated with a genuine laugh.

Irritated at her mistake, she replaced the rose attar lavender concoction with something less scented.

'Renard told me about Ralf,' Adam said into the uneasy atmosphere. 'I'm sorry. He was a good man, and I know you loved him.'

Heulwen straightened up like a warrior preparing to resist a blow. Yes, Ralf had been a good man: a fine warrior and superlative horseman, all that men would admire. But he had been a poor husband and an unfaithful one, rutting after other women the way his stallions did after mares on heat – and then there was the matter of all that unaccounted-for silver in their strongbox. 'It is never safe to build on quicksand,' she said with a hint of bitterness, and fetched him a shirt and tunic of her father's, his own baggage still being below in the hall.

'What about Ralf's stallions?'

Heulwen shrugged her shoulders. 'I thought I might sell them, but two of the three are only half trained and could be worth much more if they were properly schooled.'

He returned to his ablutions. Women and warhorses. Le Chevalier had been expert in the art of taming both. Adam only had the latter skill, learned out of a jealous need to prove that he was as good as the man Heulwen had chosen to love, a skill in which, as a mature man, he now took a deep and justifiable pride. 'I could finish Ralf's work,' he offered diffidently.

Heulwen hesitated, then shook her head. 'I couldn't take advantage of you when you're so recently home.'

'You would be doing me a service. I haven't worked on a horse since leaving for Germany, and it will give me space to relax between curbing the Welsh and organising my lands. I am the one who would be beholden.'

His eyes met hers and then he averted them. 'Well then, thank you,' she capitulated with a nod. 'There are two half-trained stallions as I said, and one that Ralf was hoping to sell at Windsor this Christmas feast.'

Adam stepped from the tub and dried himself on the towels laid out. Turning his back, he quickly donned the clothes she had found for him. Struggling with a sense of hopelessness, he felt like a fish caught by the gills in a net. Oh Heulwen, Heulwen!

'They're stabled in the bailey. My father and Renard

have been exercising them since Ralf died.' Her expression brightened. 'You can see them now if you like – if you're not too travel-worn. There's time before dinner.'

'No, I'm not too travel-worn,' he said, glad of an excuse to leave this chamber and their forced proximity. Although she had made the initial suggestion, he was the one to move first towards the door. 'I'm never too tired to look at a good horse.'

She smiled with sour amusement. 'That's what I thought you'd say.'

Hands on hips, Adam watched Eadric and two undergrooms lead the three destriers around the paddock at the side of the stables. There was a rangy dark bay, handsome and spirited, a showy piebald, eminently saleable but of less calibre than the bay, and a sorrel of Spanish blood with cream mane and tail and the high-stepping carriage of a prince. It was to the last that Adam went, drawn by admiration to slap the satin hide and feel it rippling and firm beneath his palm.

'Vaillantif was Ralf's favourite too,' Heulwen said, watching him run his hand down the stallion's foreleg to pick up and examine a hoof. 'He was riding him when he died.'

Adam looked round at her and carefully set the hoof back down. 'And the Welsh didn't keep him?'

'I don't think they had time . . .'

'I'd have made time if I were a Welsh raider.' He nodded to the groom, and with a practised leap was smoothly astride the stallion's broad, bare back. The destrier fought the bit, but Adam soothed and cajoled him, gripped with his thighs and knees, and urged with his heels.

17

Heulwen watched him take Vaillantif on a circuit of the paddock and her stomach churned as he went through the same routines as Ralf had done, with the same assurance, his spine aligned to every movement the horse made. Even without a saddle, his seat was easy and graceful. Vaillantif high-stepped with arched crest. He rapidly changed leading forefeet. A command from Adam and he reared up and danced on his hind legs. Another command dropped his forefeet to the ground and eased him into a relaxed trot and then a ground-consuming smooth canter. A quick touch on the rump and he back-kicked.

Adam brought him round before her and dismounted, pleasure flushing beneath his tan. 'I've never ridden better,' he declared with boyish enthusiasm. 'Heulwen, he's worth a king's ransom!'

'God send that you should ever look on a woman thus!' she laughed.

His face changed, as if a shutter had been slammed across an open window. 'What makes you think I haven't?' he said, giving all his attention to the horse.

Heulwen drew breath to ask the obvious question, but was forestalled by the noise of the hunting party clattering into the bailey, and turned to shade her eyes against the slant of the sun to watch their return.

Her father sat his courser with the ease of a born horseman. He was bareheaded, and the breeze ruffled his silver-scattered dark hair and carried the sound of his laughter as he responded to a remark made by the woman riding beside him.

A packhorse bearing the carcass of a roebuck was being led away towards the kitchen slaughter shed where the butchering was carried out. The houndkeeper and his lad were taking charge of the dogs that enveloped the humans knee deep. A white gazehound bitch clung jealously to the Earl's side, nose thrusting at his hand.

'Yes, he's still got Gwen,' Heulwen replied to Adam's raised brows. 'It's the first time since her pups were born that she's left them to run with the hunt. If you ask Papa nicely, he might give you one once they're weaned.'

'Who says I want a dog?'

'Company for you at Thornford.'

He angled her a dubious look and started across the crowded bailey.

Lord Guyon, alerted by a groom, lifted his head and before Adam had taken more than half a dozen paces, was striding to meet him. His wife gathered her skirts and hastened in his wake.

'We'd given you up for a ghost!' Guyon clasped Adam in a brief, muscular bearhug.

'Yes, graceless whelp, why did you not write!' This reproach was from Lady Judith, who embraced him in her turn and kissed him warmly, her hazel-grey eyes alight with pleasure.

'It wasn't always easy to find a quiet corner, the places and predicaments I was in, and you know I have no talent with parchment and quill.'

Lady Judith laughed in wry acknowledgement. Her foster-son was literate through sheer perseverance – hers and the priest's – but he would never write a fluent hand. His characters had a disturbing tendency to arrive on the parchment either back to front or upside down. 'No excuses,' she said sternly, 'you could have found a scribe, I am sure.'

19

Adam tried without success to look crestfallen. '*Mea culpa.*'

'So,' said Judith with a hint of asperity that reminded Adam for a moment of her half-sister the Empress, 'what brings you to the sanctuary of home comfort when you could be preening at court?'

Adam spread his hands. 'My task was fulfilled and the King gave me leave to attend my lands until Christmas.'

'Henry is back in England?' Judith took his arm and began to walk with him to the keep. 'Last we heard he was in Rouen.'

'Yes, and in fine spirits. He gave me letters for you and your lord. I have them in my baggage.'

Lady Judith sighed and looked ruefully at her husband. Letters from Henry were rarely social. Frequently they were commands or querulous complaints, and usually they elicited ripe epithets from her husband who had perforce to deal with them. 'Can they wait until after dinner?' she asked with more hope than expectation.

Guyon gave a caustic laugh. 'They'll either spoil my dinner or my digestion. What's the difference?'

Judith shot him a reproving scowl. 'The difference is that you can decently wait until Adam has settled himself. If the news was urgent, I am sure he would have given it to you immediately.'

'Scold!' Guyon complained, opening and shutting his hand in mimicry of his wife's jaw, but he was grinning.

Her eyes narrowed with amusement. 'Do you not deserve it?' Turning her attention from him, she looked around the hall. 'Where's Renard?'

'Training the falconer's daughter to the lure I very

much suspect,' Heulwen replied. 'That new hawk of his is past needing his full attention.'

Judith cast her glance heavenwards. 'I swear that boy has the morals of a tom-cat!'

'He'll settle down soon enough once the novelty of what he can do with it wears off,' Guyon said, unperturbed. 'The falconer's lass is no innocent chick to be devoured at a pounce. She'll peck him where it hurts if he dares beyond his welcome.' He nodded down the hall at the knot of men clustered at a trestle and deftly changed the subject. 'Sweyn and Jerold are still with you, I see, but I don't recognise the other two or the lad.'

'I'll introduce you,' Adam answered. 'The boy's my squire, Ferrers's bastard. His father had him marked out for a career in the church, but he was thrown out of the noviciate for setting fire to the refectory and fornicating in the scriptorium with a guest's maidservant. Ferrers asked me to take Austin on and fit him for a life by the sword. He's shaping well so far. I might ask to keep him when he's knighted.'

Guyon, thirty years of winnowing wheat from chaff behind him, looked the men over with a critical eye. Sweyn, Adam's English bodyguard, was as dour and solid as ever, his mouth resembling a scarred, weathered crack in a chunk of granite. Jerold FitzNigel had been with Adam for more than ten years – a softly spoken Norman with rheumy blue eyes, a sparse blond moustache, and the lankiness of a sun-drawn seedling. His appearance was deceptive, for he was as tough and sinewy as boiled leather.

The two new men were a pair of Angevin mercenary cousins with dark eyes and swift, sharp smiles. Guyon would not have trusted either one further than he could throw a spear. Ferrers's lad was a compact, sturdy youth with intelligent hazel eyes, a tumble of wood-shaving curls, and a snub nose that made him look younger than his seventeen years and a good deal more innocent than his history.

The group also numbered a dozen hard-bitten men-at-arms, survivors of numerous skirmishes across the patchwork of duchies and principalities lying between England and the German empire. A motley collection, but all wearing the assurance of honed fighters.

'They're good men to have at your back in a tight corner,' Adam said, as they left the soldiers to arrange their belongings out of the way of the trestles that were being set out ready for the evening meal.

'Were my doubts so plain?' Guyon looked rueful. 'I must be getting old.' He glanced sideways at Adam. 'Will they not grow restless without battle?'

'Probably, but I don't foresee a problem. I'm not expecting there to be much peace.'

The glance hardened. 'In that case, you had better let me see that letter now,' he muttered.

Adam shrugged. 'I can tell you and spare my squire's feet. I know what's in it because I was there when Henry dictated it to his scribe. You are summoned to attend the Christmas feast at Windsor, and your family with you.'

Guyon relaxed, and with a grunt led Adam to the small solar at the far end of the hall, which was screened from the main room by a fine, carved wooden partition and a curtained archway. 'Not just for the joy of seeing his grandsons, I'll warrant,' he said cynically as he sat down on a pelt-covered stool. 'Since the death of his heir, Henry's been so eaten up with envy of my own brood that it hasn't been safe to make mention of them, let alone set them beneath his nose, William in particular.'

Hardly surprising, thought Adam. King Henry had fathered over a score of bastards, Lady Judith among them, but his only legitimate son had drowned and his new young wife showed no signs of quickening. The *White Ship* had been a magnificent vessel, new and sleek when she was boarded in Barfleur on a cold November evening by the younger element of the court, intent on catching up with the other ships that had left for England earlier in the afternoon. The passengers were well into their cups, the crew also, and the ship had foundered on a rock before she even cleared the harbour, with the loss of almost everyone on board. Guyon's firstborn son and heir had also been a victim of the *White Ship* disaster, but there were four other boys to follow, the last one born only a month after the sinking. 'He's inviting everyone else too, for the purpose of binding their allegiance to Matilda as his successor.'

Guyon rubbed at a bark stain on his chausses. 'Bound to come I suppose,' he sighed. 'She is, after all, his only direct heir, but it won't be a popular move. Is he expecting a rebellion?'

'Reluctance, yes. Rebellion no.'

The lines at the corners of Guyon's mouth deepened. 'Some will come very near to it,' he said, frowning. 'It's going to stick in the craw to have to render homage to a woman – a foreign woman at that – and from what I hear of her, Matilda won't offer them a sweetener to

23

help them swallow their bleeding pride. She'd rather see them choke on it.' He cast Adam a speculative look. 'What about William le Clito? He's the King's nephew by his older brother, and certainly has prior right to Normandy, if not to the throne.'

'Are you one of le Clito's supporters?'

'God's balls, no!' Guyon gave a short bark of laughter. 'What do you take me for? The lad's no more set up to rule than a blind hawk's capable of bringing down prey! He's done nothing all his life but dance to the French King's schemes! If I favoured anyone, it would be one of Henry's other nephews, Stephen of Blois, and even then I'm not so sure. He's too good-natured and not enough iron in his soul to be strong like Henry.'

Adam nudged a sprig of dried lavender among the rushes with the tip of his boot. 'What about Robert of Gloucester? He's Henry's son, and he's got the stamina that Stephen lacks.'

Guyon dismissed Adam's candidate with a wave of his hand. 'If we allowed ourselves to think of him as our future king, we'd have to consider all the other royal by-blows, and they number as many as the years Henry's been on the throne, and include my own wife. Besides, Gloucester's not like that, and I know him well enough to trust one of my sons in squirehood to him. He's not the kind to desire the weight of a crown on his head, and he used to worship the ground Matilda trod on when they were small children.'

Adam dipped his head. 'Point taken.'

Guyon looked shrewdly at Adam. 'But, if we swear for Matilda, then we also swear for her future husband, whoever he might be – or do we have a say in that?

24

Knowing Henry for the slippery creature he is, I think not.'

Adam took a mental back-step, realising from whom Renard had inherited his sudden thrusts of perception.

'Do you know who he might be?' Guyon pursued. 'No clues on your long tramp from Germany?'

Adam felt his ears burning. 'No, sir.' He watched his toe crush the strand of lavender and all the little dried balls fall off into the rushes. A pungent, herbal smell drifted past his nostrils.

'Fair enough.'

'It's not that . . .'

Guyon shook his head. 'If you cannot speak, then so be it. Doubtless I'll learn soon enough. Suffice to see that you are keeping your fighting men. I know what to expect.'

'I'm not keeping them so much for that purpose as for the Welsh.' Adam uttered the half-truth, half-lie with what he hoped was plausible sincerity. After all, it was only what he had inadvertently overheard between the King and the Bishop of Salisbury, whose tentative discussion had been more an examination of possibilities than anything solid. 'Heulwen said that there is a new lord across the dyke causing trouble?'

'Davydd ap Tewdr,' Guyon said with a grimace. 'And trouble is not the word. Either that or I'm slowing down. He's been running rings around me and the patrols. He claims that my tenants and Ralf's have encroached beyond his boundaries. Well, you can't stop the farmers grazing their beasts where they see good pasture, and the animals can't tell the difference between Welsh grass and English grass – it all tastes the same. There's bound

25

to be some encroachment, and I'd be a naïve fool if I believed it was all one-sided. I suppose I should take my troop across the border and hunt him down, but he's skilled in woodcraft, and I'd not be assured of the victory. I've even toyed with the thought of offering him a marriage alliance now that Heulwen's a widow. She's Welsh on her mother's side and part of mine through her namesake my grandmother, but I've as good as committed myself to de Mortimer's offer when it is made official.'

Adam was horrified. 'Jesu – you surely don't mean to accept!'

Guyon shrugged. 'Warrin's father is a personal friend. He mooted the idea of a match between them more than ten years ago, but Heulwen had already drawn her bow at Ralf and I turned the offer down. Since then, Hugh's been trying to pair off his infant daughter with Renard, but I have no intention of accepting. This will ease the pressure on me. Besides, with the Welsh being so troublesome, we need authority like Warrin's along the border. Widows don't stay widows long in the marches. It is too dangerous, and Heulwen accepts the fact of an early remarriage.'

'You are willing to sacrifice her in the name of policy?'

Guyon looked irritated. 'Grow up, Adam. How often are matches made without a practical reason behind them? It's hardly a sacrifice. She likes him well enough, and Warrin's matured since those early days. Still likes his own way and has the will to get it, but that happens to be an advantage when it comes to dealing with my daughter. She'd walk all over a man of less character. You know what she's like.'

'Not the kind to live in amity with a man of de Mortimer's ilk for long,' Adam said thickly. 'What will you do if he thrashes her? As I remember, it was his every remedy for those who baulked his will or answered him back.'

'I told you, he's learned control since then. People change as they mature. She is my only daughter, and precious for the memory of her mother as well as for herself. I would never put her in a situation where I thought she would be unhappy.'

Adam said nothing, but his lips thinned.

'I realise that you and Warrin hate the sight of each other, that it goes gut-deep, and I know you are tired from your journey, so I make allowances. Suffice to say the final choice is my daughter's. I won't constrain her to anything she does not desire of her own free will, and she knows it.'

Adam pinched the bridge of his nose. Gut-deep, so Guyon said. Yes, it affected him thus: a quivering tension in the belly, but it also ran bone-deep and soul-deep, and was not something he would ever be able to discuss with detachment. Better to change the subject before there was a rift.

'How fares Lord Miles? Is he still well?'

'Fit as a flea considering his years!' Guyon laughed with relief in his voice, equally anxious not to quarrel. 'The damp plagues his bones and he tires more quickly than he used to, particularly since Alicia's death. She was a full ten years younger than he was and he always thought he would go first. He's taken William into the hills for a few days. The boy wants to learn to track like a Welshman, and my father's obliging, although I don't believe the lad's capable of keeping still for longer than the time it takes to blink. They're due home tomorrow or the next day.'

Adam said ruefully, 'I keep thinking of William as a babe in arms, it hardly seems a day since his baptism.'

'Three months after the *White Ship* went down and our future security with it.' Guyon's expression was suddenly harsh. 'God grant the lad a warrior's arm and a lawyer's cunning when he comes to manhood. He's going to need both.'

2

Adam snapped open his eyes and listened to the darkness with pounding heart and straining ears. The air in the small wall chamber was as thick as black wool and as difficult to breathe. Sweat crawled over his body like an army of spiders. Uttering a groan, he bent his forearm across his eyes.

At the foot of his pallet the straw rustled. 'Sire?' his squire said anxiously and Adam heard the youth fumbling about for tinder and flint, then striking a spark on some shavings and lighting the candle. Jagged shadows flickered on the walls and made him think of the descriptions of hell that zealous priests sometimes fed their congregations.

'Sire?' the squire said again.

Adam lowered his arm and saw the frightened glitter in the youth's eyes. 'I'm all right, Austin, nothing but a bad dream.' Sitting up, he motioned to the wine jug.

The youth splashed a half-measure into the cup beside it and anxiously handed it across. Adam drank thirstily, then looked over the rim at the youth. 'Oh in God's name, stop staring at me like that, I'm all right. With the sort of life we've led recently, the wonder would be if I did not ride the nightmares!'

Austin chewed his lip. 'Sorry, sir. It is just that you seemed troubled earlier before we retired.'

Troubled was not the word. Adam shook his head mutely at the youth and thought of Heulwen in her tawny gown, the curves of her figure outlined by the tight lacing from armpit to waist, and the belt of pearls and gold thread encircling her hips. He had been hard pressed to keep his eyes on his meal and his thoughts upon what people were saying to him.

He lay down again, hands clasped behind his head and, closing his eyes, saw her belt once more in his mind's eye. It had been Ralf's bride-gift. Ralf, whose taste in trinkets, horses and women had never been less than impeccable.

Sleep had flown. His mind blew hither and yon like a bird on a storm wind. The stiff linen sheet scratched his skin. The boy's anxiety was tangible and stifling, and he began to wish he had made him sleep below with the other men of the escort. He was well aware of the heroic qualities with which the lad had imbued him as his saviour from the cloister, and was both amused and irritated. He was only human, and the sooner Austin grew out of treating him like a god and grew up, the more comfortable they both would be.

Adam sat up again, reaching for his clothes. 'Go back to sleep, lad,' he said, and began to dress with swift economy of movement. 'It's still the dead of night. I'm going up on the wall walk for a breath of clean air.'

Lying on his pallet, Austin watched his lord fasten his

cloak and slip quietly from the room. Austin knew something was badly wrong and that it had a connection to the handsome flame-haired widow who called Lord Adam 'brother'. He was sure his lord had groaned her outlandish name as he threshed about in his dream. It was not something he could ask about, nor did he have the scope to understand, for as yet, women were no more to him than a passing carnal interest. Puzzling and worried, he lay back down and shut his eyes, but it was a long time before he slept, and still his lord had not returned.

The night was clear and cold, more than a hint of autumn on the breeze blowing from the River Dee. Adam paced the wall walk and inhaled the scents of starlight and water. In the stables a horse neighed and the sound carried up to him, as did the laughter of the men on watch as they warmed their hands at a fire in an open part of the bailey.

Adam remembered the numerous nights he had spent as a squire, taking his turn on watch, eyes skinned upon empty moonlight. Henry's reign had been mostly peaceful and Ravenstow was impregnable to Welsh assault, but guard duty was still taken seriously. It was a practice for the warfare which might be visited upon them if the King's robust health failed, or if strife arose from this swearing of allegiance to his daughter, Matilda.

He thought about his own lands. His father's possessions had been confiscated by the crown during the rebellion of 1102, but Thornford and its dependent manors were his, and there was another manor near Shrewsbury. He was by rank of land a small fish in a wide ocean, but his connections nonetheless made him an important one. He was the lord of Ravenstow's foster-son, had spent his late adolescence as a squire in the royal household, and had made influential friends and contacts while attending there. Henry trusted him – as far as Henry trusted anyone – and had promised him reward for his loyalty and service. Adam was wise enough not to anticipate the event too eagerly: promises were one matter, their fulfilling, where the King was concerned, another.

A guard ascended the wall walk, a huge fawn mastiff padding beside him on a leash. He saluted Adam, who acknowledged him, admiring the dog's armoury of teeth from a wary distance before turning to pace the battle-ments. Another guard in a cowled cloak was leaning against one of the merlons, his face in shadow. When he failed to salute, Adam paused in surprise and stepped back. Ravenstow's constable took the keep's discipline seriously and would lean hard on a man neglecting his duty.

'Look sharp, soldier!' he snapped, realising too late as the figure turned with a startled gasp, that it was not a guard at all. 'What are you doing here?' he demanded, almost angry that even up here on the wall walk in the dead of night there was no escape.

Heulwen stared at him, her eyes wide with surprise. He could see the starlit gleam of their whites. 'I came here to think,' she said a little breathlessly. 'It's open here; your thoughts are not squashed by walls.' She considered him, her head cocked on one side. 'And you?'

'I came for solitude,' he said harshly, then swore beneath his breath. 'I'm being a churl again, aren't I?'

He sensed the deepening of her smile. 'Yes, you are.'

'I – I had a nightmare, and my squire was making a fuss.' He looked down. 'I don't remember what happened, and I don't believe I want to.' He shivered, the hairs on his forearms standing straight up.

'At least yours was only a dream.' She turned, putting down the hood of her cloak so that her face emerged, framed in the silvery nocturnal light.

Adam swallowed. Her hair was exposed, braided in a thick plait ready for bed, its glorious colour cooled and muted by the starlight. His mind and body blended into one dull ache. 'I know you grieve deeply for Ralf,' he said unsteadily.

One side of her mouth turned up. 'Ralf!' she exhaled mockingly. 'Jesu God, I've been grieving for years, but not for him.' She glanced at him quickly. 'I had to have him, Adam, whatever the cost. Do you know what it is to burn? I don't suppose you do. Well, I burned until everything turned to ashes, and if I have taken it badly, it is because that is all I have left.' She rubbed her arms within her miniver-lined mantle.

Adam, who knew precisely what it was to burn, could only stare at her, burning still, barred from touching. 'Heulwen, I . . .'

'No, don't commiserate.' She laughed bitterly. 'I don't think I could bear it, and besides, it doesn't suit you.' She laid an impulsive hand on his sleeve. 'Look Adam, I know it's late, and I know you came here for solitude, but there is a matter sorely troubling me, and I need to talk to someone.'

He gnawed his lip, desiring to deny her and bolt for the safety of the restless bed from which he had so recently absconded, but he was powerless to refuse the pleading note in her voice He looked down at her hand gripping his. It was slender and long-fingered, the feminine image of her father's and adorned on the wedding finger by a ring of braided gold.

'How could I refuse?' he asked with a grim smile, and wished he knew the answer.

The wine made a musical sound as she poured it into two goblets of trellised glass. The candles were reflected in the bronze flagon, which had a handle shaped like a dragon's head, the eyes inlaid with garnets and the tongue curling between sharply incised fangs. An embroidery frame stood near the brazier and he went to peruse the boldly worked pattern. It was the hem of a man's tunic, sewn with couchant leopards in thread of gold on a dark woollen background. Lady Judith's work, he thought, recognising the style. Heulwen had never owned the patience for more than the most rudimentary needlecraft.

'It's a new court robe for my father.' She handed him the wine. 'He'll be needing it, if what I heard is true.'

'That all the tenants-in-chief are summoned to swear for Matilda, you mean? Yes, it's true.'

'Ralf said something about it before he was killed. About Matilda being our future queen.'

Adam swallowed a mouthful of his wine to be polite, and put the cup down. 'It was fairly obvious once Henry summoned her from Germany.'

Heulwen gave him an appraising look. 'There was more to it than that. He knew something, and it was setting him on edge. I asked him to tell me, but he laughed and said that it was nothing – patted me on the head like a dog, and rode away to his death.' She paused as if debating whether to take the final step, then drew a swift breath. 'When the funeral was being arranged, I had cause to check our strongbox. Ralf always kept the keys himself; he wouldn't let me near it, so I never knew until he was dead how rich we actually were – too rich for our standing. I know he made a good profit from the horses, but not to the tune of what was in that chest.'

Adam looked at her sharply. 'You mean it was ill come by? Heulwen, how much?'

'Two hundred marks.'

Adam whistled. 'Christ, if I had that much to my name, I'd be a happy man! That's more than an inheritance relief on some baronies!'

'A great amount for a "nothing",' she said savagely.

Adam's lips remained pursed. 'But,' he mused, 'was he being paid to keep it a "nothing", or was he being paid to reveal it in all its glory? Or perhaps both?'

Her voice was alarmed. 'What do you mean?'

'Ralf travelled far and wide. He was renowned for his skill and valued for it by men of much greater estate than himself. I know for a fact that on more than one occasion he carried messages between Henry and Fulke of Anjou . . .' He paused. Her eyes had gone wide with shock. 'You didn't know?'

The wine shook in one hand, while the other was clenched in the folds of her gown. 'I was ever the last one to know,' she said bitterly. 'I suppose it is common knowledge.'

'Not common knowledge,' he said gently, 'except to those of us involved in that kind of game.'

'Adam?'

He gave her a quick, vinegary smile. 'It's a night for surprises, isn't it?'

'You are saying that you and Ralf were – are spies for Henry?'

'I wouldn't quite say that. We have occasionally carried messages – verbal ones that could not be entrusted to parchment.' His look became thoughtful. 'But the payment for such was never a tenth so high.'

'Then betrayal . . .' she whispered, appalled.

Adam shrugged. 'I'd certainly say he was dabbling his fingers in a murky broth, but how deep I don't know.' He rubbed his chin. 'Have you spoken to anyone else about this?'

'No, I've kept it to myself – half the reason my temper has been so foul. Papa has too much on his trencher already, and it was easier to pretend it didn't exist.' She shivered. 'But it does, and I'm frightened.'

It was the lost, forlorn note in her voice that finally undid him. Until then he had succeeded in maintaining a neutral front, but the sight of her so close to tears, trembling with fear, her spirit subdued, was unbearable and before he could rationalise the move, think better of it and step away, he had put his arm around her and drawn her against him. 'It's all right, Heulwen,' he said with a mingling of tenderness and desire, 'I won't let any harm come to you.'

A sob wrenched from her throat, followed by another. She pressed her face into his chest, stifling her grief in the dark wool of his tunic. Adam murmured reassurances and stroked her braid. Her hair smelt faintly of herbs and he was intensely aware of her body pressed

36

to his. He slipped his arm down to her waist. 'Heulwen . . .' he muttered and lowered his head, seeking sideways, finding and kissing her cheek and temple, and then, as she raised her head in surprise, her mouth. It opened beneath his, pliant and warm, sweet as wine. His hand slipped down over the curve of her buttocks, moulding her closer. For less than the space of a heart-beat her body undulated and yielded to his, and then she jerked like a skittish horse fighting a saddle, tore her mouth from his, and shoved herself violently out of his embrace.

'Adam no!' She dragged her sleeve across her mouth. 'Dear God, no!'

'Heulwen . . .' He took a step towards her, hand outstretched in entreaty. 'It's not . . .'

Quivering, she backed away, grabbing her cloak off the stool where she had flung it. 'I'm not some wide-legged slut to be tumbled at your whim. If you want that sort of pleasure, you know where the guardroom is!'

Adam's eyes darkened. Torn between fury that she should bring it down to this base level, and shame at his own loss of control, he could only stare at her, bereft of words. Heulwen stared back. The air between them trembled. Then she turned from him and fled.

'Oh blood of Christ!' he snarled and plunged after her, but in the darkness he stumbled over someone's pallet and came down hard among the rushes, the disturbed sleeper cursing him in English. Adam snapped a scalding reply in gutter French, and struggled up again. In the dim light from the banked fire he could see the snoring servants and men-at-arms, the polished brown highlights of the lord's oak chair set on the dais, a dreaming dog twitching its paws, but no Heulwen.

Adam swore again, this time at his own stupidity, and dug his fingers through his hair. He had meant only to comfort, had not realised until he held her how precarious was the line between the need to comfort and the need itself, and his lack of judgement had just cost him dearly. The memory of her frightened anger filled him with chagrin. What if she loathed him now?

He returned to the solar, found the garnet-eyed flagon and his cup, and set about seeking oblivion in lieu of the sleep that he knew would not come.

3

Miles, lord of Ashdyke, watched his youngest grandson leap and turn and, with his wooden sword, cut beneath the defences of an imaginary foe. The old man sighed deeply and propped his aching legs on the footstool that Heulwen attentively fetched for him.

'It's a long time since I was even half so agile,' he told her wistfully. 'He's faster than a flea.' In his eyes there was pride, for he recognised much of himself in the slight, elfin boy, or as he remembered himself in the unfettered days of a long-distant childhood.

Heulwen watched her half-brother too, wincing as he clipped the laver and almost sent it crashing over. 'I suppose you let him wear you out, Grandpa,' she scolded gently, bringing him a cup of wine.

'Not in the least.' Miles grinned. 'It has been a pleasure to have him with me. He's deadly with a slingshot. Brought down two big pigeons that had been damaging the seedlings in the garth – and very tasty they were too.'

Heulwen smiled dutifully, the expression not quite

reaching her eyes which were full of care. Miles sought her fingers and squeezed them. She looked down at his hand. It was brown and mottled with a twisting blue rootwork of veins, but it was hard and steady and it was her own young unblemished one that trembled. She cast him an anxious look, which he returned with the serenity of long years. 'We had a visitor while you were away with William.'

Miles slowly nodded and smiled. 'I know. Young de Lacey. Eadric told me when I arrived. I dare say when I've rested these old bones enough to want to sit a saddle again, I'll ride over to Thornford and welcome him home.' His gaze was shrewd. 'Are you going to tell me what's wrong?'

Heulwen looked down. 'I've quarrelled with Adam,' she said in a small voice and swallowed, thinking of the incident of two nights since. She had asked him to the solar, forced her dilemma on him, and then, when his sympathy had turned into something far more dangerous, she had reacted like a wild animal striving to break free of a trap. Even worse, she had accused him as though it had all been his fault, when she knew to her shame that it was not. Her own body had quick-ened readily to desire, and when she had run from him, she had been running from herself. The following day she had pleaded a megrim as an excuse not to come down to the hall, and Adam, without personal invita-tion, could not go above. He had asked to speak to her and she had sent her maid Elswith to tell him she was unwell. He had taken the hint, gathered his men and ridden out, and the silence left behind weighed heavily on her conscience.

40

'There's nothing new in that, as I recall from your childhood,' Miles said wryly.

William danced up to them. Heulwen opened her mouth, but said nothing. Panting, the child paused to regain his breath, and bestowed upon her a dazzling, impish smile. The youngest of her father's sons, he had a profusion of bouncy black curls, green-blue eyes like her own and their grandfather's and a way with him that could charm the birds from the trees.

'Heulwen, can I go and see Gwen's pups? Papa's gone into the town to talk to the merchants and Mama's busy in the dairy. Eadric said I had to ask you.' He put on his pleading face, managing to look almost as soulful as Gwen herself, so that Heulwen was forced to laugh.

She tousled his hair. 'Go on then but be careful, and don't get too close. She's still very protective.'

'I won't, I promise. Mama says I can have one for my very own when they're old enough to leave Gwen. I've seen the one I want – the black dog with the white paws. I'm going to call him Brith.'

Heulwen felt a pang for childhood's earnest enthusiasms, the passionate joy in small things, the blissful ignorance of wider concerns, and the tragedies forgotten in the time as it took to wipe away the tears. William gave her a brief, tight hug and, sword still in hand, ran off down the hall.

'And Judith worries about Renard and women!' Miles chuckled. 'William is going to outstrip him a hundred-fold when the time comes. I can only be glad that I won't be here to wince as the sparks fly!'

'Don't say that!' Her tone was sharp.

'It's the truth, girl, and we both know it. I'm borrowing

time hand over fist these days, and when I do go, I dare say I'll be glad.' He leaned back against the carved oak chair and steepled his fingers against his lips. His eyes were still keen, his voice steady without the quaver that so often affected the elderly, and his face betrayed to Heulwen none of the fatigue that was inwardly sapping him. He could not however sustain bursts of energy for long periods these days, and had to husband his strength like a housewife coddling a contrary tallow flame. He was more than four score, an age seldom attained and, slowly but inexorably, his body was failing his will.

'Now then,' he said comfortably, 'what about this quarrel of yours. Can it not be mended?'

Hesitantly at first, but gaining impetus, Heulwen told him the tale, omitting the details about the suspect silver in Ralf's strongbox. 'I know I should have been more tactful, Grandpa, but I was frightened. One moment he was comforting my grief, the next he was kissing me . . .'

Miles closed his eyes and conjured up the image of Adam de Lacey. A quiet young man of serious countenance and direct gaze. A superlative horseman, good with a sword, even better with a lance, and not given to the kinds of folly just described to him. He looked thoughtfully at his granddaughter, well aware that she had not told him the whole tale, and she knew he knew, because she had lowered her eyes and her cheeks had turned pink.

'Foolish,' he snorted, 'but not to be wondered at. In part you brought it on yourself. You do not need a gazing glass to know you are attractive to men. Their eyes have always told you.'

42

'I didn't bring that on myself!' she objected.

'You interrupted me,' Miles said with a shake of his head. 'I was going to say that any young man who found himself alone with you, at your invitation, in the darkest hours of the night might well be pushed over a brink he didn't even know was there. His first intention probably was to offer comfort. As far as I know, Adam de Lacey is no womaniser. Your father never had trouble with him the way he did with young Miles and his lechery.'

'Do you think I owe him an apology?' she asked with a sinking heart.

'Not necessarily, but I think you were a little harsh with him. You have created a mountain out of a molehill.'

Heulwen looked down and fiddled with the raised embroidery on the belt at her waist. Her grandfather's great age had in no way incapacitated his wits, and his shrewd scrutiny was making her uncomfortable. She said quickly, 'Grandpa, I think you're right. I'll make amends as best I can.'

The light caught the silver tips of stubble on his throat as he swallowed. 'You could do worse than consider Adam de Lacey for a husband. Obviously he is attracted to you, and he's well thought of by men who recognise honour in other men.'

She dropped to kneel beside him, her knees weakening at the very suggestion. Her mind scurried, necessity making it nimble, finding an excuse out of what had once been the truth but was now the truth no longer. 'Grandpa, I couldn't, it would be like marrying one of my own brothers. Anyway, I'm as good as spoken for already.'

'I see,' he nodded wisely. 'So you are still set on accepting de Mortimer's offer?'

'Yes, Grandpa. After Ralf, I'll be grateful for a man whose absences are not going to send me into a jealous frenzy.'

She had known passion, he thought, and been burned by its heat, but there had been no healing balm of love to temper its destructive force, only lies, deceit and self-delusion, and she had been too young to understand. A marriage that was purely a business arrangement would suit her very well for the present, but what of the future? Her braids were the colour of liquid fire and they reflected her spirit. No good would come of trying to squash herself into a niche for which she was not made – but how to explain it to her when for the nonce she could not see the wood of the future for the trees of the past. 'Heulwen . . .' he began and then subsided as a seeping weariness overcame him. He felt as if all the marrow was trickling from his bones and soaking away.

'Grandpa, are you all right?' She leaped to her feet in fear. 'Here, drink some more wine.'

Miles watched her fumble for the flagon and then closed his eyes. When she pressed the cup back into his hands, he forced his lids open again, feeling as though the death pennies were already weighing them down.

Her voice trembled. 'Grandpa, I'm sorry, I shouldn't have bothered you.'

He put out his free hand and lightly touched her face as she bent over him. 'Nay, love, don't fret,' he said with a forced smile. 'I'm all right, just very tired. We'll talk again when I've had a chance to rest.'

'It doesn't matter, Grandpa. I'll make my peace with

Adam, and as soon as Warrin returns from Normandy I'll accept his offer, and that's the end of it. I'll go and get Mama.'

'Child, never mind the end, what about the beginning?' he whispered, but to thin air, for she had gathered her skirts and was running down the hall.

4

Sweating, Adam closed his eyes against the glare of the sun and gulped wine straight from the costrel. Opposing him, Jerold FitzNigel rested his swordpoint in the dust and wiped his forehead upon the back of his hand.

Red juice trickled down Adam's chin. Finished, he handed the costrel back to the knight, wiped his mouth, then, bending over, hands on knees, blew out hard through puffed cheeks.

'You're out of practice,' grinned FitzNigel, who drank heartily, then, gasping with satisfaction added, 'I'd have killed you then if we'd been using sharpened blades instead of these whalebone pretences.'

'You wouldn't,' Adam retorted with the surety of self-knowledge. Practice was practice, a repetition of various moves in a shifting dance of aggression and avoidance until perfection was accomplished – necessary, but devoid of the deadliness that gave true battle its edge. There was devastating exhilaration in pitting your skill against another man and knowing that the stake was either your life or his. But as he had no intention of murdering his marshal, Adam's edge was as dull as the rebated sword he was using.

Jerold finished drinking, stoppered the costrel and tossed it over to Austin, for whose edification this bout was partly taking place. 'Care to wager?' he challenged Adam and, spitting on his palms, raised his shield and dropped behind it to a battle crouch.

Adam wiped his right hand down his hose and applied it once more to his sword-grip. 'I'd not part you from your hard-earned coin,' he retorted, shifting his stance on Thornford's gritty practice-yard floor. As Jerold attacked, he leaped over the low swing of the blade and beneath the knight's guard, feinting at the shield and sweeping under it. Jerold sprang backwards like a startled hare and a breath came hard between his teeth. Laughing, Adam pressed his attack.

Horses clattered through the main gateway and into the bailey. Grooms went out and a servant came running in and spoke to the squire.

'Lord Adam,' Austin called, 'Miles le Gallois is here. He's brought you some horses and craves a moment of your time.'

Adam misjudged his stroke, lost his balance, and found himself once more looking down the fuller of Jerold's sword and into the knight's laughing eyes. He pushed the blade aside in disgust.

'Sorry, lord,' said Austin, biting his lip.

'My own fault, lad, I'm not concentrating.' Adam thrust the blunted sword at the boy. 'Here, take my place and see if you can improve on my performance.'

'Shouldn't be too difficult,' Jerold mocked.

Adam made an eloquent English gesture, dropped his shield and wandered into the main bailey.

An elderly man was dismounting with care from Ralf's bay destrier. Behind him, an expression of wistful pleasure on his face, Renard was loosening the sorrel stallion's girth, while beyond on a leading rein, the piebald sidled friskily.

'Lord Miles!' Adam strode forward with genuine pleasure and held out a calloused palm. 'This is indeed a surprise!'

Miles clasped the proffered hand. 'Indeed it is,' he answered, smiling as he gazed upon Adam's state of sweaty déshabillé.

'I've been practising my swordplay in the tilt yard – not with any great success. It's a relief to leave it.' Adam pushed his wet hair off his forehead.

'Grandpa has brought you these on his way home, since you forgot them in your haste to leave us.' Renard gestured towards the horses, his mouth curving with mischief. 'My sister doesn't usually have that effect on men, rather the opposite.'

Adam gave Renard a sour look. 'Perhaps I know her too well,' he retorted.

The youth shrugged. 'Or not well enough.' He fondled Vaillantif's whiskery muzzle and glanced at his own grey crossbreed. 'It's like riding silk. Old Starlight's going to seem as rough as sackcloth by comparison.'

Miles smiled at his grandson. 'You're developing expensive tastes, boy.'

'Why not – I'm the heir, aren't I?' Renard's spoke flippantly, but there was an almost bitter expression in his eyes. The sound of weapon play drifted across from the

48

direction of the tilt yard. Leaving the horses, Renard sauntered towards it.

'Too sharp for his own good sometimes, that one,' Miles said, as the grooms set about unsaddling the destriers and leading them and the remounts to the water trough. It had once been a coffin, so the priest said, undoubtedly Roman, for there was a vague weather-beaten inscription in Latin just visible on its side. 'With a tongue like that in his head, he's got to learn when to keep it sheathed.'

'Most lads of that age are indiscreet to some degree,' Adam said, thinking of his own squire's recent mis-demeanours.

'Or that's what you tell yourself in lieu of throttling them.' Miles eased himself down on the mounting block with a sigh, and spread his palms upon his knees.

Adam laughed in wry acknowledgement and signalled to a servant. 'You'll stay to dine?'

Miles thanked him for the hospitality, then added, relenting, 'Renard's a good boy really. They've sent him to see me home. Partly it's to be rid of him for a while, and he needs the responsibility and experience of commanding men. Partly it is because I wasn't well a few days ago.'

Adam looked concerned. Miles waved the air in dismissal. 'It was nothing, my own fault. I exhausted myself trying to keep up with a child of five. They say the old return to their infancy. Well by God, I paid for my foray. Judith and Heulwen had me posseted up in bed for two days and wouldn't let anyone near me.' A mischievous spark kindled in his eyes. 'I told them I'd have more company laid out dead in the chapel, and

49

made myself so difficult a patient that in the end they saw sense and just about pushed me out of the keep!' He looked over at the horses snuffling around the trough, their shadows mingling in the dust. 'Heulwen told me why you quarrelled,' he said quietly.

Adam tossed his shirt on to the ground and sat down beside it, his back to Miles so that the latter did not see his frown. 'Did she?' He twisted his fingers around a clump of grass growing near his feet, uprooting it from the dry soil.

Adam's back might be turned, but Miles could see the tension in his neck and shoulders, could feel it in the quality of the atmosphere, and thanked Christ that Renard had gone to investigate the training. He nodded towards the three stallions and said, 'She sent them by way of an apology. She knows she treated you unfairly.' The wrinkles deepened around his mouth and eyes. 'She's also very stubborn.'

Adam looked round at Miles. 'Did she tell you everything?'

Miles spread his hands. 'As much as any woman. A carefully adjusted version of the truth, I hazard. She did not explain what the two of you were doing in the solar at midnight in the first place.'

Adam lowered his gaze to the grass clod dangling between his fingers. 'We spoke of another matter too, concerning Ralf and what may be an affair of treason. Heulwen was worried, and so was I when she told me – and one thing led to another.'

'Do you want to tell me? About Ralf, I mean?'

Adam threw away the grass and stood up in one lithe movement that made Miles envious. 'No.' He rotated his left arm to ease a muscular ache and eyed the horses. 'Not yet. Not until I know more.'

Miles inched far more circumspectly to his own feet, pain knifing through his knees.

Adam went to the three stallions and began to look them over again with a knowing hand and admiring eye. He stroked Vaillantif's muzzle. The stallion butted him and mouthed the bit. He took the bridle and led him towards the training ground, a deep frown knitting his brows. He had his truce. Now all he had to do was find the grace to accept it and forget.

'It's a great pity,' Miles added, limping beside him. 'If only you hadn't grown up with her, she wouldn't be thrusting the obstacle of "brother" under your nose, and in my opinion, you're far more suited to her needs than the strutting cockerel she's determined to wed.'

They passed between the shadows cast by the corridor of two storesheds and Adam did not see the quick, calculating glance that Miles shot his way. 'I am not and have never been a brother to her,' Adam said curtly. The word sent a shudder through him. 'But it does not mean your opinion is right – with respect. I am not some willing hound to come at a whistle and be leashed because it suits the need of others.'

'That is not what I meant, and you know it. You are as difficult as my granddaughter.'

'Let it be, sire,' Adam said stiffly. Gathering the reins, he mounted Vaillantif and trotted him across the training yard to a bundle of lances that were stacked against the far wall.

The men paused in their sword practice and turned to watch him. Jerold took another swig of wine from the skin and passed it to Renard, who was now stripped to his shirt and in possession of a whalebone sword and a kite shield.

Adam leaned over the saddle and took up a lance, then rode Vaillantif to the quintain course down the long edge of the ground.

Smiling slightly, Miles strolled over to the knot of expectant men and paused beside his grandson.

'He's using the French style,' Renard said with interest as Adam couched the lance under his arm and fretted Vaillantif back on his hocks.

'Well that's because it's a French sport,' said Jerold. 'Besides, underarm's better than over. More thrust behind it when it's positioned like that.'

Renard shook his head. 'I've tried, but God's life, it's difficult.'

'Watch,' said Jerold, giving him a silencing look. 'Hold your tongue, and learn.'

The quintain was a crossbar set on a pivot, with a shield nailed to one edge and a sack of sand to the other, the objective being to strike the shield cleanly in the centre and thus avoid being struck from the saddle or severely bruised by a knock from the bag of sand.

Adam crouched behind the shield and positioned the lance across his mount's neck. He tightened the reins and Vaillantif's forefeet danced left–right on the ground. 'Hah!' he cried, and drove in his heels. Vaillantif arrowed down the tilt run, dust spurting from beneath his hooves, sunlight flashing on the bit chains, stirrup irons and bright sorrel hide. He moved effortlessly, eating the ground, and each stride that he took hammered the word *brother* into Adam's skull. The tip of the lance wavered and

52

readjusted. Adam hit the target precisely where he intended and cried out in triumphant rage as he ducked over the pommel, his face buried in Vaillantif's flying blond mane. The sandbag kicked violently on the post and grazed the air over his spine.

Vaillantif galloped on to the end of the tilt. Adam sat up and reined him round, set heels to his flanks again and repeated the manoeuvre, swirled in the dust, and charged back down the tilt. The lance cracked the shield and the sandbag hurtled round. Adam ducked, drew on the bridle, and hurled the lance point-down into the dust. There was no sense in foundering a good horse just to take the edge off his frustration. No sense in anything. He looked at the quivering ashwood shaft, wrenched the tip free of the ground and walked Vaillantif over to his audience.

'Christ!' declared Renard, eyes round with admiration. 'I'd hate to face you across a battleground!'

Jerold FitzNigel was watching his lord with a peculiar look in his pale eyes. He knew Adam playing and Adam for real, and just now they had been permitted a rare, deadly glimpse of the latter.

Miles kept his own eyes lowered and his thoughts to himself, but when Renard began to demand enthusiastically to be shown how it was done, he cut him short with an elder's brusque prerogative.

'It's all right.' Adam managed a smile as he slid down from Vaillantif's back. 'We all have to learn some time – don't we?'

5

France, Late Autumn 1126

William le Clito, claimant to the Duchy of Normandy and the English crown, both currently held most firmly by his uncle Henry, shoved the girl impatiently off his lap and scowled across the room at the immaculately dressed man sitting on the hearth bench drinking wine. 'You said it would be simple,' he complained, and pitched his voice in singsong mimicry, 'An arrow from the rocks above, or a sudden ambush in the forest, or even a second *White Ship* – but there she is, safe at her father's court in London without so much as a scratch to show for your efforts, and all the barons and bishops preparing to do her homage!'

Warrin de Mortimer stroked his close-cropped beard and regarded the petulant man opposite with an irritation that did not show on his heavy, handsome features. Le Clito – the Prince. Prince of nothing. King Henry had robbed le Clito's father of England, Normandy and his freedom in that order; but stung by conscience and the protests of his nobility, had left his son at liberty.

The boy, now grown to manhood, had a genuine claim to the English crown. His father was the King's older brother and William the Conqueror's eldest son. King Henry was the youngest son of the Conqueror, and the Empress Matilda his only surviving legitimate child. 'Yes,' he said to the glowering young would-be king. 'And it would have been simple if she hadn't had so vigilant an escort and you had provided me with more than fools. We made several attempts, but de Lacey was ready for each one.'

'He knew?'

Warrin gave an irritable shrug. 'For the most part I would say he was too experienced in that sort of warfare to be caught out. You don't grow up with men like Miles le Gallois and Guyon of Ravenstow for tutors and emerge a simpleton in the art of skirmish. The Empress's escort did take wounds, but none of them fatal.'

The girl sat down on a rug before the hearth and, piqued at being ignored, hitched one side of her gown up her leg. Unfastening a garter, she began to roll down one of her hose – slowly and provocatively. Le Clito's focus faltered and swivelled to his mistress. She curved a triumphant smile at de Mortimer.

'So much for all the silver paid out to get the information,' le Clito said angrily. 'We might as well have saved ourselves the time and expense.'

King Louis's time and expense, Warrin thought cynically. William le Clito had no serious funds of his own, but relied on Henry's enemies to provide them for him so that he could continue to be a thorn in his uncle's side.

'I intend recouping some of it before next Candlemas,'

Warrin said with a smile, as he contemplated le Clito's mistress. Her hair was as brown and glossy as a palfrey's hide, her face dainty, with clear grey eyes. A tasty morsel, but not the remotest challenge to the feast awaiting him at home.

Le Clito raised his brows. 'How?'

'I'm taking the next galley to England and once there, I'm marrying our informant's widow.'

Le Clito started to laugh, realised that his companion was not jesting, and leaned forward, his mouth hanging open. 'You're what?' The girl extended her toes and wiggled them at the fire.

'That way I can legally lay my hands on the silver and whatever else is bestowed in his strongboxes. I'll get a castle, three manors and a blood bond with Guyon of Ravenstow whose daughter the widow happens to be – and a very fetching widow at that.'

Le Clito stared at him. 'You sly bastard!' he chuckled.

'God helps those who help themselves, sire.'

'And is the lady in question agreeable?' Le Clito picked up his wine and grinned at him over the rim of the goblet, beckoning the girl from her sulky pose on the rug.

'I don't foresee any difficulties.' Warrin rose, extending his tall, powerful frame in a luxurious stretch. 'I've trodden very softly around her these last few months and spoken her father fair. My own father's a personal friend of his and anxious for the match, so there's been some persuasion from that side too. All there is left to do is obtain your uncle Henry's permission, as le Chevalier's lands are in his gift. I have no reason to think he will refuse me.'

The girl snuggled herself down beside le Clito and rubbed her hand over the V-shape of dark chest hair exposed by his loosened shirt laces. 'All well and good for you,' le Clito grumbled. 'A fat purse and a warm bed, but what of the future? I'm the heir in direct male tail to my grandsire the Conqueror, the eldest son of the eldest son. Are you going to abandon me and bow to my uncle's will? Are you going to accept that high-handed bitch to rule you – and whatever cur he drags from the gutter to be her husband?'

Warrin grimaced. 'My father will give his fealty for our lands, not I. You know I'd rather sit in the stink of air from the devil's fart than put my hands between hers in homage. I'll be at Windsor for the swearing because I've got to be. I'll let you know what happens and find out who we can depend upon to renege at the first opportunity. I had to get rid of le Chevalier, he was playing both sides of the coin, but I've still got some contacts at court.'

The girl's expert hand wandered lower and le Clito shifted on the settle to accommodate her ministrations.

'You ought to get married again,' Warrin advised as he lifted the curtain to leave. 'No good begetting bastards. Ask your uncle. He's got twenty-two of them, and not one of them can inherit his crown.'

6

The pied bitch yawned and scratched vigorously at a tender spot behind her ear. Four pups, bright-eyed, fat-bellied and inquisitive, tumbled and played beside her. Sunlight shafted down from an unshuttered window and bathed their fuzzy infant fur. Judith pushed the shears through the crimson wool marked out on her sewing trestle, the tip of her tongue protruding between her lips as she concentrated. It was to be a court robe for Renard and there was precious little time left to sew it, for they were well into November now, the slaughter month. The boy kept on growing; his best tunic, stitched only this midsummer, now revealed his wristbones and barely touched his knees, when it had been made to hang below them. Flanders cloth it had been, of an expensive, bright deep blue, lavishly embroidered with scarlet silk thread. It would do for Henry later on, so all was not lost, but the new garment had still to be stitched, and prayers said with the sewing that Renard would not grow again for a while at least.

The curtain clacked on its rings. Heulwen exclaimed as she tripped over a curious pup, then swore as it dug its sharp little milk teeth into the hem of her gown, intent on a growling tug-of-war. With some difficulty, she persuaded it to let go, and toed it gently sideways towards its dozing dam.

'Have you finished?' Judith deftly turned a corner. Crunch, crunch went the shears. She looked a brief enquiry across the richly coloured cloth.

'For the moment.' Heulwen picked up a small pot of scented goose-grease salve from the coffer, took a dollop and began to work it into her dry, cold-reddened hands. Several pigs had been slaughtered for salting, and the supervising had involved a certain degree of demonstration. Washing excrement from pigs' intestines, scraping them and then packing them down in dry salt for later use as sausage skins was a form of purgatory, but then so was needlecraft and, on balance, Heulwen thought that she would rather wash sausage skins.

'I've left Mary filling the bladders with lard and Gytha and Edith making a brine solution. I'll go down and check it in a while, but they've done it a hundred times before and should be all right. Thomas is dealing with the hams. We'll need more salt before Christmas.'

'I know.' Judith worked her way to the end and laid down the shears. 'You can help me pin this now you're here.'

Heulwen screwed up her face. Judith began to smile. 'You need the practice,' she teased gently. 'Soon you will have a man of your own to sew for again.'

Heulwen felt heat warm her cheeks and brow. She picked up a pincushion. 'Nothing is settled yet,' she muttered defensively. 'I know Papa's had Warrin's letter formally asking for me, but the King has yet to approve – and for that matter, so have I. Besides, Warrin's still in Normandy.'

'But due home any day now?' Judith started to pin the cut edges together, working nimbly. Then she paused and looked thoughtfully at her stepdaughter. 'In some ways the sooner the better for you, I think.'

'And you too, Mama.'

Judith's scrutiny sharpened, but she took no offence. Several weeks of each other's company had begun to rub the amity a little threadbare. Much as Judith was fond of her stepdaughter, she did not possess the calm, maternal patience that would have served in her best interests. Instead she was wont to snap, or say something tart, and Heulwen would bristle and retort in kind. It was hardly surprising that there should be friction, Judith thought. Heulwen had married Ralf at fifteen, and had been a chatelaine in her own right for more than ten years. Adjusting to the codes of her former life for no matter how temporary a time must be difficult, especially when faced with an older woman who smiled, but resented the intrusion. 'Yes,' she laughed. 'For me too. I will relish the peace and quiet!' And then she sobered. 'But daughter, you must be certain this match with Warrin is what you truly want for yourself. You know your father and I would never push you against your wishes.'

Heulwen drew breath to say that yes, it was what she truly wanted; her mind was made up, but what emerged from her mouth was different. 'Mama, do you think Warrin is a suitable match?'

Judith pondered the matter while she set half a dozen more pins into the fabric. 'Suitable, yes,' she said at length. 'But whether he is the right choice, only time will tell. You have known him since childhood. He's ambitious, self-opinionated, and about as sensitive as a wall. He'll expect you to decorate his bed and board as befits a man of his standing.' She straightened up and glanced at Heulwen's anxious face, seeking something to say that would even the balance. 'You certainly won't lack for anything. Warrin's always been generous. I dare say you'll even have maids enough to do all your sewing.' She smiled briefly, then grew serious as she added, 'But if you have a need to go beyond the gilded trappings, then I advise you to think again. To Warrin de Mortimer you will be a trophy, cherished for how highly others will envy him, rather than cherished for your own sake.'

'I realise that, Mama, and it does not bother me,' Heulwen said determinedly, 'In fact I—'

'Heulwen, you've got a visitor,' Renard announced as he sauntered into the bower. He was eating a cinnamon and apple pasty filched from beneath the cook's nose, and his narrow grey eyes were alight with mischief.

'Warrin?' She abandoned the pincushion and raised her hands to check the set of her veil and the tidiness of her braids.

'Wrong,' he said cheerfully, coming further into the room. Having crammed the rest of the pasty into his mouth, he stooped at the hearth to pick up one of the hound pups. It wriggled and sought to lick him with an ecstatic pink tongue. 'Adam de Lacey.'

Her hands fell from her braids. 'Adam?' she repeated weakly. 'Why does he want to see me?'

Renard gave her a mocking grin, head flung back to avoid the strivings of the pup. 'Perhaps he wants to arrange another midnight tryst in the solar,' he suggested.

'Renard!' snapped his mother, glaring at him with disfavour. 'If you spent as much time exercising your brain as you did your tongue, you would have a wit to be feared indeed!'

'Sorry,' he said with the graceless joy of one who is not sorry in the least. 'He's brought you your horses. You did say you were going to sell them in Windsor, didn't you? And you'll have to face him sooner or later.' He held the pup in the crook of his arm like a baby and wandered over to the sewing trestle to look with idle interest upon his mother's endeavours.

Judith frowned at him, although she was secretly proud. His height dwarfed hers, although childhood was still stamped on the features of the emerging man. There were crumbs on his upper lip amidst the dark smudge of a soft moustache line. The crimson wool would suit him very well. He was tall like Guyon and dark-haired, but his eyes were the grey impenetrable ones of his grandfather the King. He also possessed his grandfather's sleight of tongue, married to a lethal adolescent lack of tact. The future lord of Ravenstow and the responsibility, God help her, lay at her feet.

Renard kissed his mother's cheek and looked across at his half-sister, eyes dancing. 'Do you want to send me back down with a message and tell him you're too busy sewing?'

The thought of what Renard might say spurred Heulwen out of one kind of panic and into another. She put the pins carefully aside, resisting the temptation to stick them in her brother instead of his new tunic. 'No, Renard, that would be a lie, and anyway, I'd be pleased to see him. One misunderstanding does not make for a lifetime's enmity.' She widened her eyes sarcastically. 'What do you imagine happened in the solar? Or perhaps, knowing your mind, I shouldn't ask. The pup's just pissed on you.'

'What?' Renard looked, swore, dumped the puppy on the floor, and dragged off his tunic to his mother's stern reprimand about his language. Heulwen made her escape.

It was stupid to be so afraid, she thought as she twisted her way down the turret stairs and entered the great hall. Stupid to feel so tense and queasy. 'He is my brother,' she repeated to herself but to no avail. That part of her past was gone for ever, banished by the sight of a lean-muscled warrior in a bathtub. No, she amended, it was not stupid to fear danger or to panic when forced to greet it face to face.

Adam was in the courtyard talking to Eadric, his furred cloak thrown back from his shoulders, the cold sunlight reflecting off his hauberk and the silver pendants studding his swordbelt. The groom had custody of two fine horses – a bay and a piebald. Vaillantif's reins were held by Adam himself, and as he spoke to the servant, he caressed the bright sorrel neck, thick now in its full-grown winter fell.

Heulwen took a deep breath, gathered her courage in both hands, and walked across the ward to greet him.

'You wanted to see me?' she said to Adam. 'Will you come within to the hall?'

He hesitated, then inclined his head. Having given

63

Vaillantif's bridle to Eadric, he followed Heulwen back across the ward. A woman accosted her with a question about the pigs that were being dissected. While Adam waited, he stared around. A serjeant was drilling his men. The spear butts scraped on gravel and clacked in forested symmetry as their owners responded to bellowed commands. The woman departed with her instructions. Against the forebuilding entrance, two small boys were playing marbles. One of them raised his head and flashed a brilliant blue-green glance at his sister and the visitor.

'Why aren't you at your lessons?' Heulwen demanded sharply. 'Where's Brother Alred?'

'Gone into the town with Papa.' William made a face. 'We've to do our lessons this afternoon.' His gaze lit covetously on Adam's ornate gilded scabbard and the contrastingly austere sword-hilt protruding from it.

Heulwen said to Adam, 'William wasn't here last time you visited.' She turned to the boy: 'William, this is Adam de Lacey, my foster brother. I don't think that you'll remember him.'

Adam crouched down and picked up one of the round, smooth stones, his expression carefully impassive, aware that she had said 'foster brother' deliberately.

'Can I look at your sword?' William's eyes were avid with longing. Belatedly he remembered to add 'please'.

Adam shot the marble at a larger one near the wall. He heard the crack of stone upon stone and briefly closed his eyes, fists clenched upon his knees. Then he stood up and, smiling down at the boy, drew the weapon from its fleece-lined scabbard.

'William, you shouldn't be so . . .'

'He's all right.' Adam's voice was relaxed, concealing

the tension that gripped him. 'I was the same at his age about your father's blade – about any blade come to that, because they were real and mine was made of wood, or whalebone.'

William took it reverently. His small fist closed around the leather-bound grip and he held it up to the light so that the iron gleamed bluishly. Inlaid along the blade in latten was the Latin inscription *O Sancta*, repeated several times to make a decorative pattern. The pommel was an irregular semicircle of inlaid polished beechwood. 'Papa says I can have a proper sword of my own next year day,' William said eagerly.

'With a proper blunt blade,' Heulwen added. 'You do enough damage with the plain wooden one you've got now!'

Adam chuckled. 'I can imagine!' Gently, with more than a hint of poignant understanding, he took the sword back from the child, slotted it home, tousled the tumbled black curls, and continued with Heulwen into the keep.

She sent a servant to fetch hot wine and offered him a chair on the dais set close to a brazier. He unfastened his cloak and draped it across the trestle; unlatching his scabbard, he placed it on top.

'Do you want to unarm?' Heulwen indicated his hauberk as he stretched out his legs to the warmth.

He shook his head. 'Thank you, but no, it's only a passing visit, I won't keep you long.'

Heulwen looked down, wanting to apologise for the way their last encounter had ended but unsure that a reconciliation was in her own best interests. White-hot physical attraction frightened her. She had sat at its blaze before, watched it go out, and shivered over the ashes.

The servant brought the wine and a dish of the cinnamon apple pasties, and returned to his duties. Across the hall at another trestle, Adam's men sat around a basket of loaves, bowls of salted curd-cheese, and flagons of cider. Watching them Adam said, 'I've returned Ralf's stallions so you can decide whether you want to sell them at Windsor.'

Heulwen poured wine for them both, keeping her eyes on her task. 'What are they worth? Have you had time to find out?'

'The bay is almost fully trained and sufficiently well bred to fetch you around forty marks,' he said, his tone brisk and professional. 'The piebald's not of the same calibre, but because of his markings you should get around twenty for him. If I continue to school him over the winter, he could fetch a top price of twenty-five.'

'And Vaillantif?' she matched his tone.

'That's really why I came.' He transferred his gaze from contemplation of his men and fixed it on her instead. 'I want to buy him from you, Heulwen. I'll give you a hundred marks.'

She forgot her circumspection and stared at him in astonishment. 'How much?' she gasped

'It is what he is worth.' His eyes were bright and intense as he leaned forward in the chair.

'Adam, no, I cannot accept such a sum from you!'

'But you would accept it from a complete stranger at Windsor,' he pointed out.

'I wouldn't feel guilty about taking a stranger's coin.'

He set his jaw. 'Heulwen, I'm asking you as a boon – as a favour to me. Let me have him. You've slapped me in the face once. In Christ's name, leave me some small shred of pride. Do you know what it cost me to come here today?'

She opened her mouth to speak, changed her mind and drank her wine instead. 'Yes, I do know,' she said after a swallow. 'The same that it cost me to come down from the bower to face you.'

Adam considered her across his own cup and eventually he smiled. '*Pax?*' he said gravely.

'*Vobiscum.*' She returned the smile, feeling as though a great dark cloud had been lifted from her horizon. 'Very well. For the sake of our mutual pride, you can have Vaillantif, but I won't accept the full price – and before you start arguing, let me say that I owe you for the training and stabling of the other two horses. Eighty marks I'll take for him, not a penny more.'

'And if Warrin thinks that you have undersold a part of his future property?' he asked with an edge to his voice.

'Then Warrin can go whistle. I'm not . . .' Her voice trailed off and she put her hand to her mouth.

'What's wr—' Adam followed her gaze down the hall and saw, as if conjured from thought, Warrin de Mortimer advancing towards them in the all too solid flesh, his cloak bannering behind him with the vigour of his stride and his brows slanted down in a black scowl.

'Adam, I will kill you myself if you start anything,' Heulwen hissed from the side of her mouth, as she rose and prepared to greet her husband designate.

'Me?' he said sarcastically. 'Why should I want to start anything? Do you think I want to be on your conscience for the rest of your life?'

Heulwen stumbled and Adam had to lunge and grab

67

her elbow before she fell headlong down the dais steps. At their foot, Warrin de Mortimer regarded Adam with a mingling of irritation and strong dislike. Heulwen freed herself from Adam's grasp and went to take Warrin's cloak with a smile of greeting. As she reached for the fastening pin, he circled her waist with his hands and stooped to claim her lips. The kiss did not linger, but it signalled possession.

'Home and unscathed from your jaunt with the Empress, I see,' he said to Adam.

'So it would seem.' Adam leaned across the table for his scabbard, and without haste began to belt it on.

De Mortimer gave him a look of contemptuous amusement, as though he were watching a truculent child over whom he had a clear and confident advantage. 'You know,' he mused, 'it doesn't seem a moment since we were sparring in that tilt yard out there.' He grinned nastily. 'I hear you have learned from the drubbings I gave you.'

'A great deal more than you, Warrin,' Adam answered evenly, and turned to Heulwen as if the other man did not exist. 'The money is in my saddlebags. I'll have Austin bring it to you. What about the piebald?'

'I – I don't know,' she stammered, floundering in the currents of hostility swirling between the two men. 'I will have to think about it.'

Adam sent a jaundiced glance in de Mortimer's direction. 'I'll leave him, then. If I'm any judge of character, you'll not be selling him at Windsor either. As to the other matter, leave it in my hands. If I hear anything, I'll let you know.'

She nodded and raised her chin. 'Thank you, Adam.'

'Think nothing of it.' His mouth was wry as he swept on his cloak and, leaving his wine, brushed past her and de Mortimer to summon his men.

'Aren't you going to congratulate us?' needled de Mortimer. 'I'll almost be your brother-by-marriage, won't I?'

Adam did not turn round, and he had to swallow his gorge to answer. 'Congratulations,' he said stiffly, and strode down the hall, away from the temptation to do something utterly stupid.

Once outside in the cold, clean air of the bailey he let go, crashing his fist into the solid forebuilding wall in lieu of Warrin de Mortimer's handsome, contemptuous face. His skin peeled away from his knuckles in small grated strips. He looked at the thin welling of blood and welcomed the pain that blotted out thought.

'He affects me like that too,' Renard said strolling down the stairs to join him. 'He's so damned patronising – he treats me as if I were no older than William.'

'You act that way sometimes.'

'Are you going back to Thornford now?'

Adam examined his raw, bunched knuckles, the price of holding on to control for too long, then shot a dark glance at Renard. 'Why?'

'Oh, no reason.' Renard shrugged. 'I thought I'd ride with you. Starlight needs the exercise and I'd rather not stay here while Warrin crows and struts before Heulwen like a dunghill cock longing to tread a hen. Did you see all the rings he had on his fingers?'

Adam looked at his ally and found a brief smile. 'He was somewhat over-endowed.'

'He's wearing spikenard too. I could smell it on him

a mile away!' Renard wrinkled his nose. 'There's not going to be much room for Heulwen in his heart. He's madly in love with himself!'

Without comment, Adam went to Vaillantif and unlatched a saddlebag. Withdrawing a leather money pouch, he handed it to his squire. 'Go within, Austin, and deliver it to Lady Heulwen. Tell her that the other twenty are her wedding present. She will know what you mean.'

'Yes, sir.'

Adam watched him lope off, then turned back to the horse, and unslinging his helmet from the pommel, put it on. 'You'll need armour,' he said to Renard. 'Do you have a hauberk?'

'I have the one that was my brother's before he drowned. It fits me better than it used to fit him. Will you wait for me?'

Adam nodded at the dun stallion resting slack-hipped beside Vaillantif. 'You can use my remount instead of your own horse if you like. I noticed you were outgrowing that grey when you came to Thornford.'

Renard's dark eyes kindled. 'Adam, you're a friend!' He embraced Adam in a fervent hug that almost squeezed the breath from the latter's body.

'What do you do to your enemies?' Adam asked weakly.

'What's this for?' Warrin de Mortimer lifted one of the bags of silver just delivered to Heulwen by the snub-nosed squire, and jinked it back down on the trestle.

Despite the offhand tone of his asking, Heulwen could tell he was irritated. 'I sold him Vaillantif.'

Warrin flicked his forefinger against the side of the bag. 'For a goodly sum, by the looks of things.'

'He insisted on giving me more than was due. He was very stubborn. I didn't want it.'

'So stiff-necked that one day someone is going to snap it for him,' Warrin muttered.

'You?'

He laughed and shook his head. 'Is it so obvious?'

'You were like a pair of dogs circling each other, waiting for the right moment to leap at one another's throat.'

'I don't like the bastard, I'll admit that outright.' He extended his hands to the brazier. 'Never knew his place as a junior squire, and I doubt he does yet.'

Heulwen watched him, her stomach a mass of tiny butterflies. His hands were steady over the heat. Broad and powerful, they did not suit the various rings with which he had bedecked them. Her father very seldom wore jewellery and neither did Adam.

'What was the other matter of which he spoke?' he asked into her silence.

She shook her head, knowing a grievous mistake when she saw one. 'It was trifling,' she dissembled. 'Ralf sold a horse and I want to buy him back.'

'You could have asked me to do that.' He looked at her reproachfully. 'There was no need to involve Adam de Lacey.'

'You were in Normandy, and besides, Adam knows the owner.' His jaw tightened, but so did hers in determined response. 'Warrin, don't scowl at me like that. Adam has been my foster brother since I was two years old. If you cannot tolerate his occasional presence on mutual ground like Ravenstow, then you might as well seek a different woman to wife!'

Immediately he was contrite, turning from the brazier to take her hands in his. 'I'm sorry. It's just that I arrived here eager to greet you, and I did not expect to find Adam de Lacey sprawled in your father's chair . . .'

'And you are accustomed to having your own way in all things,' she agreed with an arched brow.

'Yes, I am!' Before she could rebel, his hands had slipped around her waist again and his breath was warm on her cheek as his head descended and he claimed her lips, imprinting them with the will of which he spoke. His arms tightened and his tongue probed. Heulwen stood passively within the embrace, neither welcoming nor resisting it, but it was sufficient for him that she was warm and pliant in his arms, and he persisted, driven by the anxiety to possess, and a more basic need.

The smell of spikenard was too powerful to be pleasant. It irritated her nose and made her want to sneeze. He was wearing his hauberk and the links began to bruise her arms where they were trapped by his. A small, inner voice asked her if she would have noticed such discomforts if Adam had been holding her. She tried to respond to Warrin, but the heaviness of his jaw grinding on hers made it impossible and she broke the kiss. 'Warrin, you're crushing me.'

He was breathing hard and his eyes were opaque with lust, but he had sense enough to realise where he was and what was at stake. Taking a grip on himself he released her and folded his long body into the chair that Adam had previously been occupying. 'In Christ's name, Heulwen, let us soon be wed,' he said roughly. 'I know you're still mourning Ralf, but time doesn't stand still – well, not unless I'm abroad talking cheeses with some stuff-witted steward on my father's Norman lands and counting the hours until I can come home and gladden my heart with a sight such as you.'

'Flatterer,' she said lightly, sitting down beside him.

'It's true though. Heulwen, you're driving me mad.'

His arm was resting on the trestle and she rubbed her index finger upon his wrist, stroking the wiry golden hairs the wrong way. 'Once you and Papa have formally agreed the terms and you have asked the King for Ralf's lands, we can be married without further delay,' she said.

'It cannot come quickly enough for me,' he said, thinking of her ripe body beneath his in the marriage bed, and of a chest full of recently minted silver.

'Nor me,' she said, her own tone more grim than eager, her mind upon Adam and the lessons learned from her time with Ralf.

'No chance of a hot bath?' he asked hopefully, his glance becoming decidedly lustful.

Heulwen stopped stroking his wrist and stood up. 'A cold one might suit your need better,' she laughed. 'I'll see what the maids can do.'

It was only when she reached the haven of the tower stairs and stood alone in the cold, musty silence, that she realised how much she was shaking.

'Snow,' grumbled Sweyn, twitching his powerful shoulders and glowering at the massing banks of greyish-yellow cloud piling in from the direction of the Welsh mountain ranges.

Adam's troop had emerged from the forest and on to the drovers track that would lead them in a few miles to the Thornford crossroads. Behind them the trees swayed like dancers striving to shake off the last vestments of parchment-dry leaves. The grass at the edge of the road was pale and limp, the road itself a ploughed morass of hoofprints and deeply gouged cartwheel tracks. Come full winter, it would qualify for the title of bog.

Vaillantif snorted and dipped his head to explore the unappetising fare at his hooves. Adam let the reins slide and turned in the saddle to look at Renard. 'Do you still want to come with us?'

Renard contemplated the threatening clouds with wind-stung eyes. He was wearing a thick tunic, topped by a heavily padded gambeson and mail hauberk, all overlaid by a fur-lined cloak, and was thus, despite the wind, warm enough. The stallion beneath him was a pure joy to ride after the shortcomings of poor Starlight.

'I'd far rather be snowed in with you than Warrin de Mortimer.' He smiled and, shaking the bridle, urged the dun on to the road.

'It's only November. It won't come to that.'

The smile became a mocking grin. 'Why take that chance? I notice you didn't linger.'

'If you're coming, shut up,' Adam snapped.

Renard shrugged, but let the grin fade as he rode forwards.

'He's still a boy,' murmured Jerold, joining his lord as they headed into the sharp wind.

'For which I'm making allowances.'

'I'd noticed,' Jerold said, 'but then he's like his sister, isn't he? Likes to season a stew just for the mischief of seeing others grimace when they taste it. I know how you were, and still are over the Lady Heulwen. And it's no use looking like that. It's the truth and you know it. I was there at her wedding, remember? Who do you think fetched Lady Judith when you sank all that wine? Who do you think sat by your pallet while you recovered your wits, or what was left of them? And now she's free to wed and she's done it again. How far will you go when it's Warrin de Mortimer who takes her to bed?'

Adam's fingers jerked on the reins. 'Jerold, let me be, you're worse than the boy,' he growled, while beneath him Vaillantif danced and tossed his head, rolling his eyes to show their whites.

'Sweyn and I were only saying to each other last night that you need to take a wife. There are bound to be barons at court this Christmastide with daughters for sale, and it's time you thought about settling to the yoke and breeding up heirs instead of living on dreams.'

Adam's temper snapped. He rounded on the knight to snarl his displeasure but got no further than, 'When I want your opinion I'll—' And then his breath locked in his throat and his eyes widened in horrified astonishment as an arrow sang through the narrow triangle of space between his hand on Vaillantif's reins and Vaillantif's neck, burying itself in the horsehair pad of Jerold's saddle flap. The heavy sky began to precipitate not snow, but death-tipped arrows. Welshmen, either afoot and armed with bows or astride their small, tough mountain ponies, were pounding in the wake of their missiles, mouths agape to yell their war cries.

'God's bleeding eyes!' Jerold blasphemed and, trying to control his plunging stallion, groped for his sword.

Adam wrestled his shield on to his left arm. 'Close formation!' he bellowed. 'And don't give them a chance to hamstring the horses! Sweyn, get to Renard and guard him with your life!' It was all he had time to say, for the battle closed its gaping jaws and swallowed them whole.

The first Renard knew of the rapid Welsh assault was the arrow that ripped a hole in his cloak and slammed into his stallion's belly. The animal screamed and reared, forehooves tearing at the clouds, then came down stiff-legged and bucked. The high saddle and Renard's own swift reflexes kept him astride, but that was all that could be said. Of controlling a gut-shot horse there was not a hope in hell. If the dun went down, he would be crushed to death; and if it threw him in its frenzy he faced being trampled or killed by the force of the fall.

There was no time to think, only to act on instinct. He released the reins, kicked his feet free of the stirrups, and as the dun came down on all fours between twisting bucks, he used the high pommel to vault down from its back. He stumbled and felt his ankle wrench, but was able to duck away from the destrier's pain-filled madness and draw his sword. His shield still hung from the saddle and there was not the remotest possibility of reaching it without being brained by the plunging shod hooves.

Battle clashed around him. A burly, black-eyed Welshman who looked as though he ate horseshoes for breakfast came at him with an iron-studded oak mace. Renard dodged the first vicious swing of the weapon. His enemy was laughing. Battle took some men that way, and obviously this one saw his opponent as a mockery of opposition. '*Cenau!*' he said contemptuously. A whelp indeed Renard might be, but of a warrior breed, trained from the cradle to fight. As the Welshman swung his mace for the kill, Renard ran under the blow and slashed at his enemy's bare thighs. Blood sprayed, spattering Renard's face as the honed edge sliced muscle, tendon and artery. The mace caught him glancingly on the shoulder, but it was the off-balanced blow of a mortally wounded man going down.

'*Yr cenau gan dant!*' Renard gasped, breathing hard as he finished it. 'A puppy with teeth!'

'Renard, ware behind!' roared Sweyn.

He spun quickly, but was not fast enough to avoid the thrust of a spear. Frantically he twisted as he felt his hauberk rings give and splay, and a vicious iron point tear his gambeson and score his ribs. He was caught like a fish on a spit and in a moment he was going to die, the last thing he saw the snow-bound sky and the frightened, triumphant young face of his killer.

The thrust home was never executed because Sweyn reached him, and cursing, rose in his stirrups to bring the full weight of his axe down upon the young Welshman's skull, which was only protected by a cap of stiffened leather and thus split open like a carelessly dropped egg. Violently jerking, the body fell, tearing the lance head free as it went.

'You bloody young fool, where's your shield?' Sweyn howled.

'On my saddle,' Renard said hoarsely.

The Englishman glared round and saw the foundered, threshing dun with Renard's shield now rolled to splintered remains beneath him. 'Here, take Morel,' he said gruffly and swung down from the saddle.

'I couldn't . . .'

'Hell's death, boy, do as you're told. We're not in a damned tilt yard today! You're a liability on foot, one we can't afford!'

Colour flared across Renard's cheekbones. He opened his mouth to retort, thought better of it and instead seized the black's bridle and leaped astride. The pain in his side burned like fire, but he set his jaw and refused to think about it; indeed, within the space of ten heartbeats he did not even have the time to pay it any attention as the fighting redoubled in fierceness, and all that stood between himself and certain death were the lessons learned by rote in the safety of a courtyard, and the grimly determined Sweyn wielding a great axe at his stirrup.

* * *

It was over. Adam slid down from Vaillantif's back, wiped his sword on the cloven corpse at his feet and stared into the spectral November silence that the retreating Welsh had left in their stead. The road was strewn with bodies, most of them Welsh, but among them were two of his own men, and another who had taken an arrow in the belly and would not last the night. Bare sword in his hand, he studied the corpses and brushed at a persistent thread of blood running from a bone-deep nick in his jaw.

'This one's still alive. Shall I kill him, lord?' One of his Angevins was kneeling over an unconscious Welshman, hand grasping the cropped black curls to jerk back the head.

Adam walked over. It was a young man whose life hung in the balance, barely twenty years old, to look at him. His tunic was of undyed wool, and his short leggings were bound with crude strips of leather, but his boots were of embossed leather and his swordbelt was set with carnelians. 'How badly is he wounded, Thierry?'

'Bad enough. This lump on his head's bigger than a gull's egg, and he's taken a deep slash to the thigh.'

Adam dabbed again at his bloody jaw and made a swift assessment of the youth's chances. 'Bring him with us. He may be of some value if he doesn't die of wound fever.' He looked round. 'Sweyn, where's Renard?'

The English knight jerked his head towards the side of the road. 'Sick,' he said. 'First taste of hard battle, but he came through well in the thick of it. Are you all right, my lord?'

'I'll do.' Adam glanced up and blinked as a snowflake landed on his lashes. He sheathed his sword. The Welsh youth was draped unceremoniously over the back of a hill pony someone had captured. Adam took Vaillantif's bridle and walked him over to Renard. The lad was wiping his reddened dagger upon the bleached grass, but when he saw Adam approaching he stood up, and with trembling hands sheathed the weapon. His face was tear-streaked and ghastly white, his teeth chattering uncontrollably, and not because it was cold. Death had breathed on him – his own and other men's, and even after the Welsh retreat he had been forced to kill again.

'I'm sorry, Adam.' He swallowed. 'Your dun. He was gut-shot, I had to do it.'

Adam followed Renard's gaze to the dun. A Welsh arrow protruded from its flank and the blood ran in rivulets from its slit throat. A faithful, sturdy companion, the stallion had carried him in safety to the German court and back. 'Nothing else you could have done,' he said steadily. 'Just thank Christ it was his gut and not yours.' He glanced briefly over his shoulder to where Jerold and another knight were gently lifting the dying man on to his horse. Mercifully, he was unconscious.

Renard wiped his hands together. There was blood on them, darkly crusted beneath his fingernails. 'I've never killed a man before,' he said, throat working. 'In a tilt yard it doesn't matter. The swords are blunt, and if they are not, then your opponent is made of straw. He doesn't cry out and bleed and die at your feet with his eyes on you . . .' His voice shook.

Adam set one arm compassionately across Renard's shoulders. 'I felt like that the first time too, and the second, and the third. Everyone does, but it is a lesson you have to learn for yourself. No one can tell you.'

Renard's dark grey eyes went blank. 'It gets easier then?' he said through stiff lips.

'No, but you learn to shut it out; you have to. If you had not killed him, he would have killed you.' Adam tightened his grip and shook Renard slightly, imparting reassurance. Renard winced and drew a hiss of pain through his teeth, his hand clutching his side. Adam released him, eyes sharpening. 'You idiot, why didn't you say you were hurt?'

'It's not serious – well at least I don't think so. Sweyn killed the man before he could put any weight behind his thrust.' Renard closed his eyes and fought the urge to retch as he saw again the axe cleaving down and the head splicing apart beneath it.

'Are you fit to climb into a saddle?' Adam indicated Vaillantif. 'You'll have to sit pillion like a wench, but the way this snow's starting to come down I'd rather reach Thornford before dusk, and the Welsh may well have re-inforcements close by. We couldn't withstand another brawl like this one.' He mounted up and extended his hand. Renard grimaced through clenched teeth, but hauled himself competently astride, and only when secure did he hang his head and let out his breath in a gasp of pain.

One of the men-at-arms stripped the dun stallion of its harness and loaded it on to the horse bearing the two dead men. The Welsh bodies they left where they had fallen and where they would presently be taken up and borne away by their own people. The snow floated down, covering the land in a white healing blanket, curtaining the horsemen as they rode away, muffling the beat of hooves to silence so that the only sound was the keening of the wind.

8

'Do you believe that I should have approved the match between Heulwen and Warrin?' Guyon asked his wife.

Judith ceased grooming her hair, put down her comb and turned to her husband. He was sitting before the hearth, looking indolently at ease with a cup of wine in his hand and his feet stretched out resting comfortably against Gwen's firelit rump, but she had been married to him for too long now to be deceived.

'What reason could you have had to refuse?' She rose and came to him. Placing her hand on his shoulder she felt the tension there, and began to work on the knotted muscles. 'Both of them seem eager for the match. She's not a child any more, Guy; she's long been a woman grown.'

He closed his eyes and gave a low-pitched sigh of pleasure at her ministrations, but his mind remained sharp. 'I know that, love. I also know it hasn't been easy for you having her here at Ravenstow.'

'And you wonder if you have given in too easily in

the hopes of having a return to peace in your house-hold?' she said archly.

'Most assuredly that is part of it,' Guyon acknowledged with a laugh, then sobered. 'I just wonder why Warrin should be so keen to wed her. Men of high estate do not marry for love. Well and good if love grows from a match, but it is not the foremost reason for tying a knot. There have to be others.'

'Heulwen married for love the first time,' Judith pointed out.

Guyon snorted. 'What she thought was love. Moonstruck lust in reality, and I was dotingly led by the nose to arrange a disaster.'

'Tush, it was a sound business arrangement,' she objected, leaning round to kiss the corner of his mouth. 'Ralf's skills and our horses. It wasn't just Heulwen's pleading that caused you to make the offer.'

'Perhaps,' he conceded. 'But it has given me cause for doubt. Am I doing the right thing this time? Where Heulwen is concerned, I stand too close to see clearly.'

For a time, Judith continued kneading his shoulders in silence while she considered. 'The blood bond with you and her dowry are reason enough for him to seek her in marriage,' she said at length. 'He's known her for a long time, and he did offer for her before.'

'Perhaps,' Guyon said without conviction. 'But there are other heiresses of similar, if not greater value.'

'Then mayhap part of her value to him does lie in personal attraction, and that is all to the good. After the way Ralf treated her, Warrin's pride will be like balm on an open wound.'

Guyon was silent. Judith eyed the back of his neck

with exasperation, recognising this mood of old. He would sit on his doubts like a broody hen on a clutch of eggs, and nothing would move him until they either hatched or went stale. How to send them stale? She pursed her lips: after twenty-eight years of marriage, she had several diversions in her armoury – short-term at least. She slid her hands down over his collarbone and chest, leaned round to kiss him again on throat and mouth, let her hair swing down around them, bit him gently . . .

'It was snowing on our wedding night, do you remember?'

Guyon's lids twitched but did not open. He caressed Judith's hair with a languid hand. 'Yes, I remember,' he said, with a smile. 'You were scared to death.'

She propped her chin on one hand and traced her index finger lightly over his chest. 'I was too young and badly used to know better,' she said softly. 'You gave me the time I needed and for that I'll always be grateful.'

'Just grateful?'

'What do you think?' She sought teasingly lower and giggled to hear him groan.

'Jesu, Judith, I'm not young enough to game all night any more!'

'What would you wager?'

'Doubtless my life if I made the attempt!' He laughed, and half lifted his lids to study her. The rich tawny hair was stranded with silver now, and fine lines webbed her eye-corners and spidered around her lips. But she was still attractive, her body trim despite the bearing of five sons and two miscarriages between. Theirs had been a political match, forced upon them both, and begun with mistrust and resentment on both sides; but out of the seeds of potential disaster had grown a deep and abiding love. His pleasure in her was still as keen as it had been in the early days, for Judith had an extensive store of devices and surprises to keep him interested, and he was essentially of a faithful nature, seeing no point in going out to dine on pottage when there was a feast at home.

'The trouble with Ralf was that he enjoyed pottage,' he murmured.

'What?' Bewildered, Judith stared at him.

'Nothing. Foolish thoughts aloud. I told you, you're flogging a dead horse.' Laughing, he pushed her hand away.

'Speaking of which, Renard will need another mount before we go to Windsor.' She kissed his jaw and laid her head on his shoulder. 'He bids fair to outstrip you in height and he's not sixteen until Candlemas.'

'So I'd noticed,' Guyon said with rueful pride. 'Starlight can go for use as a remount. There must be at least another five years left in him. He was only a youngster when Miles first had him.'

Judith felt the familiar pang strike her heart as he spoke the name of their eldest son; her firstborn, drowned with his cousin Prince William when the *White Ship* went down. How long ago was it? Six years, and still as if it were only yesterday she could see Guyon riding into Ravenstow's bailey with the disastrous news received in Southampton, and she eight months pregnant with William, the wind raw on her face, turning her cheeks as numb as her mind. No grave at which to mourn, just a wide expanse of grey, sullen water.

She nuzzled her cheek against Guyon's bicep seeking

to blot out the pain, and thought of her father the King, whose every hope and scheme had foundered in that vessel. Not only the loss of a son, but the loss of a dynasty in male tail. Miles could never be replaced, but at least she and Guyon had the grace of four surviving sons.

'I haven't seen Matilda since she left to become an empress,' she remarked, thoughts of Henry leading her to thoughts of the small, truculent half-sister whom she had last seen at the age of seven, stamping her foot at Queen Edith and shrieking in a tantrum that she was not going to Germany, that no one could make her.

'Apparently you are fortunate,' Guyon said drily. 'Adam was not impressed.'

'I feel sorry for her.' Judith defended Matilda. 'There cannot have been much joy in her life. A little girl adrift in a strange country, forced into different customs and language, and cut off from her family. I know her husband was kind to her, but to a child of her age he must have seemed ancient.'

'A replacement for her father then,' Guyon said sleepily, and yawned.

'Probably,' Judith agreed. 'So when he died, and her real father started making demands on her to come home when it was he who had packed her off in the first place, is it any wonder that she should turn mulish and diffi-cult? After all, he hasn't recalled her out of loving concern, has he? I'll wager he rubbed his hands with glee when her poor husband died! She knows very well that if her brother were still alive, or if Queen Adeliza had proved a competent brood mare, she'd still be in Germany, the Dowager Empress and highly respected by people whom she knows and suits. As it is, all the barons are eyeing her with suspicion and muttering into their wine. A mark to a penny there's another husband being chosen for her, strictly of her father's choosing.'

She paused to draw breath, aware that her indignation on Matilda's behalf had carried her too far. Her words, by association, might lead back to the niggling treadmill of the match between Heulwen and Warrin de Mortimer, the very thing she had sought to distract Guyon from in the first place.

'Anyway,' she said, adroitly changing the subject, 'it will be a pleasure to see Henry and discover how he's progressing in Robert of Gloucester's charge, and it's a long time since I've had a good gossip with Rob's wife.' Her tone warmed with anticipation. 'That little booth's always there at Christmas, you know, the one that sells attar of roses, and I need to buy some more thread-of-gold for that altar cloth in the chapel, and we've almost finished the saffron . . .'

'Enough!' her husband groaned, laughing. 'You will clean me out of silver!'

'But in a good cause.' She nibbled his ear. Her hand strayed downwards again, teasing, knowledgeable.

'Wanton,' he murmured, shifting to accommodate her further.

'For a dead horse, you're remarkably lively,' she retorted.

'. . . A dead horse,' said the serjeant as Guyon gestured him to his feet. 'A dun stallion with an arrow in his belly and his throat slit wide. Our patrol came across him in the middle of the drovers' road; he was crusted in a night's fall of snow.'

'Any other signs of a skirmish?' asked Warrin de Mortimer, speaking around a mouthful of bread and honey.

'I couldn't rightly tell, my lord. The snow had blown and drifted. At first we did not realise there was a horse there at all, until one of the dogs found him.'

'A dun.' Heulwen put her cup down, her colour fading. 'Adam had a dun with him yesterday, and it was the road he would have taken to Thornford.'

Warrin gave her a sharp glance, a hint of irritation in his ice-blue eyes, then dropped his gaze and took a gulp of cider to wash down his bread, hoping that the Welsh had done to Adam what they had done to Ralf. It would stop Heulwen agitating over the witless sod, and he would be able to comfort her as only a husband could.

'And Renard went with him,' Judith said, one hand at her throat, the other gripping the trestle.

'He was riding a dun; I saw him leave,' said William. He had been sitting quietly at the end of the dais, a wooden soldier in one hand and a heel of bread in the other, only half understanding what was being said, but alerted enough by the fear in the adult voices to be frightened himself. 'It was Sir Adam's remount. He had a black mane and tail and a blaze.'

The serjeant swallowed and nodded. 'Yes, that's the one.'

'Holy Christ . . .' Judith closed her eyes.

'Mama, Renard's all right, isn't he?'

Judith turned a blind, terrified gaze on her youngest son, changing it swiftly, but not swiftly enough, and gave him a meaningless smile. 'Yes, of course he is, sweetheart . . .' After all, there were no corpses saving that of a slaughtered horse. William came to her and she drew him close, holding on to his small, warm body.

'Eric, get the men saddled up,' Guyon snapped at his grizzled constable. 'I want to see this for myself. We'll ride on to Thornford along the drovers' road.'

'I'll come with you,' offered Warrin, gulping down the last of his cider and standing up. 'You can use my men to swell the ranks of your own. Safety in numbers, I think.'

Guyon nodded brusquely and left the trestle to go and arm, beckoning the serjeant to come with him so that he could be further questioned as to what he had seen.

Judith bent over her youngest son, reassuring him, her heart clogged by dread. The November sacrifice, she thought: two sons paid, three still to lose. She shuddered.

'Take care,' Heulwen said to Warrin, grasping his sleeve.

'Don't worry,' he answered with a tight smile and bright eyes. 'I'm not going to be cheated out of what is rightfully mine.'

She frowned.

'Look,' he said with heavy patience, 'Adam de Lacey is too experienced a fighter to fall prey to a piddling band of Welsh – *more's the pity* – and if Renard's with him, then Renard will be all right. Trust me, sweeting.' He silenced her intention to speak with a hard kiss that took away her breath, released her, and went after Guyon, pausing only to squeeze Judith's shoulder reassuringly as he passed.

Heulwen watched him stride across the hall and from her sight, his pace assured and arrogant. A shard of ice lodged in her heart. She remembered a soft summer day and the dismayed cries of the servants as Warrin rode into her bailey, Ralf's blood-soaked body draped like a dead deer across Vaillantif's back. She remembered the dull, sightless eyes, the wounds that had bled him white, and the void expression death had set on his face. Warrin telling her then not to worry; telling her again now, like a foretaste of doom. With a small cry she gathered her skirts and fled the hall for the sanctuary of the chapel and cast herself down on her knees before the altar, and there entreated God to keep Renard and Adam safe, and to forgive her sins.

Adam paused, hands on hips, breath steaming into the clear, frosty air, and watched the men from Ravenstow ride into his bailey. A snort rippled from him when he saw Warrin de Mortimer astride the piebald stallion. 'That's two marks you owe me,' he said to Jerold.

The knight squinted against the cold glare of the sun. 'That's two marks more than he's paid out over that horse,' he said acidly. 'But then what need when it's part of his future bride's dowry and you are fool enough to have trained him for love, not money?'

Adam gave Jerold a hard stare, but the knight was not for retreat and returned it full measure and Adam was the first to disengage. 'What need indeed?' he said, and turned to crunch across the snow and greet the horsemen.

'Adam, thank Christ!' Guyon said sharply as he dismounted. 'What in hell's name happened?'

Adam shrugged his shoulders. 'What you would expect. The Welsh must have had their scouts out yesterday morning and seen me pass on the road to

Ravenstow. We weren't laden with travelling baggage, so it wouldn't take a great intellect to deduce we'd probably be returning soon that same way.' Gingerly he touched the clotted slash on his jaw. 'They bit off more than they could chew, but we didn't have it all our own way. I lost three good men and sixty marks' worth of destrier, not to mention those wounded.'

'Where's Renard?' Guyon stared anxiously round the bailey for his son. 'Was he injured?'

'No more than grazes,' Adam reassured him as they turned towards the hall. 'He danced too close for comfort with a Welsh spear, but Sweyn got to him in time. He's still abed, but only because I sent him there last night with a flagon of the strongest cider we had, and a girl from the village. I don't expect to see him this side of noon.'

'You did what?' De Mortimer looked at him in disgust.

'Oh don't go all pious on me, Warrin!' Adam snapped. 'The lad fought well – accounted for two of the bastards on his own and got himself clear of a gut-shot horse in the middle of a pitched battle – but it's a violent baptism for a youngster raw from the tilt yard. He took sick afterwards. In the circumstances, I thought it best that he drown his dreams in drink and the comfort of a woman's body, and Christ alone knows why I am justifying myself to you!'

'Calm down, Adam.' Guyon touched his rigid arm. 'I'd probably have done the same with him. Just thank God you're both safe. When I saw that horse in the road . . .'

'I was going to send to you this morning, but I've not long risen myself.'

'Did you take to drink and dalliance too?' de Mortimer needled him.

Adam's jaw tightened, making his wound hurt. He thought of several sarcastic replies but decided that to utter them was to play into Mortimer's hands. 'We took a prisoner,' he said to Guyon, half turning his shoulder on the other's galling presence. 'He's got a nasty head wound and a slashed thigh, and he's still out of his wits. The village herb-wife had a look at him and says he'll mend, but doesn't know how long it will be before he recovers his senses.'

'You had reason to make of him a prisoner then?' Guyon prowled forward to the hearth. The snow on his boots became transparent and slowly melted into the rushes. A dog came to sniff at the cold air on his cloak.

'He was wearing gilded boots and there were jewels in his sword-hilt. Someone of note among his people, I would say. If we had left him in the road he would have died.'

'What's one less Welshman except a blessing?' de Mortimer said moodily and kicked at the dog as it came to snuffle him.

'Not in this instance. It may be that we can barter him for peace.'

'And we all know a Welshman's notion of peace!' de Mortimer scoffed. 'If it had been me, I'd have left the whoreson to die!'

'I know,' Adam said tightly. 'Either that, or helped him on his way. You're good at that.'

It had been an insult flung like a wild blow in battle, but it certainly hit its mark. De Mortimer whitened and recoiled as if he had been physically struck. 'You stand need to speak so when your own father . . .'

'Christ on the cross let be!' Guyon said sharply. 'You're like a pair of infants. For all the heed you've taken of the manners drilled into you at Ravenstow, I might as well have saved my breath!'

There was a difficult silence while the two antagonists glared at each other. Then Adam broke eye contact and cleared his throat. 'Do you want to see my Welshman?' he asked. 'It may be that you will know him.'

Guyon inclined his head, noting wearily that neither man was prepared to apologise.

He lay on a pallet in one of the upper wall chambers, a maidservant tending him and a footsoldier posted outside the curtained doorway. 'Although God knows, with that leg, he's not going far,' Adam said as the woman curtsied and withdrew a little. A brazier had taken the chill from the room and was positioned near the pallet to afford the stricken man the best of the warmth. The room had no access to daylight, and the constant use of rush dips and candles had streaked the walls with soot.

Guyon stared down at the captive on the bed. The youth's face was blue with bruises and hollow in the cheekbones. The black curls had been cropped away from a nasty contusion the size of a gull's egg high on his forehead. His cheeks were oily with the bloom of late adolescence. 'He's only a youngster,' he said, surprised into compassion. 'No, I don't know him. What about you, Warrin?'

De Mortimer shrugged. 'They all look the same to me. I haven't been much on the borders these last three years, and by the looks of him, three years ago he would still have been taking suck!'

'Someone's bound to claim him,' Guyon said. 'The Welsh kinship bond is sacred, and he's well-bred, you say, perhaps even the leader of this escapade?'

'Could well be,' Adam nodded, 'the Welsh blood their young men early.'

'How bad is the leg wound?'

'He's stitched up like a piece of Bishop Odo's embroidery and likely to take the wound fever, but Dame Agatha is doing her best for him.'

Guyon started to turn away. Warrin made to follow him, but his cloak pin had worked loose and the brooch dropped to the floor with a soft clink. Muttering an oath, he stooped to retrieve it, and at that moment the patient stirred with a groan and opened his eyes.

Immediately Guyon and Adam turned to him, but de Mortimer was the nearest, his square, strong bones illuminated in the light of the rush dips, and it was upon these that the young Welshman focused. A look of sheer horror crossed his face and he shrank back into the pillows, crying out in Welsh.

'It's all right,' Guyon said quickly in that same language. 'No one is going to harm you. You are here to be healed and returned to your family.'

The youth shook his head, panting hard, his eyes on de Mortimer.

'You say you do not know him, but he certainly seems to know you, and well enough to be afraid,' Adam said, drawing Warrin away from the bed while Guyon continued to soothe the patient.

'I've never seen the whelp before in my life!' Warrin

snapped. 'It's obvious. He's taken a blow to the head and his wits have gone wool-gathering. Anyone who looks even remotely Norman is fodder for his nightmares.'

'Perhaps,' Adam said noncommittally and eyed the prisoner who had subsided against the pillows, his eyes once more closed. He was either exhausted, or too frightened to look upon Warrin de Mortimer again.

'What are you going to do about him?' Guyon asked as they returned to the hall. 'You're due to leave for Windsor within the fortnight.'

Adam pursed his lips. 'I don't know. Perhaps ask your father to come here. He's acquainted with most of the Welsh families of the region – related to half of them come to that. He's competent to deal with whatever arises, and I can leave Jerold here with him. If the lad's family come to negotiate, they can take the first steps without me, and I should be home by January's end to conclude them.'

Guyon nodded agreement, eyes thoughtful.

'What was all that gibberish he was babbling?' asked Warrin as the men gathered to warm themselves at the hearth.

Guyon's tone was neutral. 'He said he never meant to eavesdrop and that if you let him live, he would not tell a living soul.'

'Tell a living soul what?' Warrin looked blank. 'What does he mean?' A pulse throbbed hard in the base of his throat.

'I suppose we'll find out in good time,' Adam said evenly, then turned away to view another black-haired young man in shirt and chausses who had just collapsed on to a trestle bench at the side of the hall dais and now sat groaning and rumpled, his head clutched between his hands.

'Your heir, my lord,' Adam grinned to Guyon, 'safe and sound.'

Despite the sables lining her travelling cloak, Heulwen shivered as she stood beneath an overhang and waited for the grooms to lead her saddled palfrey out from the stables. The snow had become sleet, needling silver and white from a sky the colour of a dirty hauberk – and hauberks were in evidence everywhere as the final preparations were made for the journey to Windsor – and from the look of the weather, a wet, uncomfortable journey it was going to be.

Renard squelched across the bailey, furred cloak already mired at the hem, armour glinting as he strode. She was about to call out to him, but a young woman came running out of one of the bailey buildings and accosted him. Renard glanced round, set his free arm about the girl's willowy waist, and whisked her into the darkness of a doorway, where Heulwen saw his cloak swirl around her to enclose, and his head bend to her offered lips. The falconer's daughter, she thought with the glimmer of a smile. Amazing what prowess in war did for a man's standing with women. Renard's pretence at manhood was swift becoming reality.

Heulwen had been hysterical with relief at his safe return, but only a portion of it had been on Renard's account. The thought of Adam sprawled somewhere in a frozen puddle of his own blood, like Ralf a victim of the Welsh, had terrified her beyond all coherent thought. Nothing had been the same since. She was still reeling and uncertain, balanced on a see-saw of want and denial. She clenched her fists and fixed her gaze upon Warrin's broad, solid frame as he stepped out into the sleet, his face twisting into a grimace of discomfort. He was her betrothed in all but the pledge now that she had consented. All that prevented their union was the formality of the royal yea-say and there was no reason for that to be denied.

He came towards her, blowing on his hands, caught her gaze and smiled. She managed a wan response.

'Chin up, doucette, you look as dismal as this godforsaken weather!' He stooped and kissed her cold lips, then stood back to look at her.

'This journey is hardly going to be a jaunt to a fair,' she responded, trying to draw some inner glow of feeling from his presence, but the only warmth that came was because he was shielding her from the wind.

'I've brought you a present,' he said with a smile and placed a small drawstring bag in her hand. 'It won't ease the misery of this weather, but it might lighten your heart, and it will certainly gladden mine to see you wear it. Call it your betrothal gift.'

Heulwen loosened the string with fumbling, frozen fingers and slid a circular cloak pin on to her palm. It was an ornate, spectacular piece, wrought in gold and inset with glowing jewels of sapphire, ruby and rock crystal.

'Thank you, it's beautiful!' She turned it over, thinking to herself that it was also ostentatious and indicative of her future husband's attitudes and tastes.

'Here, let me pin it on for you.' He reached eagerly to pluck loose the pin that already held her cloak. It was a simple thing by the standards of the gorgeous object she now held, a braided silver circlet given to her by her father on her seventh year day. It made her feel uneasy to see it so summarily dismissed. Carefully, tenderly, she dropped it in the empty leather bag.

'Is it not a risk to display such wealth as this on a long journey?' she asked doubtfully. 'Surely it would be more sensible for me to wear it when we reach Windsor – perhaps when you ask the King for me?'

Warrin snorted with patronising indulgence, making her feel in truth no more than seven years old. 'You worry too much over trifles,' he said, as he forced the new brooch through the thick Flemish cloth. 'We are armed to fight off any chance attacks on the road. We could even deal with a horde of Welsh if they came at us. No, beloved, it pleases me that men should see the high value I set upon my prize.'

'Not your prize yet,' she reminded him, nettled at his superior tone.

'Well then, my future prize.' He finished securing the pin and lowered his hand, as if by accident brushing the curve of her breast. 'My future wife.' His voice thickened and his mouth fastened on hers, demanding. Feeling like a whore who had been paid in advance to show gratitude, Heulwen responded with the unthinking expertise taught to her by Ralf, her heart numb and her fingers frozen as she linked them around Warrin's neck.

The Welsh prisoner opened his eyes to full consciousness and stared in bewilderment at the limed white
chamber walls surrounding him. Rushlight flickered.
Beneath his fingers he could feel the grainy texture
of a linen garment, and under that, the rapid beat of
his fevered body. His throat was as dry as scoured
parchment and when he tried to speak, no words
emerged.

'He's awake,' Adam said softly, and touched his companion's knee.

Miles grunted and his head jerked up from his chest.
Rubbing his eyes, he turned to the youth on the pallet and
saw that, despite a slight fever, he was lucid and aware.
Miles reassured him in Welsh that he was meant no harm.
The youth's dark eyes remained puzzled and suspicious,
but he drank greedily of the watered mead that Adam set
to his lips. He listened in silence while Miles introduced
himself in the proper Welsh fashion, naming all his
antecedents and relatives before telling him of Adam's

identity, where he was, and how seriously he had been wounded.

'It was foolish to attack Lord Adam's troop,' Miles added with a shake of his head. 'He might not speak the *Cymraeg* beyond a smattering, but that does not mean he is an idiot in matters of border warfare.'

The youth's mouth twisted. 'I don't need lecturing,' he said. His voice was hoarse and rusty from lack of use.

Miles nodded benignly. 'Perhaps not from me, but your kin will be only too delighted to point out the error of your ways, once they know you are alive, I am sure.'

The down-turned mouth was joined by a heavy scowl.

Miles translated what had been said so far. Adam put the mead down. 'Ask him who his kin are.'

Miles began to speak but the youth cut across him and said in halting French, 'My brother won't be delighted, he'll be furious. You needn't have gone to the trouble of saving me. He'll murder me with his own hands when he finds out.'

'Your brother?'

'Davydd ap Tewdr.' He looked down again. 'I'm Rhodri, and younger than him by ten years. We're born of different mothers.'

A slow, beatific smile lit up Adam's face. 'Worth your weight in Welsh gold then.'

'Or a peace treaty,' Miles said. 'He's ap Tewdr's heir as matters stand.'

'Yes, gloat,' said the youth miserably. He shifted angrily in the bed and his body jerked taut, his breath locking in his throat.

'You've made a regular mess of that leg, lad,' Miles pronounced. 'You're lucky it's not festering.'

'I'll send to your brother.' Adam offered him the mead again. 'There's a Welsh carrier plies his trade through here once a month. He's due next week and he'll know where to take word. And I'd be an innocent if I did not know that your brother has his own ways and means of discovering your whereabouts.'

The youth drank and said nothing, but colour crept up into his face.

Adam frowned, eyeing his captive. 'Tell me how you come to know Warrin de Mortimer.'

The colour vanished from the youth's complexion. 'He was really here then?' he said hoarsely. 'I thought perhaps it was just part of a bad dream.'

Adam's mouth twitched. 'So did I,' he said half under his breath. 'No, I am sorely afraid he was here, but he said that he did not know you.'

The lad shivered. 'It may be so.' He looked down at his fingers and interlaced them on the sheepskin coverlet.

'You said something about eavesdropping?' Adam pressed. 'That you promised not to tell a living soul?'

Rhodri dug his fingers into the springy fleece. 'He came to visit my brother under a banner of truce. They spoke together for some time . . .'

'And you overheard?' Miles guessed.

'Yes.' Rhodri swallowed and looked at the older man. 'Davydd never gives me any responsibility. He sends me out hunting or on petty scouting trips like a child.'

'Sometimes it is hard to know when a fledgeling is ready to fly,' Miles nodded sympathetically.

'And sometimes a fledgeling's wings are clipped!' the boy snapped. His mouth compressed to a single narrow line.

Adam folded his arms. 'So,' he prompted, 'what did you overhear?'

Rhodri continued to work on the fleece and watched his fingers in motion. 'De Mortimer offered my brother silver to kill one of your barons – Ralf le Chevalier. He said that he had a loose tongue and had to be silenced. Davydd agreed. Le Chevalier was no friend of ours, and on more than one occasion he had trespassed with our women. I . . . Is there any more mead?'

'Yes of course.' Adam exchanged shocked glances with Miles as he poured a fresh measure into the cup and gave it to the lad.

Rhodri swallowed deeply and then leaned back against the pillows, his eyes closed and his hair sweat-soaked. 'De Mortimer arranged the ambush and set le Chevalier up to be killed by us – but only Davydd knows that – and me, but I'm not supposed to. The rest of the men all thought it was sheer good fortune when we encountered them in the woods. De Mortimer was watching us, waiting until le Chevalier was down from his horse and bleeding his life into the ground before he made his move. He came down on us with his full force. If Davydd hadn't been expecting just that kind of treachery, we'd have been dead too. *Rhaid wirth lwy hir i fwyta gyda'r diafol.*'

'One needs a long spoon to sup with the devil,' Miles translated grimly.

'My brother was furiously angry about losing the chestnut stallion,' Rhodri added. He darted a sheepish look at Adam. 'I was going to gall him into a red rage by returning from this raid astride the very same horse he had missed, and instead he's got to ransom me and thank his enemies for saving my life.'

102

'Perhaps under the circumstances, he'd prefer to let you rot,' Miles said drily.

Rhodri parted his lips in an expression midway between grimace and smile. 'Brotherly love usually wins by a hair's breadth,' he said.

Adam paced across the solar until he reached the brazier, held his hands to the warmth and looked at Miles. 'You know what this means?'

Miles moved his shoulders. 'It could mean a lot of things, the main one being that my granddaughter is about to pledge her life to her husband's murderer!'

'Sir, she cannot be allowed to do it.'

'Then stop her.'

'How?' Adam spread his hands. 'She knows I hate even the taste of de Mortimer's name on my tongue, and anything I try to tell her, she'll dismiss as raving or fantasy. What do you want me to do? Abduct her over my saddle?'

'Worth a try if all else fails,' Miles said. 'I'm past four score years, lad. Do I have to spoonfeed it to you? Go to the King, put the matter in his hands, and while you are about it, ask of him a boon.'

Adam eyed him suspiciously. 'What sort of boon?'

'Has he rewarded you for your tireless efforts to keep his delightful daughter alive? Knowing Henry, you've had a bagful of promises and a pocketful of nothing.'

'And he's unlikely to change!' Adam growled. 'If it's going to hit his purse, then he'll refuse.'

'It is no concern of his purse,' Miles said. 'Ask him for Heulwen to wife.'

Adam's tawny eyes widened. 'Ask him for Heulwen?'

103

he repeated, voice rising and cracking as it had not done in ten years.

'You hold your tenure direct from him, as did Ralf, and I shouldn't think after the first shock Guyon will object to your suit. In a way, he may be relieved.'

Adam shook his head and walked away from the old man to stare at a hanging on the wall. It had been worked by his mother long before his birth and the moths had eaten it bare in places. His thoughts raced to the erratic thudding of his heart.

'You need a wife,' Miles added mischievously. 'This place frequently resembles a midden.'

'I can't,' Adam said in a flat voice. 'I'm her foster brother.'

Miles said something very rude in Welsh, then reverting to French asked, 'Is that how you feel?'

Adam swung round, sat down on a stool and placed his head in his hands. 'Once, yes, when I was small, I did love her like that, but it changed a long time ago, for me, anyway. Heulwen still thinks of me as a brother.'

Miles raised a sceptical brow. 'You know that for a fact?'

'It was rammed down my throat when I brought her the horses.'

'With more fear than conviction, I'll warrant.' Miles pursed his lips. 'Of course, you don't have to ask Henry at all, just tell him about Warrin and Ralf and hope he will act on it and that Heulwen will find a better mate in time. The choice is yours.'

Adam sat in self-contained silence. The candle fluttered in the sconce and light rippled suddenly on the fittings of his belt as he drew a shuddering breath and

104

raised his head. 'What if she turns on me with hatred?' he said, recoiling from the thought of being rejected by her yet again.

'Then I would call it a disguise for other feelings.'

Adam shook his head and looked away, but within him the hopes and terrors aroused by Miles's suggestion jousted with each other for dominance. Heulwen. He could have Heulwen at his board, living day to day with him, sharing his bed in the great chamber above. Heat rose in his face. Heulwen looking at him in disgust, fighting him, derision on her tongue, and unlike Warrin de Mortimer he did not think he could find it in him to strike her silent if she baulked him, even if it were a matter of life and death. *Life and death.* He thought of what the Welsh boy had told them, its implications. Whatever the reasons, Warrin de Mortimer was guilty of murder. And likely he knew about the silver in Ralf's strongbox, and had set out to gain it for himself by the simple expedient of marrying his widow.

'I'll leave you to think about it.' Miles pushed himself out of the hard, high-backed chair. 'I'd like to see the lass settled before I die, so you'd best make haste.'

'I don't know whether to kiss or kill you!' Adam said ruefully.

'Save the kiss for Heulwen and the killing for where it belongs,' Miles advised him. Legs stiff from having sat so long, he limped carefully from the room.

Adam stared at the archway through which Miles had disappeared, and slowly rose himself, a bemused expression on his face, his thoughts walking a mental tightrope. After a while, he began to realise that the rope was strung across a gorge that stretched into a distance he could not see, that behind and below snarled the demons and serpents of self-doubt and cowardice, and that the only possible way was forward. That understanding made his burden suddenly seem much lighter. He straightened and squared his shoulders, and strode from the chamber, calling for Jerold and Sweyn.

10

Down in the south, the snow had turned to freezing rain and the ground was a morass of puddles and melting, muddy slush. The court was keeping Christmas at Windsor, and almost every royal tenant-in-chief was present in answer to the summons from the King. The lesser but still important barons were here, the high clergy and the King of Scots with his retinue – all present to swear allegiance to the Dowager Empress Matilda, King Henry's daughter and designated heir. Banners and shields adorned the balconies of the wealthy, and the evergreen bunches outside every alehouse welcomed the swollen ranks of Windsor's temporary population

Heulwen shivered and tried to huddle deeper into the folds of her cloak as the wind flurried her garments and blustered rain into her face. She struggled to display an interest she did not feel in the bolts of cloth laid out for her inspection upon the counter of a cloth merchant's booth. Dutifully she rubbed the fine, white linen between her fingers and agreed that it would be perfect for making shirts and shifts, trying to smile as lengths were cut and folded to one side.

'Now,' Judith said with a note of satisfaction, her discerning gaze on the merchant's displayed bales of cloth, 'your wedding gown. What about that green silk over there?'

Obligingly the merchant reached for the bolt indicated.

'I don't know, I had not thought.' Heulwen shivered, her face pinched and pale.

'Well in the name of the saints do so now!' Judith snapped with the exasperation that came of having trailed around the market-place all morning with a limp rag in tow. 'Heulwen, you're to be betrothed tomorrow morning and married at Candlemas. You haven't time for vagueness!'

'I'm sorry, Mama. It's just that I'm cold and out of sorts,' Heulwen excused herself, giving again that wan, forlorn smile that made Judith want to scream. 'The green will suit me very well.'

'God in heaven, child, you haven't even looked at it!'

The merchant lowered his eyes from the irate lady of Ravenstow and the woebegone young woman at her side, and busied himself unfolding the bolt and rippling the grass-green silk across the counter.

Heulwen's lower lip trembled as she fought with tears. Fine sleet stung her face like flung shingle. Behind, two accompanying men-at-arms were stamping their feet to keep warm, and Helgund, her stepmother's elderly maid was grimacing at the pain from her chilblains.

'I trust in your judgement, Mama,' she said in a subdued voice and stared at the muddy hem of her cloak.

Judith closed her eyes and swallowed. A packhorse laden with brightly coloured belts was led past, and someone else's servant scurried by clutching a cloth-covered pie dish, the savoury steam teasing the nostrils and torturing the empty stomachs of those freezing at the draper's booth. 'Very well,' Judith said with commendable calm for one who was so sorely tried. 'The green silk, and some of that gold damask over there for an undertunic and trim. Have them brought to my lodgings and my steward will pay you.'

The merchant bowed, and started to refold the bolt of silk, his face expressionless.

As the women left the booth, Judith's exasperation gave way to concern, for Heulwen was following her with the vapid docility of a sheep. 'Perhaps this betrothal should be deferred until you are feeling better,' she said with a frown.

'No!' That response at least was sharp and swift and so at odds with Heulwen's mood that Judith stared at her stepdaughter with widening eyes.

'No,' said Heulwen in a more controlled voice. 'I'm not ill, Mama. I need this betrothal to take place tomorrow. It is the waiting as much as anything else that is dragging me down. I cannot take an interest in my wedding gown when I have this dreadful fear that something will happen to prevent the marriage.'

'Nonsense!' Judith said brusquely.

'I know, but it does not make the fear go away.'

Judith allowed her man-at-arms to boost her into the saddle of her waiting mare. The frown remained on her face. Heulwen might be more than half Welsh, but her nature was essentially practical, without the eerie sense of premonition with which so many of her race were gifted. If she was having brooding foresights, it was because she felt like a condemned prisoner who sees the moment of execution approaching, and is impatient for that moment to have come and gone and have the peace of darkness.

She and Guyon might not have pushed her into this marriage, Judith thought grimly, but neither had they done anything to stop her, and if you let a boat drift with the tide, frequently it smashes to pieces on the rocks. Perhaps the betrothal should indeed be cancelled until Heulwen had had more time to settle down. After all, there was no rush.

'Your father and I were forced to marry,' she said as she shook the reins. 'I was unhappy and terrified and there was nothing I could do short of killing myself to prevent it from happening. It took a long time and a great deal of patience on your father's behalf before I learned to trust, even longer before love grew out of it – for both of us.' She looked across at her stepdaughter. Heulwen's mouth was stubbornly set now, but whether to resist Judith or tears was uncertain.

'It was different for you and Ralf,' she continued. 'You wanted him from the beginning, and he wanted you – but I think it was your dowry and the thought of having a nubile fifteen-year-old in his bed whenever he chose to sleep there that decided him, not love.'

'Mama, what are you trying to tell me?'

'Oh, I don't know. Perhaps that you should not let your experience with Ralf sour your future expectations.'

'It hasn't.' Heulwen grimaced. 'Not soured, but lowered. I no longer think that the stars will fall down into my hands just because I reach for them. Was that how my mother felt about Papa?'

Judith reined back her mare as a laden cart splashed past them. She had never concealed the past from Heulwen, but it was seldom the girl asked, and some parts were too painful for Judith to broach without direct demand. 'Yes,' she said. 'I suppose it was. Your mother knew it was impossible for them to wed – a Welsh merchant's daughter and a marcher lord – so she guarded her heart from him. I met her only once, on the day before she was killed. She came to tell Guyon that she was severing the old ties and getting married; it was a business arrangement like your own.'

Helwen was momentarily diverted from her troubles. 'Weren't you jealous of her? When I found out about one of Ralf's women, I was ready to take a dagger to her throat – and geld him!'

Judith's lips twitched. 'Jealous?' She urged the mare forward again. 'Oh yes, so jealous that until I met her it gnawed at me like poison, but I could not hate her. Besides, although your father occasionally visited her, he did not lie with her after we were wed.' The twitch became an open, rueful smile. 'Oh, not for reasons of moral nicety or to salve my feelings I am sure, but she was heavily pregnant with you, and by the time you were born, he was beginning to notice that he had a wife for that kind of comfort.' The corners of her eyes crinkled. 'I did once take a knife to one of the women at court though when she presumed too far on their old acquaintance – Alais de Clare. She's bound to be at court tonight. It's a long time since we met on that kind of battlefield – I wonder if she still remembers.' Her mischievous laugh lightened Heulwen's mood and she responded with the first genuine smile of the morning.

When they rode into the courtyard of their town house, the grooms were already busy tending several fine blood-horses. A squire was fondling a strawberry roan trapped out in expensive, gilded harness. The stallion's superb pinkish coat was as glossy as satin, revealing that its owner could afford to keep it stable-fed during the long winter months. The squire glanced round and a delighted grin flashed across his round face. Having swiftly handed the roan's bridle to another boy, he ran across the courtyard, to help Judith and Heulwen from their mounts.

'Henry!' Judith kissed her fourth child joyfully. He squirmed away, concealing a grimace, and smoothed down the sandy hair she had just tousled, a red flush mantling his freckled face. He was of his royal grandfather's build, stocky and compact, promising bull-like strength rather than the feline grace of his brothers, and he was the only one with his mother's tawny-hazel colouring, the others all being dark like Guyon.

Warned by his reaction to Judith's embrace, Heulwen confined herself to a swift peck on his cheek and an admiring remark about the new dagger at his belt.

Smiling proudly, he showed it to her. 'Earl Robert gave it to me last night for serving so well at table,' he said, his head high.

'You've learned something then,' Judith said, looking him over with brisk approval. Henry had been something of a scarecrow before leaving them to squire in Robert of Gloucester's household, but he had acquired a certain polish since then to judge from his spruce, outward appearance and the smooth alacrity with which he had helped her down from the mare.

'He was dining with the Empress. She smiled at me. She's very pretty and not as . . .' He left the rest of the sentence in midair and looked at Heulwen, who was staring at a particularly handsome dark bay stallion tethered among the others.

'He's a beauty, isn't he?' Henry said enthusiastically.

'Henry, what's he doing here?'

The boy blinked at the sharpness of her tone. 'Lord Robert's just been over at the horse fair. He took a fancy to this one, and it was Adam of Thornford selling and he's got a good reputation. My lord said that the price was high, but probably fair for what he was getting.' Puzzled, he looked from his mother to his half-sister. 'What's wrong? What have I said that's so funny?'

Heulwen shook her head. 'He was one of Ralf's stallions – Adam was selling him for me. What did Earl Robert pay?'

'Seventy marks in the end. What do you mean, Adam was selling him for you?'

Heulwen touched his arm. 'I'll tell you all about it later.' Biting her lip, she followed her stepmother into the house.

Before a smoky central hearth, Earl Robert of Gloucester, senior child among the cluster of illegitimate offspring King Henry had sired, was warming his feet at the fire, cup of hippocras in hand, high forehead ribbed with pleading sincerity as he addressed the dubious Lord of Ravenstow.

'We need your support. I know you have your doubts about swearing for Matilda, God knows, she'd tempt a

113

saint to commit murder sometimes, but she's capable of ruling, I swear it.'

Guyon gave him a pained smile. 'I do not doubt her capabilities. I'm married to such a one myself.' His eyes darted with wry amusement to the threshold where his wife was handing her cloak to a maid. 'But men look to be ruled by a man, not a woman.'

'Do you?'

'By preference, yes – well, in some ways anyway,' he added with another amused look at his wife, but then he sobered. 'What worries me is that she will wed someone who is going to try the crown on for size and in consequence break us all.'

'My father is wiser than that. He will look and choose most carefully,' Gloucester objected, bristling. 'And Matilda's no meek maid to give up what is hers by right.'

Frowning, Guyon stared into the middle distance, and finally back at the earnest face of his brother-by-marriage.

'It is not enough to say your father will choose carefully. He will choose to his own dictates unless he is made to swear that he will not go about the purpose of arranging Matilda's marriage without the agreement of his tenants-in-chief.'

'You have been talking to Henry of Blois, haven't you?'

'No, I haven't. It is what any sensible man would say.' Guyon's nostrils flared with impatience. 'I've only seen Henry of Blois from a distance thus far. The only man to whom I have spoken is the Earl of Leicester, and that's because my son's a chaplain in his household – and Leicester is not happy about swearing an oath to Matilda, with or without a husband.'

Robert of Gloucester scraped his hands rapidly

through his receding dark hair. Mustering support for his sister's cause was like ploughing a stony field; every few paces he met solid opposition, even from such reasonable loyalists as Guyon of Ravenstow whose own children were Matilda's nieces and nephews. 'Guy . . .' he began again, but his brother-in-law interrupted him, spreading his hands and sighing.

'All right, Robert. I'll swear to her, for her, and at her, but only if Henry promises not to tie her to some entirely unsuitable husband.'

'I am sure he can be brought to an agreement,' Robert said, with the smoothness of a diplomat, meeting the by now familiar response of a half-raised shoulder and a look of badly concealed disbelief. He judged the moment propitious to leave and let Guyon mull over what had been said. If he made haste, there was still time to visit Hugh of Norfolk and sound him out before it was time to prepare for the evening's feast and make his report to Henry.

He stood up and turning, kissed his half-sister and then Heulwen in greeting and farewell.

'We were just admiring your new stallion,' Judith said. 'If Heulwen had known you were looking for another destrier, she'd not have trailed the bay all the way to Windsor.'

'I beg your pardon?' Gloucester smiled and looked blank.

Laughing, Judith told him from whom he had actually purchased the horse.

Robert laughed too, if a little ruefully as he donned his hat. 'One of Ralf's stallions, no wonder! I did think it strange that young de Lacey should have a horse of that calibre to sell when he's only just home from the Empire. The sly fox, he never said anything!'

'Perhaps he wasn't sure you'd offer the full price if you knew it was almost in the family,' Heulwen suggested, the insult negated by the dimple that appeared at the corner of her mouth.

Robert snorted. 'Very probably. He's as wary as an undercroft cat, that one. Doubtless since I paid him seventy marks for the beast, you'll be seeing him sooner rather than later.'

Heulwen fiddled with the brooch pinned at her shoulder, heavy as a man's hand clasped in possession. She had not set eyes on Adam since the day of the Welsh attack and had managed in the interim to convince herself that what she felt was a passing lust, and that any male could as well be substituted – but a substitute was not the genuine article. She thought of Adam's dark smile, that quizzical way he had of looking, his dry humour, the gentle pressure of his hands on a horse's flank, or on her waist.

'I saw Warrin de Mortimer at the horse fair too,' Gloucester added. 'He and his father were trying the paces of a courser. I gather that the young man's soon to be wed. He's very lucky.'

'I'm very fond of him,' Heulwen said tonelessly.

Guyon eased to his feet to see their guest out. 'I hope Warrin and Adam did not encounter each other,' he said. 'Last time they were within rubbing distance I had to stop them going for their swords.'

Gloucester shook his head. 'No. They were at opposite ends of the field, and young de Lacey was making to leave even as I did.' He smiled secretively.

Guyon gave him a questioning look

Robert glanced over his shoulder at Heulwen. 'Yours

won't be the only betrothal we celebrate this feast-tide, my dear. I have it on good authority that my father intends offering Adam de Lacey a rich bride in reward for services rendered to the crown. There are one or two choice heiresses in his wardship, and he is going to give young de Lacey first pick.'

After he had gone, Heulwen realised that she must have made the appropriate responses, for no one had remarked upon her behaviour, and they were all at ease, talking among themselves. They were her family, and yet she felt like a stranger, sneaking warmth from a hearth not her own.

The thought of Adam with a wife cut her to the quick. She could mouth that it was what she wished for him; she could say it with seeming sincerity, but the truth was different. For three months she had turned a blind eye in the same way that she had turned a blind eye to Ralf's infidelities – full knowing but refusing to acknowledge. But such blindness did not last for ever, and the light when it returned was too dazzling to be borne.

She complained of a headache when at length Judith noticed her silent pallor, and allowed herself to be bundled up in warm furs and put to bed like a child, a hot stone at her feet and a drink of honey in hot water between her cold fingers, permitting everyone to think that she had caught a chill from standing too long at the market stalls. When Warrin came calling, she told Judith to send him away and curled herself into a foetal ball of misery, wishing she were dead.

11

Henry, by the Grace of God King of England and Duke of Normandy, held up his hand to silence the scratching of the scribe's quill, and stared with shrewd, flint-grey eyes at the young man kneeling before him. 'You are quite sure of this?'

'The Welsh lad had a fever, sire, but he was still well within his wits,' Adam answered steadily. 'He knew what he was saying, and I judged it to be true.'

'But then your judgement may be coloured by the known fact that you and Warrin de Mortimer hate the sight of each other.'

'Miles le Gallois was there too. He will bear out my story, and he has no axe to grind.'

Henry pursed his thin lips and continued to study Adam. The young man's father had been a rebel – violent, untrustworthy and ambitious to a fault, but a good warrior in the field, very good. To all outward appearances his son had inherited only the last trait, although it was never safe to take anyone for granted. It was a timely reminder that like did not always breed like. Old Hugh de Mortimer was steadfast and bovine without an original thought in his skull. There was nothing bovine about Warrin, and perhaps nothing steadfast either.

'Ralf le Chevalier acted the courier for me on several occasions last year,' Henry said, pinching his upper lip between forefinger and thumb. 'You had several accidents between the empire and Normandy, didn't you?'

Adam grimaced and recited, 'Two attacks by brigands, a sniper on the Rouen road, a fire at a priory where we stayed overnight, and three barrels of pitch that mysteriously exploded on the galley we were to have taken from Barfleur had we not changed our plans at the last moment. The last one was not on Ralf's slate, he was already dead by then, but I think you will find that Warrin de Mortimer was in Normandy at the time.'

Henry stared into the distance for a long time. The scribe stifled a yawn behind his hand and unnecessarily trimmed his quill. At length, the King leaned forward in his chair. 'I understand he's been paying devoted court to le Chevalier's widow?'

Adam stared at the cold tiles that were paining his knees, concentrating on a red diamond shape until his eyes blurred. 'Yes, sire.'

'On your feet. I cannot read your eyes when all I can see is the top of your head.'

Adam stood up, his expression immobile. Henry regarded him without relaxing the intensity of his stare. 'Does the widow's family welcome the match?' he pursued in a soft voice.

'Ravenstow's loyalty is without blemish,' Adam said quickly, seeing where this was leading and feeling cold.

'That is not what I asked.'

'Her family do not object, but neither do I think there would be a protest if the arrangement were broken. Indeed, sire, it is on that very subject that I desire you to grant me a boon.'

Henry raised his brows. 'Indeed?'

Adam clenched his fists and inhaled deeply. 'I desire your permission to take Ralf le Chevalier's widow to wife.'

'Ah,' Henry said with satisfaction. 'Now we come to the meat of the matter.'

Adam swallowed and held on to his composure, continuing doggedly, 'The formal betrothal between her and de Mortimer still awaits your consent. There is no legal impediment to my request.'

Henry's brows came down and levelled. 'Why this particular woman?'

'I want her,' Adam said bluntly, 'and I'd rather have her than Hawise FitzAllen or Olivia de Roche. I know her dowry is not as great, but there are compensations.'

Henry eyed him sharply. 'How did you know the girls I had in mind?'

'Your son the Earl of Gloucester bought a horse from me this morning. He thought as a favour to give me some extra space of time to decide – unaware that my decision was already made.'

Henry snorted down his nose. 'He has a tender heart and a mule's brain,' he remarked of his eldest son, but his eyes softened with a rare, genuine affection before his gaze impaled Adam again. 'I ought to refuse. You are putting me in a most difficult position.' He drummed his fingers on the arms of his chair.

For what seemed a millennium, Adam waited, unspeaking. It would be no use to remind Henry of the many debts and obligations that went unpaid on his part. To the King, a loyal man was a workhorse, and any toil performed merely his due.

'You want her,' Henry said incisively. 'Whim or conviction?'

Adam opened his mouth.

'No.' Henry gave a brusque wave of his hand. 'I can see it in your face. You're beyond redemption. What does the woman say?'

'She will refuse me at first, but she is open to persuasion,' Adam said, hoping it was true.

Henry looked at his nails and considered. 'Give me the silver in le Chevalier's strongbox, and you can have her,' he said. 'De Mortimer can be compensated by one of the other women I was going to offer you, if of course he doesn't lose his life and his lands for treason once the matter has been investigated further.'

Dismissed, Adam breathed out a hard sigh that was not so much relief as the releasing of tension now that the first and simplest of his tasks was completed. All he had left to do now was convince Heulwen and her family to see matters his way, which was definitely more daunting than facing a king who had the power of life and death at his fingertips.

Heulwen sat up in bed and, folding her arms around her raised knees, contemplated the hanging on the wall opposite without really seeing the hunting scene it so vibrantly portrayed. It had been stitched by the same group of women who had worked on Bishop Odo's tapestry and was worth a small fortune, or so Warrin said with his habit of setting a price on everything.

The shutters were closed against the bitter wind but she could hear it howling angrily against the cracks and hurling needles of sleet upon the shingles. Below in the main room, only the servants were present. Her father had business elsewhere, her stepmother had gone to visit the Countess of Gloucester, with whom she had a friendship of several years' standing, and Renard and Henry were off at the horse fair.

At last she put aside the covers and sat on the edge of her bed. A stoked brazier threw out heat. Judith said that a chill was best sweated out, but only Heulwen knew she was not suffering from a chill unless it be of the soul. Tonight she was to be presented at court and tomorrow morning Warrin would formally ask Henry for his approval of their marriage – strange how a haven could become a trap in so short a space of time. Her thoughts were as stifling as the pressure of Warrin's mouth on hers and the feel of his heavy hands on her body. The change was not in him, but in her, and was a gradual feeling, brought to its crisis by Lord Robert's news today.

Swallowing the knot of self-pity in her throat, she picked up her undergown and tunic from the end of the bed. Behind her the door opened and then gently closed. The latch rattled home. She tucked a loose swathe of hair behind her ear and turned, thinking to find her maid. 'Elswith, I want you to bring me – Holy Mother, what are you doing here!' She dropped the garments. 'Where's Elswith?'

'Below stairs . . .' Adam's voice emerged as a croak, for the short chemise she was wearing left little to the imagination, and those the most tantalising parts. 'I told her I needed a very important private word – I didn't realise that – Elswith said you were resting, I didn't think that . . .' He shut his mouth.

'You never do!' She snatched up her cloak and wrapped it around herself. 'What kind of manners do you have that you could not wait below?'

'It is not a matter of manners, Heulwen,' he said wearily.

'Then what is it?'

'A matter of murder – Ralf's.' He put down a leather money pouch on the coffer near the bed. 'Payment for your bay stallion.'

'What did you say?' She stared at him, her eyes widening with shock.

'Heulwen, sit down.' He gestured to the bed, and removing his cloak, draped it across the coffer.

She remained standing. 'The Welsh killed Ralf,' she whispered. 'Do you tell me otherwise?'

'Yes, the Welsh killed him, so much is true, but Warrin de Mortimer paid them to do it.'

'I don't believe you,' she said flatly.

'I did not think that you would.'

'Adam, if this is a ruse to blacken Warrin's name to me it won't – Oh!' She cried out as he strode round the edge of the bed, grabbed her arm, and pushed her down.

'Sit there!' he snarled, his breath ragged and hard. 'Stop running away and listen for once!'

She gasped at the force he had used, as if a tame dog had suddenly turned vicious, and gazed up at him, shocked by his harsh expression. With neither softening

123

nor compassion, he told her everything his Welsh hostage had revealed, finishing bitterly, 'Your grandfather was there, ask him if my word is not good enough.'

'I – no Adam, you must both be mistaken . . .' Her eyes were desolate, like a woman he had once seen when her house had burned down and she had lost everything. 'Why would Warrin do such a thing? Is he involved in this betrayal too? I do not believe it!'

'Then you are deluding yourself.'

'You've always been quick to see wrong in Warrin!' she lashed out, clutching at straws. 'Perhaps he had discovered that Ralf was betraying the King's trust. That would as easily explain things as your version.'

'Warrin would not give a bucket of horse shit for the direction of Ralf's allegiance, not unless it jeopardised his own standing!'

'Don't shout at me,' she said miserably, and wiped the back of her hand across her face, smearing tear streaks.

Guilt flooded through Adam at the sight of her vulnerability, and he sat down beside her on the coverlet. 'I'm sorry,' he said in a more controlled voice. 'It's just that I seem to be butting my head against a stone wall, and it's only natural to howl at the pain.'

Heulwen surveyed the ruins of her world: Warrin was Ralf's murderer by proxy, and the reasons for his courtship were thus cast in a sinister light. Ralf himself was dead, and not in clean battle, but brought down in a murk of lies and intrigue. There would be no betrothal, no marriage, nothing; the trap was sprung and she was free, but at what cost? She wiped her eyes again and looked at Adam through her wet lashes. He was gazing down at his hands, his mouth set in a bleak line.

Impulsively she leaned over and kissed his cheek. 'No, Adam, the apology should be mine.'

Adam groaned and turned his head. Their lips met, and he lifted his hands to pull her against him. He knew he ought to tell her the rest of the tale, what he had requested of Henry and what Henry had demanded of him in return, but he was afraid of breaking this moment and being brusquely rebuffed. The kiss momentarily broke as they surfaced for air. Gasping, Heulwen stared at him, but if her breathing was swift, it owed less to panic than it did to desire. She had been fighting the attraction ever since his return in the early autumn, but there was no longer any need to continue the battle. Adam was to take a rich wife of Henry's choosing, and honour no longer bound her body to Warrin – least of all to Warrin. She joined her mouth to his again, leaning into his taut, quivering body, pushing him, so that they fell backwards together across the bed.

It was wild and desperate, frantic on both sides, so hot that it immolated all reason, leaving only the touch of skin on skin and the exquisite sensations of desire aroused to an unbearable level and then released, flinging them both into oblivion.

Adam slowly revived to the sound of his own breathing. He tasted the salt of perspiration and felt beneath his lips the thundering pulse in Heulwen's throat. Her ribcage rose and fell rapidly against his own. He lifted himself a little to look tentatively into her face. Her eyes were closed, her lips parted. She licked them as if still seeking the taste of him in a gesture so sensual that, although he had peaked, he pushed forward again into her body. She gave a small moan of pleasure and rubbed

125

a bent thigh along his hip-bone. He touched a coil of her hair, felt it slide like silk between his fingers, and was filled with an overwhelming mixture of tenderness and guilt. 'Heulwen,' he murmured tentatively. 'Heulwen, look at me.'

Her eyes opened. They were misty, still glazed with satisfaction.

'I'm sorry,' he said. 'I didn't mean to go this far . . .'

She covered his lips with the palm of her hand. 'It doesn't matter,' she whispered. 'It was bound to happen, and I knew what I was doing.'

'Then you are not angry this time?' he asked, thinking back to the last occasion when he had kissed her and she had run from him.

Heulwen took her hand away and replaced it with her mouth in a slow, undulating kiss. 'Only at myself for driving you too fast. It was over too soon to be fully savoured.'

Adam stared down at her, becomingly flushed and tousled beneath him, and was startled by the sensual, frank regret he saw there.

'Does my boldness disturb you?' She tilted him a half-teasing, half-serious look.

'Disturb me?' He considered the thought for a moment, and then grinned. 'Well yes, it disturbs me a great deal, but in the sort of way I don't mind. You have my approval to be bold as often as you like!' His own look was half-teasing, half-serious as he lifted himself off her. Instead of reaching for his clothes, however, he lay down at her side and wound the strand of hair he held around his fingers. The bed was warm from the heat of their bodies and the piled skins and feather mattress made it as soft and comfortable as a glimpse of heaven. The room was silent except for the sound of their breathing, the tick of the charcoal settling in the brazier, and the occasional sputter of the rush dips. Outside the world howled, tearing cold fingers at the shutters, striving to prise apart their encapsulated haven.

Adam turned his back on it to fill his eyes with Heulwen's tumbled beauty and his hand moved to stroke the swell of her breast. 'Heulwen, would you marry me if I asked?' His voice was mild and quiet, designed not to frighten her.

'I thought that Henry was going to offer you the pick of several wealthy heiresses? Robert of Gloucester told me so this morning.' Her eyes were clearer now, focusing on him as the pleasure faded to a background sensation.

'He did, and I refused them. I asked for you instead and he consented.'

'What do you mean?' The strand of hair was jerked from his fingers as she raised herself on one elbow to stare at him.

'What I said. I want you to wife. Listen Heulwen . . .' He reached out to her as she sat up, her eyes furious.

'Did it not occur to you to ask me first!' she cried. The rough wool of his crumpled tunic prickled her thighs. She dragged it out from beneath her and pushed it at him.

'I am asking you now. You cannot deny that you want me as much as I want you.'

'That was lust, pure and simple,' she bit out. 'A mare will stand for any stallion if the time is right.'

Adam flung the tunic back down on the bed and grabbed her by the shoulders. She twisted in his grip. 'Let me go,' she spat, 'or I'll scream!'

'Scream, then – have the maids discover us like this. Peal the bells, let all of Windsor know!' But he released her and, breathing hard, sat back.

'Adam, I won't marry you,' she said on a quieter but still determined note.

'Why? And do not say it is because I'm your brother. I swallowed that one like a stewpond carp, but I've learned since then.'

She hid her face in her hands for a moment, then opened her palms and scooped back her tumbled hair, regarding him squarely. 'Because,' she said, 'I will not be bound by holy vows to that kind of hell ever again.'

'But you were willing to wed a turd like Warrin de Mortimer,' he objected. 'Perhaps I am being stupid, but I fail to see what recommends him above me?'

'Our arrangement was one of convenience,' Heulwen said in a shaken voice. 'You would want more of me than I can give. Yes, my body answers yours, but such a need is fleeting. Ralf taught me that lesson too well for me ever to forget it.'

'I am not Ralf,' he said and leaned towards her, 'and it is far more than a fleeting lust. That, I could have slaked anywhere.'

'So you say now,' she retorted bitterly and picked up her shift. 'But what will you say in ten years' time?'

'If the past ten years have not altered my heart, ten years forward will not change it either.' He touched her shoulder, slid his hand down her arm until he reached her wrist and tugged her gently against him. 'Heulwen, I love you,' he whispered against the hammer-beat of the pulse in her throat. 'Marry me?'

He felt her melt under the gentle persuasion of his

fingertips and stretched out his free hand to remove the shift that she held as a barrier between them. 'Marry me,' he said again, and sought her mouth with small, nibbling kisses.

Heulwen gasped, torn between the demands of her senses and sense itself. 'Adam, please I . . . give me time to . . .'

Outside a maid cried a warning, the sound rising to a scream and then cut off short. Heulwen and Adam sprang apart and Adam shot to his feet. Heavy footsteps pounded up the wooden outer stairs, coming at a run, and the door crashed open upon its hinges. Wind-spun snow swirled round the threshold, and over it strode Warrin de Mortimer, his face a blizzard of furious emotions as he surveyed the scene within.

'You misbegotten, hell-spawned son of a murdering pervert!' he roared, and reached to his scabbard.

'Warrin, put up that sword!' Heulwen cried in alarm. He was blocking the doorway, their only means of escape, and he was a murderer with murder in his eyes. Pale as ice they flickered briefly to Heulwen where she sat, naked and shivering, clothed only in her hair and the shield of her crossed arms. 'Hold your tongue, whore!' he spat. 'Am I supposed to believe that this is one of your foster brother's "occasional presences" that I must by necessity tolerate?'

Adam had been sidling nearer to the bed. 'I have the right,' he said. 'Heulwen has been vouchsafed to me this afternoon by the King himself.' He arched a sardonic brow. 'I am assuming you didn't know?'

Warrin roared like an enraged bull and sprang. Adam flung himself sideways and the sword slashed across the pillow which Adam had managed to grab to protect himself. As the feathers snowed down, hampering Warrin's vision, Adam dived across the room and grabbed Guyon's shield from where it was leaning against the wall. He jammed his left arm into the leather hand-holds and tried to reach the scabbarded sword standing further along the wall.

Warrin got there first, and it was only the speed of Adam's reflexes that saved him from being hacked open like a pig on a slaughterman's trestle. A splinter of wood flew up from the surface of the shield and rebounded to stick like a quill in de Mortimer's cheek. He plucked it loose and dark blood dripped down his face.

'Do you enjoy murder?' Adam asked, ducking another swipe of the blade. 'A surfeit of Welsh hospitality for Ralf, and a sword through the belly for me. My Welsh hostage overheard a certain conversation between you and Davydd ap Tewdr, and was a witness to its result.'

Warrin's guard dropped for an instant and Adam lunged, buffeting the shield boss at his face, then made a dive for the sword. The night-candle stand crashed over, and Judith's expensive cedarwood box of tapestry silks tumbled with it. A hinge splayed and snapped, and the bright silks spilled out and were trampled underfoot.

Warrin recovered from his momentary recoil. 'I'll have your life for that foul slander!' he choked, and came on fast as Adam strove to free the blade from the scabbard.

Heulwen darted for the open door and screeched at the full pitch of her lungs for help. In the courtyard, Renard and Henry, just returned from their visit to see the jousting and already alerted by the squawking of the maids that something was seriously wrong, hurtled up the stairs.

'God in heaven!' Henry's eyes were huge with disbelief. From behind his naked half-sister, there came the sound of a muffled crash and a howl of fury.

'More like hell to pay by the looks of it,' Renard said. Pausing only to gesture at two gawking serjeants, he pelted up the stairs.

'Renard, stop them, they'll kill each other!' Heulwen screamed at him.

He pushed his cloak at her. 'Cover yourself,' he snapped. Thrusting her to one side, he entered his parents' bedchamber. A hurled goblet crashed against the wall, narrowly missing his head. The air was awhirl with goose feathers, some of which had drifted into the brazier – which was, remarkably, still standing – and the room was filled with the stench of burning. At the far side of the room, as mother-naked as Heulwen, Adam de Lacey was cornered behind a badly scarred shield, and Warrin de Mortimer was swinging murderously at him.

'In the name of Holy Christ, stop!' yelled Renard, his voice cracking as it sometimes still did when pressure was put upon it. He was ignored and his jaw, which was very much his royal grandfather's, tightened. He leaped on to the bed, took three paces ankle-deep in feathers and jumped down between the antagonists, ensuring that he faced de Mortimer rather than presenting him with the target of the space between his shoulder blades.

'Renard, keep out of this,' Adam snarled at the youth's turned back.

131

'In my father's absence I have the authority here,' Renard answered, his voice once more on the level and controlled. 'Put up your swords.'

Adam shot a sidelong glance at the two hesitant but brawny serjeants standing to either side of the doorway, Heulwen shivering beside them, her face pinched and blue. He grounded his own swordpoint in the rushes, but kept his fingers wrapped around the hilt, and did not lower the shield.

Warrin bared his teeth at Renard. 'Don't get ideas above yourself, whelp! What kind of authority is it that allows your sister to play the heated bitch across the sheets with this forsworn cur!'

Colour slashed across Renard's cheekbones. 'Put up your sword,' he reiterated and nodded to the serjeants, who started forward. 'I think you should leave.'

De Mortimer stared into Renard's flint-dark eyes, then beyond them to where Adam stood poised, prepared to defend, or attack. 'I'll have a reckoning for this,' he said thickly as he slotted his blade back into the scabbard, 'on your body.'

'My pleasure.' Adam returned the sneer. 'And you had better start praying because I can see the flames of hell encircling your feet already.'

There was a tense silence while their eyes met and held, will beating against will. Warrin pointed an index finger at Adam. An ostentatious gold ring trembled on his knuckle. 'You're dead,' he said hoarsely, and turning on his heel, stalked to the door. As he reached Heulwen, he struck her backhanded across the face, knocking her hard into the wall. 'Whore!' he repeated, and slammed out into the bitter, snow-pocked wind.

Renard gestured the serjeants out after him. 'Make sure he leaves,' he said, and went to pick up his sister from the floor. Adam shouldered him roughly aside, and, dropping the shield, stooped to lift her himself. A furious red blotch was fast marring her cheek and closing one eye. Her breath came in great dry gasps.

Renard took a sheepskin from the devastated bed and threw it around her shoulders on top of his cloak. 'You've really set the fat into the fire this time.' He shook his head. 'Couldn't you have trysted somewhere less dangerous?'

'It wasn't intentional,' Adam replied without looking round. 'It just happened.'

Renard arched a sceptical brow, thinking of himself and the falconer's daughter, or that engaging little laundress at the palace who was as soft as a kitten, neither of whom had ever fired him beyond the loss of all caution. He lifted the shield and replaced it against the wall.

'The trouble is,' he said, pursing his lips, 'you are likely to burn a lot of other people too.'

'Renard, leave it alone,' Adam said with soft vehemence, and sat Heulwen down on the bed. 'Come, love, let me look at your face.'

She pushed him away. 'It's nothing, the least of my wounds,' she whispered and bent over, arms folded to her middle, her face screened in her coppery masses of hair, as she began to sob.

Adam stretched his arm around her shoulders, feeling helpless, and held her. 'Hush, Heulwen, it's all right,' he murmured over and over again, fingers smoothing and stroking.

133

Renard cleared his throat. 'I'll see if there's any usque-baugh below,' he said, and headed for the stairs, only to collide with his mother and her maid advancing up them. From the expression on his mother's face, it was obvious that the news was already on its way to scorching a path through the city.

Judith stared at the shambles of her bedchamber with a face that wore the calm expression of fore-warned disbelief. She took in her work basket and the riot of spilled silks, the overturned candle-stand, the raw slashed wood showing its flesh through the leather skin of her husband's shield, the hacked pillows and the feathers that puffed gently into the air as she trod forwards, and finally, her gaze came to rest on the bed.

Adam de Lacey looked up at her. One lean-muscled arm lay across Heulwen's shoulder and his hand was buried in her tangled hair. 'It's all my fault,' he said, meeting her eyes squarely. 'I'll make amends.'

Judith looked quickly around the wrecked room again and back to Adam. 'Indeed you will,' she said severely. 'I suppose you were caught in the act?'

'Not quite.' Adam coloured. 'I'm sorry I—'

'It's too late for apologies to be of much use,' Judith said waspishly, but having removed her cloak, she sat down at her stepdaughter's other side. 'Adam, put some clothes on before you freeze to death,' she said in a brusque tone, 'and you'd better let me have a look at that wound on your arm. It needs salve.'

He looked with surprise at the oozing narrow cut running between wrist and elbow. 'I did it on the candle-stand,' he said vaguely. 'It wasn't de Mortimer's sword.

You'd better look at Heulwen first. He struck her full force across the face as he was leaving.'

Judith contemplated her stepdaughter, or what could be seen of her through the screening swathes of tangled red hair. She was whimpering softly now, and Judith judged the pain of Warrin's blow to be the least of her agony.

'Adam, when you're dressed, I think it would be advisable if you went below to wait for Guyon,' she said in a gentler voice, and to Heulwen, 'Come, child, calm yourself. No one yet died of shame.' Under the weight of Judith's stare, Adam reluctantly relinquished his hold on Heulwen and sought out his clothes. Stony-faced, the maid picked up his crumpled shirt from the floor and handed it to him at arm's length. Awkward in the uneasy silence, he fumbled into it and struggled with chausses, hose and tunic.

'I suppose,' Judith said wearily, 'that I should have seen it coming.' And then on an angry, exasperated note, 'If you wanted each other this badly, why in God's sweet name did you not speak to me or Guyon!'

Adam stamped into one of his boots, then hunted around the room until he found its partner half buried beneath a trailing length of creased sheet. 'I was going to if you had been here this afternoon, but . . . well, the wain came before the ox.'

'Not just the wain but an entire baggage supply of trouble!' Judith said tartly as he pulled on the other boot and began latching his belt.

Renard returned with the usquebaugh flask in his hand. 'Papa's just ridden in,' he announced cheerfully. 'Good luck, Adam. I don't know what he'll do to you when he sees the state of his shield.'

'Renard!' Judith's tone was peremptory.

He gave the flask to Helgund and came to the bed, where he squatted lithely on his haunches to peer under and within Heulwen's curtaining hair. 'Come on, Helly,' he coaxed. 'I'd have hated it to happen to me, but de Mortimer's been deserving a kick in his arrogance for so long now that it's a pleasure to see him get it. I'd rather have Adam for a brother-in-law any day than that conceited pea-brain . . . All right, Mama, I'm going.' Grinning, less than contrite, he sauntered out of the door.

'You'd better go down too,' Judith said sternly to Adam.

He swallowed and nodded, but his feet drew him not to the door, but to stand and then crouch before Heulwen as Renard had done. He took her hands between his. 'Heulwen, look at me,' he pleaded.

She shook her head. He released one of her hands and parted her hair to expose her face. For an instant her eyes met his, and they were full of a furious misery before she turned her head aside.

'Heulwen, please . . .'

'Adam, go!' Judith snapped. 'Can't you see that she's in no fit state to deal with herself, let alone the burden you are trying to set on her?'

He bit his lip and stood straight, desiring somehow to set the thing to rights and knowing that what was right by his code was not necessarily right by Heulwen's.

12

Guyon looked across the gaming board at the young man seated opposite, and suppressed with difficulty the urge to lay violent hands on him and throw him out of the house. It was a gut reaction. Adam de Lacey sometimes looked so much like his father that Guyon would find himself forgetting that physical similarity was the only resemblance.

He dropped his gaze to the jet and ivory counters and nudged one gently across the squares, reminding himself that life, unlike draughts, was mostly marked out in subtle shades of grey. 'I do not know what to say to you,' he admitted. 'A part of me is so angry that I could kill you here and now without remorse, but only a part and that the lesser. I can see how it happened and how it was drawn out of all proportion, but Christ alone knows how long it will take to unravel all the tangled threads and sew them into some semblance of order – and I'm not talking about my wife's tapestry silks.' He sighed heavily. 'It goes pride-deep, Adam, and you've done the equivalent of striking the de Mortimer family in the face with a rotten fish. Are you quite certain of your facts?'

Adam's eyes brightened. 'You saw the Welsh lad's re-action for yourself when he laid eyes on de Mortimer, and your father was with me when I received from him the full tale and will bear me out. The lad was not lying or mistaken, I would stake my life on it.'

'You will probably have to,' Guyon replied grimly: 'trial by combat is almost a certainty. Warrin's not going to admit to the crime, and he's got a very personal grudge now, hasn't he?' He shook his head at Adam. 'Heulwen knows how to pick husbands,' he grimaced, 'all three of them.'

Adam felt the hostility emanating from Guyon. He was not really surprised. Guyon had shown remarkable restraint thus far over what threatened to develop into a full-blown scandal and had caused a serious rift with the de Mortimer family, formerly close allies to Ravenstow. Now and then, like steam escaping from a lidded cauldron, a spurt of anger was bound to erupt.

'If I could undo it, believe me I would,' he said.

'Even down to retracting your request to the King?' Guyon arched a sardonic brow.

Adam's eyes kindled with a harder, amber light. 'I'm sorry if I went to him first, but I did not know how much time I had, and I had to stop her from pledging herself to de Mortimer.'

A small, uncomfortable silence fell. Into it Guyon said, 'It will break Hugh de Mortimer if his son is proven guilty.'

'Perhaps you would rather I retracted the accusation, gave up Heulwen and sailed on the first ship for

138

Outremer!' Adam said, angrily as he heard Guyon's ambivalence.

'Perhaps I would,' Guyon snorted. 'But it wouldn't be justice, would it?' And then he clenched his fist and crashed it down on the board, sending the counters leaping awry. 'Christ, Adam, why didn't you ask me for Heulwen before all this blew up in our faces like a barrel of boiling pitch!'

'Because I knew she wouldn't have me!' Adam retorted bitterly. 'She wants a cold-blooded contract of convenience, not a love match.'

Guyon studied him, and gradually his fierce expression softened and he sighed. 'It is not to be wondered at after the way Ralf treated her. She loved him so hard it almost broke her when he took off in pursuit of other women.'

'I don't need other women,' Adam said intensely. 'I never have, except as a salve to ease the wound of not having her. I know we have not had the best beginning, but God willing I'll spend the rest of my life making it up to her.'

Guyon made a rude sound. 'And a fine martyr you will make!' he scoffed. 'As I have heard the tale, it was only half your fault. Granted, it was a serious breach of courtesy to go above uninvited, but I suppose your news warranted it, and Heulwen didn't scream rape, did she? If one of the maids did hear her cry out, it was certainly not for help.'

Adam cleared his throat and looked down at his hands as if their conformation was of great interest. He remembered her undulating beneath him, the sounds he had dammed against her mouth with his own as the last

139

fragment of sanity was consumed in the conflagration. Was it truly no more than a carnal matter of lust?

Guyon shook his head. 'Christ knows, Adam, for I do not. You escort that sharp-clawed termagant across Europe, rescue her from a handful of dangers, weave your way with diplomacy through the courts of barons, princes and kings, only to bloody your nose on something as simple as this!'

'Perhaps because it's been too simple for too long,' Adam said wearily, and raised the hands he had been studying to dry-wash his face. 'I haven't the ability to fathom it any more.'

Heulwen watched her father remove his thick outdoor cloak and pace to the brazier to warm his hands. Two rings winked in the light: one set with a ruby, the other with intaglio. Were it not for the need to dress in finery at court, they would have remained buried at the bottom of a casket so seldom opened that spiders had been known to weave their webs across its lock before now. Heulwen put down her piece of sewing, which was only a pretence anyway, and came to his side.

With a brief, tired smile, her father gently tugged one of her braids. It was a gesture she remembered a hundred times from childhood. It had many meanings – teasing, affectionate, conspiratorial or warning, but never anything less than love. Tears filled her eyes and she flung herself into the haven of his arms and wept against the breast of his scarlet court robe. 'I'm sorry, Papa. If I'd known the trouble it would cause, I'd never have done it – I thought Adam was going to marry elsewhere – I thought that just once it wouldn't matter.'

'Hush, *cariadferch*, hush, you'll drench my robe and shrink it,' he said, his lips at her temple. 'I thought you were supposed to be lying down. Judith said she had given you poppy in wine and that you were best left to sleep.'

'I tipped it into the rushes when she wasn't looking,' Heulwen confessed. Sniffing, she pushed herself out of his arms and looked up into his face. 'I didn't want to sleep until you returned from court; I had to know what happened.'

'You would have done better to drink the wine,' he said, and wandered from the brazier to his shield to examine its raw, splintered surface.

'Papa?' She swallowed, feeling frightened.

'What do you think happened?' he growled. 'Warrin's fast, I'll give him that. He drew first blood: accused Adam of maligning his good name by a false claim of murder, and of deceiving and dishonouring you. It shifts the onus to prove the claim from his shoulders on to Adam's, and because Warrin brought it into the open of his own will, it diminishes the suspicion against him. The King was quite content to agree to a trial by combat and I'm a cross-eyed leper if I don't know the reason why.'

'Why?' Heulwen was driven to ask, feeling sick.

'A fight to the death is going to make excellent entertainment to follow up our swearing to Matilda. It will take men's minds off their anger at having to swear to a woman. It's going to ease their frustration to see spilled blood, preferably Adam's, as he was one of the men responsible for bringing Matilda to us in the first place. Tomorrow's the swearing, and the trial's to take place the day after.'

141

'That's horrible,' Heulwen whispered, appalled.

'No, just expedient. You can't blame Henry for using it to his advantage. This reckoning between Adam and Warrin has been coming for more than ten years.' Guyon shrugged. 'It's not just over you, Heulwen, you're only the spark that ignited the dry tinder.' He removed the rings from his fingers and tossed them on the clothing chest.

Heulwen sat down again, her hands pressed to her mouth. Guyon looked at her with troubled eyes. He could see the imprint of himself stamped upon her features, mingled with those of her mother. Her hair grew the same way as Rhosyn's, and the timbre of her voice was an exact, poignant reminder of the woman he had lost to the savagery of Walter de Lacey. And Adam de Lacey was Walter's son. Guyon cast that thought from his mind. Adam was no more like Walter de Lacey than a lump of flawed glass was like a polished jewel.

'Child . . .' he began softly, and crouched beside her.

'I'm all right, Papa.' Tear-tracks streaked her bruised face as she stared beyond him into some unpleasant distance. 'Only I think I'd like that poppy in wine now.'

13

The Empress Matilda's slender body was encased in a tunic and gown of royal purple, trimmed with ermine tips at cuff and knotted hem. Apart from the colour, she might have been an effigy. Adam set his own hands between hers and received an icy kiss of peace in return for his oath of loyalty to her and the future heirs of her body. Unsmiling, tepid, she took his fealty as her due, her expression remote, declining to acknowledge how many times over she owed him her life. Had she permitted herself to smile, she would have been attractive. Beneath her gauze veil, her braids were a bright brown, and her eyes were of an arresting lake-water blue, challenging every man who dared to look into them. On all sides of the great hall, the high barons and bishops of the land stood as witnesses to each other's swearing: Bigod, Ferrers, de Clare, de Blundeville, Salisbury, Winchester, Canterbury. Adam stepped back and another lord took his place and swore allegiance.

Henry was smiling in lieu of his daughter, not just a

flimsy parchment smile to put a good grace on the proceedings, but one of deep and genuine satisfaction. Adam supposed that it was indeed gratifying to him that his barons had agreed to acknowledge Matilda as his successor, which was in part due to the tireless persuasion of Robert of Gloucester. But if they had been brought to swear, then so had Henry – that he would not seek a foreign husband for his daughter without the baronial consent. But then what had oaths of that kind ever meant to the King, except the buying of time to break them later? Adam thought. Henry would marry his daughter to whomsoever he chose; that smile said so.

The celebration feast commenced with the pomp and ceremony befitting such a grand occasion and the presence of so many important men. Adam, as a minor tenant-in-chief, was relegated to a place at the far end of the hall, for which he was grateful. He had no great fondness for these gatherings with their rife hypocrisy, everyone trying to outdo each other and glancing sidelong to see if they had succeeded. There was the back-stabbing, there were the sly insults and, for him also, the hostile shoulder-nudges of men who wanted to see him lose the forthcoming trial by combat. Men who supported Warrin de Mortimer for the sake of his father, who was well thought of and respected at court, and undeserving of the scandal visited upon his house by a young man whose own family reputation was considerably more tarnished. And then of course there was the gossip; the jests at his expense, the sniggers and the sly innuendoes. Adam bore them stoically, but it did not mean that inwardly he was not goaded raw.

'I'm either going to marry you to Heulwen or officiate at your funeral, so you might as well speak to me!' complained a rich, deep voice at his hunched left shoulder.

Adam swivelled and stared at the grinning young priest who had just squeezed his way on to the trestle beside him. He found a sudden answering grin of his own. 'John! I hadn't thought to see you here!'

'The Earl of Leicester might feel in need of a confessor after swearing to an oath like that,' laughed Guyon's second son and namesake. To avoid confusion, he had early on been called for the saint on whose eve he had been born, and only on the most formal occasions ever went by his christened name.

'So might we all,' Adam said ruefully, 'the King in particular.' He stretched out his arm and playfully patted the bald island of scalp ringed by a thick sea of reddish-black waves. 'You're ordained now?'

'Since last Martinmas.'

'So I've got to call you Father and treat you with a proper respect?'

John's dark, beautiful voice rumbled with laughter. 'Is that so much of a trial?' He folded his arms on the trestle. A serving girl dimpled at him as she leaned over to pour wine. He smiled back, but without noticing how pretty she was, not because he was unaffected by pretty women – indeed on occasion, celibacy had been a discipline he had failed – but because he simply could not see her clearly enough to know. Ever since early childhood when he had fallen over cradles, sewing baskets and hound puppies rather than walk around them, when he had been defeated in sword practice because he could

145

not see the blows coming until it was too late, he had known he was destined either for the priesthood or an early death. It was an obvious choice, and he had flourished, and already had a responsible post in the Earl of Leicester's household.

Adam glanced sidelong at the young man. 'Aren't you going to lecture me from your pulpit, then?'

John squinted at a dish of eels stewed in herbs and wine, and answered with a question of his own. 'Do you know why my Lord Leicester chose me above several others to be his household chaplain?'

Adam shook his head.

'Because he knew I wouldn't keep lecturing the soldiers about mere peccadilloes. Men will always gamble, take the Lord's name in vain, and fornicate where they shouldn't with someone else's woman, and then brawl about it. They're unlikely to take much notice of the bleatings of a mealy-mouthed priest young enough in some instances to be their grandson. I suppose I could hurl hellfire and damnation at them, but I prefer to keep that for the sins that really matter – like murder.'

Adam looked sharply at John. A soft, myopic doe-brown his eyes might be, but they bore the clarity of knowledge. 'You believe me then?' He laughed bitterly. 'No one else does.'

'That is not true,' John contradicted. 'It is just that empty vessels make the most noise, and if you've noticed, it's all coming from de Mortimer's side. Don't worry, Adam, we're not all out to knife you in the back. That's Warrin de Mortimer's particular vice.' He took a mouthful of the eel stew, swallowed, and added thoughtfully, 'I saw Warrin de Mortimer in the early spring when

146

was returning from my studies in Paris. He was a member of a hawking party that included William le Clito when they crossed our path.'

'He was what?' Adam stared.

'There were a lot of other young men present, mostly from the French court, I think. I do not suppose there is any harm in going hawking with William le Clito, it just depends what they were talking about, but I didn't hear any of that.' He reached for a piece of the fine white bread that had been baked especially for the feast. 'I saw Ralf, too.'

'What, with them?'

'No, the following day just outside Les Andelys. He was kicking his heels beside a water trough, obviously waiting for someone. I would not have recognised him, my eyesight being what it is, but my horse needed to drink and Ralf was too close for me to miss. He wasn't pleased at being discovered either, and not just because there was a woman clinging to his arm or because I'm Heulwen's half-brother.' He bit into the crust and moistened it with a sip of wine. 'He asked me not to say anything, tapped his nose and told me he was about the King's private business, and at the time I believed him. I had no reason to doubt then.' He gave Adam a reassuring smile. 'Don't worry, the King knows. I told my Lord Leicester last night as soon as I realised its significance and he took it straight to Henry, so even if this trial by combat doesn't favour your cause, it's not a lost one. Warrin de Mortimer is marked.'

'I thought that the victor's arm was aided by divine intervention,' Adam said drily, as he attempted a morsel of the fish stew himself and grimaced. A favourite dish of Henry's it might be, but in Adam's opinion, Henry was welcome to it.

'That is the theory,' John said with spurious gravity. 'But divine intervention is a fickle force to depend upon, and I should know, I'm a priest.' Then he sobered and fixed Adam with a troubled stare. 'Warrin used to be able to flatten you in the tilt yard when we were children,' he said.

'He's relying on that memory now,' Adam agreed, 'but I was only half-grown then, and he was almost at his full strength. We're much of a height now. I know that he is broader, but if so, then I have the edge on speed.' His smile was wry. 'Still, it won't do any harm to pray for me, and for Heulwen.' He reached for his cup and took a quick swallow of the wine. It was Rhenish, the kind he had lived on for several months of purgatory at the German court, the kind with which he had almost killed himself on the day of Heulwen's marriage to Ralf. 'I've loved her for a long time,' he said.

'The way she used to look at Ralf ought to have melted that ingrate's bones,' John reflected, shifting his shoulders uncomfortably, 'but he ran after other women instead.'

Adam put his drink down and tugged at a loose thread on the gold embroidery at his tunic cuff. 'I think I would call him out too if he still lived,' he muttered, and snapping off the thread, sprinkled it from his fingers where it drifted, flickering with light, into a candle flame and was consumed in a brief, bright flaring.

The morning of the trial dawned knife-cold with a slicing wind from the east. Frost gleamed like crumbled loaf

148

sugar on every rooftop and pinnacle, frilled the edge of the Thames in crackling silver praline and dredged the beached boats like sugared marchpane confections. The air was grainy with minute frozen particles, sharp as crushed ice to breathe.

Adam rose as the first streaks of dawn sparkled on the thick swatches of frost layering the shutters, broke the panel of ice in the bowl set on the coffer, and having sluiced his face, went to first Mass, his heart as heavy as lead within him but his mind composed for the coming ordeal. He heard Mass, he made confession, was absolved, and sat down to break his fast with Sweyn. Austin served them hot wine, bread and cheese, his manner both restless and subdued.

Sweyn rubbed one huge, calloused palm over his beard, loudly vibrated his larynx, and spat into the rushes. 'Watch his footwork,' he growled. 'It was always his weakest point. If you can fault him there, then you have a chance. Do not, whatever you do, lock horns with him bull to bull because he will kill you.'

'I do have eyes in my head!' Adam snapped. He broke a hunk of bread from the loaf, took a bite, and without tasting it, washed it well down with a gulp of the wine.

'What about brains?' Sweyn enquired, unimpressed. 'If you're not prepared to listen to some sound advice, then you're a fool.'

Adam inhaled to retort, saw the fear lurking behind the drawn-down bushy brows and half-lowered lids, and was silenced. 'I am listening,' he said instead. 'I just become edgy before a battle. You should know that by now.'

Sweyn's expression softened for a moment. 'Aye well,'

he muttered, 'that's as may be, but you'll need to be on an even keel before you step into that arena.'

'Have you ever known me not so when it has mattered?'

'No, but it has never touched you so closely before.' Sweyn braced his hands upon the board and shoved to his feet. 'I'll give you a workout to warm up when you've done eating – I'm going for a piss.'

Adam watched him to the door, then lowered his gaze to the bread between his hands. He did not really want it, but knew he had to eat something. It might be unwise to go into a fight with a loaded stomach, but if the ordeal were to last any length of time, then an unsustained sword arm was liable to fail. He forced another piece down, took a gulp of wine, and became aware of the intent scrutiny of his squire.

'Austin, stop looking at me as though I were already corpsed in my coffin and go and fetch my sword,' he snapped.

The youth rubbed his wrist across the dark down on his upper lip. 'They are laying bets in the alehouse down the road that you won't last more than ten minutes against Warrin de Mortimer,' he said, his young voice torn between indignation and doubt.

'Are they?' Adam arched one eyebrow. 'Because I am guilty of slander, or because my sword arm's supposedly weaker than his?'

'Both, my lord.'

Adam shoved the empty cup aside and swept his hand impatiently across the debris of bread on the trestle. 'Did you make a wager?'

The squire reddened. 'Yes, my lord. They all laughed

at me, but they were willing to take my coin.' His eyes brightened with contempt. 'Their loss. They haven't seen you fight.'

Adam snorted. 'God knows what your father will think. He entrusted your training to me, and thus far I've set you a fine example, haven't I? Drink, women and gambling.'

Austin's blush receded. He gave Adam one of his incorrigible looks. 'It was Papa who gave me the money for the bet and told me to put some on for him too while I was about it.'

'That's very encouraging,' Adam said with a pained smile, adding, 'Austin, I don't want you standing round catching your death of cold while I do battle. God knows, one fatality is enough today. Get my sword, lad, then I want you to go to your father's house and await my summons.'

Austin's throat rippled. 'My lord, I want to be there,' he said resolutely. 'It is my place as your squire.'

'It won't be pleasant, whatever the outcome,' Adam warned, watching him with thoughtful eyes, assessing the youth's degree of control and maturity. 'If I am killed, I expect all members of my household to behave with dignity. If you think your grief or rage are going to goad you into some act of folly, then I cannot permit you to come.'

'I promise to uphold your honour, my lord.' Austin stood straight, tears glittering in his hazel-green eyes. 'Please do not send me to my father.'

Adam gave him a curt nod. 'So be it then.' He left the trestle and went to pick up and buckle on his sword-belt, giving the youth time to compose himself. Austin wiped his face on his cuff, then went to lift the scabbard from its leaning place against the wall. The gilded leather sheath resting across one palm, the pommel across the other, he suddenly stiffened and stared at the woman standing in the doorway.

'My lady,' he muttered, his face burning scarlet.

Adam swung round, his own complexion as dusky as his squire's before it slowly faded to match the hue of his bleached linen shirt. Without taking his eyes from Heulwen, he held out his hand for the sword and dismissed Austin with a brief gesture. The boy hesitated, then bowed, and with obvious reluctance left the room. Heulwen stood aside to let him pass, then closed the door and, putting down the hood of her cloak, advanced towards Adam. He noticed that the ornate brooch no longer adorned her cloak but had been replaced by the simple braided pin she had formerly worn.

'You should not be here.' His voice was level, betraying none of the conflicting emotions that the sight of her aroused in him.

'I couldn't skulk behind my father's closed doors when I knew what you had to face today.'

'It might have been easier for us both.' He set his hand to the sword grip and gently eased the weapon from its sheath.

'But not the best or truest path.' She looked from his face to the gleaming steel and shuddered. 'Adam, I have to be present at this trial by combat, for Ralf's sake. It is my duty as his widow to be there whatever happens.'

'Heulwen, if I fail, it will go hard with you. You'll be branded a whore in full public view.'

She shrugged and forced a smile. 'I still have my father and Judith and family friends between me and such disaster. I am not afraid on my own count.' And then her smile slipped to reveal the terror and tension beneath it. 'Adam, in God's name, put up that sword until you have need to draw it,' she whispered.'

Carefully he resheathed the weapon and laid it down on the trestle, then crossed the three paces between them. One of her braids slipped and swung forward to brush against his hand. He touched it, using it as a rope for his fingers to climb until they reached her face. Tenderly he touched the purple and yellow swelling beneath her left eye.

'Am I then a matter of duty too?' he challenged softly.

'Adam, that's not fair!'

He stroked the other, unmarked side of her face. 'Am I more to you than a stallion to a mare?' he persisted.

'You know you are!' she said with furious reluctance.

'Do I?' Her anger sent a pang through him. He wondered how long it would take to break down the barriers she had built around herself during her marriage to Ralf.

She made an impatient sound, at whom he did not know, and raised her hand to take his away from her face. 'When I saw you at Ravenstow in the autumn, I wanted you,' she said, her voice low and intense. 'Half my mind saw you as the boy I used to know, my foster brother. The other half saw the man you had become, and between the two I did not know which way to turn. I still don't, and it's too late for choices now anyway. I'm trapped.' She turned his hand over so that it lay palm upwards in her own, the skin hard across the fleshy pads beneath each finger from the constant pressure of gripping a sword.

Ralf's hands had been fine-boned and swift in motion like the man. Adam's were those of an artisan – strong and square with spatulate, capable fingers that would have looked utterly ridiculous decorated with rings. A jolt of terror shot through her at the thought of them gripping a sword in the arena. Her breath caught and her grip tightened.

'I've been trapped all my life,' he said, 'and it's not too late. After today, it is only the beginning.' He turned his hand in hers, linking their fingers, and drew her against him. For an instant she resisted, and then he felt her body flow against his. He bent his mouth to hers, desire beginning to melt reason like a flame burning down the wick of a candle, stripping the wax.

In the doorway, Sweyn loudly cleared his throat. 'My lord, I've fetched the whetstone for your blade and you have yet to warm up for the fight.' He flicked a granite, impervious look at Heulwen and inclined his shaggy head. Adam sighed and fumbled for his grip on reality. The flame inside him steadied, receding to a glow, but his eyes were intent as they memorised her face upturned to his. And then he took a deep breath, controlling himself, and released her. 'Pray for me,' he said with a rueful smile. 'If all goes well, then we'll rejoice together later. If not,' he shrugged, 'at least we have had this opportunity to say our farewells. I'm glad you came.'

Heulwen swallowed, unable to speak for the tears crowding her throat. It was almost like being widowed again; worse, in some ways. Ralf's death had struck her like a bolt of summer lightning. This time she had the long, slow roll of thunder to warn her beforehand. And if by God's mercy Adam lived, then Warrin would die, and even if he was guilty, she could feel no satisfaction, only utter weariness.

'God keep you safe,' she managed to whisper at last, and drawing up the hood of her cloak, hurried from the room before she broke down before him.

Hugh de Mortimer watched his only son duck beneath the arena rope in the tower's ward, and clenched his war-scarred knuckles into fists.

'He is innocent,' he said in a harsh, metallic voice.

Guyon stamped his feet to keep them warm and regarded the arena and the two young men now within it. Adam was moving restlessly, trying to keep his muscles from stiffening up in the cold. 'I am afraid my foster son does not share your belief, and although it pains me to say so, Hugh, neither do I.' He looked along his shoulder at the older man standing beside him on the raised platform.

'You would take the word of a Welsh barbarian and a traitor's hell-begotten spawn above that of my own son?'

Guyon's jaw tightened. An acerbic retort burned on his tongue but he said nothing. What was the point in blistering an open wound? 'I don't wish to quarrel with you, Hugh,' he said evenly. 'This goes hard with us both.'

'If wishes were horses then beggars would ride and whores be restored their virginity!' his companion grated. 'Do you know how much store Warrin set by your wanton daughter?'

'I know how much store he set by his own vanity,' Guyon was driven to retort in Heulwen's defence. 'My daughter is not a wanton. Choose very carefully what you say to me.'

155

'Choose carefully? Blood of Christ, when I think what . . .'

'Peace, my lords,' said the King, stepping smoothly between them. 'It is grievous enough that these young men should be fighting at all, without the unseemliness of two of my senior barons turning the occasion into an open brawl.'

Guyon swallowed his anger and bowed to Henry. 'It was not my desire to cause insult or unseemliness,' he said, and held out his open palm to Hugh de Mortimer. The latter ignored it, but inclined himself stiffly to the King.

'A pity that you did not pursue such sentiments in the ordering of your own household, my lord,' said the cool silken voice of the Empress Matilda who was now standing beside her father. She was wearing a woollen gown the precise colour of fresh blood, topped by a sable-lined cloak.

Guyon regarded his wife's half-sister with a blank expression and disfavour that did not show on his face. 'I hazard we all have skeletons rattling to escape from the places where we have walled them up,' he said, his eyes seeking among the gathered nobility and resting for a pointed, benevolent moment upon Alain Fergant's bastard son Brien.

The Empress's face did not betray by so much as a flicker that she had understood what he meant, but he saw the twitch of her fingers within the fashionably long sleeves of her gown, and knew without any satisfaction that his barb had hit the mark. Brien FitzCount was a handsome and intelligent young man with a forceful personality and all the finer attributes of a courtier married to the pragmatic approach of a common soldier. He was also the illegitimate son of a popular but only moderately important Breton count, and as such stood not a chance in the darkest pit of hell of becoming Matilda's approved consort. What went on behind locked doors and closed shutters was another matter, of course. Thou shalt not be caught was the eleventh commandment of the court, and Matilda had been fortunate enough not to violate it . . . yet.

There was a brief flurry in the crowd that had gathered to witness the fight, followed by a burst of excitement. In the arena, the opponents turned their heads from their hostile regard of each other and watched a group of men-at-arms approach the dais, escorting at their centre Judith of Ravenstow and her by now infamous stepdaughter. The common folk craned to take a better look, murmuring to each other, quoting the various superstitions connected with red-haired women and speculatively admiring the picture she made as she walked the path cleared for her by the Ravenstow serjeants. Her eyes were modestly downcast and her skin so pale that it might have been moulded from ice, her pallor emphasised by her sombre garb, unadorned except for the flash of agate prayer beads glimpsed briefly through the opening of her cloak as she walked.

From somewhere in the crowd the jeer of whore went up, but it was only echoed sporadically, for she did not look like a whore, and among the common people at least, there was sympathy for a pair of lovers. Counter-cries went out, good-humoured, egging Adam on, cheering Heulwen.

'It's a circus!' Hugh de Mortimer ground out. 'Can

you hear them? Thank Christ I didn't bring my little Elene to Windsor.'

'Why else do you think they are here?' Guyon said, a hint of disgust in his own voice. 'They want to be entertained.' He shouldered across the dais to his wife and daughter and helped them up the steps.

Hugh de Mortimer, who had smiled upon Heulwen and embraced her as his daughter on the last occasion they had met, now stared at her with loathing, the word harlot in his eyes if not on his tongue.

Feeling as if she had been spat upon, Heulwen curtsied first to Henry and then the Empress. The latter gestured her to rise, subjected her to a thoughtful, thorough scrutiny, then bestowed on her the kiss of peace. 'Come, Lady Heulwen, sit by me if you will and warm yourself at the brazier. Wine?' She beckoned to a servant. The gesture was both diplomatic and kind, but the keen glitter of Matilda's eyes first on Hugh, and then Warrin de Mortimer, dispelled any illusion Heulwen had that the Empress was being pleasant. Matilda was a cat patting a captive mouse between her paws.

Heulwen let herself be guided and sat down beside the Empress, feeling like a player in some monstrous show. She looked down at her bleached knuckles while the charges and counter-charges were read out and refuted, then raised her head to risk a glance at Adam as he made his denial and accusation. He was bare-headed, his hair curling and dark with hoar droplets, and like Warrin he wore no mail, only a padded tunic that ended wide-sleeved below the elbows and beneath it his ordinary robe. He had a shield, his sword and his skill, and Warrin possessed the same. Two living men had entered that arena; only one would emerge.

Adam glanced once and briefly at her, and half raised his sword in salute; the edge shivered with blue light that cut her to the heart. Behind her, her father set his hand on her shoulder and gently squeezed. 'Courage *fy merch fach*,' he murmured in Welsh, the language of her birth and first few years. She swallowed and put her own hand up to grasp his, as Henry nodded at the steward beside him, and the man inflated his lungs.

'*Au nom de Dieu et le Roi, fait votre bataille. Laisser-aller!*'

Adam crouched behind the shield and felt the ground delicately. Each blade of grass was a knobbled white spear, slippery with potential death. Warrin sidled, sword and shield extended like pincers. On his cheek, the scabbed-over deep scratch was a remnant and reminder of the brawl in the bedchamber.

He attacked. Adam parried the blow with a swift, economical move and twisted out of range. Someone jeered, but he was oblivious, his whole being taken up in the concentration of battle. This was no tilt yard session where their tutor would separate them before damage was done, no courtesy match where the victor would accept the yielding of the vanquished with good humour. This was kill or be killed, simple and conclusive.

Warrin had a negligible advantage of height, although Adam had the leg length whereas Warrin's was in the body. Warrin was more powerfully developed, but not quite so fast, and both men were skilled fighters.

Warrin came on again and Adam parried. The blade bit his shield and rebounded with a dull, metallic thud.

159

Adam struck his first blow and Warrin's shield was immediately there to catch it. The shock rippled along Adam's arm, jarring it to the shoulder socket. Warrin pushed and Adam leaped backwards, half turned and, shield presented, swiped backhanded and low at Warrin's unguarded right knee. Warrin jumped and skidded on the frozen grass. The crowd roared and surged and were forced back by the Marshal's men. Adam followed through, but Warrin took the blow on his shield and behind its protection regained his balance and attacked, driving Adam back towards the stakes in a savage flurry of hacking blows.

The men fought each other forwards and back across the arena. Their swords crashed and thudded on the shields, biting gouges in the wood. Occasionally the grating sound of steel upon steel rang out as they parried blade to blade. They began to breathe harshly and hard. First blood went to Warrin, and second too, both of them minor cuts but signs that Adam was losing the edge of his speed.

Heulwen half turned her head, her soul shrinking, her body constrained to remain and witness. Beside her, Matilda was tense, her blue eyes gleaming. She resembled some ancient goddess presiding over a rite of sacrifice and appeared to be enjoying every moment.

'Ah,' she breathed softly and leaned forward a little. 'He has him now, I think.'

Heulwen swallowed and willed herself to look at what her incautious tongue and body had wrought. There was another wound bloodying Adam's gambeson, more serious she judged from the way he was holding himself, scarcely managing to parry the blows raining down on him, and the more enfeebled his defence, the more vigorous and confident grew Warrin's attack. His left arm dropped another degree, and without awareness, Heulwen cried out.

'God's death Adam, be careful,' Guyon muttered, his hand tightening on Heulwen's shoulder.

Warrin's sword flashed and bit down again. Adam gave ground, staggered, and slipped to one knee, his shield splaying wide in an invitation that the other man could not resist. The crowd roared.

Guyon's grip became a vice on his daughter's shoulder as she made to jerk to her feet. 'Be still,' he commanded against her ear, 'can't you see he did that apurpose?'

Warrin drew back his arm for the death blow, and in that split second Adam launched himself in a move so fast that Warrin had not time to recover and guard. His surprised grunt became a shriek of agony as Adam's sword took him across the ribs and abdomen and brought him down.

Gasping, bleeding, his stance as unsteady as his swirling vision, Adam laid the point of his blade at Warrin's throat, knowing that all he had to do was lean on it to cleanse away in blood the years of abuse he had suffered as a squire, the resentment, the insult to Heulwen. For Ralf's murder, or for himself? He squinted at the dais and through a blur saw Hugh de Mortimer gesticulating in agitation at the battleground and speaking rapidly to Henry. The King was listening, his expression impassive.

Adam forced himself beyond fatigue and pain to think with the speed of necessity. He had Warrin de Mortimer at his mercy, a single, short sword-thrust from death. Already his case was proven. To kill Warrin as he deserved was to gratify himself and end one small feud at the expense of beginning a far greater one that Heulwen's father could not afford.

Henry's eyes were inscrutable as slate while Hugh de Mortimer pleaded for his son's life, but his right hand started to move as if to make a command. Adam did not wait, for whatever it was would have to be obeyed. He stepped quickly away from his fallen opponent and moved unsteadily to the stand.

'My claim is proven,' he panted. 'Let him live with his dishonour.' He sheathed his sword.

Henry gave Adam a calculating look before dipping his head the briefest fraction and turning to the man beside him. 'My lord, your son has seven days' grace to quit my lands. After that his life is forfeit.' He looked at Adam again and said in a tone as frosty as the weather, 'Adam de Lacey, your cause is upheld; God has found in your favour. You have leave to depart and seek attention for your wounds.'

Adam opened his mouth to give the formal, customary reply, but his tongue refused to serve him as his vision darkened, and his last awareness was of Heulwen's cry of consternation, and the ground rushing up to strike him.

14

'It isn't far now.' Heulwen laid her hand on Adam's sleeve, her eyes anxious, for she could tell from the awkward way he sat in the saddle that his wounds were paining him.

'I'm all right.' He tossed her the semblance of a smile. 'Sore and tired. Nothing that Thornford's hospitality cannot cure.'

'You should not have set out so soon,' she remonstrated, not in the least reassured, for although his main injury was not mortal, it was too serious to be treated with the lack of respect he was affording it. The wind was bitter, stinging their faces, the sky the colour of a dusty mussel shell and full of fitful rain, and he had been forcing the pace. 'It was Warrin who was given seven days to leave the country, not us.'

'I have explained why it was necessary Heulwen, stop fussing.' He pressed his knees to Vaillantif's sides. She bit her tongue and threw an exasperated glance at his back. In her ignored opinion they should still be in

London, allowing time for his flesh to knit properly and his strength to return. But Adam, as stubborn as ever, and a querulous patient, declared that he was surfeited with the city and the whole damned circus of the court; that he had cauldrons simmering in the marches that he could not afford to let boil over – his Welsh hostage for one, his Welsh hostage's brother for another, his new wife's lands for a third – and nothing his new wife had been able to say or do had shifted his resolve.

They forded the river and clopped through the village, the dwellings huddled together beneath the lowering sky. An urchin with a sling at his waist lifted a stone and contemplated folly until noticed and clipped around the ear by his horrified father, whose back was bent under a load of kindling for their croft fire. They passed the carrier with his train of pack ponies making for Shrewsbury via a night's lodging in Oswestry, and greeted the reeve astride his sturdy black cob descending from the keep. The news had gone ahead of them with their messenger, and they were congratulated upon their marriage.

Heulwen smiled and thanked the men whose eyes were frankly curious. Adam said nothing, but stiffly inclined his head. As they rode on up the low slope, her gaze remained anxious as she thought back to their wedding four days ago on the morning that they had departed Windsor. As in all her dealings thus far with Adam, convention had been thrown to the winds. They had made their vows at the convent of St Anne's-in-the-Field, whose abbess was her father's widowed half-sister Emma. The ceremony, performed by John, was witnessed by immediate family and thirty nuns. Following a hastily organised wedding feast, they had left their guests to finish the celebration, if such it could be called, and set out at Adam's stubborn insistence on the road home.

It had taken them four nights, and their marriage had yet to be consummated. Adam was too sore and saddle-weary to take advantage of his altered state, and there had been no privacy on their nightly stops. They had bedded down among his men in the halls and guest houses where they had been given hospitality, rolled in their cloaks around the hearth for warmth.

Heulwen had begun to notice an air of constraint in him. He scarcely addressed a word to her, and only met her eyes for the most fleeting of wary glances. If she had not been so concerned for his physical well-being, so unsure of her ground, she would have rounded on him with the honed edge of her tongue. As it was, she kept that weapon in its sheath and tried her best to be meek, gentle, and attentive – the perfect wife.

Had Heulwen yielded to her first impulse and berated him, she would have been spared much anxiety. Adam, beset by the pain of his injuries and bodily weakness, was an easy prey to doubt. He reasoned to himself that Heulwen had been forced into this marriage by circum-stance, and the anxious, fussy concern that was all she seemed capable of displaying towards him smacked of guilt and was more than he could bear.

He could feel her watching him now but knew that if he turned round, she would be gazing at the forelock between her mare's ears and would not look up again until his eyes turned elsewhere. Giving vent to his frus-tration, he kicked Vaillantif with more force than was prudent as they reached the gatehouse and in consequence received a jolt of speed from the horse that whiplashed pain through his body and made him gasp.

The guards saluted him and a groom ran to catch the stallion's bridle. Adam gripped the pommel so hard that the oak leaf design carved upon it was imprinted on his palm. Before anyone had time to help her from her own saddle, Heulwen was down from her horse and hastening to her husband.

'I knew we should have rested up in Shrewsbury for another day,' she said with self-recrimination. 'Look, there's blood on your tunic!'

'Hush, Heulwen.' He glanced around the busy ward. 'Do you want my people to think I have brought a shrew to rule them?'

'Adam, it's no light matter!' Tears filled her eyes. 'You have been very fortunate. You could still take the wound fever or stiffening sickness, or perhaps just die because you have pushed yourself too far.'

His tension eased a little and a hint of natural colour returned to warm his face. 'I admit to folly, but there is no need to publish it abroad.' He touched her cheek and saw her own colour come up. Her eyes were luminous and he could have drowned in them. Abruptly he said, 'Your grandfather is waiting,' and removed his hand to command Austin to help him down.

She saw that his face had closed again, every plane taut and resisting, and with a feeling of helplessness she turned from him, lifted her skirts and cloak free of the bailey floor and almost ran to the old man who stood expectantly at the foot of the forebuilding steps. With a cry of relief, she cast herself into the haven of his embrace, and hugged him tightly.

'How now, child,' he said softly. 'It is a smile that I thought to see on your face, not these floods of tears!' And then with a lightness that covered serious concern, 'Do not tell me, you and Adam have quarrelled again?'

'Worse than that, Grandpa,' she gulped. 'I've married him on the heel of disgrace, and it's been a terrible mistake. I know it has!'

'Wandering in the wood again looking for the trees,' he answered comfortably, patting her shoulder, and looked over the top of her head towards Adam who was advancing on them slowly and stiffly, his face wearing the guarded, defensive look that Miles knew of old. 'What's wrong with him?'

Heulwen dragged the trailing end of her sleeve across her eyes and turned in his arms to study her husband. To her own eyes Adam was moving a little more easily now, only his tight jaw muscles betraying his pain. 'He took on Warrin in a trial by combat,' she said and felt her grandfather's hand grip her in surprise.

'Warrin's dead then?'

'No, but severely wounded and accounted the loser and banished from Henry's domains. It's been horrible, Grandpa. I don't want to talk about it, not now. Can we go inside?'

He looked at her bruised face, seeing more than just the fading marks. Hugging her against him, he turned to the forebuilding.

Adam eased himself carefully into the high-backed chair, closed his eyes while he mastered the pain, then opened them again upon Miles and the cup of usquebaugh-spiked wine he was holding out. He managed to give the old man the semblance of a smile. 'It's not as bad as it looks. I'm just stiff from the saddle, that's all.'

'How serious are your wounds?'

Adam drank and felt the usquebaugh hit his stomach like a swallowed hot coal. 'Not mortal, but sore. I'll wear a lifelong scar from hip-bone to lower ribs. I made a mess of things in Windsor, not just my body.'

'A trial by combat was always a possibility,' Miles said.

'Well, yes, but you do not know the half of it.' Adam glanced at Heulwen. Her back was turned and she was talking in a low murmur to Elswith her maid as they unpacked the travelling chests.

Miles looked too. 'Like that, is it?' he asked, remembering Heulwen's distress in the bailey.

'Worse.' Briefly, Adam gave him the flesh-pared bones of the tale.

Miles pursed his lips. 'No wonder you headed with such haste for the marches rather than make a prolonged feast for those vultures at court.'

'I was an idiot. If I had not raced head-first into the thing I would not have come such a cropper, would I?'

'Probably not,' Miles admitted, 'but at least Ralf's murder is avenged and you have your heart's desire.'

'Yes.'

Adam's tone of voice caused Miles to raise his eyebrows and then, after a moment's hesitation, reach inside his tunic. 'I warned Heulwen against walking in the forest looking for trees, and if you are doing the same thing at the opposite end of the same forest, how are you ever going to meet?' he demanded gruffly, and held out on his shiny, age-creased palm a piece of cunningly worked gold.

'What's this?' Adam reached out, winced, and completed

the movement to discover a circular cloak brooch of intricate English craftsmanship – a wolf curved round, chasing its own tail, its eyes set with red garnets.

'It belonged to Heulwen's grandmother, my first wife Christen. She was English, and it had been in her family time without memory. She treasured it the most of all her jewels, not for its beauty, but because it represented a new beginning. I was going to give it to Heulwen as a wedding gift, but perhaps it might be more appropriate coming from you when the time is right.'

Adam raised his head to meet Miles's shrewd, patient gaze. 'Is there anything you don't see?' he asked ruefully.

'Put it down to my ancient years,' Miles said with a like smile in reply. 'That and knowing you are both more stubborn than mules, and I do not have much time.'

Behind them the noise of two stalwart servants tipping buckets of hot water into a bathtub filled the small silence of words unspoken, and when all was quiet again, Miles changed the subject.

'It has been as peaceful here as a nest when the swallows have flown – neither sight nor sound of Davydd ap Tewdr in search of his fledgeling.'

'Does he know we have the boy? Are you sure the news has reached him?'

'The last two market days have been bustling with Welsh faces. He knows, all right.'

Adam's brows twitched together. 'Then what is he waiting for? Why hasn't he come?'

Miles spread his hands. 'Perhaps Rhodri's expendable. Perhaps he wants to put the fear of God into the boy by making him sweat awhile. You could always arrange to hang him in public on market day and find out.'

Adam flashed him a look. 'You are jesting of course!'

'Bluffing,' Miles said with a gentle smile. 'It is one way of testing brotherly affection.'

Adam snorted. 'And if my bluff is called? What should I do? Let him swing? Or prove my word is so much chaff and keep him neck-whole?'

'At least you would know whether to change the direction of your attack. If Rhodri ap Tewdr is no good as bait, he may yet make an excellent pawn.'

Adam narrowed his eyes. Their captive's attitude to his older brother had been ambivalent when he had spoken from his sick-bed, and if Davydd ap Tewdr chose not to negotiate for Rhodri's life, it was hardly going to increase the love side of the balance. 'You mean replace Davydd ap Tewdr with someone a little more receptive to Norman ideas?' he murmured. 'Someone who has reason to be grateful he was picked out of the road and restored to health rather than being left to die of cold among the corpses of his own folly?'

'Something like that. The lad's got a practical head on his shoulders, and while he might dislike us, he's not yet progressed into hard-bitten hatred. I estimate him redeemable.'

'So all I have to do is remove Davydd ap Tewdr and unleash Rhodri to replace him.' Adam drained his cup and sighed heavily. A dull ache pulsed behind his lids. 'I don't feel much like confrontation just now. I could sleep for a year.'

'At least a couple of days,' Miles amended cheerfully. 'Which is more than most newly married men ever get, you must admit.'

Adam looked down at the glittering brooch in the

hand not holding the empty cup. 'Yes,' he said more wearily than ever. 'But then most men don't have to fight their way to the altar and take for their bride a woman who would rather run in the opposite direction.'

Through half-closed lids, wound newly dressed, Adam lay on the bed and watched Heulwen pick up his abandoned garments, consigning some to be taken by the maids for laundering and others to be folded away in his clothing chest. His limbs were lethargic, but his mind was as restless as a confined animal. He was home, should have felt at ease and relieved, but perversely he was tense and on edge.

Heulwen set about removing her travel-stained garments and pinned up her braids, then waited beside the tub, shivering a little, while a maid heaved a fresh bucketful of hot water into it.

Adam perused the generous contours of her body. He knew now how it felt, pressed against his in the act of love, knew it within as well as without. Taking her to bed was no longer a darkness of the imagination, but a reality barbed with doubt. Even now there was no satisfaction.

Heulwen dismissed the maid and stepped into the tub, which was constructed from a large barrel with a bench lodged across its width. She seated herself upon it and pensively contemplated the bed and its silent occupant. 'Adam, are you asleep?'

'No.'

'Do you want me to mix you something to ease the pain?'

'No, it's not necessary.'

She gnawed her lower lip, wondering how to cut through this frosty reserve of his when all her compliance and concern were rejected as though she had offered him an insult. She tried again. 'Adam, is there something wrong?'

'No.'

She heaved a sigh. 'It's impossible to talk to you when you keep pushing me away like this.'

Suddenly he was no longer recumbent, but struggling to sit up, eyes wide and amber bright with indignation. 'Is it any wonder? I haven't needed a nursemaid since I was a brat of six. I've been coddled and swaddled and scolded like some puling infant, and every time that I've baulked, you've either wrung your hands or sulked!'

The bath water swished as Heulwen grabbed the sides of the tub. 'I am not the one who has been sulking!' she flashed in return. 'How dare you accuse me! If you are going to behave like a brat of six, then expect to be treated like one! You should be grateful for my care, not hurl it back in my face as though I had cursed you!'

'Grateful!' he choked. 'Grateful, when it makes me feel like a leper receiving charity from the hands of a guilty patroness!' Tears of frustration and rage glimmered in his eyes.

Heulwen clenched her fingers on the side of the tub, throttling the wood in lieu of the man on the bed. 'Should I then ignore your wounds?' she spat at him. 'Abet your stupidity by pretending they do not exist? Adam, you have been worrying me sick the way you drive yourself!'

Abruptly, the anger drained out of him. He slumped back against the pillows, pain etching two deep lines between his brows. 'Perhaps I do it because I dare not stop,' he said wearily.

Heulwen finished washing then left the tub and dried herself on the linen towels that the maid had left to hand. She donned a loose gown and said in a voice as weary as his own, 'You should have taken one of those other girls that Henry was going to offer you. I will only make you unhappy.'

He conceded her words with a lift and drop of his brows. 'It's a risk I'll have to live with. Are you done? Don't stand there shivering; come to bed.' He shifted, making room for her.

She hesitated, unable to fathom his mood.

'Please.' He raised his lids.

'Oh, Adam!' What she saw there brought her to the bed before she was aware of having moved. There was a lump in her throat. She leaned over and kissed him on the mouth. It was meant to be a conciliatory gesture, contrition for hot words scattered abroad, but Adam's arm banded hard around her waist, pulling her down and the kiss deepened possessively before he broke it to investigate her throat, pulling down the fabric of her gown, parting the deep opening to seek the swell of her breasts.

Heulwen gasped, for this was not what she had bargained for in his tired, weakened state. His weight came clumsily down on top of her and her gasp became an exclamation as he entered her, because she was not ready and he was eager. She closed her eyes and made herself go as limp as a piece of tide-rolled flotsam. Instinct moistened her body and the discomfort diminished. Deliberately she arched and subsided to his rhythm, fanning her hands down over his narrow flanks. He was breathing in harsh, agonised gasps. Without fuss she increased her pace, urging him on, was touched by the edge of the maelstrom herself and felt pleasure burn within her, but before it could intensify or culminate Adam cried out and gripped her to him, his body shuddering with the violent ripples of climax.

She listened to his breath whistling past her ear, felt the sharpness of stubble scraping her throat and the rapid rise and fall of his ribcage inhibiting her own attempts to breathe. 'Adam, you're squashing me,' she told him in a calm, practical voice, and when he did not move, pushed at his broad shoulders, trying to lever herself out from beneath him.

Through the numbness of aftermath and the zigzagging renewal of pain, Adam became aware of Heulwen's struggles, and gathering himself withdrew from her. He rolled over on his back and with a groan bent one elbow across his eyes so that he would not have to look at her, for he was ashamed.

'You're bleeding again and no wonder!' she reprimanded him. 'Adam, you need not have been in such haste. If you bolted your food in the same way you'd have terrible indigestion, and serve you right!'

Cautiously he took his arm away from his eyes, drawn to look at her but terrified of what he might see in her face. Her expression was cross; no, exasperated, and the look she returned him was speculative, assessing, as if an item taken for granted had suddenly sprung a hidden compartment. Nowhere did he read anger or revulsion. She adjusted her gown, left the bed to fetch bandages, then returned to him, shaking her head. 'If only you'd taken the time to ask, I'd have shown you a way that would not have put pressure on that cut.'

Shocked surprise replaced the bleakness in his eyes as he stared at her. For a woman to admit to such superior knowledge of the bedroom arts was beyond his experience, and probably that of most men. Whores, or at least the high-paid ones he had occasionally bought, were usually all soft, urgent compliance, begging and breathless in praise of his skill – and totally dishonest, he thought wryly. He had never owned a more permanent mistress to make him aware of anything different . . . until now.

Heulwen lifted her shoulders in a gesture that strove for nonchalance but didn't succeed. 'I was married to Ralf for ten years. He was the kind of man who grew bored without novelty. Once the freshness of my virginity had paled, he amused himself by teaching me all the other devious little paths to the centre of the maze, and when I was accomplished the boredom set in. I was his mare and I was saddle-broken. He moved on in search of a new mount. In the end, the times he came back to me I could not bear it, knowing that I was just a "good ride" among countless others.' Efficiently she rebound his wound with a roll of fresh bandage. Her hands were steady. It was her chin that wobbled.

'Your father was right,' Adam said gently after a moment. 'You do know how to choose your husbands. We've all been bastards.' He touched a tendril of hair that had uncoiled from her pinned-up braids. 'If I behaved badly just now, forgive me. It was because I was afraid and overwrought. Starving men and feasts do not go very well together.'

She blinked hard and turned away to remove her gown, surreptitiously wiping her face on it as she did so.

She had cut through the protection of his indifference and seen what was layered beneath, but in doing so had revealed more of her own self than she wished to see. She felt soul-naked, vulnerable and frightened. Adam was watching her – she could feel his eyes boring into her spine. Quickly she pinched out the night candle so that abruptly there was darkness, but when he drew her against him, she went unresisting into his arms and rested her head upon his breast.

He felt her cheek cool and damp and, stroking her hair, wondered if he was in heaven or hell.

15

Miles felt the grey's pace falter for the third time in as many minutes, and with a worried glance at the encroaching clouds, drew rein and stiffly dismounted, the pain in his joints a gnawing ache. He removed his gauntlets, to run his hand carefully down the stallion's suspect near foreleg and, as he felt the hot, swollen cannon joint, knew the worst.

'Trouble, my lord?'

He faced the knight in command of his escort who was himself dismounting, and spread his hands in a helpless gesture. 'It's an old strain. I thought he'd rested up enough after these weeks at Thornford, but obviously I've misjudged it. You'd best fetch the remount from the back of the wain and hitch him there instead. He'll not bear my weight for the distance we've to cover before dark.'

'Yes, my lord – are you all right?'

Miles smiled at the young face, so earnest behind the helmet's broad nasal. 'Naught that a warm fire and cup of hot wine won't cure, Gervase. My blood's running as sluggish today as the Dee in midwinter.' He struggled to pull his gauntlets back on and clapped his hands together to try and revive the feeling. There was pain today, a thin knife wedging itself between his joints and grating them apart. The biting damp and cold shredded his lungs as he breathed it in, and sent a chill shuddering through his body. He wondered briefly if it was the homing instinct of a dying animal that had filled him with the urge to travel down the march to his main holding, denying the weather and the exhortations of his granddaughter and her new husband that he remain with them at least until Candlemas. He went slowly towards the wain where Gervase's squire was saddling up the brown remount.

'You could always sit within, my lord,' the young knight said, indicating the cart with its load of travelling chests and supplies pressed on him by Adam and Heulwen.

'The day I cannot straddle a horse and take to one of those contraptions will be the day of my funeral,' Miles said grumpily. Yes, he was feeling his years, but was not yet prepared to admit defeat.

He set his foot in the long stirrup and allowed the squire to boost him into the saddle; suppressing a grimace of pain, he gathered up the reins. Expression blank, Gervase signalled to the wain driver and turned to remount his own destrier, but paused half-way into the saddle, his eyes widening in shock.

'Ware arms, the Welsh!' he cried, his voice whiplashing the cold air.

Miles's escort closed around him. He fumbled with his shield strap, swearing at the clumsiness of his gnarled, frozen fingers.

The Welsh wasted no time on the niceties of battle. Arrows were the means of destruction, arrows aimed at the Norman destriers to bring them down. A shaft struck one of the geldings harnessed to the wain, but obliquely in the rump, causing pain but little serious damage. The horse threw up its head and, with a shrill whinny, tried to bolt. The driver cursed and strove to control its panic, but the horse was insensible to all save the instinct to escape from danger and the pain. Another arrow hit the driver, pinning his arm to the structure of the wain. He shrieked, and the reins were torn from his grip by the jerking of the injured horse. It shied into its companion, which, terrified by the lack of a guiding hand and the stench of fear and blood, skittered sideways and tried to bolt.

Miles saw it coming, but could do nothing about it. He was aware from the corner of his eye of Gervase's squire leaping to try and grab the reins, a warning shout tearing hoarsely from his throat, his eyes wide and appalled. As if in slow motion the baggage wain swayed and rocked like a drunkard caught out after curfew, and as the horses plunged and strained and kicked, it lurched and tipped over on its side, smashing its wooden-base frame into jagged spars, wantonly hurling its contents forth like tossed rags.

The horses threshed free and with harnesses trailing bolted into the midst of the panic. A flying sliver of wood shot into the eye of Miles's stallion, and with a scream of agony it reared, forehooves pawing the sky. Miles tried to cling on to the reins and pommel, but a lifetime separated his reflexes from Renard's and he was flung from the saddle, landing hard against the shattered carcass of the wain.

Outnumbered and outmanoeuvred, it was quickly and bloodily over for the Normans. The Welsh leader, big and broad, with the legacy of the Irish Norse revealed in his sturdy bones and bright blue eyes, nudged his horse around a mailed corpse and drew rein before the smashed ruins of the wain where a dead youth, his neck broken, sprawled close to the stallion's hooves. He pressed his knees and let the horse pick its way delicately around the body to the other side of the wain. For a moment he was filled with a sickening disappointment, thinking that his scheme had come to nothing, but then the man on the ground moved feebly and groaned.

Davydd ap Tewdr dismounted and bent beside the old man to examine him with the swift thoroughness of one accustomed to doing battle on the run and dealing with its casualties. 'Naught save cracked ribs and bruising,' he announced with relief in which excitement trembled, 'but he's bruised and badly shaken. Twm, bring a blanket. We've got to coddle him as tenderly as one of our own until we can exchange him for Rhodri.'

Adam couched the lance beneath his arm, held the shield well in to his left side leaving no gap, clapped his heels into the stallion's belly and shouted, 'Hah!'

Vaillantif leaped from his hocks like an arrow from an arbalester's wound bow and sped down the tilt yard. Adam's lance struck the quintain a solid blow. He ducked as the sandbag flung round and parted the air over his crouched frame. He turned Vaillantif in a compact swirl of hooves and repeated the move with an effortless liquidity that had the spectators envying him his accomplished grace, and the young Welsh hostage viewing his own imminent attempt at the quintain with trepidation.

Adam lit down from the saddle with only the slightest hint of stiffness to mar his movement and suggest a recently healed wound. Walking Vaillantif over to the youth, he handed the lance up to him. 'Remember to keep your head down, your shield in tight, and don't sit up too soon afterwards or you'll get your skull well and truly rattled.'

'And I aim for that red triangle in the centre?' Rhodri sighted down the tilt, voice matter-of-fact, mouth nonchalant, eyes dubious in the extreme.

'That's right.' The corners of Adam's eyes crinkled for a moment before he schooled his expression to a teacher's benign neutrality. 'Not just the red triangle, but the dead centre of it, your enemy's heart. Good fortune.' He slapped the borrowed black destrier's glossy shoulder and stepped back.

Beside Adam, Heulwen paused on her way back from the somewhat neglected plesaunce where she had been planning some new herb beds. Linking her arm through his, she felt the small, unseen ripple of laughter make his body tremble.

'What's amusing you?' she demanded.

The fact that she had spoken to him gave him the excuse he needed to break into an open grin. 'I know what's coming next.'

'What?' She watched the young man's throat move as he brought up the lance.

'It takes months and months of practice at the quintain to avoid that sandbag. The beginners can't divide their attention between aiming and ducking. They can't

181

co-ordinate it all. He's in for a bruised back at the very least. Most likely he'll end up on the ground.'

'But I was watching you. It looked so easy!'

He chuckled. 'It is when you know how, but you learn the hard way, believe me.'

'As in all things,' she said with a small, almost sad sigh, and fell silent to watch Rhodri ap Tewdr gallop down the tilt to a rendezvous with his inevitable fate.

More by luck than judgement, he almost succeeded in being one of the elite few to cheat the sandbag on their first occasion – nearly, but not near enough. The spear tipped the target just slightly off centre, its impact unbalancing him, so he was a fraction too slow when he ducked and the sandbag fetched him a buffet across the back of the neck that swiped him out of the saddle and jarred him to the ground.

The black destrier jogged to a halt, and after one curious look over its shoulder, bent to nose at a tuft of grass. A grinning Austin ran out to catch the bridle.

'Not bad,' Adam admitted judiciously as he bent over the groaning, bruised young man. 'We'll have you jousting in Paris yet.' He took the reins from Austin and enquired with the faintest hint of challenge, 'Want to try again?'

The Welsh youth threw him a burning glance, then turned aside to spit out a mouthful of bloody saliva. 'Go to hell!' he snarled, but struggled unsteadily to his feet. He caught his horse and pulled himself into the saddle, and prepared to attack the quintain once more.

'Bravo, lad,' Adam murmured, watching with calculating eyes the strike, the mistimed duck and the way he strove to stay aboard his mount before finally conceding defeat and sprawling on the tilt yard floor, the last of the wind driven from his lungs.

Adam collected horse and spear and brought them back to him. Rhodri braced himself on his elbows, retching and fighting for air, wasted some of it on cursing Adam, but nevertheless got doggedly back on the horse as soon as his body was capable of obeying his will.

Rhodri turned the stallion in a quarter-circle and galloped not at the quintain, but straight at Adam, the lance levelled and deadly. Heulwen screamed. Adam's whole body tensed to move faster than he had ever done in his life if he had misjudged his man. At the last moment, the spear tip changed direction and the horse swerved. A string of foam globbed Adam's gambeson. He smelt the strong odour of stallion sweat and was swept by hot breath as the destrier passed within a fraction of trampling him down.

'Jesu God!' Heulwen cried furiously. 'He might have killed you!'

'I don't think so.' Adam turned to where two of the watching knights had seized Rhodri's horse and were dragging him out of the saddle, pinning his arms and ramming them behind his back.

'All right, Alun, leave him be.' Adam gestured.

They let him go, but almost as roughly as they had seized him. The young man shook himself like a dog and rubbed one of his bruised arms. Blood smeared and stained his chin. His lower lip was swollen and dark. 'How did you know I would stop?' he demanded belligerently.

Adam smiled briefly. 'A gamble on your nature and a guess that you wanted to live beyond a brief moment of glory.'

Rhodri spat blood at Adam's feet. 'Rumour says that if my brother does not come, you are going to hang me from the highest tree on the demesne.'

'Does it?' Adam gave the youth a bland look, and taking Vaillantif's reins from Austin, swung smoothly into his own saddle.

'He won't swallow it, you know. He'd rather see me swing.'

'Then you'll have to hope the rumours aren't true, won't you?' Adam took up a lance and turned from his hostage to canter with negligent grace down the tilt and lightly rap the shield in the dead centre, avoiding the sandbag with insouciant ease and swerving to an elegant halt at the end of the run. Rhodri scowled at him and touched his swollen, tender mouth.

'Why did you bait him? I thought you were dead for sure.'

Adam threw down the balled-up wisp of hay he had been using to rub the horse down, wiped his hands on his tunic, and looked round at Heulwen. 'I wanted to test his mettle. I was curious to see if he would get up and try again after that first humbling in the dust.'

'Your life would have been a high price to pay for finding out!' she snapped. 'Did the King know how rash you truly were when he sent you to fetch his daughter?' Fear gave her voice a shrewish timbre, and hearing it, she clamped her mouth shut and glared at him.

Adam slapped Vaillantif's ruddy satin hide. 'Never buy a chestnut horse or have truck with a red-haired woman,' he quoted with a grin. 'They're both nags. I appear to have committed both crimes, don't I?'

'Adam . . .'

He looked at the brimming temper in her eyes, their colour dazzling and sea-tinged against her flushed, furious face, and set his arm across her shoulders. 'Oh Heulwen, don't be such a scold for so small a crotchet.' He kissed her cheek.

She wrenched free of him. 'You're just as irresponsible as Ralf,' she snapped. 'And when I complain, you make light of it, put me at fault!'

Adam opened his mouth to defend himself, saw how rigidly she was standing and realised that in a moment she was going to run from him and they would reach another impasse. Before she could bolt, he grabbed her resisting hand and drew her around the stallion and into the empty stall next door, where he dumped her down on a mound of dusty hay, evocative of the scent of summer and the memory of thundery sunshine.

'Look,' he said, throwing himself down beside her, 'I did not know for certain that he was going to ride at me. If I had turned and run, it might have tipped the balance and made him drive that lance straight between my shoulder blades.'

Her anger was unassuaged. 'You should not have goaded him into that state in the first place.'

'I was testing his character. If he had remained down that first time, I'd have considered him short on guts – no staying power. The fact that he kept on getting up tells me he's got courage and a stubborn streak,' and then wryly, 'and the fact that he rode at me is proof that he's foolhardy.'

Heulwen sniffed. 'That sounds like a pot calling a cauldron black!'

He conceded a shrug. 'It was a calculated risk. A man

is always wise to study the temper of a weapon before he puts it to use.'

She frowned at him. 'What do you mean?'

A groom led another horse into the stables, peered over the partition and, clearing his throat, apologised and went out again.

'Miles and I had several discussions before he left – about replacing Davydd ap Tewdr with his younger brother.'

'So what will you do, kill him when he comes to ransom the boy?' she enquired, her lip curling.

'It's a nice thought,' he admitted, 'but it wouldn't work. Rhodri would turn on us as you saw him turn just now, and he wouldn't stay his hand. Even if I killed him, it wouldn't be the end of it. We'd just have all the other big fish crowding the pool to feed on the small fry. No, if Davydd comes, I drive a hard bargain, as close to the bone as I can get. If he doesn't, I foster the doubts in Rhodri's mind and start needling my way into Davydd's territory.' He stopped speaking and studied her almost desolate expression. 'What's wrong? What have I said now?'

Heulwen shook her head. His eyes had lost their ruthless gleam and were filled with nothing more dangerous than anxiety. She could not say that she had just seen his father's legacy in him and that it frightened her far more than his rashness to hear him plan like this, his gaze as bright and impersonal as that of Renard's hawk. It was still bright now as he looked at her, but far from impersonal. Lowering her lids, she was aware of the rapid rise and fall of his chest and knew that it was not just an anxiety of the mind that awaited her response.

'Nothing,' she said. 'It is a side of you I have not seen

before.' She gave him a guarded look. 'Although we grew up together, I don't really know you, do I?'

'You could learn,' he said hoarsely, and touched her cheek, then before it was too late, withdrew his hand and started to get up. That particular avenue was fraught with pitfalls. They had made love several times since the first night of their homecoming, and while the experiences had not been disasters, neither had they spoken of overwhelming success.

Heulwen was a willing enough partner – willing but not involved – happy to pleasure him, but reticent with her own responses. Part of it, he suspected, was that after Ralf she was wary of giving too much of herself away unless surprised into it. Certainly she seemed relieved rather than frustrated by his faster, more open response, but it did nothing for his pride. Give her time, Miles had said to him, but Adam did not know how long he could be patient.

As he reached Vaillantif's headstall, her arms suddenly came around his waist from behind, and he felt her cheek press hard against his back. 'I could try,' she murmured so quietly that he had to strain to hear, 'but Adam, I'm frightened.'

He turned around, reversing the embrace, and tipped up her face to study it. 'Surely not of me?' His heart lurched.

'I don't know.' A small shudder ran her length. She could not say to him that with Ralf the learning had led her out of love and into misery, and she was terrified of it happening again. 'No . . . but of what the future holds.' She tightened her grip on him and stood on tiptoe to reach his lips.

'Sire, come quickly!' Austin tore into the stables, his eyes so wide that the hazel iris was completely ringed by white.

Adam and Heulwen jolted apart and started at the squire. 'The carrier's here and he's got a wounded man with him – sore wounded.'

Adam released Heulwen and set his hand on the youth's quivering shoulders. 'Take your time, lad.'

Austin swallowed, gulped more air, and added, 'The wounded man's the driver of Lord Miles's baggage wain. They were hit by the Welsh, so he says, stripped and massacred, saving Lord Miles whom they took away with them.'

'No!' cried Heulwen. 'No, oh no!'

'All right, Austin,' Adam said evenly. 'Fetch Father Thomas, then tell Sweyn to get the men mounted up. Tell him also that we'll need pack ponies and ropes.'

'Yes, sire.' Austin ran. So did Adam, but in the direction of the gatehouse, not the keep, with Heulwen struggling behind him and cursing her skirts as they hindered her.

The injured man had been brought in slumped across one of the carrier's ponies like a half-filled sack of cabbages. Now he lay on an oxhide stretcher, his face the colour of grey clay and his breathing rapid and shallow.

'He's done for, poor bugger,' muttered the carrier from the side of his mouth. 'That wound in his arm's mortal nasty.'

Heulwen knelt beside the stretcher, gently raised the covering blanket, then winced. The man's right arm was bare to the shoulder, the sleeve ripped away and nothing to see of the muscle below it but a shredded, clotted

188

mess, inflamed and swollen. Torn between anger and sick pity, Heulwen bit her lip. 'Couldn't you have washed and bound it better than this?' She shot an accusing look at the itinerant merchant.

The carrier sucked the few yellow stumps in his mouth that passed for teeth and shrugged. 'I did me best. I worn't going to linger in case any o' them Welsh bastards came back. Poor sod was pinned straight through to the wood behind. It were the devil of a job to free him and if it worn't for me happenin' by, he'd still be there.'

'Everyone was dead apart from him?' Adam demanded.

'Far as I know. I didn't stop to look too closely. Leastways nobody groaned, and the ones I saw had arrows and sword cuts that no man could survive. Proper mess. They must have ridden straight into an ambush.' He stopped to cough and lick his lips.

Adam snapped his fingers at a goggling servant. 'Where was this?'

'Heading down Ledworth way, close on Nant Bychan near that border stone that's always being disputed. Even going at full lick, you'll not make it there much before prime.'

The man on the stretcher groaned again, this time with more awareness. Heulwen laid her hand on his brow and his lids fluttered open. 'Mistress Heulwen,' he croaked weakly, then coughed. Adam took the ale that the servant had been about to give to the carrier and handed it down instead to his wife. Carefully she tilted up the injured man's head so that he could drink. He did so, after a fashion, the golden liquid spilling into his beard and staining his rough tunic.

'It was so sudden,' he gasped. 'We could do nothing.

They slaughtered us like spearing fish in a barrel. Lord Miles they took alive – it was him they wanted. The rest of us didn't really matter save as practice targets for their bows.'

Adam swore. Heulwen looked up at him with brimming eyes.

'What else do you do but find a bargaining counter of equal worth to barter?' he said flatly.

Surreptitiously the carrier reached down to the half-full cup of ale that Heulwen had put down beside the wain driver, then stepped back with it clutched triumphantly in his hand. Father Thomas arrived at a trot and, kneeling beside the stretcher, began to prepare the wounded man for confession.

Heulwen rose unsteadily to her feet. The sound of the destriers being saddled up drifted across the ward from the stable enclosure and mingled with the words of the priest and the hesitant replies of the wain driver. Adam swung towards the more distant noise, his face taut like a hound anticipating the hunt. Involuntarily, Heulwen put her hand on his sleeve as if she would leash him.

Adam looked down. 'Come and help me arm,' he said, turning her with him towards the keep. 'I want Rhodri ap Tewdr confined to the hall. No need to lock him up, but keep a close eye on him.'

'His brother is responsible for this, isn't he?' she demanded.

They had to separate to negotiate the twisting stairs to the upper floor and their bedchamber. 'I'd wager all the silver in Thornford's strongbox on it,' Adam said grimly. 'He's taken your grandsire for ransom.' On reaching their chamber, he lifted his hauberk from its pole.

'If you hadn't taken the boy prisoner in the first place—' she began, then clamped her mouth on the rest of the sentence.

Adam eyed her sharply and said nothing, but his anger showed in the bunching and release of a muscle in his jaw.

'Adam, I'm sorry.' She touched his shoulder. 'Oh, curse me for being a shrew. I know it's not your fault. It's just that . . .'

'You know I'll stand there and take it,' he finished for her. 'Just be careful how far you go. Do you think I do not care? Do you think the thought has not crossed my own mind?'

Her chin wobbled. She struggled with tears and, losing, began to weep. He swore and drew her down on to his lap and kissed her. 'Heulwen, don't.'

'He's not well!' she sobbed. 'He's old and sick. I've seen how he struggles to mount the stairs and climb on a horse. It will kill him!'

Adam did not seek to deny her fears. What she said was true. He had noticed the change in Miles himself, as if everything was going forward to meet the spring, leaving Heulwen's grandfather in a winter limbo. He pressed his lips to her temple and held her tightly until he felt her shuddering abate, then he drew away to look at her. 'Come on, love, help me arm up. I've got to go to the scene and see for myself what has happened.'

She sniffed, wiped her eyes and got off his knee. Ralf would have laughed at her and ruffled her hair, or else would have wanted to bed her for the novelty of watching her tears as he took her. Warrin would have blustered and fussed and flexed his muscles. Adam was full of a checked restlessness, eager to be gone, but for her sake containing it with admirable fortitude.

She lifted the hauberk from the bed and helped him to don it. Since its last wearing it had been scoured in a sack full of vinegar-dampened sand to remove all the dirt and rust, and had then been dried, carefully oiled and hung on its pole to await further use. The rivets made a whispering, silvery noise as the hauberk slid down over his body, and when he stood up in it he looked twice as broad as he actually was. As he buckled on his swordbelt she stepped back to look at the whole of him. A cold shiver ran down her spine. The man who had merely played at being the warrior was transformed into the warrior in truth.

'Adam, be careful,' she said unsteadily. 'I don't want to lose you too.'

He stooped to take his helmet from where it lay at the foot of the hauberk pole. 'I'll send word by messenger ahead of me,' he said. 'I know it is as hard to wait as to be doing.' Coming to her, he curved his free arm around her waist, holding her carefully so that she would not be bruised upon the rivets. His kiss was fierce and hard, speaking all that his grip could not, and then he left her for the bailey and the men assembled there.

16

Miles opened his eyes and stared with exhausted indifference at the black forest trunks. The pain in his chest and down his right arm was a dull, gnawing ache. Every breath drawn expanded his broken ribs and was pure agony. He was aware of the damp, cold air seeping into his marrow – or perhaps it was just the bony finger of death.

Welsh voices flitted among the trees – the language of his childhood, learned in the green forests of Powys at his Welsh grandfather's knee so long ago, and now suddenly so close that he could almost see the shadows of men, smell the damp woodsmoke of their fire and hear their bright laughter. But of course he could; he was their hostage. He was eighty-two years old, not eight, and his body was still earth-chained to pain. The laughter ceased and one of the shadows resolved itself into the tall, broad Welshman who had led the raid and was now holding out to him a leather costrel of mead and a heel of dark bread.

Miles shook his head, feeling neither appetite no thirst, feeling nothing save a distant sadness that he had not been permitted the indulgence of a last look at so many familiar things. 'You are being very foolish,' he said in Welsh.

Davydd ap Tewdr shrugged. 'How so, old man? bargain you for my brother. Where is the folly in that?'

'Corpses have little value.' Miles gave him the exhausted travesty of a smile. 'Oh not the lad . . . yet. He's in fine fettle, but what happens when you put a failing candle in a draught? I haven't got long, and neither have you.'

The wind laboured through the bare January branches which snagged over their heads, striving westwards. Rain spattered through the sparse canopy. The Welsh prince looked down at his frail means to an end really looked, and saw that Miles le Gallois was not lying for his own sake. Part of it was the dull forest light emphasising the grey-blue patches beneath the seamed eyes, but the rapid rise and fall of the old man's breast owed more to a struggle for air than to any fear or anxiety.

'God rot you in hell, you won't die on me, not until you've served your purpose!' he muttered.

'Do not wager on it,' Miles said, and closed his eyes welcoming the darkness.

Heulwen, in the midst of a dutiful ave at the bier of the dead wain driver, was disturbed by FitzSimon, commander of the garrison in the absence of its other senior members

'My lady, a group of Welsh are approaching the keep,' he said. 'They have a litter with them.'

Heulwen rose from her knees and beat at the two

lusty patches on her skirts. 'There is no news from Lord Adam?'

'Not yet, my lady,' he said and added, with ill-concealed irritation, 'it is too soon for that.'

Heulwen gave him a swift glance of similar irritation, but bit her tongue on her temper. 'Very well, I'll come aloft,' she said, and having made her obeisance to the altar, left the small chapel and followed him out into the grey afternoon. The wind swirled around her woollen skirts and tugged at her veil; she held the former down with her right hand, the veil on her head with her left, and ascended to the gatehouse battlement.

Between twenty and thirty Welshmen had stopped just beyond arrow range, all of them decently mounted on shaggy mountain ponies. They wore the native garb of stitched fleeces and knee-length tunics, bows slung at their shoulders and the short swords they favoured at their hips. Narrowing her eyes, Heulwen could make out a blanket-shrouded form on a litter to the forefront of their array.

One of their number detached from the group and rode forward immediately below the walls of the keep to request in accented French to talk to Adam de Lacey. Heulwen peered down between the merlons. 'Ask him who wants to talk and why,' she told one of the keep soldiers who had been summoned aloft for the use of his deep, carrying voice. The question was relayed, there was a pause for consultation, and then the reply floated back to her.

Despite the fact that she had been half prepared to hear it, it still hit her solidly in the gut. Davydd ap Tewdr desired to exchange her grandfather for Rhodri.

'Dear God,' she whispered, for there was now no doubting that the form on the litter was her grandfather – and the litter meant that he was too weak to sit on a horse, the bastion of his stubborn will and pride.

'Delay him until we can get a message to Lord Adam,' FitzSimon said and turned to command one of the men.

'No!'

He swivelled to gape at Heulwen in disbelief. Accustomed to taking orders from men, and by his position in the keep hierarchy to giving them too, he was possessed of an arrogant certainty that women should defer to their male superiors, and was unpleasantly astounded by her denial.

'My lady, with all respect, this is too serious a matter to be judged by us,' he said, recovering his dignity and twitching his shoulders within his cloak like a hawk settling ruffled feathers.

To be judged by a woman – a flighty, red-haired woman of more than half-Welsh blood. As if his head were transparent and the words written on his brain she could read his mind, and her chin rose a stubborn notch. 'It is also too serious a matter to leave until my husband's return!' she answered. 'That is my grandfather down there on that litter. Have Rhodri ap Tewdr brought up here to me now.'

He hesitated until he could hesitate no longer, then inclined his head in scant formality and left her. Heulwen swallowed, bowed her head, and leaned it for a moment against the gritty stone behind which she sheltered. 'Holy Christ, what do I do?' she murmured into the shadow created by her body. 'Adam, help me, what do I do?'

Rhodri, hands corded behind his back, was thrust into

her presence, his eyes anxiously wide, his mouth set in a thin, tight line. She straightened, adjusted her cloak, and faced him with a cold expression.

'Your brother has come for you. I wish my husband had left you to die in the road.'

He returned her a measured gaze, for he had heard the news of his brother's raid and watched Thornford react to it like a disturbed anthill. 'My lady, I am sorry, believe me,' he said in Welsh. 'Even knowing that your lord intended using me for his own purposes, I could have wished myself free in different circumstances.'

'Spare me your condolences,' she snapped, 'you are wasting your breath.' She turned from him to the soldier with the voice. 'Tell him that Lord de Lacey is not here, and that in his absence Prince Davydd will have to deal with his wife, who is of Welsh blood herself and the granddaughter of Miles le Gallois.'

Heulwen collected the reins and thanked the man who helped her into the saddle. Her mare, sensing her tension, jibbed and sidled, and she had to put a soothing hand on the damp neck and murmur soft words.

'My lady, I still say you are making a mistake in going out to treat with them,' FitzSimon muttered beside her, and curbed his own restless stallion. 'It is much too dangerous. They might attack us.'

'I doubt it, but if they do, I trust in the might of your sword-arm to deliver us.' Her voice was both dulcet and biting at the same time. She set her heels into Gemini's sides and the mare moved anxiously forwards.

Feeling belittled by her scorn, FitzSimon glared at Heulwen's back, knowing that if she had been his to

beat, her body by now would have matched the slate
blue shade of the cloak pinned across his breast. Starting
after her, he dragged viciously on the hostage's reins.
Rhodri ap Tewdr sat his dun gelding in silence, his hands
lashed to the pommel, his feet joined by a double loop
of rope slung beneath the horse's belly, surrounded by
an escort of six serjeants.

As Gemini paced away from the safety of Thornford's
outer bailey and palisade, Heulwen felt sick with apprehension and fear. She swallowed valiantly, hoping that
appearances and emotions were not one and the same.
It was easier for the men, for their faces were half
concealed by their helms. Hers was open, vulnerable to
Welsh eyes and whatever they might read into it – her
fortune and her grandfather's. The responsibility was
terrifying.

Davydd ap Tewdr watched warily as the group from
the castle approached the prearranged meeting place,
marked by a Welsh lance thrust point-down in the turf.
'All right,' he said over his shoulder. 'Bring him.'

The woman who drew rein and faced him across the
wind-quivered shaft was striking – not classically so, her
bones were too strong, but in an earthy, tempestuous
way, appealing entirely to the senses. 'Lady Heulwen?'
He gave her a wolfish smile and looked beyond her to
Rhodri, who flushed and averted his gaze.

'I hope we need not waste time on the formalities?'
she responded frostily. 'Surely there is no more to be
done than to make the exchange?'

Davydd ap Tewdr brushed his hand over his moustache and refused to be frozen by the ice in her gaze.
He noticed that not by so much as a flicker had she

acknowledged the presence of her grandfather lying on the pallet. 'He's still alive,' he said, and then, provocatively, 'and we have treated him with more courtesy than you appear to have extended towards my brother.'

'That was my own fault,' Rhodri said quickly. 'I fell off a horse this morning.'

Ap Tewdr gave his youngest brother a sharp glance. 'Last time you fell off a horse you were three years old!' he commented, but let it rest and turned smiling to Heulwen. 'My lady, by all means let us make this exchange. I have no desire to linger here, and I am sure you will want to take your grandfather within to warmth and comfort.'

Heulwen nodded stiffly, unable to speak, knowing that if she so much as looked at the litter, then, like a piece of ice bearing too much weight, she would shatter apart. She raised her hand and gestured to FitzSimon.

Disgust evident in his every movement, the knight drew the sharp hunting dagger from his belt, dismounted and stooped to slash the ropes that bound Rhodri to the dun, then pulled him down from the saddle.

Rhodri rubbed his wrists. FitzSimon pricked the dagger longingly through tunic and shirt. 'Don't try anything,' he growled.

'I'd have to be as mad as a *saeson* to do that with freedom so close,' Rhodri retorted, and the daggerpoint punctured his skin. The Welsh stiffened in their saddles, and hands flashed to sword-hilts.

Heulwen flung herself down from her mare and rounded on FitzSimon. 'Give me that knife!' she cried, then snatched it from him and pitched it as far away as her strength would allow. 'Is your pride everything that you cannot take a childish jibe without responding in similar wise?' She made a furious gesture of dismissal. 'Return to the keep and wait for me there.'

FitzSimon recoiled as if from the venom of a striking snake. He was aware that the anger of the Welsh had subsided and that they were watching the scene with amused curiosity, so the pride she had spoken of with such scorn must either be swallowed or choked upon. After a precarious moment, he chose the former, but with a very bad grace. Lord Adam was going to hear of this, by Christ on the cross he was! 'My lady,' he acknowledged, making the words sound like an insult. He went to his dagger, picked it out of the grass and wiped it meticulously before sheathing it, then mounted his horse and spurred it to a canter.

Heulwen watched him leave, then turned again to Davydd ap Tewdr. 'I apologise for him,' she said stiltedly, and swallowed. The rage had begun to drain from her. She wanted to burst into tears and knew she dared not, for then they would see her as just another hysterical woman rather than an authority with whom they must reckon.

'Don't,' said ap Tewdr with a laconic shrug, 'a Welsh arrow will put an end to him sooner or later.'

'I know all I wish to know about Welsh arrows,' she snapped. 'Let us have this exchange over and done with.'

'By all means.' Ap Tewdr's tone was mockingly expansive and Heulwen hated him for it. 'Give your lord my regards and regrets that we could not deal directly.'

'I will do so,' she said through her teeth, 'be assured of it,' and gestured the two serjeants forward to raise the litter. Still rubbing his wrists, waiting for a mount to be brought through the Welsh ranks to him, Rhodri looked down at the man lying there, and then quickly away, but it was too late. His eyes had already fixed the image in his mind.

'Be careful,' Heulwen cautioned the men, and as the Welsh took charge of their leader's brother, slapping him on the shoulder, crowing over him and their success, she took her own first look at her grandfather.

He was awake and aware, watching her, and he gave her the ghost of a smile. 'You did well, *cariad*,' he whispered. 'Proud of you.' His hand twitched beneath the blanket, emerged after a brief struggle, and stretched towards her. She swooped down to take it, and the men stopped as she bent over him, her body racked with shudders of grieving and relief.

'Come, *cariad*,' Miles said hoarsely, 'no tears, not now . . .' He stroked her braid, then, assailed by weakness, his hand dropped back on to the covers and he closed his eyes. Crying freely, distraught, but not to the point of being incapable, Heulwen tucked her grandfather's cold hand back within the covering of sheepskins, drew them up to his chin, and went to retrieve Gemini. Half blinded by tears, she watched the Welsh ride away in the opposite direction, their triumphant cries fluting the cold wind. One of the riders hesitated and looked round. She thought it was Rhodri, but through the distorting blur of tears could not be sure, and neither did she care.

'Christ, but I really thought he was going to die on us!' Davydd ap Tewdr laughed with the jubilation of relief. 'If we'd left it until dawn tomorrow, it would have been too late. He'll not last out the night.'

Rhodri swallowed bile and said nothing. He was remembering the sunken, blue-tinged flesh and hearing the old man's dragging fight for breath.

'You didn't have to do it this way,' he said when he had control of himself.

The wide shoulders twitched irritably within the encasing half-hauberk. 'Not developing a conscience are we, Rhod?' he scoffed. 'Would you rather have swung from a gibbet on Candlemas eve?'

'It wouldn't have come to that. It was only a ruse to get you to come. De Lacey wanted to treat with you.'

'A ruse, hmm?' Davydd ap Tewdr chuckled with sour amusement. 'Well, de Lacey got more than he bargained for, didn't he?'

'And sweet Christ so might we. Do you know how much outrage this will cause? We'll have every marcher lord between Hereford and Chester down on us for this!'

Davydd reined to a halt and slewed around to glare at his slight, dark brother. 'You dare to lecture me, whelp!' He fetched Rhodri a buffet that reeled him in the saddle. 'You dare to preach at me like a belly-aching priest, when it was your idiocy that brought about this whole predicament. Christ on the cross, I should have left you to rot on a *saeson* gibbet!'

The blow had opened Rhodri's cut lip, and dark blood dripped off the end of his chin and soaked into his mount's coarse winter fell. 'I'm not ungrateful,' he muttered thickly, 'I just thought you could have gone about it in a different way. There's enough bad blood already. We killed Lady Heulwen's first husband, and now you've as good as murdered her grandfather.'

Davydd let drop the reins he had picked up and stared hard at Rhodri. 'What do you mean, her first husband?'

'Ralf le Chevalier, don't you remember?'

'Le Chevalier? She's *his* widow?' He leaned on his pommel and stared, and suddenly surprise gave way to laughter. 'God, she ought to be eternally grateful to us that she's rid of him. I wish I'd known!'

Rhodri studied his brother, a new maturity stripping the scales of childhood from his eyes. Davydd was only aware of the ground directly beneath his feet, without a thought for the looming horizon. It had been his own shortcoming until his wounding and imprisonment had taught him a different, wary discretion. He twisted his injured lip. 'Why couldn't you have made peace with de Lacey? All right, he's a Norman and out for his own gain, but he's no glutton. He'd have listened to reason, and he's the lord of Ravenstow's own son-in-law now.'

Davydd spluttered at the notion. 'I'd as soon invite a pack of wolves to kennel among my flocks!'

'You probably just have. Miles le Gallois is respected on both sides of the border. His son's wed to the English King's own daughter, and he has Welsh connections on the distaff side with half the nobility of Gwynedd and Powys!' This time Rhodri jerked his mount sideways, avoiding the intended blow.

'A wolf in sheep's clothing!' Davydd roared, thoroughly beside himself, spittle flecking his moustache. 'And fostered at my own hearth. You've gone soft, turned into a Norman lick-arse!' He dug his heels into his pony's flanks and, cursing, swept on ahead, leaving Rhodri to blink after him, unexpected tears stinging his eyes.

Had he turned into a 'Norman lick-arse'? He cast his

203

mind back over that jousting episode this morning, the superior, good-humoured amusement quickly becoming rage as the pet animal rounded on its captors with a snarl. The calculating stare of Adam de Lacey and his deceptively smiling mouth. Davydd did not know what he was facing.

Rhodri thought of the old man, Miles le Gallois: Miles ap Heulwen uerch Owain of the line of Hwyel Dda. There was Welsh blood there, as good as or better than his own. He had grown fond of the old man during the months of his confinement, perhaps more than was wise. Miles had been perceptive and tolerant, compassionate without pitying, for he understood Welsh ways having been born to them himself, and despite the plentiful opportunity had never mocked or belittled Rhodri. He deserved better than he had received. Rhodri wiped at his eyes and swore because he was moved to grief for a man by tradition his enemy. Then he touched his cut lip, and glowering at his brother's broad back, kicked the horse and cantered to join him.

It was late afternoon when Adam and his men came upon the remains of the Welsh raid. The jingle of their harness, the snorting of their mounts and the creak of men shifting uneasily in their saddles broke the silence of the grave, sending small animals scuttling for cover and birds winging with calls of alarm.

One of Adam's Angevins leaped down from his destrier and examined a soldier's sprawled corpse. His leather hauberk had been stripped and a pale band of skin upon one of his fingers showed where a ring had recently been worn. Stony-faced, Adam nudged Vaillantif forward through the wet grass. There were no weapons beside the bodies. Swords, axes, lances, shields, all had been taken, including the harness from the dead horses.

'The bastards,' Sweyn muttered at Adam's shoulder. 'I wish I had been leading this escort.'

'Be thankful you were not,' Adam said shortly, and dismounted to prowl across the devastation to the overturned cart. Miles's destrier was there, belly-up. Adam stepped over its corpse and squatted beside the stripped body of Gervase de Cadenet. He did not try to press the eyelids shut, for he could see that the body was well into the stiffening stage. A wild, dark rage against the perpetrators of this outrage filled him. He made the sign of the cross over the young knight and murmured a short prayer, then beckoned to Austin and another knight to bring a pack pony.

They loaded the bodies on to the animals they had brought and draped them with blankets, then moved slowly back up the march.

'I will write to Lord Guyon as soon as we reach Thornford,' Adam said to Sweyn as they splashed through a shallow, swiftly running stream. His mouth tightened bleakly. 'God knows how he will take this news.'

'Lord Miles isn't strong enough to bear rough treatment,' Sweyn said. 'I saw the way you helped him on the stairs the other night. He's failing swiftly.'

Adam grimaced. 'Was I as obvious as all that? I thought I did it with subtlety.'

'You did, sir, but it is not your way to put your arm across a man's shoulders in conversation, even when you are fond of him and have the right.'

'Now I know why Jerold calls you my watchdog!' Adam said with rueful humour.

'And you can't teach an old dog new tricks,' Sweyn retorted, his fierceness masking deep affection. 'I've had my eye on you since you were a puling babe!'

'And I haven't changed, don't tell me!' Adam rolled Sweyn a sarcastic look and slapped the reins across Vaillantif's neck, increasing the pace.

They cut across the woodland using the carriers' well-worn track, and with the dusk hard upon them reached the common grazing land that Thornford shared with a neighbouring village – and there encountered the Welsh, riding out of the damp twilight mist in the direction of the border.

A mutual moment of shock held both groups immobilised, and then Adam issued several sharp commands to his own men, delegated Austin and an older knight to take care of the burdened pack ponies, and grouped the rest into a tight phalanx of iron and horse. His lance swung smoothly to the horizontal. The Welsh saw what was happening and tried to break and run, but got no further than the first splintering before the fury of the Norman charge engulfed them. Adam had singled out his man as Vaillantif galloped down upon the Welsh, marking the place to strike as clearly as he always marked the four nailheads on the quintain shield.

Davydd ap Tewdr's bodyguard was carried from the saddle by the impact of the honed battle lance and died as he hit the ground. Adam pivoted Vaillantif, drew his sword and engaged the man on his right. Behind him, swearing, Sweyn hacked and manoeuvred to stay with him.

Adam's opponent had no shield, and the grating shriek of steel on steel as the Welshman parried made Adam's bones shudder. The second blow shattered the inferior Welsh steel, leaving the man a broken hilt for defence. Adam swept it aside and concluded the matter, moving on like a reaper through ripe wheat.

The shield that was butted forward in protection by his next adversary was a Norman one, raided from Miles's escort, good and solid, but its new owner wore no armour, only an ill-fitting helm to guard his skull. In the split second before Adam struck him down to hell, he recognised the horrified young face partially concealed behind the helmet's broad nasal, and with an explosive oath changed his grip on the hilt: with a rapid flick of the wrist he sent Rhodri's blade spinning from his hand.

'In the name of Christ's ten fingers, what are you doing here?' Adam roared, saw the dark eyes widen, heard Sweyn's choked warning, instinctively crouched behind his shield and commanded Vaillantif sideways. The blow came in hard from the left, clipping the top of his shield and jarring his left arm to the bone as he strove to hold against it. He brought his right arm over in a solid retaliation and had the satisfaction of hearing his enemy grunt with pain, but the retort was fast and determined, and the short Welsh blade ripped open Adam's surcoat and splayed a diagonal line through the rivets of his mail.

He pricked Vaillantif with his spurs and the destrier reared up against the Welshman's mount, forehooves slashing. Adam swung his sword backhanded from shoulder height. Trained from infancy, there was so much power behind his blow that it almost severed the

Welshman's head. The body crumpled from the saddle and the Welsh pony bolted, stirrups hammering against its belly.

Breathing rapidly, Adam looked around. The Welsh were in retreat now, fleeing for the safety of the forest. 'Where's the lad?' he demanded.

'He ran for the woods, sire,' replied Sweyn. 'And the others with him.'

Adam scowled in the direction of the trees. Behind them, the sky was as grey as steel.

'If the lad's loose, and they were coming from Thornford . . .' Sweyn began.

'Then the exchange must have already taken place,' Adam finished, a knowledge that had been with him since the first impact of the charge. His chest expanded on a deep breath. 'They didn't waste much time, did they?'

'Do we go after them, my lord?'

Adam shook his head. 'No. They'll split up the moment they hit the forest and it is their own ground. We'd be picked off one by one that way. Anyone hurt? Go and find out, will you?'

'What about the Welsh?' asked Jerold. 'The bodies, I mean. What shall we do with them?'

Adam glanced down. His last victim returned his look balefully from his muddy bier, blood crawling from severed flesh and sinew. 'Leave them. They'll be claimed when all is quiet.' He wiped his sword on his thigh and sheathed it, looked up and said tersely to the man who had come to ask instructions of Jerold, 'What are you staring at?'

'My lord, that is Davydd ap Tewdr, I would swear an

oath on it. I saw him at a fair in Shrewsbury last year, and quite close to. I was going into an alehouse as he was coming out with some of his people . . . He was laughing.' His eyes flickered with unwilling fascination over the hanging jaw, the stained teeth exposed in the eternal grin of death that threatens the living with their own, inevitable fate. Shuddering, he crossed himself.

Adam gestured the man away. 'I was wondering to Heulwen how it would be without ap Tewdr breathing down my neck,' he said to Jerold. 'It seems as if I'm about to find out. Go on, muster the men. There are still three miles ahead of us and it's nearly dark.'

On first sight of her husband, Heulwen almost fainted, for as he stepped into the torchlit hall, the brownish-red colour of drying blood almost obliterated the rich blue of his torn surcoat. His face too was liberally spattered in the areas where it had not been protected by helmet and ventail.

'Holy Christ!' she cried, and stopped short of running into his arms. 'Adam, what happened? How badly are you hurt?'

He followed her eyes down. 'It's not mine, love,' he reassured her. 'It's Davydd ap Tewdr's. He's dead.' His voice was matter-of-fact, as if he was discussing a mundane, everyday occurrence. He kissed her awkwardly. 'They told me at the gatehouse that Miles is here. Where is he?'

'I had him carried up to our bedchamber. He's very weak – barely conscious. He took a fall and I fear that perhaps a piece of broken rib has pierced his lung.'

'Yes, we found his horse.' His mouth tightened as he

remembered the scene they had come upon. He decided not to tell Heulwen, and plucking at his surcoat grimaced and said, 'Do you think you could organise a bathtub?'

'Yes, of course.' She snapped her fingers at a waiting maid and issued a brisk command.

Adam took the cup of wine that was given to him and, drinking it thirstily, made for the stairs.

'Sir, can you hear me? It is Adam. Davydd ap Tewdr is dead. We met his war band coming away from here and there was a battle. Rhodri took to the woods with the survivors and I let him go . . . Sir, my lord?'

Miles struggled up through a floating, weightless darkness towards a burden of light and pain. There was a hand gripping his own, and the voice, although low-pitched, was anxious, almost pleading.

'It's no use!' he heard his granddaughter say on a soft sob. 'No use, Adam, he's too far gone. Elswith, run and fetch Father Thomas.'

Miles forced his leaden lids to open. The candles burning on the coffer were a yellow blur; everything was a blur. His granddaughter's hair merged with the candle flame, and link mail silvered his vision with shifting discs of light.

'Adam?' he breathed weakly, vaguely puzzled until he remembered. A faint smile. 'Don't go chasing your tail lest you catch it. My will lies in the dower chest at Ashdyke . . . Guyon knows.'

'I am going to write to him this very night. He should be here within the next few days.'

Miles moved his head from right to left on the pillow. 'It doesn't matter. I'd rather die without a host of weeping relatives around my bed. Guyon knows that too . . . No great tragedy for me, I'm glad to go . . . I've stopped fighting it . . .'

'Grandpa, no!' Heulwen let out the words with an involuntary cry, then pressed the back of her hand across her mouth.

'Child, it is a blessing. You have your life before you . . . Do not grieve for me. I have lived mine to the full and beyond.' He closed his eyes again, and seemed to sink down into the bed as if only his shell remained. His hand relaxed in Adam's.

'Adam?' Heulwen's voice was thin with fear. She clutched his mail-clad arm. 'He's not . . . ?'

'No, not yet.' Adam removed his hand from the dead-leaf texture of the old man's. The aftermath of hard battle was in his bones, making him feel as limp as a rag. 'But it won't be long – certainly before your father can get here. You have to accept it; he wants to die. Let him go.' He took hold of her shoulders, kissed her forehead and became aware again, as she stood resisting in his embrace, of the state he was in. 'Where have you lodged us for the nonce, Heulwen? I'm reeking in blood, and in no fit state to comfort my wife or let her comfort me.'

Heulwen stood a little back from him, his words dragging her from her grief to the realisation that there were things to be done; that she had a husband who needed her attention and her ministrations.

'The wall room that was Rhodri's.'

Adam paused at the door to let the priest enter and spoke to him for a moment before continuing on his way. He stopped again as he caught sight of his squire

211

whispering to one of the maids, his hand in the act of curving around her waist. 'Austin, go and fetch me parchment, ink and quills, and bring them to the wall chamber!' he snapped. 'You girl, about your duties!'

She blushed, and bobbing a curtsy fled, the empty bath pail banging against her skirts. Adam shook his head. 'That boy!' he muttered beneath his breath, but with more irritation than anger, and shoved aside the curtain to enter their temporary bedchamber. Another maid finished emptying her pail into the tub and flitted from the room. The steam from the bath was laden with the scent of bay and rosemary.

'Adam, I had to ransom him, I had no other choice,' Heulwen said, beginning now to feel nervous as he reached to the buckle of his swordbelt. 'FitzSimon wanted me to send to you first, but I was too frightened for my grandfather.' She rubbed her hands together, watching him. 'I think I wounded FitzSimon's pride.'

'You're good at that,' he said. 'You find the sore spots in a man's soul and prick them sometimes until they run with blood.' He fetched her a look from under his brows. 'I know all about your behaviour towards my designated constable. He was waiting in the gatehouse for me to ride in, and as full of righteous indignation as an inflated bladder. I heard him out, and then I deflated him to a manageable size.' He clinked the swordbelt across the coffer.

Unable to discover from his tone whether he was annoyed at her or at FitzSimon, she said, 'For my sake?'

His smile was slight and sour. 'Not entirely. FitzSimon hides his inadequacy in arrogance and the belief that he's always right. He's a good soldier when directed, but he doesn't enjoy surprises such as women who snatch his authority and make ransom deals with Welsh brigands.'

'Adam, there was no other way. By the time I had sent for you . . .'

'Did I say that I wholeheartedly agreed with him? You might have handled him with more tact, although I doubt that's in your nature, but in the matter of the commands you gave you were right. My own would have been the same. No harm done, except that Rhodri is loose sooner than I expected, and I still don't know him well enough to be sure which way he'll jump next.' He pulled off the torn surcoat, tossed it to one side, and waited for her to help him remove his hauberk. Half a day since she had aided him to don it. Now the once gleaming links were spotted with mud and splotches of blood where it had soaked through the surcoat. There was also on his left side a line of splayed, warped rivets, showing how close he had come to being riven himself. Heulwen stared at the discarded, ruined surcoat and suddenly her hands were icy, unable to take the hauberk's weight so that it slithered to the rushes at her feet.

Adam had turned his back on her and was removing his gambeson and shirt. When he turned round and sat down on the bed, she stared at the comet-shaped bruise empurpling his ribs in the precise position of the damage to surcoat and hauberk. The livid mark was concealed from her as he leaned over to unwind his garters, and Heulwen gazed at his bent head, her stomach churning.

At Windsor, the trial by combat had seemed like stiff and gilded play-acting, he and Warrin just characters in

213

some monstrous charade, real, but only half real, and herself another player watching it all through a dark mirror. Over the space of the past two months, the charade had receded as she lived with Adam and had begun to see unknown facets glinting under the surface, with herself reflected in them. Now, staring at the tear in his hauberk and the bruised flesh above the new pink scar of his fight with Warrin, the dark mirror shattered and exposed her to the reality of how much she stood to lose.

Adam glanced up. 'Have you . . .' The look on her face stopped him. She was so pale that her skin seemed translucent and he thought for a moment she was going to faint. 'Heulwen?' He dropped his leg bindings and stood up, but before he could reach her, she had reached him. One arm went hard around his neck and she fastened her mouth on his, not just offering, but wildly demanding. He tasted tear-salt, felt her shudders, and her other hand was stroking him intimately, kindling a blaze. He broke away from the kiss with a gasp like a drowning man and clamped his hand upon her working one, holding her away before his control snapped and he took her to the bed and used her in the way she was demanding.

'No, Heulwen, not this time,' he said hoarsely. 'I'll not deny that I want you, but not like this. If you want to rage against your grandfather's dying, do it some other way. Go and kick the wall, or slaughter a pig, ride a horse into the ground, but do not bring it into our bed. God knows that's a haunted enough place as it is.'

Heulwen shook her head, her eyes brimming. 'You don't understand, Adam. It's not my grandfather I fear to lose, it's—'

There was a discreet cough outside and, hard upon it, Austin came into the chamber, sheets of parchment tucked under his arm, quills and an inkhorn in his hands; behind him walked a maid bearing food and wine.

Adam set Heulwen gently to one side and directed the squire to put down the writing implements and then go. While Austin did his bidding and the maid set down her tray, Adam finished undressing and set about the matter of a perfunctory bath. Heulwen lifted the flagon to pour him a cup of spiced wine, her hand shaking on the handle.

Presently, Adam put down the sponge, set the soap dish out of reach and said with quiet decision, 'Heulwen, go to my chest and bring me the casket you'll find at the bottom.'

She handed him the goblet and, giving him a curious look, went to do as he asked. The casket lay beneath his summer cloak and lighter linen tunics – a small, but exquisitely executed box made of cedarwood overlaid with enamelled copperwork depicting the signs of the zodiac – not a masculine possession at all.

'It belonged to my mother, so I'm told,' Adam said, watching her from beneath his eyelids. 'Brought back from the east with a host of tall tales by one of her brothers. I meant to give it to you some time ago, but it slipped my mind until now. The jewels inside are yours. They were my mother's personal ones, not bound to be passed on with the estate titles.' He gave a deprecatory shrug. 'There isn't much. Apparently her first husband saw no reason to deck a woman in gauds when he could better use the money elsewhere, and my own father – well you know all about my own father.'

Heulwen sat down on the bed and after one glance at Adam, raised the casket lid. A modest collection gleamed at her from the interior. Two intricate necklaces in the Byzantine style, probably gifts from that same brother, a girdle stitched with thread of gold, and a silk purse that matched it. There was an ancient torc bracelet of woven gold, several cloak clasps, some of silver, some of bronze, and some rings, one set with three garnets. She thanked him reservedly, wondering why he had chosen to give these things to her now: a sop to her pride? A comfit to an upset child?

Adam left the tub, dried himself, donned his chemise, then sat down beside her. 'You haven't opened the drawer at the bottom,' he said, nodding to the copperwork panelling the base of the casket. She narrowed her eyes to look closer and saw that what she had thought were decorative knobs were there for a purpose. When she gently pulled them, a drawer slid out. She made a small sound of surprise, and picked up the brooch that lay within.

'Your grandfather said that I was to give it to you when I deemed the time right,' he said, studying her pensively.

She stared at the piece. 'Grandpa gave you this? The wolf brooch?'

'On that first night we returned from Windsor, together with a warning to beware of futility, which we haven't heeded very well, have we?' He gave a self-deprecating shrug.

'He set great store by this.' She traced the figure of the wolf with a gentle forefinger.

'And by you.' He touched her braid. 'Are you going to sit in vigil with him tonight?'

'Yes,' she said through a tear-constricted throat.

'Then wear it for him.' He leaned round to kiss her, but did not linger, and crossed the room to the onerous duty of parchment and quill. She listened to him setting out the materials, heard the wine splash into a cup and the soft sound of tearing bread. The brooch took on warmth from her hand and the garnet eyes seemed to flicker with a life of their own in the candlelight. She thought of Ralf. Charming, irresponsible Ralf, who would have long since bolted for the safety of another woman's arms rather than face such an emotionally charged passage as this. Then she thought of Warrin, who would have comforted her with a superficial show of concern and then expected her to rally. Behind her a quill snapped and Adam cursed through a mouthful of bread; more wine trickled into the cup.

He had withdrawn to a discreet distance, giving her space to think and recuperate: there if she needed him, but not intruding. She looked round to where he was laboriously toiling on the letter to her father. Already there were ink stains on his fingers and when he rubbed his hand over his face in perplexed thought he left black streaks upon forehead and cheekbone and nose. A wild tenderness stirred within her, as different to her feelings for Ralf as a caterpillar was to a butterfly: an awakening, an acceptance of wings. She rose and, going behind him, put her arms around his neck and rubbed her cheek against his. 'Adam, thank you,' she said softly.

Her words were greeted not with a smile or an acknowledgement, but with an oath as the second quill split, splattering ink everywhere. He hurled it down in disgust and in so doing, sent the inkhorn flying. A spreading puddle of ink rapidly obliterated the few words that had straggled onto the parchment. His profanities caused Heulwen to gasp and giggle. She had thought she was aware of every last soldier's curse this side of Jerusalem, but this was an education. She scrambled for one of the bath towels and used a corner to blot up the ink. It was too late, the parchment was ruined. She bit her lip and looked at him. 'Shall I do it? I know that you and quills have a mutual enmity.'

'Would you?' A look of abject relief crossed his face. 'I didn't want to burden you more . . .'

The feeling increased, soaring aloft, unfettered. She smiled up at him and he caught his breath at the expression in her eyes, dazzled by it. 'I was going to say earlier, before we were interrupted, that it was not my grandfather I was afraid of losing – it was you.' She slipped her hand inside his shirt and traced the livid bruise above the scar. 'And if our bed has been haunted by Ralf's ghost, I do not believe it is haunted any more.' She rested her palm lightly on his flesh, but went no further. The next move had to come from him. 'Ralf used to mouth words of undying love to me at the same time as he was mounting another woman. Empty words – anyone can say them. Actions speak the louder.'

Adam's eyes were stinging. He swallowed hard, and knowing that his voice would not serve him, set his arm around her waist and bent his mouth to hers. The first kiss was long and gentle, as was the second. The third was deeper and its impetus carried them towards the bed, but without undue haste, for this time there was no wish on Heulwen's part to force the pace, or on Adam's to possess elusive quarry.

He left her mouth, to investigate the hitherto unknown delight of her eyelids, her earlobes and the soft, tender hollow in her collarbone. He unwound her braids and played with her hair, a cool, streaming river of fire, drew off her gown and undertunic, discovering the white nape of her neck that gleamed between a parting in the rich copper-gold strands. Heulwen gasped at that, her throat arching.

Adam swallowed again, this time against a different primal emotion, and sought to distract his mind. He concentrated on the lacings, which were difficult enough to make him swear beneath his breath, but when they were undone and the tunic removed, there was only her short shift and the light shining through it, outlining the contours of her body. She turned in his arms and put her own around his neck, and those contours were fitted intimately against his own, two halves of a puzzle becoming a whole.

For a moment he almost yielded to the surging greatness of his need. He thought about tilting at the quintain. If you went at it too soon, all the power was wasted and you ended flat on your back on the tilt yard floor. It was all a matter of balance and timing – of controlling your lance. That thought, so irreverently appropriate, made him shake with silent laughter and the tension eased. An image of the tilt yard in his mind, he took her to the bed.

'That was wonderful,' Heulwen murmured breathlessly, and slanted him a rich green-blue glance, replete and provocative at one and the same time. Adam kissed the tip of her nose and nibbled her throat, loath to relinquish the moment's triumph and tenderness for what lay beyond. 'Only wonderful?' he teased, finding it enjoyable now to touch her body without having the urgency of desire to contend against.

'I would not want your head to swell out of all proportion to the rest of you,' she retorted.

'I wasn't thinking of my head,' he gave back promptly, laughter in his voice, then yelped and was out of her and off her quicker than a pickpocket at a fair as she dug her fingernails into his buttocks. He looked at her reproachfully. 'Vixen,' he complained, but marred his protest with a grin, and then a kiss. She responded. Her hands slid down over his shoulders, tangled in the sparse golden hair on his chest, and it was with a sigh of genuine regret that she broke away. 'This is not getting your letter written is it?' She looked round for her shift.

'You had better use the tub before you go to your grandfather,' he said, still grinning, eyes raking her from head to toe. 'I may not be any use at writing letters, but I seem to have written my love all over you.'

Heulwen followed his gaze down. Breasts and belly, ribs and thighs were haphazardly smeared and streaked with ink transferred by sweat from his fingertips. She giggled mischievously at him. 'Knowing your talent with a quill, I suppose this is the only love letter I shall ever receive. It seems a pity to wash it away.'

He slapped her rump. 'Baggage! And it's not a love letter.' He stretched out his arm for his half-finished wine.

'No? What is it then?'

'A receipt for dues paid.'

She made her eyes round and wide. 'But I thought you kept that kind of account with a tally stick?'

He choked. Laughing, she ruffled his hair and went past him to the cooling tub.

Silent, keeping vigil by candlelight, Heulwen sat at her grandfather's bedside, holding his hand and watching his last moments slip away. The letter to her father had been written and dispatched and the dead victims of the Welsh raid had been composed, their bodies now waiting in the chapel for the dying to join them.

She glanced across to Adam. He was sitting on a stool, his back propped against the wall, his head nodding as he dozed. She had said he should sleep, but he had refused, insisting on keeping this vigil with her; but as the hours passed in silence, so had the strength of his will to remain awake.

The hand beneath hers stirred, and the eyelids strove like moths beating at a window to reach light.

'Grandpa?' She leaned over him.

Her voice, soft but frightened, woke Adam. He jerked upright with a start, saw her leaning over the bed, and was immediately on his feet, cursing himself for having fallen asleep. Quickly he went to her, expecting to see a corpse; instead he looked down into lucid, knowing eyes. The faintest suggestion of a smile was upon Miles's livid lips.

'The brooch,' he mouthed, for there was no strength in his breath to make a sound. His eyes were upon the gleaming circle pinned to Heulwen's gown. Almost imperceptibly, he nodded approval.

Adam set his hand on Heulwen's shoulder. 'The brooch,' he confirmed. 'I can't promise not to go chasing my own tail, but I'll try.'

221

Miles made a sound that might have been a chuckle but was never completed, as his last breath sighed into silence.

'Grandpa?' Heulwen said again.

Adam leaned in front of her and gently used fore-finger and thumb to close the half-open eyes which in their youth had been the same glorious colour as Heulwen's. 'He's gone,' he said gently, and making the sign of the cross stood back. Then he looked at Heulwen, and drew her into his arms. She pressed her face against his breast and clung to him, but only for a moment, Damp-eyed yet composed, she released him and looked up into his face. 'I'm all right,' she said. 'I can accept it now. It was my own fear that would not let him go.' She drew a deep, steadying breath. 'I will do whatever needs to be done. This is women's work now. I'd rather you sent in Elswith and Gytha to me and went to bed. I'll join you when I've finished.'

He studied her intently, then gave a brief nod, recognising her need to be alone with her thoughts, upon which the maids would not intrude but his own continued presence might. 'Don't be too long,' was all he said as he headed for the curtain, 'the living need you too.'

17

A scowl blackening his brow, mouth set in a thin line, Adam strode across Milnham's moon-washed bailey, oblivious of his destination, only knowing that if he had stayed in the great hall for one moment more he would have committed the act of murder on at least one if not more of the gathered funeral guests. *Guests*, hah! They were a flock of kites descending to eat, drink, mouth empty regrets and platitudes, and declaim fulsome eulogies that were naught but hot air.

Slowing his pace, he breathed out hard. No, that was an injustice born of his own foul temper. Most had attended out of genuine respect and affection for Miles and it was only men like Ranulf de Gernons, who had never really known him, who came out of curiosity and the desire to make mischief. De Gernons was heir to the vast earldom of Chester whose borders blended into Ravenstow's, and could hardly be turned away.

A fire burned in the ward; guards stamping beside it while they warmed their hands and talked about the torchlit feasting within. Cold began to seep through Adam's tunic and shirt. He wished he had stopped to pick up his cloak, but there had been no time for rational thought, only the need to escape before he leaped on de Gernons and violated the laws of hospitality. He paused by the welcome heat of the flames. The soldiers acknowledged and withdrew a little, their expressions curious. He held out his hands, rubbed them together, blew on them and shivered.

'Here,' rumbled John's rich deep voice, 'you forgot this.'

Adam turned to his brother-in-law and took the cloak he was holding out to him. 'Thank you.'

'Pay no heed to Lord Ranulf, he does it apurpose,' John said. 'Papa's just given him the bladed edge of his tongue and Gloucester backed him to the hilt. I don't think he'll open his mouth again – at least not this side of the curtain wall.' He gave a cynical shrug.

Adam swung his cloak across his shoulders and fumbled with the pin.

Frowning, John rubbed one finger over the bald, slightly prickly skin of his tonsure. 'You don't believe what he said, do you?' he asked sharply. 'Oh come on, Adam, he was winding you up like a rope on a mangonel just to watch you let fly. Everyone knows that Grandfather's death wasn't your fault. You couldn't have prevented it.'

'Yes I could,' Adam said woodenly. 'I could have hanged Rhodri ap Tewdr higher than the man in the moon long before it happened. I could have left him in the road to die on that first encounter. I could have given Miles a larger escort or made him take a different road home.'

'Hindsight is a wondrous thing,' John said with more

than a hint of his mother's asperity, 'and de Gernons certainly knows how to turn it into a weapon in your case. If you had left Rhodri ap Tewdr lying in the road, Heulwen would now be Lady de Mortimer, wedded to her own husband's murderer.'

Adam's head jerked up.

'Yes,' said John with an emphatic nod. 'Think about it. God's will is oft-times strange.'

Adam snorted and looked away into the flames. Greedy tongues of fire wrapped around the wood and scorched his face.

'Are you going to go after the boy?'

Adam sighed and shook his head. 'If it was left up to me, no. Davydd ap Tewdr's dead and Miles wouldn't have wanted it. He liked the lad, had high hopes for him. Your father understands that. It is men like de Gernons who worry me. They have the scent of war in their nostrils and they're doing their utmost to flush it into the open.'

John lowered his arm. 'De Gernons might be trailing the scent of war with our Welsh, but that is as far as he will get. When Papa stands his ground, there's no moving him.'

'I hope not,' Adam replied, 'because I think de Gernons is testing our strength for the times to come. If I were your father, I'd look to strengthen Caermoel and Oxley against future assault, and I don't mean from the Welsh.'

John gave a bark of startled laughter. 'Don't be ridiculous, Adam! De Gernons might not be everyone's view of a *preux chevalier*, but he's hardly going to start a war with his neighbours!'

'Not in the present situation, no,' Adam conceded. 'But what if the King died tomorrow?'

'All the barons have sworn for Matilda,' John said, but the laughter left his face.

'And how many would hold to their oath – de Gernons? de Briquessart? Bigod? de Mandeville? Leicester? You tell me. With William le Clito to look to and his father still alive, not to mention the claim of the Blois clan, Henry's dominions would explode into war like so many barrels of hot pitch!'

John crossed himself and shivered with more than just the damp cold of the February evening. 'Then I must pray wholeheartedly for the King's continued good health,' he said, and looked round with relief as Renard emerged from the forebuilding ushering their youngest brother before him together with a half-grown brown-and-white hound.

Renard was laughing so hard that his face was suffused and tears were streaming down his cheeks. 'Sorry,' he spluttered. 'I know it's no occasion for mirth, but Will's dog just did to Ranulf de Gernons what we're all desperate to do but dare not!'

'He bit him?' guessed John, beginning to grin with an unholy delight.

Renard shook his head and sleeved his eyes. 'No!' he gasped. 'Pissed up his leg! It was Will who bit him when de Gernons went for his dagger. I hauled dog and boy out by their scruffs before anything worse developed and left Papa to deal with it. Christ Jesu, you should have been in there!'

'He was going to stick a knife in Brith!' William sniffed indignantly, his own tears those of anger and distress as he squatted beside the dog, his arms around its shaggy shoulders. The hound whined, and swiped a pink tongue over the boy's wet face.

Renard tousled William's profuse black curls. 'Don't worry, fonkin, no one's going to harm you or Brith. Mama might scold your manners and Papa might be annoyed because it's dishonourable to bite your enemy, but I doubt anything worse will come of it. Perhaps Papa might even give you that sword you've been craving for the past year and a half!'

William's face brightened and his eyes sparkled. 'Really?'

Renard winked. 'Just wait and see . . .' He held out his hand. 'Come then. I'm supposed to be marching you off to bed in disgrace.'

'I'm hungry,' William protested, looking pathetic.

Renard flashed a white grin. 'So am I, being as I left half my dinner behind in there. I dare say we can find some honey cakes in the kitchen on our way – better fare at least than Ranulf de Gernons's leg!'

Adam burst out laughing and waved him away.

'Nothing to do with that little yellow-haired kitchen girl?' John asked with a knowing smile.

'Well, yes,' Renard retorted, looking seriously innocent, 'you should sample her honey cakes.'

Adam and John watched the youth, the boy and the dog cross the ward and go down the steps into one of the auxiliary kitchen buildings. John's shoulders shook with laughter. He folded his arms, the smile still on his lips, but his eyes were pensive. 'The new lord of Milnham-on-Wye and Ashdyke by the terms of his grandfather's will, and only just six years old.'

Adam fiddled with a loose piece of fur on the lining of his cloak. 'I can understand it not going to Renard,' he said slowly. 'He stands to inherit an entire earldom so he's not in any need of these estates, and you being a priest aren't likely to continue the line by legitimate means, so you're not in the bidding.'

John inclined his head.

'But what about Henry? He's the third son. Why did Miles pass him over in favour of William?'

'Henry gets Oxley when he reaches his majority,' John explained, unperturbed. 'Like Ashdyke, it came into the family through our English grandmother. It isn't a large holding, but enough to keep body and soul together. Apparently Grandpa gave it to my father when he was knighted, and Papa intends doing the same for Henry. If Ashdyke and Milnham-on-Wye had gone to him too, there'd have been nothing left for Will except a sword, hauberk and horse. Besides, Grandpa always had a special place in his affections for Will – and for Heulwen too.'

Adam tugged the fur loose and scattered it from his fingers. 'A man worries about breeding up sons to follow him, and when he has them, he worries about how he is going to furnish their helms,' he said, with a pained smile.

John darted him a quick look: in ten years of marriage to Ralf, Heulwen had quickened only the once and miscarried early, and although these were still early days, she had shown no signs of breeding with Adam. He was unsure of Adam's attitude to the likelihood of her barrenness and decided that now was not the best moment to probe lest he make a misjudgement and say the wrong thing.

A baron crossed the ward to one of the storesheds that had been cleaned out and provided with braziers and mattresses to accommodate the guests who over-spilled the capacity of the main keep. He nodded a curt good-night to Adam and John. Adam stared wide-eyed after Hugh de Mortimer. He had ridden in at the last moment to attend Miles's funeral, ignoring the surreptitious nudges and speculative stares of his fellow barons and mourners. The atmosphere at first had been strained to say the least, but gradually it had eased. De Mortimer had not once mentioned his son or alluded to the painful events at Windsor, and an attempt by de Gernons to bring them into the conversation had immediately been squelched by Guyon. De Mortimer had pointedly avoided Heulwen and Adam, but had been at pains to extend the olive branch to Guyon and Judith.

'He's still after a blood bond with us,' John said quietly. 'Hugh wants Renard for his youngest daughter, Elene, and he's willing to let sleeping scandals and feuds lie in order to get him.' John grinned at the look on Adam's face. 'It's not as stupid as it seems. Renard's blood-related to the throne, and every marcher lord with a daughter between the cradle and thirty years old is looking at him with the word "son-in-law" shining in their eyes.'

'God's life,' Adam muttered, shaking his head. 'How old's the girl?'

'Just coming up to six. She's from his second marriage, obviously.'

'What does Renard say?'

John chuckled. 'You know my brother. He just smiles and says that practice makes perfect, and hasn't he got a lot of time?'

229

'And your father?'

'Keeping his head down. Ren's right, there is plenty of time yet and at least a dozen interested parties. Papa will let Renard do the initial winnowing and make a decision from there. Mind you,' he reflected, 'a match with the de Mortimer girl would heal the rift caused by you and Heulwen, and the dower lands he's offering would be very useful. The girl herself is a real heart-melter. Mama fell for Elene straight away when she saw her at a wedding last year.'

'Perhaps because she has no daughter of her own,' Adam suggested. 'I know she raised Heulwen, but she was still very young herself then, and Heulwen married at fifteen. It must be lonely for her sometimes, particularly now that William is growing up.'

John looked startled. 'Mama lonely?' The thought had never occurred to him, for she always seemed so composed and brisk and capable. 'I suppose so,' he said doubtfully, 'but even if the betrothal does take place, Elene won't come to Ravenstow until she's at least ten, and there'll not be a wedding for another two years if not much longer. Anyway . . .'

'Anyway,' interrupted Heulwen, 'Ranulf de Gernons is snoring drunk across his trencher because Mama's been giving him raw ginevra, and everyone's going to bed, including me. Adam, are you coming?'

She was wearing a very fetching green silk gown that shimmered like the surface of a lake, and her braids in the firelight were a warm, rich red, where they showed below her veil, catching on the curve of her breasts and reaching to the braid girdle encircling her hips.

'How could I refuse an offer like that?' he murmured,

slipping an arm around her waist and drawing her sidelong against him.

Heulwen elbowed him in the ribs. 'Your mind is a treadmill,' she remonstrated, but smiled, knowing that he was teasing her. There was barely any standing space in the small keep, let alone the room for privacy to indulge that kind of need.

'And who could blame me?' Adam answered, not in the least set down, and he planted a kiss on her raised eyebrow.

John smiled. 'Three's a crowd,' he said, and bid them good-night.

'Is de Gernons really asleep in his dinner?' Adam asked, as arm in arm they went back towards the keep.

'He was, but Mama got two of the servants to stretch him out on the floor and put a sheepskin over him – and a bowl beside him for when he wakes up.' Her eyes glinted at the memory and then hardened. 'If it had been left to me, he'd have spent the night blanketless in the midden.'

'Now, Heulwen, you can't do that to the future Earl of Chester,' he admonished her.

'Couldn't I? It is where he belongs, rooting with his trotters. He has the manners of a pig; not only that but he looks like one. If this was Martinmas, I'd be salting him down for the winter by now.'

Adam spluttered. His mood lightened and his head came up. 'Belike he'd go rancid on you,' he said.

'Very likely,' she agreed, then said, 'By the by, Earl Robert of Gloucester said that he wanted a word with you, but that it could wait until tomorrow.'

'What about? Did he say?'

231

'No, but from the way he spoke to me it is not something he wants to air in public.' She slipped him a look along her shoulder, but his face was bland, no expression on it to reveal what he was thinking. 'Have you any ideas?'

Adam shook his head. 'Not an inkling, unless it is something to do with Ralf. The King was going to investigate the matter. Perhaps Robert has news.'

Heulwen shivered. 'I don't think I want to know.'

Adam squeezed her waist. 'It might be nothing of that, love. No point in conjuring ghosts out of thin air.'

No,' she said, and leaned against him.

They went into the keep, where Ranulf de Gernons was snoring stertorously in the straw near the door. Adam was very tempted to tread on him, but discretion won out at the last moment. 'I wish that I was a dog or a small boy,' he murmured, as he stepped delicately over de Gernons's scuffed, ceiling-pointed toes. 'There's so much more leeway for lack of manners.'

Heulwen's upper lip curled with disgust. 'Why not just be a pig?' she said.

18

Rhaeadr Cyfnos cascaded like a white mare's tail over fern-edged rocks and foamed into a basin a hundred and fifty feet below, where the water became as dark as polished onyx before it trickled like liquid silver over the lip of the basin and into the stream beneath. Adam drew rein at the head of the falls and stared, half hypnotised by the roar of the water and its wild beauty. His skin was damp, his hair and garments cobwebbed by droplets. Vaillantif bent his neck to snatch at the grass, which even this early in the season was a lush green. The bit-chains jinked, while the stallion's teeth tore rhythmically at the grass. Munching, he raised his head and looked round, ears pricked curiously, nostrils flaring to catch the new scent.

Adam laid one hand on the crupper and turned. Robert of Gloucester, astride his rangy dark bay, was picking his way carefully along the narrow track and then down over the shallow leap of rock to join him. The two knights with him hung back to speak with Austin and Sweyn so that he reached Adam alone. The Earl looked briefly at the tumbling water, then away. He had an aversion to heights: looking over battlements was a necessity to which he had schooled himself, but staring at waterfalls for pleasure was a different matter entirely.

'Spectacular,' he said dutifully, and backed his stallion from the spray.

'There are better ones in Wales,' Adam said, exhilarated by the wild, foaming power of the water.

Gloucester smiled sourly. 'I'll take your word for it.'

Adam laughed. He nodded at the other destrier. 'Is the horse all right?'

'Excellent.' Gloucester slapped the elegant bay neck. 'The Empress tried him out while we were at Windsor – he suited her very well. I might make of him a betrothal gift.'

Beyond the damp black tree trunks a watery sun was trying to break through the clouds. Adam squinted up, then looked along the foxfur collar of his cloak to his companion. 'Is that a means of introducing what you wanted to talk about?'

'In a way, I suppose.'

Adam laughed. 'I can just see the Empress astride a destrier, she likes to have firm control of the male. What sort of way, my lord?'

Gloucester tugged gently at a short stalk of straw that had become tangled in his stallion's mane. 'The King wants you to take letters of enquiry to the father of the prospective bridegroom.' The words bore a slightly pompous ring, as though he had been rehearsing them.

Adam watched the pheasant feathers in the Earl's cap begin to droop in the fine water vapour from the falls.

The news was not unexpected, but even so, he felt queasy. What makes you think I am the man to be the King's herald in this matter?'

'You know how to keep a close mouth. You've done his kind of work before and know its dangers and pitfalls.'

Adam shook his head. 'I have the Welsh to deal with, my lord, and I am an English baron. I witnessed the King's oath to us all that he would not seek a foreign husband for his daughter, and Geoffrey of Anjou is not only foreign, he's Angevin – an enemy.'

Gloucester blinked rapidly. 'How did you . . . ?'

'I overheard the King and the Bishop of Salisbury talking about it last autumn.'

'And you said nothing to anyone?'

'They were only discussing the possibilities at the time and, as you say, I know how to keep a close mouth.' He turned his head towards the falls.

'Geoffrey of Anjou is an excellent choice.'

'Is he?' Adam felt the cold beginning to seep beneath his cloak, chilling him. 'Convince me.'

'He's young and strong . . .'

'He is fifteen years old,' Adam pointed out.

'With his life before him,' Robert argued, 'and likely to be a sight more potent than her last husband who apparently had, er, difficulties.'

'You surprise me,' Adam said sarcastically. 'She would shrivel any snake to the size of a worm with the way she has of looking.'

Robert's face reddened. 'You will keep a civil tongue in your head when you speak of my sister.'

Adam gave him a look and gathered the reins. 'Why?

235

She never extended that courtesy to me.' He clicked his tongue to the horse.

Gloucester caught at his bridle. 'Wait, my lord, at least allow me to finish what I have to say. It avails us nothing if we each ride away in anger.'

Vaillantif started to plunge and sidle. The Earl took his hand off the bridle. Adam checked the stallion and in so doing, mastered his own anger. Robert of Gloucester had always had a blind spot where his sister the Empress was concerned, and Adam liked the Earl who, despite his royal blood and high status, still managed to be as genuine and honest as a plain rye loaf. He slapped Vaillantif's neck, and said, 'You are right, it avails us nothing. I apologise.'

Earl Robert removed his hat and looked dismally at the dripping feathers. 'I leap to her defence because no one else ever does,' he said wearily. 'Like you, everyone sees a bad-tempered bitch who needs a whip taking to her hide to teach her humility, but that's just a façade. If you knew her as I did, you would be more charitable.'

Adam raised a sceptical eyebrow but forbore in the interests of peace to comment.

The Earl sighed, cast him a doubtful look from beneath hoary brows and said, 'Geoffrey of Anjou is far more than a champing young stallion bought to prove his worth at stud. I grant you that he's tall and handsome to look upon, but he's also well-educated, and certainly no political innocent. His father has taught him well and he has the makings of a fine warrior and general. If we make Geoffrey Matilda's consort, then Fulke, as his father, won't be as eager to stir up the mud using William le Clito as his stick.'

'Ah,' said Adam, beginning to understand. Henry's obsession. 'It has to do with le Clito again.'

'It has to do with a very dangerous thorn in our side,' the Earl corrected him. 'Pluck out the root from which it draws sustenance, and it will wither and die.'

'You are gambling for very high stakes.' Adam leaned down to adjust his stirrup. 'If you succeed and your father can hold the reins until he has grandsons old enough, then it will be a gamble well repaid. If it fails . . .' He straightened and looked bleakly at the cascading water without finishing the sentence.

'It won't fail,' Gloucester said forcefully. 'Can I give my father your yea-say that you'll go herald in payment of your forty days' service this year?'

'I'll think about it,' Adam said neutrally.

'I need to know within the week.'

Adam inclined his head, but refused to give more response than that.

'My lady.' The Earl inclined his head to Heulwen as he guided her grey mare carefully down to join them.

'Sire.' She slackened the reins to let Gemini crop at the grass and looked at the Earl. 'Mama wants a word with you – something about getting Henry to learn English. She thinks it will stand him in good stead when Papa gives him Oxley, and she also wants to ask you the name of that stone carver from Bristol you mentioned yesterday.'

The Earl smiled at her, but in a distant way, his mind obviously not on such day-to-day trivia. He looked hard at Adam. 'Within the week,' he repeated, setting his cap back on his head at a rakish angle. 'Is de Gernons still at the keep?' he asked Heulwen.

Her lip curled. 'Just preparing to leave. His temper'
about as vile as the headache he's nursing; I shouldn'
go near him.'

'I won't. I think I'll take the long way back. The horse
needs a good workout, anyway.'

They watched him leave. The hoofbeats and the voices
of his escort faded through the trees. The falls roared
Adam's face felt stiff. He slid his fingers along the reins
and applied gentle pressure.

'Trouble?' Heulwen followed him back to where Austin
and Sweyn were waiting.

He turned his mouth down. 'Only to my conscience
I have known this has been coming for a long time.
should have been better prepared, but I'm not.'

Vaillantif's hind legs slithered on mud, but he lunged
powerfully with forequarters and neck and recovered
The woods enclosed them, smelling of damp and fungus
Dormant bramble bushes snagged at their cloaks as they
rode through the forest in silence. Heulwen let the reins
hang slack, for Gemini was placidly following the stal-
lion's lead. She stared anxiously at Adam's back, knowing
that she could not force him to tell her what was on his
mind.

The trees thinned and they came suddenly upon a
clearing and the mossed-over remains of a once-proud
building, now reduced to chunks of tumbled stone. Some
white edges only just beginning to rethread with green
gave evidence of pieces having been recently cut.

Adam dismounted and tethered Vaillantif to a young
tree. A weasel leaped over his boot and streaked away
through the damp grass. The sunlight broke through the
clouds and trees to stroke weak fingers over the ruins

Heulwen jumped down from the mare and tied her beside the destrier.

'Why have we stopped?' Shivering, she stooped under a low hanging branch. Twigs stretched like fingers. She felt as if hidden eyes were watching her every movement.

Adam caught her hand in his. 'Whimsy,' he smiled. 'I used to come here sometimes as a boy when we visited Milnham-on-Wye with your father.'

'You never brought me!' she said half indignantly, for in childhood she had thought to share every secret and experience of Adam's – the still, clear backwater of the Wye so wonderful for summer swimming, the haunted well at the farmstead where the Welsh had raided, the rock upon Caermoel ridge with its strange carvings.

He tightened his fingers around hers and raised them briefly to his lips. 'It was in the days when you did nothing but dream about Ralf and scheme how to get him,' he said without rancour, and drew her around an outcrop of masonry and between some broken stumps of rock. 'I wasn't good company myself, then. I think it's Roman. Look, you can see where they've taken pieces recently for that new section of curtain wall.' He rubbed his hand over a jagged white edge, then wiped away the smear on his cloak.

'Was I really so heedless?' Heulwen asked.

He shrugged, trying for lightness and not quite succeeding. 'You had other matters on your mind, and I had long been a piece of familiar household furniture taken for granted – your foster brother.'

'Oh, Adam!' Her throat tightened and her eyes began to sting.

'Everyone blamed my moods on my growing body not on jealous sulks – and this was an excellent place to come and sulk alone, opportunity permitting.' Abruptly he tugged at her hand. 'Come.'

He led her onwards until they came to a short avenue overgrown with brambles, straggling grass and tree saplings. Out of the tangle grew jagged slender pillars of grooved, weathered stone, and at the end of the avenue was a section of tessellated mosaic floor depicting a hunting scene. Fragments here and there were missing or displaced by tree roots, and chunks of stone from what had once been a roof married one edge, but the overall effect was still magnificent.

'There's another one over there,' Adam nodded, 'but it's more broken than this one. I would come here and work on it – clear the debris so I could see what lay beneath.'

Heulwen picked her way among the ruins to look. He followed her. A spring of icy water bubbled up near their feet and meandered away in the rough direction of Rhaeadr Cyfnos. Rooks cawed somewhere above the dark trees. Behind them the horses snorted and champed. Adam returned to Vaillantif; unslinging the wine costrel from around the cantle, he brought it to Heulwen, who now sat on a block of lichened stone regarding the hunting mosaic.

'Drink?' He withdrew the stopper and held it out to her. Companionably they shared the wine and contemplated the ruins.

'I wonder who lived here?' Heulwen mused.

Adam wiped his mouth and shrugged. 'I don't know. Some of the stones have inscriptions, but they're either

o weathered to read or parts are missing. I had thought
make a copy of the hunting mosaic at Thornford
the plesaunce. What do you think?'

Heulwen nodded approval and swallowed her
outhful of the rich, tart wine. 'And the herb beds
nning out from it.'

Adam gave her a bright amber glance. 'I thought I'd
ange some of the animals, though – wolves and vixens
stead of boar, perhaps a leopard or two since they are
ur father's device, and most certainly some horses.'

'A sorrel with cream mane and tail,' she smiled.

He raised one eyebrow. 'In pursuit of the vixens?'

She laughed and swiped at him. He ducked and
ragged her down off the stone and into his arms. Cold,
sting of wine, their lips met and through the laughter,
esire rippled suddenly like a bright thread decorating
garment.

'I think you should also include a priapus,' she
urmured against his mouth.

'Only if there are nymphs in it too!' he retorted. 'Stop
at, you hoyden. Austin might not bat an eyelid, but
weyn's more set in his ways. You'll shock him for
ertain!'

She glanced over his shoulder. 'They can't see us from
ere.' She kissed him, her tongue flickering as delicately
s a serpent's. His hand strayed down to the curve of
er buttocks and squeezed her against him. Despite his
rotest, he began to wonder hazily where they could lie,
r failing that if it would be possible standing up, for
ere was no great discrepancy in their heights. The
ovelty of that thought increased his arousal and his
reath caught and shortened as Heulwen tightened and

relaxed against him. What had started out as a jest w
swiftly becoming a desire-driven imperative. 'Heulwe
let me . . .' he said hoarsely, but the jingle of harne
and the noise of horses pushing through the trees ma
him look up and then stop what he was doing and swir
her hard around, so that she was shielded by his bod

'Adam, what's the matter, why are you—?'

Behind them a sword cleared its scabbard. 'Swey
put up,' said Adam without taking his eyes off the m
who were moving through the trees and surroundi
them. The sword grated back into its sheath, but the o
warrior moved closer to Adam, as did the squire.

Rhodri ap Tewdr drew rein and contemplated t
small group before him, while at his back, his men shift
restlessly.

'Welcome to the tryst.' Adam performed a mockir
bow. 'May I enquire what you are doing so far fro
home?'

'A matter of unfinished business.' Rhodri levelled t
spear he was carrying and directed it at Adam's brea

Heulwen stiffened, her thoughts flying to Thornfor
tilt yard and the moment when the Welsh prince ha
almost ridden Adam down. She took an involuntary st
forwards, but Adam gestured her back. 'Such as?' I
said and, as before, stood his ground, matching Rhod
look for look.

The latter held the moment for a long time befo
tossing the spear to the soldier beside him. Ada
breathed out, cold sweat slicking his palms. Rhodri smil
as he saw the tell-tale trail of vapour coil the a
Dismounting, he tied his horse to a sturdy beech saplir

'I want a truce,' he announced. 'There has been to

uch blood spilled already and I don't want to see this
mmer's harvest go up in flames – mine or yours.'

'I'm in full agreement with that,' Adam said, steadying
e euphoria of relief into a careful neutrality. He reached
r the costrel lying on the stone and handed it to Rhodri.
' you cease raiding over the dyke and making a nuisance
 yourself among my father-in-law's tenants, I'll try to
rsuade him and the rest of the funeral guests that
xterminating you is not the next best thing to going on
usade.'

'I am sorry about Lord Miles.' Rhodri drank from the
in and returned it. 'I learned respect and fondness for
m during the time that I was your prisoner. If I could
ido the manner of his dying I would. Davydd went
o far.'

'And paid for it,' Adam said with grim satisfaction.

Dull colour suffused Rhodri's skin. His cloak brooch
ashed as he took a deep breath. 'Yes, he paid for it,'
 said, his voice over-controlled. 'But our raiding began
 revenge – we were provoked. Our grazing lands are
ing ruined by Ravenstow's tenants, and yours too on
e southern side. Only last autumn one of your villages
eared an assart on our side of the border, and on le
hevalier's former lands the boundary stones have been
oved. I know they have. I came down that way to be
ere. We are only taking back what is ours!' His dark
es burned as he looked from Adam to Heulwen, half
cusing, half defensive.

Adam inclined his head, acknowledging Rhodri's argu-
ent. 'I will talk to my bailiffs and stewards, and I'll
de out and see for myself what liberties have been
ken. Send a witness to attend on me if you want. Peace

243

never flourishes on half-measures.' He frowned and folded his arms. 'As to your complaint with the Earl Ravenstow, you'll need to talk to him yourself. I cann vouchsafe for him or his tenants.'

'That is the reason I am here,' Rhodri said sombre 'I knew he would be here . . . and also I want to pay n respects to Lord Miles. I need you to give me safe esco to the keep.'

Adam sucked in his cheeks and looked dubiously his wife. 'Did you say that de Gernons was leaving?'

She nodded. 'He should have gone by now.'

'Yes,' he confirmed, 'I can give you safe escort.' Ar then he looked at him curiously. 'How did you know would be here?'

Rhodri smiled slyly and stroked his stallion's shagg neck. 'I knew that sooner or later you would be out fro the castle to exercise your horse or hunt. It was only matter of keeping my eyes open and myself out of sigh I've been watching you for the past hour.' The smi deepened into an open grin.

Heulwen blushed. Colour darkened Adam's face.

'How much did you hear?' he asked quietly.

Rhodri deliberately misunderstood the questio 'Enough to know how much you were enjoying you selves,' he said, his gaze running over Heulwen wi appreciation.

'You know what I mean.'

Rhodri opened his palms. 'Not a great deal. The roa of the falls unfortunately concealed most of what yo and that other Norman were saying. Still, I suppose fro the look on your face that if I were to bellow the new abroad, you'd cancel my safe escort.'

'You know the strength of my sword-arm.'

Rhodri's face was unreadable. The smirk, however, had gone. 'You Normans,' he said contemptuously, 'always conspiring in corners against each other.' He looked round at his war band. '*Fe fynn y gwir ei le eh?*'

Adam's colour remained high. *The truth will out*: he knew enough Welsh to understand that simple saying. He was aware of Heulwen watching him and that he could not deny Rhodri's words. 'That's rich coming from a Welshman,' he retorted, and added shortly over his shoulder, 'Austin, stop gawping like a turnip-wit and get our horses. We're returning to Milnham.'

Heulwen picked up her sewing, grimaced at it with extreme disfavour, and uttering a sigh started to push the needle through the fabric. It was a shirt for Adam, a basic, simple garment within her scope, but a genuine and literal labour of love since needlework of any kind was to her a form of purgatory, and it was a mark of her desperation that she was tackling it beyond her daily allotted stint.

There was nothing else to do. Father Thomas, Adam's chaplain, had said he would give her a copy of *Tristan* to read, but the howling storm outside had kept him the night at the monastery five miles away. A visiting itinerant lute-player had left them at dawn before the weather took a turn for the worse, hoping to make Ledworth by nightfall. The carrier was not due for at least another week with his budget of news and gossip, and Adam's mood was fouler than the weather that kept them huddled so close to the hearth. She darted a glance to the trestle near the fire where he sat, flagon and goblet

245

close to hand. The last three days he had scarcely been sober, drinking as if to exorcise some demon. He was not drunk now, but the evening was still young, only just past dusk and the flagon full. By the time they retired it would be down to the lees.

She jabbed the needle angrily into the linen, pricked her finger and swore. He looked up at her exclamation and half raised one eyebrow. Heulwen sucked her finger and regarded him gravely. 'Why are you brooding like a moulting hen?' she demanded.

He did not deny it, but lifted the flagon and, pouring the wine, took three long swallows. Then, carefully, he set the cup back down at arm's length and sighed. 'I've a decision to make. I've been trying to drown my conscience in my cup, but it keeps surfacing to preach at me, or else it mocks me from the dregs and I have to fill up and start again.'

'What sort of decision?' Without regret she put her sewing aside. 'Certainly you cannot think straight sitting in a fog of wine fumes.'

He tilted his head slightly to avoid the scorching heat that came from sitting so close to the fire. 'I've been trying not to think,' he said wryly.

'Is it about Rhodri? The Welsh?'

'Hardly.' He rubbed his forehead and winced. 'Since we all agreed a truce at Milnham and I've seen to my part of the bargain, there's been no trouble from that quarter and I don't expect any. Rhodri's got enough ado keeping his own people together without bothering mine and your father's – for the nonce at least . . . Christ Jesu, Heulwen, do you have a remedy for a megrim? My head feels as though it's going to explode.'

'Your own fault,' she said without sympathy. 'What do you expect when you drink for three days solid?'

He gave her a sour glance. 'I asked for the remedy, not the cause.'

'Remedy? Leave the wine alone.' She stood up and brushed some cut ends of thread from her gown.

'If my head is aching, it is for reasons far more complex than the downing of too much Anjou,' he snapped.

Heulwen gave him a single look more eloquent than words, and stalked away down the hall. He followed her with brooding eyes as she went, then swore and pressed the heels of his hands into his eye sockets, feeling as though a lead weight were crushing him from existence. Ralf might have thrived upon intrigue, but Adam found the conflict of loyalties almost more than he could bear. What was he supposed to do? Follow Henry's desires and have the barons all call him traitor, or tell his peers and face banishment, perhaps even death? The King had clandestine ways of dealing with men against whom he could not openly move.

Adam groaned. His responsibility was not only to himself. He had Heulwen to consider and her family – his too by foster-bond and marriage. Tell Guyon and risk being condemned by the King; or not tell him and be slighted. Somewhere, amid the wine fumes, the shadow of his long-dead father mocked his honour with brimstone laughter.

'Here.' Heulwen bent over to hand him a cup of some cloudy substance that smelt revolting and tasted on the first, tentative sip even worse.

'Faugh!' He pulled such a face that she laughed.

'Drink it,' she commanded, and added in a barbed tone, 'pretend it's wine.'

Adam glared at her, but held his peace and gulped the concoction down. Shuddering, he plonked the cup upon the trestle. 'Torturer,' he complained, and struggled not to retch.

From behind her back, Heulwen brought forth a small comfit dish. 'Honeyed plums,' she said, her eyes sparkling. 'Do you remember? It was the way Mama used to bribe us to swallow her potions when we were little.'

Adam scowled at her but was unable to maintain the expression and with a reluctant grin, took one. She put the dish on the trestle and sitting down again, picked up one of the glistening, sticky fruits herself and bit slowly into it. Adam regarded her through narrowed eyes. She returned his scrutiny and licked crystals of honey-sugar delicately from her fingers. His crotch grew warm. 'It was sweets of another nature I had in mind,' he said softly.

Heulwen leaned over her husband and pinched out the night candle. Before the light was extinguished she saw that Adam was already asleep and that the frown lines between his brows were for the moment but vague marks of habit rather than present distress. It was one of the few positive lessons she had learned from Ralf – how to ease the tension from a man's body and leave him in a state of physical, if not mental well-being. As to what was troubling his mind to the point of him drowning it in drink, only he could resolve that one.

She gave a soft, irritated sigh and lay down beside him. He had ever been one to stopper things up inside silently simmering like a barrel of pitch too close to a cauldron, giving no real indication of how volatile the mixture was until it exploded.

She pressed her cheek against his warm back, closed her eyes and tried to sleep. She must have succeeded, for when she opened her eyes again it was to hear the bell tolling for first Mass and to find the bedside candle lit, with Adam watching her by its flame. Sleepily she stretched her limbs and smiled at him.

He leaned across to kiss her tousled, inviting warmth, but it was a brief gesture, not a prelude to further play. 'Heulwen, if I asked you to come to Anjou with me, would you?'

'Anjou?' she repeated, eyes and wits still misty with sleep. 'Why do you want to go to Anjou?' She yawned.

He traced small circles upon her upper arm and shoulder with a gentle forefinger. 'I don't *want* to go to Anjou,' he qualified ruefully. 'I wish the damned place did not even exist. Henry wants me to go there as a messenger.'

Heulwen was silent, digesting this surface information and wondering what nasty currents flowed swift beneath it. Three days of heavy drinking for one. She looked at his downcast lashes and waited for them to lift so that she could see the expression in his eyes. 'Yes, of course I'd go with you.'

'Without even knowing the kind of message I was bearing?'

Thoughts of Ralf scurried through her mind. She banished them and sat up, tossing back her hair. Adam's character was totally different. To break his honour you would have to break the man. Perhaps that was the deepest, most dangerous current of all. 'Yes, even without knowing.' She cocked her head. 'Was Anjou the reason the Earl of Gloucester wanted to speak to you so privately?'

Silence. 'Yes,' then more silence. He drew a slow, considering breath. 'The King is breaking a promise he made to us all, and I am to carry the message breaking it.'

'Oh Adam, no!' Heulwen cried with indignant sympathy, and her eyes grew angry as she understood his dilemma. 'Why couldn't he have sent Gloucester himself?'

Adam shook his head. 'And have everyone wondering what the King's eldest bastard was doing in Anjou? I will be considerably less conspicuous.' He turned his head on the pillow. 'I keep thinking of Ralf and Warrin and wondering if they were so wrong. Henry uses men. Time and again I've heard your father say it, time and again I've seen him do it and been used myself. Is it any wonder that I begin to feel like a whore?'

She leaned over him and smoothed the lines that had reappeared between his brows. He laced his fingers in her bright hair and told her the nature of the message he was to bear.

Heulwen was momentarily surprised, but hardly shocked. Henry had attempted a marriage alliance like this before, between Geoffrey of Anjou's sister and the son he had lost on the *White Ship*. 'As I see it,' she said, 'it is on Henry's conscience, not yours. It doesn't matter what his letter says, you are only its bearer.'

'So I keep telling myself,' he said woodenly.

'And if you renounced your allegiance, which would

be the only honourable alternative, you'd have to sell your sword for a living, and I warrant that Henry would still have his way in the end.'

'Principles do not put bread on your board. Is that what you are saying?'

'I am saying there is no point going breadless for an inevitability. If your conscience troubles you, it is a sign you still have your honour. I don't think Ralf ever suffered from either, and therein lies the difference.' She assessed him, trying to decide whether his expression meant that he had heard her and was considering, or if he was just being obdurate. She folded her arms upon his chest. 'You had better tell me how long I have to pack my travelling chests, and do I bring a maid, and is Geoffrey of Anjou really as handsome as they say?'

Adam sighed and pulled her mouth down hard to his in a kiss that was as much a reprimand as a token of affection. 'What would I do without you?'

'Brood yourself head-first into the nearest firkin of wine!' she retorted.

It was not so far from the truth, he thought, letting her go and watching her as she picked up a comb and began to work her hair into a straight skein ready for braiding. She knew exactly how to cozen him out of a bad mood, although at the present, new as it was and so long waited for, just the sight of her was enough to raise his spirits and everything else. He glanced down at himself, but it was the need of his bladder rather than the need for his wife that was making him tumescent right now.

He stretched, heard the familiar sinewy crack of his shield-arm and sought out the chamber pot. He felt almost cheerful now that he had made the decision to to take Heulwen with him. The notion of leaving her behind had been part of his reluctance to go on this journey he had been asked to undertake. Her reaction had been important too when he told her the reason for his going. No scorn or revulsion, just a practical acceptance and words of common sense that put his fears into their true perspective. He had been tail-chasing again.

'Be sure to pack the wolf brooch,' he said over his shoulder with a wry smile.

19

Anjou, Spring 1127

The cockerel was a jewelled image cast in living bronze, and looked as though he had just stepped down from a weather vane to strut in the dust. Alert topaz eyes swivelled to study his surroundings. His coral comb and wattles jiggled proudly on head and throat as he paraded the circle, his tail a light-catching cascade of green-tipped gold, legs cobbled in bronze and armed with deadly spurs. Here in the city of Angers he was without rival, for all his rivals were dead.

He stretched his throat, raising a ruff of bright feathers, and crowed. Bets were laid. His owner rose from a lithe crouch, and with his hands on his exquisite gilded belt, he looked round impatiently.

'He's late,' grumbled Geoffrey Plantagenet, heir to the Duchy of Anjou. He was almost as fine to look upon as his fighting cock, being tall with ruddy golden curls and brilliant frost-grey eyes. Thread-of-gold crusted the throat and cuffs of his tunic, and the dagger at his narrow hips blazed with gems; like his bird's spurs it was honed to a wicked edge.

'Have you ever known William le Clito not to be late?' snorted Robert de Blou, watching the bird which had originally been his gift to the youth at his side. 'He'd miss his own funeral, that one.'

Geoffrey flashed a white grin, but his fingers tapped irritably against his belt. 'He will need to shape better than this if he wants my father's continued support against the English King.'

'My lord, he's here now!' cried another baron pointing towards the river. Geoffrey turned his head and with a cool gaze watched the approach of William le Clito and his small entourage of mongrels – Norman malcontents, Flemings and Frenchmen, and the tall yellow-haired English knight who had been banished from his own country for the murder of a fellow baron.

'You are late,' he addressed the would-be Duke of Normandy who had recently married the French king's sister. Geoffrey passed an indifferent look over the women they had brought with them. Not obviously strumpets by their appearance, but strumpets nevertheless. Le Clito might be a new husband but it was no reason for continence when a diplomatic visit to Anjou offered the chance of easy sin.

Le Clito gave Geoffrey a smile of blinding charm which, because he used it so often, had lost most of its impact. 'My apologies. Our barge was held up. I'm not that late, am I?' He touched the younger man's shoulder with familiarity. Geoffrey stepped aside, nostrils flaring with controlled choler and regarded the bird that Warrin de Mortimer was holding under his

254

arm – a handsome black, the feathers emerald-shot in the spring sunlight.

'You wager that sorry object can beat my Topaze?' he scoffed.

'Name your price and we shall soon see,' le Clito answered jauntily. 'Warrin, put him down.'

Someone scooped up Geoffrey's bird so that men could look at the form and condition of the black and make their wagers. The cockerel shook its ruffled feathers and preened, and stretched on elegant tiptoe to crow defiance.

Warrin de Mortimer leaned against the wall and rubbed his side where the thick, pink ridge of scar tissue was irritating him. He looked at the black and knew full well that Geoffrey's bird would win because Geoffrey of Anjou always won. He had never had to beg at other men's tables for his meat. His fingers paused directly over the scar: his own fault. He had underestimated de Lacey's speed, forgotten to allow for the years of experience that followed squirehood. For that particular error of judgement he was now an outcast in the land where he had been his father's heir, reduced to the status of plain household knight in the pay of a man whose own luck was about as reliable as a whore's promise.

'Are you not wagering, *chéri?*' A woman linked her arm through his and admired him with melting brown eyes. 'I say Lord William's bird will win – he's bigger.'

Which showed how much Héloïse knew about cock-fighting, or indeed about anything. All her brains were between her legs – which had not seemed such a bad thing last night. A pity she had to open her mouth as well as her thighs.

'No,' he said with a sullen half-shrug. 'I'm not

255

wagering.' These days money was too important to fritter away on the fickle prowess of a fighting cock. His father haphazardly sent him funds and assurances that he would have him pardoned and reinstated in England by the time of the next Christmas feast, but neither money nor promises were reliable.

The girl pouted and turned away. He wondered if she was worth it and decided she wasn't – no woman was – and it was at that point that he looked up and across the thoroughfare spotted Heulwen.

The cocks struck together in a rattling flurry of bronze and black feathers. Beaks stabbed, spurs flashed. They danced breast to breast in midair and the men danced too, yelling, exhorting; and over their heads, ignoring their noise, ignoring the birds, Warrin de Mortimer stared and stared, not believing his eyes, not wanting to believe his eyes. His heart began to pound. His breath grew shaky and the hot scar pulsed against his ribs.

The birds parted, beaks agape, wings adrift in the dust, circling each other and clashing together again. Dark blood dripped into the ground. Warrin left his leman, and ignoring her querulous enquiry skirted the circle of raucous, intent spectators to step out into the open street.

Adam glanced across briefly to the cockfight, drawn by the bellows of the crowd rather than by any real interest in the sport. Nobility, he realised, for the sun flashed off jewelled tunics, belts and weapon hilts.

'Miles – my brother I mean, not Grandpa, used to own a fighting cock,' Heulwen reminisced. 'Mama never liked the sport. She used to scold him deaf the times he was home, but all the young men at court had them and he did not want to be any different.' She sighed and shook her head. 'Poor Chanticleer. He didn't even come to a glorious end. Run over by a wain in the ward while chasing one of his wives, and his corpse consigned to the pot.'

Adam chuckled and hastily drew rein to allow a cart to lumber past. It was laden with barrels of wine, the oxen drawing it sleek and well muscled. Dust rose and puffed beneath their shod cloven hooves, and Heulwen covered her face with her veil and coughed.

Southampton, Caen, Falaise, Mortain, Roche au Moins. Most of the time she had enjoyed the different scenery and customs. The land through which they had passed was gentle and pastoral, much flatter than her own Welsh hills, and dominated by its rivers, the Mayenne, the Maine, the green Indre and the majestic Loire itself. There were vineyards in abundance and great swathes of yellow broom, providing shelter for small game. There were fig trees, prickly sweet-chestnuts and elegant cedars silhouetted against a washed-blue sky, and the people spoke a purer, stronger French than the kind spoken in her native marches. Now, at the end of their journey, she was sweat-stained, gritty and so saddle sore that once down from her mare she thought she would never want to ride again.

'Not far now,' Adam said, as if reading her mind. 'Just over the bridge, isn't it, Thierry?' They had sent half their escort on ahead to purchase and prepare them lodgings, and Thierry, one of the advance party, had been waiting for them this morning at the city gates to show them the way.

'Yes, my lord.'

Heulwen looked at the bustling wood and stone structure spanning the Maine. Beyond it and above, Count Fulke's keep thrust at the sky, banners fluttering on the battlements. 'I hope Austin has been busy,' she said, the thought of a feather mattress devoid of vermin pushing all other lesser considerations to one side.

Adam tilted her a smile. 'I will say this for you,' he teased 'you're a better travelling companion than the last woman I had the misfortune to escort any distance.'

'I'll warrant she was not so sympathetic to your needs,' she said and saucily poked her tongue between her teeth.

His look narrowed and smouldered. 'Not by half,' he said softly.

With heightened colour, she laughed at him, and heeled Gemini forward.

The lodging Thierry had rented belonged to a merchant absent on pilgrimage to Jerusalem, and although small – Adam nearly brained himself on the door lintel when first entering – there was adequate stabling for the horses and a well-tended orchard garden going down to the river's edge, where it ended in a private wharf complete with rowing boat. The house had the added benefit of being close to the castle.

Indeed, later, looking out of the unshuttered upstairs window into the street below as she combed the tangles from her damp hair, Heulwen saw a party of horsemen returning along their thoroughfare to the keep. Laughing young men with a few older nobles sprinkled among them, a seasoning of armed guards sweltering in quilted gambesons and half-hauberks, one of them clutching a tattered but victorious bronze cockerel. For added spice here were gaily clad women of the highest rank of the oldest profession.

'Adam, come here,' she called.

'What is it?' Minus his tunic, shirt laces dangling loose, Adam braced his arm on the window frame and leaned behind her. Suddenly his tension was as palpable as the spring sunshine pouring in on them. 'William le Clito,' he muttered, his surprise tinged with more than a hint of displeasure.

'Who, the one with the red-gold hair?'

'No, he's far too young. The dark one on the roan. I'll hazard just by looking at his clothes that the other one is Geoffrey of Anjou himself.'

Heulwen craned forward.

'What's William le Clito doing in Angers?' Adam said with a frown. His question was purely rhetorical and the answer already known: he must be seeking Count Fulke's support so that he could stir up unrest in Normandy. A pity for him that Adam came not seeking, but offering a prize beyond refusal. He touched Heulwen's shoulder. 'Come away from the shutters, love,' he murmured. 'You'll have their eyes popping out and rolling until they reach the river . . . and besides, I don't want half the court boasting to have seen the wife of King Henry's messenger in her undergarments.'

'Too late for that,' she laughed, although she was aware of the warning beneath his light remark and withdrew from the window, latching the shutters. It was one thing to behave as she pleased at home, quite another when she and Adam were out to make a good impression upon the Count of Anjou.

The last man in the cavalcade rode past. Attached to

his cantle by a leading rein was a fine, riderless pied stallion. In the shadow of a doorway across the street, Warrin de Mortimer stood and stared at the dwelling opposite and marked it with burning eyes.

Fulke, the son of Fulke le Rechin, Count of Anjou, was a man of middle height, middle build, and middle years. He was robust and florid with hair that would once have rivalled Heulwen's for colour, but had faded with the years to a softer, ginger hue, thinning at the crown. Set above a bulbous wide-pored nose, his eyes were a bright steel-silver and they missed nothing.

Adam kept his responses modest as he presented Fulke with Henry's gifts of an English embroidery and a goblet set with sapphires and crystals. For Geoffrey there was a copy of Bede with illustrations in gold leaf and a cover of ivory panels. The young man accepted it graciously and smiled, but not as broadly as Fulke, and his own eyes, bright mirrors of his father's, were not only vigilant but cold.

Both father and son took an interest in Heulwen and Fulke insisted she join them at the dais table. 'It is not often that we are graced by company so fair,' Fulke said.

William le Clito was a guest at the table too, making his apologies as he arrived late, and hastily taking his place near the Count and his son.

'Heulwen . . .' he said when introduced. 'What does it mean?'

She gave him a quick smile. 'It is Welsh for sunshine, my lord. I take it from my great-grandmother Heulwen uerch Owain. She was a princess of her people.'

'I see you have pride,' said le Clito, a bitter twist to

his mouth, 'I can understand that.' The twist became malicious. 'It is an unusual name; surely you must be the same Heulwen to whom one of my knights, Warrin de Mortimer, was betrothed?'

Heulwen felt heat seeping into her cheeks. 'No, sire.' She pitched her voice low for control. 'I was never betrothed to him. He was accused of conspiracy and murder and found guilty . . . as surely you must know.'

'Warrin de Mortimer?' Fulke of Anjou frowned in question.

'You know,' Geoffrey said. 'The big yellow-haired one who wears more rings than he has fingers. Down there look, on your right, just sitting down.'

'Ah, yes.' Fulke stroked his beard.

Heulwen's heart began to pound. Her vision blurred, but not enough to blot out the sight of the man taking his place at one of the lower trestles where le Clito's men were settling to eat, nor the fact that he was watching her with steady, hostile eyes. Blue was not a hot colour, but his gaze was scorching a hole right through to her spine. Warrin here in Angers. Please God no, it could not be true!

William le Clito said, 'I took him in when he was banished from my uncle's domains. I understand, my lady, that Warrin and your husband fought a trial by combat last Christmas feast over a somewhat cloudy issue?' He gave her a mocking look. 'I do not suppose the more lurid details carry any tinge of truth?'

'It would be ill-bred of me to respond, my lord,' she replied stiffly.

'I like a woman with spirit,' Geoffrey said with appreciation.

261

She wondered if he would be so amused once he was married to the Empress. Ignoring him and le Clito, she looked beseechingly at the Count. 'Sire, I would rather not speak of this matter.' She did not need to feign the catch in her voice, but she dropped her head and dabbed at her eyes with the trailing sleeve of her gown.

'Come now, my lady, do not distress yourself.' Awkwardly Fulke patted her hand and gave le Clito a warning look. 'Lord William meant no harm; he did but tease you a little too far. He will apologise if he has offended.'

William le Clito did so, his words about as sincere as a holy relic bought at a fair, and Heulwen accepted it with comparable sincerity and forced herself to eat a morsel of the delicious herb-roasted venison. It was almost impossible to swallow, knowing that Warrin was watching her.

She looked along the board at Adam. He was eating as if there were nothing wrong, but she noticed that he had recourse several times to his cup to wash his own food down. His attention was no longer on the priest, but centred on Warrin and the brooding, thoughtful expression on his face was one that Heulwen had begun to know very well. Becoming aware of her scrutiny Adam turned, his eyes meeting hers, and his look changed, becoming a wry grimace accompanied by an infinitesimal shake of his head. Heulwen bit her lip. Fulke touched her arm and spoke to her, and she had to turn away to listen to him. It took all her fortitude and skill to smile and respond as if nothing was the matter.

The meal progressed through several courses and entertainments. Tumblers tumbled; a lute-player sang two heroic lays and then one of the love songs composed by Duke William of Aquitaine, its contents blazingly explicit.

Finger bowls were brought round again, the water infused with herbs, and fruit and nuts were served with a sweet wine. Fulke retired from the table and summoned a page to light him to his private apartments, commanding Geoffrey and Adam to attend him. He thanked Heulwen for the pleasure of her company and gave her the kiss of peace in dismissal. Women, like the entertainment, were excellent side-trappings with which to gild a feast. They beguiled away idle time, but that was as far as it went. A messenger's wife did not share the messenger's function.

'I will be all right,' she said, as Adam took her arm, one eye on the waiting page, the other on le Clito, who had joined a dice game near the hearth. As Fulke's guests he and his men were sleeping within the castle itself.

'Are you sure? Christ, I could well do without this particular twist of fate.' Scowling, Adam sought Warrin de Mortimer and saw him still sitting at the trestle, wine cup beside him, a red puddle slopped around the base, and upon his knee a black-haired woman with sultry eyes. Her arms were around his neck, her fingers in his hair. His hand was on her thigh. She was whispering in his ear, but he was only half listening, all his attention focused on Adam and Heulwen.

'Yes, I'm sure.' Heulwen suppressed a shudder and kissed her husband, shutting out the sight of Warrin's accusing stare against Adam's cheek, drawing reassurance from his familiar individual scent.

Adam squeezed her waist and took her across the hall to give her into the care of his bodyguard, saw her on her way, then returned to his duty. Warrin de Mortimer he pointedly ignored, but he was still aware of him in the periphery of his vision, unpinning the neck of the woman's gown.

The squire poured wine, left the flagon and a plate of small marchpane confections to hand, and bowed out of the room. One of Fulke's dogs circled several times, then flopped down before the hearth.

Adam gave Fulke the sealed parchment that had been his responsibility for the past several weeks and sat down at the Count's gesture on a chair that had been made comfortable with cushions.

Fulke broke the seal, opened out the parchment in his stubby hands and started to read. Geoffrey picked up a marchpane comfit and decisively bit it in half. 'Interesting?' he asked as he chewed.

Frowning, Fulke shook his head, took the document nearer to the candle and started to read it again. Geoffrey raised one eyebrow, but after a calculating glance ignored his father. He picked up another piece of marchpane and tossed it to the dog. It leaped and snapped and licked its jaws. 'Do you joust, my lord?' he asked Adam.

Adam blinked at him, taken by surprise. 'Occasionally, sire,' he said cautiously.

'More than occasionally, I think,' Geoffrey contradicted. 'I saw your stallion in the stables earlier, and when I spoke to your squire about him he said you could hit a quintain shield dead centre ten times out of ten.'

Adam looked across at the Count whose lips were moving silently as he read. 'Austin tends to exaggerate, my lord.'

'There's a mêlée organised for tomorrow, le Clito's party against mine. I'd be honoured if you'd take part . . . on my side of course.'

It was tantamount to an order, no matter the manner of its phrasing. Behind a neutral mask, Adam considered the young man who was obviously accustomed to having his own way and probably dangerous if he didn't get it. 'Sire, the honour is mine,' he responded gracefully. The English barons were going to love Geoffrey of Anjou, he thought wryly.

Geoffrey smiled. 'Weapons *à plaisance*, my lord. No sharpened edges, whatever personal grudges you might harbour.'

Adam inclined his head and took a drink of his wine. 'No sharpened edges,' he repeated after a moment when he was sure of his control.

Fulke looked at Adam with cold, shrewd eyes. 'Do you know what is written here?'

'Yes, my lord.'

'What is it?' demanded Geoffrey. 'A bribe from King Henry to stop us getting too friendly with his favourite nephew?'

Fulke snorted. 'You might say that.' He handed the parchment across, and put both palms up to cover his mouth while he watched his son read.

'God's death!' Geoffrey choked as he reached the relevant part of the document. 'She's old enough to be my grandam!'

'She is also the Dowager Empress of Germany and King Henry's designated heir,' Fulke's voice was sharp with warning, 'and she is but five-and-twenty.'

Geoffrey's first high flush of colour had receded to a

dirty white. He swallowed and reread the parchment a
if willing the words to change before his eyes.

'A crown and a duchy,' Fulke said, watching hin
intently.

Adam quietly drank his wine, observing them from
beneath downcast lids. They were like two stags, one in
its prime, at the peak of its powers and recognising tha
the only way was down, and the other young, unsure
but gaining rapidly in strength and experience with the
occupied peak as its goal.

'I don't want it.' Geoffrey tossed the parchment down
His throat worked.

'Think with your head, boy, not your heart. We'll no
better an offer like this, not in a hundred years. Think
of the power! The woman's only a means to an end
God's blood, once you've planted a seed in her belly
you can sport wherever the fancy takes you. Surely a
few nights in Matilda's bed is a cheap enough price to
pay!'

Turning away, Geoffrey paced heavily to the narrow
window slit and leaned his head against the wall. The
dog left the hearth and padded across to nuzzle its mois
nose against his thigh. After a short silence the youth
rubbed his face and drew a shuddering breath. His back
still turned, he said, 'You told me, Father, that Henry o
England was like a spider weaving a web to entrap al
men. Why should we be lured into its strands?'

'Is the answer not obvious?' Fulke said impatiently. 'We
too are spiders.' Fulke crossed the room to reach up and
squeeze his tall son's shoulder with a firm, paternal hand
'And these matters are better discussed in private.'

Adam drained his cup and stood up, neither slow no

oath to take Fulke's warning to the boy as reason to depart. 'With your permission, my lords,' he said.

Fulke looked round and nodded. 'Yes, leave us.'

'Sire.' Adam picked up the parchment from the rushes, put it carefully back down on the trestle and made a courtly obeisance as he departed.

Jerold and the men of his escort, other than those who had seen Heulwen home, were waiting at the stables for him. A convivial game of dice was in progress and a flask of wine and a giggling kitchen girl were being passed from hand to hand.

Adam secured his cloak and strode across the ward. 'When you've finished, gentlemen,' he said, his sarcastic tone redeemed by the merest glint of humour.

Thierry's teeth flashed. He pocketed the dice. 'I was losing anyway,' he said disrespectfully and stood up. Wiry and light, he was at least two handspans smaller than his lord. He caught the girl by the arm, murmured something in her ear and slapped her buttocks to send her on her way.

Adam narrowed his eyes at the Angevin and paused, his hands on Vaillantif's neck, one foot in the stirrup. 'You'll lose a week's pay on top of it if you don't look sharp,' he warned.

Thierry tilted his head, unsure whether to take the words as threat or jest, and opted for caution to the extent that he knew it. Saluting smartly he took a running jump at his bay and vaulted effortlessly into the saddle. 'Ready, my lord,' he announced, cocky as a sparrow.

Adam's mouth twitched. 'Spare such tricks for tomorrow. Young Geoffrey's got a mêlée organised, and we're fighting on the Angevin side.'

The news was greeted by cheers all round, for when not actually involved in a war, Adam's men enjoyed nothing better than practising for it. The mêlée was a dangerous game, sometimes crossing the narrow line between war and mock-war, but the hurly-burly was fun and offered the chance to gain rich prizes, for a man defeated had by the rules to yield the victor his horse hauberk and weapons, or their value in coin.

Adam listened to their eager banter and felt the excitement stir his own blood. It was his sport: he excelled at it, and the prospect of decent competition was exhilarating, or would have been had not the presence of Warrin de Mortimer buzzed like a huge black fly in the ointment.

Thierry was watching him with a tense, speculative gaze. Adam returned the look sharply and the mercenary quickly wheeled his horse into line and made himself busy with a loose piece of harness.

'A mêlée!' Heulwen exclaimed, throwing down her comb on the bed and whirling round to face him, her hair a flaming swirl around her shoulders and waist. 'Have you run utterly mad?'

Adam spread his hands palms upwards. 'Warrin is no match for me on horseback,' he said defensively. 'On foot at Christmastide it was a little too close for comfort I admit, but not astride.'

Heulwen laughed in his face. 'You do not seriously believe that Warrin will play by the rules?'

He sat on the bed and looked at her. 'Heulwen, understand this, I *want* to fight in this mêlée.' He hesitated searching for words that were difficult to find because it was a feeling that came from the gut, not the mind. 'It is . . . oh, I don't know, bred into me, blood and bone. A sword is still a sword no matter how much you cover it in gilt.' His palms opened wider as he spoke, displaying to her the calluses of his trade and the thick white scar of an old battle wound bisecting his life line. 'Even if I didn't want to take part, it is expected of me. Henry's honour as much as mine is at stake.'

'Honour!' Heulwen choked on the word, fortunately too overwhelmed by fear and rage to say more.

Adam's eyes narrowed and the light shivered on his tunic as he took a swift breath. 'Yes, honour,' he said and lowered his hand to pick up the comb she had thrown down.

'Warrin doesn't know the meaning of the word!'

He ran his thumb along the ivory teeth. 'No. He just digresses from it when it's a choice between his honour and something he wants. Then he conveniently forgets he ever lapsed.'

She exhaled hard, not in the least mollified. 'Is that supposed to be reassurance?'

Adam sighed. 'It was supposed to tell you I'm not entirely naïve.' He pulled her down on to the bed beside him and gently began to draw the comb through her hair. 'Would declining to take part guarantee my life? I think not. A swift thrust from a dagger in the crowd could as easily be the manner of dispatch. In a mêlée I will have Sweyn to my left, Jerold to my right, and Thierry and Alun thereabouts; and if it has worked before a dozen times in battle, there is no reason to think it will not work on a tourney field.'

She felt his palm following the course of the comb

269

down her hair, smoothing, coaxing. Men, she thought with contempt. Willing to die for the art of showing off their prowess in the killing arts and calling it honour; fighting cocks strutting in their fine feathers. She could still see the eager gleam in Adam's eyes when he had first come to her, could hear the laughter of his men.

Adam set his palm to her jaw and turned her face to him. She looked down but he exerted pressure so that she had to meet his gaze. 'Look, sweetheart, I will avoid him if I can, that much I swear to you. Not because I don't want to separate his head from his neck, there's nothing I'd like more, but I cannot allow personal enmity to stand between myself and what I am here to do for Henry.' He stroked her cheek. 'It will be all right, I promise you.'

She shook her head, her eyes filling with tears. 'You stubborn, pig-headed . . .'

'Tail-chaser?' he suggested with a raised brow, and bent his mouth to hers.

'In God's name Adam, do not chase it too far!' she whispered against his mouth. 'I will die if I lose you.'

20

The chosen site for Geoffrey's mêlée was a broad green field just outside the city walls, and it was here, shortly after dawn, that the court assembled either to watch the sport, or prepare to partake. The early March morning was mild with the promise of warm sunshine, and although furred cloaks were much in evidence, there was no real discomfort from cold. If people gathered around braziers, it was because they served as a focal point over which to discuss and anticipate the fighting to come.

Heulwen listened to the bright chatter surrounding her and was aware of an overpowering feeling of dread and isolation. She tried to smile and respond to the tide of enthusiasm, agreeing with a baron's wife that yes, the weather was fine and that the sport should be well worth watching. She bought ribbons from a huckster to tie around Adam's lance, clapped and laughed emptily at the antics of a dancing bear, and pretended to listen with attentive enjoyment to the ballad of an itinerant lute-player. Her mouth ached with the strain of forced merriment and her head with the strain of the pretence, when all she wanted to do was run away, dragging her husband with her, and not stop until she reached the haven of her own Welsh marches.

She looked for Adam across the wide expanse of virgin grass which was soon to be despoiled. He was over at Geoffrey's pavilion with the Count. Austin was outside keeping a half-hearted eye on Vaillantif, his main interest reserved for a dancing girl who was playing a tambour and flashing her ankles at him. A ragamuffin child with the girl was feeding a wrinkled apple to the stallion.

Adam ducked out of the tent, talking to Geoffrey of Anjou. He pointed to the helm tucked under the young man's arm and made a comment. Geoffrey laughed and replied, and both of them paused to examine and admire the powerful sorrel stallion. The child made himself scarce, as did the dancing girl. Adam playfully cuffed Austin into awareness, took his leave of Geoffrey and, unhitching Vaillantif, walked him across the field towards Heulwen.

Man and horse were all prepared for the mêlée. Adam was accoutred in his hauberk and a fine new surcoat of blue silk, stitched with a gold lozenge on the breast to match that on his shield. Vaillantif was also trapped out in blue and gold, and both man and horse were bursting with such exuberance that Heulwen's heart turned to ice.

Halting the stallion, hand held close to the decorated bit-chains, Adam gave her a slow, measuring look that took full note of her pallor and the false curve of her lips. 'Listen,' he said gently, 'Fulke has promised to give me his written reply by tomorrow afternoon, so we'll be able to start home before the week's out, I promise.'

272

He was doing his best to allay her fears, she thought, but he had not a hope in hell of succeeding. No point in tarnishing the shine. Instead of saying that tomorrow might be too late, she patted Vaillantif's glossy neck and brought out the ribbons.

'I chose them to match your surcoat,' she said, and bit her lip. 'I'm sorry if I'm being a wet fish, Adam. I will make it up to you, I promise.'

He arched one brow and the corresponding mouth corner tilted up. 'I can think of several ways,' he said, 'and I am sure you can think of several more.'

'At least a dozen . . . I wish today was already over.'

Adam ran the fairing ribbons through his fingers and looked over his shoulder. Men were warming up with short practice charges and courtesy raps of lance on a companion's shield. Hoarse, joyful cries floated across the field. The leathery smell of harness and horses pervaded the air.

Heulwen gave him a gentle push, the most difficult thing she had ever done in her life. 'Go. If you linger here with me you won't be ready. Just don't take too many risks.'

He hesitated, aware of her pretence, but not knowing how to reassure her any more than he already had. It was the element of danger in this kind of sport that made it so exhilarating. He took her face in his hands and set his lips upon hers. Vaillantif snorted and butted his muzzle into the centre of Adam's spine, jarring him forwards. Their mouths jolted apart. He turned to the horse. 'It seems I have my orders,' he laughed, and set his foot in the stirrup.

Heulwen stared up at him astride the destrier: tensile

273

strength and agility coupled to smooth power. Try as she might, she could not prevent the misgivings that clouded the pride she felt in the picture they made. Despite the increasing warmth of the spring sun, she was shivering. Brusquely she told Elswith to go and buy some hot broth from one of the hucksters, knowing in her heart that it would do nothing to melt the block of ice at her core, for it was fashioned of fear.

Vaillantif danced with eagerness as Adam adjusted his stirrup-leather and made himself comfortable in the high saddle while Austin handed up helm, shield and the blunted jousting lance festooned with blue silk ribbons. Adam rode out on to the field and trotted Vaillantif over it, testing the feel of the ground and examining it for any obvious pot-holes or snags of stone that could bring a horse down in mid-charge.

On his right, Geoffrey of Anjou was cantering and turning his own destrier – a lively Spanish grey, well-sprung in the ribs but a little short of bone in Adam's estimation. Still, the lad was handling him exceptionally well, and although his constant laughter revealed his underlying excitement, he seemed otherwise steady enough.

Adam came round past Heulwen and the other women. He dipped his lance to salute her and she smiled at him, one hand leaving the bowl of broth she held to wave back. She was trying hard, he thought, his sense of joy dampening slightly. In childhood she had got them both into some dreadful scrapes, had egged him on to all kinds of folly and resultant punishment, always snapping her fingers in the face of danger. But then in childhood it had all been a game. It was frightening to realise, when you grew up, that the game was a reality you could not stop when it grew dark.

He slowed Vaillantif to a walk as they passed the assembling knights of William le Clito. Warrin was among them, leaning against the piebald stallion whose price had never been paid, arms outspread upon withers and rump, looking for all the world like a blasphemous crucifix effigy. He was talking lazily to le Clito, but broke off what he was saying to stare at Adam with a contemptuous smile.

Le Clito spoke and Warrin ceased slouching and turned his back on Adam to check and hitch the piebald's girth. Adam swung Vaillantif away and trotted him back to his own end of the field where his men were warming up.

Gradually, the opposing lines of knights began to assemble. Horses snapped at each other and were reined back hard, or sent round in a circle to attempt a place in the line again. Men jostled, struggling to position their shields and lances as well as control the reins. It was disorganised chaos out of which, after much bellowing, cursing and energetic waving of arms, Geoffrey finally succeeded in bringing about a reasonable battle formation.

There were several seconds of silent, strung tension: all down the line, men fretted their destriers for the charge. Adam tucked himself down behind his shield, rested the weight of his lance upon his thigh, and stared across the expanse of field at the opposing lines. The pied horse stood out boldly among the bays and browns and chestnuts, an easy target either to attack or avoid. He glanced briefly at Heulwen. Whereas all around her people were craning on tiptoe or bending sideways to obtain a better view of the proceedings, her stance was rigid. He wanted to shout a reassurance to her, but it was impossible, and in the same moment as his thought, the attack horn sounded along the line and all his attention was swept back to the charge.

'Hah!' he cried, and slapped the reins down hard on Vaillantif's neck and used his spurs. The stallion lunged at the bit and spurted into a gallop. Grass tore up in great moist clods. Sun flashed on armour and blunted spear tips and gleamed on straining horsehide. Adam singled out his man – a solid knight upon a squat dun, and guided Vaillantif with the pressure of his knees, his lance held loosely and his body relaxed as he counted down the strides of space.

Timing his move to the last inch of ground, he adjusted his aim, gripped the lance and thrust forward. The strike was true. The knight's lance wavered awry. He had closed his eyes against the impact and gone a fraction too high; Adam's lance, striking true centre on his shield, sent him sailing over the crupper to crash in a heap on the muddy ground.

Adam caught the dun's bridle. The knight's squire had dismounted and was helping his dazed lord to his feet. Adam asked if he was all right, received a grudging assent, and with a curt nod of his own told the defeated man where to pay his debt, before wheeling Vaillantif in pursuit of another opponent.

He and a knight with a bronze-decorated helm traded several sword blows until they were separated by another group of four knights hacking desperately at each other. Adam recognised Geoffrey's grey stallion; blood was rickling from a minor wound on its near forequarter and its nostrils were flared wide. Geoffrey was holding his own, but making no real impression on his opponent, an older thickset man who was obviously trying to wear him down. Adam gathered his reins and prepared to join and turn the balance.

'My lord, to your right!' warned Sweyn, warding his shield and sidling his bay nearer. Instead of spurring forwards, Adam pulled his right rein and turned Vaillantif to face a group of five young men, working as a team and obviously determined to take a prize like Vaillantif for their own.

Adam grinned wolfishly, twisted the reins again, and charged Vaillantif at the centremost knight, leaving Sweyn and Jerold to deal with those on his left, and Alun and Thierry with those on his right. The sorrel was sluggish to respond to his command and he had to use the reminder of spurs to bring his head up.

The two horses snapped together. Adam's opponent struck and his blade rebounded off Adam's shield. Adam's powerful backhand stroke slammed the young knight's shield inwards, clouting him in the mouth with its rim. Adam followed through immediately giving no respite, and the shield gave way again to a howl of pain. The man groped for his reins and missed them as he tried frantically to disengage. His horse plunged, went back on its haunches, and fouled the mount of the knight who was engaging Sweyn. The latter took immediate advantage and redoubled his efforts to belabour the opposition.

Detached from Adam by the pressure of battle, Thierry and Alun were too far away to prevent what happened next and Jerold, although he tried, was unable to fight clear of his own encounter and come to Adam's aid. 'Ware arms, my lord!' he bellowed at the full pitch of his lungs, 'in the name of Sweet Christ, ware!'

In the crowd, Heulwen screamed her husband's name and started to run towards him but was caught back by one of Adam's serjeants who had the presence of mind to know that if she ran on to the field among the milling and trampling of the great warhorses and the swinging weapons, she would be killed. She fought him like a wildcat, but he held on grimly, begging her to stop, and at last she did so because she could not break his grip and all her strength had gone. Sobbing, tear-streaked and panting, she turned in his hold to face the field, and by that time it was all over.

Adam, his sword lifted to strike at his struggling adversary, commanded Vaillantif with his thighs to meet the new challenge. The sorrel pivoted and staggered badly just as Adam's raised right forearm took a vicious blow from a morning star flail. His sword became snared in the ricocheting chain and was jerked from his fingers, while some of the steel points in the weighted ball at the end of the chain caught in the mail rivets of his hauberk sleeve and the gambeson beneath, splaying iron and shredding fabric. The impetus of the blow tore him sideways and down from the saddle.

He landed hard, but rolled as he fell, and presented his shield to his enemy's next assault. *Enemy*, not opponent, for the man cursing at Vaillantif and striking him out of the way with his shield was mounted on a foam-spattered piebald stallion. The morning star flail was certainly not a weapon of courtesy, nor was the manner of Warrin's attack: slamming in from the side while Adam was still engaged and omitting to utter the obligatory warning of challenge.

Gasping, with black stars fluctuating before his eyes, Adam strove to his feet. His right arm was numb, he could not feel his fingers and his shield was about as much protection as a flimsy sheet of parchment against the man who was about to ride him down.

Cursing, Sweyn fought to disengage. Jerold had succeeded, but could see that it was futile – he was going to be too late.

With the flail swinging suggestively on its chain, gathering impetus, Warrin sent the pied stallion into a dancing rear. Adam watched death tower over him, mane rippling against the sky, the shod hooves showing two bright arcs that were the gates to the underworld. The rear blazed to its zenith, and Warrin de Mortimer prepared to strike.

The horse came down but twisted, crashing sideways, barged by the blood-streaked shoulder of a grey Spanish stallion. A descending forehoof clipped Adam's shield. He staggered but kept his feet, and Warrin in turn was torn down from his horse and flung to the ground as Jerold reached him and held a blade at his throat.

Vaillantif was trembling and sweating, head hanging, tail limp. Moving gingerly, Adam went to examine him. The destrier was as wobbly as a newborn foal. Adam's face was chalk white with fury as he stalked back to de Mortimer. 'What have you done to my horse?' he snarled, seizing the sword from Jerold.

'I haven't been near the spavined beast!' Warrin stared

up the blade and Adam stared down it, a muscle ticking in his cheek. 'Belike he took a blow on the head in the fighting!'

'Do you know why this groove in a sword blade is called the blood gutter?' Adam said through his teeth. He began to lean on the hilt.

'Enough!' commanded Geoffrey of Anjou, dismounting to thrust Adam aside from his purpose. 'This mêlée is an affair to prove valour, not an extension of your trial by combat. You both shame yourselves!'

'Shame?' Adam cried incredulously. 'Look at the way this whoreson came at me, choosing his moment and full intending to do murder. The shame is not mine!'

'Do you know for certain that he has interfered with your stallion?' Geoffrey demanded. His face was flushed, translucent with his own anger.

'God's blood, it's obvious!' Adam snapped. Geoffrey stared. Adam fished for control, netted a semblance, and setting his jaw returned the sword to Jerold. 'Seek for proof and you'll find it, sire,' he said on a quieter but still vehement note. 'I know when I have been set up like a quintain dummy.'

'What's the matter here?'

They all turned to face William le Clito who was leaning down from his champing black destrier. Pink runnels of sweat streaked his face and he wiped at them with the leather edge of his gauntlet.

'A breach of honour from one of your side,' Geoffrey said. 'Best if you withdraw him and keep him confined until we decide how serious the breach is.'

Le Clito shrugged. 'Personal grudges are bound to make this kind of sport more dangerous, and in the heat of the moment men tend to forget their manners,' he said with complacence.

'Is this the result of impulse?' Adam gestured at Vaillantif. Austin had appeared and was very gently trying to coax the wobbling horse towards the edge of the field. 'Is this the kind of weapon used in courtesy?' He nudged the flail with his toe.

Le Clito took in the evidence and looked down at Warrin who was now sitting up, his helm on the grass beside him. His face was ashen, and against it a pink scar high on his cheekbone stood out like a brand. 'What have you to say?' le Clito asked with a raised brow.

'I never touched his precious horse. I wanted to tumble de Lacey in the dust and bloody his pride as he did mine, and I took it too far.'

'Horseshit!' Adam rasped.

Geoffrey looked around. The mêlée was winding to a halt as men drifted over to listen to the altercation. 'My lord?' he said to le Clito.

Le Clito saw that he had no choice and gestured to the knight beside him. 'Etienne, escort Warrin from the field and keep him confined in my quarters until I come.'

Geoffrey nodded curtly and remounted the grey. To Adam he said in a low, furious voice, 'Is this a sample of the kind of behaviour I can expect from English barons?'

Adam made no reply, which was the best he could manage in his present mood. He stared at a thick streak of mud on his surcoat, and forced his limbs into rigid quiescence.

'I suggest you go to your lodgings and have yourself and your horse tended.' Geoffrey wrestled his horse around.

Adam watched him ride away, le Clito beside him, and became aware of the pain thundering through his arm. Warrin de Mortimer did not look at Adam as he straddled the piebald and departed from the field with le Clito's knight. The flail hung down from his saddle, catching glints from the sun.

'Will he be all right?' The straw crackled.

Adam turned to regard his wife in the swinging light of the horn lantern. She was carrying his fur-lined mantle over her arm and also the morning's abandoned picnic basket. 'I thought you were abed?'

'I was, but I couldn't sleep knowing you were down here alone. How is he?' She knelt beside him and laid a gentle hand on Vaillantif's stretched red-gold neck. The horse was spread out in the straw, his breathing regular but noisy, his limbs twitching now and again in strange muscular spasms.

'No real change, but if he was going to die he would have done so by now, I think.' He compressed his lips and looked at her from the corner of his eye. 'You warned me, didn't you?'

'It is no comfort that I was right.' She took her hand from the horse's neck to set it over his. 'When I saw you go down this afternoon . . .' She swallowed. 'Oh Dear Jesu!'

He felt her shudder and, a little awkward because of his bruised arm, drew her against him and kissed her. She began to cry then, burying her face in his chest, her fingers clutching his tunic and shirt.

Adam was taken aback by this sudden outburst of emotion. Saving an incident with one of his serjeants, who now sported a badly scratched face and the beginnings of a black eye in recompense for his efforts to prevent her from hurtling herself into the midst of the mêlée, she had been as remote as an effigy. When he had walked off the field she had neither cast herself hysterically into his arms nor turned the termagant, but had greeted him with about as much warmth as a stone. She had seen efficiently to his injuries, which consisted mainly of heavy bruising. That he had no broken ribs or fingers was a miracle, and she had said so a trifle tartly, but there had been no more reprimand than that. She had treated him with the dutiful courtesy she might yield to a stranger.

'Come, sweeting,' he said tenderly, 'it's over now. There's no need for tears.'

Sniffing, she drew away to wipe her face on her cloak. 'Blame my stepmother,' she said, and suddenly there was an undercurrent of laughter in her voice. She busied herself finding a wine costrel and two cups from the depths of the basket.

He looked at her in puzzlement.

'She trained me – drilled it into my head that in times of crisis the worst thing you can do is panic. When that crisis is past, then you can weep and turn into a jibbering half-wit if that is your need.' She sniffed again and handed him the wine and a hunk of bread topped with a slice of roast beef.

He looked wry. 'That sounds like the lady Judith,' he said, and took a hungry bite of food. He had not eaten since the breaking of fast that dawn, indeed had not realised until now that he was ravenous.

'I've never been so near to a blind rage as I was this

morning,' he said as he ate. 'If Geoffrey of Anjou ha[d]
not prevented me, I'd have killed Warrin there and ther[e]
Jesu God, all those high words about not jeopardisin[g]
my errand, and then I go and lean on my blade.' H[e]
shook his head in self-disgust and took a swallow of th[e]
cold, sharp wine. 'Austin says one of the city's begga[r]
children fed Vaillantif a couple of wrinkled apples. H[e]
saw no harm in it, and I don't suppose I would hav[e]
done either – only in hindsight. A beggar child woul[d]
not feed apples to a warhorse unless paid to do it. He'[d]
eat them himself.'

'You think that was what brought Vaillantif to this?'

'Assuredly. What better way of evening the odd[s]
than to have Vaillantif founder at the wrong moment[.]
All Warrin had to do was watch for the comin[g]
opportunity.'

'What will happen to him?'

'Not a great deal, I suspect. For the sake of politica[l]
diplomacy the whole thing will be forgotten as quickl[y]
as possible. Le Clito will go back to France with hi[s]
retinue, and we'll return to England and the ripples i[n]
the pool will drift to the bank and disappear.' He mad[e]
a face. 'Christ's blood,' he said softly as he put the empt[y]
goblet down, 'I wish we were home now.'

She leaned her head upon his shoulder. A shiver o[f]
foreboding rippled down her spine. 'So do I,' she sai[d]
in a heartfelt whisper. 'Adam, so do I.'

'How could you be such an idiot?' snapped William l[e]
Clito and glared at the man stretched out on the bed[.]
'All right, Adam de Lacey owes you a debt that can onl[y]
be paid with his life, but what's your hurry? Surely yo[u]

ould have arranged something a little less obvious? is no wonder my cousin reached England in safety if his is the level of your ability!'

'It was not supposed to be obvious,' Warrin said, sulkily, and folded his arms behind his head, revealing armpits tufted with wiry blond hair. 'There was nothing wrong with the idea. It was just pure mischance that the help interfered at the wrong moment. If he hadn't, the world would now be rid of Adam de Lacey and no one any the wiser.'

'You think no one would notice his horse staggering about like a drunkard!' Le Clito scraped an exasperated hand through his thinning hair. 'You think no one would notice the hoofprints all over your victim's corpse, or not recognise that piebald you were riding? God's balls, you truly are an idiot!'

'Accidents happen in tourneys all the time. His horse was struck on the head. I could not prevent mine from trampling him. I got carried away in the heat of battle. It frequently happens, and I had a witness to corroborate my version of the truth, one of de Lacey's own men, the little Angevin with the red boots who likes the dice more than he should.'

Le Clito snorted contemptuously. 'Be that as it may, you are more than fortunate to be lying on that bed and not on the straw of a cell floor. I had the devil of a task persuading Count Fulke not to throw you in his oubliette. Indeed, the only thing that saved you was the fact that we're returning immediately to France.'

Warrin jerked up on his elbows. 'France?' he repeated, startled.

'You weren't there in the hall to hear it, were you? A

messenger arrived from my father-in-law. Charles ᴏ Flanders has been murdered at his prayers, and min have been answered.' A grin split le Clito's round fac 'I've been offered the vacancy – William, by the grac of an opportune knife, the Count of Flanders. How d you fancy settling down to a Flemish fief and a broac beamed wife with yellow plaits?'

'You have been offered Flanders?' Astonishmer increased, verging upon incredulity.

'By Louis of France as the overlord of the Duchy. Bu there are others who have a claim, and that's why w have to go back straight away. There's some hard fightin ahead, but when I come through it, I'm not just goin to be a thorn in my uncle Henry's side, I'm going to b an enormous barbed spear.'

Warrin closed his eyes and lay back again. A fief i Flanders. A Flemish wife. Earning his bread by the swor His eyelids tensed in pained response to the particula barbed spear in his own side. 'It is wonderful news, m lord,' he said, meaning it, but not having the enthusiasr to colour the words.

Le Clito looked at him speculatively and grunted. 'Ye isn't it?' he said in Warrin's tone. He picked up a drie fig from the dish on the low trestle and bit into it. 'Wh₂ I do wonder is what my uncle Henry wants with Cour Fulke. Nothing he desires the world to know, that muc is certain.'

'The Count has given you no hint?'

Le Clito chewed and swallowed. 'Not a word. Eve when delicately pressed he changed the subject, so it obviously to his advantage and not ours.' He eyed th bitter-mouthed knight on the bed. 'You could of cours

286

make amends for your behaviour today and do yourself great benefit at the same time.'

Warrin eyed his benefactor warily. 'My lord?'

'I want you to find out why my uncle has seen fit to send a messenger here to Anjou and I want you to find out before de Lacey and his wife leave for England. They're bound to have some communication with Fulke, even if it's a verbal one. I want to know what it is, and as long as I'm not implicated I don't care how you go about getting it.'

Behind the bitterness, something else uncoiled in Warrin's eyes, exultant and savage. 'Money, my lord,' he began. 'I will need—'

'You will be given what you require, and more by way of appreciation when you bring me some proof of your success.' Le Clito rose smoothly to his feet and went to wash his hands and face in the laver. 'The details are yours to command. I trust you not to fail – this time.' He stretched for the towel and dried his hands thoroughly, the gesture almost symbolic.

'I won't,' said Warrin, and then softly on a breath that scarcely stirred the air, 'by Christ on the cross, this time I won't.'

21

'Hot pies, hot pies!' a vendor bawled close to Heulwen's shrinking ear. 'Fresh lily-white mussels!' another exhorted in counterpoint, a laden basket balanced on top of her head, her wide-brimmed hat protecting her wimple from the dripping shellfish. Her wares did not smell particularly fresh to Heulwen, or perhaps it was just the fact that down here near the wharves the air was more pungent anyway, replete to surfeit with the watery aromas of a busy river and the numerous vessels plying their trade. Fishing craft in various stages of decrepitude, inshore cogs, larger merchant galleys, sleek nefs with striped sails and rows of decorated oar-holes.

Heulwen paused beside Adam to watch sailors rolling barrels of wine on to one of the galleys. Water slapped against the stone. Rain had been in short supply that year and a green weedy line showed how far the river level had fallen, although the lowering sky and the damp warm wind suggested this was soon to be remedied. She looked at the water, thought of the Channel crossing and

imaced to remember the cold choppy sea. That she
ad not been sick on the first crossing was owing to the
lative calm of the waves and her own iron determin-
ion not to burden her husband or put him off wanting
 take her anywhere again. Adam's travel-hardened
onstitution was impervious to most discomfort, and he
eated those who suffered with surprise and mild
apatience.

Adam set his good arm across her shoulders. He was
earing his injured one in a sling. 'Not long now, love,'
 said, as if he had caught the drift of her thoughts.
Once I have Count Fulke's reply, we can be on our
ay.'

'Tomorrow dawn, then.' She wrinkled her nose, and
ot just at the sudden stink of hot pitch as they passed
me men caulking a galley's strakes.

'Too late to set out today,' he confirmed with regret.
 don't go to him until this afternoon and it's bound to
 vespers at the earliest before I can get away, if not
ompline and full dark . . . Are you hungry?'

Arm in arm they left the blended stenches of the
harves and warehouses and found a space to sit and
at hot mutton pasties, bought from one of the ubi-
uitous street vendors and surprisingly good, washed
own with a costrel of the local wine. Adam had
urchased several barrels to take home with them, for
eing bought at source, it was of high quality at an
ttractive price.

The sun was a warm white halo beyond the clouds
nd the breeze blew the market-place smells at them.
pring came earlier to Anjou than it did to England.
ere the trees were preparing to blossom; in the

289

marches the snow was still skittering in the wind Heulwen found herself longing to put out her tongue and taste it.

Repast completed, they moved on through the seething mass of humanity. A woman, her teeth rotten stumps tried to sell Heulwen a caged bird and was rejected with a shudder, for Heulwen had never been able to tolerate the sight of a creature in a cage. She did, however succumb at Adam's insistence to some new hairpins and a pair of beautifully worked silver braid fillets from haberdasher's stall.

Adam looked critically at the horses that were for sale A young black Flemish mare caught his eye. She was compact and solid without being overly thickset and possessed of a bold, confident carriage. Her winter coat was coming away in handfuls, making her look patchy but this was no detriment save to appearance and probably the reason she was still for sale. He ran his good hand down her legs and found them well formed and sound.

'Adam.' Heulwen touched his shoulder.

He turned at the warning in her voice and looked at the entourage winding its way through the market-place. William le Clito with an escort of knights in their fine array. No women this time, their presence replaced by a string of laden pack ponies, and all headed in the direction of the city gates.

'Well well,' he said, lips curving into an arid smile 'What a pretty sight, and Warrin doing rearguard duty It's a pity I've never been much use at left-handed knife-throwing.'

The piebald was limping from a hip strain incurred

e previous day. Straight-backed, Warrin rode him
mpetently. Beneath his helm, his square jaw jutted
th determination and his left, ring-bedecked hand was
nched hard on his thigh, hinting at the violence that
s so much a part of the determination.

After one hard stare Adam deliberately turned his
ck to continue his examination of the black mare.
though he affected indifference, his body was rigid.

'I will sleep easier in my bed tonight,' Heulwen said
a relieved note.

The group moved on. Warrin glanced once and briefly
Heulwen and Adam, his expression blank. Then his
ze fixed on the Angevin Thierry, who was whittling a
ece of wood with his meat dagger, tiny slivers and
avings dropping on to his tunic. Thierry raised his
ad and returned Warrin's stare blandly, then returned
his whittling.

'He's gone,' Heulwen murmured.

'*Deo gratias*,' Adam said through his teeth, some but
t all the tension leaving his body.

'What's wrong?' she asked, sensing the residue.

Adam shook his head. 'Nothing.' He twitched his
oulders. 'A knife's echo between my shoulder blades.'
e spoke abruptly to the horse coper. 'How much do
u want for her?'

Heulwen chewed her lip and considered him with
asperation. Tail-chasing again, she thought, and to no
od purpose.

He bought the black mare for twelve marks, haggling
e coper down from the fifteen he had first asked.
argain struck, he turned to his pensive wife. 'Can you
ke her home with you if I go to see the Count now?'

'Yes, of course.' She forced a smile. 'Compline, y
said?'

He grimaced. 'Most probably . . . I'm sorry, love, I
I cannot bring you with me. I wish I could.'

Heulwen pouted. 'You've taken a fancy to one of t
court whores,' she accused him, 'and you want me o
of the way.'

'They are rather engaging,' he admitted, his face
straight as her own, but then his eye corners crinkle
marring the deception. 'But I'd rather share a bed w
you any day.'

'I'm glad to hear it.' She stood on tiptoe to kiss hi
'For your sake.'

When Adam arrived at the castle, Geoffrey of Anjou w
tilting at a ring that had been set up on a quintain in t
bailey, and he was making a commendable job of it. Ada
joined the gaggle of spectators, among them the kitch
girl with whom Thierry had been so familiar two nig
before. She blushed and giggled behind work-roughen
hands. Adam ignored her to concentrate on Geoffre
performance.

Geoffrey lifted the ring on the end of his lance a
came away cleanly without encountering the sandb
Turning the grey at the end of the tilt he saw Adam, a
having handed the lance to a squire, jogged over to hi
'What do you think?' He was panting slightly, his lips par
in a grin that only just fell short of being smug. He kn
he was good.

A rainy gust of breeze flurried across the ward. Ada
hooked the fingers of his uninjured hand in his belt. 'N
bad, my lord,' he nodded in reply, 'you check yours

ightly before you go for the strike. It would be better if
ou could maintain the pace.'

Geoffrey favoured Adam with a glittering look. 'I'll
ear it in mind,' he said, and then gestured at Adam's
ung arm. 'How do you fare?'

'It is sore, my lord, but no lasting damage, I think.'

Geoffrey dismounted gracefully. 'And your horse?'

'He's got his legs back and took a handful of oats
om my hand this morning, but he's still subdued. A
litting skull, I hazard.' His lips tightened. 'God knows
he kind of potion he was given.'

Geoffrey snapped his fingers at a groom, and as the
rey was led away drew Adam across the bailey in the
irection of the hall. 'We found the lad who gave him
hose apples,' he said, watching Adam through eyes half
hut against the rain.

Adam checked. 'Did you? What did he say?'

'Nothing. They took him dead from the river this
horning and by the looks of him he'd been all night in
he water. He must have slipped on one of the wharves.
t's easily done. We've had three drownings already, this
ear.' He spoke without inflection.

'I see,' Adam said softly.

'I thought that you would.'

They went into the hall. Smoke from a badly tended
earth stung his eyes and caught in his throat. He
oughed and blinked. 'Where does it all end?' he said.

'William le Clito told me all about your quarrel with
e Mortimer.' Geoffrey balanced on alternate legs as he
moved his spurs.

Adam's lip curled. 'How generous of him.'

'Not at all. He was explaining why we shouldn't clap

293

the whoreson in irons and leave him to moulder in
cell. Said the man had a right to be aggrieved by wh
you had done.'

Adam's expression became intractable.

'Is it true?' Geoffrey asked, persisting where an ang
would have feared to tread. Between his thick golde
lashes, his eyes were very bright.

'That he was responsible for Ralf le Chevalier
murder? That he was involved with le Clito in plottin
against the Empress? Yes, both counts are true.'

'And the other?'

Adam gave Geoffrey a hard stare that told the yout
he was walking a very dangerous edge, then he tran
ferred it to the banners above the dais and said quietl
'When he discovered myself and Heulwen together, Kin
Henry had already vouchsafed her hand in marriage t
me.'

'But snatched from beneath his nose,' Geoffrey sai
as they mounted the stairs to the private rooms abov
'Was that the reason you did not kill him?'

Adam's anger, caught in mid-stream by surpris
submerged into thoughtfulness. He disliked Geoffrey
Anjou, but then he was not particularly fond of Kin
Henry, and the latter's ability to rule had never been i
dispute. Geoffrey, it appeared, read men as easily as h
read the vellum-bound copies of the romances whic
were currently so popular. 'One of them,' he answere

Geoffrey paused on the stairs and glanced over h
shoulder. 'Is the Empress really as beautiful as they say

Adam struggled to keep pace with the fluctuatin
levels of Geoffrey's mind: mirror-bright shallows, tepi
mid-waters and opaque, cold depths. 'She is handsom

294

he heard himself respond. 'Rich-brown hair and milk-white skin.' *A mouth to make your loins ache and when she opens it, the venom to shrivel them.*

'And a temper?'

Adam smiled faintly. 'A royal temper, my lord, but then you said yourself that you liked spirit in a woman.'

Geoffrey continued up the stairs. 'A mare too spirited to permit a man in the saddle is a waste of time . . . is she?'

There was a hint of satisfaction in Adam's tone as he said, 'You called her old enough to be your grandam, but the difference in age is a double-edged blade. She is hardly going to run with enthusiasm into the arms of a boy barely out of tail clouts. Believe me, you will have to catch and saddle her before you can even think of mounting.'

Geoffrey threw him an angry stare, but eventually it dissolved into a snort of reluctant laughter. 'I thought you were supposed to be a diplomat?'

'I am, my lord. I did not say that the Empress was unridable. When she is not being haughty and impossible, she makes interesting company, but you will need curb and spur and God's own patience to deal with her.'

Geoffrey made a noncommittal sound. 'And your barons?'

'They will hope you get a son on her, the sooner the better – those of them that do not will hope that you fall off and get trampled in the act.'

The neutrality became another smothered ripple of amusement. 'So that the child can grow to manhood before Henry dies and your barons change their fickle minds?'

'You have nailed the shoe to the hoof, my lord.'

'The mare's hoof,' Geoffrey compounded with a mischievous twinkle as he swept aside the heavy woollen curtain and led the way into his father's rooms. 'You have heard I suppose that le Clito's gone to claim his own destiny?' He took an unlit candle from the holder on the trestle and kindled it from another wavering in a wall bracket.

'Yes, my lord.'

Geoffrey eyed him thoughtfully now, the mockery flown. 'William le Clito's going to be too busy to look to England for a long time. Flanders is a bubbling stew of trouble, and it will take all the housewifely skills he does not possess to simmer it down.' He returned the candle to its holder. 'Mind you, your King is not going to like this promotion one small bit. He has a better claim himself through his mother. She was Count Baldwin's daughter, and le Clito is a generation removed.'

'Flanders depends on English wool,' Adam said. 'Therefore Flanders depends on King Henry's goodwill.' He pushed his hair back from his brow. 'I'm glad I'm not William le Clito.'

'We are all pawns.' Geoffrey shrugged and picked up a sealed package from the trestle, turned it over in his hands, deliberating, then gave it to Adam. 'Here, take it. It is my father's reply to your King.'

Adam lowered his hand from his hair to accept the document. 'Does the Count not wish to give it to me himself?' he asked doubtfully.

Geoffrey gave him a twisted smile. 'It's more appropriate coming from the sacrificial pawn, don't you think?'

Adam frowned.

Geoffrey forced a laugh. 'Don't worry, it's not treason. My father should be here any time now. He's busy with an envoy from the Holy Kingdom of Jerusalem and a couple of papal messengers – arranging another appointment with destiny.' He sprawled gracefully on a chair and considered his exquisite gilded boots. 'Have some wine, and tell me more about my delectable future bride.'

22

'I'll leave the fur-trimmed overgown out, shall I m'lady?'
Elswith held up the said garment for her mistress's
inspection. 'You don't want to catch cold on the road
tomorrow, especially now it's raining so hard.'

Heulwen considered the gown of blue Flemish wool,
the hanging sleeves edged with marten fur, then glanced
towards the sound of the rain on the shutters. The candles
had long been lit and outside a wet, blue dusk was settling.
'No, Elswith, pack it with the others,' she said. 'Last time
I travelled in that it was raining and it got so waterlogged
I nearly drowned. I've never been so uncomfortable in all
my life.'

'But my lady, what will you wear instead?'

Heulwen turned to a pile of garments on the bed.
'These,' she said with a smile that quickly became a
splutter of laughter as she saw the maid's horror.

'By the Virgin, my lady, you cannot!' Elswith squeaked.
'It's ungodly, it's not decent!'

'But a sight more comfortable and practical. Come, unlace me, I want to try them on.'

'What will Lord Adam say?' Elswith protested as Heulwen discarded her gown and undertunic in favour of a pair of Adam's braies and chausses and one of his tunics. She was tall for a woman; not as tall as Adam, or as broad, but her breasts took up some of the slack and a firmly buckled belt dealt with the rest.

'Lord Adam?' She sat down on the bed and neatly tied the leg bindings, her eyes dancing with mischief. 'I don't know what he will say, Elswith. I think that his eyes might pop out of his head, but then it's useful to keep a surprise or two up your sleeve!' She laughed at her own weak joke and lay back on the bed, her arms folded behind her head, one knee bent sideways.

Elswith made a shocked sound and Heulwen giggled again. 'Do you know,' she observed, 'men have by far the fatter end of the wedge. Could you imagine me lying like this in a skirt . . . or like this?'

'My lady!'

Heulwen's giggles transformed into gales of laughter. Her face suffused with colour and tears poured down her cheeks, but at last she took pity on her maid's suffering, rolled over, and sat up on the edge of the bed. 'It's true, though!' she said defensively, wiping her eyes. 'Men's clothes are a deal more practical to wear.'

'My lady, tomorrow . . .' Elswith's eyes bulged with dread, 'you're not really going to . . .' She could not bring herself to say it.

'Yes, I am!' Heulwen said stoutly. 'I'll be wearing my cloak over everything and a wimple and pilgrim's hat to

cover my braids. Don't be such a goose. If you . . .' She
stopped and stared at the door as it shook to the violent
thumping of an agitated fist.

'My lady!' Thierry cried, voice urgent. 'Come quickly,
it is Vaillantif. He's down and threshing in the straw and
I fear he's dying!'

Heulwen shot to her feet, all merriment flown. 'Jesu,
no!' She grabbed her cloak. 'All right, Thierry, I'm
coming!' She fumbled about, found and donned her shoes
and struggled to tie on her pattens.

'My lady, you cannot go out dressed like that!' Elswith
held out an imploring hand which Heulwen pushed
impatiently aside. Her eyes flashed, anger making their
colour vivid.

'God's blood, if I'd known you were going to be so
prim and purse-mouthed for a trifle, I'd never have
brought you to attend me!' She tossed her braids over
her shoulders and stood up, adding as she went to the
door, 'I expect you to have finished packing that trunk
by the time I return, including that fur-trimmed gown!'

Elswith's chin wobbled; she bit her lip and looked at the
floor. Heulwen unbarred the door to the wet, windy night.
Water dripped from the brim of Thierry's hat which was
dipped low, concealing his eyes in shadow. The rushlight
made dark spangles of the raindrops on his cloak and
caught the quick glint of his teeth as he spoke.

'Quickly mistress, I beg you!' He took hold of her
arm and, drawing her out of the room, began to help
her down the stairs. He did not appear to have noticed
her strange attire but she felt him trembling and his face,
caught for an instant in the full light before Elswith barred
the door, was a tight mask. Her anxiety increased as she

300

repared herself for a gruesome sight. Having come to
now Thierry in their weeks of travel, she had found
is nature to be quick and fox-sly, with a propensity for
vomen and dice and a devil-may-care attitude to life
hat left very little room for trembling distress over the
leath of a horse.

'What has happened to him? When did it start?' She
hook her arm free as they reached the foot of the stairs.
Ier wooden pattens squelched and stuck in the mud
nd an unswept mulch of horse droppings, loudly sucking
ree as she moved.

'About half a candle-notch since, mistress. His legs
ust suddenly buckled and down he went . . . I do think
e ought to be put out of his pain, but I need your or
_ord Adam's yea-say.'

Heulwen looked up at the sky in supplication and
eceived a face full of rain.

'Perhaps I should send to the keep?' Thierry said
loubtfully and took her arm again.

'I'm all right,' she said. 'I'm not about to take a fit of
he vapours.'

His grip tightened and his teeth flashed again in a
rimace. He hooked one leg neatly behind hers and
rought her down hard on a pile of wet straw sweep-
ngs outside the stable door.

Heulwen screeched and struggled, but Thierry, fifteen
ears the trained mercenary, adept at brawling and un-
listurbed by any feelings of moral nicety concerning her
vomanhood, efficiently set about immobilising her
hrashing limbs and trussing them as though she were
_ hunted deer he was preparing to carry home from the
orest. She succeeded in biting him, clamping her teeth

301

into the fleshy part of his hand between the base of h
little finger and wrist. His skin punctured and she taste
his blood. He gave a smothered exclamation of pain an
pressed the arch of his free hand across her windpip
until choking, she was forced to let go.

He wadded a piece of rag brought for the purpos
into her mouth and bound it tightly with a length
cross-garter, then sat back on his haunches to study he
and regain his breath. Blood was still trickling down h
hand. He stanched the wound on a fold of his cloa
'Vixen,' he panted, but without too much rancour, an
his smile flashed briefly when he took his eyes from he
face to admire the rest of his handiwork and realise
that the reason she had given him such a hard tim
was that she was wearing men's garments instead of tw
layers of heavy, encumbering skirts.

'I always did wonder which of you wore the chausses
he chuckled maliciously. 'Now I know.'

Heulwen writhed, frantic with anger and fear. Sh
was trussed like a fly caught in a web, but somehow sh
did not believe that Thierry was the spider. His appetit
was not of that kind.

He stooped over her now, grinning cheerfully at he
ineffectual struggles, and laying one hand on the belt
her waist, hauled her up and over his shoulder in tru
huntsman's style, setting off with her across the path an
down through the dark, rain-sodden orchard.

His gait was slightly uneven, for Heulwen was no ligh
weight. Hanging upside down, her breath foreshortene
by his shoulder butting into her mid-section, by her bruise
throat and the clogging wad of fabric in her mouth, sh
felt consciousness recede to a dark, striving undulatio

Her wet braids slapped across her cheek. Momentarily her eyes flickered upon tree trunks darker than the sky, and a crack of lantern light from a loosely fitting upstairs shutter in the house they were leaving behind.

Unbalanced by her weight, Thierry staggered and bumped against one of the trees. A deluge of fat, cold droplets struck the exposed nape of Heulwen's neck, arousing her with a jerk from the edge of oblivion. Thierry cursed good-naturedly. She wondered hazily what he was receiving to make all this worthwhile. Adam paid all his immediate retinue two shillings a week, plus extra when they were on active duty such as now. Good wages, but a man like Thierry had his eyes set upon a sudden sunburst of gold rather than a steady trickle of daily silver – probably the reason he gambled. In many ways he was like Ralf.

He lurched again, almost missing his footing on a moss-covered step, and then they were down at the river's edge. Heulwen heard the water lapping on stone and saw a wheeling, glittering darkness of solid water and rain-slashed sky as he swung her down off his shoulder and dumped her on the wet timbers of a merchant's small private wharf.

'Don't do anything stupid,' he warned. 'If you roll, you'll go into the river and I'm not going swimming in the murk to fish you out.' He stepped over her, executing a neat leap as she tried to trip him up. 'Tut tut,' he said, wagging his forefinger and shaking his head, 'you ought to know better than that.'

She glared at him and fought her gag, jerking her body as he picked her up again and with an effort heaved her into a small rowing boat, where she lay at his feet wriggling like a new-caught salmon. The small craft see-sawed precariously as Thierry cast off the mooring rope and sat down on the bench. Water puddled the planks on which Heulwen lay and the wood bore the ingrained stink of fish and stale riverweed.

'It's hardly a royal barge, my lady,' Thierry mocked as he positioned the oars and began sculling out into the current, 'but I can promise you a royal welcome when we get to where we are going.' And then he laughed, but it was a strained sound, like the whinny of an anxious horse.

The journey downriver was a nightmare. The boat was leaky and every now and then Thierry had to cease rowing and bale out the water with a large leather tankard. The river was choppy and water kept slopping over the sides, drenching her. While Thierry was capable of rowing, he was not an expert oarsman.

Frozen to the marrow by shock and exposure, Heulwen shivered violently at Thierry's feet while her fear crystallised and took human shape. Warrin had obviously not left Angers this morning with le Clito and his retinue. It had been a ruse. Somehow and somewhere he was still here and she was being taken to him. This thought paralysed her mind as surely as Thierry's efficient binding had paralysed her limbs: bound and at Warrin's mercy, and no one aware of her predicament. Water slapped over the boat's bows again and Thierry had to ship oars and bail. Heulwen closed her eyes and prayed to drown. Her brother Miles had drowned. They said that it was an easy death, but perhaps that was just to comfort the living.

Thierry started rowing again. After a little while, he started to sing softly – a soldier's ditty that Heulwen knew although she was not supposed to. She had been en years old when caught singing 'The Coney Catcher's Ferret' for a dare during Mass. Her stepmother had marched her to the laundry by the scruff of the neck and there scrubbed out her mouth with disgusting tallow soap, the near-apoplectic priest as a witness and Adam and Miles, who had put her up to it, hovering in the background, terrified that she might tell. Public penance done, she was taken in disgrace to the bower where Judith had given her a dish of sugared comfits to take away the taste of the soap, and then, lips twitching, had asked her if she knew all the words because she had never been able to discover the entire version herself!

The memory scalded her eyes. Tears oozed from between her lids, grew cold and seeped sideways into her soaked braids. She wondered how her resourceful stepmother would deal with this situation. Her shoulders shook. She thought of Adam and her throat wrenched, making the ache there unbearable.

'Feeling sorry for yourself?' Thierry broke off singing to ask. 'Aye, well I hazard you've got cause. It's a pity for you I don't have a conscience. Rather see gold than a woman's gratitude any day.' He winked at her, tilted the brim of his hat against the sweep of the rain, and continued to row in time to the words of his song:

> *'I kissed her once, I kissed her twice*
> *I kissed her full times three*
> *I let her feel my ferret bold*
> *As she sat on my knee*
>
> *And when I popped him in her ho—'*

305

The boat bumped and grated against a larger bulk and he stopped singing to guide the fishing boat along side a small, fat Angers cog that was anchored at one o the main wharves close on one of the wine warehouses

'Hola!' A pale moon-face appeared at the side and stared down at them. 'What's your business?'

'Promised cargo for Lord Warrin de Mortimer! Thierry called back. 'Delivered on payment of agreed sum, of course.' Removing his hat, he performed a brief sarcastic flourish.

The face withdrew. There was a short pause, the sound of voices, a thumping, dragging noise, and then the face was back and a rope ladder was tossed over the side.

'I'll wait here for my money,' Thierry announced narrow-eyed and watchful. 'It's a mortal long way to fall especially with a cut throat.'

There was a pause. Thierry folded his arms and sat down. The face disappeared again. More muttering, a raised impatient voice, and then two faces materialised and stared.

'Christ on the cross!' Thierry's good nature began to show ragged at the edges. 'Is this going to take all night Perhaps I'll just row away and barter my goods some where else, eh?'

'All right, I'm coming down.' The second man lifted himself over the ship's side to take purchase of the swaying rope ladder. He paused on the final rung, judged carefully and stepped into the small boat, but he still caused it to wobble violently from side to side. Thierry fought to balance it and prevent it from capsizing.

'Careful, my lord,' he said on a rising note, 'you'l have us all in the water and I've no mind for a swim.'

'When I want your opinion, I'll let you know,' growled Warrin de Mortimer and transferred his interest to the bottom of the boat and its bedraggled occupant. Heulwen turned her head aside and tightened her closed lids. 'Why is she wearing men's clothing?' he demanded suspiciously.

Thierry shrugged. 'How should I know? It hasn't been the kind of journey for pleasant chit-chat. Ask her yourself. Perhaps she and that husband of hers like to play games.'

Warrin's eyes snapped up again, his anger burning bright and dangerously. 'Don't go too far,' he snarled.

'Pay me what we agreed and I'll leave you in peace.' Thierry held out his hand.

Warrin fished beneath his cloak and brought out a leather purse, its contents promisingly musical. His lip curling with scorn, he handed it over, fastidiously ensuring that their fingers did not touch.

Thierry noticed this with a scornful amusement of his own. 'Mind if I count it?' he grinned, not caring if de Mortimer did or not, and tugging on the drawstring he poured the coins out into his palm. 'Jesu, but for a man exiled you're mortally rich,' he observed. 'Or you were . . . I congratulate you, it's all here.' Thierry trickled the money back into the purse and remained on his guard. He was fully aware that were it not for the precariousness of this tiny fishing boat, de Mortimer would long since have leaped on him with dagger drawn.

Warrin swallowed his anger and bent carefully to lift Heulwen from the bottom of the boat. The craft tipped and reeled. Heulwen kept her eyes closed but could not feign unconsciousness, for when he laid hold of her, his fingers were bruising and her body contracted from the pain.

Thierry started bailing the boat out again as Warrin manoeuvred himself and his burden carefully on to the rope ladder. 'What about her husband?' Thierry asked curiously as he worked. 'He is bound to scour the city for her.'

'He won't find her.' Warrin paused on the ladder to gain his breath. 'Not until I'm ready, and by then he'll be glad to die.'

'I wouldn't be too sure of that,' Thierry said. 'A word of advice: don't think you've won until you're standing over his body.'

Warrin's knuckles whitened on the ladder rung. 'Get you gone,' he said through his teeth, 'now, while you still have the chance.'

'There speaks a man of decision,' Thierry retorted. Performing a mocking salute at Warrin's turned back, he sat down and took up the oars.

Warrin puffed a hard breath and completed the journey up the ladder. Stepping over the vessel's side he took his burden to an aftward awning – a somewhat flimsy affair of oiled canvas and wooden struts, where he threw Heulwen down on a leaky straw mattress at the far side.

Cursing the rain and hoping that it would have emptied its worst and moved on by dawn, Adam squelched into the house and hung his dripping cloak on a clothing pole near the fire. The men-at-arms were organising to bed down for the night, but the rush dips were still kindled against his return and a trestle stood close to the hearth

pon which a platter of cold meat and fruit and a pitcher
f wine were laid out.

Adam glanced at the repast and then ignored it. The
are at Fulke's table had been rich and spicy and the
vine potent. Although not drunk, he was not entirely
ober and had no wish to begin the morrow's journey
vith a blinding headache and churning gut.

He left Sweyn and Austin peeling off their sodden
arments and went back out into the downpour and up
he outer stairs to the floor above. Elswith opened the
loor to his knock. 'My lady, thank the Virg— Oh it's
ou, Lord Adam!' The maid wrung her hands and looked
t him with a mingling of relief and consternation.

Adam removed his sling, and picking up a towel from
eside the small laver began to rub his hair dry. 'Where's
our mistress?' He looked round the room. The travel-
ng chests were packed, all save one small one of oxhide
or their personal effects, and the room was tidy, almost
s bare as a monk's cell.

'Lady Heulwen went down to the stables more than
candle notch since with Sir Thierry. He begged her
o come quickly, said that Vaillantif was dying!'

Adam's hands stopped. 'What?'

Elswith burst into tears. 'Oh, my lord, she was cross
vith me, ordered me to stay here and finish packing . . .
said it wasn't decent, but she wouldn't heed me. I didn't
nean to be insolent, truly I didn't!'

Adam stared at the maid, thoroughly bewildered.
What wasn't decent? What are you babbling about?'
Ie threw the towel down.

'My lady was japing. She tried on some of your
lothes and said that she was going to travel in them

309

tomorrow – I begged her not to – and then Sir Thierr
came and she went with him without even botherin
to change.' She buried her face in her palms and shoo
her head from side to side.

'To the stables?'

Elswith peered at him through her fingers and gav
a loud, mucus-laden sniff. 'Yes, my lord, but it has bee
a long time now . . . I was wondering whether to go down
but I did not want her shouting at me again.'

Adam began to feel cold, and it was nothing to d
with his wet clothing. 'Stop snivelling and go and tel
Sweyn and Jerold not to unarm,' he said with quiet inten
sity, and went back out into the rain.

Vaillantif raised his head from the manger. Munchin
noisily, he stared at Adam with alert liquid eyes. Hi
cream tail swished softly against his hocks and he pricke
his ears. In the next stall, the new black mare was dozin
slack-hipped, and beside her Heulwen's dappled grey
was asleep. Except for contented, normal horsy sound
there was silence. Adam stared round, eyes wide, ear
straining. Nothing. The cold sensation in the pit of hi
belly crystallised into a solid lump of fear.

He turned to the groom who had emerged from
empty stall in the stable's far reaches, knuckling his eye
and yawning. A woman's voice complained, calling hin
back, and he gave Adam a sheepish grin. 'Thought I'
have an early night ready for tomorrow, my lord,' h
said to Adam's set features.

'Have Lady Heulwen or Thierry been here tonight?
Adam demanded curtly.

'No, sire. Not since your mare was settled in. Is ther
some trouble?'

Adam ignored the query. 'Has Vaillantif been all right?'

'Yes sire.' The groom gave him a gappy grin. 'Dancing on all fours he were when we brung the mare in. I reckon as she'll come into season before long.'

'Saddle him up.'

'Now, my lord?' The man's eyes widened in dismay.

'No, in three years' time!' Adam snarled. 'Of course I mean now, you idiot! And you can do the same for Sweyn's and Sir Jerold's. Be quick about it. You don't get paid for doing nothing!'

The man's face became as blank as a dunce's slate. He tugged his forelock and scuttled off to find the harness. Adam stalked back to the hall.

Thierry's cousin Alun was all numb astonishment. 'Thierry? Take Lady Heulwen?' He shook his head emphatically. 'I know he has his wild moments but he would not do such a thing, I know he wouldn't!'

'And you have no idea of his whereabouts?' Adam pressed his hand against the doorpost, his knuckes showing bone-white with pressure.

'My lord, if I did, I swear I would tell you, if only to prove his innocence.' He shifted his feet and cleared his throat nervously. 'Perhaps Lady Heulwen had an errand and he went to escort her?'

'Then why did he need to use the pretence of a sick horse to lure her from the room?' Adam retorted.

'Perhaps it was just an excuse for the maid to hear.'

Adam's hand flashed down to his sword-hilt, then stopped. Carefully, breathing hard, he transferred his grip to his belt and squeezed the leather as though it were a man's throat.

311

Alun said, 'Thierry has a girl at the keep, a kitchen lass called Sylvie. Probably he's with her. I know there has been a mistake.'

'So do I,' Adam said grimly. 'Sweyn, Austin, come with me. Jerold, take the men and search the streets.'

'Yes, my lord.'

Adam collected a brand and set off for the back of the dwelling.

'It's Warrin de Mortimer, isn't it?' grated Sweyn, pacing beside him.

Adam did not answer, but Sweyn received his reply in the rapid increase of Adam's stride as though he were propelling himself away from the very thought. Passing the stables, Adam slowed his pace to wait for his body guard and said, 'You've had more command of Thierry than I have. What do you think of him?'

Sweyn grunted and gave Adam a sideways look. 'You've seen him fight, my lord.'

'He's damned fast in a tight corner,' Austin contributed.

'Usually of his own making,' Sweyn growled. 'Got no moral backbone. He wenches, he drinks and he gambles. Christ's balls, how he gambles! And then he gets into a fight.' The old warrior cleared his throat and spat. 'Alun's the steadier one, covers up for him when he can. If you recall, when you took them on it was Alun who did most of the talking.'

'Is he covering up for him?' The question was half-rhetorical. They reached the edge of the garden. The rain pattered and dripped. Beyond the orchard, unseen but heard, the river lapped at the wharving.

'No, I'd say not,' Sweyn said to his master's silence.

312

out probably he will try to find him and warn him what's foot.'

'Send one of the men to follow his movements and make sure Alun's given the chance to break away. Austin, take the message back to Jerold.'

Hunching into the collar of his cloak, the youth saluted and left. Adam paused and leaned against one of the trees and said quietly to the older man, 'Sweyn, if I stopped to think what might be happening to her, you'd be dealing with a madman.'

Sweyn hesitated, then set his huge hand on Adam's shaking shoulder and gripped it. 'We'd all go mad if we stopped to think, lad,' he said gruffly.

Adam acknowledged Sweyn's attempt at comfort with a stiff nod, and holding the torch aloft, started off again. His right foot came down on something small and hard that made him catch his breath and swear. He thought it was a broken twig, but the torchlight reflected off a shiny surface instead of the matt darkness of bark. Sweyn stooped and picked up a small metal object and gave it silently to Adam.

It was an engraved silver braid fillet, one of a pair that Heulwen had bought that morning in the market, and Adam recognised it immediately since he had made the final choice for her. 'It is Heulwen's,' he said hoarsely to Sweyn. 'She would not have come down here in this rain unless she had solid reason – or was forced.'

'The river . . .' Sweyn began, but Adam had already moved off in that direction at a brisk pace.

The merchant's wharf was deserted. Adam rested his hand on the weed-slippery mooring post and stared out across the dark water at dark nothing. The torch hissed

and sputtered and the wind wavered streamers of hea
back into his face. 'The boat isn't here,' he said over h
shoulder to Sweyn. 'There was one moored here whe
we took these lodgings, and it's gone. It would be th
safest means of abduction; no guards to pass.'

'What now? He could have taken her anywhere.'

'We alert the Count and turn Angers inside out,' Ada
said, tight-lipped.

'Where do you want me to start?'

The smell of the river was very strong. Adam's nostri
clenched. 'Try the wharves and warehouses along th
waterfront; start on this bank and work your way acros
to the other – I'll join you as soon as I've seen the Cou
– try the drinking dens too. It may be that we can ru
Thierry to ground. He can't get out of the city until th
gates open.'

'What about by boat?'

'The chain is down across the river until dawn.'

'My lord . . .'

Adam turned. Sweyn closed his mouth. 'Nothing,' h
muttered into his beard and trudged back towards th
house. Adam stared down at the small silver fillet in h
hand, then closed his knuckles over it and clenched the
so hard that he distorted the shape of the ornamen
Then he set off after Sweyn.

For a moment Warrin stood panting, the pounding
his heart almost blinding him as his vision throbbed wit
each beat. Heulwen lay where she had fallen, face presse
in the straw, waiting and wanting to die.

'You can stop pretending,' Warrin said betwee
breaths. 'I know that you are aware.'

314

The canvas billowed in the wind. She heard the scrape of his feet on the planking as he moved and with difficulty turned to stare at him. He stared back and, chest still heaving, slowly drew the dagger from the tooled sheath at his belt. 'Wondering what I'm going to do with this?' he mused, flipping it end over end like a juggler. 'Well, so am I.' And his cheeks creased into the mockery of a grin as he squatted down beside her.

Heulwen flinched and tried to back away from him.

'There's no cause to be afraid,' Warrin mocked. 'If you're a good girl, I am sure we can come to a bloodless agreement.' Setting to work, he cut the cords that bound her ankles.

Heulwen stared at his rain-darkened pale hair, thinning at the crown, and wondered queasily if this was an appetiser to whet his hunger for rape. However, after he had freed her legs, he cut the ropes at her wrists and released her mouth from the foul gag. She watched the rings sparkle on his fingers as he worked and found herself fixing on them with unnatural concentration, for she dared not look at his face and see what was written there.

He frowned down at her as if unsure of what to do with his prize now that it was in his possession. Her chin was trembling, not with distress, but with cold, and her flesh was a pinched bluish-white. He thought of her in the Lacey's arms last Christmastide – her hair a lustrous copper swirl, skin flushed with a satisfied glow, eyes both brilliant and misty – and contrasted the memory with the shivering, half-dead creature lying at his mercy now.

'Sit up!' he commanded harshly, disturbed by the ambivalence of his thoughts.

When she did not move, he seized her by the wrist and dragged her up. 'I said sit up!' he snarled.

Heulwen screamed as his fingers dug savagely into the weals left by Thierry's expert binding. Her hair, heavy with water, had begun to untwist from its braids, and hung about her face in sodden strands. She bent her head, breathing in shuddering gasps and keeled sideways. He slapped her across the face and her eyes opened but they were barely focusing, and in the next moment she flopped limply forward against him.

Warrin swore and shook her to see if she was feigning but she jerked back and forth in his grip like a child's rag doll.

'Bitch,' he said, but with more irritation than malevolence, and laying her back down on the straw he studied her with a scowl. He had sufficient experience of cold season battle campaigns to know the signs and what would happen if he just left her, and he did not want her dead . . . at least not yet.

Methodically, quickly, he stripped away her soaked garments and then, starting with her dripping hair, began to rub her vigorously with the coarse woollen blanket from the pallet. Her flesh was goose-pimpled and ice cold to the touch, but under the rapid friction it began to warm and turn a scrubbed red.

Her breasts were full and firm, tipped by taut pink nipples and they undulated against the wool as he worked. Lower down at the juncture of her thighs, a red-gold triangle drew his eyes and for a moment his imagination ran riot as he thought of it tangling in a lovers' knot with his own flaxen bush. He quelled the image sharply. De Lacey's father had been the one to pleasure himself uttering corpses; such a desire had never been the core of his own need.

Heulwen moaned and stirred, her eyelids fluttering. He dragged the pallet into the middle of the room, close to the brazier, and wrapped her in his own fur-lined cloak before fetching from his belongings a flask of aqua vitae and a small horn cup.

One of his men-at-arms poked his head through the opening and he snarled at him to get out. When he tried to pour the aqua vitae from flask to cup he discovered that his hands were shaking. He set the cup down abruptly and turned round to Heulwen. Her eyes were open now, heavy-lidded, watching him with awareness and apprehension.

'Is this in the cause of revenge?' she asked weakly.

'Revenge?' He knelt down beside her and drew her towards him to tip the contents of the cup down her throat. He felt her tense and try to resist him, applied pressure to the back of her neck and felt a small flicker of triumph as she was forced to yield and, choking, swallow it. 'It's more than revenge, sweetheart,' he said with satisfaction, 'much more.' He refilled the cup, his hand steady now. 'Drink,' he commanded.

'I can't . . . I don't want to.'

'Shall I force it down your gullet?'

Heulwen looked at him; saw that there was no way out except to comply. Shuddering, she gulped the stuff down in two fast swallows. It hit her stomach and exploded into her blood. She gasped for breath. Tears stung her eyes.

He adjusted his cloak around her shoulders and drifted his hand casually down the midline of her body within

317

the folds as he arranged it. His palm brushed the cres[t]
of her nipple, paused, travelled lower. Heulwen recoiled.
A wry smile twisted his lips. 'You might be a whore, bu[t]
you're still a beautiful one,' he said.

'Why did you murder Ralf?' she asked.

His head reared back at that. 'I didn't,' he said.

'As near as makes no difference.'

He waved his hand. 'He was playing a double game[,]
selling information to us and then selling us back t[o]
Henry. I put a stop to it because he had gone too far. [I]
had to.'

'And you are not playing a double game?'

Warrin shook his head vehemently. 'It is my fathe[r]
who owes his allegiance to King Henry and then to th[e]
Empress. I have given my oath to neither of them, s[o]
how can I be forsworn? William le Clito has more righ[t]
to England and Normandy than that sulky bitch wil[l]
ever have. He is the eldest son of the eldest son.'

'I see,' she said in a small, distant voice.

'No you don't, you never have!' Goaded by her tone[,]
he pushed her down on the straw with her arms brace[d]
either side of her head. 'You promised yourself to m[e]
then played the whore behind my back. How dare yo[u]
talk to me of double games!'

'You murdered Ralf and your honour to get me!' sh[e]
spat. 'I counted that promise null and void.'

The distance receded. He saw her eyes begin to flas[h]
with anger, felt the resistance of her body and his ow[n]
flamed hard in response. 'Come, Heulwen,' he muttered[,]
'kiss me . . . Kiss me like you kiss de Lacey.' His mout[h]
descended, hot and avid.

All her senses rebelled, but were whipped into line b[y]

the common one, aided by an instinct for survival. If she fought him, he would beat her. She could see the wildness in his eyes, as if he were more than half hoping for her to do just that, and if she was going to escape, she needed her wits and her limbs in functioning order. She parted her lips to the greedy demand of his and responded with all the superficial expertise taught to her by Ralf, using it as a shield.

What followed was unpleasant and painful, but not beyond the limit of her endurance. She understood a part of what drove him and was therefore prepared to permit him his petty victory. Without love or even a seasoning of lust, the act was meaningless. She closed her eyes and ignored the exultant sound he made as he thrust into her – a dunghill cock treading a rival's hen to mark his ownership.

She wondered if it would have been like this had she married him. Probably. Instead she had married Adam. The thought of her husband darted across her mind like a flare of lightning and made her gasp aloud in anguish. Warrin, conceited, took an entirely different meaning from the sound. He panted something obscene in her ear, his hips grinding powerfully back and forth. Heulwen bit her lip and stifled a cry behind her tongue. It could not last for ever, she told herself, not at this level of fury.

His mouth crushed down on hers, his fingers twisting in her damp hair, gripping convulsively as his whole body stiffened and shuddered in the throes of climax. She stared over his shoulder at the brazier's glow, the heat blurring her eyes as he collapsed on top of her.

After a while, when his breathing had eased, he withdrew from her and lay down at her side, drawing the

319

fur-lined cloak up and around them both. One hand reached out to fondle her breast. Heulwen folded her lips in and pressed them together, clutching at the dry straw lining the floor so that she would not strike him away.

'I've been waiting a long time for this,' he said lazily, and with obvious self-satisfaction. 'Don't tell me it wasn't good for you too.'

'Where would be the point?' Heulwen said in a tired voice. 'I doubt you'd listen.'

'And still she bares her teeth,' he smiled, his fingers still caressing. 'Tell me then, vixen, how much do you hate me?'

She drew a sharp breath to spit at him that words could not describe the depth of her revulsion, but looking into his face she caught the fleeting glimpse of another expression behind the mockery – a child peeping out from behind a wall to survey the ruins of a prank that had gone monstrously wrong.

'I don't hate you, Warrin,' she said instead, wearily. 'God help us both, I pity you.'

The fleeting glimpse vanished, obliterated as he hit her open-handed across the face – not enough to really hurt, but sufficient to give due warning of what was to come if she dared too far. 'Careful,' he said gently. 'De Lacey might be soft enough to let you insult him, but don't expect it of me.'

Heulwen met his gaze then quickly looked away before he should see her loathing. Warrin smiled and stretched with languorous satisfaction. 'Do you want a drink?'

She tossed her head and willed herself to smile. 'Why not?'

He sauntered over to the flagon and splashed wine into the cup. 'There's only one,' he said, raising it to her. 'Never mind, we can share it like a pair of lovers.'

She sat up, the cloak tucked around her breasts, and reached out sideways for Warrin's discarded shirt and tunic.

He looked at her sharply. 'What are you doing?'

'I'm cold,' she protested, 'and these are warm and dry.' She flashed him a look full of wide innocence. 'Surely you don't believe I'd be so foolish as to try and run?'

He grunted. 'I don't know. That Welsh blood of yours is too fickle to be trusted.' He took a gulp of the wine and returned, but despite his words he did not prevent her from pulling on the garments, amused by the novelty. When she reached for his chausses, however, he rubbed his index finger gently along her naked inner thigh. 'What are you doing here in Angers?' he asked softly.

Thierry took a cheek-bulging mouthful of wine, swilled it round his mouth, swallowed and sighed with enjoyment. Then he picked up the waiting dice, blew on them and threw. They landed in his favour. Grinning from ear to ear, he scooped up his winnings amid the groans of his fellow gamblers.

He had been here longer than he should, he knew that, but outside it was still pouring down, and he was winning hand over fist. He promised himself that as soon as he started to lose he would leave. A girl who was filling up jugs of wine kept smiling at him. She had sparkling eyes and dimples. He winked at her and wondered if he could spend the rest of the night comfortably bedded

321

down in the hay store with her breasts for a pillow. Just as he was about to call her over and explore the possibility, his cousin strode into the room wearing an expression as black as the weather.

'Alun!' Thierry strove to his feet, staggered, and planted his legs wide apart to hold his balance. 'What the devil are you doing here?'

'A murrain on the devil!' Alun spat, grabbing a handful of his cousin's tunic and dragging him face to face. 'What kind of stew have you been stirring your fingers in? Where's Lady Heulwen?'

'I don't know what you're talking about!' Thierry tried to push him off, but without success. 'Let go of me. You're mad!'

'Mad, am I? What's this then?' Alun had felt the bulge beneath Thierry's tunic and snatched out the bag of silver from its nestling place against Thierry's breast. 'Winnings from dice?' He flung the silver down on the table. Men turned and looked. 'Christ Jesu, you're in dead trouble, and you'll soon be just dead . . . Come on!' He dragged at his cousin's arm.

Thierry belched. 'Stop panicking,' he said, belligerent with drink. 'I was as cosy as a clam in a shell here until you came bursting in.'

'Idiot, if you don't—' Alun stopped. 'Christ's balls,' he muttered under his breath, and stared at Jerold who was blocking the doorway.

'You tripe-witted dolt, you've led them straight to me, haven't you!' Thierry spat, and drew his sword.

Jerold moved equally fast, but was tripped by Alun.

'Run, Thierry!' Alun bellowed.

Jerold scrambled to his feet. 'Keep out of this!' he

growled at Alun, and plunged out of the drinking den in pursuit of his quarry.

Water spurted from beneath Jerold's boots as he ran. He tripped over a startled cat and almost fell again. The cat yowled. He cursed, narrowing his eyes, and licked water from his scrubby moustache. After a pause to listen, he hurried down the narrow black throat of an alleyway running parallel to the waterfront. Before him, faintly, he could hear lurching, staggering footsteps. Thierry's, he hoped, and his stomach knotted at the thought that he might only be pursuing a worthless drunk.

The footsteps ceased. Jerold stopped, his heart threatening to burst as he drew his breath shallowly, the better not to be heard. Further up the alley a shutter was flung open and someone peered out amidst a dim splash of candlelight. He saw a rope of dark hair hanging down.

'Who's there?'

Silence. Jerold flattened himself against the wall and side-stepped softly along it, gently drawing his dagger.

'Come away,' commanded a querulous, sleepy voice from the depths of the room, 'it's only cats.'

The shutter slammed. Jerold shot out of the shadows, grabbed the man hiding half slumped in the darkness of the recessed doorway, and laid the blade at his throat. 'Where is Lady Heulwen?' he hissed.

Thierry's larynx moved convulsively against the knife. A shudder ran through his body and his weight started to sag against Jerold. 'The *Alisande*,' he croaked.

'Louder, whoreson, I can't hear you.'

Thierry responded with a bubbling choke and Jerold realised that it was not rain on his hands but the heat of blood, and that the man he held was badly, if not mortally wounded.

'Waiting for me outside,' Thierry gargled, 'tried to run . . . Too much drink. Can't always throw to win . . . She's on the *Alisande* . . .' The last word was an indistinguishable choke that faded to nothing.

'Listen, you poxy Angev—' Thierry's head lolled, and Jerold found that he was holding a literal dead weight. A soft oath issued from his lips. He was in a pitch-dark alleyway with a freshly stabbed man and, most probably, his murderer. He backed up against the door, every sense straining. There was silence, but that did not mean it was safe.

His alertness gave him a split second's warning; enough time to sense the direction of attack and to thrust Thierry's body towards the dark shape that came at him. He heard a grunt of surprise, saw the faint gleam of light along the edge of a knife, and ran sideways out of the doorway which was protecting his back but giving him no room to manoeuvre. He transferred his dagger to his left hand and drew his sword in a shiver of steel.

His attacker leaped and struck. Jerold felt the dagger tip prick through his mail, but the hauberk was triple-linked and the rings held off the force of the knife. He tried to swing the sword, but a gauntleted fist crashed into the side of his face, making him reel, and the long dagger flashed again, striking not for his body this time, but for his throat.

Jerold got his arm up in time, and again the hauberk saved him from certain death, but he was stunned, his vision and reflexes impaired. Light blossomed, contracting his pupils; he had a momentary impaired glimpse of the ace of his assailant, staring upwards at the shutters above, which once more had been flung open, and recognised him for one of Warrin's men.

'Drunkards, go and brawl in someone else's doorway!' shrieked the woman with the dark braid, and accompanied her abuse with the well-aimed contents of a chamber pot. The other man involuntarily recoiled. Jerold reversed his sword and buffeted the hilt into the other's diaphragm with as much force as he could muster. He heard the air retch out of him, saw him double up, and was feverishly upon him, fingers winding in the rain-and urine-soaked hair to jerk back the head and expose to the sword a pale expanse of throat. Above him, the woman screamed more abuse and banged the shutters closed again.

More footfalls splashed in the darkness coming at a soft run, and voices echoed. Breathing hard through his mouth, Jerold stared towards them. Torchlight flared against the slick alley walls; horses' hooves rang on stone.

He gave a great gasp of relief and the wildness went out of his face as he recognised first the sorrel and then, half concealed behind a pitch-soaked brand, his lord. Sweyn and Austin were with him and half a dozen serjeants on foot. 'She's been taken to a ship or a boat by the name of *Alisande*,' Jerold panted. 'If we can make his whoreson sing, he'll tell us precisely where.' And then, eyes flickering sideways to one of the men on foot who was crouching over the form in the doorway, 'It's no use Alun, Thierry's dead for his sins. One gamble too many.'

'I know where the *Alisande* is moored, I saw her today,' Adam said, the quietness of his voice betraying how

close to the edge of reason he actually was. 'Jerold, dea
with this. You can have the footsoldiers.' Backin
Vaillantif, a difficult feat in the narrow alley, he turne
him and spurred towards the wharves at a speed tha
would have been considered reckless in the light of day
and was pure insanity in the middle of a black, rain
night. Sweyn spat an obscenity and struggled after him
Austin not far behind.

Jerold closed his eyes for a moment. There was bloo
running from a deep cut on his cheek. He wiped at i
with the back of his hand, looked at the dark smea
then lifted his weight from his semi-conscious assailant

'Bring him,' he said tersely to one of the gawpin
footsoldiers, and rammed his sword back into its sheath
before he gave in to temptation and used it.

Vaillantif skidded on a patch of mud and almost los
his hind legs. Adam clenched the reins and clung on
He lost a stirrup and had to fumble with his foot to fin
it. Bubbling pitch from the torch oozed on to his han
and burned – solid pain – practical considerations. Th
stallion was sweating and trembling. He patted the sati
sorrel neck and murmured soothingly, and in so doin
brought himself under control.

It was several hours since the search had first begun
and as building after building had been scoured an
found empty, black imaginings and the self-indulgen
guilt of 'if only' had clawed at the bulwarks of his sanity
Then one of Jerold's men had come running to find hir
with the news that Thierry was found and being followed
Desperate hope, desperate prayer, desperate bargain
with God. If only.

* * *

So this was it, Heulwen thought. If her submission to him had been the heart of the matter, then this was the cold blade of reason. She avoided his gaze. 'Adam wanted me with him,' she said in a subdued voice.

Warrin splayed his hand on the soft, tender skin and dug in his fingers. 'Not just half the truth, Heulwen, all of it,' he said, 'and do not plead innocence because I won't believe you.'

She swallowed. 'Adam had messages from King Henry to Count Fulke. I do not know what was written, I swear it.' Which was the literal, if not the perfect truth.

'Try harder.' Warrin's lip curled. 'As you value your life, Heulwen, try harder.'

'What more do you want me to say? How can I tell you what I do not know?' She made her voice sound tearfully puzzled. It was not difficult.

'You're lying,' he said savagely and his hand left her thigh and snaked to her throat.

'I'm not, I'm not!' She choked, flailing against him, panicking as his grip tightened on her windpipe.

'My lord!' cried one of his men-at-arms, poking his head through the canvas flap. 'There are soldiers searching the wharves upriver and their lights are coming down towards us.'

Warrin swore and shoved Heulwen down on the straw. 'How far away?' he demanded, and wrapping his cloak around his nakedness, hastened outside to see for himself.

Heulwen dragged air into her starving lungs. It still felt as though his fingers were squeezing the life from her. When she was able to move, she rolled over and scrambled to her feet. The flask of aqua vitae lay on its side nearby. She picked it up, pulled out the stopper with clumsy, shaking fingers and choked down a mouthful, her eyes on the canvas flap. Outside she could hear Warrin talking to his men, his voice quick and agitated.

He ducked back into the shelter and she took an involuntary step backwards, the neck of the flask gripped tight in her hand.

'I'll give that whoreson husband of yours his due, he's fast,' Warrin growled, 'but not fast enough. By the time he arrives, there'll be nothing to find except his own death. Do you want to watch?' His arm reached out. 'Come here.'

She shook her head and moved sideways. He came after her, moving with the heavy grace of a hunting lion. 'There is nowhere to go,' he said. 'Do not make me lose my temper.'

Heulwen circled the brazier. He followed and made a sudden lunge. She swooped from his reach so that his fingertips just grazed the ends of her hair, and then she flung the contents of the flask into the brazier.

A blinding, white pyramid of flame whooshed upwards and Warrin reeled back, his eyebrows singeing, forearms crossed to shield his face. Heulwen kicked over the brazier and ran for her life. Warrin roared a warning to the men without and sprang after her.

The flames licked experimentally at the straw, nibbling delicately at first, beginning to chew and then greedily devour.

A soldier made a grab for Heulwen and caught her right wrist. She used her left one to snatch his dagger from its sheath and slash at him. He howled and let her go, the arch of his hand gashed to the bone. Breath sobbing in her lungs, she dashed for the side of the vessel

328

Warrin seized her as she reached the ladder and spun her round, his hand reaching for the dagger, his eyes on its deadly flash. He did not see the sudden, violent jerk of her knee until it was too late, and doubled up retching as she caught him straight in the soft base of his testicles. She wrenched herself free, scrambled and jumped.

The black, cold water closed over her head and rushed into the fibres of her makeshift garments, weighting her down. She lost the dagger. Blind and deaf, encapsulated, she kicked for the surface and broke it, gasping, trod water, sank a little, and choked on a gulped mouthful of the river. Through blurred eyes she saw the outline of the wharf and struck clumsily out towards it. Her clothes hampered her. The water was cold and leached her strength, as did sheer terror as she heard a splash behind her and realised that Warrin was coming after her.

He was a strong swimmer, as she knew only too well. Ravenstow overlooked the Dee, a large, commercial and dangerous river and her father had insisted that his children and his squires learn the art. In childhood, she had been taught beside Adam and her brothers in the backwater shallows . . . and so had Warrin.

She floundered frantically towards the wharf which never seemed to come any closer, although it could only have been a matter of a few short yards. She swallowed water again. The back of her throat stung as the river washed up her nose. Her fingertips grazed weedy stone and her knees jarred into it. She was beyond feeling pain, knew only relief as she started to drag herself on to the rain-washed dockside.

A hand fumbled at her ankle. She screamed and kicked hard. The hand lost its grip and with the strength of

panic she pushed her body to its limit. Stars burst befor
her eyes, maiming her vision, but she reached soli
ground, got her feet beneath her, and began to shambl
towards the distant, bobbing torchlight.

Warrin came after her. He was frighteningly fast an
he still had breath to spare for curses as he ran to catc
her. She heard his footsteps right behind, and then h
was level with her. She twisted away, but he twisted too
caught her arm and spun her off her feet, a knife flashin
in his other hand.

Heulwen saw the blade descending and screamed ou
all the breath that remained in her body before th
world darkened beyond darkness.

'Steady now,' Adam said softly to the horse, an
eased him forward again. Sweyn and Austin joined hin
and they rode at a jog trot towards a group of moore
merchant cogs. Austin rose in his stirrups and pointe
'God's bones, look, one of them's on fire!'

Adam followed Austin's finger towards the deck of
merchant cog that was well ablaze. They could hear th
roar of the flames fanned by the wind and the cries
men who were frantically trying to bail them out wit
buckets. Reflected fire danced on the water. 'It's th
Alisande!' Adam said with a sureness born of the gut, n
the mind.

As they watched, momentarily frozen with shock,
figure half rolled, half dragged itself out of the river o
to the wharf, thrashed blindly to its feet and started towar
them at a stumbling run: a woman, for the streaming ha
was as long as the tunic she wore. Adam stared, and th
disbelief gave way to a heart-stopping jolt as he recognise

330

s wife, and saw behind her Warrin de Mortimer in hard
ursuit, drawing a knife from his belt.

'Hah!' Adam cried to Vaillantif, and once again risked
urring him. The stallion's hooves struck blue-white
arks from the cobbles. Adam drove him straight at his
nemy. Warrin was as preoccupied with Heulwen as a
ider with a trapped fly as knelt over her, the knife at
er throat.

Adam did not hesitate. He drove the burning brand,
nce-fashion, straight into Warrin's shocked, upturned
ce. Warrin screamed and reared up and back, the knife
attering to the ground. His shrieks rent the air and he
ll to his knees, arms over his face, then rolled over, writhing
 mindless agony. Adam dismounted and dropped the
rch into a puddle, where it sputtered out. With the same
eliberate purpose that had carried him through thus far,
 followed Warrin's contortions, drew his sword, and
plied the *coup de grâce*. After he had watched him die,
dam jerked the blade free, wiped it meticulously clean
 Warrin's blood-sodden shirt, and without looking back,
eathed the weapon and turned to Heulwen.

Round-eyed, Austin gaped. Sweyn, of a more prac-
cal mind, dismounted. 'Come on, lad,' he jerked his
ead at the ground, 'help me throw this fish back whence
 came. We can't leave him in the middle of the street.'

Adam knelt beside his wife. 'Heulwen?' he said tenta-
vely and examined her quickly for signs of injury. His
outh tightened as he saw the blue and red fingerprint
ruises lacing her throat. Lower down on her thigh there
ere marks too. He swallowed bile and lifted her up
gainst him, and knew that he would never be able to
e Warrin's death as a confessable sin.

'Sweyn, get me a blanket,' he commanded over h
shoulder.

Heulwen's throat moved. Her eyelids shuddered a
half opened. She felt a strong arm supporting her he
and another gently around her shoulder blades, but the
Warrin had been gentle and violent by turns, and s
remembered that he had been about to kill her. She sti
ened and struggled.

'Lie still, love, you're safe,' she heard Adam's voi
say, easy and calm and familiar.

'Adam?' She drew back to look into his face to ma
sure it was not her imagination playing tricks. Torchlig
marked out golden-hazel eyes and thick, bronze-brow
hair. She touched his face and, bewildered, look
around. 'Where's Warrin?'

His hand tightened across her back. 'Dead.'

'Dead?'

'Dead,' he repeated, dropping the word like a weight
body into the river, and taking the blanket Sweyn ha
managed to find, he wrapped her in it and then in h
own fur-lined cloak.

Heulwen closed her eyes and shuddered. 'He want
to know why we were in Angers,' she said faintly as h
mounted Vaillantif and she was handed into the sadd
before him. 'I didn't tell him.' Her teeth were chatterin
She turned her face into his tunic and clung tightly
him like a child beset by a nightmare. Adam kissed t
top of her head and blinked hard, then pressed Vaillan
to a gentle walk.

23

Thornford, Summer 1127

dam curled his fingers around his belt and contem-
ated the mosaic that the two craftsmen were so
ainstakingly working on. It was a copy of the ruined
oman one in the forest beyond Rhaeadr Cyfnos with
few adaptations of his own, and when finished it would
ansform Thornford's plesaunce from a merely func-
onal herb garden into a delightful place to sit on warm
immer evenings.

He sat down on the turf seat and studied the mosaic
om a different angle. The colours were autumnal –
eam and bronze, russet, gold and brown. His attention
andered towards his wife, who was discussing the siting
' the new mint and sage beds with the gardener and
hether they had room for another patch of stavesacre
combat the current epidemic of lice.

Busy, he thought with a twist of his mouth. In the
vo months since their return from Anjou she had not
opped. She was not just busy but frantic, and she
ould not talk to him – at least not beyond any trivial,

meaningless chatter masking God knew what. He cou
not get close enough to find out. He watched the tilt
her head as she listened to what the gardener was sayi
and the gesture of her arm as she pointed to the so
bed at their feet. Superficially there was no differenc
but it was like skimming the surface froth off a bubbli
stew and never reaching the meal itself.

She had not spoken of her time as Warrin's prison
on board the *Alisande* – not one word, but he had be
able to deduce much from her actions. In the early da
she had lived in a bathtub and scrubbed herself ra
and it did not take great alacrity of mind to realise th
Warrin had done more than just question her.

He had opted for time and gentleness to bring h
round, but they seemed to be having the opposite effec
Heulwen retreated further into her shell with each da
that passed, and nothing that he said or did seemed ab
to draw her forth. The nights were difficult too. It wa
not that she rejected him: on the contrary, she frequent
demanded more of him than he was capable of, ar
with such desperation that there was no real pleasure
it for either of them.

He looked at the wolves that made up the centrepie
of the mosaic. Black wolves chasing their tails surrounde
by a ring of red vixens. The men were working on th
huntsmen now. The gardener had gone. Adam rose ar
strolled across the plesaunce to join his wife. She wa
pressing her hand to her stomach and her complexic
was the unhealthy shade of whey.

'Heulwen?' He put an anxious arm around he
'What's wrong?'

'Nothing.' She gave him that vapid, closed look th

334

was learning to hate, and smiled brightly. 'It's those
salted herrings we bought last month. They've been
disagreeing with me. Cuthbrit says the mint should go
here and the tansy over there, but I don't know. There's
more sun . . .'

He tightened his hold, silencing her. 'Heulwen, for
God's love, I cannot bear any more of this hoodman's
blind! We have to talk about Angers. When I look at
you, I feel as though I'm looking across the Styx at a
being from the underworld.'

'Angers?' She drew a deep breath, let it out again
shakily and looked around the plesaunce, which was
taking graceful shape from the silver of Henry's gratitude. A king's price. Cheap. She felt laughter rising in
her throat, and then the nausea. 'It is with me every
waking moment without having to talk about it as well,'
she said stiffly. 'I . . . I don't feel well. I'm going to lie
down.' She pushed herself out of his concerned embrace
and ran from him.

Adam stared vacantly down at the prepared herb bed.
He wondered if he ought to go after her, but the thought
daunted him. He was still wary of rejection even when
he knew it was not personally intended. He chose the
coward's way, and deferring the confrontation went to
tell Austin to saddle up Vaillantif.

He took the men out on a wide-sweeping patrol. After
a few miles he paused in a village to speak to the reeve
and accept a cup of new ale from the beaming, flustered ale-wife, and then rode on. The open spaces and
the silken gait of the stallion eased him. He drew rein
on the crest of Thornford Dyke, looked across to Wales,
and inhaled deeply of the sweet spring air.

He found himself wishing that Miles was still alive. He could have confided in him. Guyon had lost Heulwen's own mother to rape and butchery, and Heulwen's situation was too close for him to broach it. Countess Judith would offer him abrasive advice in her usual forthright manner, and just now, that thought was unpalatable. All Miles had left them was the wolf brooch – a light in the darkness, but a light did not show you which path to take, it only illuminated the way you chose.

He shook the reins and paced Vaillantif along the top of the dyke, examining its state of repair. Not that he expected to clash with the Welsh this year, thank Christ for small mercies. It was rumoured that Rhodri ap Tewdr was getting married to the daughter of another local Welsh lord; he wondered how true the rumours were and if it would alter the delicate balance along the borders.

He moved down the dyke to visit a fortified manor held by one of his vassals and sat down to meat with the man while they discussed the need to put more of the forest under plough. Having declined his invitation to hunt, Adam then set out for home.

It was a little before vespers when he rode into the bailey, and although the slanting sun was still warm and golden, he felt the hairs prickle erect on his spine at the atmosphere as he dismounted. He started to ask his groom what was wrong, decided he would rather not know in so public a place, and hurried towards the hall. There was no sign of Heulwen or Elswith. His steward, Brien, was busy at a trestle with tally sticks and a exchequer cloth, an inky quill between his fingers, but when he saw Adam he rose and came quickly to him

'Lady Heulwen was taken ill while you were out, my
rd.' He looked anxiously at Adam. 'We did not know
ere you had taken the patrol, so we put her to bed
d my wife took it upon herself to fetch Dame Agatha
m the village.'

The information struck Adam like a fist. Dame Agatha
her capacity of wise woman and experienced midwife
s a frequent visitor among the keep's women. Adam
d known her literally since his own birth. White-faced,
pushed past his anxious steward and took the tower
irs two at a time.

Dame Agatha was emerging from the outer chamber,
e comfortable folds of her face marred by a frown as
e dried her hands on a clean square of linen. Like the
st of her they were pink, plump, and capable. 'My
rd,' she said deferentially, but blocked his way, forcing
m to stop his headlong stride towards the bedchamber.

'Where's my wife? What's happened?' He stared at
e drawn curtain behind her.

'Be at ease sire, it is nothing serious.' Her French was
angled by a heavy English accent and hard to under-
nd. He had to concentrate and it brought him off the
mmer. He breathed out once, hard, and held himself
patience. 'She is sleeping now; I have given her a
ane. What she needs is plenty of rest with her feet
ll raised. The bleeding has stopped, but she will need
be careful.'

'Bleeding?' Adam said stupidly, clutched by the horri-
d thought that Heulwen had perhaps attempted her
n life while he was gone. 'What do you mean?'

Dame Agatha gave him a curious look, then her face
tened into comfortable folds. It was not the first time

she had come up against this kind of stunned disbelie[f].
Men might profess themselves the stronger sex, but the[y]
were frightened ignorants when it came to this particu[u]-
lar arena. She patted his arm solicitously. 'It sometime[s]
happens. With rest I do believe she will settle down[.]
Leastways she hasn't lost the child.'

'Child?' Adam reeled. 'What child?'

Dame Agatha sucked a sharp breath between the ga[p]
in her front teeth, and stared at him in dismayed surpris[e].
'Forgive me, my lord. I did not realise she had not tol[d]
you – perhaps waiting to be sure, eh?'

'You're telling me that my wife is with child?' he aske[d]
unsteadily.

'Somewhere between two and three months alon[g],'
she nodded. 'Sometimes bleeding happens at this tim[e].
It is my opinion we'll see a healthy babe this side of th[e]
Christmas feast.'

Adam stared at her blankly. *Somewhere between two a[nd]
three months along.* Christ's sweet wounds, no!

'My lord, are you all right? Shall I get . . . ?'

He looked down at her sympathetic hand on his slee[ve]
and swallowed. 'Yes, he said stiltedly. 'Just taken [by]
surprise, that is all.' He withdrew his arm. 'Thank yo[u]
for coming.' He fumbled in his pouch, found a silv[er]
penny and pressed it into her hand.

Dame Agatha folded her several chins into her che[st]
and looked puzzled. There was the same checked, wi[re]
tension about him that there had been in his wife, as [if]
this pregnancy was a disaster instead of a boundless jo[y].
It took some people that way, usually those who alrea[dy]
had a dozen offspring to feed and no hope of nourishi[ng]
a thirteenth beyond the breast. A man in Lord Adam[']

338

sition was usually delighted at the prospect of an heir; wife too, at having proved her ability to conceive.

She dropped her gaze to the coin and folded her gers over it. 'I'll come back in the morning – sooner you need me,' she said, made her obeisance and left.

Adam eyed the thick curtain separating him from the dchamber. He did not need to master his feelings, for t now he did not have any. He was numb. At last, he ced his limbs to move and drew aside the heavy wool. swith was in the bedchamber, folding up some strips absorbent linen. She darted him a quick, frightened ok and her industry increased.

'Did you know?' he demanded.

Elswith blushed and fumbled. 'My lady said naught me,' she answered defensively. 'I suspected a month ce, but it weren't my place to speak . . .'

Adam went to the bed. Heulwen was sleeping deeply, r breathing natural and even, as if nothing had ever ubled her life before. Still numb, disbelieving, he ndered what he was going to say to her when the ects of the tisane wore off and she woke up. He sat wn on the stool beside the bed and unpinned his light mmer mantle. 'Elswith, go below and tell them not to it the dinner hour for me. You can bring some bread d pottage up later.'

He watched her curtsy and leave, then leaned his chin his laced fingers and stared at Heulwen.

eulwen opened her eyes and gazed vaguely around the dchamber. Her feet were propped up on a swaddled ck and the blankets were tucked up to her chin. The ht in the room was dim and grey: morning or evening

she could not tell, nor understand what she was doin
in bed. And then her stomach churned queasily as
had done for the past several weeks, causing her t
remember, and turning her head in discomfort on th
pillow she looked straight into Adam's eyes and flinche
with a small cry like a wounded animal.

Adam flinched too, then with a soft oath leaned quick
over the bed and gathered her to him. 'Heulwen, don'

Tears filled her eyes and overflowed. Through the
she saw that Adam wept too. He swore again, dashe
his sleeve across his face and left her to fetch the fla
of aqua vitae. Heulwen watched him tremble a measu
into a cup, watched as the fine russet hairs upon his wr
became in her mind's eye blond and wiry. The smell
the drink was evocative and more than her stoma
could bear, and she lunged from the bed, scrabbled f
the chamber pot and was violently sick.

Adam flung down the cup and flask and hastened
her, but he was floundering in quicksand, did not kno
what to do. 'Shall I send Elswith for Dame Agatha?'
said anxiously.

Heulwen shook her head. 'It's not because of that
she panted weakly, 'it's the aqua vitae . . . Warrin forc
me to drink it before he . . .' She broke off, retchi
uncontrollably.

'Christ Jesu!' Adam held her shuddering body, braci
her up until the spasms had ceased, and spent, she lean
wearily against him.

'I set fire to the ship with it too,' she gulped. 'I thre
the flask on the brazier when I saw my chance . . .'

'Hush, love.' He squeezed her shoulders, kissed I
bright hair.

'You asked me about Angers . . .'

'It doesn't matter, truly it does not.'

She heard the hint of panic in his voice and wondered it was for her or for himself. 'But it does,' she insisted. ve been trying to deny it ever happened, but I can't w, can I?' She laid her palm against her belly. Haltingly, using for respite when the narrative became too inful, she told him everything.

Listening, Adam was scalded by pity and love and a ge too still and deep to express. It held him immobile, cry of anguish jailed inside his head. When she ished, there was an absolute, frightening silence.

'I do not expect you to acknowledge the child,' she iispered when he said nothing, just sat staring at the nging on the far wall as though it were of vital portance.

Slowly he dragged his eyes from it and focused them her. 'It could as easily be mine as Warrin's,' he said. /e lay together several times in Angers – and beyond.' e grimaced, remembering.

'Yes.' Heulwen turned her head aside. 'It is the not owing that tears at me. Dame Agatha says I must not le a horse or run up and down stairs if I want to keep is child. All I need do is disobey her instructions and I miscarry.'

'No!' he said clenching his knuckles. Taking hold of mself he said on a calmer note, 'No, Heulwen. Mine Warrin's, the child at least is innocent. What would ve happened to me if your father had deemed me countable for my father's sins? If you deliberately lose is babe, you exchange one burden for another much avier to bear.' He dug his fingers through his hair and

gave a short, bitter laugh. 'God, I'm sorry, I sound li
a priest!'

'You have the right,' she said and her lips curved in
the travesty of a smile, 'and the right of it too. I cou
not bring myself to ride a horse over rough ground
dash about the keep like a maid at Martinmas. It
just seeing a way out and knowing I cannot take it. O
it is such a mess!' She clutched at him in misery a
frustration.

He held her, tried to gentle her, but was too unsettl
himself to succeed. 'All those years with Ralf you we
barren,' he said against her hair. 'And now this. God
heaven, we pay for what we want, don't we?'

Heulwen dropped her head against him. 'I was barr
of my own choosing,' she said, her voice so low that
had to strain to hear it.

'What do you mean?' He held her away so that
could look into her face.

Heulwen met his gaze and then slid hers away. '
the early months of my marriage to Ralf I quicken
and miscarried. I was in my third month like now, b
I lost so much blood that Judith said another child t
soon would kill me. She knows as much lore as any her
wife. If I did not conceive, it was by the artifice of spong
soaked in vinegar and daily portions of gromwell
wine.'

Adam gaped at her. He stood on the threshold of
room that very few men were permitted to enter a
suddenly he did not want to be numbered among t
privileged. 'If Ralf had known . . .' he began uncertain

'He would have beaten me witless. I don't think Judi
ever told my father. Safest not to, and besides, it doesı

vays work, or else my brother William would not be
re.'

Adam struggled to set reason over his instinctive
asculine reaction. 'Did you . . . I mean, have you
er . . . ?'

'Practised that deceit on you?' she finished starkly for
m. 'No, Adam. That was an easy choice to make – or
I thought.' She laid her hand upon her belly, and a
b caught suddenly in her throat. 'Jesu, I wish I had
ne that night . . .'

'Heulwen, no . . .'

There was a discreet cough outside the curtain and
swith came in with a wooden platter of bread and a
sh of pottage. Behind her a younger maid carried a
sh pitcher of wine and some new candles. The women
sitated, obviously discomfited by his presence. A
man's domain; he was trespassing. He looked at
eulwen, saw that she was shivering, and picking her
, tucked her back into bed.

Elswith removed the chamber pot. 'Still sick?' she
uttered to him, looking worried.

Adam shook his head and indicated the flask. 'It was
e smell of the aqua vitae.'

'My sister was like that with cheese,' volunteered the
her maid, and subsided with a blush as Elswith threw
r a look.

'Don't go!' Heulwen implored him in a frightened
ice as he moved away and the women closed around
r.

'I'm not,' he half turned to reassure her, 'but it might
as well if I eat over here where it won't disturb your
mach any more.'

343

She lay back against the pillows and stared at th
candle flame flickering as the new life flickered withi
her body, and watched her husband by its light, feelin
so wretched she would have been glad to die.

24

Wales, December 1127

'Try this,' said Renard, handing a pasty to Adam, who took it and sniffed suspiciously.

'Leeks again? Jesu I'm starting to feel like one of the things!' He took a bite and discovered he was not wrong. There was curd-cheese in it too and a lethal dose of sage.

'When in Wales,' Renard reminded him with a grin and held out his cup so that it could be replenished with mead. 'You must admit, this is excellent.'

'Until it kicks you in the skull tomorrow morning,' Adam qualified. 'That girl over there keeps looking at you.'

'I know. Do you think she's available, or would I be offending the laws of hospitality if I tried to find out? I'm supposed to be on my best behaviour. No fondling forbidden fruit to test how ripe it is.' His eyes sparkled with self-mockery. He would never be handsome in the classical sense like his father. His maturing features were plain in repose, but he had striking quartz-grey eyes and possessed charisma by the barrel-load.

Renard was here in Wales at the hall of Rhodri ap Tewdr, representing his father at Rhodri's wedding to a neighbouring Welsh lord's daughter. The truce had to be seen to be functioning; the reason Adam himself was present. Were it not for the political necessity of attending, he would have remained at Thornford with Heulwen. She was very near her time – 'as huge as a beached whale', she had said ruefully to him on the morning that he left. Judith was with her to attend the lying-in, and Dame Agatha. She would have the best possible care, but Adam was anxious.

From somewhere, during the past six months, he had found the fortitude to stand against the storm, but sometimes in the stillness of the night, listening to Heulwen toss and moan, or holding her while she wept, he would stare into the darkness and find himself filled with fear. She thought him strong, was leaning upon that strength, drawing from it, and it frightened him. If the child was born with blond hair and blue eyes – which was possible even without Warrin's paternity – then he did not know if he would have strength enough, and if he broke . . . he took a jerky gulp of his mead, spilled some down the front of his tunic and swore.

'It's not me who's going to have the kicked skull in the morning,' Renard said with a swift grin.

Adam scowled at him. 'Just because you have to curb your tongue with the Welsh, do not think you can let run riot with me!' he snapped.

Renard sucked in his cheeks and gave Adam a speculative look, wondering whether to make a remark about the latter's short temper and link it to Heulwen

minent motherhood, but decided against it. The
Welsh would revel in an open brawl between their
Norman guests. 'Sorry,' he said, making his tone genuinely
apologetic.

Adam rubbed the back of his neck. 'No, it's me who
should be sorry, lad. Pay no heed. I'm not fit company
just now.'

Renard cradled his mead. 'Heulwen's as strong as an
ox. I know you'll think I'm just saying it to comfort you,
but it's true and I should know, some of the slaps I've
had.' He smiled at Adam and was rewarded by a token
stretching of the lips in response.

'Change the subject or shut up,' Adam said, watching
the energetic footsteps of the dancers stamping around
the fire.

Renard shrugged. 'All right then. I'm getting betrothed
at Whitsun to the de Mortimer child, God help me. Papa
and Sir Hugh are discussing dower details and the like.'

Adam bit the inside of his mouth. Renard was not to
know that the very mention of the de Mortimer name
was like a burning sword in his side. 'Congratulations,'
he managed to murmur after another swallow of mead.

'No need to say it like that!' Renard laughed. 'The
chit's worth having. Now that Warrin's dead, she's Sir
Hugh's sole heir, and there's some prime grazing land
and flocks attached to her inheritance.' He eyed up a
smiling Welsh girl. 'Warrin's death hit Sir Hugh hard,
you know. He was hoping to have him pardoned.'

'Was he?' Adam strove for indifference, but the words
for all the flatness of his tone were vicious.

'A street brawl in Angers. Not the most glorious exit
to hell, is it?'

347

Adam's flatness became a rough snarl. 'He got le
than he deserved!'

'Is that what happened? Did he really get into
drunken fight on the dockside with some sailors and er
up in the water?'

A muscle bunched in Adam's jaw. 'How should
know?' he snapped. 'If that is the official version give
to his father then that must be the truth.'

'I just thought that with you being in Angers at th
same time—'

Adam shot out his hand and grabbed Renard
shoulder with bruising force. Mead tilted and spille
'Well keep your thoughts to yourself!' he hissed, puttin
emphasis on each word.

His face was close, the firelight burning in his eye
Renard held him look for look, but felt his innard
dissolve. He was reminded of a wolf. Adam made
sound in his throat, thrust Renard aside, and having rise
to his feet, stalked away from him.

Renard smoothed the mark of fingerprints from th
crushed fur on his shoulder and deliberated whether
go after him or not. Did he owe Adam an apology? I
pursed his lips and decided he didn't. It was Adam
reaction that was at fault, not the imprudence of h
own tongue.

The Welsh girl lifted a pitcher and came to repleni
his cup. He watched the flow of her body within th
simple linen gown and decided that whatever w.
troubling Adam, he was best left alone until he was co
enough to handle.

It was cold outside the hall, a crisp frost driftir
upon the twilit air. Adam watched the vapour stea

m his breath and his urine. Laughter floated out to
m, and singing, and the warm greasy smell of
asting mutton. He finished and went slowly back
thin the hall and leaned his shoulder against a
pporting pillar to watch the roistering. He not only
t like an outsider, he knew that he was one. Renard
is thoroughly occupied in persuading the Welsh girl
sit down beside him. Adam thought about making
iends and decided that keeping his distance was
obably the best way.

'He's on a promise there!' grinned Rhodri ap Tewdr.
Adam turned to the young Welsh leader who had
me to stand at his side. Rhodri was flushed with mead,
hough only to the point of merriment, but then he
d a vested interest in remaining sober tonight. 'Seldom
time when he's not,' Adam snorted. 'Do you mind? I
in't want some enraged husband or father leaping on
m and starting up the war again.'

Rhodri guffawed. 'There's only one kind of war I
int to wage on my wedding night, and it's certainly
it with you Normans. No, there's no objection.
anwen's husband threw her out a year ago when he
ught her in the bushes with a wool merchant. I tell
u, the path to her door is so well trodden that I'm
iazed there's any grass left growing round it – not that
iave any personal knowledge.'

'Of course not,' Adam agreed gravely.

'*Duw*, she'll wring him dry!' Rhodri chuckled, and half
rned as another dance started up and people shouted
d beckoned to him. 'I'm sorry your wife couldn't
.end, but for a good reason eh? I'll pray for her safe
livery and wish you a fine son. I only hope my own

bride's as quick to vouchsafe me an heir!' He slappe
Adam's arm and shouting, ran to join his bride in th
centre of the dancers, sparing Adam the need to mak
a reply, which was just as well.

The girl had her hand on Renard's lower thigh an
was leaning forward, affording him a perfect view dow
the front of her gown. Adam found a pitcher of mea
and went off to court oblivion.

Heulwen caught her breath and, screwing her eyes shu
braced herself against the wall and gripped it, pantin
The pain tightened and squeezed until she was awar
of very little else. Beneath her shift, her belly was
taut mound, a burden of which she longed to be ri
and at the same time feared to do so because of th
outcome.

'Come on lass, don't tense yourself up,' scolded Dam
Agatha, taking her arm. 'It makes it worse. Scream
you want. There's only me and my lady to hear. That
it, gently now.'

Heulwen gasped with relief as the contractio
diminished. 'I wish I was somewhere else.'

Judith straightened from putting a hot stone in th
bed and looked round, humour glinting in her eye
'When I was having Miles, I didn't scream once,' sl
said.

Dame Agatha raised a sceptical brow. 'You had a
easy birth then, my lady?'

'No. I was a day and a half in labour and I swore th
vilest soldier's curses through every single minute of
Guy said it was a good thing for the sake of my mort
soul that the others were quick into the world.'

350

The midwife chuckled. 'Best way. Nowt like a good bit o' swearing to help matters along . . . Is that another one, lass? Come on, breathe through it now, slowly . . . good, good.'

Heulwen subsided, gasping. It was no use saying that she could not go on; she had no choice, but the niggling pre-dawn pains had increased their intensity down the hours until now, near noon, they were rapidly becoming unbearable.

Judith went to the brazier and set about making her a posset containing beaten egg to keep up Heulwen's strength, and powdered raspberry leaf to aid and ease the pains. 'It's best that Adam is away at Rhodri's wedding,' she said practically as she worked. 'He'd only be wearing a hole in the floor and getting underfoot. Men usually do, especially with a first one.'

Heulwen burst into tears and Judith turned and stared at her. She was totally baffled by the changes this pregnancy had wrought in her bright and lively stepdaughter. Yes, the carrying was a burden towards the end, and the labour a time of anxious prayer and endeavour, but Judith had expected Heulwen to weather it with a shrug and a smile, impatient to have the child in her arms. Instead she was acting like a martyr in the act of being martyred.

Dame Agatha crooned and soothed. At a loss, Judith made Heulwen drink the posset and went below to see how the keep was faring in the hands of the steward's wife. Emerging from the turret entrance into the hall, she was just in time to witness the arrival of Adam and Renard home from Wales, and raised her eyes heavenwards in a silent plea for patience.

351

Fine sleet filled the wind and as she drew nearer th men her nostrils were accosted by the pungent stink wet wool. She forced a smile of welcome on to her lip

'Where's Heulwen?' Adam demanded without eve bothering to greet Judith. 'Is she . . . ?'

'Her time is here,' Judith answered calmly. 'All is goir as it should. Dame Agatha is in attendance, but my gue is dusk at least before you'll meet your heir.' She too his cloak and stood on tiptoe to kiss his cheek in a ra gesture of affection.

'Can I see her?'

Judith in her time had scandalised the rules of conve tion, but she was more than taken aback by his reques Men simply did not go near a birthing chamber un well after the event. It was forbidden, a mystery, ar jealously preserved that way. 'Adam . . .' she began, tryir to phrase the refusal kindly, but something in his expre sion stopped her before the words were spoken. Sl sensed he was asking her yea-say, but did not really ca whether she gave it or not. It was his keep and she cou not prevent him.

'Look, she is in some pain. If it is going to overs you, then you had best wait without.'

Adam nodded curtly. 'I'll manage,' he said.

Judith gave the ghost of a smile. 'I suppose you we there at the sowing,' she said, and did not understar why he gave her such a peculiar look.

Renard, ignored by his mother aside from a abstracted peck on the cheek, approached the heart blowing on his cold hands, and crouched down the heat.

Dame Agatha was horrified to see a man enter th

rthing chamber and would have driven Adam out again
ammediately, her sleeves rolled up, had not Judith dragged
er forcibly to one side and begun whispering to her
gently.

'Adam!' Heulwen gave a great gasp, ran into his arms
ad clung to him. He took her face between his hands,
agers laced in her loose hair, and kissed her wet eyes,
er cheeks, her lips, tasting the salt of sweat and tears.
he swell of the imminent baby intruded between them.

'I cannot stay, sweetheart, but I'm here,' he said with
catch in his voice. 'Judith says that all is going well?'

She heard the anxiety in his voice. 'So I'm told, but
's no consolation.' She rubbed her face on his cloak,
ad realised that it was damp and cold. 'Is it snowing?'

'Sleet.'

'How did your wedding feast fare?'

He snorted. 'The same as all wedding feasts. I've got
splitting headache for my indulgences and Renard's
ot some rare bite marks that I hope his mother never
es!'

Heulwen actually laughed through her tears and
agged him. Her burden was suddenly lighter. 'Oh
dam, what would I—' She broke off and cried out,
utching him as the contraction gathered with savage
eed and crashed over her, and for a moment she was
st in primordial pain. He bit his lip, utterly helpless as
e clawed at him.

'They're coming closer and harder,' Dame Agatha
uttered to Judith. 'He shouldn't be in here now. It isn't
ecent!'

The pain receded. Heulwen pressed her forehead
gainst him, panting.

'I think,' Adam said against her ear, 'that any ma
who objects to vinegar-soaked sponges should be mac
to spend some time in the birthing chamber.'

'Wrong!' she managed to jest shakily. 'He should I
made to bear the baby himself.'

'I would take your place if I could.'

'And I'd let you . . . Oh!' She grasped him again wi
a cry that rose with the peak of the contraction towar
a scream.

'Heulwen!'

Dame Agatha was not to be thwarted any longer ar
thrust herself forward between them, taking Adam
place. 'My lord, you must leave!' she said forceful
'There is nothing you can do here except get in our wa
We will send word out as often as you need it.'

Judith, seeing the anguish on his face, took his ar
and drew him firmly to the door. 'Adam, please!' sl
hissed. 'You have overstepped the bounds far enoug
already.'

The contraction was easing. Heulwen slumped wi
relief and raised her head to look with glazed ey
towards her distraught husband. 'I'll be all right,' sl
said, her voice breathless but level. 'Go . . . please.'

'Are you sure?' He turned, still resisting Judith's pu

Heulwen nodded and clenched her jaw, trying
hold off another surge as it gathered like an incomir
wave. It was impossible and she dissolved into th
cramping pure agony. Dame Agatha soothed and he
her, massaging her back. 'Come on, lass, let's ha
you walking again, round to the flagon, that's it, goc
girl.'

Judith dragged Adam out of the room. 'You've gor

reen,' she snapped. 'The last thing I need on my hands
st now is a sick or fainting grown man.'

'Is she really all right? You're not just saying it as a
op to keep me comforted?'

Judith's features gentled from their exasperation. 'No,
m not just saying it. Heulwen's a healthy mare and the
ains are coming good and strong, just as they should.
ow, get out from under my feet. Find yourself some-
ing to do. I promise you'll be the first to know any
ews!'

'My lord, you have a son,' Dame Agatha said, placing
blanketed, bawling bundle in his arms, her expression
nsorious, for she had not yet forgiven him for tres-
assing on forbidden territory.

He looked down into the baby's scarlet face. A tiny
st had found its way out of the blanket and was waved
ately beneath his nose.

'A healthy pair o' lungs and no mistake,' the midwife
dded with satisfaction as Renard came to peer over
dam's shoulders at his new nephew.

'He looks as though he's been boiled,' Renard
ommented unfavourably, then gave Adam's shoulder a
ruising thump. 'I don't suppose you want to celebrate
Welsh mead?'

Adam took no notice. 'Heulwen, is she all right?'

Dame Agatha saw the fear in his face and relented,
er mouth softening. 'Your lady is exhausted and some-
hat bruised, the child was big and strong, but she's
ken no lasting harm.' Her smile deepened. 'Do not
or Jesu's sake tell her what my own husband told
ne after our first – that the next one would be much

easier, not unless you want a piss-pot emptying ov
your head!' She stood aside and gestured towards th
stairs like a sentinel indicating the throne room to
menial.

Heulwen slowly lifted her lids and rested heavy eyes c
her husband and the bad-tempered bundle he wa
holding so awkwardly in his arms.

'I'm sorry it isn't a girl,' she whispered, and easy tea
of exhaustion filled her eyes. 'It would not have mattere
so much then, would it?'

Adam glanced quickly towards Judith, but she wa
busy in the far corner of the room, well out of hearir
range.

'As long as you are safe it does not matter at all,' l
said, and meant it. 'I don't think I've ever been so afrai
not even on a battle eve, as I have been these last fe
hours.' He leaned down and kissed her, then with
grimace carefully placed the baby in her arms. 'H
sounds like a set of Hibernian pipes. Do you suppo:
he's hungry?'

Heulwen slipped down the shoulder of her bedgow
and dubiously offered the baby her breast. He screeche
bumping his face against her until by accident he foun
the security of her nipple and covered it with a despera
gulp. As if by magic the wails ceased, replaced by smal
gratified snufflings.

'Thank heaven for that,' Judith said tartly, givin
Heulwen a steaming cup. 'Bugloss to promote the flo
of milk. It looks as if you have a glutton on your hand
I haven't heard such a noise since Renard was born, an
he still hasn't learned to be quiet. I'll go and fetch yo

mething to eat. You'll need to keep up your strength: ther that, or get a wet-nurse.'

It was an excuse to leave them alone for a time. eulwen knew she would be quite unable to eat what- er was brought. She touched the baby's hair. It was ft and dark. His eyes were closed now, the lids lined ith brownish-gold lashes. The waving arm was still, gers fanned on her breast as he sucked. She felt his lnerability and it tugged at her heart as much as the oubts.

At the exact moment of his birth, when he had slipped om her body, she had only been able to think of the pe. Now, alongside that memory, others warmed her. erself and Adam and some ink stains that wrote their wn story; a dish of sugared plums; a stable in Angers d the straw prickling her naked thighs as the bedstraw ad done while she laboured.

She looked from her son to her husband. Adam said at it did not matter, but he had been quick to put the aby into her arms. It could be a natural male response something so feeble and tiny. She could not tell from s face and she could not ask him.

'How would you have him named?' she asked into his ence.

Adam watched the busily working small jaws drawing fe and comfort from her. His son or a changeling, the ild was still Heulwen's, and as he had said, an inno- ent. He played with a strand of her hair. They had nbraided it, following the superstition that twists and nots of any kind could impede the smooth passage of child into the world. 'There is only one possible name,' e murmured. 'He has to be Miles.'

Heulwen's throat closed on a sob. Her body jerked
she tried to control herself, and the baby, losing his gr
on security, bawled his indignation, rooted frantica
until he found it again, and settled, sucking at doubl
speed. 'Yes,' she managed huskily, 'he has to be Mile

25

Ravenstow, Summer 1128

Elene de Mortimer, seven years old, stretched out her hand and considered with pensive pride the enamelled gold betrothal ring shining on her finger. Renard would one day place her proper wedding ring there when she was a woman and old enough to be married to him. As of now they were only betrothed – pledged to each other as in the tales of the romances that her nurse sometimes read to her. He had given her another ring too, to be worn when her hand grew, but too big now. It hung on a silk cord around her neck for today, but her father said that she must put it away in her coffer when they went home.

All the grown-ups were still eating and drinking in the hall and talking about another wedding. Someone called Matilda had got married to someone called Geoffrey, and there seemed to be some kind of disagreement about whether they should have got married at all. Elene had become restless, then bored, and used the need of the privy as her excuse to leave the high dais and climb the stairs to the apartments above. Then, although knowing that she should return the moment she had emptied her bladder, curiosity had overcome caution and she had begun to explore this stout border keep that would one day be her home.

One of the rooms contained a sewing bench and two looms. A dog was asleep in a pool of sunshine near the window, but it raised its head and growled when it sensed her presence. Startled, she hurried out and came to a small wall chamber which she knew was reserved for herself and her nurse tonight. It smelt musty and dried lavender was posied everywhere to combat the odour of the stone.

A short turn up another spiralling set of stairs brought her to the lord's chamber that one day she would share with Renard, as Lady in her own right.

A small round gazing glass was propped up on a coffer and she stopped short with a small gasp that was half awe, half delight. She had heard of such objects of course, even seen a poor imitation of one at a fairing, but they were rare and vastly expensive. Picking it up and holding it this way and that, she studied the reflection of a child with hip-length, blue-black hair, wavy and strong, a crown of fresh flowers pinned grimly in place and still defying the pins. It showed her wide-set golden-green eyes, a milky skin, a smile made gappy by missing teeth, and a mischievous expression emphasised by a small snub nose. Her father had smiled sadly at her before the ceremony, and said in a voice rough with emotion, 'Child, you look just like your mother.'

She had never known her mother, her father's second French wife and much younger than he, for she had died a miscarriage a year after Elene's birth. Her father was often sad, more so these days since the news of Warrin's death.

Elene wrinkled her nose at the mirror. She had never really liked her much older half-brother. He would bring her presents, expect her to enthuse over them, and then ignore her. Her father had ignored her too when Warrin was at home, telling her to go and play or find her nurse. A sudden sound made her gasp and whirl round guiltily from the mirror, and for the first time she noticed Renard's older half-sister sitting in a chair nursing a baby.

'Don't worry, I won't eat you,' said Heulwen with a smile, and lifting the baby from her breast, she covered herself.

Elene tiptoed to the chair. Unable to resist, she put a curious finger on the brown spiky fuzz crowning the baby's head. 'What's his name?' she asked.

'Miles, for his great-grandfather.'

'Oh.'

Heulwen studied the child. She was impishly appealing and bore no resemblance whatsoever to her late brother, but it be a suggestion of stubbornness about the small, round chin. 'Do you want to hold him?'

Elene's whole face lit up. 'Can I really?'

For answer, Heulwen placed her son in Elene's arms, showing her how to hold him, not that he needed as much support now. He was able to sit on his own, and turned his head frequently to take note of what went on around him.

'I'm going to have lots of babies when I'm married to Renard,' Elene confided seriously. 'How many teeth has he got?'

'Two.' Heulwen put her palm across her mouth conceal her amusement lest she hurt the child's feeling

Elene sighed. 'I wish I had brothers and sisters. Warr was lots older than me, and he never wanted to play.

Heulwen stiffened at the mention of the name. Th smile left her expression. 'Never mind,' she heard herse sympathising. 'You have a whole family by betrothal no

Elene nodded and gave Heulwen a beaming smi then looked down at Miles who was studying her wi round, curious eyes. 'I like babies. Are you going to ha any more soon?'

Heulwen coughed. 'That lies in God's hands,' she sai and sensing a change in the light, looked beyond th absorbed little girl and saw, with a clenching of h stomach, that Elene's father stood in the doorway.

'There you are!' he said harshly to Elene. 'What do you mean, running away from your own betrothal fea Do you know how bad-mannered that is?'

Elene caught her lower lip in her teeth. 'I wasn Papa,' she said in a small, forlorn voice. 'I just went the privy and, and . . .'

'. . . and then came to watch me feed Miles.' Heulwe rescued her quickly and gave a brief, reassuring smile Elene. 'It is my fault for keeping her.'

Sir Hugh grunted and looked from his daughter the copper-haired woman now lifting the baby back in her own arms. The infant almost dislocated its neck it swivelled to stare at him.

'She still should not have run off,' he said, and the cleared his throat and added with abrupt gruffness, 'Wh you did to my son was wrong, but I accept that he to compromised his honour in more ways than one. For th success of this betrothal, I'm prepared to let the past lie. I've spoken to your husband already and he says . . .'

'. . . And he says he will do his best,' Adam said, following de Mortimer into the room. Going to Heulwen, he kissed her cheek. She stood up, Miles struggling in her arms, met Adam's eloquent look and although she felt cold, managed a half-smile at the older man.

'The servants are setting out the trestles in the plesaunce for the afternoon. Are you coming down? You can put Miles on a fleece among the women.'

Sir Hugh stared at the two of them together, the swaddled infant held between them. There was a bitter taste at the back of his throat as he thought how, given different circumstances, that baby could have been his own grandson. Elene ran to him, the garland askew on her unruly raven curls. He set his arm around her narrow shoulders, squeezed them hard, and turned to the doorway. On reaching it he paused and looked round. 'You have a fine son,' he said heavily. 'I congratulate you. May he bring you more joy than mine did to me.'

There was a taut silence after he had gone, broken by Miles, who gurgled and held out hopeful arms to Adam. After a hesitation, Adam took him from Heulwen and walked to the window to look down on the somnolent, sun-steeped bailey. Ranulf de Gernons was being dragged across it by a huge black alaunt, choking against its leash. 'It's a pity de Gernons had to spoil the gathering,' he remarked.

Heulwen murmured something and pretended to tidy away the baby's things from the bed. Surreptitiously she looked over at the window. Adam was holding Miles gently now in a relaxed pose, and the baby had stilled,

363

eyes agog on the dust motes drifting in a band of sunlight. He leaned out to try and grab them and his hair took on a red-gold tint as it was touched by the sun.

Heulwen swallowed a painful lump in her throat. She was never quite sure how Adam felt about Miles. While carrying him in her womb, she had been afraid of rejecting him, but after the first difficult moments her doubts disintegrated. He was helpless, dependent on her. The feel of him at her breast filled her with love and a pang too powerful to be understood. Adam did not have that closeness of the body to bind him to a child perhaps not of his siring, and it fretted at her for she dared not search beneath Adam's outwardly calm exterior to see what lay beneath. He had acknowledged Miles as his heir, but sometimes she feared that it was only for her sake, and the child's; doing what was right rather than what he personally desired.

To distract herself she asked, 'Has my father said anything to you about the Empress's marriage?'

Adam turned from the window and came back into the room. 'No, Guyon's been avoiding me, biting down on words he'd like to utter but knows he can't without risk of a rift. I suppose we'll come to it soon enough – discussion I mean, not a rift.' He went towards the door. Heulwen followed him, pausing in front of the mirror to adjust her circlet and veil. Adam stopped beside her. Miles reached out a chubby hand and patted the glass, laughing at himself.

'He looks like you,' she said softly. 'Adam, he's yours. I know he is.'

For a moment Adam stood silently, watching the baby and the man and the woman; one joyfully innocent, and wo balanced on a knife-edge. 'Do you think it would nake any difference, whatever I saw in the mirror?'

Heulwen swallowed. His tone was gentle, but it frightned her. 'It might,' she said, her mouth dry, and saw is jaw tighten and his eyes narrow the way she had seen hem do on a tilting ground. 'Adam . . .'

'Don't say anything else,' he said, still gently, and eturning Miles to her arms, walked out.

Heulwen put her head down; eyes stinging, she nuzzled er son's fuzzy hair. All unwittingly she had just offended Adam's honour, and she would only dig herself into a leeper pit if she went after him and tried to explain. he knew that look of his by now.

Sniffing, she wiped her eyes on the turned-back anging sleeve of her gown, balanced Miles on her hip, nd went slowly downstairs.

he plesaunce smelt of grass and the spicy, slightly eppery scent of gillyflowers. Bees throbbed among the lossoms. Bream cruised the surface of the stewpond in earch of mayflies. The sky was a glorious, soft blue, the un hot, but tempered by light ripples of breeze.

Adam watched Heulwen join the other women and ut Miles down on his tummy upon a thick sheepskin. Ie was chewing on a ball made of strips of soft coloured eather, and the women were cooing over him and making fuss. As if drawn by a magnet, Elene left her father's ide to crouch beside him.

Two servants carried some trestles past on which to ay out the food and drink. Adam met Heulwen's gaze cross and between them and turned sharply away. It lid not make any difference, or so he had told himself a thousand times over; and a thousand times over the doubt crept in, and she had seen it. He was more angry at himself than her.

Ranulf de Gernons was showing off his dog. Slab-muscled and glossy, it lunged on the leash and snarled at Brith, young William's own small pet hound.

'Owning the biggest horse, the biggest dog and the biggest mouth does not necessarily command you the respect for which you had hoped,' Guyon said wryly from the side of his mouth as he joined Adam beside the rose bushes that climbed the wall.

'It also makes you the biggest fool if you can't control any of them,' Adam qualified. 'Why's he here in the first place? Surely you did not invite him by choice?'

Guyon snorted. 'I didn't invite him at all. He's on his way to Chester and sought lodging and hospitality on the way. That it happened to be the eve of Renard's betrothal was unfortunate.' He gave Adam a look. 'The seeking of hospitality is not I think his main motive.'

'No?'

'His father wants to know what we are going to do about this illegal marriage between Matilda and Geoffrey of Anjou, and Ranulf's gone bloodhound for him.'

'Illegal?'

'Oh don't play me for a fool!' Guyon snapped. 'You know what I mean. Eighteen months ago at Windsor we were guaranteed a say in the choosing of Matilda's husband, a say which has been utterly ignored. As usual Henry has quietly connived behind our backs to get his own way.'

Adam felt his face begin to burn. 'So what are you going to do? Get it annulled out of pique and start a war? And who will you put in Geoffrey's place? Ranulf de Gernons, perchance?' His voice was harsh.

Guyon arched one brow at Adam. 'I am not an inexperienced hound to run yelping after a false scent. If the truth were known, I'd prefer not to run with either pack. You knew about this marriage, didn't you?'

Adam breathed out and pushed his hair back from his forehead. 'I'm sorry,' he said, exasperated with himself. 'I should have curbed my tongue but Heulwen and I have just had a disagreement, and my temper's still hot. Yes, I did know, and for the sake of my honour, which God knows is frequently a millstone around my neck, I could not tell you.'

Guyon grimaced. He knew all about King Henry and the knots he tied in men's honour. 'And is Geoffrey of Anjou likely to be a millstone too?'

'He has the ability to control his wife and all of us if given the chance. For good or bad, I don't know. By God's will, he'll breed sons upon Matilda who will be of an age to succeed their grandfather when his time comes.'

'It has caused much ill-feeling,' Guyon said. 'Henry might have solved his problems across the Narrow Sea, particularly now that William le Clito's done the honourable thing and got himself killed in Flanders, but I'm not so sure about England. Many of us are far too insular for our own good.' He watched Renard, Henry and a group of laughing young men head towards the tilt yard. Henry's voice sounded like a creaking gate; it was on the verge of breaking. Suddenly he felt old.

Adam had turned to watch them. Guyon laid one hand on his shoulder. 'If you have quarrelled with my

367

daughter, I should go and set matters to rights now. If you disappear with my sons you'll only make it worse for yourself later,' he said with wry experience.

'Easier said than done.'

Guyon grinned and pushed him. 'Go on . . .' And then, while Adam still hesitated, reluctant, 'The babe's shaping well. He has eyes like Heulwen's mother, but he looks like you. Wolves breed true, as my wife's maid was always saying darkly of you when she rocked your cradle.'

Adam gave him a sharp look and then laughed between his teeth. 'I don't need force-feeding, but I'm certainly having it rammed down my throat today.'

Guyon gazed at him, puzzled. 'What?'

'Nothing.' Adam shook his head and, still smiling, took a step towards the women.

De Gernons lost his grip on the black hound's leash and the mastiff tore from his hands and hurtled across the plesaunce to leap among the women and attack Brith. The two animals rolled together, snarling and snapping. Elene screamed and ran to her father, hiding her face against his tunic. Shouting, William tried to grab Brith's collar and recoiled with a shriek, a dripping red slash bisecting his knuckles. De Gernons bellows at the mastiff to heel went unheeded.

Heulwen, who had been talking to Judith at one of the trestles, cried out and picking up her skirts started towards her son, who was lying in direct line of the biting, frantic hounds, about to be rolled upon or worse, for de Gernons's mastiff was in a state of frenzy, black gums bared on a ferocious snaggle of teeth.

The women screamed. Miles wailed. William's young hound, lighter of build and gentler of nature, was striving to disengage, blood-drenched and yelping. Adam, running, snatched Miles out of harm's way as the mastiff, victorious but still full of fighting rage, snarled and launched himself at the nearest thing that moved.

Unable to defend himself because he held the baby, Adam went down beneath the massive forepaws. He smelt the dog's rank breath, saw the white-rimmed eyes and froth-spattered jaws, and tried to roll and avoid the savage array of teeth. Something splashed over him. He tasted wine and realised that someone had emptied a flagon over the dog to try and drive it off him. Heulwen screamed and screamed again. Above him there was a solid, vibrating thud and a dreadful howl suddenly cut off. The dog's weight slumped on him and then was dragged off. He breathed again, and rolling over, slowly sat up. Miles screeched in his arms, a trifle rumpled and red with indignation, but otherwise unscathed.

To one side the dog lay in a puddle of blood, a jousting lance pinning it to the turf of the plesaunce through its ribs. Heulwen threw down the empty wine pitcher and dropped to her knees beside Adam, sobbing with reaction and relief. Behind her, face bleached, eyes as dark as flint, Renard was facing a sputtering, furious Ranulf de Gernons.

'You . . . you have killed my dog!' he howled with the disbelieving fury of a spoiled child who has had a favourite toy confiscated.

'Have I?' Renard said through clenched teeth. 'What a shame, and before he'd finished performing for us too.'

De Gernons's jaw worked. 'Do you know how much he was worth?'

'Oh yes,' Renard answered. 'The length of a jousting

lance at least.' Turning his back on the enraged heir to Chester's wide domains, he gestured to two gawping, frightened servants. 'Get rid of this. Throw it on the midden.'

Too breathless to speak, Adam stood up, his tunic splattered with wine and blood and glared at de Gernons in lieu of actions. Guyon stepped quickly between his son and son-by-marriage and the 'guest' before a situation too volatile to be contained developed. The laws of hospitality might be inconvenient, but they were also sacred. 'Only a fool brings a beast like that among company,' he said, each word soft but distinct with scorn. 'It is too much to expect your apology, I know, but that you should try to turn the blame around astounds me beyond contempt!'

De Gernons looked around the circle of accusing, hostile eyes, at hands that hovered above dagger grips, leashed by custom but straining to break free. He hawked and spat, and without another word pushed past Guyon, roughly nudging his shoulder, did the same to Renard, and stalked out. They heard him yelling for his horse to be brought.

'Like dog, like owner,' Renard muttered.

Guyon grimaced. 'We have just made a powerful enemy, and one who will harbour a grudge beyond all reason.'

'Who wants him for a friend?' Judith said acidly as she bathed the slash on her youngest son's hand with wine. William tugged away from her, anxious to see to his wounded dog.

'That depends on how matters develop at court,' Guyon said bleakly. 'Adam, are you all right?'

370

'Bruised,' Adam said with a brief nod and watched the servants dragging the mastiff's body away. 'Thank Christ it's nothing more serious. I thought I wasn't going to reach Miles in time.' He kissed his son's cheek and hugged him close for an instant before handing him, fretting, to Heulwen. A mutual look passed over the baby's head, but for now there was no opportunity to explore it further.

One of the women handed Adam a cup of sweetened wine.

Guyon shook his head. 'He didn't find out what he wanted to know.'

'I think,' Adam contradicted over the rim of his cup, 'that he found out more than he bargained for – and so did we.'

The night was as still as a prayer. Heulwen's gilded shoes whispered softly over the grass of the deserted plesaunce. In the pond a fish plopped ponderously. Moths blundered among the flowers. A bat was outlined briefly against the green-streaked sky. She looked down at her hand linked in Adam's as they stopped beside the pond. The water near their feet boiled as a frog dived in panic.

Adam pulled her against his side and squeezed her waist, lightly palming the curve of her hip. 'You were right this afternoon,' he said, staring out over the dark, glassy water. 'Sometimes I have found it very difficult indeed.'

'Adam . . .' She half turned, meaning to say that she did not need an explanation, but he took the hand she meant to lay against his mouth and held it prisoner.

'I suppose I should thank de Gernons,' he said. 'Until

371

I thought that hell-hound of his was going to kill Miles, didn't realise what he meant to me.'

'He is yours, Adam.' She laid her hand on his sleeve 'I wasn't just saying it this afternoon.'

His smile was ghostly, like the last of the light. 'Well that's a welcome blessing along the way, but it won't alte the depth of my feeling for him – enrich it, perhaps. He dipped his head and kissed her. She responded, arm tightly around his neck.

'Lie with me?' he said between kisses.

Surprised, she looked up at him. His eyes were as dar as the glitter of the pond beside them. 'Here? Now?'

He was unpinning her cloak and his and spreading them on the summer-scented grass. 'Can you think o a better place? The keep's crowded.'

Her breathing caught. A delightful warmth contracted her loins and she returned to his arms.

The horizon was dark and the moon had risen, a fa white crescent silvering sky and land. Adam stretched lazily, and sitting up, reached for his shirt.

Heulwen sighed and extended a languorous forefinge to run it down the knobbled ridge of his spine, smiling to feel him quiver. 'I suppose,' she said regretfully, 'tha Miles will be roaring to be fed, and Elswith will come seeking me before he rouses the whole keep.'

Adam laughed at the thought of the maid's face shoul she seek them here and find them like this.

Heulwen sat up beside him, her unbraided hai tumbling down, and pressed her lips to his shoulder 'Adam, can we go home tomorrow?' She helped him tu his shirt down.

'I don't see why not.' He turned his head to kiss her,
d continued dressing. 'Any particular reason?'

'Not really.' She began shrugging into her own clothes.
d like to see our own plesaunce finished before the
mmer's end.' There was a sudden hint of mischievous
ighter in her voice.

'It would be more convenient than visiting Ravenstow
ery time,' he agreed.

She nudged him with her foot in retaliation, then
bered. 'I want to dedicate a chapel too, for my grand-
her's soul . . . if you are willing?'

Adam stood up and said quietly, 'How could I not be
lling? We owe him more than we can ever repay. Of
urse you can have a chapel.'

'Thank you.' She kissed him warmly.

He donned his cloak and then swung hers around her
oulders. The moonlight caught the wolf brooch into
brilliant, white glitter.

'No more tail-chasing?' she said as he fastened it.

'No more tail-chasing,' he agreed, and smiling, turned
th her towards the keep.